mothers to work all day … ,
to behave like men—ac… r
with her youngest brothe… ,
so like Mathilde's, the … ,
so like hers.

That curve of cheek, that sweep of hair, opened the gate he had wedged so tightly shut when the impact of Winslow's words had first hit. Behind the gate lay Mathilde, and Claude Louis, and all that he held dear. He saw Mathilde as he had left her that morning, going at the first break of dawn to his fields. She had roused when he did, had brewed his coffee, cooked his meal, and held herself against him in a last moment of parting. She smelled of milk; he had opened her loose gown and put his lips to the firm breasts crowned with nipples that now swelled on the crest of a white sea. Her stomach was firm again, the muscles a strong wall that could hold another babe and keep it safe until time to come out into the world he was building. And Claude Louis, his son, for whom every thrust of his ax was made, every swing of his scythe. A sound wrenched from him, a groan, a cry. "I must go home," he said, and began pushing his way to the doors.

The wall of flesh before him would not yield, even as he pushed and tried to force his way through. Then a tremor ran through the crowd, and Claude saw Winslow and his aides, their red coats cutting a path through the gray-clothed men like blood trickling across a rock. Winslow kept his eyes straight ahead; he stared past the four hundred eleven pairs of anger-darkened eyes focused on his smooth, round face. As the small party filed through the doors, Cavendish, who had been standing at Winslow's side, turned. "You are cruelly wronged," he said. Then he, too, vanished into the bright air of afternoon.

Impatience to leave this deserted place pushed Claude once again into the crowd ahead of him. When it did not yield, he felt impatience give way to panic—what was holding them here? He tried to look through the shifting, desperate web of bodies that stood between him and the door; Now he could not see the door; he could only see red and white uniforms and bayonets gleaming, the slanting rays of the failing sun.

"You are the king's prisoners," a voice shouted, a harsh joy making the words a curse. "You will be kept in this church until the vessels which are to take you away are ready. You will be dealt rations regularly, but may have no other indul-

gence. And any of you who think restlessness will help you—
know that it will not. You remain quiet, or you will be punished
on this spot."

The darkness of despair has one blessing—it is so heavy it
crowds out thought. In that first hour, there were few sounds,
only faint scrabbling noises as brother sought brother, parent
sought child. It was not until the watch outside cried the sixth
hour that someone said, "We must pray."

From the back of the crowded church, a church in which
the bitter smell of fear was already replacing the smell of
incense and candlewax, a voice, once strong, now reed-thin
as though the very vocal cords were imprisoned, began: "The
angel of the Lord declared unto Mary . . ." Across the church,
like the sound of leaves first rustling, then gathering and rising,
whistling in front of a long wind, voices picked up the old
familiar words. "Hail Mary, full of grace, the Lord is with
thee." Not a man but could remember the last time today he
had prayed the Angelus, pausing in his fruited fields, sweat of
his toil cooling his brow, the cold cider and thick cheese and
bread waiting under a nearby tree. Then, the bell of the church
had been a chime, not a toll. And that morning, when the bells
of dawn had sounded and each had turned from his wife's body,
or stopped grinding coffee beans, or paused in the act of thrusting arms into shirt, to pray, what meaning had the words had?

"Holy Mary, Mother of God, pray for us, now, and at the
hour of our death. Amen." Claude crossed himself and squatted
on the stone floor. Pierre Boudreaux, his father and brothers
circled around him, sat. He nodded toward the statue of Mary
in a niche near the main altar. "She's a dear saint—but too
sweet to understand these sons of dogs. Best pray to Saint
Paul."

"She's God's mother, Pierre," Claude said. "What son re-
fuses his mother?"

That was a dangerous word. The younger boys, frightened,
hungry, exhausted, gave way before its magic. At the first sob,
drawn through a throat rough with pain, the shell of age fell
away, and throughout the church, the honest weeping of children rose over the murmur of talk, of prayer.

Pierre cast a look at two guards standing near the door.
Moments before, they had made plain their contempt for the
prayers they heard, hoisting their weapons high and shouting,
"These are the only prayers that help you!" Now, they were

silent. As the sound of weeping grew stronger, as the pain in the hearts of those openly weeping and those who wept inside became more evident, the guards turned and faced the wooden barred door.

The night in the church was long, its hours marked by the prayers, the sighs, the cries of men who, for the first time since they had settled in Acadia, were not at home with their women and infant children. Each man who had such thoughts had a heavy task—to close out, if he could, the horror that engulfed his soul when he thought of his defenseless women, the prey of marauding and angry Britishers. "They're not all gentlemen, the Britishers," Pierre whispered to Claude. "And when they don't look on an Acadian woman as anything but a convenient hole—"

"Shut up!" Claude's eyes burned into Pierre's face. Pierre gripped Claude's hand, his own eyes filled now with pity. Claude let his face fall forward on the arms crossed over his knees. He began to say the little prayer his mother had taught him, the little prayer that came to his lips in times of great joy, great pain, great grief. It was his mother's voice behind the words, the feel of her hand on his brow, the softness of her dress, the scent of verbena she put in her clothes press. "Christ Jesus, you are Faith, I have faith in thee. Christ Jesus, you are Hope, I hope in thee. Christ Jesus, you are Love, I love thee." Over and over his lips said the words. His breathing slowed, his heart stopped its frightened pounding. His mind left one candle of consciousness to watch; the rest of Claude Langlinais slept.

The evening did not begin to seem long for Mathilde bathed Jeanne until after Claude Louis had been suckled for the last time, rolled into his warm shawl, and laid in his cradle by the fire. While they fixed and cooked their own supper, while Mathilde bathed Claude Louis, while Jeanne mended a tear in one of Claude's big work shirts, they kept an eye toward the road. But not until the last light had been gone from the sky for half the time between two strikes from the mantel clock did they begin to worry.

"Where could they be?" Mathilde had tired of looking from the window—she had taken a lantern and walked down to the gate, holding the light high to see if the empty dust in the footpath had something to tell her.

She watched Jeanne pull the heavy wooden shutters over the windows and slide the bars into place across them, watched her bolt and bar the doors. Then Jeanne sat by the low fire, her tongue clamped between her lips, her fingers flying through her crochet. It was no good trying to get Jeanne to talk to her, not when she looked like that. Mathilde sat in her rocker, picked up the linen she was making into a Sunday shirt for Claude. She tried to force her mind to think of the needle pushing in and out of the heavy cloth, but all the rumors she had half listened to all summer rushed past that flashing bit of metal and pierced her brain as easily as the needle pierced the work in her hands.

She remembered in July, when Claude Louis was five months old, and smiling all the time, that Claude and her brother Pierre had talked in heavy voices about what had happened to some men they called deputies. She hadn't paid attention—counting how many times she could make Claude Louis smile was far more important—but there had been something about these men, these deputies, going to talk to the English for all the Acadians. They had been put in prison, or something. And hadn't they lost their lands? Maybe she remembered that their wives and children had been sent away—it had all been too awful. She'd finally put her hands over her small ears and told the men to stop talking about all that, to come play with the baby. Her Claude had taken her hands from her ears and kissed the inside of each ear with his tongue. She had forgotten everything he had said, then.

"Is it like it was with the deputies, in July?" Her voice sounded strange, she had never said anything so serious in all of her life.

Jeanne put down her crocheting. She looked at the girl sitting across the fire from her. Time enough later for her to learn whatever there was to learn. Certainly Jeanne would not say that unless something terrible had happened, surely someone, if not Claude then one of Mathilde's brothers, one of Jeanne's family, would have come to tell them where Claude was.

"Men do stay out all night," she said. "Even when they have wives as soft and willing as you."

Mathilde's eyes met Jeanne's. She had almost forgotten that Jeanne, sleeping in the loft so close above their bed, knew very well that Mathilde found the duties of the marriage bed a pleasure to be repeated as often as Claude's good strength allowed.

Unconsciously, she tossed the dark curls from her neck. Jeanne was good to them, a fine nurse for Claude Louis,—but she, Mathilde, was a woman. Claude's woman. Madame Langlinais! Jeanne would be Tante Jeanne forever, borrowing babies because no man had ever given her any of her own.

"Let's go to bed," she said. "It's late."

But when they had washed in front of the fire, and dropped the softly gathered nightdresses over their heads, and brushed their braids out—Mathilde's dark hair catching the firelight as it bounced away from the tight formation that held it all day, Jeanne's gray softening to silver in that same light—Mathilde turned to Jeanne as she prepared to climb to the loft.

"Will you sleep down here? With me?"

Not since she married Claude eighteen months ago had she slept alone; she must be enclosed in arms, held against a warm body that cared for her, protected her, even if that body was her son's nurse.

The night breeze off the bay that caught the last smoke from the Langlinais chimney skipped across moonlit fields, touched down to see baskets of fruit forgotten under laden trees, and swept through the open window of Colonel Winslow's barracks to flirt with candle flame and quicken the fire. The colonel reached out a hand to catch a paper sailing with the wind, then sank back into his chair, an untouched glass of claret at his elbow. The roast venison lay congealing in its sauce, the salad of fresh cress wilted. He could eat half-raw hare in the field, could pull dandelion leaves and munch them as he rode, but he had no stomach for this well-cooked meal. He pulled his journal to him—perhaps writing the day's events would reduce them to what they, after all, were. Following the orders of his king.

The smart tap at the door, recognizably Cavendish's, was a relief. But the lieutenant had not come to share more tales of the underside of court life.

"Ugly business, that," he said, gesturing toward the church.

"It gets worse." He held out a paper to Cavendish, watched while the younger officer read it. Cavendish's face contorted—as though he had just stepped into a charnel house. No need to ask why. When he had first read the orders, he hoped he had looked the same way. He had ridden over the district just last week, taking pleasure in the bountiful crops, the bursting orchards, the scenes of happy industry. These Acadians were a neat and busy people, pious, strong in their family life—he had never believed they would betray their neutrality. The results of their industry had been tallied, the figures were all recorded. Forty-three thousand five hundred horned cattle, 48,500 sheep, 23,500 pigs, and 2,800 horses. When these 13,000 people had been deported, laden onto ships helter-skelter, set upon the hostile surface of a British sea, who would then own that livestock, that land? Winslow thought that it must be easy to harvest as the king did.

"So now we pillage and burn." Cavendish's voice was at least five years older than it had been moments before.

"Lawrence is afraid some of them will escape, come back. If their land is burned, if their harvest is destroyed—they'll starve."

Cavendish looked at Winslow, a look that seemed to see past that smooth forehead under its powdered wig to the convoluted brain behind. It was a brain that had, over the years, learned to carry out orders without question. Winslow lifted a hand as though to screen his eyes from the fire's glare; he sought to screen the clear light he saw in Cavendish's eyes, a light that threw this whole shabby business into awful relief against the plain dailiness of other duty. He watched as Cavendish strode to the desk, sat astride a chair placed there, pulled paper toward him, dipped the quill in the thick black ink, and began to write. The scratching of the pen, the whisper of sand blown across the page to dry it, fell in with the soft greedy sounds of the fire as it consumed the fat pine knots—music for a peaceful night. He handed the paper to Winslow, saluted and went out into the night, the door slamming behind him.

Winslow rapidly read the few lines Cavendish had scrawled. He noted the flair of the signature beneath the stark words with which Cavendish had resigned his commission. Another door seemed to slam, a door that left Cavendish honorably extracted on one side, and Winslow, harnessed in mindless service to a vengeful king, on the other. Perhaps it wouldn't be too bad. They could find other land, other homes. But he had seen evacuations of civilians before. Even when a friendly army was trying to keep families together, the inevitable separations took place. With a hostile army, ready to punish, to harass—Winslow sighed and, taking a fresh piece of paper, wrote a document of his own.

The next morning, the sergeant read Winslow's order to the troops without comment. No soldier or sailor could be absent without leave, under pain of severe punishment, in order that there be no opportunity for distressing this distressed people. The colonel's getting soft, the sergeant thought. Him and that fancy lieutenant. But there are more of us than there are of them.

After handing the order to the sergeant, Winslow went to the church. He stood outside the barred doors, willing himself to face what lay beyond. Two of the armed guards fell in step ahead of him, loosened the doors, swung them open, and ushered him inside.

A field of men lay before him, cut down in midharvest like the wheat on their own lands. Where yesterday he had seen pride, determination, resistance, today he saw only grief. The faces that turned toward him each held, to one degree or another, signs of a universal language of mourning that knows no nationality, no religion. Slowly, as though a wind from heaven—or hell—had risen and was bringing them to their feet, the waves of men who had lain in desperate closeness through the night rose and faced him.

For a long moment, Winslow thought that the silence in that church would not be broken in his lifetime. Then he saw a man working his way through the crowd, gently pushing aside those who listlessly blocked him, until he stood before the colonel.

"My name is Claude Langlinais, Monsieur Colonel. I am an Acadian."

And a proud one, Winslow thought. A night of hunger, thirst, fear, and loss hasn't broken him—may nothing that follows succeed.

"We all understand now what has happened to us, that we must leave our land, our homes. We know that we must accept this. We have faith that God will open another door even as this one is closed. But, Colonel Winslow, there is something the bon Dieu cannot do for us, that you can do. Let us go to our families, speak to them, tell them what has befallen us. I pray you—they must not hear of this calamity from strangers!"

Not only proud, but brave. Turn them loose? That could never be. But Langlinais was still speaking, proposing that each day a few men from Grand Pré, a few men from Rivière aux Canards go to their families. Their return would be guaranteed by the lives of those who remained. Winslow assayed the mood of the men before him. Well, why not? He nodded his assent and spoke to the guards. Ten men from each group were to be allowed to leave each day. They were to return by sundown, or the lives of the others would be forfeited, one for one.

Now Winslow wanted to be gone from this evil place, this place dedicated to the worship of God which now seemed a temple of Satan himself. Surely, the only love in that place was what these poor people could feel for each other. Their God had abandoned them—He had blessed their harvest then snatched it away. He had brought them to this land, then allowed them to be thrown from it, even as Adam and Eve had been thrown from Paradise. And still they called him the bon Dieu! Winslow's God was much less capricious. He required, Winslow believed, only that his followers live as officers and gentlemen.

The business of selecting the first twenty to return home was quickly settled. Claude they chose automatically. Others were chosen because they represented many families, or could visit clusters of farms, the better to bring news, not rumor, to the anxious watchers.

Perhaps never again would Claude Langlinais experience the sensation he felt when the church doors swung wide, and he, with nineteen others, walked out into the September morning. The sky was no different than it had been the day before, the sun still the same.

But the clarity of his vision was changed. It was as though a sharp, bright glass had been drawn over the world, almost a magnifying glass, calling attention to details—the red veining in a yellowing leaf, the quick scent of a crushed wildflower— that yesterday Claude would have ignored.

"Don't forget we're out on an English leash," Pierre said when they parted at the footpaths that forked up to their own farms. Pierre quickly climbed until he disappeared behind a stand of flaming maples. At first Claude moved as fast as his brother-in-law. Then, when the path broke out of the woods and ran along his fields, he slowed. He had been thinking of Mathilde, nothing but Mathilde and Claude Louis this whole weary time. Now he would see them, and hold them—and have to tell Mathilde that they were to be parted again, perhaps forever.

Claude had no faith in British promises. How many times in the past forty years had trusting Acadians tried to leave Nova Scotia, as the treaty promised them, only to have ships strangely delayed, papers lost, orders changed? He didn't believe for a moment that Acadian families would be kept together—what did those sons of dogs care? The sailing date for the men in the church had already been set, but there had been no mention of their wives, their children.

Claude thought of the small hoard of coin money hidden under the kitchen floor. He would divide that, giving more to Mathilde than to himself. He, Claude, had other ways of getting the necessaries. While Mathilde—

Now he did quicken his step, running when the path curved. He left the last field, and ran along the little home yard he had fenced around their cabin. Smoke rose in a thin straight line from the chimney; nothing else stirred. The shuttered windows were strange to his eyes; he had left a home and returned to a fortress.

He strode to the front door, lifted the wooden knocker that hung on a leather thong. "Mathilde! Mathilde! It's Claude!"

The sound of a bar being pulled, a bolt being released. A door creaking. And then a cry—"Claude! Oh, Claude!" And an armful of warm woman, close against him, lips soft with worry taking from his own lips all the dryness fear and a long night of thirst had put there. "Claude, where have you been? Claude, what's happened?"

"Shh!" Enough for now to hold her, to run his hands over every swell of that dear body, to pull her to him, to think, for a few moments, that she was his, that she would not be taken from him. He knew that if he stood longer, his resolve to honor his promise to return would weaken, and that it would take all the strength he had just to go back.

He needed much of that strength for what lay before him now. "Come inside, Mathilde. Is there breakfast still?" He drew her inside the door, closed it behind them. But he bolted it again, let down the bar, and did not open the windows. Jeanne stood behind him, ready to engulf him in her own great embrace.

"People who are late for breakfast can't expect much," she grumbled, but she smiled broadly as she went to the fire, put the skillet on the grill, and tossed in ham and squares of cold mush.

"Where have you been, Claude?" Mathilde would not leave his side; when the baby wailed, she picked him up, changed his napkin, and sat on the low stool next to Claude's chair, one smooth breast offered to the infant while she clung to Claude's hand.

"Let the man eat, child," Jeanne said, handing Claude a mug of coffee.

She knows it's something terrible, he thought. We may as well have this time of peace. Why not?

And so he drank his coffee and watched Mathilde feed his child and ate the good ham from his own pigs, the mush made from his own corn. He spooned liberal portions of Mathilde's apple jelly onto his plate and twisted bits of ham around in it.

"You're hungry enough," Jeanne said, her voice filled with questions.

Claude handed the empty plate and mug to Jeanne. She set the plate in the pot of water heating over the coals and filled the mug with coffee. "Now tell," she commanded, bringing him the mug.

He told, trying to soften the force of the devastation that had been unleashed. The cold and monstrous facts could not be softened, not to ears as loving as Mathilde's, not to ears as sharp as Jeanne's.

"We're Catholic, we're French, and we have fat farms. That's enough, isn't it?" Jeanne said.

Mathilde said nothing. After one terrible cry, she had thrown herself across Claude's lap, where she lay almost lifeless. They heard no weeping, no sound. When Claude raised her face, the eyes that stared back held all the tears in the world, but none fell. The soft mouth was drawn in a tight line of denial, the skin had lost the flush of autumn sun. She will look this way in her grave, Jeanne thought.

"Mathilde, Mathilde, you must believe that we will be all right. The bon Dieu—"

Those eyes flashed to the crucifix hanging above their bed. Slowly, Mathilde rose and went to stand beside the bed, her eyes fixed on the cross. Her hands moved to it, took it from the wall, held it for one moment, and then hurled it against one of the shuttered windows.

"Sacrebleu!" Jeanne crossed herself, then scurried to pick up the crucifix where it lay, the Christ figure loosened by the fall and hanging away from the wooden cross.

"Mathilde, don't be angry at God. This is not God's will." Claude's arms were around her, he could feel the passionate beating of her heart, a heart usually so tranquil, so happy, so calm. Only in their bed had he felt that kind of beating—to think that she was learning the angry passions that destroy! One more sin on those English heads—

"God knows everything. It is His will." Mathilde was stubborn, a child where he needed a strong woman. He had thought it would be years before Mathilde must have that kind of womanly strength—now he had but hours to help her find it. He drew her to the chair set near the fire, sat and pulled her gently onto his lap. Jeanne, her own lips set in a line, bent over the cradle and picked up the sleeping baby.

"I'll take him upstairs," she said.

Claude watched the broad back disappear into the opening in the ceiling, then tightened his arms around Mathilde. Her head was on his shoulder, her face pressed into the rough gray wool of his shirt. She was moving her face back and forth, whispering, almost chanting, one word, "Non, non, non."

"Sweet child, you'll rub that lovely face all raw," he said, and he lifted her face in his big hand and turned it to his. "Now, listen, Mathilde, all isn't lost. We'll be all right, you'll see, we'll be all right."

The eyes, so close to his own, were beginning to spill their load of tears; the first were runneling down her cheeks, leaving small traces like a snail path in the garden. "I'm young, I can begin again. That land—" His arm made a sweeping gesture over the air around them, bringing the memory of the wide fertile fields in beside the quiet fire.

"That land is all we have," she said, and now the tears were flowing like a spring freshet, a torrent of pain, a torrent of fear and anger.

"But it is not all the land in the world! Mon Dieu, do you think we will not find land somewhere else?" Even as he spoke the words, Claude felt as though it were crumbling between his fingers, the good loam that made his fields so fine.

"But where, Claude? Where are they sending us?" She fell against his neck, and the warm tears melting from her skin onto his would serve for him, too; men did not cry.

"Oh, any of a dozen places. New England, the Carolinas, places that lead to other places, yes?" A feeling of hopelessness that he had somehow managed to hold at bay until this moment overtook him, as the flying hawk overtakes the small gray hare. He felt pounced upon, enveloped; the sharp fangs of fear bit at him and he felt the breath of death.

He tightened his hold on Mathilde, felt the small warmth that crept from her body through her dress. His hand began to stroke her, moving over the gentleness of her body, feeling it stir beneath him. He glanced up toward the loft. Jeanne had let the trap down; they were alone. He began to untie the ribbons that held her bodice closed: Mathilde, feeling cold fingers on her warm breast, lifted her head and put her mouth over his. They stood up, his hands removing her clothes until she stood naked in the dusky light from the fire. His eyes moved over her as he stripped. He was both delighted and shocked. Never had Mathilde forgotten her modesty and stood before him; even in bed, she kept her nightgown on. But now—

"You are beautiful," he said. He bent to kiss her breasts, knelt to kiss the soft stomach, the inside of her thighs. When they were in bed, the fierceness of her almost frightened him. What savage had this news released?

As though reading his thoughts she said, low in his ear, her breath carrying the scent of cinnamon: "We must make today count for a long time."

He raised himself on an elbow, looked down into the face flushed now with feeling for him. "Listen, Mathilde, you must believe that we will be all right. You must work with me to see that we are."

And then he held her close, and told her where to hide the coin money he would leave with her. He told her to dry fruits and meat so that they would have food on the long sea voyage; he told her that when the day of departure came, she was to wear many layers of clothing, and use her bundles for blankets and food.

"How do you know so much, Claude?" she asked. Her voice sounded almost like his own Mathilde, the child-wife who looked to him for love, for guidance, for life. He felt the hawk loosen its grip.

"Because I am one hell of a smart Acadian, that's why," he said. And he laughed and kissed her nose and tickled her bare belly under the covers until they were both laughing, laughter that changed into small sounds of passion and desire.

"I will love you always, Claude," she said. "No matter what happens, I will never love anyone else."

"Nothing's going to happen," he said.

When he left later that day, looking back once, he felt that perhaps the worst was behind them, and that the voyage to a new life would not, after all, be so bad. He would not look at his fields, though his way ran beside them until he reached the road. That part of his life was over, those fields were dead to him; he would bury all memory of them, as though they had never been his, and start anew.

In the church that night, he heard much the same sort of resolution in other voices, saw the same sort of determination in other eyes. As he listened to the men around him, Claude's heart became lighter than it had been at any time since the colonel had read their terrible judgment. "We're not beaten, not yet. Not ever." Claude turned to look at the crucifix that hung high over the altar. Raising his hand, he crossed himself. "By the honor of the Cross, good Jesus, I swear that I will not rest until once again my wife, my son, and all my children to come after him are safe on land that is mine. And may the devil take any man who stands in my way."

The September sun continued its slow march to the autumn equinox. Inside the church, the rhythm of life was set by the departure each dawn of twenty men and their return at twilight. That rhythm quickly took on the deadly beat of the funeral march; the news the prisoners brought back was a poison that stole into the blood of those who heard it.

"The British are hunting fugitives down—they are shooting at those they hunt, they are saying to mothers and to wives that families will be shot to death if they do not turn husbands and fathers in." The rumor marched from mouth to mouth, acquiring force as it went. It was fed each day by tales of new horrors, new woes. Fields burned, homes pillaged. Fugitives condemned to death.

Within the space of but a few days, the ugliness of fear had replaced the shimmering beauty of faith. Men prayed, not for strength for themselves, but for their families.

"Our families are worse off than we are, and we're in prison," Pierre said. He had long since emptied his tobacco pouch; the cold empty pipe was something to gnaw on, something to hold. "Mon Dieu, I'm going mad. Every time I close my eyes—"

Claude reached out, clasped Pierre's arm. "Don't say it. Don't think it. They're all right. We've got to believe they're all right." He thought of the shutters, the barred door. Would wood and metal keep soldiers from Mathilde, from her softness, her curving nakedness? He thought of her moving under him, of how her breasts felt beneath his chest, of the wetness that ran out of her. "I'll kill—" He stopped the word, stopped the thought. The worst thing that could happen was to become less of a man because of this. He could not fill his mind with hatred and vengeance, and still trust in good. "They'll be all right," he said. "They have to be."

Five days after their captivity began, the church doors were thrown wide. The sudden blaze of light sent them falling back like sheaves before the scythe; the bright edge of the sun moved over them, grim stubbled faces, stained and dirty clothes, gray and grieving faces.

"They're beginning to look like the dogs that they are," Claude heard a sergeant say, and he stood up and straightened his back and fastened his eyes onto that hated British face. When Winslow stood once again in the center of the church, once again unrolled a heavy sealed document, once more began to mouth those incomprehensible words, Claude knew he was in a nightmare where horror after horror comes in a flood of darkness and finally snuffs out all light.

"We are in the hands of madmen," Pierre said when the last word had been read and seemed to hang before them like a sword, its bloody tip fresh from killing.

"I do not think they are mad," Claude said. The horror had been cold; now his anger was colder. He felt that somehow it had been forged in all the anger and loss, he knew it would cut his enemies down like the sword of God, he knew that he would fight no longer against hatred and vengeance; vengeance was his and he would take it. "They mean to destroy us as a race. This is the way they choose to do it."

Names were being called now, the English tongue making mockery of the soft French sounds. Soldiers with bayonets were pushing the boys into line, grabbing them from their father's arms, their brother's protection. Next to Claude, Pierre was sobbing, great sounds that welled up from the darkness in him to meet the other sounds of grief that filled the church. "Mon petit frère, mon petit frère." Over and over those words, grinding out of him, tearing at him. Claude stood frozen. Even as he saw them roughly thrown into that bleak line, even as he saw them moving from the church, he didn't believe what had happened. Why would the British send these children, these boys as young as ten and twelve, on ships by themselves? They were sending them to their deaths.

As the line of boys and young men moved forward, hands reached out to touch, to hold. Claude turned from the look on Pierre's face as he watched his youngest brother stumble by. He could stand his own pain well enough, but the pain of others . . . He would not think of Mathilde; he would go mad if he thought of her, of what this news would do.

Even as he fought that torment, a new sound, a keening wail of grief as old as creation, reached his ears. The women who daily brought rations to the prisoners and who remained close to the church most of the day had seen the crowd emerge. They must have had hope, Claude thought. They must have thought we were being set free. And then they learned the truth.

He shut his ears to those terrible cries, shut his eyes to those terrible faces, crushed with a grief they had never thought to bear. If he could shut it all out, he would be with Mathilde— not the sweet and gentle Mathilde, whose feelings were only now taking on the strength of womanhood, but the Mathilde who was being modeled by all of this pain, all of this hatred, all of this suffering. That woman, he knew, would be one he had never thought to know, one she had never thought to know.

"And for no reason! Mother of God, for no reason." He had never been a political man. He had never cared who sat on what throne, so long as he had been able to till his fields, marry his wife, breed his heirs. Kings, queens, princes royal—what did they have to do with him? Today, finally, he had learned. What they had to do was everything. They could take his wife's virtue, his fields, his cottage, his hopes.

How could those men have such power over him? Who decides something like that? Not God, he thought. God doesn't have time or thought for such things. Well, whoever had decided this hell for him, he would undecide it. He turned again to the crucifix. His earlier vow, to have fields again, a home again, was not enough. "Jesus, by Thy Holy Cross, I swear I will not rest until no man on earth can order me or mine to do his bidding, until no man on earth can take what is mine, until no man on earth can bring harm to me or to those I love."

"Why are you not crying?" the man standing beside him said. "Do you not share this loss?"

"Mon vieux," Claude said, clasping his hands on the old man's shoulders, bent and small in the loose gray shirt, "I have no strength to spend on tears. Nor should any of us. I will not weep for what these devils do. I will not weep until I stand on land I own, with my wife beside me and my son in my arms."

"You'll weep in hell then," the man answered.

Two hundred fifty young men, fifty to each of five ships, were sent into exile that September tenth. One hundred forty-one were unmarried; these were lads who cried for their fathers, their mothers, their brothers and sisters as troops with bayonets fixed marched them toward the river. There began that day a flood of exiles that would rush over more than six thousand Acadians, bear them forward on its tumultuous tide, and deposit them throughout the English colonies scattered along the North American Atlantic Coast.

Before it was over, scenes played out that bitter day would become commonplace: a young son, unable to reach his mother, kissing his religious medal, removing it from his neck and flinging it to her to be as tenderly kissed and returned; a mother fainting as her son boarded the ship, riding with such deceptive peace on the swells of their own familiar river; sisters younger than the brothers torn from them trying with clumsy words and fear-filled hearts to comfort those so desolate around them.

Until now, the immensity of what was transpiring had not fully struck the prisoners. Occupied with fears for their own safety and that of their families, strained by lack of sleep, of food, of cleanliness, each man and boy had had more than enough to do simply taking care of his own concerns. Today, as they peered out over soldiers' heads to watch the line of prisoners join other Acadians outside, their hearts accepted what their minds had known but denied. The British soldiers had been rounding people up from all over the district, rounding them up as though with a giant rake, pushing debris before it, to remove them from the land of the terrible British king.

Claude, pushing his way through to the front of the crowd, standing on tiptoe to see out the door, saw Jeanne standing with a group of women from Grand Pré. As they had arranged on his visit hours, at the beginning of this incredible travail, Jeanne had been bringing food in to him. Unlike many of the women, she did not stay near the church, but brought the rations, gave them to the guard, and went hurriedly back to

Mathilde as Claude watched from the church window, his daily ration of hope dwindling as she vanished from sight.

That she was staying today troubled him. Of all days, this one was a poor one to choose. Mathilde would learn soon enough that her brother was gone. And would begin to think, as he did, of what this day foretold for the future.

As Claude looked out, the door to Colonel Winslow's quarters across from the church was suddenly thrown open and the young lieutenant who usually accompanied Winslow came striding out, his face masked with fury. Looking neither to the right nor to the left, he moved rapidly through the crowd to the rail where a black mare stood pulling late summer grass, her graceful neck curving against the dark woods and light blue sky. The sergeant Claude had come to hate sprang forward. Through the clear September air, almost crystalline in its brilliance, Claude heard the sergeant speak. "Lieutenant Cavendish, sir, aren't you coming to the river?"

Cavendish, one foot lifted to mount, turned his face to the sergeant. Such anger Claude had not seen on any man's face. It was unlike the rage that tore at him, a rage that covered pain. The lieutenant looked as though he had finally journeyed through innocence. He looked—betrayed. His voice, loud over the low sounds of the crowd, filled the space over all their heads.

"Come to the river? To see the soldiers of Our Majesty's Empire do today's brave deed? Thank you, no, sergeant. I've no stomach for your sort of courage."

He was in the saddle, had lifted his crop and slapped the mare lightly on her shining ebony rump. She wheeled around and moved into a trot. By the time they cleared the square, she was cantering. Claude watched the black and red and white blur vanish down the road.

"Too bad he's not in charge," he said to Pierre. But Pierre had left his side. Claude turned and looked over the men clustered behind him, blinking as he tried to focus his eyes in the dimness of the church. He finally saw Pierre kneeling over something near the pulpit. The line of Pierre's body, the final defeat of it, told Claude even before he reached the scene that this day had not yet unleashed all its dreadful arrows.

"It's father," Pierre said when Claude leaned over him, thrusting his head forward to better see the figure crumpled on the stone floor. "He's dying."

So that is how a voice sounds when there is no grief left,

no rage left, no hope left, Claude thought. Only the desolation that pain has come, and, having come, will never, never leave.

"There must be something—" Even as he said the words, Claude heard the rattling breath, saw the heavy work the chest made of taking in air, letting it out.

"He is beyond anything we can do, thank the bon Dieu," Pierre said. "He is beyond anything but our prayers, and I think we need them far more than this good man ever will." The flat voice, tired, beaten, frightened Claude. Much more lay ahead of them than the loss of a brother, a father. If they were despairing now—

"He has led a long life, Pierre. He will be with God very soon. Let him go to God with our prayers in his ears." He began the rosary, automatically chanting the mysteries, saying the Aves, counting on the small black beads he kept with him during his working day. Other voices took up the prayers. Soon the old, old words rose above the gray mass that seemed overwhelmed by the walls around them. As Antoine Boudreaux breathed his last, those last breaths coming easily now, like a child going into a sleep, careful hands straightened limbs, placed his worn beads in his folded hands, and smoothed his disordered hair.

I must report this, Claude thought. There must be a burial, a service—even English devils must honor the dead, that surely was a covenant known to all men. If I could see that lieutenant—he would understand. If any of these dogs are not completely given over to Satan, it is that lieutenant. He moved through the clusters of men who were trying to settle themselves into some sort of ease and took a post at a window. The rail was empty; the lieutenant had not yet returned from his ride.

The sun had fallen out of the sky, disappearing with a sudden drop into a cloud bank low on the horizon, before the pounding hooves sounded down the road. Claude peered through the haze of twilight, saw the large black animal move into sight. He pushed himself up into the window and shouted. "Lieutenant! Lieutenant!"

A soldier turned, alerted by the cry. "What the devil—" The sharp prick of the bayonet's point at his throat sent a burst of fever through Claude's blood. This man dared threaten him? His hand went to his side and came away empty. Of course his knife was gone. His bare hands, then. As he lifted them to grasp that shining blade, he heard a hiss, saw a blurring dark line cross his vision and disappear. He heard a grunt, saw that dark blur again, and realized that someone was whipping the soldier. He looked up and saw the black mare, her rider's arm raising and lowering rhythmically as the lieutenant's riding crop curled down over the retreating red back. "Do you add murdering the defenseless to your other valorous acts?" that terrible voice cried after the running soldier.

They faced one another, Claude and the lieutenant, in that moment just before the last light is pulled from the sky by the weight of the vanished sun; the space of the church wall that separated them was as vast as the coming night.

"And darkness came upon the land," the lieutenant said softly.

"What?"

"A quote—almost a quote. The Bible—something about the dark that falls on a land. You are learning that, I know."

Startled, Claude realized that the lieutenant was speaking French—and decent French at that. His heart lifted for one small beat. It would be easier to tell of Antoine's death, to ask the favor of his burial, in the dear, beloved tongue. It proved easier than he had hoped. After the first few words, the lieutenant had leaned into the window, listening with the whole length of his body. At a wave of that mighty red arm, soldiers had appeared, had heard brusque English orders, had left to return with a stretcher.

"The women will lay him out?" The question was to Claude.

"Yes—"

"They'll carry him to my quarters. There's a room there—would your brother-in-law want to go, go tell the family?"

Mathilde! For another small beat, his heart forgot pain and remembered sweetness. He would see Mathilde. No matter that he would see her grieving, bent under the loss of first brother, then father. He would see her face, feel her hands in his, perhaps for a time hold her.

"He can leave at dawn," Cavendish said. "For tonight—will you watch with him?"

So the English did know something of civilized ways. When they reached the room where the soldiers had laid Antoine, they met new proof that death did cross all barriers, make all quarrels foolish, for some men, at least. Someone had straightened Antoine's body, seen to it that the hands holding the rosary were comfortably at rest. The body was stiff now, its sharp outlines under the rough wool blanket ungainly. The women would not wash and dress it until morning. The face, in life so full of humor, so full of the knowledge that life was very often a riddle to which one would never know the answer, was drawn up in the seizure of death. Claude drew the blanket up gently. "Give him peace for now, Pierre," he said.

On a low table near the bed stood a decanter of wine and two glasses. There was a plate of cheese and bread, and a bowl of autumn fruit. Someone knew how long the hours go when one watched at that final twilight between life and death. There were guards at the door, yes, but in the room the solemnity of this last attention overrode all that. Those small moments when his heart had known hope seemed to come together and make a little seed. Something in him loosened. He knew that he would live his vow, that he would one day make himself and all he loved proof against the will of any man. But now there was room again for love, and for hope.

The prayer he had not said for days, the prayer he had tried to forget as the church around him had each day become more and more of an English prison and less and less the temple of his God, that prayer his mother had taught him rose fresh and young to his lips. "Christ Jesus, you are Faith, I have faith in thee. Christ Jesus, you are Hope, I hope in thee. Christ Jesus, you are Love, I love thee."

Pierre left at first light, two soldiers marching with him. Claude, watching from the window, saw Pierre's back become straight and tall with each step away from this English garrison, with each step toward his beloved countryside. He knew the prayers in Pierre's heart, the strength he asked for. How tell his mother that the last child of her marriage had been torn from his brothers, his father, and sent alone onto the black, black sea. How then tell her that his father was also gone. It was more than a man could bear, more than a woman ever could. He thought again of Mathilde, and, kneeling beside Antoine's body, wept.

There was a knock at the door, and a voice. "Sir, I ask your pardon for intruding—but I have brought the women."

Even as he went to the door, the effect of that "sir" began to work on Claude. Never again would it matter that another man offered him that small courtesy; it had been offered now, and that would serve for a lifetime.

He stood outside the door while the women laid Antoine
out. He could hear the soughing sounds of the rosary they
chanted as they worked, the rise and fall of the prayers of each
line of beads like the wind rising and falling in a meadow. The
rise and fall of the voices lulled him. His eyes closed and he
slumped against the rough wall and slept.

"You need a decent bed." The voice came from the other
side of memory. He tried to think whose voice that was. Who
cared that he slept, that he was human? But he was past caring,
he felt himself led across the floor, knew that he was guided
to a bed, helped to lie down, felt wool scratch his chin as a
blanket was drawn over him. And then he knew no more.

The bells of the Angelus woke him. Six o'clock! Why had
he slept so long, there was hay to cut, apples to pick—and
Mathilde already up! Why had she not wakened him? He sat
up, blinked in the half-light that seemed to be leaving rather
than coming into the room. And then of course he knew that
it was the bells of evening that he heard, not morning, and that
although he would see Mathilde, it would not be at breakfast
where she pridefully set out the good things she had cooked
for him, but at her father's grave.

They buried Antoine on a small hill in the grassy pasture
that lay behind the church; the hill looked past the ships riding
in the harbor out to the open sea. "From here he can watch
my brother," Mathilde said. She was standing close within the
circle of Claude's arms. She had not left him since they had
met in the church the night before. Pain and lost hopes had
struggled to conquer the rush of love, of faith, that filled them
in that moment. But feeling her heart beat under his, Claude
believed love and faith might win.

"We will find your brother," Claude said. They had talked
the night through, whispering under the repeated prayers,
speaking with their eyes, their hands, their whole beings speaking, making up for all the time of separation behind them.
Having his wife at his side, watching his baby son suckle, gave
back to Claude the strength the days and nights of imprisonment
had drained from him.

In the days that followed, Claude began his plan for survival.
The rumors that reached their ears, rumors so terrible they
could only hope they were exaggerations, spoke of farms burned,
wells poisoned, the old and feeble dying of exposure as they

were rounded up and taken to ships lying like hungry sharks to devour them. Fear battled with despair in the confines of the church; neither was a good companion. By early October, most of the men in the church had fallen into a stupor from which only food could rouse them.

"Look at them," Claude said to Pierre, his gesturing arm sweeping over the desolate figures around them. "Could you believe these men ever lifted a hand to work? Ever sang, or laughed? Look at them!"

"There is no work for them to do. Their homes are gone, their farms destroyed, their families—who knows? As for singing, laughing . . ." Pierre's voice trailed off as his hands fumbled with the long-empty pipe.

"But there will be work again. Homes, fields, families. Yes, and there will be singing again—and laughing! Pierre, for God's sake, you believe that, don't you?"

Pierre shrugged. "All things are possible for God."

"God! We've got to give him something to work with, by heaven." And then he told Pierre of his plan. "We must learn English. We must be strong again. Those things first. With those tools—who knows what we will build?"

From the eighth of October until the twenty-seventh of that terrible month, when the stench of burned rotting crops lay over the land and the sound of weeping never quite left the sullen air, the people of Grand Pré and Rivière aux Canards were herded toward the river and loaded onto the ships. The fleet did not sail until October 27—and so there was new grief to bear, for families were separated, women put pell-mell in one ship, their husbands in another. While still on shore, there had been some hope for new lives in another land. Now, there was no cause to hope, no cause to live. It was then that the old, the feeble, the invalid, began to die.

Claude knew almost all that was happening with his people. He had managed to form a kind of servant-clown image—with rough jokes on his tongue and forced mischief in his eyes he had won over one of the soldiers who stood guard, and from him he learned not only the English he so badly wanted but the news of what was being done at the harbor.

"If it was the army now, it'd be going better," the man said one afternoon when he had come back from a burial detail. "Those sailors, they've got no hearts."

Claude was silent. Each time he saw sand on a soldier's boots, he knew that more of his people had died on that barren shore and had been buried there. Thank heaven that Antoine, at least, had had the burial of a man. As for the sailors being responsible for this infamy—Colonel Winslow was no sailor. Those ships were there at his request, it was his soldiers who went through the district searching out the Acadians who were still desperately trying to hide, his soldiers who burned fields and houses and barns, his soldiers who had taken the happy land and made of it a bitter place.

But prisoners do not have the luxury of speaking their hearts; they may only speak what serves them. "You mention sailors," Claude said, his face twisted into the mask he wore as clown. "You mention sailors—have you heard this little story?"

Claude managed to learn a few new English words each day. "And not all of them filth," he reported to Pierre as they were exercising behind the altar one day, arm-wrestling, lifting the heavy candelabra high above their heads—any movement they could devise that would stir blood, challenge muscles. "I asked him about Lieutenant Cavendish—the one who helped us? He said Cavendish is a gentleman, that even Winslow doesn't ask him what he is doing. But that Cavendish holds himself above all this."

"Which is why these things happen," Pierre said through clenched jaws. He was pressing his arm against Claude's, trying to force it down to the soft brick floor. "Gentlemen hold themselves above it, while we are buried."

"You waste life being always angry, Pierre. Be angry when you can act. What you are feeling—it will destroy you."

"You know what is happening at that river and you ask me not to be angry?"

"I ask you not to have useless anger. If you live with anger each hour of your life, it becomes your master. My anger—it is my servant. It will make me stronger when I can fight." And in a surge of strength he forced Pierre's arm down and held it. For a moment, the anger that had been Pierre's familiar during the past weeks blazed. The arm struggled. Then, it rested. As did Pierre's face. For the first time since Antoine's death, the Pierre that Claude knew looked back at him. He released Pierre's arm, reached and clasped Pierre. "We will not fail, Pierre. You know that we will not."

*   *   *

But as the days of October marched by, the beat of the march a slow funeral dirge, even Claude's discipline began to give way. By now Mathilde and Claude Louis and Jeanne must be on the shore, might be loaded onto one of those treacherous ships. The soldier knew nothing of where the people came from, only that each day another mass of people came through the village on their way to the river, sometimes singing hymns, sometimes praying, always clinging to each other in inconsolable despair.

"I found this along the line of march," the soldier said one day. "Here, what does it mean?" He thrust the fragment of paper at Claude. Claude's eyes went over the familiar words before him, penned with difficulty by some awkward hand.

"Vive Jésus! Vive Jésus! Avec la croix, son cher portage. Vive Jésus! Dans les coeurs de tous les élus! Portons la croix, Sans choix, sans ennui, sans murmure, Portons la croix! Quoique très amère et treès dure, Malgré le sens et la nature, Portons la croix!"

"It's a song—a hymn," he said.

"So what does it mean? That's a change, hearing holy words from your mouth! Tell it to me—no, sing it!"

A remembered sound in Claude's ear. His mother used to sing those words in a low humming voice, making the harshness of the phrase, "Carry the cross," sweet with her quiet acceptance. When had she not done the duties that God had sent her? When had she not risen each day to meet its trials, its troubles, with gentle trust? And now her son would scar her memory forever by making mock of the hymns she loved.

"I will not sing it," Claude said. He turned away, knowing that he would find the priest when he made his daily visit, and confess. A heavy hand dropped on his shoulder and he was spun around.

"You will sing it. You forget how little choice you have."

Claude waited for anger to strengthen him. He would flatten that hated British face with one blow from his fist; he would, for one moment at least, be a man again. And then he heard his own voice saying, with a strength that did not spring from anger, "He is your Christ, too. Do you wish him scorned?"

For a space of two heartbeats, the hand kept its grasp. Then Claude felt it loosen, saw the derision in the soldier's eyes replaced with a look that might even have been respect.

The soldier spoke with him in a new way now; no longer did Claude have to trade rude jokes for a precious word of English. "You need to learn the language, yes. No telling where you'll end up." A kind of pained embarrassment came over the man's face whenever their attention turned to the river. "At least it's almost over," he said one afternoon. "The fleet sails day after tomorrow."

So this part of their ordeal was ending. No matter what the next stage brought, at least it would be new. He needed the exercise of dealing with new pain, he was quite worn out with this old one. He had never mentioned Mathilde's name to this Englishman; he had steered away from casual questions about his wife, his family. In the beginning, when he had learned that all the ships would sail at once, convoyed by three war ships as though to a prison colony, he had told himself that he would find Mathilde and Claude Louis and Jeanne when the men from the church joined the miserable cargo at the river's edge. He had kept to that hope for many days, until he could no longer hide from that terrible chaos of deportation. Unless a miracle almost as great as the parting of the Red Sea occurred, he would never see his family again. Well, with every one of them needing a miracle, he should not count on his prayers being heard—unless all he asked for was a small bit of luck.

"Do they keep passenger lists for those ships?"

"Lists? Yes, of course."

"Then it is possible to know where one's ... one's family is."

He knew that all the desolation of his soul lay naked on his face.

"Man, there are over thirty ships out there."

He saw the sympathy in the other man's face, knew that the first allegiance of kind to kind was stronger now than any false division made by man. "But if one had the lists—"

The soldier shrugged. "Yes, if one had them. Colonel Winslow, now, he has copies. But—" Another shrug. A shrug that meant, *But the Winslows of this world care nothing for you. The names on that list are evidence only, evidence that he has performed his task, and rid this Nova Scotia of the Acadian blight.*

Hateful to feel his mind clawing at the walls around it, seeking futilely for some opening. Hateful to feel that his tiny weapons, his growing knowledge of a rough but usable English, his growing physical strength, had failed at the first obstacle. And then he thought of Cavendish. The man had been kind to him once, had seen Claude as a fellow human being, who needed comfort, food, sleep.

"Lieutenant Cavendish—is he still here?"

The soldier shot a look at him. "Yes. He keeps to his quarters a lot. Rides that horse of his. I've heard he refused to sail on the flagship of the fleet. Winslow is angry—but what can he do? Cavendish's father has the ear of the king."

"Will you help me see him?"

How well Claude understood the look that crossed the soldier's face! Don't do anything that calls attention to yourself. Obey orders, follow the lead of the man in front of you. Keep your bayonet sharp and your powder dry. Let someone else be the hero; you stay alive. And then the only miracle he would need. Another look. "Yes."

Cavendish, when Claude saw him, seemed cold, remote. The swing of grace which had marked his every move was leaden now; he had been marked by the horror around him, and that mark showed in every line of his face. He will not have the strength to do what I ask, nor the interest either, Claude thought. And yet he was here, he would ask.

"You were so kind when my father-in-law died, sir. And so I make bold to ask—if I could see the ships' lists, could find my wife—"

The cold eyes that had been roaming the room fastened themselves on Claude's face. They stared at Claude, the ice that filled them chilling the cold autumn air with an arctic breath colder than any wind from the pole. "Your wife—" The voice was cold, too. The man is dead, he's a corpse, this is the chill of death.

"Your wife—she was the pretty one, wasn't she? With the baby?"

As though it had happened ten years ago rather than just weeks, Claude remembered the afternoon of Antoine's burial. A breeze from the open sea had plucked at Mathilde's skirts, her shawl, her curls. It had brought color to her cheeks, so that even in her grief she had been radiant. Yes, she was the pretty one. Whom he now knew he would never see again. He must have lost his senses and not known it. The weeks of captivity had robbed him of his reason, or else he would never have ventured here. "I'm sorry for bothering you, sir." He turned toward the door.

"What?"

Some faint warmth crouched at the edge of the chill. Without turning, Claude repeated, "I'm sorry for bothering you."

The laugh was a sound from hell. Claude froze in the blast of that terrible sound, then slowly turned. Cavendish broke off laughing, began to speak, the words coming with great gasps. "You are sorry for bothering me. And I, I sit there knowing that almost three thousand people are crowded into those ships, that the fields they loved are burned, their homes destroyed, the goods they so trustingly packed scattered on the shore. And you are sorry!" The gasps had turned into sobs. "If you had seen what I have seen—" the voice went on. The face before Claude was more ravaged than ever the face of a Christ on His cross. For the first time since September 5, when this long passage began, he was seeing a pain more terrible than his own. The hatred he had struggled against rose in one last surge, then lay vanquished. He, at least, could forgive those who persecuted him. While the persecutors had no one to forgive but themselves.

"What is your wife's name?"

"Mathilde—Mathilde Langlinais. And there is Jeanne, her sister. Boudreaux is her name. Jeanne Boudreaux. And my son, Claude Louis."

Cavendish rose, went to the door. The returning warmth had melted some of the lead. His body, still heavy, had some swing of grace, some quickness of pace. He pushed the door open, spoke to the sentry outside. "Get me the ships' lists." When the sentry stood, not moving, Cavendish's voice rose. "You heard me! The ships' lists. Now!" He slammed the door shut.

They stood waiting, silent. Claude had never felt such tension, such a tightening of every nerve and muscle. In a few moments, the heaviest burden of his bondage could be lifted. He would know where Mathilde and Claude Louis were—and he knew that Cavendish would see that he reached them. A knock at the door, then the sentry entered, a sheaf of long papers in his hand. He took them to Cavendish, hesitated, then, seeing that Cavendish ignored him, was already scanning the long lines of names, looked curiously at Claude, and left.

"They're on the *Endeavor*," he said. "Bound for South Carolina. Well, that's not so bad. The governor there is a gentleman in deed as well as title—James Glenn, a friend of my father's. You should be decently welcomed."

"But it's English?"

"South Carolina? Yes."

"I cannot live on English soil."

Cavendish put down the list. The clarity of reason had come back to his eyes; his face, thrown into floating shadows by the flickering firelight, was less ravaged. "No, of course not." The lieutenant moved to a map that hung behind the worktable. His finger targeted a spot, then rapidly walked across the map. "Come here." Claude, standing in the center of the rough-walled room, felt as though he had suddenly been released from the monstrous fist that had slowly been squeezing his way of life, his family, his very manhood, out of him. Flesh that had been pressed tight against muscles, muscle that had crowded twisted nerves, now had room to stretch—room even to grow.

His eye followed the moving finger until it rested. He saw the familiar French spelling, recognized the word. "Louisiana."

Cavendish swung around. "That's where you should go. Where you must go."

Something was happening in Claude's heart. A feeling he had not known for a long, long time. Then he recognized it. It was hope.

Never would Claude forget the hours that followed his meeting with Cavendish. From a man verging on disordered madness, Cavendish had become the vigorous lord who took it as his right that those around him would obey him. Food had been ordered, and wine. A heavy wool jacket was produced, boots put on Claude's feet. "I would give you money," Cavendish said, "but it would never stay with you aboard the ship."

And then they had gone to the river, where Claude had seen for the first time those harrowing scenes which had been whispered about for weeks until they had assumed almost the quality of stories with no truth in them. He stood, his gaze wandering over the miserable landscape before him. He knew the faces, the names, of these wretched people, but he knew that the beings that had once answered to Clothilde, Marie, Paul, Henri, were no more. Many of them had lost their reason, driven into madness by grief for children torn from their arms, for husbands executed, for wives who died on that cold beach. Many had lost their health on the rack of that terrible month. And all had lost their homes.

He looked at Cavendish's face. It was white, as white as that of any invalid woman. The lips were bitten into so fine a line as to leave no room for words. Cavendish grasped Claude by the arm, pulled him down toward the shore. Not until they reached the sentries guarding the boats that carried this battered cargo out to the ships did he speak. "Take me to the *Endeavor*."

The sentry hesitated. The figure before him was tall and imposing in the well-cut uniform of an officer of his Majesty's army. And the man who wore that uniform made it more imposing still; he was obviously one who had been born to command. "Do you have orders, sir?"

"I have my order to you; that is all you need to know." Before the cold in those blue eyes the sentry gave way. He beckoned to a sailor who idled in one of the boats, whittling a reed from the river.

The ride to the *Endeavor* was the longest part of that voyage into exile. Claude would not think that Mathilde might be dead, he would not think it—he did think it. The faces of the women on shore, many as young as Mathilde, had shown him what despair and hunger and terror and exposure to the elements can do to even the freshest face, the ripest body.

The wait on the deck was interminable. There had been a brief dispute with the ship's captain, a dispute settled when the name Cavendish was spoken. Then the captain had shrugged, the same thing the soldiers used when confronted with this young officer who apparently did not need military channels, as he had more expedient and powerful ones of his own.

A sound behind him. A cry. He turned, and saw Mathilde. In the moment before they embraced, his eyes had etched all the changes in her on his memory and in his heart. As the color gradually leaves a fading rose, so the color had left her face until only the softest shading ivoried the pallor. As fog and mist obscure the brilliance of the stars, her early disbelief that this was happening, her later panic, her final despair, had obscured the brilliance of her eyes, so that only the color and shape of them were the eyes he once knew. The weeks of hunger had eroded the curves of her body. Her dress hung away from her; bones he had not thought to see unless she lived to be ninety strained against their light covering of flesh. "Claude—" It was the voice that finally broke his heart. There was no laughter in it, no hint that it had ever known how to laugh, or tease, or whisper love in his ear. He went to her, took her in his arms, held her so close that each pulse in his body could speak to her, could tell her that she was safe, that whatever lay before them, he, Claude, would conquer; that whoever tried to harm her would give his life, that he would put the light back in her eyes, the color in her cheeks, the flesh on her bones—the laughter in her voice.

The sailors around them were silent. It is perhaps easier to ignore horror than sweetness, to detach oneself from the desecration of humanity than from reminders that humanity will triumph. To men who had watched 121 wretches crowded into that ship, to men who knew that on the month-long voyage ahead there would be little food, no sanitation, not enough places to lie down, little fresh air, and many, many deaths, with no more burial than is given garbage tossed over the rail, the sight of these two clinging to each other was harder to bear than anything they had yet witnessed. Each man had clung to a woman as Claude clung to Mathilde, each man had known the passion that forged Claude's arms so solidly around her, each man had known the reverence a father feels for the woman who had borne him a child. And when Jeanne moved forward, her mouth bravely smiling, to put his son in his arms, the sight of Claude's face became an amulet for those who saw it, an amulet against ever again forgetting what it is to be human.

"My God, this is terrible!" It was Cavendish's voice that broke the silence, that set the frieze of men, temporarily halted in their tasks, back to swabbing the deck, mending ropes, weaving nets, all the while not looking at each other, but at the little family that stood in their midst. "Thank heaven I have choices, though I question my right to have them when I see what happens to those who by accident of birth do not." He turned to the ship's captain. "Perhaps we shall meet again, captain. If we do, I'll not be in this uniform!"

Claude, his right arm around Mathilde, his left cradling his son, heard Cavendish speak his name. The lieutenant was standing before them, the gold braid on his hat glinting in the sunlight as he swept it off. "Lieutenant Cavendish, Madame Langlinais."

In a swift movement, Mathilde crossed the space between them. She took the lieutenant's hand, lifted it to her lips, kissed it. Tears were giving quick brilliance now to her eyes, and over and over again the murmured thanks were offered: "Merci, monsieur, merci, merci, merci."

"I have done nothing, madame, nothing."

"You have done everything," Claude said. He reached out a hand, was met by Cavendish's firm clasp.

"There is an older allegiance than to King George," Cavendish said. And then he turned and disappeared over the side. They heard the thud as he dropped into the waiting boat. The boat came into sight, bobbing on waves whipped up by a freshening breeze. Cavendish sat in the bow, his eyes fixed in some distance beyond the shore. Claude pulled Mathilde around to where they could look past the crowded harbor out to the open sea. "This ship will take us to South Carolina. But we will not stay there." He was his own man again. He had his wife, his son, and a place ahead of him where French people were free.

"Where will we go?" Her head was on his shoulder, a light curl drifted across his skin.

"To Louisiana," he said.

"Louisiana." She said it hesitantly. "And when we get there?" To have those eyes looking up at him again! He could do anything.

"And when we get there, we will build another happy land."

# PART ONE
## *Renascence*

# CHAPTER 1
## *Attakapas*

The insistent, sure sound of a young cock filled the dawn stillness, vibrating it with the promise of the life of the day. Claude Louis Langlinais, pulled from sleep by that bright shrill call, automatically chanted the Angelus to himself, using the words to bridge his night dreams and the morn. Standing, he reached for the heavy gray cotton workshirt hanging near his bed, then paused, strong young hand still stretched before him. Today was no work day. Today was the fête to celebrate his approaching marriage to Cecile—and there, laid carefully across the end of his bed, was the new shirt his mother had made, each strand of cotton that made it grown by her, picked by her, spun by her, woven by her. His mother's face came before him—the weight of the heavy work of resettlement had pulled at her cheeks, drawn lines around her quick eyes, touched her hair with the frost of age; it had not slowed her constant response to her children, to her duties.

As he splashed water on his face, pulled the new shirt over his bare torso, some of the fresh softness seemed to go out of the May morning. There was no way he could remember the four terrible years of pilgrimage from Nova Scotia to Louisiana, no way he could know what his parents Claude and Mathilde Langlinais felt when they finally made their way to this piece of land that stretched along the Bayou Teche in a place the Spanish called the Attakapas Territory, named for the Indians who once held it. That had been twenty years ago, he had been but four years old. But he had grown up on tales of the hardships his parents, all the Acadians, had suffered as they fought, struggled, endured years of exile in New England, along the Atlantic Coast, in Santo Domingo and Texas, always looking toward this Louisiana Territory, which, no matter if the Span-

43

iards now ruled it, had at least been discovered, colonized, first by the French.

Claude Louis went to the small window cut into the heavy clapboards split from cypress logs that formed the sturdy house walls. His eyes followed the low swell of pasture and fields stretching away to the horizon. They were not so wide, his father said, as the fields left behind in Nova Scotia, nor the roads that passed along them so well marked. "But there is one thing, Claude Louis," his father said, bending over and picking up a lump of rich black dirt. "These fields are ours, granted to us." Sifting the black rich dirt through his work-rough fingers, watching that slow, fine fall. "I cleared them, I dug the drainage ditches back to the bayou, built the dikes. I said—corn here. Cotton here. Cane there. You know?" And the black eyes, veiled sometimes with pain, but never dimmed, never dulled, gazed at him. "It is our land, Claude Louis. We are bound to it."

Now, seeing the green spikes of cane, the reaching stalks of young corn, the thick clusters of cotton plants, Claude Louis felt a stirring in himself not unlike, perhaps, the stirring of life in the seeds that had become those flags of green before him. Working along with his father, with his younger brother Julian, either in the fields that provided them with food, cotton fiber for clothing and household needs, or in the swamps trapping the animals whose fur turned into, through the alchemy of the New Orleans traders, money to buy coffee, spices, and other goods that could not be grown from seed or taken with snares, he had been bound up in his own thoughts, his own dreams. The land he conquered with his constant struggles was not, after all, his own. He could walk over it, his sisters Suzette and Bernadine at his side, with little feeling other than that these were long rows to hoe. But when he married Cecile—then he would have a plot to call his. Small, of course. His father would not carve up the large grant the Spanish had given him. But his. His and Cecile's.

Julian was already out in the fields, he saw. At eighteen, Julian thought a man who waited, as Claude Louis had, until he was twenty-four to marry was either a fool or blind to the attractions of the girls in their district. Suzette, whose engagement to Raoul Hebert the summer she was seventeen had been ended when he died of lung fever, became as angry as she ever could when she heard Julian's teasing. "To marry, one sometimes needs more than just anyone who happens along, Julian," she would say. And turn before they saw her tears. She was almost twenty-two now. Claude Louis, who had decided a long time ago that Suzette, a year younger than Bernadine, would never marry, still hoped Suzette would somehow throw off her fears and risk listening to one of the farmers who still paid courting calls on Sunday. "It's hard to hope again, when a loss has been so great," his mother said when he worried about her. And what to say to that? Mathilde spoke almost never of the agony of the four-year passage from Nova Scotia to Louisiana, hardly at all of the difficulties they had faced, new ones, it seemed, with every year and season, as they had made a home in this land.

"But how did you know how to plant crops? A new climate, different soil—"

A shrug. "We just did. We learned. We tried. Sometimes what we did worked—sometimes it didn't."

"And food—how did you know what in the swamp was good to eat? The roots, the plants."

Another shrug. The Indians. Lessons gleaned from other settlers when the men went in to a trading post, or to a gathering where cattle were being swapped.

Now it seemed as though more struggles were in store for him. Claude had said they were bound to his land. But did that matter? Had it mattered to the British king who first drove them from Nova Scotia? Would it matter to the British king George III, whose angry American colonists had taken their grievances to the field?

The men in the settlement had talked, more and more as the early months of 1779 greened into spring, of what would happen if the Spanish king decided to take sides. Claude Louis hung at the cluster's edge, silent, respectful, listening. On Saturdays, when Chevalier Alexandre, commandant of the Attakapas District, held court to settle the minor fusses between neighbors which could be adjudicated here, the size of the crowd in his low rooms had little to do with the number of complaints to be heard. What brought the Acadians together was the concern that their land was, once more, not safe against the rapacious carelessness of kings at war.

The young smell of his mother's climbing rose, which trailed over pegs to frame the windows, tickled Claude Louis. Sacrebleu! Kings could wait. Cecile LeBlanc was even now curling her black hair around small, slender fingers, tossing the ringlets so that they framed her face in ruffling wisps that begged a man's hands to touch them. She was settling a dress over her petticoats, tying the bodice over those curving breasts, the sight of which had kept him from the communion rail more than once. His own fingers seemed not to want to obey him, he felt his body seem to go away from him, to become weak—zut! If just thinking about Cecile did this, what would being her husband do?

Mathilde slid a bowl of couche-couche in front of Claude Louis, put a pitcher of milk, a bowl of raw sugar, near. "I thought you'd forgotten what day this is and had gone on out to the fields," she said. Claude Louis saw the teasing laughter in her eyes, caught the reflection of it in his father's, who was sitting at the end of the table drinking coffee.

As he looked at them, Claude Louis saw his parents as not only papa and mama, but as Claude and Mathilde Langlinais, known throughout the Attakapas District as among the earliest settlers, the ones who had offered guidance and support, food and comfort, to their exiled brethren who had followed them over long decades of privation and pain. His mother had once been as young as Cecile! His father as young as himself! He saw the droop of his mother's body, a droop that had been set by years bending over a hoe, a spinning wheel, a low hearth cooking fire. The fatigue that pulled at her face, so that though Mathilde laughed more frequently now, though her eyes were filled with light again, her smiles had to lift against deep lines left by hard work and harder suffering. Claude seemed, to his eldest son, made almost of the same tough hide that grew stronger the longer it was left in the beating sun, the penetrating rain. His age showed only in the even gray of his hair and brows. Though Claude Louis had never heard his parents speak of that first young home in Grand Pré, or heard his mother mourn all she had lost, he knew that those early strokes of pain had indeed left wounds that were open still.

Claude Louis' thoughts turned to his new life. Cecile had had quite enough struggle in her life already. He would see to it that her freshness was not stolen by work beyond her strength, troubles beyond her endurance. To have a wife whose eyes remained young, whose voice never lost laughter—now that was something to strive toward! He bent over his breakfast, his energies concentrated now on the food before him.

"When you've finished breakfast, I want to show you something," Claude said. He went to the open cabin door, stood framed by the blue light that stood tall above the thin green of the pastures. "I think we'll put the table under the big oak," he said to Mathilde. "And put blankets out for the little ones to sit on. Claude Louis, all the LeBlancs are coming, yes?"

Claude Louis forked ham into his mouth. There was a small pause in the busy sounds his mother was making at the hearth, where great pots of gumbo and stew were already simmering. His mother did not like Cecile. She was not enchanted by soft black curls, not charmed by quick brown eyes. She had come back from an afternoon of trousseau sewing at Madame LeBlanc's recently with lips as thin as needles. Claude Louis had heard his mother talking with Suzette and Bernadine. "She is pretty, yes. But who is young and not pretty? While we sewed sheets, she made flowers on pillow covers." The strength of his mother's voice was punctuated by her great eyes, which were, he knew, wide with expressive shock. "Flowers on pillow covers! When she doesn't have enough sheets to half fill an armoire."

"But, maman—" That was Suzette, ever the peacemaker. "But maman—you know what a terrible life she had—all the LeBlancs—in Massachusetts. Maman. If a few flowers make her happy now?"

"Life is not all flowers," his mother said. But the anger was gone, only a weariness left. And Claude Louis thought, once more, how much he owed that gentle sister.

"Yes. They are all coming. Even the old aunt who arrived just last month." He drank the last of his coffee. "This won't take long? What you want to show me. I told Cecile I'd come get her . . . she doesn't like . . ."

Again the small pause in the busyness—then his father spoke. "No. Not long. There's time."

They walked along the hole-pocked road that late May morning, past a ditch filled with buttercups, past a red-winged blackbird whirring up from the tall pasture grass. An image of Mathilde flashed before Claude. At every wedding, every birthing, every death, the grace and ease of Mathilde's sure instinct increased joy, softened grief. Her courage, the way that straight spine was held, those smiling lips, sent shadows of fear back into the darkness from whence they came, and made all promise bright. She did not like Cecile LeBlanc, did not think she would know how to be a wife—nor want to. But she would not let her son—or herself—down. Claude's breath eased into the scented air. Men who saw her now for the first time saw only the energy, the decisiveness, that made their own wives turn to her. He saw her as she was before the weight of childbearing had pulled at her stomach and breasts, he saw her as she was when he had taken her, twenty-five years ago, shy, trembling, yet curious and trusting enough to forget her fear, to the bed he had carved for them. May the good Lord make Cecile such a wife!

They stopped at the opening in the hedge that surrounded the first field of what had been the Gaspard farm. "This is a rich farm, yes," Claude said.

Claude Louis pulled a stalk of sweet grass, chewed it idly. His eyes swept over the land before him with the appraising, searching look of the born farmer—never would his plow break on an overlooked stone, never would his cows drop calves carelessly in the field. "Too bad the Gaspards couldn't keep it—though with the last of the men gone—who will buy it, do you know?"

"It's already been bought." Why was he dragging it out so? Why was it so hard to simply tell his son that this farm, fertile, cleared, waiting for his hand upon it as a woman waits for her lover, was his? He knew the answer. When a man brings his children into a world of loss and deprivation, when each meal is wrenched from the resisting forest or bartered for during a four-year pilgrimage, then giving up is a habit, giving is not. Too many times his children had gone without, been hungry, been cold. They had borrowed his courage, their mother's laughter, tested themselves against hardship, and won. His voice could not get around the love that filled him, he knew that he would weep.

He felt Claude Louis' hand, the warmth like that of the sun-drenched soil that holds its memories of the day's heat long after moonrise. "Papa—have you bought it?"

"Yes. For you."

It was fine when a son became a man; you could weep with a man as you could not with a woman. They walked into the first field, bending over to crush the earth between their fingers, lifting it to smell its promise of harvest. "This will be a farm to make you proud, papa! Cecile and I will have many sons, they will work with me, and when you are tired of working, you will sit under that big oak and watch us continue what you have begun." He is as tall as I am, Claude thought as his son's eyes looked at his from so exact a level that a surveyor's measure might have been laid between them. Again the large hand closed on his shoulder. "Papa. Cecile will have good sons. She will be a good wife."

Claude broke from that trusting gaze. "Good husbands make good wives," he said. "Unless a man is blessed enough to marry a woman like your mother. She came as she is from God's hand, and I have thanked Him every day of my life."

"As I thank Him for Cecile," Claude Louis said, and Claude heard a voice that came from a new place in his son's young body. He is ready for a wife, for land, he thought.

Suzette and Bernadine were setting out plates and mugs on the long table under the big live oak tree in front of the cabin. Mathilde's finest cloth, the lace and linen one she had brought from Nova Scotia pinned like a petticoat under her skirts, covered it; someone had placed a pitcher of roses in the center, and their sweet pinkness echoed Bernadine's cheeks.

"Pretty," Claude Louis said, gesturing to the roses. "Cecile will like that."

Bernadine straightened her blue cotton apron and lifted a moist tendril of hair from her forehead. "Are you frightened, Claude Louis?"

"Of what?"

"Of getting married?"

Claude Louis looked at his sister. Her body was slim, pliant with youth. He had not really seen how pretty Bernadine was until he had known Cecile, cared about a woman's beauty. Some man would want Bernadine for a wife, why hadn't he seen that? He remembered the boys who somehow found their way to the path Bernadine walked to church, or who hung over their fences when she went by. A sudden jealousy of the man who would wed Bernadine, take this sister out of his life, swept over him. Zut! Cecile's brothers probably felt this same way about him.

"It doesn't take courage to marry," he said.

"It doesn't? Then if the funny feeling goes away, a feeling of being scared, you know? If that goes away, does that mean you should marry?"

"Now what does that mean?" he asked to the quickly empty

air. Bernadine, laughing, had darted into the house, where he could hear her light, happy voice making his mother laugh.

"I think Bernadine will marry, too, Claude Louis. Soon, maybe." Suzette's calm gray eyes rested on Claude Louis' face. Some of her quiet drifted over Claude Louis, slowed his heat-warmed blood. Suzette was already the steady, dependable spinster she would no doubt remain. Mathilde often said, with the only heartfelt sigh she allowed herself, that were there an order of nuns to take her, Suzette would have become a bride of Christ. As it was, Claude Louis saw a coventlike routine in his sister's life. She marked the hours of her day with prayer, spending leisure time before the little grotto her father had built in a far corner of the kitchen garden. And Claude Louis knew that many of the little services that eased his life, made it go more smoothly, he owed to her.

"And you?" Did his words hurt her? But the gray eyes were calm still, smiling.

"I think not."

Claude Louis bent, kissed her thin cheek. He could smell the good aroma of roasting pig, pushing its way into the moist air that made the region one great hothouse, so that seeds sprouted almost as soon as they were put into the rich black earth. "I'll go help papa," he said.

Rounding the corner of the cabin, Claude Louis paused to watch his father carefully lift the broad palmetto leaves that had been laid over the pit, wetted down with bayou water, making a thick layer to keep the slow heat deep in the leaf-lined hole. Earlier, when he had clasped his father's shoulder, he had been startled, dismayed, to feel the small looseness in those hard muscles. Now, seeing his father move, Claude Louis knew that Claude was old, worn; the still easy strength was like a last beam of powerful light shot up by a dying sun. He lifted a hand, brushed his eyes.

"Smells good, huh?" Claude said. He stood back from the pit, sniffed the rich smell of roast pork that drifted upward. "I hope those LeBlancs bring empty stomachs, yes."

"They will. And possibly little else." Claude Louis looked around him. Had he said those words? They seemed to hang in the smoke before him, waiting for him to grab them back.

Claude patted his son's arm. "Now, Claude Louis. The LeBlancs, they're good people. A little close with what they have. Stingy, even. But you know, they didn't have it as easy as we did. They've not been here so long, been able to do so well."

"I know that. But sometimes, papa, when I'm with them, I wonder almost where Cecile came from. No one else in her family knows how to have a good time, to laugh—"

"She makes up for that," Claude said. He looked at the sun's shadow, casting now only half the length of the young pine he marked the time by. "You'd better start out, son, if you're not going to keep Cecile waiting."

He watched Claude Louis go, moving a little slowly at first, then quickening his step, then almost bounding in leaps across the rain-scarred mud. Claude's own heart remembered well the restlessness that turned a young lover's steps into leaps, his pulse beats into thunder. There was no question that the doll-like Cecile, small, playful, pretty, was more than enough to stir that restlessness into passion. But he feared Mathilde was right. Claude Louis was not the first man to be so enamored of promised pleasures that he did not serve himself well when it came to choosing a wife. Cecile had, after all, been spawned by that dour man, raised by that bitter mother, grown up with those solemn brothers. Whatever she knew about family, she had learned there. And no matter how much one would like to stay in bed forever, one could not really do so. Well! He would find Mathilde.

Claude Louis stood with Cecile to welcome their guests to the fête. Cecile had woven daisies and roses into a wreath and crowned her dark hair; the deep flush in her cheeks challenged the color of roses, and the brightness in her eyes took its sparkle from the radiance of sun caught in the droplets from yesterday's rain that still clung to grass blades.

As Claude Louis looked about him he saw Chevalier Alexandre, finished with his official duties, mixing with the other guests. Despite the immense humanity and compassion he brought to his dealings with the Acadians who filled his district, his first responsibility was to the governor in New Orleans— and beyond that, to King Carlos III in far-off Madrid. As he walked toward the engaged couple, hands tugged at him, voices hailed him. "Alexandre! What news from New Orleans?"

Then a louder voice, one forceful and at the same time light, rose above the women's chatter, the men's questions. "The news is that Carlos the Third has declared war against England.

He's come out on the side of the American colonists."

Claude Louis' head jerked in the direction of that familiar voice. Uncle Pierre, by God. And if anyone besides Chevalier Alexandre would know what the Spanish king was doing, it would be Pierre. He went frequently to New Orleans, taking furs from the trappers in the district, returning with store goods they couldn't grow or find in the woods and swamps around their farms. Now Pierre was the center of a circle of men; Claude Louis could see the feathered cockade that topped Pierre's broad-brimmed gray hat bobbing like the cork on a fishing line as he fed news to the hungry ears around him. Claude Louis strained to hear his words. "New Orleans is full of it," Pierre said. "And although the king has said nothing about fighting on this continent"—the feather bobbed more violently as Pierre's head felt the force of an elaborate shrug—"where, in all of America, are the Spanish and British closer neighbors than in Louisiana?"

Claude Louis' mind saw the stretch of the Mississippi River, with British forts rising at Baton Rouge and Natchez, two other posts guarding the approaches to the river between these points. He had always stayed in Attakapas, helping his father; he'd not had contact with the redcoats. Nor had anyone else. But Pierre occasionally ventured north up the Mississippi after a foray to New Orleans to trade with the soldiers at Fort Manchac near Baton Rouge. A sorry place, he had called it, after the civilized life in New Orleans. But then, what could you expect of the English?

"Will there be war here?" His father's voice, low, steady, cut under the crowd noise.

Pierre shrugged again. "Who can say? But they talk of Galvez as one to want war."

"Alexandre!" His father's voice rose again, demanding. "Do you know more than what Pierre has said? Will the war be carried to Louisiana?"

Alexandre's shoulders, eyebrows, lifted. "Only what my soldier's bones tell me. If you are Galvez—a young general, eager to make a name, a career—if an old enemy of your country is fighting for her life, and has a few outlying posts around your territory—what would you do?"

"But has it been ordered?" Claude Louis heard the sword of pain cutting the edge of his father's voice. He knew that his father—as he was—was thinking of the militia. That Claude Louis belonged to it. And that it might be called.

The look Alexandre gave Claude had the length and breadth of years behind it. He had come to Poste des Attakapas to bring, like the first chevalier before him, assurance, advice, and help. He would like to help these people now. But if the strong-willed Galvez wished to seize British forts with one hand while he seized his rising fortunes with the other, what assurance, what advice, what help, could save them? "Not that I know."

Pierre stepped forward, circled his brother-in-law's shoulders with one great arm. "Come! This is a fête! Let kings play games—we have serious business today. Dancing, singing, feasting. Kissing pretty girls!" he said, leaning over and kissing the forehead of a young cousin standing near.

"That's right!" Cecile cried. She broke away from Claude Louis took the center where Pierre stood, began chanting one of the songs they'd all learned as children. As her light voice sang, her feet began to move to the song's rhythm; soon she was making a small weaving dance, alone, the sun lifting golden lights from her dark hair, bobbing up and down in the center of a circle of eyes. "Dansez, mes enfants, tandis que vous êtes jeunes; Bientôt arrivera que ma fille me fera grandmère; Au lieu de danser la gavotte, dans un grand fauteuil on radote!" (Dance, my children, while you are young; Soon my daughter will make me a grandmother; Instead of dancing the gavotte, one gossips idly in a big armchair.) Others began to dance, fiddles were brought out, partners chosen. Claude went to find Mathilde. "Today we forget the king," he told her. "All kings. After all, we beat the first one, didn't we? We found again our happy land."

"I wonder if the LeBlancs think so," Mathilde said. Claude followed the pure line of her gaze; she was watching Madame LeBlanc watch Cecile and Claude Louis. Cecile was dropping her wreath of flowers over Claude Louis' head. He had bent down toward her so that her small length could stretch up to meet his—their bodies were silhouetted against the bright earth behind them, and knowing that they were to wed, one could take that silhouette into closer darkness, into naked sleep.

"Their life has been hard," he said. "That marks people."

"The LeBlancs' life?" Where had that note in Mathilde's

voice come from, she who never complained. She caught his hand, held it to her breast. "Their life? Claude, do you remember our life?"

"Claude Louis has chosen, Mathilde. The LeBlancs must know Cecile could have no better husband."

"True, she could not. But Claude Louis could, perhaps, have a much better wife!" Then she closed her full lips down, made them into a firm line that held her words back. She went, deliberately and slowly, to where Madame LeBlanc sat, observing but not part of, judging but not entering, the scene before her. The low rocker Claude had made from a huge cypress he felled the first week they'd been in Attakapas had been set, with other chairs, under one of the big oaks. Madame LeBlanc was enthroned there, the impatient motion of her foot against the grass rocking the chair across the root-heavy earth. Mathilde dropped into a straight chair next to her, began talking.

Claude Louis touched Cecile's arm. "See the chair your mother is sitting in? That's the first piece of furniture papa made, once we got here. Hearing maman tell about it was one of my favorite stories, when I was little." His eyes were not on the bright face beside him, a face that gradually dimmed as Claude Louis' voice took on the warmth of his own family lore. "We were living in a lean-to, with hides covering the opening. There was me, and Bernadine and Suzette—they'd been born on the way here—and then Gaston he'd been born in New Orleans while papa and maman waited to be assigned to a settlement. So when maman nursed Gaston she had no chair, nothing but a pallet of hides on the floor. Papa says he will never forget the way she looked at him when he pushed aside the hide covering the door and put the rocker beside her, and lifted her and Gaston into it."

"I guess not," Cecile said, sunlight shimmering in her tossing curls. "It's so rough—it's not a bit pretty."

"Pretty!" The word burst from Claude Louis, almost a shout. "I guess not! Papa had all he could say grace over just to make it, much less decorate it." He looked down at Cecile, saw the quick fright in her eyes. He took one small warm hand in his. "But, Cecile—what I make for you—or buy for you—there's time, money, for things to be pretty, too."

He felt the flutter of Cecile's hand, the whisper of her breath on his neck as she spoke: "Oh, Claude Louis—I don't know why it matters so much—but I do like things nice!"

The two fathers were standing, readying the toasts to the bridal couple. Claude Louis allowed himself to be pushed forward, Cecile laughing and blushing beside him, to a position directly in front of the table where the wine was set out. His eyes went to the rocking chair Madame LeBlanc had just left. Its rockers were still moving, bumping on the rough ground. He felt a shiver chase down his back, and wondered where it came from. There could be no chill in the May air, that wasn't possible. He looked at the girl beside him; her promising smiles and hinting curves surely bespoke joy, felicity? The shiver chased again. He called it lust.

"Papa sounds as though he were reading at a funeral," Cecile said. Claude Louis watched her lower lip droop into a pout, her little sulky manner creep over her fresh body, giving each movement a rebellious twist. That had been her second attraction, after her beauty. Unlike the girls who smiled and giggled and blushed at the least word, the smallest attention, Cecile LeBlanc remained quiet, pouting. It had been a challenge to make her laugh, see her happy. And he had succeeded. Would succeed.

"But it is not a funeral," he said, taking her warm hand and squeezing it. "It's the beginning of our life. Our happy life."

"I hope so," Cecile said. "I like to be happy!"

Papa's toast isn't much better, Claude Louis thought. He heard the stilted, almost formal words, heard his father try to make love gild the edges of those solemn sounds. Heard him hasten to finish so the musicians could start up again. Claude Louis knew his father wasn't purely glad about this match and couldn't pretend to be. Claude Louis lifted his own glass, began his response to the toasts. His eyes sought Cecile's. No one was marrying Cecile but himself. And he thought she was perfect.

"It was a lovely fête, maman," Suzette said when the LeBlancs were gone, putting gentle arms around her mother. "Your bread was wonderful, some of the lightest you've ever made."

A smile began to work itself through the frown in Mathilde's eyes. "I hope Cecile thought so. A bride should like her mother-in-law's cooking, no matter how good her own is."

"Don't tease, maman," Claude Louis said. He sat opposite his father, a pipe like Claude's clamped between his lips. The mild smoke was like his voice: he had a pretty bride, a lovely bride, a young bride. Old women thought of bread, young men thought of love. "You know that if Cecile makes bread at all, it probably has lumps. Or doesn't rise."

"Which is wonderful!" Suzette said. "See, maman, she will learn from you. After all—" Suzette laughed, a coaxing laugh, asking Mathilde to remember that anyone who lived under any influence not Langlinais had not yet lived at all. "After all, she will want to be like you, you will see." Now Mathilde was smiling, now she could enjoy discussing the fête with Suzette and Bernadine, going over each detail, remembering each triumph, each near catastrophe.

"Where's your brother?" Claude asked Claude Louis.

Claude Louis laughed. "Julian decided that the Marcantels couldn't possibly get home unless he walked with Charlotte. Didn't you see him making big calf's eyes at her all day?"

"And you, you don't make calf's eyes at Cecile?" Bernadine said. She shook the big wooden spoon she was holding at her brother. "You'd think no one ever was going to get married before in the whole world!"

"They aren't," Claude Louis said. "This is the most important wedding in the entire world—the most important thing that will happen this whole summer."

"Have you forgotten what your uncle Pierre said?" Claude's voice came from behind the cloud of pipe smoke, from a face hidden in shadow. But the voice, the words, were clear. And the fear.

Claude Louis turned. "Do you think Galvez will fight? Call the militia?"

Claude signaled to his son to move closer, away from the women's busy talk and busier ears.

"You heard all that I heard. Even if Galvez doesn't start something—can the British be trusted?"

Claude Louis spat into the hearth. "Not from what you've told me. Sacrebleu! They drove my parents from fields that would have been mine—they sent my mother, my old nurse, onto a crowded, leaking ship, out to a sea that nothing had but storms, illness, death. Trust them! How?"

"We can't. This declaration of war by Carlos could be just what they've been waiting for, those English. More land to rape and plunder. More fields to ruin, more wells to poison." Claude stopped. The smoke was thick in front of him, hiding his eyes, but Claude Louis knew that the pain he sometimes caught in his father's face was gathered there now, huddled against the threatened onslaught.

Claude Louis' thoughts went to the farm his father had shown him, those cleared and fertile fields. His hands itched to till that soil almost as much as they itched to touch, to stroke, Cecile. Now he might not live to sow seed in his bride's soft belly, much less in those fields that would lie fallow until spring. Mon Dieu, this business of being a man was hard cheese sometimes!

"Papa." He leaned forward, put big hands on Claude's knees. "There is more to being a man than taking a wife. More than farming one's land. A man defends what is his. You, my uncle, other men of Grand Pré—you fought in your own way. Do you not think I can fight in the way given to me? And if that way is with a gun—can't I handle a gun? Shoot as well as any man?"

"You have never killed a man, Claude Louis." The shrug moved through the smoke, wafting it closer to Claude Louis. "A deer, a wild pig—but a man?"

Claude Louis stood, his shadow black and large against the wall behind him. "When a man wishes to plunder my land and terrify my wife—he is not much of a man, papa. I should have no difficulty killing him."

They set the wedding for the third Saturday in July. Mathilde and Suzette and Bernadine joined the LeBlancs in completing Cecile's trousseau, which, because of the short time the LeBlancs had been in the settlement, seemed, to Mathilde, pitifully inadequate. "We'll add to your dower chests, too," she told her daughters. "Perhaps when Cecile sees what a bride should bring to her husband, she will use those fingers to weave blankets instead of garlands."

While the cotton and cane and corn grew high in the fields around the cabin, petticoats and bed linens and tablecloths grew on every available surface inside. Cecile and Madame LeBlanc came one afternoon to sew with the Langlinais women. Claude Louis, coming in at midafternoon for black coffee and biscuits, felt the storm of tension in the air of the close-ceilinged room. Madame LeBlanc's chair—Mathilde's rocker—had been pulled away from the others. She sat stiffly, her neck angled over the work in her lap. Cecile was on a low three-legged stool near the hearth, something lacy in her small hands. Her tongue,

Claude Louis could not help but note, flew faster than her needle; every once in a while she would look at the work in her hands as though she were not quite sure what it was. Mathilde was sewing in earnest, her needle flashing in and out, each long pull of thread making a web to more tightly weave her own around her. Bernadine sewed as she lived, enthusiastically, with great flair. While Suzette was the quiet center, untangling knots, matching thread, pulling out crooked seams.

"Madame LeBlanc, you would like some coffee?" He held out the big pot, letting the steaming aroma make its own invitation.

"I am not accustomed to coffee in the afternoon," she said, the angle of her neck never changing. "When we were in Massachusetts, we often did not have it even for breakfast."

"But you are not in Massachusetts now," Mathilde said. Then her lips bit down over the words as though she were biting thread.

"No, we are not, and isn't that fine?" Cecile said. "I would love coffee, Claude Louis, with lots of sugar, please." She hopped up from her stool, her work sprawling behind her. "I want everything I could not have in Massachusetts, and I want lots of it."

"You have always wanted everything," her mother said. The angle of the neck seemed to bend her words, make them crooked, not good to hear. "You would want everything if you were the queen of France and had her palace."

"And why not?" Cecile's lips cushioned the edge of the cup she drank from. Claude Louis could imagine that softness against the hard surface, how the surface wanted to sink into the softness. "Why should one live badly when one can live well? Why should one sleep on plain pillow slips when one can have them embroidered?"

"Perhaps," said her mother, neck and words still angled, hard, "perhaps because all this frivolousness takes one away from one's real work."

"Zut! Real work. All you think of is cooking and washing and scrubbing. Well, that is not what I like to do, and I shall not do it." She drained the last of her coffee, put the cup down on the table. She lifted her rounded arms over her head, sent a stretching movement down her lithe spine like that of a supple young cat. "I think I'll go back to the fields with Claude Louis and pick some flowers," she said.

While the women watched, she untied the apron that had protected the dark stuff of her skirt from threads and lint, tossed it aside, and danced through the open door. The sound of her high round voice against the bright May air was the only sound in the room. Claude Louis quickly chewed the last biscuit and swallowed his coffee. He looked at his mother, saw the darkness in her face, and left, following the path Cecile had taken from that nerve-taut room.

She was waiting for him, her face lifted to the sun, her light voice lifted in happy song. She reached her hands to him. "Was I very bad, to leave that hot old room and that sticky work to be in the fresh air with you, Claude Louis?" She pulled him next to her, skipped along to keep pace with his long strides. "After all, it isn't my idea to have so many sheets, so many blankets. We'll keep each other warm, won't we, Claude Louis?"

"But there is work, Cecile," he said. The darkness of his mother's face, the quiet silence of Suzette's, the quick darting frown of Bernadine's, still colored his thoughts. "Cooking, cleaning, washing—it does have to be done."

"Don't be such an ogre," she said. "Of course it has to be done. By someone."

While the women sewed, drawing on the stores of cloth woven from their own cotton, dyed with peach leaves, and with indigo from the Natchitoches settlement, Claude Louis built his house. Claude and Julian helped as they could; at the height of the growing season, when weeds pulled in the morning seemed to have sprung back doublefold at night, there was little time to spare. "A man should marry in winter when there's not so much to do," Julian grumbled one morning as he split clapboards for the house. By rising when only the gradually graying sky spoke of dawn, they managed to give Claude Louis an hour before their own chores pulled them back to fields and pasture.

"I'll help you when it's your turn," Claude Louis said, slapping his brother's rump. "We'll get the roof on tonight. Uncle Pierre and his boys are coming."

"Good. Uncle Pierre puts a roof on to stay, isn't that right, papa?"

Claude, hefting a stack of clapboards to carry to the almost-finished wall, paused. "Your maman and I'd have had no place to live if Pierre hadn't shown me what to do." It was another often-told tale. Pierre had arrived at Attakapas before Claude and Mathilde. His wife, his two infants, had died on the voyage. When he reached South Carolina, he had bullied his way through any difficulty, had been among the first to make the journey halfway across a dangerous continent to the river that would take him home.

"It was home I was going to, I knew that," Pierre told them. "I let nothing stop me, I was driven as though by hunter hounds. It was not until I reached this place, had my land, built my cabin—and married again—that I knew peace." Like all children growing up in Poste des Attakapas, Claude Louis, his sisters, his brother, could recite the way stations of the Acadian exile like the Stations of the Cross. Massachusetts, Connecticut, New York. Halifax, Maryland, Pennsylvania. South Carolina, and Georgia. Those that had reached Virginia had been allowed to remain only four months before being shipped to England; in Pennsylvania, a law was passed forcing Acadian parents to give up their children to the service of private families. But the Acadians sent to Massachusetts had fared by far the worst; Cecile had been born there, and even her shimmering life was weighted by the darkness of her early years.

That night, Claude Louis felt a bursting joy as he helped his uncle, his father, his brother, and his cousins roof his house. The walls were strong and sturdy, the chinks between the clapboards filled with a mixture of clay and moss, a paste almost like the mud the children delighted in playing in down at the bayou's edge. There was nothing left but to smooth that paste over the inside walls to make an even surface, fit shutters and doors into the waiting frame—and take Cecile home.

"It's a good house," Claude Louis said, watching Pierre put the last few split shingles in place.

Claude, standing beside him, looked not at his son but at the smoke that did not so much rise from his pipe in the heavy night air as waft gently through it, thickening it for a moment, then dissolving. "And Cecile? Will she like this house?"

"Why would she not? It's what we all live in."

"She seems to like—fine things. And I'm not sure she— wants to take care of a house, Claude Louis. Your maman doesn't gossip, mon fils."

Claude Louis remembered Mathilde's heated reports, kept from him at first, but finally filtered to him through his sisters' concern, his brother's wonder. "Maman said when Madame

Gaudin was dying and her daughter couldn't leave the new infant to nurse her, Cecile wouldn't take a turn sitting with her. She said she doesn't like ugly old women. Claude Louis—" Suzette, questioning. "At the Heberts' today, we were shelling beans to dry—and Cecile did nothing! Not one bowlful!" Bernadine, angry, worried. And Julian. "Claude Louis, if Cecile doesn't cook—what will you eat?"

"Papa! You must remember—Cecile has to make up for all those years in Massachusetts. She didn't have the kind of childhood Suzette and Bernadine had." But even as he heard his own words, meant to convince his father, he heard their falseness. Suzette and Bernadine had not been cruelly treated, badly used—but they had worked, like everyone in this struggling settlement, from the time they were old enough to toddle to a hen's nest and carry eggs in a small apron. "Anyway, we're not married yet," he said. "When this is her house, when she doesn't have her mother . . ." He turned from the soft understanding in his father's eyes.

Two weeks later, standing beside Cecile in the nave of the church, Claude Louis saw the enchantment of the curls falling around her face, the enticement of the bodice that hid and yet revealed her full breasts, but saw nothing of the art that arranged both. With so pretty a face across the table, why care what one ate! And with so rich a body in bed, what mattered the number of sheets in the armoire? He looked out over the people in the church, their clothing dark against the summer-blooming flowers that were massed in bouquets. Alexandre's military uniform stood tall and bright against the civilian garb around him; the gilded sword riding low on his hip was secure in its scabbard now—but for how long? For the first time in weeks, Claude Louis really thought of war.

He looked down at Cecile. Did that sword shadow her, too? But like all brides, she of course did not expect disaster to be a witness to her wedding. She did not know that in forts along the Mississippi River redcoated soldiers might even now be readying their guns, white-breeched legs could be moving in marching order. Could the greed for conquest that made these kings, be they French or English or Spanish, look ever on a neighbor's land, swallow this new Acadia as it had devoured the old?

Claude Louis felt his spine grow straight and firm. He had

cut his teeth on the hard memories of his father of those terrible days in the church at Grand Pré. His father had told him of his vow, when he stood and faced the Cross and said he would not rest until no man on earth could bring harm to him, or to those he loved. And his father had done that. Shepherded his family across miles of wilderness, supported Mathilde through the first grief of burying Jeanne in that wilderness, of later losing an infant son to the cold damp of his first Louisiana winter. Turned away from the ruin the English had wrought, turned toward a new land. Claude Langlinais had lived his vow.

And now, if war came? If the forts along the river held, if Galvez could not after all drive the British from the territory, send them to whatever hellhot-blooded Spanish generals conjured up for old enemies, what then? The Acadians were not unarmed, this time. They were not dupes, this time. Like the colonists in those faraway towns and villages and farms and fields who had finally risen up to throw off their false lord, the Acadians would rise up. They would call the Indians from the swamps, they would go against those lines of redcoats, not in lines, but like shadow-spirits among the trees. They would hunt down and trap the British as they hunted and trapped the low-lying swamp. Because though Cecile did not like to think of it, though her lower lip was never so full, never set in so drooping a pout, as when someone spoke of coming war—she would have to understand that he was a man, and there are things a man must do.

Father Jean François stepped forward, put Cecile's hand in Claude Louis'. The words that bound them together for all their lives seemed short and small indeed—how could so great an adventure begin so quietly! Cecile's eyes seemed as large as the round window high over the altar, her small frame seemed tiny against the columns soaring to the roof. Her tongue trembled, stammered her vows. Only the touch of her smooth hand made her seem a woman. His own hand was callused with work, some of it building this very church. The Capuchin who first traveled the territory had spurred the men of Attakapas on, telling them that civilized men build churches, barbarians build forts. Their children would be baptized here, his and Cecile's. Married here. And if he had to kill a regiment of redcoats to keep it safe, he could!

Later, watching Cecile dance with his father at the wedding fête, watching the lithe movement of her small body, Claude

Louis tried to imagine those quickly moving feet walking the fields, that slender body big with child.

His eyes went to his sister Bernadine, who was standing with Mathilde and Madame LeBlanc. The late sun of the July afternoon was screened by the branching oaks around the church, but the light that filtered through the green shading touched Bernadine with gold. She stood with her dark hair gilded, the cream of her skin brushed with rose. At the end of the day, she and Etienne Aucoin would announce their engagement— "I'm not scared anymore," she had told Claude Louis. "Now that's a woman who can laugh and work, too," he said.

"Not like your bride," a voice behind him said.

He turned to find André LeBlanc at his elbow, a glass of wedding wine in his hand. The look on LeBlanc's face was a strange one—pride in Cecile's beauty, embarrassment at her uselessness? The man must have taken many glasses to say such a thing about his daughter—to her husband. "She's been spoiled, I'm afraid," LeBlanc said. "Perhaps you don't care?"

"She is my wife," Claude Louis said, and went to claim her.

The flower-decked wagon waited for them, horses patiently pulling at the long summer grass. "Let's go," Cecile whispered, a light inside her glowing as through the open shutters of a lantern. She looked eager, excited, as Claude Louis lifted her to her place in the wagon, and as he climbed beside her, he heard a matron mutter behind her hands that no bride should look so ready for the marriage bed. His eyes went to his mother, standing in the circle of his father's arm. Seeing them, he knew that the rites he and Cecile would soon celebrate his parents celebrated still—as he picked up the reins, whistled to the horse, he wondered if he and Cecile would last so long, if the young passion he felt now would become richer, better, as their marriage aged. He glanced at the girl beside him. The sun still filled the sky with light. It was high summer, dark would come late. In that clear light, Cecile's face seemed to be no age at all—not that of a child nor yet that of a woman. Her lips were parted, her eyelids half hid those glowing eyes. "Cecile!" She turned, staring. "Cecile!"

Then she laughed, a puppet, a doll, suddenly alive. "Claude Louis! Can't you make these horses go faster?"

They lay in the bed Claude Louis had built, on the mattress Madame LeBlanc had made. Moonlight had only been moonlight until Claude Louis saw it on Cecile's slight body; he watched the moonshadow fall across her nakedness, in the very act of hiding it, revealing it more. And though he knew that Father Jean François had this morning pronounced them man and wife, made holy the things he did with Cecile, and the feelings that had so long demanded this release, he wondered why he felt that he was lying, not with his wife, but with a stranger.

# CHAPTER 2

## *Manchac*

During the first week of their marriage, when Cecile slipped back into sleep when Claude Louis rose, leaving the making of his breakfast to him, Claude Louis said nothing. When a woman has brought you such joy, the least one can do is indulge her. After all, Cecile was not accustomed to having a husband. As he was not yet accustomed to the astonishing fact of having that delicate, graceful body in his bed. He had known nothing of women: now he thought that if everyone had a woman like Cecile, the world's work would not get done because no one would get out of bed to do it. As it was, it took all the discipline he had to leave that soft body with all the delightful places he was still discovering, to dress and go out to the fields.

When he finally did speak to her, toward the end of the second week, she fastened her huge eyes on him and said nothing. "Aren't you accustomed to getting up early?" He tried to keep his attention on what he was saying, knowing almost without knowing that if he did not win this first point, the course of their life was set. But his eyes and then his lips and hands kept straying to Cecile's breast—she slept naked, complaining of the heat, though he knew Madame LeBlanc would have allowed no nudity in her house. Then he forgot everything but that lithe body moving under his. After that, he said nothing about Cecile getting up.

The summer days boiled by on the heat that rose from earth and water and the swamp that was both: the vegetation grew as though blown up like tall thin balloons by the stream of heated air that got hotter and hotter as July became August. There was no resting, then. Each day brought its own measure of chores, each week its tasks. Roofs had to be tightened against the coming storm season, preparation for the harvest had to be made. The women had vegetables to dry, fruit to put up. Busy in his fields, Claude Louis could forget everything but his crops—and Cecile.

He walked over to his father's one afternoon to sharpen his hoe on Claude's big grindstone and found his mother sitting in the open door with her hands full of mending. "You should give me that shirt," she said. "That's an old tear on the shoulder, you'll rip the whole back if it's not fixed." She reached out a demanding hand. "Here. I'll sew it while you visit with your father. He's down at the bayou, cooling off." The hand stayed, cutting through the heated air, rigid, waiting. Claude Louis peeled the shirt off and handed it to her. He saw her studying the stains on the front, hallmarks of careless washing. "You can visit a little today, can't you, Claude Louis?"

"Maman, there's so much to do always—"

"On Sunday?" Mathilde clamped her lips in a way Claude Louis seldom saw. He knew the words behind them. That two miles was not so long a road. That Cecile didn't have to give every Sunday to her family—could she not put her feet under the Langlinais table once in a while? Except that those who ate with the Langlinais helped in the kitchen, too. Better go back to her own parents, where she had grown accustomed to doing nothing, to being spoiled.

"Maman—"

"Go see your father," she said between those thin lips. The very thinness of the line her mouth made, shut over words she would not be able to take back, told Claude Louis how angry Mathilde was.

He walked back to the bayou, his shoulders feeling heavy. Picking his way through the rows of his mother's kitchen garden, he unconsciously sorted out the smell of ripening tomatoes from that of okra and beans; he leaned over to pull a radish which he wiped on his trousers and then ate, the white hot flavor waking up taste buds dulled by the heat. He had of course laid out a plot for Cecile's kitchen garden when he cleared the land for the cabin—didn't every housewife have a garden where she grew the vegetables, the herbs, for her kitchen? Already she should be setting out the cauliflower and greens for fall harvest.

He saw his father sitting on a rough bench made from a cypress log, staring out over the rich brown water. The heat of July, August, was heavy. Nothing stirred against that heaviness; small animals, drying grass, hugged the earth, seeking the last bit of winter-moist cool. And in August, there could be hurricanes, mighty storms that tore out of the Gulf of Mexico and raced over the low-lying land that bounded the coast, sucking everything up in terrible fast winds and drenching the earth with pounding dark rains. By the timed the storms reached Attakapas, the winds had usually lessened, but the cane could still be beaten flat in the fields, the harvest ruined.

"You all right, papa?" And when Claude looked around, startled. "I don't know. It's not like you to rest before it's so dark you can't see to work anymore."

"I'm all right. Tired, maybe." He patted the bench next to him. "Sit, son." They sat in silence, watching the smooth water crawl by, burdened by the dirt that washed into it from the fields and slowed its pace. The bayou was named "Teche," the Indian word for snake; one tribal legend told of a great snake that had been killed here. The territory was full of reminders of those earlier people, the Chitimacha and the Attakapas, who still lived nearby. Attakapas meant "man-eater"—supposedly, they ate their prisoners of war. The men traded with them, came to know them, heard their lore, knew their gods.

"Damn the British," Claude said.

"Is that what you're thinking about?"

"They're like a stone in front of my plow, a stone I can't roll away." A long deep sigh, pulled up, it seemed, from the earth at Claude's feet. "You think you're going to reach a place where life will be a little easier, you know? And then—more stones!"

"We Langlinais have never let stones stop us, papa. No matter how many or how big."

"But that takes everyone working, helping. Claude Louis ...I don't like to speak of it... but I cannot help but see it ...and your mother sees also..." He turned his eyes to the fields that ran beside the bayou. The tall corn, waving cane, gave him courage. A man could not build such goodness by himself! "We see that Cecile shirks her duty. She does not cook, she does not clean... your sister Suzette tells us that Cecile spends her days singing, braiding flowers in her hair— while that old aunt does her work." He could feel Claude Louis stiffening beside him, but he would not stop. "That is not the way of our women, Claude Louis. She is making mock of you."

"I know you speak from love for me, papa." The words, coming from that stiff pose, were stiff also, the tone one would use to a stranger. "But you do not understand Cecile. Not even a little bit."

"No, I don't. But if you do, Claude Louis—if you do, I guess we let it go."

"What I understand is that we might even now be at war. After all, it was three weeks after King Carlos declared war on England that we knew of it. All the time we're hoeing weeds and keeping an eye out for hurricanes, New Orleans could be under attack. All right, papa. The work is important. But so is play. And now—when there may not be much time—"

Claude Louis heard the tension in his voice. The atmosphere of August, already heavy enough, stifling enough, had seemed charged with a different tension. Since late July, rumors from New Orleans had first floated like debris on the bayou, then become more active, until now talk of war had pulled ahead of all other interests when the men gathered. It was generally known, though not in any great detail, that early in July, the King of Spain had authorized his subjects in America to join in the war against the English and their possessions. Alexandre, when questioned, shrugged in a way that said what he knew he could not tell, and what he did not know he would not make up. The most he would say was that Galvez's advisers wanted to wait for reinforcements from Havana before doing anything—the province was poor, an offensive campaign sure disaster.

"Maybe Alexandre will have definite news when he gets back from New Orleans," Claude said. "Pierre told me this morning that Galvez has called a public gathering in New Orleans. Alexandre rode out yesterday to attend."

"Maybe he's ready to call the English bluff. Why wait for them to call the steps?"

"It's more than a bluff. Pierre knows those forts—and he has friends in New Orleans. He says the British are stronger in force than Galvez. Even if Galvez is trying to save the Mississippi, keep the English from taking over both banks down to the mouth—even if he were fighting for all of New Spain itself—a small force can only do so much."

"He may very well be fighting for all of New Spain, papa. Let the English have the river, and their way to the Gulf is clear. From there to Mexico—papa, there's no other way. He'll have to call the militia."

They looked at one another across the heat that steamed the earth, making cotton pods swell, corn husks fill, cane juice rise; they could feel something else in it now, feel the heat of anger and powder and hate and blood. "At least, papa, it's the English I'll be fighting."

Some light seemed to flicker at the back of Claude's dark eyes, flicker, flame, then die. "These British are not the same soldiers who were at Grand Pré, Claude Louis."

Claude Louis' head jerked up. He looked at his father's eyes, searching for that flame. "The flag is the same," he said. "The uniform is the same. They're still up to their old tricks. Look what they're doing to their own colonists."

"Flags and uniforms don't make a cause," Claude said. "Men do that. And like all men who war, you must make your own cause, Claude Louis."

Claude Louis stood, pushing the heat away from him. "That's easy. My cause is to hold this land. And to protect my wife."

Claude heard the conviction in Claude Louis' voice, a conviction as easy as the naming of his cause. And as unknowing. "Until you have seen what fields look like when enemy soldiers have finished with them—until you have seen the eyes of a woman whose husband has been locked away from her—" Then the flame of his anger burned, a bright burning that was stronger, more intense, than the August sun. He knew what happened to him when his anger ruled—bitter rage was a poor legacy to give his son. Far better to let Claude Louis learn, in his own way, what is, is not, worth fighting for, than risk his life to try to heal old wounds, old scars. He put an arm around Claude Louis. "I hope you never see those things. But, Claude Louis, you—and Cecile—you come to us this week."

"I meant to bring a pot of peas I cooked," Cecile said when they gathered that Sunday. "But I fell asleep and they burned up." She said this as though she had not just admitted to two terrible crimes—to fall asleep when work was to be done was unthinkable, and to let good food burn was never, never done. While the rest of them sank beneath the heat, Cecile skimmed through it. The quick movement of her body was accented by the questions her hands made in the air, the exclamation point of her face. When Suzette and Bernadine began to set the table under the trees, Cecile, with a pouting glance in their direction, went to Claude Louis, pulled at his arm and began asking to be taken down to the bayou, where there might be a little breeze. "Perhaps you should help my sisters—" he began. But with each word, Cecile's lower lip seemed fuller. And as always, Claude Louis was lost in the fullness of that pout.

"I want to be with you," she said. She leaned forward, whispered in his ear. Claude Louis could feel his mother's eyes on him, knew she saw the sudden brightness in his eyes, the way his hand moved down to Cecile's. For a moment, he held. Then, Cecile laughed, pulled away and darted ahead, her un-plaited hair falling from under her bonnet in a waterfall of glinting black almost to her waist. Claude ran after her, stiffly at first, as though he knew he was letting his wife show his family how easily she had her way, then freely, until the two moving figures were caught together in a frame of leaves and sunlight just at the edge of the small woods fringing the bayou.

Mathilde pulled the lettuce for the salad with firm, quick strokes that seemed angry only to those who knew her well enough to know the rhythm of each thing that she did. The bitter chard was not as bitter as the knowledge that Cecile would insult her husband's sisters and mother by choosing to play rather than help them. She rose, her apron full of thick, green leaves. Her eyes were on the woods where Cecile and Claude Louis dallied; the sweat collected on her brow, shimmered on her lips heat and filled the lines the sun seemed to etch so deeply.

"Cecile will have to grow up if Claude Louis is called," Claude said. "Someone will have to see to things while he is away."

"Zut!" Mathilde replied. "I didn't tell you, why bother? But last week, when that rain came up so quick? Claude Louis had some of his best seed corn drying—and Cecile, little ninny that she is, didn't get it in! She told him lightning scared her." Her voice was as heavy and thick as the leaves in her hands. One should fear God's judgment, that was all. And to let fear ruin good seed!

At table, Cecile helped herself to bowls before even Mathilde had been served, took the choicest part of the hen—and yet chattered on so gaily, humming little tunes, telling a funny story, that Bernadine and Suzette and even Julian were soon

laughing, too, their young voices rising lightly above the weight
of their parents' solemnity at either end of the table.

When it was time to clear, wash the dishes, Cecile was
tired. "Take me home," she said. Claude Louis lifted her onto
his mare, climbed behind her, tried to make his good-byes
without looking into his mother's face. "I'm glad we left early,"
Cecile said, leaning against him, curving herself into his body.
The feel of her along his length and the rhythm of the horse
made him want to hurry; he wanted to get her inside their
house, strip her clothes from her, enter that small body that
seemed to grow large enough to take all of him in.

On Monday Claude came to Claude Louis' farm to help mend
the pasture fence near the main road. They had been at it for
most of the morning when the sound of a hard-ridden horse
came to them. The sound of the pounding hooves, like a drumbeat of death, quickened their already tight nerves; they ran to
the road, peered down its dusty length. As the horse and rider
came into view, they saw that it was Alexandre, disheveled,
exhausted. He reined his horse and dismounted, flinging himself onto the grass bordering the road.

Claude Louis handed Alexandre the leather bag they carried
water in; he took a long drink and then poured the rest over
his dust-covered head and neck. Claude Louis felt the morning's
sweat grow cold on his neck; he could not look at his father.
They would know within minutes if war had spread to Louisiana—a Spanish officer did not half-kill his horse just to get
home for dinner! "Well, do I fight?" Claude Louis' voice was
deep, coming from some place of resolve within himself. The
single word, "I," seemed to be the only one his father heard.
A choked sound, like a father's cough when he follows the
plow across dust-ridden fields, broke from Claude.

"If you . . . we, do, it will be with our bare hands," Alexandre said, and told his grim story. Galvez had intended, at
the meeting called for Friday, to announce his plans for defense
of the colony against the rapacious British poised to overtake
her. Ships were gathered in the river at New Orleans, preparations being made. Then, on Wednesday, a hurricane had come
up it seemed from nowhere, and in less time than it takes to
eat a decent dinner had swept buildings, crops, cattle—everything—before it in a forty-mile swatch on either side of the
river, done terrible harm to New Orleans itself, and sent every

Spanish ship to the bottom of the Mississippi except one frigate, *El Volante*, which had been saved only because of her commander's skill and courage.

"That storm we had—that must have been the tail of the hurricane," Claude said. "But with the ships and their guns gone—what will Galvez do?"

Alexandre looked at Claude Louis, the old soldier's pity for the untried in his eyes. "Survive," he said. "However we can."

When Alexandre left, "to sleep a hundred hours," he said, they tried to talk of other things. Claude Louis sought to distract Claude: "I still think we should build our own moulin à gru—Antoine Landry takes a whole fifth of our crop to pay for grinding it at his mill. We could use that to advantage!" He picked up a stick, began drawing a design in the dirt. "If you and Uncle Pierre and I work together, we could get the mill built very quickly. Then, even if..." He left the "if" unfinished.

Claude focused on the drawing in the earth. A kind of shudder went over him; he reentered the world of August heat. "Perhaps we will charge a little less than Antoine does. After all, they say he will take all your corn and chase you for the sack—we don't want that said of us!" The fear, the near panic both felt was pushed down as though with a strong hoe, packed beneath a will to keep going.

Then day followed day, the sun in a contest with them to see if it could burn the crops before the farmers could get them in. Working in the fields, the men of Attakapas could almost convince themselves that a world which held blossoming cotton and tall corn rows and swaying cane could not also hold, not two hundred miles away, blossoming cannons and tall rifles and swaying lines of soldiers.

Alexandre drilled the militia daily, waiting until the men had their day in the fields, and then marching them in the square in front of the church. If he had any word from New Orleans, he did not speak of it, but patiently answered the questions that were fired at him with the regularity and repetitiveness of the drill itself. At the end of an evening of drilling, Claude Louis joined a few of the others around Alexandre, determined to have an end to rumor and uncertainty. Their determination was backed by the presence, in Alexandre's room, of a stranger, a man wearing a Spanish uniform and the insignia of high rank. "Chevalier—it is our lives. Please, does that man bring news?"

Claude Louis saw Alexandre's long look go over them, resting now on this face, now on that one. A softening of his expression, a weakening of his resolve. Then—"Come. He'll tell you himself."

Inside the low-ceilinged room, the Acadians clustered while Alexandre spoke in Spanish to his visitor. The man's face darkened, then, with obvious reluctance, he came to where Claude Louis and the others stood. His French was halting, not pure, but the clarity of Claude Louis' excitement, the depth of his need to know, seemed to make even the most accented syllable plain.

"You must understand that Bernardo Galvez is not an ordinary general—even for a Spaniard," the man began. "When the storm was over, he reassessed his position. We were, after all, nearly prostrated by that hurricane. And the English, with their Indian allies, can put fifteen hundred men into the field and have an easy victory. So!" The man shrugged, reached for the open bottle of wine on the table behind him, poured more in his glass, drank. "He ordered Don Juan Antonio Gayarre to do the impossible—put the defenses back together. Though there are those who whisper that what Galvez has ordered, what Gayarre is doing, looks more like preparation for an offensive march than for mere defense."

"Is there anything left for Gayarre to mobilize?" Alexandre asked.

"Well! Perhaps he thinks it would be better to die of exhaustion attempting to carry out Galvez's orders than to defy him and be shot by either his angry general or the victorious British. He is finding men, equipment."

"And Galvez? What does he do?" the man standing beside Claude Louis asked.

"General Galvez? Why, he is firing up the people to defend themselves. What a ragtag crowd they are! Were. The man's a genius," he said to Alexandre, and poured more wine.

"He held a public meeting, you see, and finally made official what everyone already knew. Spain and England are at war. Then, before anyone could finish muttering that he knew that, what news was that, Galvez told them that they, we, were under grave threat of attack by the English who occupied forts along the river." The few men in the gathering who had actually known of those forts nodded—of course, the English did not build forts for no purpose! One man spat, a hard, ugly sound.

"Then, having hooked them with his frightening words, Galvez brought them in. 'You will not face this storm of war defenseless,' he said. And then he announced he had been commissioned as permanent governor of Louisiana under the royal patent, and that it was his sworn duty to defend them. Ah! That made them feel better. You must understand, this young general has a reputation before he has yet made one.

"The next words were crucial to his purpose: 'Gentlemen,' he said, 'I cannot avail myself of my commission without previously swearing before the cabildo that I shall defend the province; but, although I am disposed to shed the last drop of my blood for Louisiana and for my king, I cannot take an oath which I may be exposed to violate, because I do not know whether you will help me in resisting the ambitious designs of the English. What do you say? Shall I take the oath of governor? Shall I swear to defend Louisiana? Will you stand by me, and conquer or die with your governor and for your king?' Of course, they answered him in a storm of sound. So, gentlemen of Attakapas, prepare then to march!"

Claude Louis went home in a daze that shut out the sounds of evening and blocked everything from his sight but one face— Cecile's. She had become the most important thing in his life, truly a part of his body. He carried her curving warmth with him to the fields each morning, returned to touch, to be with that warmth each night. The light stroking of her slender fingers against his tired muscles, the sweet smell of her hair, the soft-ness of her skin, had formed a kind of circle that kept him safe from everyone and everything else. To leave that! To leave her, march with these other farmers whose guns shot animals for food, whose anger dissipated itself in a few harsh words, per-haps a blow or two—and was then absolved in the confes-sional? Damn! He would not know an Englishman if he met one, so long as he did not wear that red coat.

Cecile was sitting under a large oak tree that hovered at one corner of their cabin; she had woven a fan of palmetto leaves and was moving it slowly through the heavy air. Light from the last sun's rays broke over her, screening her face with a pattern of leaf shadow. Claude Louis had a vision of her as his mother must have looked at the end of that long pilgrimage from Nova Scotia to Attakapas. He saw her slim body worn to skeletal thinness, saw those huge eyes made small with sorrow and pain. A surge of feeling rushed through him, gathered in his heart. If it took marching to Galvez to keep those monstrous changes from taking her, march he would.

When Galvez left New Orleans on August 27, 1779, for the German and Acadian coasts to recruit more men, he had raised one schooner and three gunboats from the river, called down to New Orleans boats which had been in a safer harbor when the hurricane struck, and could boast of ten pieces of artillery mounted on these assorted vessels. His small army, consisting of 170 veterans, 300 recruits, 20 carabiniers, 60 militiamen and the American Oliver Pollock with 9 volunteers, plus 80 free blacks, was marching toward Fort Manchac, believing it was defending New Orleans by meeting the attacking British forces in the field.

"That's when I knew Galvez was truly brilliant," Alexandre said later. "He had not even seven hundred men, and he was ready to march against a British fort! Not only march, but attack!" By the time the army was bolstered by the 600-odd men who joined it along the 115 mile march, and by 160 Indians, it could boast of just over 1,400 men—a number that would hardly put the fear of God into the English, but that could very well put into them the fear of Galvez.

When time came for the militia to join Galvez, families throughout Attakapas gathered to watch fathers, husbands, sons, go off to war. The LeBlancs and the Langlinais came together at Claude Louis and Cecile's; seeing that large group, Mathilde hoped that, for once, their common concern might draw them into one strong circle.

"You must not worry about Cecile," she said to Madame LeBlanc. "We will see her every day, help her as we can."

"Help! She needs more than help. How can Cecile take care of that house, that farm, with Claude Louis away? Men always have their games, their sport. They begin well, oh, yes, they do that. But sooner or later, they fall away."

"Claude Louis did not make this war, Madame."

"But he made Cecile his wife. Knowing all the while that she does not take to work the way others do. Well, if he comes home to find everything in ruin, that is hardly my affair."

In the end, the old aunt moved in with Cecile, to take care of both house and girl. Claude Louis went to his father-in-law.

"My father, my brother, will do a large share of the chores on our farm while I am away. I expect you to do the same."

"And is she worth it?" André LeBlanc asked, but turned away before Claude Louis could answer.

"Oh, I don't care about all of that," Cecile said, tossing her black curls. "Of course someone has to feed the pigs, milk the cows. But Claude Louis—what I wanted to say—" She moved closer, clinging to him, holding her face up to his. "You will get to New Orleans, won't you? To buy me something pretty?"

Claude Louis' arms swung down around that small body. He bent and kissed the forehead, so fresh, so clear. "Of course. Now, what would you like? Something like Uncle Pierre picks out, bright colors and many feathers, many ribbons?" They moved apart, the little space separating them from the others assuming the width of an ocean.

"He loves her very much, maman," Suzette said, touching Mathilde's arm.

"And she? Does she love him?" Mathilde's firmness would not soften, her judgment of this daughter-in-law was final. When Claude Louis came to her to say good-bye, some part of him stood back. He felt the tug of Cecile's eyes on his back, felt all the strands that pulled him to his wife's side. The strength of his arms could not break those strands, not even for the moment that he held his mother. He saw the pain in her eyes, and knew that she, too, felt that distance.

The long waiting for the call to war, the exhaustion of putting a good face on his leave-taking, the relaxed fatigue of fervent love in Cecile's arms, combined to put Claude Louis into a sleep as deep as the bayou current that cut steep banks as it ran out to the bay. When something, a sound half heard, awakened him, he half sat, fighting off the heavy, satiated sleep. Then, like an echo of the first terrible cry came another, not so loud, but still with the chilling note of terror vibrating through it. It was Cecile making those cries. He took her face gently in his hand and turned it to him, at the same time moving so that he could cradle her in his arms. Though asleep, her eyes were wide open and staring at some sight so awful that even the shadow of it he saw in her gaze melted his young strength. Her lips were set in a grinning grimace that made him understand, finally, what a devil might look like when celebrating a fallen soul. The white light of the moon cast that terrible face into high relief, like a face carved on a headstone. He knew he was seeing death in Cecile's face, the death of a spirit.

She had told him, from time to time, some of the things that had happened to those Acadians who landed in Massachusetts. Public floggings were the least of the penalties for those who broke the multitude of laws governing them; he had thought she exaggerated, or perhaps was repeating stories half overheard and magnified by a fearful child's mind. Later, when other members of her family confirmed what she said—eyes being plucked out by the barbed end of the cat-o'-nine-tails, burnings, hangings—he realized that the light laughter, the eyes that darted restlessly in search of pleasure, the high, rapid voice, all made a mask that Cecile wore to keep the horror of the world away.

Until tonight, he had thought she had always worn that mask, that the horror had not touched her. She had lived in its midst, but surely she had been too young to have faced it herself? Now, watching her, knowing that in her sleeping mind she was going through some tortured time, he felt the knife pierce him, too. Someone in another place in another time had cut away Cecile's youth and left only her childish play. He saw those frantic efforts at gaiety as the only weapon she had to fight the monstrous thing that engulfed her. He could almost see her child's mind grasping at every butterfly, every trinket, as proof that the world could not indeed be as bad as she knew it was. He held her close and crooned the old lullaby Mathilde had sung to all her children. "Fais do-do, Minette, Trois petit cochon dulaites; Fais do-do, mon petit babe, Jiksa l'age de quinze ans. Quan quinze ans aura passés; Minette va se marier." (Go to sleep, kitten, Three suckling pigs; Go to sleep, my little baby, Until the age of fifteen years. When fifteen years have passed, Kitten will marry.)

Claude Louis resolved to show her that the world she had with him was a world filled with things good and beautiful, all meant for her. As the last notes of the lullaby drifted out into the moonlit air, Cecile's mask melted; her body became lax in his arms, and her breathing came deep, slow, even. He laid her back among her pillows, those foolish lace-trimmed rose-embroidered pillows she loved so well. If foolish pillows brought her happy sleep, she should have a boat full!

The next morning, marching with the others on the road toward the Mississippi River and their rendezvous with Galvez,

Claude Louis was glad he had spoiled Cecile, if that is what he had done. As the dust in the road began to rise in great smothering puffs under the thrust of their marching feet to hang in the air layer by sifting layer, he faced the knowledge that he might never see Cecile again—at least her memories of him would be happy ones.

But thoughts of home were banished by the thud of marching feet; by the time they reached the meeting place on the river, more Acadians from the settlements at Opelousas and Pointe Coupée had joined them. Banded together by their memories of all that their people had suffered at the hands of the British, they were eager for battle, ardent and disciplined as any of Galvez's regulars. Claude Louis felt in his own body the sudden hunger for conflict—these Acadians would not be vanquished. If in Nova Scotia thousands of Acadians had been overcome by a small English force, this time one Acadian would be worth five or more redcoats.

Galvez imposed order on his motley troops as his country imposed order on the raw American continent. He sent a troop largely made up of Indians and free Negroes three quarters of a mile ahead of the rest of his army as they began the march upriver to Fort Manchac. Familiar with the woods, the forward contingent would reconnoiter and guard against surprise attack by the advancing English. The veteran troops marched next, protected by the artillery of the small fleet that kept pace with the march on the broad face of the river, and by the thick forest which grew near the riverbank. The militia was the rear guard; already they were beginning to feel like seasoned troops, despite the fact that their field baptism was being conducted without tents, horse-drawn supply carts, or any of the other items of war usually considered essential to a prolonged campaign.

"I think it is good we know how to live off the land," Raoul Landry, one of the militiamen from Attakapas, said to Claude Louis. "This Galvez either thinks we will die so fast he doesn't have to feed us or that we indeed fight like angels and need no food."

Except for the men marching on either side of him, ahead of him, and behind him, Claude Louis could almost have put himself back in the wooded lands of Attakapas, hunting dove on an early September morning. Galvez had warned them the British were bringing up some four hundred troops—every bird call, every branch whipping against a careless face, put him on the alert. At any moment, the woods would lose their innocence, would know violence and death.

But the day wore on with the only flash of red the scarlet back of a cardinal as it flew to its high, safe nest. Galvez halted them a mile and a half from the fort; when the troops were gathered before him, he announced in that proud Spanish voice that his instructions were not merely to defend New Orleans, but to attack the English who were entrenched along the Mississippi and drive them from Spanish territory in the name of King Carlos III. Shouts went up from the troops like the multitoned notes of bugles and trumpets, and the hoarse challenge in those voices asked, not for honor for the king, but vengeance.

Claude Louis' mind flew back to that last night with Cecile, to the horror that marked her beauty. His mother's tales of the evil voyage on the *Endeavor*, of being deprived of the means to answer the most primitive human needs, of watching corpse after corpse thrown carelessly into the sea, came back with a force they had never had when told beside a bright fire on a quiet hearth. The soldiers lying in wait at Fort Manchac, and farther up the river at Baton Rouge, might not be the same as those who could look at a tender young Acadian mother, her dying infant clasped in her arms, and tear it from her, herd her on one boat, her husband and children on the other. But they served the same army, the same line of kings. Such men should be helped to what awaited them in eternity, and helped with all due speed. Kill such men? Easily. Gladly. His voice raised with the others in resounding declarations of loyalty to the general God had sent to lead them against this British army that would sweep over them, pillaging, raping, devouring.

They camped where they stood, sleeping on the thick ground cover that cushioned the rich earth of the riverbank. Claude Louis felt that he had slept many nights rather than one, so many wakings and dozings marked the passage of the dark hours. When the call to formation came, the entire camp had been ready for hours; the restless troops, thinking perhaps that the battle they fought that day would not be so frightening as the one they fought in their night dreams, moved quickly to follow Galvez's orders.

The sun, that seventh day of September, burned straight up into the heavens on rising, scorching the wet air and filling the space between earth and treetops with steaming mist. The birds, weary now of nesting and feeding fledglings, thinking perhaps already of the migrant birds that would soon come to share their winter food, chirped in a lazy chorus as the sun cleared the misted edge of the horizon. Claude Louis, standing with two Attakapas men, shivered. His abstract thoughts of vegeance fell away. He had never even seen a man killed; how was it done, and how, he wondered, did you bring yourself to do it, when the phantom ogres fled and only the live enemy faced you?

The veteran troops were in the fore; Claude Louis, with a dozen other militia, was ordered to a small rise on the riverbank from which they could watch the progress of the battle and be prepared to join it on signal. Then the familiar trees surrounding the fort, the oak, the gum, the pecan, burst forth into strange fruit. Blossoms of smoke carried on stems of exploding sound suddenly appeared; though the watching men could not see their own troops, they could see quick movement in the embrasures of the fort as the British responded to the attack. Under that canopy of exploding parasols, the Spanish regulars came into view, storming the fort. Galvez's bright figure darted everywhere; by the time the militia had been waved down to converge with the others, the British were already vanquished—the reinforcements had only to enter the fort, where the Spaniards were taking prisoners.

"Not much of a test of our strength," Raoul grumbled. "One captain, two lieutenants, twenty privates—a British insult to a general like Galvez!"

"Then hope for more insults," Claude Louis said, sprawling next to Raoul amidst the resting troops. If the British had no more strength than that in any of their river forts, they might go through the entire campaign with no more bloodshed than today—one British private hardly presented the soul-tearing scenes of war that taunted Claude Louis with their unknown horror. "I wish we'd seen more of it," he said.

Raoul looked at him. "And gotten it over with. Yes."

Claude Louis rolled over, plucked a blade of grass, began to tear it in thin strips. "What are you fighting for, Raoul?"

"To keep what I have. And to have time to earn more."

"Not against the British? Because of what they did to our people?"

Raoul shrugged. "If not the British, someone else, eh? Twenty-five years ago, it was the British. Now, it is still the

British. But truly, it is the land. All—French, Spanish, English—all want this land. You and I—we have some of it. And we have a general who wishes to keep it." He shrugged again. "In Acadia, we also wished to keep it. But we had no army. You understand?"

"You talk like my father. He speaks of his land as though it isn't even part of the territory."

"It isn't," Raoul said.

The rest after that skirmish lasted a full six days. "Mon Dieu, even another long march would be better than this," Claude Louis complained to Raoul on the fourth day. They had seen little of their general; while his men inventoried the fort, arranged to get the prisoners to New Orleans, Galvez closeted himself with his staff to plan the strategy that would drop the fort at Baton Rouge into ardent Spanish arms. When they marched, finally, it was the thirteenth of September, and air that morning held, at the rim of day when the separation of dark and light stops time and movement, just one small edge of chill promise. Though the sun would reign throughout the rest of the month, and even into the early days of October, the earth could breathe again. Autumn would come stealing down from the northern reaches of the river, bringing ducks, bringing cool winds, touching the summer green with gentle painted fingers. I want to live to go back to Attakapas, Claude Louis thought, to be there when fall comes, I want to hunt ducks for Cecile and bring her red and gold leaves from the swamp to wear in her dark hair, I want to make a red and gold bed for her, and for me.

As Claude Louis fell into ranks for the march to Baton Rouge, some fifteen miles away, he hefted the weight of his musket which rested as easily as the weight of his farm tools when he took up his day in the fields; he joined the Americans, Indians, Negroes, Spaniards, and Frenchmen determined to wrest these river forts from the hold of that globe-encircling English arm, and, having loosed the clutching fingers, administer, with the swift kick of war, the thrust that would expel the British from this land forever.

Though the pace of the march did not slow, the air surrounding them seemed to become heavy with deliberation. A need for stealth crept over the moving force, the cadence of boots became muffled, the rattle of weapons dulled, and the occasional voice raised in a cry of encouragement slipped back into cautious quiet. When they broke for the noon meal, their eyes remained on the march, searching for sudden movement, the flushing of birds, the scurry of small game, that signaled human presence.

"Something's going on," Claude Louis said, standing to better view the officers gathered around Galvez. A runner, dusted with the fine soil that seemed to hang in the air like particles in heavy water, stood in front of the Spanish general, talking with great arm movements. A shout went up, and, as the word went from officers to soldiers, in a ripple of sound, the shout widened its circumference, until the whole camp resounded like a great brass gong to the victorious strike against the British made by Charles de Grand Pré, a Spanish commandant who had taken a force north of Baton Rouge.

Raoul, who had scampered over the rough ground to a better listening post, returning grinning. "Well, Grand Pré's made our job easier. He's taken those two posts between here and Natchez—is holding both garrisons prisoner. There'll be no help for the British from upriver."

"So if we win—there remains only Fort Panmure at Natchez—" Claude Louis said.

"We won't lose."

When they were near enough to the fort for a reconnoitering foray to be made, Galvez took a few of his officers and disappeared into the thick woods that flanked the approach to the fort. The men, strewn over the landscape like statues in a military park, were quiet, but a kind of vibration in the air seemed to be moving everything else: the earth that puffed up at every footfall in summer-dried plumes of dust, the leaves that shivered in a dancing movement that made each tree seem ready to shake loose from its roots, the moving glint of sunlight on metal blades, metal gun barrels. "The earth feels our pulse," Raoul said. "It is anxious for us."

The afternoon had many hours. Raoul whittled some of them away, making whistles. He put one between his lips, blew softly, then handed its mate to Claude Louis. "We will try to stay together, when it begins. But if we are separated, or one needs the other—we have these."

Claude Louis tucked the little wooden fife deep in his trouser pocket, and for the first time since beginning this campaign, felt something like peace enter his spirit.

Galvez assembled his troops late in the afternoon to hear

the plan of battle. The veterans had speculated throughout the day that, with the woods that formed a wedge pointing toward the fort like a giant funnel, Galvez would pour his troops through the narrow end, the element of surprise giving the extra thrust to their attack. Claude Louis had been measuring himself against what he thought would be asked of him: to run across open ground, to dodge shot, to see friends die. To kill another man.

But when they stood before Galvez, he rearranged their minds in swift words, sketching his idea in the air before them. He told them of the ditch that ran around the fort, a full eighteen feet wide, and taller than a man stands by a good four feet. Making ragged points with his quick hand, he described the chevaux des frises that guarded the fort walls with their tall spikes. The British fort held almost four hundred regulars, besides over one hundred militia.

"I tell you," Galvez said, "I would not be doing my duty to my troops if I led you in an assault against such strength." His eyes went over the troops, restless, anxious to begin. "I know your courage, and I honor it. But if we were to make direct assault on that fort, we would suffer many, many losses. Many of you are heads of families—can I take so many husbands, so many fathers? We must capture this fort—but we must not do it by losing the men who build our land."

Galvez's plan was simple enough. A detachment of militia, with the companies of freemen, and the Indians, would take a position in the woods that made such a tempting path to the British fort. they would behave as though readying for an attack, staying just beyond the range of the British guns. "Now," said Galvez, "while this diversion is going forward, the regular troops will move around the fort to a garden that lies behind it. They will build gun batteries while the men in the woods fire at the British, drawing their interest—and their ammunition. There will be much ammunition fired throughout the night—most of it British, and all of that, pray God, falling short of its mark. Then, at dawn—"

"At dawn, we will finish pulling the teeth of a weakened lion," Raoul said.

The men around Claude Louis straightened, growing taller where they stood. Galvez was coming to inspect the troops. As he walked up and down before them, he reached out a hand to take a musket, inspect it, test the blade of a sword. Fingers fumbled at buttons, boots were wiped against the tall grass. "He'll make a polished army of us yet," he whispered to Raoul.

"Proud men fight better," Raoul said.

Galvez finished his inspection, turned to give them a last word. "If all goes as I believe it will, by tomorrow morning the British will not only have wasted a great deal of their store of ammunition by firing into those woods—but they will have become more and more anxious, as the night wears on, waiting for the charge they know must come. They will not, I think"— and he allowed himself a smile—"be able to recover from their shock when suddenly guns are opened upon them from quite another direction. Nor do I think they will have sufficient ammunition left to do us much damage. Gentlemen, it is my intention to take this fort without ever getting closer to it than that garden—and without spilling my soldiers' blood."

Claude Louis felt as though he were standing on a tall stream of air that carried him upward with a lightness of feeling he had experienced only twice before—when he shot his first large buck, and when he married Cecile. Galvez's words gave him hope that he might be an observer in this battle, too, and that this adventure would, after all, amount to not much more than a detour on his way to New Orleans for the present he had promised Cecile. He could almost feel her warmth against him, could almost see her small figure darting ahead of him. He shouldered his musket, fell in with the men who were being sent to create Galvez's little diversion. He felt in his pocket for his little whistle, tested the sharpness of his knife with a careful thumb. Then, with Raoul at his side, he moved from the clearing that held the afternoon's golden light like a rough cup holding China tea into the woods where the dark-cool air swallowed them.

# CHAPTER 3

## *Baptism*

The soft leaves, the soft bark, the soft dirt underfoot dropped a cloth of softness over the small sounds of moving the militia made as they worked their way through the trees and scrambling undergrowth to a place nearer the fort. The Spanish captain Galvez had put in charge of them halted their forward passage where the width of the woods began to diminish, and where, if one looked closely, one could see that the trees had somehow been stripped away, layer by layer, so that only the sharp point of the triangle remained. The captain jerked his head in Claude Louis' direction. "You, Langlinais, you and Landry come with me. We must find the exact range of the British guns."

Raoul cocked an eye at the chevaux des frises rising stark against the sky. "If we are not chickens on a spit we are targets on a range," he said. They pushed through the low-slung branches that barred their way to the spot the captain thought close to the range of the British guns. He ordered them to cut the small saplings that sprang beneath the spreading branches of older trees, and to pile them as though for a barricade behind which to secure a gun. They worked until a rough sort of small wall had been built.

The captain then poured gunpowder along the ground behind the barricade, lay a wick to it, and lit it. They ducked low behind a dead oak whose trunk tilted toward the ground on its last majestic fall to earth. Then the bright spot of red-gold-orange, the flash of light, the thunder. Chunks of wood spewed up into the close-held air like refuse tossed up by churning water. The captain signaled to Claude Louis and Raoul, then began to fire his own musket. The other guns followed upon his, the three muskets sending up shot after shot in such rapid succession that even Claude Louis thought more men must have joined them. Then the sudden parting of air over their heads, the thud as metal hit earth, the light, the thunder, the bits of metal flying as the chunks of wood had flown.

The captain grabbed Claude Louis' arm, pulled him back. A second parting of air, again the thud, the light, the thunder, the bits of metal flying. "The shot is falling beyond us," Raoul panted as they ran.

"Their range is a bit deeper than I'd thought," the captain said. "We'll bring the others to here—" And he marked a large sycamore with his knife, cutting a deep gash in the fine white bark. "Then we'll set up our attack." When he saw them looking at him, trying to determine if they were, after all, really going to attack, if Galvez's plan had been part of an elaborate trick too complicated to explain to novice soldiers, the captain laughed. "Do you think the British won't send scouts? Do you think we can only play at attacking? No—we must build our barricades, throw up simple earthworks, put out patrols—not as a game, you must understand that, not as a game. As a battle."

With quick, terse orders, the captain brought the other militia up to a clearing near the sycamore that marked the range of the fort's heavy guns and dispersed them throughout the woods. The Indians were divided into several groups; each had its war drums, and, when they were positioned through the night, becoming ever more insistent, ever more a part of the pulse of fear beating in the naked throats of the soldiers inside the fort, would serve almost as effectively as the fusillade of shot to weaken the British resolve.

The militia and the free Negroes were ordered to make more barricades, to keep alert for British patrols, and to fire at anything that moved that did not give the countersign. An advance patrol was organized to keep watch toward the front of the woods throughout the dark hours; while the men on patrol would be forward of the British artillery, they were almost certain to sight British soldiers scouting the strength of the attackers.

"You and Landry take first watch for scouts," the captain said to Claude Louis. "You can take cover near the tip of the forest—you'll have a good view there." Each cell of his body seemed to have an independent life, to be clamoring as though it were one of an army of eager soldiers, ready for the fighting to begin. He felt quick envy for the Indians, with their drums and chants—they could release that clamor, that desire of the body to get the waiting over with.

"Remember there well may be enemy soldiers already in these woods," the captain said. He was busy cleaning his musket, rubbing grease on all its parts, polishing the worn stock.

"It'll be a lucky redcoat who sees me first," Raoul said. "Unless they have hunted in the swamps of Attakapas as I have—" And then he melted into the woods, his carefully placed feet carrying him as silently as though he floated on a small wagon of air. Claude Louis, his knife unsheathed and tucked in his belt, followed Raoul. Daylight had long since withdrawn from the woods, refusing perhaps to take sides on this eve of battle. But the moon, now three-quarters full, held a lantern over the night, and the soft light diffused the shadows in the trees, the brush, so that they could pick out shapes, find landmarks. And, when they reached the thin edge of the point, it was as though a shutter over the lantern had shifted, and they could see the open area between woods and fort clearly.

"No wonder the general chose not to attack that," Raoul said.

"It looks a million leagues tall," Claude Louis said.

In the moonlight that seemed not so much light as an absence of darkness, the parapets of the fort loomed almost to the sky. The rough spikes of the chevaux des frises were ready to impale anything that attempted to get past them, man or horse. The open ditch yawned blackly; only the very brink of it was lit by the moon. The rest was an abyss that promised pain and death. A gleam of light on metal betrayed the placement of the guns— and even as the two men watched, the gleam was lost in the sudden flare of exploding powder. They could see a missile projected from the blackness; it sailed past them to the left, and then they heard the thud, the thunder.

Claude Louis crossed himself. "They know we're here, that's for sure." The exploding shells sounded much like August thunder—the knowledge that men who would kill them were making that thunder charged the sound with threat.

"If I were a redcoat scout, I'd come up from that ditch," Raoul said.

Now the militia were in place; they were firing their muskets in rhythmed volleys that made their small number grow until they were a size to be reckoned with. The drumbeat of the Indians grew louder, stronger. Claude Louis could picture the thick muscles on their arms moving with the beat of their hands. Their bodies would begin to sway to that savage sound—when each brave was at one with his war chant, he would be ready for battle, massacre.

"If I were a redcoat scout and heard those war drums, I'd go the other way. Those Indians don't take prisoners."

"They're under the Spanish command, they'll do what they're told," Raoul said. His eyes were still in the open area ahead of them. He held a hand out, signaling silence. Claude Louis turned to look where Raoul was staring. Then he saw it, too, a shadow that moved across the ground.

"There's another," he said to Raoul. "There, just coming from the mouth of the ditch."

They watched the two British scouts crawl over the open ground that lay between the ditch and the edge of the woods. Watching them move, Claude Louis could also feel the hummocks of dirt and September grasses scratching at the face, the hands. He could feel the moist breath of a cooling earth on the cheek, and the marching beat of the heart. Did they know they were watched?

Claude Louis signaled to Raoul to follow him to a position that would block the scouts. He felt the cold of his unsheathed knife against his hand. There was a small nick in the blade; his thumb found it and lingered there. The handle was smooth, worn by the rub of calloused skin against wood. "We mustn't lose them," he whispered to Raoul. They began working their way carefully to the stand of holly that grew thick beneath the thin poplars reaching through the leaves of taller and sturdier trees toward the sun.

The scouts had crawled into the woods now, but three yards from each other. Raoul and Claude Louis parted, one to creep behind the farther scout, one to take the nearer one. Claude Louis, moving ahead of Raoul to meet the scout who was still crouched low just beyond the holly, felt his legs become those of an infant, not nearly strong enough to carry his weight. His belly was draining strength from him, he could feel it running down into some immense hole that had replaced the strong muscles of his torso. And his hand gripping the thong-wrapped shaft of his knife was crippled; it had no grip, could not hold.

Then he felt a warm flow and wetness on his trouser legs. His face, too, was suddenly warm, signaling shame. Mon Dieu, I've wet myself like some mewling babe, he thought. And then the hole plugged itself up, and sent flooding back, like an underground spring filling a lake, his strength, his will. His hand grasped his knife as though they were grown together; he lifted his arm and made ready to cut the throat of the scout who had just raised himself to a standing position and was now finding cover behind a thickish oak.

Behind him, Claude Louis heard a faint grunt, like that of a surfeited piglet. But he knew what that grunt was, it was the grunt of the dying scout Raoul had now taken. The other scout, his scout, heard the grunt, too. He turned his head, and in one wide-eyed moment stared straight at Claude Louis. But before his hand could move, before his mouth could do more than begin to open, could hardly have had time to so much as take in breath for a saving shout, Claude Louis had pulled his head back with one swift grab, arched the throat, and pulled the thin-honed blade of his knife across it.

He felt the blood pour out onto his hand and the weight of the man lie heavy against him. So did a deer feel when he slit its throat to bleed it before hanging the meat. But a deer did not mean to take one's land, rape one's woman, poison one's fields. He had more feeling for the deer, who did not realize that while it fed itself, it was making good meat for hungry hunters. He let the scout's body slide to the ground. Then he pulled the leaves from a low-growing bush and wiped his blade clean. He wasn't even breathing hard, and the fear that had attacked him was gone, had slunk back to its cave and gone into hibernation.

He slipped past the dead man and found Raoul.

"Did you hide yours?" Raoul asked.

"He's behind that stand of holly, between it and the oak. He can't be seen from the place they enter the woods."

"Do you think they'll send more?"

Claude Louis shrugged. Either they would or they wouldn't. If they sent more scouts during his watch, he would kill them. The British inside the fort must never know what a small force was laying siege to them, must never be so undistracted as to find time to look to their rear, where even now Galvez was directing working parties to erect the Spanish batteries beyond the garden outside the fort. But nothing stirred, neither ahead of them nor behind them, and when they were relieved at the end of the watch, all they had to report was that two British scouts had been sighted, and had been dispatched.

"What did it feel like, to kill a man?" one of the militia asked Claude Louis as he poured wine from a leather pouch and drank.

Claude Louis looked at him as though he did not quite understand the question. "Feel?" He had had more feeling when he was cleaning the blood from the knife with a swatch of sycamore leaves, seeing the dark patches stain the thick leaves, than when he had felt the first resistance of the cartilage in the scout's throat, then the heavy cut of the knife against tendon and tissue. "It is better, maybe, to think of it as removing an enemy instead of killing a man." A thought struggled against the immense fatigue he felt, something about what happens to a man, to his person, to who he is, when he puts on a uniform that many men wear. He took another long drink of wine. "But—it is—tiring. I'm going to sleep now." For the first time since he had left Cecile's smooth softness, he slept without dreaming, without waking. He slept, Raoul told him at dawn, when the rousing bugle sounded over the camp, as though his soul had been snuffed and only a loglike body remained. "At least I am rested," he answered, splashing water from a trickling stream over his face.

And then, just as the face of the sun unveiled itself to look upon the earth, a contradictory storm of sound echoed throughout the woods. The captain crossed himself. "Thank the good God our guns are in place. The attack begins in earnest. Come, move up to the edge of the woods, let us watch this."

They filtered through trees whose leaves were hanging still in the night-cool air. The sun reached out long fingers, prying through the thick branches to seek out each pocket of early autumn chill. Claude Louis shivered. His skin was cool now, his clothing dry upon him. Moving quietly through these woods, with trees like those he knew in the Attakapas swamp, he could think he was hunting dove, was going to bring home a sack full of them for breakfast. The guns that filled the morning could be hunters' guns—but then the angry answer of the British artillery came up under the lighter sound of the Spanish muskets and field guns, the dialogue between the two forces grew louder, more insistent, seemed to build to a long hanging moment of sound before falling, only to begin again.

"They can't have much ammunition left," the captain said contentedly. He had taken a post near the edge of the woods, had found a fallen log to hoist himself upon. He beckoned to

Claude Louis and Raoul. "Come—from here you can see what is happening."

Peering across the sunlit open ground, past the ditch that by morning light still yawned with awesome threat, they could see running figures passing between the tall spikes of the chevaux des frises in a frenzied minuet. "They're trying to get all their guns around to the rear," Raoul said.

"Have they forgotten us entirely?" Claude Louis asked.

"The rear wheel is squeaking more loudly," the captain said. "I'll post a watch here—but I think our part of the battle is over."

At first, the constant sound of the guns took over Claude Louis' mind so completely that he couldn't think of anything else. When Raoul pulled out dice and offered to play a game, Claude Louis shook his head. Who could see or hear anything with that roar, that confusion of sound, going on and on? But when it continued, when by noon it was still roaring on, he found that he could push it to the back of his mind. He leaned against a pine tree and pulled out the whistle Raoul had made from his pocket, put it between his lips, and began to blow softly.

By midafternoon, the British guns had clearly begun to lose the argument. The Spanish guns pressed their point continuously and definitely; the British became more and more sporadic, and finally lapsed into total silence. All over the camp, men roused themselves from their heat- and dust-wrapped sleep. Sudden quiet in battle could mean many things. The soldiers reached for their guns, moved uneasily, testing the air for the presence of danger with animal instinct.

Tension began leaping from man to man; they were like so many metallic poles, and the current of energy produced by fear and anxiety charged them. The captain broke out of the woods into the clearing where they were gathered. "That's a large force in the fort. They might be counterattacking from another point—" He sent them to their positions of the night before, waving away their questions. Claude Louis and Raoul, slipping forward once again to take the watch, saw only the quiet open ground, the ditch stretching out its treacherous length, the strong walls of the fort. There was no movement along the parapet, no sound.

"Are they all killed?"

"It looks like a ghost fort," Raoul said. "This silence is worse than all their noise."

"Every time a twig snaps, I want to shoot."

"We should separate," Raoul said. "English soldiers could have left the fort under cover of all that noise, be making their way to the river to escape."

"We've had a watch set the whole time."

"I trust no eyes but my own," Raoul said. "I'll go up that way a little, see if anything is there."

When Raoul had left, disappearing into the brush like the Indians he learned his swamp ways from, Claude Louis took up a better position himself. There was a large live oak about ten yards from the edge of the woods; its branches had dipped toward the earth until they were almost like stairsteps, leading up to the place where several branches grew away from the main trunk and made a wide place about twelve feet from the ground. Claude Louis climbed swiftly into that green bower, pulling curtains of gray moss in front of him until, he knew, he could not be seen.

It was comfortable in the tree, the even bark felt good across his back, and he rubbed against it, scratching the places where mosquitoes and gnats had bitten him. And still the quiet was unbroken, still the guns were silent. Perhaps everyone, English and Spanish, had been killed. Or perhaps all Galvez's force was gone, and the English were resting before marching out to finish off the small band of men who had so deceived them.

A different quality in the bird song and squirrel chatter alerted Claude Louis; something alien was near. He peered through a gray-green screen of moss and leaves, but saw only the empty woods. Then, above the angry protest of birds tired of having their routine disturbed, Claude Louis heard an urgent piping, a sound both familiar and strange. It took almost a full minute for him to realize that what he heard was Raoul's whistle, that Raoul was obviously in trouble.

He checked the blade edge of the knife tucked in his belt, quickly went over his musket, checked powder and shot. Then, swinging down through the branches, he dropped lightly to the ground and began his silent path to the place the sound had come from. After that first shrill piping, there had been nothing. But to survive in the swamps around Attakapas, to enter them and come back with game, one needed a memory for the crash of a large animal through brush, the whir of wings rising from a nest. As though a flag were planted, guiding him, Claude

Louis moved steadily forward to where that sound had been made.

Just beyond three pines that grew together in a tight circle, he glimpsed a flash of red. He slowed, bent into a crouching position, and crept on. Ten paces farther on, and he could see clearly. Four British soldiers, two of them holding Raoul in a rough grasp, stood screened by a thicket of wild hedge. Some kind of argument was going on; even without knowing the language, Claude Louis could tell that the argument was over Raoul, and what to do with him. The tallest redcoat's long rifle was pointed at Raoul's head, and his voice seemed to become louder and more definite. Raoul stood quietly, seemingly lost in fear-drenched apathy. But Claude Louis could see that the muscles of Raoul's neck were hard, that he rested lightly on the balls of his feet, that his entire body was strung on a rack of tension as he waited for an opportunity to break.

Almost without knowing what he had decided to do, Claude Louis raised his musket and fired. The red-sleeved arm holding the rifle jerked, then dropped. The soldier shouted a curse, grabbing at his limp and bleeding limb. Before the other three could move, look for the source of the shot, Raoul had leaped forward, wrested a rifle from one of the redcoats, and taken a position just opposite Claude Louis. At the same time, Claude Louis had entered the clearing, his musket reloaded and at the ready.

"Mais, you took time to pick flowers, yes?" Raoul said.

With Raoul's gun on them, the British soldiers were willing enough to let Claude Louis take their weapons, tie their hands behind them with long vines he pulled from the undergrowth. He then tied the four men together, binding leg to leg so that they made a great eight-legged beast. "What were they doing, do you think?" he said to Raoul.

"Getting to the river. What else?"

"If we only spoke their tongue—"

Raoul spat. "Savage language. Tongue of barbarians."

"Better that than the tongue of pigs."

The words, spoken in their own dialect, came from one of the bound men. "What, you speak like a man?" Raoul asked.

"I have known your people a long time," the soldier said. He as the oldest of the four, a battered face that had withstood all the ills of soldiering, a hardened body that expected nothing more than the ground for a pillow and the roughest forage for food.

"You were in Acadia," Claude Louis said. The words were an indictment, a judgment, a sentence.

"My first post," the soldier said.

"And did you learn to speak the language from the words of those dying on that beach? Or from the pleas of women that you not burn their homes, kill their babes?"

The fury in Raoul's voice spoke for the fury in Claude Louis' heart. Until the soldier spoke, they had had but one course, to march the prisoners back to camp. Galvez, regardless of the fact that this ragtag army was all that he had, imposed on them the same discipline he imposed on his finest troops. And, as that discipline became a part of their lives, they began to attain a faint gleam of the polish that distinguished those proud regiments that followed the flag of King Carlos III.

But now—now at least one of the Britishers admitted to being part of that terrible month that had so dishonored his army and his king. Now, in a small green place in a remote woods far from those death-barrened beaches, two who had been helpless infants when their people had been ripped from home were helpless no more. They could dispatch these descendants of that disgrace to quick—or slow—death. Claude Louis turned and stared into Raoul's face. It mirrored what was in his own.

"How many did your people lose?" Raoul said in a voice softened by the blood passion he felt.

Claude Louis shrugged. "Enough. Too many."

"Yes," said Raoul.

"We have cause to kill you," Claude Louis said to the soldier.

The soldier stared at him, those old eyes showing no fear, no feeling. "You always have to kill an enemy," he said. "And—this is not Nova Scotia."

"It would be, if you were to win," Raoul said. "Our new fields, our new homes—you would take them. Claude Louis, I think we kill them."

The sun-moved minutes went by, the air in the small glade closed around them, shutting them into a pocket of silence. Raoul's hands moved restlessly. "But there was Cavendish," Claude Louis said. The soldier's eyes showed something, something Claude Louis let slip by.

"Cavendish?" Raoul's tongue put a twist in the English sounds.

"That lieutenant who saw to it that my parents were on the same boat." Claude Louis' voice was flat. The first time his mother had told him the story, trying to overcome the hatred his small heart had for those terrible British soldiers, to lead him to compassion for all human beings in their misery and folly, he had looked at her in clear disbelief. "You tell me a fairy tale," he had said, and had refused to believe her until his father assured him that yes, there had been an English officer named Cavendish who had been a friend, more than a friend, a savior. He had not only seen to it they were on the same ship, but he had advised them how to get out of South Carolina once they landed. And gradually, Claude Louis had accepted Cavendish. But still as a myth, part of a legend, the moral dropped into a fable.

"I knew Cavendish," the soldier said.

Claude Louis said nothing. His hands were too restless. They must decide something soon, they could not stand here while the sun dropped down below the horizon, the last of its movements so quick that it seemed to plunge from the sky.

"Cavendish beat me once because I almost killed one of the men in the church."

Claude Louis stared. "He rode up behind you on that black mare of his. His riding crop fell on you as though he were an angel sent from God. And my—my father's life was saved."

"Your father." Now the soldier's voice was also flat. One of the other soldiers, pulling fitfully at his bonds, said something sharp. Another, knowing not what was said but knowing still that their lives were at forfeit, signaled him back into silence.

"Are you frightened?" Claude Louis asked. He asked it almost without caring about the answer. Though his voice showed nothing, the frenzy in his body pushed at him, wanting release. He could avenge his father his torment at the hands of this man, avenge him so easily. He remembered how, after the first small resistance, that other English throat had so quickly and effortlessly been slit.

"I cannot afford the luxury."

Raoul stirred, shaking himself into readiness. "Claude Louis, we get this over with." He raised his musket, but Claude Louis' hand came down, closed over it, pointed it to the ground.

"These are men, not animals. We don't shoot bound men."

"We don't avenge our people?" Raoul's eyes were hot, black, like two dark rocks tossed up from the molten center of the earth.

"We don't become like our enemies to defeat them," Claude Louis said. "Now we take them back to camp."

He motioned the tied soldiers forward with a sweep of his musket; falling behind them with Raoul, he stared at those red backs ahead of him. He had, he thought, probably saved them at the expense of some poor enemy in battles yet to come— they would be sent back to their army, given another fort to hold, another territory to defend. A chain of death, was it, no matter what? He shrugged. He knew about himself that he could kill when he had to. When he did not have to—pray God he would never learn that.

The camp, when they reached it, was in a state of disarray. Soldiers were hurriedly thrusting food and ammunition into packs, fires were being covered, the area cleared. "The British have surrendered," someone shouted as Claude Louis and Raoul came into sight.

They tied the prisoners to a tall gum tree, then found one of the militiamen from Attakapas. "The British have given up— and not just this fort, but also Fort Panmure at Natchez! Galvez is sending troops up to occupy it—the river is in Spanish hands, and the militia can soon go home!"

Claude Louis was filled with the lightness of his relief. His thoughts turned to Attakapas, and Cecile. "Thank God we didn't kill them," he said to Raoul. He had bought the right to his fields, his wife, with only one killing—"That Galvez is the kind of general to have."

"You're right, yes," Raoul said. "I don't think much of war, no, but if I have to be in one, this is the kind, I tell you that."

"We should thank the bon Dieu for his favors to us," Claude Louis said. As they knelt, men throughout the camp followed; voices roughened by fatigue became smoother, younger, as they murmured old prayers. A soldier next to Claude Louis rose, brushing the already fallen leaves from his knees. "The good Ursulines in New Orleans will have been in their chapel all these days," he said. "They prayed away fire, now they pray away the British."

"Ursulines?"

"The sisters. They have a convent in New Orleans, do you not know it? You are Acadian? Some of your women have become Ursuline nuns, it is strange you do not know of them."

"Acadian girls are nuns? In New Orleans?"

The soldier laughed. "You are a pious people. Why should not your young women choose Christ as their bridegroom? Besides, the Ursulines took in many women and children driven from Nova Scotia with no husband, no father, to protect them. Some of these remained as sisters."

Claude Louis thought of Suzette, who worked a full day at home then trudged down the road to his farm, where she took another set of chores. If these nuns would have Suzette—"How can I learn more about the Ursulines?"

"Go to New Orleans, speak with the superior." The man stretched, reached behind him to scratch his neck. "I won't be sorry to get back to New Orleans—hot water and hot food!" He looked at Claude Louis, hesitated, then winked. "And a woman."

Claude Louis thought of Cecile. Her skin, always warm, became so heated when he was lying with her that he sometimes felt he carried its imprint on him, that he was etched with the lines of her body. If he went to New Orleans to speak with the Ursuline nuns, he would be that much longer delayed from being with Cecile. But she had asked him for a present. The shops there had the frivolous trinkets she loved—with one trip, he could please two women he cared about. A vision of her round and naked breasts, draped with lace, came before him. What woman in New Orleans could match his Cecile!

Galvez gave the British twenty-four hours before their formal surrender; during that time, those watching the fort saw burial details laboring under the still powerful September sun. The fort itself seemed as ready for burial as its fallen defenders; the massive chevaux des frises had many gaps, as though an iron-hard fist had driven through, dislodging those giant teeth from that grim mouth. The heavy artillery was harmless, its power drained away through the gaping holes Spanish guns had put in the fort's walls, through the diminished stock of shot and powder. The British flag hung limp, collapsed upon itself, and even the occasional breeze lifted from the river's surface did not stir it.

The next afternoon, the fort flag, along with the battalion flags and all arms, were delivered to the conquering Spaniards.

"They still have style," Claude Louis said to Raoul as they stood with the rest of Galvez's army, waiting for the surrender ceremonies to begin. The English marched from the fort with flags carried high, with pipe and bugle and drum playing. Three hundred seventy-five veteran troops were made prisoners of war; the militiamen and free Negroes found in the fort were set free. "How could we be so few that we can't even keep these prisoners, yet we won?" Claude Louis asked.

"Numbers are never everything," Raoul said. "We were, after all, fighting for our homes, our families. While those"—he gestured to the British troops—"they are here because the king told them to be."

"One man should not have such power," Claude Louis said.

"Exactly what the Americans say," Raoul said. "But hush, we are under a king also."

"At least he has the good sense to give us Galvez."

The entire territory would agree with Claude Louis. With the capture of the British forts along the Mississippi River, and with the seizing of several vessels bringing supplies to the English, the Spanish forces in one short week had freed this portion of the continent, at least, from fear of being taken into the circle made by long red-sleeved arms.

Getting to New Orleans was easier than Claude Louis could have hoped; instead of a long walk, he found a place on a flatboat taking supplies downriver. Sinking into the bottom of the low-lying skiff, he learned how tired he was. Accustomed to a life of regularity, of sleeping and waking and eating and working at the same hours each day, the last month had wearied him with its laissez-faire carelessness. The only order in a day was the order imposed by military demands, the only routine the sureness that there would be no routine, that one's nerves and muscles and mind be always ready for the unexpected. Now, resting against several sacks of ground corn, he luxuriated in having nothing to do except let the river and its thick, lush bank slip by him while the sun bent over him, warmed him. It was like being rocked against a woman's body, this slow journey on the brown breast of the river. He slept, a sleep that lacked only Cecile to heal over the pinpoints of fear and blood lust and anger that were all that now remained of his first encounter with war. Galvez, his first campaign completed, had sent them home. While Claude Louis slept, the roads of the colony were filled with men. And though the cabins they returned to were just as raw as when they left, these rough homes were seen through eyes newly wise. What was worth shedding blood for was worth having.

New Orleans was a city in a frenzy. Citizens who had thronged the streets in the days before the battle, pressing for word, any word, as to how Galvez was faring, now thronged the streets to celebrate his victory. And every hour brought another influx of Indians, as though the minute hand on its sweep had gathered up the various tribes of the territory, dumping them in the midst of a city already full of English prisoners. "Mon Dieu, did we win or lose?" Claude Louis asked a Spanish soldier on guard at the square near the river landing. He pointed to the numerous British uniforms.

"By the time Galvez posted troops at all the captured forts, he had but fifty of us left to garrison New Orleans—even a general who works miracles in battle cannot make more soldiers from straw! And so he had to put the British prisoners on parole—they are free to move within the limits of the town. They are guarded, our general says, by their own good faith and honor." The soldier shrugged. "One hopes the English will have the same idea of good faith and honor as does our general. Otherwise—" another shrug, a careful touching of his musket. "Honor must sometimes be—reminded."

"But the Indians?"

"They have come to thank Galvez, to tell us what great warriors the Spanish are. They have no liking for the British."

"And they also are on good faith and honor not to fight among themselves, or pillage the citizens?"

"Galvez sent a message telling us that the Indians showed the greatest restraint while in battle. Prisoners were as safe with them, it seems, as with their own kind."

"That's true. I was placed with some of the Indians, they were a credit to the men who commanded them."

"Even so," said the soldier, "I advise you to take leave of New Orleans as quickly as you can. Galvez's reputation is strong, but man's memory is sometimes weak."

Claude Louis went first to the Ursulines. When he asked directions to their convent, the shopkeeper gave him other directions as well—to find a watering trough and wash himself. "And your shirt as well, that would not hurt, it will dry quickly, and these are ladies, you understand, they are ladies!"

Not only ladies, but great ladies; a building as splendid as the Ursuline convent must house the daughters of the mighty— how could he think of asking that his sister be taken into this order? Claude Louis stood in the carriageway across from the convent, thankful that at least his body and shirt were clean. The convent, its pale blue-gray walls absorbing the September heat, cooling it, defying it to wilt the linen cowls and wimples of the nuns who lived behind them, rose two stories above the street; the roof, tall enough for more rooms to create themselves beneath its cypress rafters, was lit by dormer windows. Claude Louis had never seen a fanlight; he stared at the graceful curve, watching the gleaming dance of sun rays on the glass.

Sitting on the low wooden chair, facing the iron grating, peering through the dimness at a white face fenced from him by yet another iron grating set into the wall six inches from his own, Claude Louis felt that this mission he had taken upon himself was far more difficult than following Galvez to the field. But the nun on the other side was kind and quick to understand.

She asked questions about Suzette, her life, her piety, that drew from Claude Louis thoughts about his sister he had not known he had. Finally, with a swift nod that he saw only as a flash of white against the dark veil, dark room, the nun signaled that he had told her all of importance. "Wait," she said. He heard the sibilance of her skirts as she moved through the dark, opened a door that let in a wide line of light, a glimpse of a garden rich with plantings. Then the door closed. Darkness and silence. Would Suzette really want this life? He almost fled into the crowded streets. What business of his, to put Suzette behind these high walls? But the nun was back. This time she left the door slightly open, and the deep light from the walled garden filtered through the dimness, picking out the details of her face. Claude Louis tried to put Suzette's plump face into the frame the white wimple made, tried to think how she would slow her quick feet to the pace those heavy skirts demanded. He saw the large rosary hanging from the cord belt, and again he wondered—did Suzette really want to count beads instead of babies?

"There is no way of knowing if your sister is truly called until she has been with us. Mother Superior says she may be admitted as a student now. If that goes well, if her vocation grows—then, we will see."

"The fees—"

"I told Mother Superior you fought with Galvez. She says there will be no fees for your sister. If, from time to time, you have an extra pig, some hens—"

"That is easy," he said. He saw the dip of her head as she bowed it; he bowed his, and repeated with her the Aves and Paters that were the voice of those round beads. Prayers for victory, prayers of thanksgiving, prayers for a vocation, for a good death, for health, crops—prayers that perhaps reminded man of his priorities rather than God, who surely already knew them.

Buying Cecile's lace was difficult only because he could not decide between a fine piece of Belgian work and a larger, but not as delicate, piece from Normandy. It would be her marriage gift, paid for with the money he had slowly saved over seasons of trapping. Each son who helped build and set the traps, skin the animals, cure the hides, received a portion of fur that was his own. When Pierre returned from selling the furs in New Orleans, that money was given to its owner. Claude Louis had already purchased a good horse, some utensils for his household. Never that he could remember had he spent money earned by dealing with cold mud in the swamps, warm bloody bodies, soft furry hides, on something that could not be used. But holding the lace over his hand, watching how the design veiled the skin underneath, his heart quickened. How Cecile's fine skin would look veiled by this lace! That was worth more, even, than the shopkeeper was asking. He put the Normandy lace back, handed the Belgian piece to the man to fold and wrap in a protective cloth. Counting out the coins, he felt as rich as any man who lived in one of the fine houses that were growing up in the Quarter.

Cecile's welcome, when he reached Attakapas, made him richer. He had deliberately slowed his steps when he neared the settlement, turning into the woods to find a stream where he could bathe. In the late evening, a chill from the upper reaches of the Mississippi Valley was beginning to put out cold fingers, reminding the Acadians that even this semitropical climate had another face. But the water was warm, he splashed and ducked his head, letting the running stream take the dirt and sweat of the campaign, the dusty marches. He wanted only Cecile, and by waiting until night came, he could slip home, have her in all the ways he had wanted her these long weeks.

Until he saw his cabin, huddled under the moonlight as though trying to cover all he loved with loving wings, he had not known how completely he had left the house of his parents and become a husband, a man, on his own. The roses he had planted for Cecile were bleached by the moon, and that same light made the small trees grow tall by the length of their shadows. He walked faster, his feet matching his pulse. A low knock, a hoarse whisper: "Cecile!" Not to wake the old aunt, never to wake her, who might be chaperone for even man and wife. And then a soft answer, a question, the rattle of the bolt, the lifting of the bar with its leather thongs, the heavy door moved back—Cecile, Cecile in his arms, her eyes spilling tears, her arms demanding, her lips soft enough to sink into forever.

"I will never leave you again," he said. And the next morning, for the first time in his life, Claude Louis did not rise when the cockerel outside announced the dawn, but, turning to his wife, said, "That cock has made a mistake. We have an hour yet before the sun gets up."

Over breakfast, cooked by the old aunt who took Claude Louis' return as calmly as she had taken her sudden removal to Cecile's house, Claude Louis listened to Cecile's rapid tongue, darting in and out as she wove for him the tale of all that had happened in the settlement since he had gone. "You should have seen the excitement the day a wild pig got after old Monsieur Gautreaux's best dog! Oh, but he was so mad! He took his gun and went chasing after that pig, and the pig was chasing after the dog—" Cecile leaned back in her chair, her light laughter sailing over her. "Then when he killed the pig, of course there was a big feast." She shrugged. "They fussed because I wouldn't help make sausage, but then—I don't like all that blood."

"Nor should you," he said. He had been waiting for the brook of her voice to slow, find a quiet place, where he could tell her about himself. Listening to the way her voice tried to skip over, skirt, the word "blood," he knew that for Cecile, his absence had been a space of empty time only. Nothing he had done, not the fear, the panic, nor, finally, the resolve to kill was real for her.

"Why do you look so solemn? Aren't you glad to be home?" She came and sat on his lap, teasing his hair with her quick fingers. "And weren't you going to bring me a present?"

He caught her wrists. "Cecile—petit chou—I was at war. You know?"

"But you came home." Her voice, flat, solid, barred any knowledge of war, or what it meant. "Why does it matter where you were? You're here now. And you did bring me a present, I know that you did."

The happy trust in her voice calmed him. "I did," he said. "And I brought news, also." He would not speak to Cecile of war, of even the small part of it he had seen. They would keep the pretense between them that he had simply been away, and had returned with lace, and with a hunger for her that would take many nights to fill. Beneath the morning glory grace and the fragile shell of creamy silken skin lay still the beasts of destruction. They were just beneath her hurried smiles, her eyes that glanced away from anything ugly, sad. "I have found a convent for Suzette."

The intensity of Cecile's happiness for Suzette surprised him. She seemed to think it the most wonderful thing Claude Louis had ever done, or would ever do. "To think she will be a nun! Behind those big thick walls? Never to look on the world again!" His thoughts, too, but when Cecile said the words, it was with a wonder that one person could find so much joy.

"You sound almost as though you wish you were to be a nun," he said.

"Oh, no, I could never be a nun! But it is a—a safe life, is it not?"

I will build walls around Cecile, not the pale blue-gray of the Ursuline convent, but walls of love and caring. She will feel safe, I vow that she will feel safe.

# CHAPTER 4

## *Hélène*

"But I don't want to live in the country." Noel watched his wife lift her wine goblet, hold the crystal globe so that the flame from the candelabra burned through the burgundy, drowning its golden light in those ruby depths.

"You've lived in the country before."

"At the château. For hunting. And country weekends. Not quite the same, cher Noel, as being buried in—what did you call it?—Attakapas?" Hélène's laugh, which when he had courted her a decade ago had seemed like the sound of chimes forged by wood sprites from the finest silver, now had an alloy of harder metal beneath the surface shimmer. She rose, her slender body following the high rise of her laughter, the shrill notes at the top of the scale pulling her up as though light fingers were grasping at her blonde hair. She glided across the floor to the sofa where Noel sat, leaned over him, put her arms around him and kissed his neck. He was enveloped in her, in the deep lace that fell back from her soft forearms, in the deep scent of her musky perfume. "Noel, we must stay in New Orleans. We simply must."

He felt the lace, the softness, the scent, withdraw. He heard the rustle as Hélène removed her gown, the rustle as she unlaced her corset, stepped out of her chemise. He knew that in moments, he would be enveloped in the softness that was a naked Hélène. He watched her come toward him ready to surround him and make him surrender to her. He determined that this time, it was Hélène who would surrender.

Afterward, with a small cruelty he almost never indulged, he watched her dress again, letting her see that he was watching, letting his eyes strip her even as she covered herself.

"I don't like being watched," she said, and the hard alloy pushed through the silver surface.

"Then go behind your screen," he said. He saw the small dark mole on her right buttock disappear as she pulled up her undergarment.

His thoughts turned to France, to Provence, on an April weekend just a scant seven months ago in 1789. They had gathered up a party of friends, people from the court, a particularly notorious actress, two amusing poets, and gone pell-mell from Paris to Beau Chêne, the de Clouet château in the south of France. Both the countryside and Hélène had been at their best—the hills, pastureland, roadsides, were bursting with fevered bloom; Hélène had been touched with that same passion, and had bloomed throughout the long weekend with a gaiety that had brinked, finally, on indiscretion.

He had been going over the grounds with his head gardener, making a list of plants and shrubs needed for the formal garden Hélène wanted to put in near the drawing room. They had been some thirty yards from the small summer house that marked the halfway point between the terrace and the fruit orchard when that unmistakable silver sound had chilled the spring air. The heavier sound that came just afterward weighted the space between the summer house and the two listeners. Noel had taken the gardener by the shoulder, pulled him over toward the terrace, talking loudly of roses and espaliered pear trees. But all the time that he discussed the merits of this yellow rose or that one, this tulip bulb or the other, the words he had heard grew and grew in an already fertile field. "What an enchanting beauty mark," that heavy voice had said. "And what an enchanting cheek it graces. How fortunate that so few men see it, my dear. You should be quite exhausted."

When Hélène and de la Houssaye had strolled onto the terrace an hour later, Noel had seen, not purple silk and blonde curls and fair skin, but Hélène stripped, handing over her body to the man who strolled beside her, surrendering herself to him as she never surrendered herself to Noel. He had told himself then that if it were not for the children, for LéLé and Noel André, and Marcel, he would charge his wife with adultery and put her away from him. That night, he had gone to Hélène's room, and for the first time in the years of their marriage, he had not allowed her to say no. He had used her, putting her resistant body into positions learned from the whores of Paris, and when he had left her, he had left also a gold piece, tossing it at her as he closed the door.

He realized that she had been talking for some time, that she had been putting the case for remaining in New Orleans, this place that was hardly livable, but that at least had the advantages of cafés, theater, shops—and other French Royalists like themselves.

"The de Gravelles are already settled," she was saying. "Their house is not grand, but by the time Juliette is through with it, it will be at least passable."

Noel looked at her then, studying her as though she were a painting he might or might not choose. She stared back at him, and in the fleeting moment of thought before he spoke, Noel saw what she saw, and what he saw as well. Hélène, not tall, slender still in her thirty-second year, fair-haired, dark blue eyes, skin that could blush from, almost, head to toe. Noel, taller by a good six inches, lean, dark haired, dark eyed. "I have already accepted the land," he said. He said it as idly as though he had not, that same December afternoon, decided the destiny of the de Clouet family in Louisiana. "The money and valuables we have with us will serve us much better invested in developing land."

"Developing? Does that mean you are going to become a farmer?" When did we begin to hate each other, Noel mused. Was it two years ago, last year, this spring? Or was it when the world came apart this summer? When we heard that the Bastille had fallen, and knew we were doomed. Or was it when the revolutionaries stormed Paris, hanged Bertier de Sauvigny and Foulon de Doué from the nearest lamppost, and we knew again we were doomed. Or was it, finally, when we fled to Beau Chêne, thinking our chêteau, far from that frenzy, would be safe, only to find a revolutionary committee in charge and the king's army defected?

"A gentleman farmer," he said. He poured cognac, willed himself to let that hot liquid fill his mouth rather than the hot words he knew were there.

"A real man would have stayed," Hélène said. "I'm going out. Give me some money, please." She put her hand out, holding it just under his face.

"You have enough frivolities," he said. For a minute that seemed to take at least twice as long as it took for the minute hand on the porcelain clock on the mantel to tour itself around the hours, Hélène looked at him. Then she ran her hand down his body, beginning just under his chin, and letting it come to rest just under his belly. He felt himself hardening, saw the silver laugh being formed in her eyes. He heard the laugh releasing itself as Hélène went out, slamming the door behind her.

Noel went to the window and opened the long shutters that sheltered it. He stepped onto the balcony overlooking Calle de Real and watched Hélène slip through the crowded street. The sky had held itself low over the earth throughout the day, keeping the wet cold of mid-December pressed against the brick streets and plastered houses. The people in the streets were wrapped against the cold, and against the winter ills it brought. Perhaps she goes to visit the de Gravelles, Noel thought.

There were sounds of children on the stair. An older, but still childlike voice was corralling the smaller voices. And then the door opened, spilling small bodies into the room, as a larger body herded them in, closed the door, removed coats, caps, shawls. They climbed over him, Noel André and LéLé and Marcel, putting their small lips against his cheek, digging into the pockets of his coat for sweets, putting their arms around him. At least she had given him children.

Gertrude, her rough country face made more red by the cold wind that ripped up from the river and tore through this small quarter of civilization in a bewildering new world, began heating water for the children's toilette on the iron stove. "News from France," she said. "News a vulture brought."

"What is a vulture?" Noel André's five-year-old tongue played with the strange word.

"A big black ugly bird that eats dead things," Gertrude said, unbuttoning LéLé's bodice.

"I am getting too big to dress with my brothers," LéLé said.

"You are nine," Gertrude said. "When you are ten, you have a screen."

"When do Marcel and I have a screen?" Noel André asked.

"Men do not have screens," Gertrude said.

"But why do we not?"

"They should have them. Men are ugly undressed," LéLé said. She had taken the large sponge from Gertrude's hand and was squeezing it, letting the warm water run down her bare arm. The only sound in the room after she had spoken was the hiss of water from the steaming kettle as it boiled onto the hot stove.

"How are they ugly?" Noel asked his daughter. He knew that if he looked at Gertrude, standing still, very still, he would go on talking, say something else, make LéLé forget what he had said. He did not look at Gertrude, he looked at LéLé, who still squeezed water from the sponge down her arm.

"They have something awful-looking hanging down. And they have a lot of hair." She looked back at him then; the face that she presented was only nine years old, but the look that came from her eyes seemed older. "At least, Monsieur de la Houssaye does. Maybe others don't."

Noel got up, thrust his arms into the sleeves of the coat hanging on the stand near the door. "I'm going out, Gertrude. To learn the news you spoke of. When Madame de Clouet returns, tell her—I may be late."

Gertrude's face was bent over the children. She was drying their faces and arms, dropping an embroidered gown over LéLé's head, stuffing the two boys into nightshirts. "Yes, Monsieur de Clouet," she said.

Noel thought, not for the first time, that silly women like Hélène had done as much to start the revolution that was racking his beloved France as the feudal economic policies that persisted long after that system had, theoretically, died. Why would women like Gertrude, whose families scraped a living from the earth, and who then had to tithe to bishops, render up seigneurial dues to nobles, or slave so that Hélène could have silk and lace, perfumes and lovers?

The café where the French Royalists gathered to exchange rumors, fears, news, was four blocks away on the corner of Calle de Real and Calle de San Felipe. The mood of the men who met there in the late afternoons wavered between unity and competition—already, some of them were faring better than others in this new world, and the ranking order that had prevailed among them in France was not holding true here any more than it had among the voracious peasants and the bourgeoisie who were lighting up the words and spirit of the Declaration of the Rights of Man, proclaimed and adopted by the Constituent Assembly in August, with the fires of burning châteaus and the flames of growing revolution.

As his feet carried him forward to the café, his mind carried him back to the weeks following the incredible fall of the

Bastille, which, like one small wedge at the base of the heavy trunk of a tree, had been the fulcrum that levered the power of the revolutionaries into a force that would, he knew, finally topple the entire structure he and generations before him had known. It had seemed wise to go to the château. They always went there in August anyway, and certainly, no one who could leave would choose to stay in a Paris being manhandled by country bullies who did not appreciate the beauty they violated.

Hélène had fussed, of course. It was her fault—or responsibility, the result of her wish—that they were even in Paris. They should have been in Normandy, at the country house of Noel's brother. But Hélène had insisted on going to Paris so that she could take certain garments to her dressmaker there for refurbishing. She had told Noel, and her tongue flew like the very blades of the scissors, the flashing needle, her modiste wielded, that it was bad enough that she had to build her wardrobe for the season around a few new gowns and many old ones turned, or with new collars, or a different sleeve which would, she hoped he understood, fool no one. That was bad enough. But to be seen going into Mademoiselle Anastasie's establishment with bundles that bespoke of old gowns being renewed, even if her personal maid did carry them—that she would not do. No, they would sneak into Paris, live behind shuttered windows and with slip-covered furniture and bare floors, while Mademoiselle Anastasie decided what miracles she could perform. Noel, Hélène had said, could take the children to the park, on walks, and to his café.

He would remember until the final moment of his life—at least he feared that he would—Hélène's voice climbing up and up a column of thin metal, becoming ever more shrill as it vibrated, protesting that he was mad, they could not leave Paris, her gowns were not ready. She had continued to protest until they were almost stopped on their way out of the city in a closed carriage by a revolutionary patrol. Only the coachman's quick tongue and quicker horses had saved them. From then on, Hélène had said nothing.

But as they traveled farther and farther from Paris, as the countryside taking its rest under the summer sun seemed unaware of the terrible visions being drawn against the Parisian sky, they had both begun to relax. Because the three children and their country nurse, Gertrude, traveled with them, they had conversed in broken sentences, using silences as much as spoken words to communicate to one another their fears.

Noel remembered that he had been the first to mention emigrating. Hélène had turned to him, the fine skin of her heated face dusted, not with the expensive perfumed powder she kept in great crystal jars on her dressing table but with the upper layer of earth that rose and rose and rose under the horses' hooves to make the air between road and top of carriage uniformly beige. "Emigrate?" It had been but one word, but that one word had told Noel all he needed to know. Hélène would be almost as difficult an obstacle to their safety as any member of the revolutionary forces.

And though emigration was clearly the only way out, Hélène complained, fussed, protested, commanded, until the very end. Until the very day they left the château, jewelry, silver, coins packed tightly in wooden chests, clothes thrust into leather trunks.

They had taken only Gertrude, the maid-nurse who would have accompanied them to Normandy. Hélène's maid, his valet, and any other servants who had not yet abandoned them to join the committee ruling their area had been left behind. When Hélène had finally understood that Nina was not to accompany her, her protests had been sufficient, Noel thought, to fuel several revolutions. Where he had found the strength to remain silent, to supervise the packing of the clothes, to himself unlock the cabinets where the jewelry was kept, the drawers and armoires filled with silver, the money box in his office, he did not know. Though the thought did intrude itself that a man who kept silent while his wife consorted with other men might be expected to keep silent about almost anything and everything else.

His way was suddenly blocked; his mind jerked itself back from that time and place no sea voyage would ever bridge to confront the woman who stood before him. The lamp crowning the tall post near Noel had just been lighted, and in the cone of brightness it forced down over the descending dark, making a glowing pyramid, he noted the woman's dark hair curling coarsely over her forehead, her honey-toned skin, the slight thickening of her upper lip as it came down over the curving lower one. He pushed his way past her, saw as clearly as if he were staring at her the slender arms propped on rounded hips, the dark eyes stating challenge. His friends taunted him that he would not take one of these coffee-cream women to bed;

there was nothing, they told him, like a woman whose heritage
was barbaric but whose father was civilized. Born of black
concubines, sired by Spanish nobles, these women, and their
brothers, were set free. Most of those thus freed were as carefully reared and educated as though they were not outside the
blanket. Occasionally, the sheltered life became a prison. Rebellion followed. But for a woman, rebellion against one form
of protection usually meant bartering herself for another form.

"I'm not one for these casual encounters," he said shortly
to a compatriot also going to the café, who, joining Noel, asked
if he had turned the woman down because he was satiated
already or because his appetite was too discriminating for a
diet the rest of them devoured. His eyes were still filled with
the naked body of his wife; though he had taken her but an
hour ago, he was full, leaden. "Then you have something
better," the man said.

"The children's nurse said there is news from France," Noel
said. They were at the café, finding seats, ordering wine, settling themselves among the men who met to assure themselves
they could still banter, gather to drink wine, compare women.
And to discuss and confront the news from home.

A newspaper, weeks old, was put under his nose. "You see
what they've done to the clerics," a man to his right said. A
finger pointed, the well-manicured nail tracing across the black
letters of the headline. Noel scanned the words, and read that
400 million livres' worth of clerical lands had been put up for
sale on December 19. His eyes moved on. "Mon Dieu." He
said the two words quietly, as though praying. The Department
of Aisne, in which his brother had his country home, was being
torn with violence. The bocage country of Normandy, that
peaceful and bucolic place where he had spent so many hours
almost holy in their harmony with the natural serenity around
him, was under siege by insurrectionists. Though the populace
spoke of government by vote, the vote was being delivered
more often than not by the sword, the rope, and the pistol.
Aristocrats in Anjou, the Franche-Comté, Dauphiné, Vivarais,
and Roussillon were faring no better. His godfather lived in
Anjou.

He reached for his glass, filled it. "My brother—his family—
if they stayed in Normandy—and my godfather—in Anjou."
The glass was stiff in his hand, like lilies held by a corpse.
"What madness is loosed upon the world?"

"Madness?" A man new to the gathering spoke from the shadows of the next table, scraping his chair on the rough brick floor as he rose. He took a stance at the table, peering down at Noel with eyes filled with the kind of rage Noel was becoming familiar with. "Why, the madness of rabble gone wild. The madness to be expected when the descendants of the Gallo-Romans our ancestors reduced to serfdom are trying to take privileges that have been ours for centuries, privileges ours by right of conquest."

"Are we to relive 1788? All that debate?" Noel said. He was suddenly weary. When the Estates General, meeting for the first time since 1614, could not solve his country's problems, he alone certainly could not.

He heard the voices around him, cresting as the sea roar crests with the cyclic ninth wave, take up the old, old arguments. "The peasants have use of the land, possess that—why should they object to the traditional dues?" "And why object that we maintained our exclusive hunting rights—what peasant properly knows how to hunt?" "The problem, of course, is that peasants are stupid."

Noel drank the last of his claret, stood and fastened his coat against the deeper chill of the lowering night. He would not, he knew, be missed. Though these compatriots had had the vision or audacity, or courage, or grace, to emigrate, to chance life in a country not even ruled by people of their own nationality, they had not weaned themselves from the terrible need to go over and over their own grievances, grievances which became more justifiable and reasonable the further distant in time they were from the stage upon which all grievances were finally being balanced.

Two weeks later, when they arrived at Poste des Attakapas, Noel felt, for the first time since his world had begun to disintegrate, despair. For the first time in four centuries, the de Clouet heir had not welcomed the new year at the Château in Provence; for the first time in six centuries, the de Clouet heir could not know what heritage his firstborn son would have. Behind were the de Clouet lands in Provence, the de Clouet town house in Paris, the de Clouet position at the French court. Ahead of him, surrounding him, pulling his feet into their spongy surface, were the lands upon which his children's future depended.

"This is a bad joke, Noel." Hélène's voice, which was made of hard metal now, and that not very often veneered with silver, cut across his despair, separating it into one portion which would vanish as he learned the ways of this new land, and into a second portion which would vanish into his soul, there to live.

The sleeping brown earth, stretched before them, covers of knotted swamp grass pulled across it. December had emptied its skies and put pockets of brown water across the fields; these lay idle, waiting to be filled with spring seed. Rising in the middle of the field closest to the road, a cabin of roughly cut clapboards stood soaking up the wet iced air.

"At least they have finished the house," Noel said. He was aware that in the wagon behind him Gertrude and the three children were silent. Three-year-old Marcel had chattered for a while, intrigued by the farm animals he occasionally saw as they wound from the settlement out to their new home. The trip from New Orleans, made on a boat that plied the bayous, had not been bad. They had, after all, been dry. Noel thought of Marie Antoinette, playing at being a dairymaid. There would be little playing here.

"That is our house?" The word "house," as Hélène uttered it, was etched deep with disgust. "Noel, have you gone quite mad? Do you remember, if your brain has not entirely turned to calf's jelly, the barns in Provence? They were palaces, Noel, compared to this."

"Hélène, this is not permanent. I have told you that. It is a roof over our heads, only that. Of course we will build something more suitable." A weariness entirely new had come into his life these last months. Never had he spent so much time in the presence of his children. The quarters on the ship coming over, the rooms in New Orleans, the tiny cabin on the boat bringing them to Attakapas—there had been little opportunity for privacy, for the kind of adult life he had been long accustomed to. Did Hélène think that he did not also want better living conditions? Good heavens, a man begot children, but surely it was up to the women, the nurses, the governesses, to rear them. Loving children, he was learning, took on a dimension unknown when one had to be with them so constantly.

"Standing here will not get us settled," he said. He climbed back into the wagon, picked up the reins of the team that pulled it. The wagon, the horses, the house, were his first purchases for his new land. A Spanish official in New Orleans, the same man who had steered Noel through the complexities of obtaining a land grant, had arranged for the house to be built, the wagon and team to be waiting. "I advise mules, not horses," the official had said. He had looked at Noel with eyes that seemed to see back through the centuries to all the proud de Clouets who had ridden with their king. Noel had said nothing, and the official had not mentioned mules again.

He guided the horses over the track that led from the road to the cabin. Though the rain had stopped, drawing itself back into the sky as their sloop had touched the landing at the settlement, the gray air, settled over the brown earth, was more dismal even than rain. Looking at the mud, Noel wondered how any seed could be kept from rotting long enough to sprout.

The workmen who had put the cabin together had made a trestle table, two benches, and platforms for their bedding. There was even, Noel noted with unfamiliar gratitude, a fire laid in the hearth. He went to it, knelt, struck flint until it sparked and lit the fine pile of tinder beneath the kindling-sized branches that were the foundation for the long dry logs someone had carefully built into a well-drawing pyramid. He had, he realized, so taken for granted fires that were laid, hearths that were swept, chimneys that were cleaned, that this was perhaps the first time in his life he had even thought to be surprised, or grateful, that some human being had taken time, given effort, to provide him with warmth.

Hélène stood beside him, holding hands over the growing flame. "I'm taking the next boat back to New Orleans, Noel. When you have a house built for me, I will return."

The fire had caught the kindling now, and was beginning to eat the bark that flaked away from the logs. Behind them, Gertrude was spreading quilts and pallets on the low wooden platforms, shaking out blankets and shawls. The children were exploring the second room of the cabin, their voices diminished by the thick plastered walls. Keeping his voice low, in that quiet register which was now almost automatic, so conscious was he of the ears other than Hélène's that could, willy-nilly, hear his every word, he said, "You go to New Orleans now, Hélène, and you may as well go back to France. To de la Houssaye, if he is not dead. Or to any other man who has time for a spoiled woman while he should be defending his lands. I—overlooked your—foolishness—in France, Hélène. That life is gone, over. In this new world, you are needed. You are young still, strong. You will, like everyone else, have to earn your way. And you can begin, my dear wife, by earning it in my bed."

He could run through all the expressions that would present themselves on Hélène's face, one after the other; he hardly had to stay there to watch them.

Being a lady-in-waiting to Marie Antoinette had been disastrous for Hélène, there was no question about that. Certainly she had not been able to handle the freedom that prevailed in the queen's salon and boudoir—if the custom of derogation, whereby an aristocrat lost his claim to nobility if he stooped to deal in trade, carried over to women who traded favors for frivolity and trinkets, Hélène de Forêt would have lost her noble name as she had already lost much more. He did not, now that he let himself dwell on it, even think Hélène had been a virgin when he wedded her. The day after their marriage, she had blamed her wanton response to his restrained and gentle overtures on the wine she had drunk. And Noel, relieved that he would not have to spend many nights in educating and awakening his bride, had accepted that. But there were certain little movements, certain gestures, that spoke of experience beyond wine-released passion.

He hefted a trunk onto the trestle table, unlocked it, thrust the top up and began taking out the clothes that had lain crushed in its damp depths these many weeks. She would find little sport here, his false lady. Even Hélène would not, he felt confident, bed with the farmers and trappers who, for the most part, were settled here.

LéLé came up to him, turning to her father rather than her mother or her nurse as though, in this new world, the old nursery traditions were forsworn, too. "Is mother to have that room, and the rest of us be here?"

"Your mother and I will have that room. You and your brother and sister and Gertrude will have the loft—up there." He pointed upward, to an opening in the low ceiling.

"Up there? Really? Like pigeons in a pigeonnier?" LéLé peered up as though expecting to see the large soft gray-and-white birds whose red beaks took cracked corn from her hands on the spreading green lawns of Beau Chêne.

Hélène's laugh was a wire that could break the soft gray-and-white necks of the feeding birds. "Like pigeons, yes, that is right, like little animals—we are living as even the peasants at Beau Chêne never lived!"

"I suggest you find the kitchen box, unpack the kettle, and heat some water. You can at least make tea."

Whatever Hélène planned to say, whatever theatrical words she had chosen to match the defiance of her pose, the angry toss of her gleaming hair, were, blessedly, never said. A rhythmical knock at the door drew Gertrude from her unpacking; smoothing her cap and her apron, she let out the latch and peered through the small opening. Noel, coming up behind her, heard a language he knew was his own and yet was not quite his own. He pulled the door wide.

The man who stood there was shorter than Noel by a good four inches, but they were much of an age. The darkness of the hair, the eyes, a certain structure of the bones, the very calm of the face that looked back at Noel, spoke of home, of France, of his beloved countryside. There are no peasants in Louisiana, Noel reminded himself. But this is surely a descendant of some French farmer.

He caught a name, two names. Claude Louis. And then a third name, the family name. Langlinais. The tongue raced on, the words Noel had learned in his nursery strangely different and yet the same, the peasant dialect of Provence mixed with phrases, words, intonations, and rhythms of two centuries of speech across the Atlantic. Gertrude was watching him, Noel saw, her expression one of—curiosity? Judgment? She's waiting to see how I respond to his caller. Standing back, Noel bowed M. Langlinais in. It was only after Claude Louis had entered, carefully shaking the mud of January country roads from his rough boots, that Noel saw the bundle he carried.

"A nothing. A little fowl, some venison. Some dried fruit and vegetables. And, I think, bread. For a welcome." But the children, crowding around Gertrude as she unwrapped the food, clearly saw these gifts as very much indeed. Only when Gertrude threatened to wrap it up again, put it away until tomorrow, unless they properly washed and brushed their hair, did they subside and follow her across the room where she hastily found sponge and towels, combs and brushes.

Hélène, after one over-the-shoulder look, a look that had sent many an advancing courtier back whence he came, had turned back to the fire. Noel went to her, took her shoulders in two firm hands, spun her so that she was confronted with

Claude Louis. "Our neighbor, Hélène. Monsieur Claude Louis
Langlinais. Monsieur Langlinais, may I present my wife, Madame Hélène de Clouet." To cover what he knew would be
Hélène's continued silence, he went on. "Monsieur Langlinais
has most graciously brought us provisions from his kitchen."

For the first time, Noel heard Claude Louis laugh. It was
a laugh unlike any he had ever heard before—open, unhesi-
tating, joyous. "From my mother's kitchen," Claude Louis said.
"My wife—well, there are other things besides cooking, yes?"
And he laughed again. "But it is a trade, you understand. My
wife puts lace and flowers on my mother's bed linens. One
makes food for the body, another makes food for the soul."

"Flowers before bread," Hélène murmured. Then she smiled.
"Monsieur Langlinais, your wife, she is young?"

Noel wanted to laugh himself, he who had thought it would
be months, years, before he found anything comical again. But
for a farmer in Attakapas to have to deal with the question of
a woman's age when that question had been raised by as skillful
a fencer, and as easily wounded a one, as Hélène!

Claude Louis' eyes went over Hélène with a swiftness that
had come from years of measuring this seed corn against that,
this hide against the other one. "Madame de Clouet, my wife
Cecile has enough years to be able to enjoy life and not so
many that she is not able to—very much as Madame de Clouet."

In the little quiet that followed, Noel saw two measures
taken. Perhaps it would not be so bad, after all, to build a new
life among men like Claude Louis Langlinais. "I should like
to meet Madame Langlinais," Hélène said.


"But what will I wear?"

Cecile's face, which had at Claude Louis' mention of Hélène
de Clouet taken on the brightness of the still distant spring,
now reflected the bleakness of the January landscape. Her hands,
those slender implements that could do the finest embroidery,
yet not chop seasonings, could pluck the mandolin Claude
Louis had picked up in a New Orleans shop, tucking it under
his cloak so that Uncle Pierre would not see it, yet not pluck
insects from a growing garden, fluttered over her apron,
smoothed down the dark material of her dress, flew up to fluff
out the curls that framed the face that still had the power to
make Claude Louis believe Cecile's frivolous ways were rare,
beautiful.

Claude Louis knew better than to suggest her Sunday silk, or the dress with the neck cut lower than that on any dress belonging to any other woman in the district. Cecile carried a vision of how she should look on any given occasion, and though that vision was sometimes indistinct, by the time she had gone over her clothes, shifted this shawl to that bodice, taken lace from one collar and made a frill for another, the vision became sharp: the image the world saw matched the image Cecile held inside.

"We will want to ask them here, I think," Claude Louis said, taking out his pipe and filling it. "Or maybe you ladies prefer to meet alone. Their children are much of an age as ours."

"Is there a little girl like me?" Madeline had been playing by the hearth, the wooden doll Claude Louis had whittled for her Little Christmas gift set in a small rush basket her grandmother Langlinais had woven. Now she looked up at her father, and Claude Louis knew again that no matter whether Cecile were frivolous or not, the sweetness of her children and the happy affection she showed them made him value her in a way that had nothing to do with that compelling body, that consuming face.

"There is one just a little older than you," he said, beckoning her to come sit on his knee. Only seven, Madeline already took her position as the eldest seriously. "So like Suzette!" Cecile would say, watching Madeline help Jean-Claude say his prayers, or take the twins for a romp in the kitchen yard. "And there is a boy, Noel André, very much Jean-Claude's age, and then a small boy, Marcel I think he is called, who can play with the twins."

Cecile's lifted eyebrows made emphatic statements. "Perhaps people like the de Clouets will not choose to have their children play with—ours."

"If they had stayed in France, that sort of distinction would possibly have cost them their lives. They would be foolish to preserve it here."

"Still—" Cecile lifted her eyebrows again; the statement this time was that people did persevere in foolishness, as he should very well know. "I wonder what they brought with them. And where they lived. Aristocrats! Claude Louis, I can hardly believe it. Aristocrats in this place!" She seemed jerked from her chair by the force of her own words; in one of those quick turns of mood that were in her like the suddenly boiling current when spring rain filled the bayous, she swept around the room, touching everything, catching Jean-Claude up in a close-armed hug, moving a small glass vase from one side of the dresser to the other, finally throwing open the shutters that barred the winds of January and leaning out into the clearing air. "Aristocrats, here! Oh, sweet Lord, perhaps I shall not die before I have lived!"

"What does mama mean?" Madeline had crept farther into Claude Louis' arms when her mother had begun her circling dance. Claude Louis sometimes caught Madeline watching her mother as though she were one of the wild plants the children found growing along the bayou, plants they would bring home for their father or their grandfather Langlinais to explain.

"Nothing. She means nothing. She is tired of the rain. But, Madeline," he said to that serious small face, "we must remember that the good God sends rain in January so that seed will sprout in March."

"What would it be like, do you think," asked Cecile, pulling the shutters tight and dropping into the chair across from Claude Louis, "never to see a vegetable until it was on your plate? Or milk until it was in a mug? Can you think, Claude Louis, how these de Clouets must have lived? To have her here? Well, I will use that coffeepot you brought me from New Orleans last trip, Claude Louis, it is not silver, of course it is not, but it is good pewter, and I have kept it wrapped in a soft smooth cloth—" When the boiling current found another, broader channel, Cecile's frustration turned to creation, her pettishness to great attention to detail. When Madame de Clouet came to take coffee with Madame Langlinais, she would find Cecile and the entire establishment at their best.

The great event was set for February 2, which, because it celebrated the Purification of the Blessed Virgin, was a feast day. Cecile tucked the candles blessed during the Mass under her cloak and climbed impatiently into the wagon, urging Claude Louis with every glance, every movement of her hands, to bid the men standing about in front of the church good-bye, and to get her home as quickly as winter-stale team and winter-muddied roads would allow. As they passed between fields lying bare beneath a sky gray and smooth as the pewter coffeepot standing in the center of their table, Cecile went over each part of her preparations for Hélène de Clouet's visit.

"I have made the fig cake already, and sweets with pecan meats and syrup. Your mother sent over some of that mild cheese she makes, and a good portion of new butter. My own mother gave me two loaves of her white bread, you know how she hangs on to that white flour, Madame de Clouet should be honored, though of course I will not let her know we do not eat fine white bread every day. And, there are preserves, and jam—and you did say you would open some of the wine you made from the muscadine. Well! That should certainly be enough, wouldn't you think?"

Claude Louis had learned long ago that Cecile would go to no end of trouble preparing what she called "pretty food." She would fuss over small tea tarts, rolling the dough out thin, cutting it carefully into intricate shapes with a sharp knife. The same woman who thought peeling vegetables and kneading bread uninteresting and tedious would spend much more time and effort on the kind of trifles that had nothing to do with the serious business of real food—making good strength for the work needed to keep them all going. That kind of cooking she left still to the aunt who had never, even when Claude Louis returned from Galvez's army, returned to her home with a married brother. And, because Claude Louis and the children were fed, because their house was as clean, as orderly, as any in the district, tongues had long ago given up busying themselves with the Claude Louis Langlinais ménage. He, after all, was so much like his father in his ability to lead, to make decisions, that if Cecile were nothing at all like her mother-in-law Mathilde, well, one could hardly have everything.

Cecile had decided that the children should meet after the mothers had had their visit. "Madame de Clouet has been much with her children," she said to Claude Louis. "Surely she will enjoy being away from them for a short space." Cecile knew nothing of life at court; her ideas of how the French aristocracy lived were made up from blurred images of great houses in Massachusetts and little stories Suzette told of the rich lives of her students. Events in France had not, in the beginning, roused much interest in the Acadians. There was little love for French kings: the one in power when some of those miserable exiles finally reached France, believing that if they had lost their Nova Scotian home, they could, at least, return to the home of their fathers, had broken each promise made for their relief, convincing them that the gulf between the powerful and the pow-

erless, the rich and the poor, was wider than could be spanned
by a mere commonality like native land and tongue. But as
émigrés arrived in New Orleans, and began to filter down the
bayous and byways of the district, Spanish land grants in hand
and chests of silver and jewels in tow, a curiosity, a kind of
sympathy for this second wave of exiles, stirred. So that now,
when fur traders journeyed to New Orleans, when dealers in
lumber and corn met buyers, news from France was sought.
The consensus was that while there were certainly grievances
to be addressed, the hatred demonstrated by pillage and murder
put those bearing the grievances in the unhappy situation of
giving their enemy cause for greater grievance still. "Nothing,"
a kind of silent consent agreed, "could be gained by making
matters worse in an attempt to make them better."

Cecile cared nothing for the grievances of the bourgeoisie
in France, less than nothing for the grievances of the peasants.
Bound into private service with a Massachusetts family in her
childhood, she had tasted enough of serfdom to know its bitterness. But she had, without having to resort to violence of
any kind, freed herself forever from such bondage. She had
watched the young men of Poste des Attakapas from under
those lowered eyebrows, those severe bonnets. She had listened
to their talk, their joking, when apparently her ears and her
thoughts had been closed away. And she had decided that Claude
Louis Langlinais was the only young man in the settlement
who would ever be able to make her life approach what she
insisted that it be. She remembered still the fine things in those
Massachusetts houses, and the way of life that had been presented to her in a series of still scenes that had been no more
real to her then than if they had been painted on canvas. But
now! Now she was mistress of her own home, and while her
home was still a log cabin, she knew that it would not always
be. Claude had been pressing Mathilde for years to let him
build a house, a real house. Mathilde had always laughed and
said she liked what she had. But, practically speaking, Claude
and Mathilde would not live forever. Claude Louis would have
the larger right to his father's farm, and all on it. She knew
that Claude Louis would give Julian something—how fortunate
that Suzette was Sister St. Paul and that Bernadine was well
married to a man with his own good farm. But with that ad-
ditional land, and the fur trading, and the mill, there would be
no reason for them to continue to live in what was almost a

hut. Someday, someday not too far distant, she would have a house.

Claude Louis took the children for a visit with their Langlinais grandparents, leaving Cecile to run a finger made even lighter and more rapid by her excited state over furniture that had already been dusted four times, to straighten for the tenth time the corners of the lace-edged cloth covering the table, to place the evergreen foliage Claude Louis had cut and brought in for her in still another container, seeking to bring before her the images that dwelt in her mind.

But the sight of Hélène de Clouet on her doorstep, that first rapturous look at a cloak made not of wool but of dark crimson velvet, with the hood faced with silver gray fox, etched over anything she had ever imagined. She stood back, feeling that she was in a masque, a play, and as though lines had been written for her, she welcomed Hélène.

Hélène, who had amused herself the last few days in constructing dialogue for this meeting, "so democratic," she had written to a friend still in France, "that surely even the revolutionary committee would honor me," felt the careful words, chosen for cold politeness, melt under the force of Cecile's dark eyes, and become warm. Stepping forward, she said with the long drawl that made her silver voice seem to become liquid, to flow in a shimmering widening stream over everything else around her, "If you had been at court, I should have hated you, for you are quite as beautiful as I am. As it is, here in this— province—I think I shall be fond of you instead."

Cecile's script, too, was not needed. Women, after all, are much alike, no matter what circumstances surround them. At least, beautiful and spoiled women are much alike. They are drawn, the great beauties, not to a woman plainer than themselves, but to one their equal. Two together can challenge any male, any group of males. Like skillful musicians who keep the counterpoint balanced, who know how to let the strengths and harmonies of one instrument take the main part before subsiding in deference to the other, a pair of beauties can change the tenor, the rhythm, and the mood of one man or many—at will.

And so before the second cup of coffee had been poured from the pewter pot, before the fig cake had been cut, Cecile had drawn the crimson folds around her, seen in her mirror her own face framed in luxuriant fur, heard from Hélène's own lips how it was to be a lady-in-waiting to the queen of France. Hélène, with an ease that was partly heritage of her blood, partly heritage of sistered beauty, took her cup in hand and moved slowly about the room, picking up the various objects that bespoke a love of luxury, examining them, measuring. "You like pretty things," she said, coming back to the table and cutting a thin slice of Madame LeBlanc's fine bread. She spread butter richly, let blackberry jam trickle across the creamy surface.

Cecile watched the lips that had just told of the queen's birthday ball close down over the bread and jam; she is almost as greedy as the children, she thought, and decided that the small-mouthed ladies of Massachusetts, high-born though they may have been, and high on the social scale as they may have perched, knew very little about how to live well.

"Of course," Cecile said, stretching her own slender arm out to cut a slice of bread. "Doesn't every woman?"

"Of course not," Hélène said. "Plain women don't. Or if they do, they are afraid to say so. Oh, they will like china, or silver, or a chair, a bed. But if you ask them if they like lace next to their skin or if they prefer it over silk, if you ask them if green suits their eyes best, or if blue brings out their color, they will toss their ill-dressed heads and tell you that frivolity is punished." Hélène's shoulders, molded by the silk of her dress, lifted. "After all, why put frills and ribbons on a poor example of the good Lord's art?"

When she saw Cecile's stare, her sudden arrested movement, she laughed. Already Hélène's laugh was part of Cecile's existence; for a long time to come, she would measure the world around her by whether or not some person, some event, in it would spark that silver laughter. "Do you not consider us works of art? Certainly, your husband, your Claude Louis does. Doesn't he worship that body of yours?"

Cecile, her head seeming enveloped in a crimson cloud as dense as the velvet cloak, felt, beneath her quick shame at hearing a woman speak so, a quicker interest. Was Hélène a woman like herself, who had become much more fascinated with the effect her body had on Claude Louis than with the effect his had on her? Had Hélène, like Cecile, managed to withdraw herself, to distance herself, so that she could watch what went on in their bed, learn from it, use it? In a rush of words that found an opening in the crimson cloud, she said,

"I cannot have any more children; he approaches me even more."

Riding home beside Noel, who called for her promptly at 5:30, Hélène was pleased. Little Madame Langlinais, she of the dark eyes and not yet fully awakened spirit, would be a fine diversion. It had proved more interesting to listen to Cecile's small offerings from her marriage bed, veiled with discreet words, hidden with blushes, than to the most ribald tales of some of her friends at court.

"Well, and how did you and Madame Langlinais get along?" Noel asked. Whatever Hélène told him, he knew that the afternoon had succeeded. She had the full look about her eyes, her mouth, that came when, like an aristocratic animal that has finally been petted and combed and fed and soothed in precisely the most perfect way, Hélène felt the world was paying attention.

"Very well," she said. "We shall spend much time together, Cecile and I." And then, with the falsely patient look Noel knew was assumed for him—"And, of course, the children as well. The Langlinais children are much of an age with ours. And there is an old aunt who lives with them, her position is one I do not quite understand—but there it is, Madame Langlinais does not have the sole care of her house and children, she will have time for some play!"

And as she thought of the games she could teach, Hélène's small red tongue made a small round center between her full curving lips.

# CHAPTER 5

## *Noel*

The following Saturday, when Claude Louis rode into the settlement for Alexandre's court, having a dispute of his own to be argued, he recognized the horseman ahead of him on the mud-rutted road as Noel de Clouet. My voice can overtake him without making mud fly, Claude Louis thought, and he shouted against the stiff air—"Monsieur de Clouet, Monsieur de Clouet! Wait up!" Noel turned his head, holding a hand up to shield his eyes from the beam of sunlight which, filtered and focused through a thick cloud cover, blinded him. He pulled his horse to a stop, and, half turning in the saddle, waved a greeting.

"Mon Dieu, this mud!" Claude Louis said, drawing up next to Noel. "Each year I forget what gumbo winter makes of our good earth. Well, March will dry it out—and by summer, by summer, Monsieur de Clouet, we will all wish for a little mud if it could bring some cool air!"

"It is hot here in summer?"

"Some of our people who have come here from the islands in the Caribbean say the climate here is like that. Of course, it makes good crops."

"What do you plant here?"

Claude Louis looked at the man who rode beside him, at the lace-edged cuffs of his shirt, the heavy gilt buttons on his coat. The boots, Claude Louis could tell without even feeling the leather, were the finest pair he had ever seen. Those boots were not made to walk behind a plow, no!

"How did you come here?" he asked, and the question hung in the stiff air between them as though it had been laid on a thin sheet of glass. The glass seemed to grow thicker, to become a wall. What, was Monsieur de Clouet not accustomed to people asking him questions? Or not accustomed to men like Claude

125

Louis, so far beneath de Clouet's rank, asking him questions? Claude Louis felt anger form like a brick in his chest; he could direct that anger to Noel, throw that brick against this wall of glass, startle de Clouet into recognizing that here in Louisiana, the old ways were no more. Claude Louis Langlinais and Noel de Clouet were two men here, two landowners, and if the truth be known, Claude Louis was better off, because he had been here longer, had made many crops. It was someone else's turn to be the newly exiled.

Now Noel broke through the glass wall, but he did it with a smile that cleanly cut the distancing silence. "Pardon! Your question made me think—how *did* I come here? Well, we had to leave France. There was no doubt in my mind, absolutely none, that our lives were at stake. Mark my words, the violence we hear about now is only the first wave—blood lust is like any other kind of lust, as it feeds, it becomes more hungry." A shrug, resigned, accepting. "Well—I did not want my wife, my children, to feed that lust. Nor myself, for that matter! As for why I chose Louisiana—" Again the shrug. "Where else? We have had friends who served France in this territory before it was given to Spain. I knew that the language, the ways, would be like home. That there were schools in New Orleans for our children."

"But have you farmed before?"

Noel laughed. Hearing that laugh, free, open, directed at Noel and his own folly in taking on this stubborn earth, this breaking climate, Claude Louis knew that, one way or another, de Clouet would make it. "Yes, I have farmed before! Sitting at my ease drinking cognac while my chief tenant reports how many bushels of apples the orchards yielded, how many bushels of pears. I have even bent over and picked young lettuce for a salad, and strawberries for my wine. Oh, yes, Monsieur Langlinais, I have farmed before!"

"You will need help," Claude Louis said. "I will gather a few of the men who know best how to proceed—we will advise you." They had reached the settlement, and could see the men of Attakapas drift by twos and threes into the building where Alexandre held court. "There—see Paul Théard? He knows what crop will go best on what portion of land. And there— the man holding the pipe? Edouard Doucet. He can tell you where to get the best stock at the best price. You have money?"

I must forget being offended, Noel thought. Each hour these

men take from their own farms to help me is money from their pockets. I must forget being offended. "Yes."

"Good. You will save much time. Many of us—" And there again the little shrug that said, God sent us our situation, He sends also the means to get out of it; for me, it was much work and barter, for you, it is money to buy what you need. Except the wisdom to know how to master that land the Spanish king so graciously gave you. "Many of us traded work in a man's fields for a new plow, or for so many pounds of seed."

There were more disagreements to be settled that morning than usual. Alexandre had commented to Claude Louis before that when winter settled itself down, crouched like a stray dog who had taken up residence and would not be encouraged to leave, men used their energy to think up reasons why this neighbor or that had transgressed a right, a right worth money.

Now in his early sixties, Alexandre was more like a father than a judge. So well did he know all the families of Attakapas that very often, when a complainant presented his case, he would be told that his father before him had often tried the same ploy, and that it would not work now any more than it had worked before. But this morning, when Claude Louis told how Émile Trahan's big tomcat had killed three of his hens, Alexandre immediately ordered payment made. Émile Trahan, of course, disputed the judgment, pointing out that it was his children who had taken the tomcat with them on a visit to the Langlinaises', that he, Émile, had been back at his farm, mending harness in the barn, and how did he know what that cat was doing?

"You knew that it was not chasing rats from your barn," Alexandre said. "Whether the cat was under your eye or not— it is still your cat. Now replace Claude Louis' hens. Next case!"

"You think we busy ourselves with small things," Claude Louis said to Noel. They stood outside the building, waiting for Alexandre. Now that the day reached toward noon, it was permitting itself to become softer, even to hint that soon it would caress the land with soft air, tickle the surface of the earth with soft rain. "I smell spring," Claude Louis said. "We will have to work hard to get your fields ready."

"First I have to build a house."

"You have a house."

"Hélène doesn't think so," Noel said.

Well, Claude mused, what was that his mother said about

visiting married children? She stayed until she could bite her tongue no longer, and then she took herself and her aching tongue home. It was none of his affair if Monsieur de Clouet wished to build a house instead of building crops. The good God did not wait for houses to be built to send spring, and planting time. But, if that is what de Clouet wanted—

"Then assuredly, you must build her a house." Claude Louis' tone dismissed the de Clouets and their strange ways. He was watching Émile Trahan approach carrying a sack.

"Here are your hens," Émile said, putting the sack at Claude Louis' feet.

"Attendez," Claude Louis said, holding up a hand. "Let me examine these chickens that have been so marvelously resurrected from your cat's gullet." The three hens that pecked and clawed their way out of the rough cloth were, in Claude Louis' emphatic words, "Ready for a long boil in a big pot, and even then, you would keep the broth and throw that old meat away!

"Émile, if I have to come back next week and show these old biddies to Alexandre, someone else's skin will be in the pot, yes! Now, Émile, let me ask you—you have still that young rooster, you know the one I mean?"

Noel, watching the two men bargain, realized that the dispute had somehow shifted. Neither man was interested in the hens, which were now scratching at the mud. The conversation became intense; while Noel could not hear the words clearly, the gestures accompanying them became broader. But both men seemed happy. Perhaps if such a system had been in effect in France, there would be no revolution and he would be back at Beau Chêne, drinking his cognac, letting someone else worry about mud and seed and plowing.

"What, these are Claude Louis' new chickens?" It was Alexandre, come up behind Noel.

"Not yet," Noel said. "May I introduce myself—Noel de Clouet."

"I of course knew you were here," Alexandre said. "You will have wine?" At Noel's nod, he led the way back to his quarters. When Noel glanced at Claude Louis, still in close-headed conversation with Émile Trahan, Alexandre said, "He will join us when he gets his new fighting cock."

"I thought he wanted three hens?" Noel took the wine Alexandre poured for him, sipped it. At least there was decent wine to be had. And other men with education. As the wine moved through his blood, driving out the damp that had been there, it seemed, for weeks, Noel felt better. After all, it was not as though he were going to build the house, plow the fields. He would have others do that. There was more to life than grubbing in the dirt. Even in a new country, men who knew politics, literature, were needed. He felt a stirring that was part wine, part the excitement of what he was thinking. There was no reason why the name of de Clouet could not be important here. No reason why the de Clouet dynasty in Louisiana could not have the honor, the rank, that it had had in France. As for the fact that many people here paid little attention to aristocratic titles—there was an aristocracy of nature, too, one more lasting than the aristocracy created by kings and conquest. To be one of nature's noblemen in this raw land—now there was a worthy ambition. Alexandre had been talking, something about chickens fighting. "Chickens fight?"

"The cocks do. One wonders if Claude Louis would have bothered to come all the way in for three hens if it were not that he knew Émile has a young cock that is quite promising—and Émile doesn't fight his chickens."

"It sounds—bloody."

"But they are only chickens," Alexandre said. "And it gives an—outlet."

Noel went to the window, threw back the shutter and stared out. He had tried, in the time they had been at Poste des Attakapas, to overlook the meanness of the buildings, the grayness of the sky, the dead brown of the earth. He had tried to decipher the patois these people spoke, struggling to pick up the sounds familiar to his sophisticated ear. He had eaten the rough food, the corn mush fried into something Mathilde Langlinais, Claude Louis' mother, called couche-couche when she had come two days before to "help Gertrude cook." If these people, settled here for how many years, accustomed to no better life, needed an outlet, what would become of them? Perhaps Hélène had been right, perhaps he should have settled in New Orleans.

"You must understand, Monsieur de Clouet. These are gentle, well-disposed people. They have a true feeling for their religion, a feeling I find unusual, though I, too, am Catholic born and bred. Many of the little—outlets—you and I might allow ourselves, these people do not." Noel shot a look at Alexandre. Well, that was news! Madame Hélène might very well have no one to play with. "And so, they fight their chickens. Innocent enough, don't you agree?"

The door was thrust open and Claude Louis strode in. "You remember I was saying you must think we busy ourselves about very small things, Monsieur de Clouet?" he said, taking a glass of wine from Alexandre. "But I tell you, the man who allows himself to overlook the small things, to overlook anything at all that will aid him and his family, that man will lose the opportunity to ever deal with the larger things!"

"I take it you have a new fighting cock," Alexandre said.

"Yes, and three old hens for the pot as well. Émile was tired listening to them squawk and he had been pecked on the hand so many times he wants nothing more to do with them—"

Alexandre opened another bottle of wine, took out cheese and bread. "Your country is having a long travail." He motioned to a newspaper lying on the table in front of him. "The *Madrid Gazette* reports that on the twenty-second of December of the year just gone, voting rights were given to property owners only—and those are divided into three classes."

"So I have heard," Noel said. He took a sip of wine, then held the glass to the light from the candle before him and stared into it as though it were an alchemist's cup that could change all that was tarnished in his life to glittering gold.

"You sound—disinterested." Alexandre, always polite, courteous, was also curious. Claude Louis' own curiosity, which he had told to go back to sleep when he realized how distasteful it was to Noel to answer questions about his life, woke up.

"Why should I be interested?" Two glasses of good claret had done nothing to soothe him, after all. Since the day they had left Beau Chêne, their last view distorted by the dust piling up in huge clouds under the pounding hooves of the horses and by the tears which, like poorly ground lens, gave now a clarity and now a blurring to the brick and stone house rising against the autumn woods, his mood had been changeable. His earlier optimism, his conviction that this barbaric land was the site for new glory to his name, had dropped as the level in the wine bottle dropped. "Why should I be interested?" he asked again, pouring a third glass of wine without waiting for Alexandre to offer it.

Noel stood, and for the first time since meeting de Clouet, Claude Louis could see how this man must have appeared in his own milieu. Tall, hard-muscled, strong in feature—what did such a man have to fear? "My family's name has been an honored one in France for more than four centuries. For more than four centuries, do you understand, we have had our land, our position. And do not think we did not pay for that land, that position. When the king raised armies, who led them? Whose swords cut down the enemies of France, enemies of the peasants as well as of the lords? Others have lived on our land, tenanted it. Farmed it. But if they farmed badly, whose land was stripped, ruined? We have minded the forests, seen to it that the game is not wantonly depleted—we have been good caretakers of the Lord's gifts to us, we de Clouets."

Claude Louis' mind heard, not Noel's voice, but that of his father, speaking of the land in Nova Scotia the Langlinaises had once owned. There was a difference in how the two men spoke of their land. What was it? He closed out the echo of his father's voice and listened hard to the mass of words pouring from Noel as though bucket after bucket were being filled and emptied.

"And how are we repaid? How do the people who buy not one plow, one bit of seed, repay us? With murder, with pillage, with robbery. They have robbed us of our lands—four centuries have gone to naught—I am here, here in a place so barren even the yards around my stables at Beau Chêne are better kept— here with a wife who knows nothing but frivolity and luxury, with children who need tutors—doctors—here with only the empty land, and not one idea of what in the devil to do with it!" Noel's voice dropped suddenly, as though all the weight of his rage had collapsed into one heavy bar.

"But you can build again," Claude Louis said. "My father did." He cut cheese and bread, offered it to Noel, who had slumped down into one of the hide-bottomed chairs drawn up to the table. "It was not easy—but he did it."

"What had happened to him?" Noel asked. His eyes were on the fire, his thought not in the room where the air was taking on the warmth of a late winter afternoon when the chimney is drawing, the wine is flowing, and tongues are moving freely.

"He is an Acadian," Claude Louis said. He said it simply, he did not need to make of those four words more than they were.

"Pardon?" Noel took his eyes from the fire, looked at Claude Louis.

"You don't know about the Acadians?" No wonder the people in this man's country are in revolt, he knows of no misery that is not his own.

Something like the glow of the slow-burning pecan logs crossed the shadowed gap between the two men; Noel put a hand on Claude Louis' arm, and said, "I'm sorry. I think you speak of something I should know."

Claude Louis' shoulders lifted, his hands moved, palms upward—gestures of forgiveness. "Whether you should or not—I will tell you now." And speaking in rapid low tones, the words carefully chosen to hide the pain, illuminate the injustice, he told to a new listener the tales of the Acadian exile.

When he had finished, a silence, like that in a cemetery when all heads are bowed to honor the dead, covered them. Then Noel stirred, poured wine into their glasses. "But I don't understand. Why didn't they just take the oath? Not at the end, of course, clearly it was too late. But earlier?"

Claude Louis thought that though Noel de Clouet did not show it, the many glasses of wine had, after all, affected his brain. "Take an oath to forswear their King in Heaven for an unworthy king on earth?"

Noel's voice, when he answered, sounded different. It had none of the rawness resulting from attempts to speak the local dialect, none of the tightness of his anger and frustration. It was smooth, liquid, coming from his throat like the mellow flow of old madeira. "But who would know? Take the oath to the king, let the furor die down, everyone forget about it— and worship in private as you please. Perhaps priests would go underground for a while as they have done before. But the land would have been saved, all that pain, that terror, avoided. Why did they not simply take the oath? Particularly since they had no liking or respect for King George anyway."

"One's honor does not change according to whom one is dealing with," Claude Louis said. "An oath is an oath—it may mean one thing to a savage, a primitive—to the men of Grand Pré, an oath meant but one thing—honor, truth." His voice, so much louder than Noel's, was larger than the small air confining them. The wine, the heat from the fire, the work of putting into words thoughts that lived in his blood, tired him. Perhaps those who had a title in front of their name, a coat of arms, a place at court, spelled honor differently. Perhaps it did not live in their blood, blood being a precious commodity that a clever skin would save.

"It's time for me to go," Claude Louis said. "Look, Monsieur de Clouet, these three hens of Émile's—they are not so old they don't lay at all. They would give you a start. And I have a rooster, he has no fight in him, but he can do his job— you could start a flock, yes?"

Noel looked at the sack lying near the door. "I can't accept those hens," he said. There was no liquid in his voice now, it had the stiffness of affront.

Claude Louis laughed, it was the laugh of his father, Claude, the laugh of astonishment that the good Lord could put so many damn fools on this earth of His, and still somehow the world muddled along. "Noel, I tell you the truth, if you want to survive here in Attakapas you better accept those hens, my little rooster, and any other thing offered you! You may have money, I don't know, but you are just one man, with plenty fields to clear, to plow, to plant—you better use your money to buy some help, and let your neighbors give you what they can."

If Noel noticed he was no longer Monsieur de Clouet but Noel, he gave no signal. For one moment, Alexandre wondered if Noel were going to laugh with Claude, or become more affronted, make the stiffness harden into a wall with the de Clouets and the others like them already moving into the district on one side, and Claude Louis and his people on the other. But Noel did laugh, an echo of the morning laugh, when he had derided his own foolishness in planning to farm when he knew nothing about it. "You are absolutely right, Claude Louis— I'd better take all the help I can get. And if those three hens and an unaggressive but romantic young rooster are being offered me, I say yes gladly."

Noel arrived home to find Gertrude, thanks to the gentle instructions of Mathilde Langlinais, who had shown her how to use game from the swamp, roots and herbs from the pastures, stirring a thick soup. Gertrude had learned to bake bread, too, and the loaves she pulled from the hole built in the brick face of the fireplace were richly golden, the crust crisp, and the insides spongy with air pockets—"Just right for dipping into Gertrude's good soup," Noel said, breaking his bread into small pieces and saturating them with the heavy broth.

"If our house is that of a peasant, I suppose I should not be surprised that your manners become those of a peasant," Hélène said. She was, however, spooning up her own soup as hungrily as though it had come from the kitchens of King Louis XVI.

Noel thought back to his conversation with Claude Louis on the ride home. He ladled more soup into his bowl, looked at Hélène. "I'm not going to spend a lot of money and effort on a larger house now." Then, as Hélène's mouth became sulky, as her hand laid down the spoon so that she could devote herself to opposing him—"We'll build a wing onto this house for you. You'll have a sitting room, a boudoir. You need not ever go into another part of the house again. Then, when crops begin to come in, when, my dear Hélène, I have somewhat established myself in this place, we shall see about the grand house you are so determined to have."

There was no use arguing with Noel the few times a year he set himself on one course—well, she would at least have a better place to live. Two rooms only, but she could furnish them well.

"And something more."

Her mind was on blue moire, pink silk, white lace. She heard Noel's voice—how had she ever thought that voice commanding, shaped by a tongue whose dexterity promised other skills as well.

"I am going to New Orleans, Hélène, there to buy three human beings. Well, have I at last caught your attention?"

"Slaves? Noel—*slaves?*"

"It is allowed. And, if there are no men to hire, one buys." Now why does that bother Hélène so? Surely, she treated every servant at Beau Chêne, in Paris, as though she were the owner. I should think she would be pleased. He said so, pointing out to her facts about this situation of slavery he had learned during their stay in New Orleans. "I should think you would like having servants who belong solely to you. Isn't that your idea of how the world should work?" And before she could quarrel with that, tell him again and again and again that if the world worked according to her ideas, she would be sitting in her queen's salon, laughing at the outrageous stories of the newest courtier, and eating bon-bons, he went on to talk of the number of slaves already in the district of Attakapas. "I was told in New Orleans that there have been slaves near the Poste since the mid-fifties—some gentleman named Masse settled here with twenty slaves. And of course they lived under Bienville's Code Noir—they received the grace of baptism, of instruction in the Catholic faith." Hélène's blond eyebrows, darkened with art, questioned his honesty; her eyes glittered at him.

"I am sure," she said, the pleasure she took in toying with him slowing her words so that she could enjoy the flavor of each one, "that the comforts of our—faith made up for all they suffered."

"Nevertheless, they lived under Bienville's Code. It had other provisions as well—the French are not so uncivilized as to abuse human beings, to ignore the well-being of those in their care!"

The glittering glance searched out each corner of the room. "As you take my well-being to heart, my dear husband"—she lifted her glass—"may I drink to the superb manner in which we now live? It quite lives up to my expectations—"

If I kill her, Noel thought, I shall surely be hanged, and then where would our children be? By carefully pouring his wine, by carefully sipping it, by taking the last piece of bread, using it to get up each bit of broth clinging to his bowl, and then chewing the bread slowly, Noel managed to use up the time he would have spent abusing her. The minutes passed and he felt the numbness that shielded him from this woman come over him. In a voice muffled by the shield, he went on. Blast it, this empty-headed woman would know something of the world she now lived in if he had to instruct her each time they met. Conversational intercourse was possibly the only kind left to them; at least that would be productive.

"As a matter of fact, I will be living up to my agreement when this land was granted to us by purchasing slaves. I will still be far short of the hundred head of horned cattle—and there is no mention of hens and roosters!"

"You have had too much wine," Hélène said. When she rose like that, drawing her soft curves into a stiff line, Noel knew that Hélène was playing the great lady who is offended by a drunken male. She used that role to stop talk, flirtation, and passion. "I am going to bed. And, Noel, I should like to sleep alone."

And so should I, Noel thought. Gertrude had come from the loft where she had been putting the children to bed, had gathered up their dirty plates and bowls and silently washed them in water heated over the well-banked fire, all the while keeping her eyes turned from Noel's face.

"Well, Gertrude, you will soon have help," Noel said. "In fact, I think we may soon find you promoted to the position of housekeeper, with someone else to do the heavy work." It felt good to stretch his muscles, he hadn't realized until he raised his arms over his head, let each long muscle pull to its full length, how coiled against themselves they had been. Zut! If a quiet evening with one's wife was more exhausting than a day in the saddle!

"I go to New Orleans on Monday to buy slaves, Gertrude. Monsieur Langlinais says I should buy two men, one woman, preferably the wife of one of the men. If Claude Louis Langlinais and the Spanish king both insist I have slaves, so be it. It is not on my head."

It was not until sleep had almost drawn over him, touching him as lightly as the featherbed covering him, that Noel realized why the idea of slavery so upset Hélène. She had never, to his knowledge, given herself to anyone. Not to him in marriage, not to the children as a mother putting their care above her own. If Gertrude had not been on shipboard to nurse the three children through the spasms of seasickness, coaxing weak tea down resisting throats, sponging foreheads with cloths wrung out in scented water, cleaning up the remnants of the violent illness that plagued them, Little Marcel, at least, would not have lived. Hélène's own stomach took the towering waves, the lurching climb of the ship to the top, the plunge into the trough, as lightly as it took her hunter's jumping in a cross-country race after game—but her nose, with its aristocratic tilt, sickened at the smell of the children's illness. She had left them to God—and to Gertrude. So if she gave herself to no one, and Noel knew very well that anything de la Houssaye and men like him had from Hélène was a token only, then she would be horrified at the idea that a self could be sold, that there could be a state of existence in which it was not up to her to say yea or nay, but to a master who owned her.

Hélène was silent on the ride into Mass on Sunday morning; it was not her usual sullen silence which pulled a blanket woven of disdain around her, but a cautious cover for whatever was going on behind that rouged and powdered face. After Mass, when Noel joined his family with that of Claude Louis', Hélène held her large leather prayer book in front of her face, shielding even the movement of her lips as she whispered to Cecile.

The elder Langlinais also lingered to talk; Noel had been in Attakapas long enough to know the esteem in which Claude Langlinais was held, and he moved to stand next to him. The idea of buying slaves still was not accepted in his brain—he had bought many strange objects in his lifetime, had, if one thought of it in that way, bought the use of female bodies for a period of time. But to buy the entire being, to own a person until the day death freed him or her?

"How did you have land granted to you without the condition that you buy slaves?" he asked Claude. Noel had had to assure the Spanish official in New Orleans that he would soon buy at least two slaves and a hundred head of horned cattle. The official, accustomed to one standard for men like Noel and another for everyone else, had agreed to a delay. He knew very well that either this coddled aristocrat would get slaves to do his work, or he would perish.

"When we came here, it was still eleven years before that rule was made," Claude said. "Madame Langlinais and I, we were among the first of our people to get to this place. They were glad enough, those Spanish in New Orleans, to turn this wild prairie over to a man with a wife and four starving babes to feed! Now, to have a whole square league—well, a man must have some substance. When I came, my substance was what my loins had produced!"

Noel clapped Claude Louis, standing between them, on the shoulder, feeling the hardness of the muscle. "The best substance a man can have, Monsieur Langlinais. Your son will teach me to be a farmer yet."

Mathilde, who had remained to gather up the Mass linens, emerged from the church, her arms laden with white cloth. "She doesn't have enough to do at home, she does the church work, too," Claude said. Noel saw the tenderness in Claude's eyes as he looked at his wife and felt something break through the sheath of hardness years of jaded experience had built up. Could a man possibly be married to a woman as long as Claude had been married to Mathilde and still look upon her in just that way? If he and Hélène dwelt in hell rather than paradise, was that choice of their own making?

"I have heard nothing but praise for Madame Langlinais since we have arrived," Noel said. And then to Mathilde, as she came up to them, "Madame Langlinais, I believe the church will have to celebrate a Mass in your honor, for truly, your good works have made you our own saint."

When Mathilde's eyes met his, Noel felt another shock go through that protective sheath. There were lines around the eyes, yes, and on the brow over them. But the eyes themselves had all the eagerness of youth, were alive with all possibility. "One does not do things to be a saint, Monsieur de Clouet. One does things because one tries to follow the example set by Christ." Then she laughed. "My mother used to say to me— 'Mathilde, if you cannot behave well and do good things for the unselfish reason of making others' lives easier, then behave well and do good things for the selfish reason that you will then be well thought of and your own life will be easier.' Now," she said, and her eyes and laugh were frankly teasing him, frankly inviting him to friendship, "can you still call me a saint? Perhaps I like being well thought of!"

"But you see, Madame Langlinais," Noel said, lowering his voice so that the others could not hear. "I know how you serve Madame Picou." The quick, closed face told him that Mathilde was not pleased at his words. Before she could speak, Noel raised his hand. "I've told no one. But I was hunting one day. I saw you some yards away—the woods were so dense, it was late." He shrugged. In so wild a country, did women go unattended? "And so—I followed you."

Mathilde looked at him for a long moment, her whole face arrested in an expression of wary curiosity. "Followed—and listened?"

"Very well. I did. And so I heard the whole tale. And saw the basket of food go from your hands to those of Madame Picou. When you have your own to feed!"

"Monsieur. It is not only hunger for food Madame Picou has. She has also a hunger of the spirit." As Mathilde spoke, the line of her body tightened, grew tall with her own pride. "You understand, to have her oldest son imprisoned by the Spaniards—and for fighting in a drunken brawl! This loss affects her far more than the loss of the only man who can keep her going."

"The other son—"

"You saw. Crippled. A good boy—but not able to hunt, to find food." Now Mathilde's large eyes met Noel's in a long moment of recognition. "But, monsieur—the brace of mallards

I found by the gate as I left madame's house—you left them?"

"Mallards provided by God in the first place, Madame Langlinais! All I did was bring them out of the sky."

"Madame Picou and Joseph ate on them for several days. She told me." Mathilde put a hand on Noel's arm, drew closer to him, looking up into his face with eyes now soft, mouth now soft, whole body bent in the earnestness of what she was saying. "I beg you to tell no one of how hard Madame Picou's life goes. She would become an object of charity and her spirit cannot take that."

"But she accepts from you . . ."

Mathilde's voice broke into laughter. "She thinks I am doing penance for my sins, but she favors me by letting me serve them."

"Your sins, Madame Langlinais? Your sins?" Noel heard his own voice rising with the height of his incredulity. "Mon Dieu, how would you even know what a sin is?" Again a long moment when her eyes met his. Then Mathilde's eyes went past Noel, to the figure of his wife standing beyond him.

"Ah, well, monsieur. What seems only a small fault to someone else might very well be a big sin to me." She pulled her cloak tight around her. "But I am grateful for your good opinion, Monsieur de Clouet."

The impatience in Hélène's voice meant that this was perhaps the third time she had said his name. He turned, thinking as he did so that he had a morning of losing encounters before him. Hélène and Cecile had joined Claude and Claude Louis; it was the first time Noel had seen Hélène and Cecile together, and he saw, with eyes that viewed things a little differently under this New World sun, that though the two women were not at all alike in many respects, they were alike in the one way that was important—they were both interested only in themselves.

Though they stood together, each woman had assumed a pose that showed off her best features. Hélène's long cape was thrown carelessly back, exposing the full curve of her breasts. Her neckline was sufficiently high for a Sunday Mass, and the decorous conversation afterwards, but the stuff of the dress clung to her—she had, Noel saw, left off her camisole, so that the nipples of her breasts were clearly visible. And one small foot was thrust out of the long folds of her skirt, out far enough so that the slender turn of Hélène's ankle, that slenderness that promised to grow fuller as the length of the leg was revealed, showed. Any man who knew women, given those small clues, could very well guess what beautiful mysteries were covered by Hélène's clothes.

Cecile's garments, her pose, told little of her body. But her movement, the way the eyes played over a man's face, the way her hands, the fingers long and flexible, described soft circles in the air, the way her body moved, made promises. When one knew a woman would bring her most primitive self to bed, one could overlook everything else. Was Cecile even aware of those promises? Noel thought not. And if Hélène, that silly wife of his who had taken the diversions of a frivolous court and made a life's work of them, corrupted the wife of Claude Louis Langlinais, she would answer to her husband. Cecile's virtue was under siege. Their friendship must be contained, it must not reach that stage of intimacy in which Cecile would follow Hélène even into the bed of a man not her husband.

So when Hélène made her request, when, with the ears of the others open to hear what she asked, with the eyes of the others open to see his response, she asked if she might accompany him to New Orleans to shop for things for the new wing on the house, he said yes, relieved that a way to separate the two women so easily presented itself.

"I mean to leave the children," Hélène said. She expects an argument, Noel thought. Always, when she expects an argument, she brings these matters up before others, depending upon my remembering that husband and wife do not quarrel in the presence of outsiders to help her gain her way.

"But of course," he said. "They do not need to shop. Gertrude can see to them." As she always does.

"And perhaps they would like to come to my little school," Mathilde said. She had not met Hélène before that morning, though she had heard enough about her from Cecile. "I have heard a sufficiency, as you would say," she had written in a letter to her daughter Sister St. Paul. Cecile had been cross with Mathilde; why did Mathilde not realize what an honor it was to have nobility in their neighborhood? And to Mathilde's quiet reply that in the eyes of God all men and women are noble, Cecile had only flashed an angry look and flounced away. Monsieur de Clouet seemed all right; there had been the business of the mallards, would she ever forget poor Madame Picou's lame son coming him with those fine birds, stammering that he had not been able to kill any game, but that a gentleman, and he had used that word over and over, a gentleman had given him these? The broth she had made from them gave strength to the sick woman, the meat had made several good meals for the son. With any luck, she could see them through the winter until the oldest son, the only one who could plant the fields, and keep them all going, was released from the jail in New Orleans and came home.

"Do you then have a school?" Hélène asked.

"It is perhaps making it grander than it is to call it a school," Mathilde said. "But with a daughter away from me who has learned to write letters, I had to learn to read and write, isn't it so? I made a trade with Father Jean. I would keep the church linens clean, would help polish the church plate—in return, father would teach me to read and write. Now I know how to read and write, but my end of the bargain continues!" She laughed and pointed to the bundle of altar linens that lay on a low bench near them. "And now I teach my grandchildren—Claude Louis' children, Julian's children. If you would like yours to come—"

Noel hoped that the others could not so easily read Hélène's face. To him, her thoughts were as clearly spelled out as though the large letters of a primer reader had written them on the smooth porcelain surface. What she was thinking was the relative advantage of having the children learn to read and write as against the not at all relative disadvantage of having the children become intimates of the children of peasants. At nine, LéLé had had some tutoring from her governess. But Noel André had had none.

"Of course we should both be most grateful to you if you would accept our children into your school," he said. "I shall instruct Gertrude to bring them to you at whatever time you say. And to remain to aid you as she is needed."

"It will be pleasant for the children to have new playmates," Claude Louis said to Cecile as they rode home. "Meeting each day, learning together—they will become good friends."

Cecile nodded, but it was plain her thoughts were not on the children, theirs or the de Clouets'. "When does Pierre go again to New Orleans?" she asked.

"He should be taking another load of furs in a few weeks. There won't be much more trapping now." Ten years of marriage to Cecile had taught Claude Louis that when Cecile asked

a question of that sort, other more pointed questions soon followed. He had been caught on those sharp points too often not
to be cautious now—what was she after, this woman who
retreated into silence not as a balance for activity, but as a
headquarters from which to plan her next campaign?

"I should like to go with him, then," she said. "I can go
see Sister St. Paul and then I can get some of the household
goods we need—Pierre is getting old, Claude Louis, he does
not always remember what it is I need!"

"Go to New Orleans with Pierre?"

"You sound as if I proposed crossing the ocean! You have
been to New Orleans, Claude Louis, many times. Why should
not I? I can stay at the guest house at the Ursuline convent.
What could be safer?"

By that evening, Claude Louis was convinced. Why should
Cecile not have a little visit? He very well knew that the presence of Hélène de Clouet in New Orleans was the primary
attraction. Never before had Cecile had any interest in visiting
Sister St. Paul; surely her interest now was her desire to see
Hélène in a setting more suited to a former lady-in-waiting to
the queen of France. And if she could see Hélène, perhaps
have tea with her and some of the ladies of her acquaintance,
what harm was there in that? Her head had been full of satin
ribbon and lace jabots for so long that the sight of more fur-
belows could hardly hurt. Besides, the mill he owned along
with his father and uncle did well; they were able to sell the
corn they received from farmers using the mill at a good price.
The fur trade also was good; if his plans to bring cypress out
of the swamp, cut it into lumber and barge it to New Orleans
worked out, he would have yet another source of income.
Before too long, they might build a finer house. And Cecile
would then go to New Orleans to shop in earnest.

In the days that remained before her departure, Cecile busied
herself about her house, going through cupboards and armoires,
counting linens, checking supplies. Her mother-in-law, coming
in one afternoon to bring the children home after their lessons,
found Cecile wrapped in a voluminous apron, so unlike the
embroidered and ruffled affairs she usually wore that Mathilde
was startled into saying—"Cecile, you have been a wife for
more than ten years and you have just now wedded your house!"

"I have never shopped for the household before," Cecile

said. "As I will now have that opportunity, I must make good use of it."

"She really believes that she is going on very serious business," Mathilde said to Claude Louis. They were standing at the fence that separated the kitchen garden from the first of Claude Louis' fields; Mathilde had come to report to Claude Louis that that very day, Jean-Claude had learned to write his own name, and that Madeline could count to one hundred.

"She is like a child, mama, I kept telling you that," Claude Louis said. Though Mathilde had, after ten years, finally accepted the strangeness of her son's household, where an old aunt acted as housewife and the wife acted as a guest, from time to time a new vagary of Cecile's would still surprise her.

"But she is not soft in the head, she is bright, Cecile is! Why then is she like a child?"

But Claude Louis could not bring his mother into his bedroom, could not show her that face that still stared unknowingly at him when the nightmares came. He had thought, in the first years of their marriage, that as Cecile felt more secure, more cared for, the dreams would cease, the haunts of her terror-filled childhood go back to sleep. Though the intervals between episodes became longer, their incidence did not stop. He learned that if Cecile became greatly excited, if she danced too long at one of the community dances, if she played too hard at a fête, her sleep would be tortured. And so his care of her grew; the wall of flowers he put around her life was designed as much to keep Cecile in those safe parameters as to keep violators of her peace out.

The night before Cecile left, Claude Louis felt fear. So accustomed was he to thinking of Cecile as within his circling protective arms that when he finally realized how far from him she was traveling, how alone she would be, he almost told her she could not go. But the silly laces spilling from her little trunk, the glow that had lit up her winter-whitened skin, shielded her. He could not make her unhappy, not if he paid for her happiness with night after night of tossing sleep until she returned. He held her close, trying to find words of caution. At last, he whispered against her silken hair—"Cecile—remember you are Acadian. You need to bow to no one." For a long time after the boat carrying her away slipped down the bayou, he remembered the large eyes, large with wonder, that answered him.

* * *

"I believe Cecile might visit me here," Hélène said to Noel. He was returning to Attakapas with the slaves; she was to remain for—"however long it takes," she told him, the eyes glittering silver, the voice glittering cold.

"Madame Langlinais?" Noel gazed at Hélène, that cream neck rising from the froth of lace at her bosom, the blonde hair coiffed into intricate curls. He remembered hearing or reading somewhere of statues being cast in bronze over the living body, so that under the smoothly perfect surface, all the work of human corruption went on. "Hélène, I warn you—"

"What?" Her entire body challenged him. In France, he could perhaps have banished her. Here, his children had no grandmothers, no aunts, no cousins.

"Keep your games here. And leave Madame Langlinais alone."

Then the silvery laugh began, the laugh that could chase him from her bed, her room, her presence. As he fled down the steps, seeking friends in the café, the notes, each one taunting, a song of scorn, followed him. Unconsciously, he found he was making the Sign of the Cross. Was he praying for Cecile—or for himself?

# CHAPTER 6
## *Cauchemar*

Pierre, long accustomed to the tedious 314-mile trip from Poste des Attakapas to Plaquemine, the village on the Mississippi where they would transfer from the boat that wound its way through the maze of bayous and lakes to a flatboat that would take them to New Orleans, was first surprised, then pleased, at Cecile's clear joy in the journey. She had hung over the map showing the way they would go, following the stabbing point of his tobacco-stained finger as it jumped from New Iberia to Lake Chitimachas, over the black network of bayous into the Atchafalaya River, through Lake Natchez on to Plaquemine.

"And then?" It took only a moment for Pierre's thick finger to wind its way through that contorted path, but mon Dieu, this boat was not a finger. She would grow old, the season would change, before they got out of this puzzle of bayous.

"Then? Then we make good time. Then we take a boat down the Mississippi. And then, little bird, we reach New Orleans."

"I don't see how I can wait," Cecile said. The excitement, which had been a flame behind her eyes, had settled into a small glow that kept her cheeks pink, her eyes bright.

"To buy flour and coffee beans and a new dishpan?"

Cecile's lower lip, which ten years of wifehood had not made less full or pink or appealing when rounded into a pout, moved slightly forward. The delicate eyelids, shadowed by the veins under that fine skin, lowered. Her head tilted to one side, pulling her slender neck into one sweet curve. "Don't tease, Pierre," she said.

Sacrebleu, he had been blind not to see what a beauty this niece by marriage was. Taken from the family circle, set in her best blue wool cape on the rough deck of the boat, Cecile glowed like a jewel which had been buried in a dull mounting and has finally been highlighted by a master craftsman. One would hope Madame de Clouet's friends were all ladies—those French lords might extend the droit de seigneur to these shores when presented with a native like Cecile. "Pull your hood around your face, little bird. This wind will chap your skin." At least the crew of this boat would not gape at her.

Over and over throughout the journey, Pierre found himself surprised by the strength of Cecile's interest in all they passed. She was constantly grasping his arm, pointing so that his eye could see what she saw. "What is that?" Birds, trees, floating plants—she was curious about each one. And then she would ask about New Orleans, which cafés did he go to, which shops were best, were the houses very grand, what did the Ursuline convent look like, what did the Spanish governor wear when he made a public appearance, what did the ladies wear?

"I know I ask too many questions," Cecile said. "But this is the first happy journey I've ever taken. I want to remember it. Then maybe I will forget . . ." Her voice dwindled as though carried on the little waves stirred up in the wake of the boat. Something closed down over those bright eyes like a drapery being pulled over a painted face. Pierre realized then that many times he looked at Cecile as though he were looking at a portrait, that the expression that came and went on her face appeared to be chosen by an artist, tried to see if they would work, discarded if they did not, with yet another one ready. Her soul does not look out of her eyes, he thought. And he remembered phrases of Claude Louis', dropped from time to time, suggesting that the days of Cecile's childhood had been told by the tips of cat-o'-nine-tailed whips.

As they walked from the New Orleans dock to the Ursuline convent, Cecile's small hand secure in his, Pierre used his pipe as a pointer, showing Cecile the places that figured in the tales he had woven for her on the long trip through the bayous.

"Madame de Clouet has rooms on the Calle de Real. I am to call on her while I am here," Cecile said, peering down a bricked street.

Pierre stopped, pulled Cecile around to face him. "You are not to walk alone in New Orleans, Cecile. Now understand that."

"I won't, Pierre, of course I won't. But I'm an old married woman, Pierre. I don't need a chaperone!"

That was true in Attakapas. And after all, what harm could come to Cecile? Staying at the convent, a few ventures into the shops with Madame de Clouet, tea in her rooms—the worst temptation lying in wait for the child was silk that cost more than she could spend. Still, he felt danger. Women who were like children, but whose eyes, whose lips, were those of a woman, whose bodies moved with the freedom of a child but with the grace of a woman—they carried danger in their very innocence. He gladly turned her over to Sister St. Paul, whose daily rosary would surely put a circle of safety around this adventurous little bird!

After nearly a decade as an Ursuline nun, Suzette Langlinais had become almost completely submerged into Sister St. Paul. The remnants of the patois of Attakapas had long since been cut from her speech by the careful pronunciation she learned from her fellow nuns. She walked with the same grace as the others, used her hands as gently. Like the others, she was well able to teach manners, all the subtle rules that governed the life of courteous people, to the daughters of the wealthy planters up and down the Mississippi and nearer bayous and of wealthy inhabitants of the houses along Calle del Maine, Calle de Real, and the other streets whose Spanish names fell so strangely on ears longing to hear only French.

"But I had no idea you lived in so grand a place," Cecile said. As a special dispensation, Sister St. Paul was taking her noon meal with Cecile in the small guest quarters that were part of the porter's lodge. Cecile had insisted on standing in front of the convent for a full ten minutes before coming in, her eyes lifted to the dormer windows shining as darkly as the glass set into those high frames. Then, scanning the long blue-gray plaster front, memorizing, it seemed, each detail, she began asking Sister St. Paul question after question. When had it been built? How did nuns have so much money? And who has designed the gardens?

Sister St. Paul had finally gotten her indoors, where there were more sights to fuel that curious tongue. But the first view of the cypress staircase that curved from the lower floor to the upper story silenced Cecile. She stood with her hands clasped behind her, staring at the stairs in front of her. Students on their way to the dining room ducked around the silent woman, ducked a curtsy to Sister St. Paul and went on, heads turned slightly to study sister's guest.

"What, you've seen stairs before, I believe," Sister St. Paul said when it seemed as though Cecile might become as one of the posts at the foot of the banister. When Cecile didn't move, the nun went to her, took her arm and pulled gently. Cecile's face swung round with her body, the eyes that had been glowing moments before were now as dull as glass painted over, the mouth beneath them was slack, slightly open. "Cecile, what is it?" There was a strange, confused terror in Cecile's eyes that alarmed Sister St. Paul. Taking her rosary from the loop at her waist, Sister St. Paul kissed the cross, held it against Cecile's lips, and began to recite the prayers that had been cradle songs for them both. She had said two decades of Aves and was beginning the Pater Noster that marked the third ten beads when finally Cecile's voice, low, strained, tired with a fatigue that seemed years old, picked up the words. By the time the Aves had been said, Cecile was moving restlessly, feet shifting on the brick floor, eyes shooting quick glances around her. The last bell of the Angelus was pealing as they finished their prayers; Cecile crossed herself swiftly, hugged Sister St. Paul and said, "Mon Dieu, Sister St. Paul, you are holy if you say the rosary each time the Angelus rings! The fields at home would never get plowed if that were the custom there." Without another look at the staircase, Cecile followed Sister St. Paul into the room where they would dine privately.

Listening to the news Cecile brought, Sister St. Paul let one part of her mind pay attention, let her voice make the proper exclamations, while another part of her mind thought about Cecile. She remembered that when she first came to the Ursuline convent, when the nuns learned that she was Acadian, of a family sent into exile, great sympathy and compassion had been given to her. The Ursulines had been sanctuary for many an Acadian woman who had arrived in New Orleans widowed, or with her husband lost to her. Into the nuns' kind ears the women had poured their cups of gall—but for some women, the quiet listening was not enough. Their souls were so marked that nothing would erase the traces of exile. How like Claude Louis not to tell them that Cecile was one of those, caught forever in a dark childhood she would spend her life trying to escape. How like him to enter that life and hold the candles high for her.

When, after the meal, Cecile asked if there were some way she could send a message to her friend, Madame de Clouet,

Sister St. Paul made the arrangements gladly. Of course Claude
Louis encouraged this visit, as he encouraged all the little
frivolous pastimes that so occupied Cecile while lettuce wilted
in the garden and the blackbirds feasted in the corn. Fill enough
moments, hours, with joy—could there be room for sorrow?
Sister St. Paul wrote the words Cecile dictated, changing them
as Cecile picked over each one carefully, substituting one for
the other, finally accepting her sister-in-law's dictum, that the
note was exactly what one fine lady would write to another.
The porter was dispatched to Hélène's rooms in the Calle de
Real, and Cecile was urged to rest. "My dispensation is not
for all day," Sister St. Paul said. "Though I may spend my
evening recreation with you."

Hélène's maid brought a response late that afternoon. Cecile
had spent several hours in the Ursuline garden, sitting under a
mulberry tree with her embroidery in her lap. The leaves and
flowers on the tray cloth did not hold her interest that day;
accustomed to the unruly growth of swamp vegetation, Cecile
could not get enough of the ordered elegance surrounding her.
She had never seen palm trees before, nor banana trees. Fig
and altheas she knew, and some of the flowers that bloomed
in symmetrical beauty had cousins in Attakapas. But the air
was different. Filtered past graceful buildings that challenged
the height of the sky, greeted by trees and shrubs that were
throwing off the memory of winter with its chill, its disease-
bearing damp, the winds of March, which rode in unbridled
fury over the prairie at home, here became fresh breezes. Cecile's dreaming thoughts were like the full leaves just emerging
from their bud casings; the order these Ursulines had arranged
promised a larger order, a larger peace, that would, finally,
make a garden of the world.

But all dreams flew away like startled sparrows when she
heard the invitation in Hélène's note. She had had to wait until
evening recreation so that Sister St. Paul could read the message
to her. The note had been tucked into the front of her dress,
she could feel the stiff paper rubbing against her. It was the
first time in her life anyone had written just to her, and the
magic of seeing marks that meant, "Madame Cecile Langlinais"
made Hélène's note an omen for good. "Madame de Clouet
wishes you to spend tomorrow with her," Sister St. Paul said.
"She will send her maid to fetch you at ten o'clock. She says
she will take you to the shops, and then you will have tea with

her and some of her friends." Watching the candles light up
behind Cecile's clear eyes, Sister St. Paul thought, not for the
first time, that if one could somehow keep Cecile's innocent
joy in such pleasures and at the same time attain mature
judgement, one would have learned how to live.

For once, everything about Cecile's toilette pleased her. Her
dark curls, springing around her somewhat thin face, were
constantly renewed by the moist air. The pallor of sleep fled
under the assault of her fingers; the hard pinches drew blood
up into the vessels just under her skin, and her cheeks echoed
the rose dawn. The new dress had a low neckline which could
be covered, for wear on the street, by a matching bertha. And
the merino shawl that Claude Louis had brought her when he
sold his first load of cypress lumber wrapped her shoulders as
softly as the spring air wrapped the streets.

Hélène's maid, a tall, dour woman, appeared promptly at
ten o'clock. And though Cecile badly wanted to ask questions
about everything they passed on the way to Hélène's rooms,
her desire to appear a fine lady was stronger. Fine ladies, she
knew from Hélène, did not converse with servants. And so she
used her eyes, her ears, even her tilting nose, to learn as much
about this city as she could. As the impressions she received
were stored away, they began making an idea, an idea she was
not yet aware of. But deep within, it was forming. A city where
she could see herself. A city made for pleasure, for joy.

Hélène stood at the door opening out onto her balcony,
watching for Cecile. When the note arrived yesterday, she had
almost been of a mind to ignore it. After a few weeks in New
Orleans, Attakapas was very far away. And her little neighbor
farther still. What did she want with Cecile anyway? An un-
educated, unmannered child like that should hold no interest
for a woman who numbered among her intimates the most
aristocratic families in France. Juliette de Gravelle's home was
almost complete, and her salon, though certainly not up to
Parisian standards, still drew the cream of the Royalists who
were arriving here weekly.

Two days ago, Hélène had met François de la Houssaye
there. That had been a shock! His wife, that insipid Charlotte,
was of course with him. She had reclined in one of Juliette's
velvet chairs, sipping wine and toying with the pastries. François had been almost rude; if anyone had heard how he spoke

to Hélène, it would have been impossible for them not to understand the meaning. His land, it seemed, was some forty miles down the Bayou Teche from the de Clouet grant. Charlotte without having any knowledge of what she was talking about, had gone on and on about their plans for a house, the richness of the land, until Hélène had quite wanted to strangle her. "And how do you like it in—what is that peculiar name—Attakapas?" On Charlotte's lips, the name sounded obscene. Hélène had left the de Gravelles' early, pleading fatigue. Let François wonder the cause of it!

But this morning, a bouquet of irises had arrived, with a note from François. Could he have the honor of paying his respects to Madame de Clouet at four that afternoon? Well, she would get rid of Cecile if she decided to see François alone. Better yet, she would not get rid of Cecile. She would allow François to come, to think that he could pick up precisely where he left off—and then let him be the plaything. She would give Cecile a lesson in flirting, one François would never forget. Remembering certain moments from the past, she felt herself blush. He deserved no mercy.

By the time they had drunk the sweet chocolate the maid prepared, Hélène and Cecile had rediscovered each other. Cecile noted with satisfaction that her skirt fell quite as gracefully as did Hélène's, that her waist was quite as small as that of her hostess. And Hélène, whose restless ways found little outlet in the narrow decorum of the de Gravelle parlor, felt the promise of gaiety in Cecile's easy delight. Between the two of them, she thought with pleasure, François de la Houssaye would be brought to his knees.

Shopping for practical goods was as much a novelty for Hélène as it was for Cecile; when she saw how carefully Cecile bargained, how particular she was about her purchases, she resolved not to tease the child by taking her to shops full of expensive trinkets. Instead they would go back to the rooms and Hélène would take out her jewels, her finery, making herself the focus of Cecile's wondering excitement.

"I made Noel get them out of the strongbox," Hélène said, pouring a necklace of sapphires set in gold into Cecile's outstretched hand. "He didn't want to, of course. But I told him I was not going to go about in New Orleans without my jewels. And this time, I am taking them with me."

"To Attakapas?" Cecile put down the sapphires, picked up an emerald ring and slipped it on her finger. "Gracious, what will you do with them there?"

"Wear them," Hélène said. "Do you think we shall always live as badly as we do now? This wing Noel is building, this addition he puts on that hut to silence me—it will not keep me quiet long! Noel! Noel has gold, he can build me a house. And he will!"

"And then you will he happy?"

The face that turned to her was so open, the voice so honest, that Hélène put down her flaring anger. This was not Noel asking her that question, Noel whose face was closed, whose voice hid all the things he knew but would not say.

"I shall never be happy," Hélène said. She had used those words often enough, playing them out as though they were a long strand of silk she used to wind about Noel, making a soft trap he could not fight free of. Today, they were not silk. They were like a strong cord, a cord that would circle itself around her. The trap was not then for Noel, it was for her. Suddenly frightened, she said again, "I shall never be happy."

"I thought I was the only person who felt that way," Cecile said. She drew closer to Hélène, the rings and bracelets and necklaces and brooches a forgotten heap of shimmering stone and metal between them. Something in the eyes that stared at her out of that porcelain face made her speak faster. "I know I will never be happy. Each time I think I am—something happens to it. It is like those little birds that come to drink from the sweet vines in summer. They beat their wings very fast, very fast, they sip as much sweetness as they can—and yet they can never stop. It is never enough."

"No, it isn't, is it?" The admission filled the space around them, crowding out the glow of fire opals, the tawny richness of topaz, the deep fire of rubies. "But still, one can have pleasure in trying to be happy, isn't that so?" Hélène drew back into her own proud isolation. There was something humbling about pain, this child should see no more of hers. "Come, let us find a gown for you to wear. A gentleman who thinks very well of himself is coming to tea. Don't you want to tease him with your beauty?"

It was a fine game, trying on Hélène's garments. Hélène insisted they begin from the skin out, she could not believe, she said, that Cecile had never been corseted. "See how that pushes your breasts high," Hélène said, standing back and observing the figure before her.

"Too high," Cecile said, when Hélène dropped a dress of crimson silk over her head. The ruffled lace at the edge of the neck barely covered her nipples; above it, her breasts rose in ivory mounds. The red glow in her face was not, she knew, a reflection from the silk, but a reflection of what her mind was telling her. "I can't let anyone see me like this."

"Of course you can. Do you think François de la Houssaye has never seen a bosom before? If you had ever lived in civilization, you would feel differently." A small stir of memory—of her life in a place that was said to be civilized, but where dresses such as this would be just cause for swift and severe punishment—worried at the back of Cecile's mind. Then Hélène clasped a pearl and garnet necklace around her throat; the heavy pendant swung into the deep cleft between her breasts, and Cecile, looking at herself in the long mirror, forgot everything but the picture before her. That splendid creature was not Cecile, she did not have to worry about things that might bother Cecile—that creature in the glass could receive a fine gentleman, could sip wine with him, flirt with him—perhaps even be happy.

Hélène had ordered her maid to arrange the cakes, the wine, the cheeses and had given her several hours to herself. "She'll go make a novena," Hélène said as the door closed behind the silent woman. "She dares not say it to me, but privately, she prays for the success of the revolution. Her brother is one of the leaders in her old village—she thinks I don't know that. But, this is the new world, isn't that so? And what happens in France cannot hurt me now! Here, I am still a fine lady. And she—she is and always will be a servant."

But I will not always be a poor farmer's wife, Cecile thought. I am not now. Claude Louis has the mill, his fur trade, this new business with the lumber—I am not yet a fine lady, but I am not a servant, nor will I ever be. Again the small stir of memory worried, again she forced it back.

The dream-play that began when François de la Houssaye arrived, bringing with him a friend he introduced as Gérome Charpentier, lasted three minutes or three hours, the length of one bottle of wine or many. The red silk dress had a will of its own, from the moment de la Houssaye and Charpentier kissed her hand. Cecile spoke words, made gestures, she had not known she owned.

"I had thought a ménage à trois," de la Houssaye murmured over Hélène's hand. His eyes were on Cecile, who stood listening to Charpentier's busy tongue. "But a quartette is equally pleasant."

"She doesn't go in for that sort of thing," Hélène said.

"Everyone goes in for that sort of thing, my dear. It is simply a matter of presenting it in the right light."

Watching de la Houssaye's eyes on Cecile, Hélène's own vision was suddenly cleared in the flash of shame that came over her. Was that the way he looked at her, his eyes lingering on each inch of bare flesh, violating it with the coldness of his appraisal? And when he spoke to her, did he use those careful tones, so sweet, so flattering, so false to any but the most self-besotted ear?

"I think you had better leave," she said. The petulant complaining her voice spent so much time on had made it like a thin reed whose high whine became weaker and less audible the longer it went on. "I think you had better leave," she said again, and this time something of the old metal was back.

"We have not even had our tea," de la Houssaye said. He moved to the table set before the hearth, studied it with his head thrown back in that pose Hélène had always before found irresistible. Then he looked at her. Now she knew what slaves on a block felt. That denial of person, of self. She felt chained by that look, each link forged from some intimacy allowed, some favor taken. His hand picked up one of the wine bottles, the other hand picked up the corkscrew, began forcing it into the cork. "How like you, Hélène. You always know just exactly what I like. Tea is enjoyed by some, of course." He looked upon her, fully. "Your husband, Noel, enjoys it, I believe? I wonder if he and I share any of the same pleasures."

A sharp crack, a sharp cry. Another sharp crack. And then Cecile's voice, released into a wholeness Hélène had never heard. "Monsieur, you forget yourself!" Charpentier, hand to burning cheek, eyes on fire with fury. "The little bitch! She slapped me!" Hélène saw his arm reach out, saw his hand form itself into a tearing claw as he grasped the top ruffle of Cecile's dress. Just as he began to rip the fine lace, the crimson silk, Hélène's hand found what it sought—her riding crop, the whip end bound in heavy silver. Her arm moved upward and then downward, over and over again. Charpentier ducked away from her, found the door de la Houssaye held open, and they both fled from the storm her fury created. She followed them, stood at the top of the stairs watching them go, the riding crop held high.

She heard sobs behind her. And knew a vast weariness. She had never cried for her innocence; did that mean she had had none? "They must have been drunk," she said, closing the door behind her. Cecile looked up. The tears seemed to have washed some of the childishness away. The eyes that struggled against the tears were older now, the mouth that tried to stop trembling not quite as young.

"They did not seem drunk." She was watching Hélène in a new way. Not looking at the cut of her gown, or the way her hair was dressed, but at the woman. "They seemed to think— to know—that they could be as—free—as they wished."

"Well, they were mistaken!"

"Then why did they behave in that terrible way?"

Sacrebleu, consort with children and one had to face the clear questions of a child! "Because they are accustomed to the ways of the court. There are always many people there, one is almost play-acting. And men have their—little friends to go to when they want to play in earnest."

Hélène felt surer. Cecile would believe what she was told, why not? "They came to talk a little, flirt a little—and the wine they had before they came made them forget themselves. Just as you said. Now, all this has made me feel very ruffled— we must be gay, have our wine, forget this ridiculousness." She finished opening the bottle de la Houssaye had abandoned, poured out two glasses. "Here, come try these pastries. They are not so good as what one had at court—but they will do, they will do!"

Cecile came slowly to the table, slowly sat, slowly sipped her wine. "This has happened before," she said. "Or something very like it."

"Don't go on and on about nothing!"

Those large eyes stared at her. "But it would have been something if you had not stopped him. He was going to rip my dress off, Hélène, you know he was." There was something about the way Cecile looked that was like being in a graveyard long after dark. Her voice, too, came from some dark and silent place, a place where there had been no light for a long, long time.

"Someone did once, you know." And without waiting for Hélène's question—"Ripped off my dress, I mean." Hélène cast a sharp eye over Cecile's face—was this some country joke? "I was maybe twelve years old. It was in Massachusetts, do you know it?" Again without waiting for Hélène's response, the voice unwound like a long reel that had been wound ever more tightly until the tension of its winding grew unbearable, and the entire reel must be loosened, played out until the end.

"Acadian children were bound into service there, given over as bound servants to those fine families. I, I was sent to that place when I was eight. It was a great house, so big I don't think I ever saw the whole of it. I remember my first chore was to scrub the stairs, a great staircase that wound up and up. Even when other chores were added, I scrubbed the stairs. Always at the same time each day. There were children in that family, too. They were older, I don't remember them all. I remember one son. He plagued me from the time I was bound to them. I didn't know why. I didn't know why no one stopped him. Those people prayed a lot, I know because I had to go to morning and evening prayers with them. They prayed a great deal, but I do not know what god they prayed to. I don't know how long I was there—but it must have been four years if I was twelve when he, the son, the one who plagued me, found me on the stairs.

"I was near the top, I was almost finished when I heard him behind me. I don't think he had been drinking, why do people say men have been drinking when they indulge themselves? He was on me before I knew—he pulled me to my feet, he put his big hands at the neck of my dress, and he just ripped it open, all the way to the hem. And then he ripped my chemise. I stood there with my clothes tattered at my feet. I didn't know what he wanted of me. He pushed me ahead of him, took me into his bedroom. He put me on the bed, and he—did things. I did not know what he did, but it made me ashamed. And then—and then, he left and got his father and came back and pointed at me and told his father I had come to his room naked and gotten into his bed like the Catholic whore that I was, and tried to do things to him. And so they took me to the town square, and I was beaten, naked as I stood."

The reel was all unwound, it had played out on one long note, even, calm. Hélène took half a step forward. She remembered stories grand nobles related after much wine—encounters with young girls, girls very much like Cecile, in open fields, in stables, in deep woods. And she remembered the shouts, the laughter that accompanied the telling. Something seemed to seize her at the very top of her pouffed and curled head, to grip her with an awful strength and shake her. The low fire, lit late to build a little wall of warmth against the lingering cold that slipped up from the river at night, threw shadows against Cecile's face. Hélène took another step. "But—but that was a long time ago, Cecile." Her voice was thin, tight. She coughed, tried to clear away the echo of horror that made her words so false. "It doesn't do to dwell on things—truly, it doesn't."

"But I haven't." Cecile's voice seemed a little more human, a little less like the dreadful tinny noise of a cheap musical toy. "I haven't even remembered it until now. Truly, I haven't." She reached back, picked up her shawl and pulled it around her, almost as though with its familiar rough weave, its scent of home, she could pull on also another Cecile.

"Then for heaven's sake don't start now!" Hélène's voice sounded better, too. She could even, she found, laugh. "After all, Cecile, you're out of all that. A whole new life—a husband—" A quick jerk of Cecile's head, quick panic in her eyes. Damn! Hélène went rapidly on. "And see how he loves you. That—what happened—couldn't have meant very much. Left any real mark. Claude Louis would know if it had."

Cecile looked at Hélène; the look was new. It was still attentive, still centered on the wonder and beauty of Hélène—but where it had never questioned before, clearly, it did now. "That's what you don't understand. If Claude Louis did know—he would never, never tell me."

Hélène's exclamation of disbelief cut the space between them. "Zut! He would. Men use any advantage they can—"

"Like your friends this afternoon?"

"Cecile, I've told you—they'd had a little too much wine, they forgot themselves." The force which had held her earlier, shaken her, had not let go. She felt gripped by a tension which, if it did not explode, if it did not release itself, she would not be able to bear. She drew a deep breath, another one. "Cecile—

they meant no harm." Hélène saw doubt in Cecile's face and
seized it. "Truly. If you were reminded of something else—
something truly terrible—I'm sorry. As they would be, if they
knew." The desire to believe Hélène fought doubt; Hélène hastened to strengthen her ally. "After all, dearest Cecile, they are
gentlemen. And you, though you are quite lovely, and have
charming manners and ways—you are still very inexperienced.
Those people who abused you so—peasants. Obviously."

"But so am I." The slow chime of the church bells sounded
the Angelus. Cecile's hand automatically made the Sign of the
Cross. "Maybe that's what's wrong, Hélène." Cecile took off
the crimson silk, patted it tenderly as she laid in on Hélène's
bed. "Your world is so very lovely—soft and wonderful colors
and easy and—and nice." Her own dress fell around her shoulders, she pulled it briskly into place. "Maybe if you're not
born in it—you get lost in it."

Only if you meet a great whore who sends you into perdition,
Hélène thought. "Nonsense. There are no peasants here, Cecile"—her lips curved in a cold smile, cutting like the metal
edge of the executioner's knife against her words—"and, of
course, no aristocrats, either."

They heard footsteps on the stairs, then the rattle of the door
latch. "My maid," Hélène said. "Returning from church. She
can escort you home now."

Cecile yawned. "What a long afternoon it's been! I am more
tired than if I had worked in the garden all day." Finally, there
was a flash of her usual gaiety. "As I would be if I ever did
work in the garden all day!"

"Sleep well, then," Hélène said. "So you'll be rested enough
to enjoy calling on Juliette de Gravelle tomorrow."

"Will—will there be many people?"

Hélène laughed. "I don't know how many—I do know that
whoever goes to Juliette's is very comme il faut, very well
mannered—and usually dull! But it whiles away the afternoon—and she does have some pretty things for you to admire." She stood on the landing watching Cecile and her maid
out of sight. Her eyes were on the vanishing figures, but her
mind was far away, back in France, when an afternoon's dal-
liance never had to be paid for—was never thought of, never
mentioned, again. She shrugged. As for Cecile's first experience—well, many women felt the same violation, the same

brutality. The difference was that, in most instances, the men concerned were their husbands.

Charpentier and de la Houssaye were not, thank the good Lord, at the de Gravelles'. Juliette was pleased to play the fine lady for Cecile, and the visit went well enough. De Gravelle showed more enthusiasm for Hélène's departure than she cared to see. He did not, she knew, approve of her, but to have it made so obvious!

"We are not in France, Madame de Clouet," he said, not taking pains to lower his voice. "You should not remain here without your husband, women do not have quite the same freedom—here." When de Gravelle could speak to her like that! She thought of the way de la Houssaye had looked at Cecile. Something else had been put to death without her even knowing it, perhaps. If de la Houssaye no longer felt bound by the old code, if he spoke about her—she pulled the hood of her cape up over those gleaming curls, wrapped the cloth around her as though putting on a garment of virtue.

"Come, Cecile, it is late." She watched Cecile's skin take on that fine overlay of rose as de Gravelle bent over her hand, spoke to her in a deferential voice he had not used toward Hélène for what? Five years? And what was that he was saying, loud enough, certainly, for all to hear? "Madame Langlinais, it encourages me that in this new land, natural beauty is cared for, cherished, kept—untouched. Your people will call us to task, I think, for all that we have so sadly forgotten. We came here expecting a primitive world, but I believe we have found a truly civilized society."

"I have decided to travel back with you," Hélène said as they walked back to her rooms, the maid behind them. "If your uncle Pierre does not mind another charge—"

"But your rooms won't be ready—wasn't Noel coming back for you?"

"I should probably never be forgiven if I took him away from the plowing, or whatever it is men do in Attakapas in the spring. Besides—" Besides if I remain de Gravelle's eyes will be everywhere—and whatever they see, his tongue will report. "Besides—I miss Noel." It must be this fretful spring weather that's in me, she thought. Else why do I feel like crying?

* * *

"Imagine Monsieur de Gravelle calling this a civilized society, Uncle Pierre!" Cecile was sitting near the rail of the boat, her fingers slowly plucking the taut strings of the lute Pierre had bought for her. She had hardly stopped talking since they boarded—if Pierre sometimes had the feeling she was fixing a story in her head, he forgot it in the rush of words, the excited laughter. Hélène, who knew very well that Pierre did not quite accept her sudden change of mind as being only a desire to be with her family again, stayed near Cecile.

"I think Monsieur de Gravelle was complimenting you on being a lady," Pierre said. "Where there are ladies, there is civilized society."

"But what have they 'sadly forgotten'? You should see how the de Gravelles live!"

"The setting says nothing about the play," Pierre said. "Now, little bird, do you think you can learn to make music with that?"

By the time they reached Poste des Attakapas, Cecile had had ample time to learn to accompany her singing with the liquid notes of the lute and Hélène had had ample time to regret her decision to return. Though spring had turned the swamps they slowly passed into tapestries of bloom, Hélène thought only of the gardens of the city she had left. The window boxes on Juliette's balcony would be beckoning to gentlemen passing by—what was more appealing than a pretty woman picking a bouquet? And the dresses of summer, sheer, light, their diaphanous folds showing the curve of a leg, the sweetness of a throat, were certainly better worn on a palm-filled patio than on the bank of a muddy bayou.

"Then why did you come back?" Noel asked a week later, when Hélène's temper had turned her entire being into one brass note that began its discord when she woke and continued throughout the day, making flat the easy harmony Gertrude had established during Hélène's New Orleans sojourn.

"I can't remember," she said. And turned her temper into hot energy that drove the men building her wing until, as Claude Louis remarked to Claude, "they work harder so they can work shorter. Madame de Clouet likes her way, yes." Noel's two slaves knew nothing of carpentry; they were out in the fields, preparing the land according to Claude Louis' directions. And so Noel had hired young men from the district who were willing to add a few hours to their chore-filled days in return for silver coins. "But Jean told me he will ask for more pay if he has to take orders from the lady," Claude Louis reported. "He holds his hammer, but she does not hold her tongue."

# CHAPTER 7
## *Requiem*

"And what do you think of Hélène's new rooms?" Claude Louis asked Cecile. She had gone to have tea with Hélène, the first in the new wing. Cecile pushed her curls back, lifted them from her damp neck.

"They are pretty." Her voice was almost indifferent. Claude Louis thought of the breathlessness with which she used to recount the amount of lace on Hélène's dresses, the number of stones in her necklaces, her tiaras.

"Just pretty? I thought they were to be the most magnificent rooms Attakapas had ever seen."

"Oh, they are lovely—really. But—I don't know. Couldn't all that work have gone into more room for everyone? There Hélène is, with two rooms all to herself—and the children still up in the loft with Gertrude."

Claude Louis reached out and pulled her to him. He kissed the smooth forehead, sweetly moist from her walk under the summer sun.

"I can see why your maman doesn't—approve of Hélène," Cecile said. Her body curved into Claude Louis, settling against the familiar breadth of his chest, the strong support of his shoulders. "She thinks Hélène wants only pleasure—and of course, that's not possible."

Claude Louis bent his head over Cecile's curls that touched his face like whispers. "Neither is it possible to only work, Cecile. That is just as bad, it seems to me, as seeking nothing but pleasure."

Cecile's hand found his. She began to stroke the inside of his palm with her light fingers. "I know. But it's so hard, sometimes, to decide between them." She sighed, a small rush of breath caught at the end with a quick laugh. "I think I have

162

put off deciding for long enough! Our house may not have a grand wing where I can put on airs, Claude Louis, but it is a fine house, a strong house, and it deserves better attention than it gets."

"The children are at my mother's?"

"Yes." Her eyes swallowed him.

"Then there is someone who will always need your attention far more than this house—than any house." He swung her up into his arms, moved toward their bed. "And, Cecile, let the dust gather in the corners if it has to—but none in our bed."

He felt the answering rise of her body under him. And wondered if it came to every marriage, this time of easy trust, when the virgin fears were stilled, the eager lust quieted, and only deep joy remained. He prayed that it would last.

The breezes blew steadily over the prairie in April, seeming to bring a fine green gauze with them that dropped over the land, slowly turning it into the deep lushes of an Acadian summer. Claude Louis, popping in to see his mother one morning, found someone else in the kitchen, a negro woman with her head tied up in a turban who nodded at him and then turned back to the big tub where the clothes were boiling. "Who's that?" he said, when he found Mathilde sitting outside, mending filling her lap.

"You know your papa. He thinks I'm getting old—tired, anyway! It's the same thing. Said I needed help."

"He *bought* her?"

"Oh, Claude Louis. No. No. She is a free woman of color. We pay her—she goes back to her home." She picked up a shirt. "Buying human beings! And if others humans are so wretched they can be purchased, how are we not judged just as wretched by someone else?"

Claude Louis bent and kissed Mathilde's cheek. For the first time, he let himself realize that her flesh had begun to fall away from her bones. He felt beneath the still plump cheek the bones that would seem to grow larger as age ate away at her substance. "I'm glad you have someone to help you. There is no longer reason for you to work so hard."

Hélène, returning from taking the children to their lessons one morning, reported to Noel as she removed her bonnet: "Madame Langlinais has a servant, can you imagine? Do you think the Langlinais are attempting to become like the de Clouets?"

Noel, who had learned just that morning how little his years of breeding fine hunters had taught him when it came to buying horses for a farm, laughed shortly and said, "When the de Clouets become more like the Langlinais, I will breathe easier. Where is Joseph?"

Hélène removed her straw bonnet, held it in front of her while she examined the silk roses that trimmed it. "How should I know? Out with those horses you bought." When Noel had hired Joseph Picou, son of the widow he had chanced upon and then come to know through Mathilde's slow revealing of the Picou troubles, Hélène had, as usual, resisted.

"Why should I not hire Joseph Picou?" Noel had said. "I cannot keep taking advantage of Claude Louis' good nature, using his knowledge, his time, when he needs it for his own work. Joseph can guide me, and he can oversee the work of the new slaves. And Lord knows that family needs some form of support!"

Hélène had shrugged. "But he is crippled, ugly. His body is all out of shape. And his brother is in jail. I don't want him to be around our children."

"Our children are better off seeing one whose body is misshapen but whose intellect and will are not than to think that perfection of the body is more important than anything else. I am hiring Joseph as my overseer, you are to leave him alone, do you understand what I am saying, Hélène, you are to leave him alone." She had given him that sullen look, the look she used on those few who knew what lay under the surface shimmer of Hélène de Clouet. Noel had not forgotten the way she had flirted, teased, a young groomsman at Beau Chêne who was not quite right in his head. She had toyed with him, raising in him passions he didn't understand and could not have expressed, only to cut him cruelly when he had waited in her path one morning with a bunch of early roses. Noel really did not want to know any more about the darkness that Hélène hid under the polish of her brilliance.

Out in the May air, he immediately felt better. The seed he had planted with such difficulty, watching as if it were money being put into that gumbo of mud, had sprouted, just as Claude Louis had assured him it would. His fields were as orderly, as green, as everyone else's. Now the fence Claude Louis had shown Jacque and Robert how to build was growing; each day its length stretched farther against the expanse of his land. He walked toward the pasture where Joseph had taken the new horses; that fence had been finished just yesterday, and he regarded it with pride. This was a remarkably effective way to build a fence, he must admit. Tall vertical posts had five holes bored at regular intervals; these were driven into the ground, and then somewhat pointed split rails were fitted into the holes to make the sides. Claude Louis called the fence a pieu. He was making a good business of selling fence parts to other farmers; his crew of men brought cypress from the swamp and then split it into the rails and vertical posts, bored the holes. Fellow farmers traded stock, tools, furs for their fences; though little money changed hands here, Noel knew that Claude Louis sold much of the barter at markets elsewhere. And so far, Noel had spent capital, not added to it. That was a concern; even for a simple farm, so much was needed!

The sight of the new horses drove everything else from his mind. Joseph had convinced him that he must have a good stallion. "If you always have to take horses someone else is willing to get rid of, then where will you be?" And Noel should also buy a decent mare. She could be the courting horse—the horse that Noel would ride, since neither Noel André nor Marcel was old enough to need to impress a young lady. She would not pull the wagon that took them to Mass, or into the Poste. She would certainly not know what a plow looked like. And, Joseph stressed, these two horses would be pastured near the road, with their troughs of feed and water always full. Passing neighbors would then know the de Clouets' prosperity was on the rise. They were good animals, Noel thought, standing with Joseph. For one of the few times he had felt just this way since coming to Attakapas, he was at home. To look at fine horses, to listen to one who knew them point out their virtues, discuss their care—and what pleasure it would be to ride a decent animal again!

"What news of your brother?" Noel asked.

"He will be released next month," Joseph said. "But he says he will not come back here—he has too much shame."

"He's not the first man to drink more wine than is good for him and get in a brawl," Noel said.

"He is the first Picou to do so," Joseph said.

"Your brother is harder on himself than others are."

Joseph looked at Noel, the puzzled look that occasionally

emerged from the politeness with which these people accepted Noel's sometimes incomprehensible ways.

"But of course. He is his own responsibility, isn't that so?"

"But what will he do?"

"He thinks to find work in New Orleans. And since I have work with you, I can take care of our mother."

Beneath the strong pride in Joseph Picou's voice, Noel heard the echo of Hélène's ". . . he is crippled, ugly . . . out of shape." He took Joseph by the shoulders that were twisted across the misshapen torso, looked into his face. "You will always have work with me," he said.


"The Langlinais are having a fête," Noel said, tossing his straw hat on the bed and reaching for the pitcher of water on his dresser. "To celebrate the feast of Saint Paul—it's ten years since their daughter went to be an Ursuline nun."

"A fête?" In France in late June cabbage-roses big as the moon would cluster everywhere. The madness of their perfume, of summer itself, entered everything—and excused everything. Still, a fête was a fête. She took light gowns from her trunks, pulled off faded ribbons, hounded Gertrude to make fresh bows, add ruffles of lace. And when the day of the fête came, she stood impatiently while Noel took half a dozen bottles of white wine from the cellar he was beginning to build and wrote out a note to Mathilde that was so graceful it created in Hélène an emotion she had never thought to feel in connection with anything or anyone Noel admired. She was jealous.

June 30 could serve, Noel thought, as a model for all that was perfect in summer. Like a huge silver cover fitted down over a round serving tray, the clear bowl of the sky, its polished surface unmarred by the slightest trace of cloud, fit down to the horizon, closing the flat prairie into its bright parameter. And like the aroma of the food on those big silver trays, the warmly scented aroma of blooming fields, growing crops, freshly running streams, filled the air. Noel stood in the center of a world so fresh, so newly come to man's firm hand, that it seemed to have a life unto itself. Feeling the strength in muscles now accustomed to daily physical work, feeling the expansion of his chest accustomed now to the deep long breathing that work demanded, Noel had a life unto himself, too. He had been forced to step from the high road his ancestors had built for him; he was no longer one of the proud de Clouets of Beau

Chêne, Provence, France. But today, June 30, 1790, he thought that he would build that fine house Hélène spoke of so incessantly if for no other reason than to have cause to name these fields, their farm—Beau Chêne, Attakapas, Territory of Louisiana.

If the entire settlement of Poste des Attakapas were not gathered at the Claude Langlinais farm, there were certainly very few missing. Noel watched, astounded, as the women of Attakapas he had come to think of as being almost as drab as the workhorses plowing the fields, moved to the rhythm of the music that was the background for all the other sounds of that day. It rose over the cries of small boys playing, over the occasional wail of a hungry infant, over the old women's gossiping voices. It was gay, insistent, filled with laughter, and Noel's feet began moving with it.

"You would like to learn our dances?" Cecile stood at his side, her beauty more sparkling than he had ever seen it. Women like Hélène could paint and powder and corset themselves, but against beauty such as Cecile's, they faded. Her skin was colored by the bright touch of the June breeze, the bright beam of the June sun. Her waist had never been confined by bone and tight lacing, and the rise of her bosom did not depend on the thrust of a corset. He had always heard Cecile Langlinais dismissed with indulgent smiles, or not so indulgent frowns, as more a child than a woman, someone who did not like to take on the duties of a woman's life. But watching the freshness before him, he envied Claude Louis Langlinais. If Cecile was a child because of her frivolous pleasures, her little joys, that distracted her from kitchen floors and spinning wheels, he would take the smiles and simple flattery of those shining eyes over the practiced art of a spoiled and jaded woman any day.

"But can I learn, do you think?"

"But of course!" She took his arm, led him into the midst of the dancers who were following the steps of a dance which had, Cecile explained, five parts, each one with music of a different mood. "This is the first part. L'Avance," she said. "Now go carefully!" Noel would dance that dance many times, going from L'Avance to the Petit Salut, the Grand Salut, Les Visites, and ending with the Grande Chaîne. But never again would it be the same as when he cautiously followed Cecile's graceful lead. At some point, he had felt himself becoming one with the music, the brilliance of the day, the enchantment

cast by his partner. He lost himself in the purest pleasure he
could remember for a long, long time. He might have been a
young chevalier in France, dancing through the long summer
with one enchanting woman after the other. He forgot his farm,
forgot the endless demands of animals and fields, forgot the
puppet he lived with and felt only the rhythm of the music as
it entered his pulse beat, the smooth flesh of Cecile's hand,
the sweet kiss of her breath on his face.

It was only at the very end, when they pulled up breathless
and he saw Claude Louis' eye on them, that he remembered
it was another man's wife who brought it to him.

"Madame Langlinais could dance at every court in Europe,"
he said, taking Cecile over to where Claude Louis stood. "She
makes even an old farmer like me think himself a fine dancer."
Noel deliberately turned away to watch the dancers forming
for the next set, made himself talk of crops and the sickness
hitting some of the cattle in the district. He owed far too much
to Claude Louis to allow the faintest shadow to come into those
clear eyes. Never again did he want to see Claude Louis looking
at him as though he were beginning to think he could not after
all trust himself and what belonged to him to Noel. Zut, the
most difficult thing about this new life might well be that he
had to make his own choices. With no court rules to guide
him, one must go back to older rules, rules abandoned long
ago. Here, Noel could very well see, coveting another man's
wife would be taken most seriously.

There was the sound of clapping from the dancers; turning,
they saw that Mathilde and Claude were leading the dance.
"She has been here thirty-one years, and look at her dance,"
Claude Louis said.

"Your mother is truly the most remarkable woman I have
been privileged to know," Noel said. He thought that those
goddesses the Greeks wrote of so exaltedly must have been
much more like Mathilde Langlinais than Hélène de Clouet.
He was near Mathilde often during the length of the day, and
he listened openly to everything she said, watched openly
everything she did. Each young wife had to bring her babies
for Mathilde's inspection, each older woman ticked off the
events of her life into those compassionate ears. And when
they finally sat to eat, he saw the tenderness with which her
sons, Julian and Claude Louis, treated her. Mathilde's manner
with Julian and Berthe and their five children, with Claude

Louis and Cecile and their four, reminded Noel of another great lady, who had said her children were her jewels. He felt a chill underneath the bright warmth of this day, and thought again that the wealth he had carried here from France would not do for the de Clouets what Claude and Mathilde's riches did for the Langlinais. Money could be lost, jewels stolen. But fine sons, devoted daughters—that verse from Proverbs was right, they would rise up and call her blessed.

"I was going to write to Suzette and tell her of our fête while it was all still straight in my mind," Mathilde said, putting her long hair into a braid for the night. "But I am more tired than I thought—the excitement, I suppose."

"The excitement? The work, as well. You never let anyone give you enough help." Claude went to her, stroked her smooth hair. "And then you played with the children, too, and danced—tomorrow you stay in bed, rest."

"Stay in bed? Because I played with my grandchildren, danced a little? Mon Dieu, do you make me to be an old woman?" She went on preparing for bed, talking about their grandchildren, commenting on how quick Julian's boys were, how pretty his girls. "And Berthe is a good wife to him, one of our sons, at least—" Her voice stopped, and Claude thought that perhaps she was going to check herself, not comment again on the utterly baffling behavior of Cecile. There was a soft sound, like the gentle exhalation of air from the lungs of a dying deer; then Mathilde's whole body seemed to gather itself into one form, one mass, and that form, mass, toppled slowly to the floor.

He was with her instantly, she had barely struck the braided rug when his arms were holding her, cradling her, while he spoke against those closed eyes, that masked face. "Mathilde! Mathilde!" Her heavy warmth filled his arms, the scent of her filled his nostrils. But that warmth was a lie, he knew that. If she were not already dead, she was dying. He heard the stirrings of birds in the shrubs outside the open window, the small sounds of night animals. As the sun had dropped under the edge of that great bowl of sky, the moon had risen, and its shadow light pulled back the darkness in patches of white. He held her for a long, long time, until even his work-hard muscles protested at holding her weight and his in that half-kneeling, half-squatting posture. He eased himself up, catching onto the solid post of their bed for balance. He laid Mathilde on the cotton quilt that covered their bed, crossing her hands over her breasts, and fitting her rosary into those fingers that would never again stroke away a child's tears, fill his coffee cup, fill his life.

He knew that he should send someone for Claude Louis, for Julian. He knew that all the things the living did for the dead, and for themselves, waited to be attended to. Yet he could not move. He pulled a chair next to the bed, sat with his hand resting on top of Mathilde's. Once he had called the others, he would have given over his grief, mingled it with theirs. In all of these long years of thinking always of others, he would now think only of himself. He would sit with his wife alone, with only the June night, its subdued sounds just loud enough to remind him that life would begin with the dawn, as company. He would allow himself all the foolishness of grief, the remembered joys that would mean nothing to anyone else, the remembered sorrows too sacred or shattering to share. He did not close the shutters against the night air; he let it caress her, bless her for this last time. The curious moonbeams slipped in, paused to light the face that was at once so familiar and remote. He saw her with two visions. The present one admitted the lines around her eyes, her mouth, the gray in her hair that even dim moonlight did not hide. That was not the real vision. The real vision beheld Mathilde as always twenty years old, always slim, always laughing. Slipping to his knees, he thanked God that after all these years together, he still beheld his wife walking in beauty and in joy. "It makes the pain of my loss a heavy cross, dear Lord. But it makes my thanksgiving for the gift of her that much stronger."

There was a moment in that time just before dawn, the time hunters and fishermen and men who work the soil know well, when Claude felt her soul leave them forever. Throughout the night, he had known she was near, could almost see her going about their home, touching now this quilt, now the rocking chair he had made so many years ago. He felt her go outside and knew she was saying good-bye to her garden, the herbs, the vegetables, the roses. And he knew when she said good-bye to him. There was a feeling of being enclosed in a great warm presence, a feeling of such peace that he never again lost his yearning for it. And then an emptiness. "She is gone."

He waited until the sleepy hens were being nudged into awakening by the crowing in the chicken yard, then got up, roasted the coffee beans, ground them, dripped the coffee. Tomorrow was a feast of Our Lady, he would ask the priest to bury her then. He wanted it to be over. He would be in pain the rest of his life, he needed solitude to learn to live with it.

After the funeral, there were many people; again, nearly everyone in the district came to the Langlinais farm. This time they brought food, this time they came to grieve. Claude only wanted it to be over, to be left alone. In the days after Mathilde's death, he spent as many hours in the fields, away from the empty house, as he could. He no longer went into the settlement for any reason except Mass, and even then, he hurried away. "Give him time," people said to Claude Louis and Julian, whose concern for their father grew as the corn and cotton and cane grew in the fields.

"They don't understand," Claude Louis said to Julian and Berthe one day. "He has lost the one thing in his life he cannot bear to lose. Because with every other loss, his strength was found in keeping her safe, whole. Now he doesn't have her to care for..."

Cecile hovered over Claude, coaxing him with the little cakes and sweet jellies she and her children doted on. "I wish I had paid more attention when Maman Langlinais wanted me to watch her cook," she told him. "Then I would know how to make food you are accustomed to." And she did try to make Mathilde's gumbo, spending a long morning chopping onions and green peppers, stirring the roux in the big iron pot hung over the coals. But even though Claude praised it, ate two bowls and said he hadn't tasted any that good since Mathilde had died, Cecile thought that all that time and all those onion tears were hardly worth it when the meal took so little time to disappear. "Zut!" she said, wiping her hands on her apron and gazing at the mound of pots and bowls, "people should live on cheese and bread and a little jam. All this cooking—it takes too much time, yes!"

Claude began to turn more and more of the decisions about the mill, the fur trade, the land itself, to Claude Louis. He seldom went into the settlement on Saturday, preferring to spend his leisure time with his grandchildren. He would gather them around him, the youngest on his knee, the others circled by his still strong arms and by the lazy fence of smoke from his pipe. Claude Louis, coming upon them one late fall afternoon, stood quietly and listened. "Now, Jean-Claude," the grandfather was saying, drawing a line of smoke toward the young face lifted to his, "remember, you must plant your beans on Good Friday. And when you plant potatoes, plant them when the moon is dark."

"But why, grand-père?"

The arms pulled the small body close, the lips brushed the dark soft hair. "Because the good God gives us the moon to guide us. Because it is the way of our people."

The old songs, the old stories, that Mathilde had sung, told, put into her children's milk at her breast, were now sung and told by Claude. "Can you say this, papa?" Madeline asked Claude Louis, and then carefully pronounced the words of a tongue twister Claude Louis himself had been teased with. "Ton thé ta ti guéri ta toux? There! Can you say it, papa? What does it mean?"

"It means," Claude Louis said, and his heart felt twisted inside him, as his tongue would twist over the words, "did your tea cure your cough? Did grand-pére teach you that?"

"Yes. And he plays games with us, too, like grand-mère did." Madeline would cry now, she of all the children felt Mathilde's death most deeply. The black armband remained on her sleeve, the black bonnet covered her curls. "I have no one to teach me now," she said, when Claude Louis found her weeping over Mathilde's cook-pots.

More and more, Claude focused his attention on his grandchildren. He is saying good-bye, Claude Louis thought. And knew they would not have their father with them much longer. The years in Attakapas dropped away. Claude was back in Nova Scotia, the children around him were his own, and the step he waited for was Mathilde's.

November closed down upon the prairie, cold, wet. "We should be like fish who can breathe under water," Claude Louis said to his father. "Wrap your throat against this air—it is heavy, it will put strain on your lungs."

"Mathilde is making me a new scarf," Claude said. "It is from her best wool, the wool from the twin lambs that died in the spring."

There was a new scarf, one Suzette sent. Claude wore it knotted carefully around his neck, its thick folds rising above his coat. But spring lamb's wool is too young yet to hold off old winter's chill. Just past the middle of November, Claude was one of the first taken by that season's lung fever.

"He is with our mother," Claude Louis told his weeping brother. "He is with grand-mère," he told his weeping children. "He is with her," he told himself, knowing for the first time in his life what it meant to lose someone forever.

He stood in the little church, listening to Father Jean's prayers. The coffin seemed so small, so small to hold so large a life. The words of the Introit rose: "The Lord, saith, My words which I have put in thy mouth, shall not depart out of thy mouth; and thy gifts shall be accepted upon My altar. Blessed is the man who fears the Lord: he delights exceedingly in His commandments."

Claude Louis' thoughts rose from the church in Attakapas and across the years that separated him from the church in Grand Pré. His father and mother had been baptized there, married there. He had been baptized there. His father had met the devil there. And turned from him. Vowed that he would find a new Acadia, vowed that no man would touch his land, harm his family, take from them what was theirs.

Claude Louis reached out, took his son's hand. As the prayers for the dead tolled throughout the church, as the muffled bell took up the prayer, he leaned down. "Listen to what I tell you. The only really bad thing about losing grand-père will be if we forget, you and I, to be like him. You understand me?"

The boy looked up. "But, papa, I am a Langlinais. How could I forget?"

# CHAPTER 8
## *Nouvelle Orléans*

The last quarter of the eighteenth century saw declarations of human rights written first in ink and then in blood both in Europe and in America. It was up to the nineteenth century to make good the promises of those declarations—without, if at all possible, creating more disturbances than were solved. And while Napoleon Bonaparte, at least at the crest of his powerful tide, might have given some semblance of order to the Europe he coveted, in the Louisiana Territory, the whims and ploys of kings and emperors that seemed to give so much pleasure to those who used them brought anxiety and unrest.

The Spanish governors, from Galvez on down to Juan Manuel de Salcedo, whose task it was to transfer Louisiana from Spain to France, had kept a wary watch on both the British and the Americans. Though Galvez had thoroughly defeated the British both along the Mississippi and the entire coast of the Gulf of Mexico, the lion had retreated only far enough for wounds to heal—one golden yearning eye was still on that river. And the Americans, stretching their unruly brawn, promised protection against the British in return for use of the Mississippi. The Spanish were most impressed. They knew well the fable of the wolf and the lamb, and that the United States, once comfortably at the Spanish gate, would soon long for the riches of Mexico. It would be but a step for that young giant to cross Louisiana, take Texas and sweep down into Mexico.

Increasingly, Spanish possession of Louisiana became less and less secure. The American Congress, working with representatives of the Spanish governor, prepared proposal after proposal that would allow the Americans the right to use the Spanish-controlled lower Mississippi for their own commerce—at one point, several American states were ready to secede, form a new nation, and enter into private agreements with Spain. While Congress planned, others plotted, and the British navy lay in wait, Americans continued to barge down the river in droves, elbowing their way into New Orleans and settling there. The French people of Louisiana were both worried—and insulted. The instability of Spanish ownership threatened their land grants—but something else was threatened more. Their civilized way of life, their love of theater, of balls, was neither understood nor appreciated by the river rats, as these wild Americans were called, who swarmed over New Orleans, using raw energy to make up for the zest of life the Creoles possessed in such high degree. "Barbarians," said New Orleans society, turning up its aristocratic nose. And went back to its Mardi Gras balls, both the public ones that gave rise to such scandal and the private ones where social hierarchies were set, to its theater, barely a decade old in that troubled year of 1803, but already commanding a wide and devoted audience, and to its gossip, which fed on both.

New Orleans was also a magnet for the peoples of the country districts. The de Clouets and the Langlinais both traveled there, though for entirely different reasons. Noel went to keep open the channel of political and financial power that had its headwaters there; Hélène went for pleasure, to spend the money Noel was surely making, and to look for suitable marriages for her children. The Langlinais, represented now by Jean-Claude, went to sniff out the source of power, and to learn what one did with it when one found it. The third generation of Langlinais and the second generation of de Clouets were about to become first generation Americans—that, they had in common.

If the ball were anywhere but Juliette de Gravelle's new house, Hélène de Clouet would have been perfectly happy. The silken bodice of her lowcut gown curved as smoothly over her breasts as though she were twenty-one instead of forty-two; between the art of her cosmetics and the soft glow of the candles in the ballroom, her face was unlined, almost fresh. Frowning makes marks, she thought, and pulled her pouting lips into a smile.

"Juliette's house is grand, is it not?"

Another cause for misery! The de la Houssayes were also in New Orleans for Mardi Gras. How intolerable to have to put up with Charlotte's gloating over her new house, too. And yes, without even waiting for Hélène to answer, Charlotte was chattering on, comparing the de la Houssayes' plantation home to the de Gravelle town house.

Hélène had now seen both. They had traveled to the de la Houssayes in early December, to be in the first group of guests welcomed to Bocage. Despite herself, Hélène had been impressed. De la Houssaye had had the vision not to try to duplicate his château in France. Instead, he had built a home with deep galleries, tall windows, long French doors. It was a full three stories high, with the top story nestling under the high-pitched roof. The one concession to Charlotte's taste was a kind of pagoda set on the roof above the front galleries. "I sit there in the afternoon and feel the breeze from the bayou," Charlotte said. She had been very much the gracious hostess, refraining from asking Hélène when the de Clouets were going to build their own fine house. The very absence of this question made it present; Hélène gritted her teeth so frequently during the fortnight stay that her jaws actually ached.

Of course the de Gravelle house was quite different. The fire of 1794 had destroyed so much of the city that their house on Calle de Real was but one of the new residences going up. Like the others, it showed the Spanish influence in its tiled roof, the ironwork balconies across the front. Three windows opened out onto the longest balcony; Hélène felt another frown forming as she saw her son Noel André and Aimée de la Houssaye standing in front of one of them. Charlotte's eyes could go one direction while her tongue went another. "I think that may be a match," she said.

Her son married to de la Houssaye's daughter. Hélène's stomach heaved. In the fourteen years that she and de la Houssaye had both been in Louisiana, she had been in his bed only once. An afternoon in New Orleans, also during Mardi Gras. The Spanish, finally offended by the violence and licentiousness covered by street masking, had banned that. But the balls, both public and private, went on. As did the violence and licentiousness, under other kinds of masks. That encounter with de la Houssaye, for instance.

Eight years ago it had been, but she could feel the heat of his eyes on her yet. Hélène had promised Cecile Langlinais she would take some gifts to Sister St. Paul. And de la Houssaye, hearing of her errand, had arranged to drive her to the Ursuline convent and then around the city so that she could

see for herself the terrible devastation the recent fire had caused.
They had driven to the convent, he had left the basket with the
porter. And they had begun a drive around the ruined city. But
the drive had ended quickly, at a small inn with a back stair.
They had wine, one glass. And then they had had each other.

Hélène knew that she would remember the rest of her life
what de la Houssaye had done then. She was naked, lying next
to him, hair loose around her face, body slack. He had pulled
the cover back from her until she was revealed to him. She
had felt his hand tracing over her, and felt herself becoming
aroused again. Then his voice, a voice as lazy and yet definite
as his hand. "I would say perhaps two years still, my dear
Hélène. The breasts are still firm, but an experienced eye can
see that the muscles are beginning to go. And the belly—" His
hand had covered its softness, then moved down to play with
the curling hair beneath it. "The belly is like a down cushion
to lie upon now, but it, too, has not many more years. And
this"—fingers moving over her—"this is still a delight. If you
can take your lovers in the dark, my dear, I think you shall
still be able to have your little games." Then he had gotten up,
dressed himself, stood watching her while she pulled on her
clothes, arranged her hair. She had wanted to kill him. She
still did.

There had been men since that afternoon. A few. And she
had made sure the rooms were dim, the carriages dark. No one
had seen her naked before him as de la Houssaye had. He still
saw her that way, she could see it in his eyes. Feel it in the
lingering touch of his tongue when he lifted her hand to his
lips in deferential greeting. Damn Noel and this terrible country! Their son undoubtedly would have to marry Aimée de la
Houssaye, who else was there?

"It would be a good match, don't you agree? Aimée knows
almost as much about growing sugar cane as her father does—
she would be a help to Noel, I can tell you that."

"My husband's plantation does every bit as well as yours
does, Charlotte."

"Of course. But remember how he fought putting in the
cane? Even when Francis told him over and over that the new
kind de Boré had brought in would granulate? I can't decide
whether your men are stubborn—or—afraid."

"De Clouets are afraid of nothing," Hélène said. Now the
warmth of the ballroom, the beat of the music, had entered

her. She wanted only to dance, to be whirled in one pair of arms after the other, to perhaps find, in an eye, a hand, a mouth, the question she looked for still. "It was a risk, to put everything in sugar. Wisdom and caution are sometimes seen as fear."

"I'm surprised to hear you use those words—wisdom and caution," Charlotte said. Hélène gave her one look, a look such as their poor queen might have cast on her executioners before her lovely neck was placed upon that awful guillotine, and turned and walked away. As though it weren't bad enough that all she had ever known was gone—to have women like Juliette and Charlotte judge her, act as though they themselves had never flirted, dallied with men—she smoothed the frown away, smiled at two men approaching her, danced away with the one who reached her first. There were still men who knew how to be discreet.

Noel had also watched his son and de la Houssaye's daughter, the way their young bodies bent toward one another, the way their searching eyes found reason to meet. Aimée was small, light-boned—the lace that fell over her shoulders seemed to have almost more substance than she did. Dark hair, so black that her long curls could have been carved from Honduran mahogany. Her skin was ivory, smooth, pale, until the excitement of the ball pinched her cheeks with color. Noel seldom had cause for gladness, but watching Aimée, he felt a rush of happiness that was as welcome as it was strange. If Noel André could marry well, marry a girl of his own kind, one, moreover, with a decent dowry, with sense—sense above everything else. He turned to the men who had gathered with their cognac and their cigars in a small room off the ballroom.

De Gravelle did have a grand house, one could almost believe oneself back in Paris. After seeing this, Hélène would give him no peace until he built her the house she had been pestering him for since the very day they arrived in the territory. Well, the last sugar crop had been one of the best. Étienne de Boré's discovery of a strain of sugar cane that could withstand the assault of the Louisiana climate and insect life and make granulated sugar as well, whatever it had been to anyone else, had been his salvation. He had not had to use capital for some years now, he could look at his children and feel that they were going to inherit something of value after all. When a man felt like that, he could think of grandchildren with joy.

De Gravelle made an expansive gesture with the hand that was not holding the cognac decanter, waved Noel into the center of the circle. Noel picked up a glass and held it out. Well! Who would have thought, when he had bundled Hélène and the children and one servant along with everything portable he owned into one carriage and hurtled to the nearest seaport, just ahead of ravening mobs, that not fifteen years later he would be on his way to new wealth, surrounded by his peers, taking pleasure in aged cognac and a well-tailored suit? When he and his compatriots in Louisiana spoke of France at all, it was as though they spoke of the Rome of Caesar, so distant did it all seem. The execution of King Louis XVI and his queen had also been the execution of any hopes they might have had that the madness would be cured, the old ways restored. Now Napoleon was emperor, Josephine his consort, France a republic—and always, it seemed, at war. Noel savored the mellow liquor, held it in the warmth of his mouth. Let someone else go cold and hungry into battle. Let someone else defend la belle France. Let those peasants, those bourgeoises, who believed they knew so well what that country needed, bleed and die for her. Napoleon, if what they read and heard was true, would brook no disobedience. He took another swallow of cognac, settled himself to listen.

De Gravelle, his tall pose showing his awareness of himself as the man in the center of things, lowered his voice sufficiently to cast a mirage of secrecy over their little group. Men stood more closely, pulled by the intimacy of de Gravelle's tone. "I have it on the very best authority that Napoleon is negotiating to sell the territory to the United States," he said.

"Ridiculous!" That was de la Houssaye. Though he was growing a fortune along with his tall fields of cane, de la Houssaye had never gotten over his isolation, not being immediately in the know. "Spain has not yet officially given Louisiana back to France—and Napoleon is already selling?"

"One does not sell an entire territory in a moment, François. Nor buy one." De Gravelle did not like to be questioned. He was one of the most important men in New Orleans, privy, it appeared, to everything that went on in government circles, as well as in the financial circles he seemed to control. His assurance had grown with his wealth; now, when de Gravelle spoke, it was as though he were speaking ex cathedra, with all the weight of one ordained by God.

"But why would Napoleon sell this territory? He may be power mad, but he does not seem stupid." Stupidity, in de la Houssaye's opinion, was the worst of sins. As delicious as he found Hélène de Clouet, it was her stupidity, not her older flesh, that finally dulled his taste for her. Other women, he knew, had educated minds as well as educated bodies, and an afternoon spent with a woman of wit and intelligence as well as passion was one of the most delightful pastimes imaginable. His disdain for Noel de Clouet was founded on one fact—that Noel had not, as far as he could tell, found other women to give him what Hélène not only would not, but could not. "This territory produces income for its owner. If Napoleon is truly going to conquer all of Europe, as it is plain he means to do, he is indeed stupid if he sells off a possession that could help pay the bills of his wars."

"If he could keep it," de Gravelle said. "Surely, François, even those of you living on the Teche know how eagerly the Americans have sought to navigate the length of the Mississippi. New Orleans is already full of them—they have begun to move in, have land granted to them—perhaps Napoleon thinks he had better sell Louisiana to them before they simply grab it. Even he cannot wage war on two continents."

"But Americans!" De la Houssaye need say no more. Every man in that little room echoed those two brief words, words said in a voice rich with displeasure and disapproval. They had all seen those rough men swarming down the river. And they had met some of the better sort, men with the American government sent to negotiate river traffic with the Spaniards. Americans might be clever, might see opportunity where others saw obstacles, but they lacked breeding. Manners. Very simply, they were not pleasant to deal with. They paid no attention to the little ceremonies of exchange, the finer civilities of business dealings. To live under their rule—barbarism.

"Well, de Gravelle, perhaps those of us living in the provinces, as you call it, might have made a better choice after all. You, sir, will have to stay and deal with them, every day of your life. Whereas Noel and I may retreat to our lands, live as we please. When Americanized New Orleans becomes too much for you, I invite you and your beleaguered family to Bocage." De la Houssaye was laughing, his well-used mouth curved in a winner's smile. So did he look at the end of a duel, when his adversary lay bleeding on the ground, or stood clutch-

ing a wounded arm. Noel wondered, and hated himself for
wondering, how de la Houssaye had won the duel with Hélène.

There was a stir of sound from the ballroom, then the clear
call of a trumpet. "They must be going to choose the next
king," de Gravelle said. "Come, there is at least one bachelor
in our little group, perhaps Olivier here might be chosen." He
herded them from the room, pushing them forward until they
were near the center of the crowd around Juliette de Gravelle
and her king. That, of course, was the primary reason for the
mood Hélène had been in all day. These Bals de Bouquet were
what attracted her to New Orleans for Mardi Gras—what better
stage for an aging courtesan than a city that threw itself into
dancing with fervor so intense that visitors could not help but
remark on it. But when she learned that one of the bachelors
serving as king of a ball had chosen Juliette to be his queen,
that the Bal de Bouquet would that night be held at the de
Gravelles', her fury and her love of dancing began a duel that,
if nothing else, kept the air in their rooms sharp with anger
and tense with desire.

She, of course, having no house in New Orleans, could not
be queen. And so she had to watch Juliette receiving the homage
of the dancers, Juliette preening under her crown of flowers,
Juliette teasing before she named the next king. She did indeed
choose the man de Gravelle called Olivier, crowning him with
a wreath of flowers and accepting his thanks with a graciousness
patterned, Hélène knew, after that of the dead Marie Antoinette.
Oliver's queen was chosen, the place of tomorrow's ball announced. And then the music started up again, a waltz this
time, with the new royalty taking the place of honor as first
on the floor. Juliette swayed by in the arms of her king, her
flowers high on her gleaming curls. Her reign lasted only until
dawn—but her glance at Hélène, mocking, triumphant, spoke
of what mattered. She had been queen of a New Orleans ball.
Hélène had not, would not, could not.

"But you, my dear, are queen in more important places."
That voice that never left her conscience. Those hands on her
wrists, drawing her into de la Houssaye's arms. "I love a waltz,
one can feel a woman's grace, envision, perhaps, how well
she moves under one's hands."

"Stop it, François." Hélène heard her voice, weak, old.
What had happened to its high commanding note, those silvery
sounds like that of the trumpet calling them to honor the queen?

"Stop it," she said again, forcing the glitter back into that worn instrument.

"Have you stopped?" he said. She looked up and saw that de la Houssaye's eyes were following another pair. "LeBrun dances well, does he not? He boasts that he does other things well. Could you confirm that?" Now he looked down at her, so quickly that she had no time to turn her eyes away. The heat was still there, the heat that stripped all firmness from her, that molded her into whatever François said, whatever François wanted. "I hope that you have not. Because I find, my dear Hélène, that though I much prefer women of greater wit, greater intelligence, there is something about you—or there was. Do you have it still?"

Was he asking to go to bed with her? Was he telling her that after insulting her, mocking her, he expected her to strip herself of her cosmetics, her clothes, put her nakedness under that searching eye, that biting tongue? But the heat of his eye had entered her, as it always had. The swirling skirts of the ball gowns, crimson, emerald green, sapphire blue, whirled around her like the crimson blossoms and emerald leaves of the trumpet vine that covered the summer house on a long-ago day when she had first given herself to him. She had had many men, but it was the feel of de la Houssaye she remembered. "You would be the best judge of that," she said. Now she had only to wait. Francis would arrange it, as he always had. A drive that ended at an inn. A walk that ended in a friend's rooms borrowed for the afternoon. A visit to Noel when Noel was sure to be away. For the first time that day, the smile did not have to be put on her face as though it had come from a jar.

Across the ballroom, Noel André danced with Aimée de la Houssaye. Within half an hour of meeting her at Bocage the previous December, Noel André had understood why his mother complained that her children might have wealth, but hardly the rich life it should provide. Aimée de la Houssaye had both. The luxurious house, the delicate pastel silks that draped the windows, the thick Aubusson rugs—all had been created simply to set off the dark beauty of this one small girl. His sisters seemed raw, countrified, almost awe-struck by their surroundings. Privately, Noel André made two decisions. He would see to it that his mother got her house—and that he got Aimée.

It was not, however, so easy. They stood in the light that

poured through the tall parlor windows that played across her bright face. Her laugh was as small and bright and gay as Aimée herself; unlike that silver sound that belonged to his mother. Aimée's laugh seemed to unfold like the panels of a fan. It could open quickly, taking in all she heard and saw. Or it could emerge and then go in again, swift as the movement of a coquette's lacy toy. As it did when Noel André questioned her, trying to learn if she had many beaux, if among them there was one she cared for most.

"You ask far too many questions of such short acquaintance, Monsieur de Clouet," she had said.

"Can't you at least call me by name?" He leaned over her, one arm braced against the window frame behind her. "My father is Monsieur de Clouet. I am Noel André."

Again that quick light laugh, fluttering, moving over her fine-drawn features, pointing up now with the dark brown eyes, now the curving mouth, now the smooth high brow. "I shall have to get to know you better. After all, once I have called you by your given name—it would be more difficult to pull back, n'est-ce pas?" Then she had taken his arm and said she would show him the grounds of Bocage. They had spent more than an hour in the brisk December air, but though Aimée guided him past camellias pink with bloom, he saw only the pink of her cheeks; though she pointed out the reflecting pond whose surface shone in the winter sun, he saw only the shine of her eyes; though she proudly explained why their house had such graceful lines, why its strength was more than its slender columns would reveal, he saw only the grace of her body, he wondered only at what strength her tininess might conceal.

Throughout the week-long stay at Bocage, he found that he was alive only when Aimée was near. Toward the end of that week, he followed her to the stables where she was inspecting a new horse. He lounged against the rail that separated the stall from the side passage through the middle of the stable, watched her as she ran a hand over the horse's gleaming back. She was in rapid, intense conversation with the stableman; at first, Noel André was intrigued at the depth of her knowledge, the expertise of her questions. But then he grew bored—and angry. "Can't you hurry?" he said. "I want to talk to you."

The dark eyes looked at him, pausing at his eyes, his mouth. A long, steady stare—Noel André thought he knew how the horse Aimée was examining must feel. "It's not a question of hurrying," she said. "It's a question of doing what has to be done. If you can wait—very well. If you cannot—" Again her eyes moved over his face. "Well, then, you can't." She turned back to the stableman, finished giving her instructions. Then she reached deep into the pocket of her skirt and pulled out an apple, which she fed to the animal standing tall before her. "Now," she said, brushing her hand against her dress. "Now I can talk with you." She ducked under the stall rail, rested one small hand on Noel André's arm and looked up at him. "What do you want to talk about?"

Noel André, caught in the clear light in her eyes, was confused—surely she knew how he felt? She could not be so innocent, no naïve, that she had not understood all the signals he sent. But if she understood, why was she making it so difficult for him? "You know very well what I want to talk about," he said. He felt his face settle into a pout and waited for Aimée to placate him as his mother and sisters did.

Instead she began to move forward, hand still on his arm. He must either move with her or be left standing in the middle of the stable, surrounded by the presence and odor of horses. "Noel André," she said, as he walked with her. "I don't play games. I haven't, not since I was a child." She seemed to come closer to him, he could feel the intensity of her whole body in the touch of that one small hand. "I like you very much—you already know that. If you want more than that—well, you won't get it behaving like a baby. Tell me how you feel right out—or keep it to yourself. But don't play games." Then she looked up at him and laughed. "And don't pout. Then you look like a baby, too. And, Noel André—I like grown-up men."

He had retired to his room to dress for dinner more confused than ever. Apparently, he could have Aimée de la Houssaye, if he wanted her. His confusion now was that, as attractive as she was, as drawn to her as he was, he was not at all sure what he felt was love—or even pure desire. There was something in Aimée that seemed to bring out that very childishness that she received so coolly. He wanted not so much to possess that small body as to burrow in it, to feel her warmth, her laughter, around him. Damn it, why could she not have been one of the girls in New Orleans who were available for an hour, an evening, a month or a lifetime? He pushed the gold studs through his shirts, stabbing each one into its hole with angry force. It couldn't matter to a woman who she went to bed with, not really. What did she have to worry about? But he already knew about himself that it made a great deal of difference to him what kind of women he went to bed with. Aimée, he had thought, would be small and compliant and easy. If he were wrong? He heard the chime strike six. Pulling on his coat, he took a final look in the shaving mirror swinging in its walnut frame. He lifted his chin, firmed his mouth. If it was a grown-up man Mademoiselle Aimée de la Houssaye wanted, a grown-up man she would have. Slamming the door behind him, Noel André resolved that she had better be worth growing up for.

After dinner, Noel André remained with the men instead of following Aimée to the music room as had been his habit. And when they joined the ladies in the parlor, he spoke longest, not with Aimée, but with her mother. As he bent over Madame de la Houssaye's hand at the end of the evening, bidding her good night, she said, "You needn't pay me court, Noel André. Aimée makes her own decisions—as long as her father agrees with her, neither of them bothers to consult me at all."

"So far, she has nothing to decide," he said. He saw a twist of a smile in Madame de la Houssaye's eyes.

"Good. Perhaps you understand my daughter after all." Charlotte de la Houssaye looked across the room, where Aimée stood on the hearth between Noel de Clouet and her father. The fire glow behind her lit up her hair, cast an aura of brightness over her deep crimson dress. "I sometimes think she has been too much in the stables—and with her father." Then Charlotte lifted a graceful hand, covered her mouth. "Pardon, Noel André. These late hours don't sit as well as they used to. Don't feel, however, that you must go to bed simply because your hostess does." She looked again toward the hearth, her eyes now on her husband. "I assure you, Monsieur de la Houssaye doesn't."

Hélène apparently felt no constraint to retire either. She ordered Noel André to pour her another brandy and patted the sofa next to her. "Sit here and tell me how your courtship goes," she said.

"There's nothing to tell," he said. He felt his mouth drooping into the familiar pout, fought it back to firmness.

"Zut! Nothing to tell indeed. Are you going to let a little tease like Aimée make a toy of you?"

"She doesn't make a toy of me. She doesn't play games."

Hélène's laughter cut across the tension in the room, a tension that seemed to come from strings woven between the members of the group on the hearth and the two sharing the blue brocade sofa. "And that's the biggest game of all. To say one doesn't play them." She leaned forward, tapped his wrist with a long finger. "Listen, Noel André. If you want to marry Aimée de la Houssaye, you mustn't ask her. You mustn't mope about and let her see her power over you. You must tell her. Make the arrangements with François, let her understand clearly that her marriage is none of her affair—that she will marry you because you wish it—and her father wishes it."

"I'm not buying a slave, Mère."

"Of course not. Simply avoiding becoming one. Comprends-toi?"

In the weeks after that visit, Noel André had not written to Aimée at all. On King's Day, a gift was delivered to her, a small engraving of an English hunt, framed in rosewood. A note accompanied the gift, announcing that he would be in her vicinity at the end of January and would call. He received a letter in return, formal, carefully phrased, thanking him for the gift and saying she would of course be pleased to see him again. When the day came, he almost forgot his mother's advice—why pretend an authority he knew was false? Games were not only childish, they were dangerous as well. If to have Aimée, he had to become someone else, at what point could he be Noel André again? But the sight of her, that small body that seemed too slight to carry the weight of curving breasts and hips, her laughing lips and eyes, strengthened him. Carry the day first, worry about the consequences later.

At the end of the afternoon, she walked down to the gate with him. "I hadn't thought it had been so long since I'd seen you, Noel André," she said. "But it must have been. Long enough, at least, for you to be all grown up."

He listened closely; was there a hint of laughter, teasing, in her voice? He heard only soft flattery, pleasing words. He put a hand on each of her shoulders and looked down at her. "Perhaps not all grown up," he said. "But certainly grown up enough to know what I want. And to go about having it. I'm going to spend a few days with the LeClercs. On my way back home, I will meet with your father. He will let you know, I am sure what the outcome of that meeting is."

"I am my father's pet," Aimée said. "I trust his judgment completely."

Riding to the LeClercs, Noel André thought that if losing one's innocence was the final step to growing up, then he was not pretending at all that he had reached that privileged state. When he compared his sentimental fancies, his romantic dreams, on first seeing Aimée and spending time with her with the actual situation, he realized what an idiot he had been. To think that love matters! That bright eyes and happy laughter weighed one small measure against money and station! Apparently, it was his good fortune that Aimée was pretty, hers that he was handsome. But had she been a cow, like the girl poor Pierre LeClerc was to marry, the match would still be arranged. He had been brought to Bocage like a bull, a stallion, to be looked over by the owners of the mare. His duty was clear—produce heirs for the de Clouet land, a spare son, perhaps, to take care of Aimée's interest in Bocage. The mask he'd worn that afternoon was, apparently, his for a long, long time.

And though he could still lose himself in Aimée's eyes, find pleasure in her laughter, there was a small chill that had settled somewhere inside him and gave no sign of going away, even in the heat and brilliance of the de Gravelle ballroom.

On Rue de San Felipe, another ball was in progress. Jean-Claude Langlinais, twenty years old and filled with the assurance of a man old enough to be sent to New Orleans alone, old enough to represent the Langlinais men with the fur traders in that port city, and old enough to have had many clearly worded invitations from the women who strolled in the streets or leaned from open windows in certain neighborhoods, was there. He had heard of these quadroon balls when he first arrived in New Orleans two days earlier. One of the men he traded with had taken him aside.

"You're a bit younger than your uncle who usually comes— you'll maybe be interested in some of the pleasures I never mentioned to him." Jean-Claude had listened in astonishment. Then he had walked about until he found a café. For a long time, he had sipped coffee and thought over all the fur trader had suggested. His father had certainly never spoken of these women, the houses one could go to, the balls where beautiful girls born of white fathers and black mothers were put on display, there to find their own protectors. Because he did not know they existed? Merde, his father was not stupid. Because Jean-Claude was left to make his own decision? And keep that

decision to himself? He beckoned to the waiter, ordered wine.
The café was filling now, men coming in and sitting at the little
tables, calling for wine, shouting to one another. Jean-Claude
could feel his blood stirring, responding to the talk, the crowd
around him. These men would not think twice about visiting
a quadroon ball saying yes to the bold invitations from women
in the streets. Nor would he. When he got back to Attakapas,
it would be time for spring plowing. And then all the months
of hoeing, of weeding, of wresting a living from a nature that
smiled one moment and sent hailstorms and floods the next.
If he were going to be buried in the country the rest of his life,
he would at least have something exciting to remember. Now,
standing on the edge of the crowd that filled the ballroom, his
eyes grew larger and larger as though to encompass the rich
scene before him. A man, ruffled shirt gleaming whitely against
the fine dark cloth of his suit, brushed against Jean-Claude.
"Pardon," he said, and then, caught perhaps by something
alien, turned and faced him. "Who are you?" he said. A waiter
passed carrying a silver tray of tiny crystal glasses, whose small
bell-shaped globes held gleaming liqueurs the colors of jewels.
"A liqueur?" Without waiting for an answer, the man chose
two, handed one to Jean-Claude.

"Your name?"

"After you, monsieur," Jean-Claude said. His hand swallowed the glass, he could crush it between his thumb and
forefinger. If this stranger did not mind his manners, the glass
was not all that stood in danger of being crushed.

"Pardon encore," the man said. A hand came out, took Jean-
Claude's. "Jean Lafitte. And you?"

"Jean-Claude Langlinais." A feeling like that he had this
afternoon, when he successfully traded the furs, slipped over
Jean-Claude. Being the representative of the family to New
Orleans was not that difficult after all. And judging from the
beauty of the women who decorated this room, there was much
pleasure to be had as well.

"You are not from here?"

"No. From Poste des Attakapas. You know it?"

"I know the bayou country."

"And you? Do you live in New Orleans?" This man was as
grand as any of the de Clouets. If Jean-Claude pretended that
he spoke, not with a tall slender dandy who was at home in
the quadroon ballroom as another man might be in the fields,

but with Noel André de Clouet, his tongue moved quite smoothly.

"My brother and I are making plans to live here. Soon." The dark eyes went slowly over the room, dividing it into squares. Each square came under the deliberate survey, each woman, each man, was taken apart, measured, kept, or discarded. Jean-Claude's eyes followed Lafitte's; he had never in all his life seen so many magnificent women, so splendidly dressed, in one room. The golden light from the candles fell on the golden lights in their skin; softly rounded shoulders and bosoms rose from dresses shimmering with richness, and the brilliance of jewels picked up the golden light, drew it in, intensified it, and threw it back against the mirrors lining the walls. Lining those walls were other women, whose proudly carried heads were crowned with turbans. They, too, had beauty, though, like aging parchment, it was darker, deeper, worn.

"Well. And how came you here?" Lafitte had apparently completed his survey; he took Jean-Claude's arm and guided him into the gaming room that joined the ballroom.

"To New Orleans? My family trades furs; I brought a load in from Attakapas."

"I meant to this ball."

"One of the men I trade with was coming. He offered to bring me. Why? Should I not be here?"

Lafitte was again surveying the room. Did he always do this? Was he like some dark animal, searching for danger at every pace, bent on doing harm before it was done to him? He moved toward a table, placing a long thin cigar in his mouth which he lit at one of the tapers burning in tall candelabra around the room. "It seems to be, perhaps, a little rich for your blood."

Jean-Claude could feel something else in his blood, taut anger that pulled his hands into fists. "Because I am young and poor?"

Lafitte looked at him now. The dark eyes that had surveyed the quadroon women, their mothers, the beaux who came to court them, now dissected Jean-Claude. In the cool depths of that long stare, Jean-Claude's anger tempered itself, calmed. "Neither of those conditions is forever." The slender hand waved. "Many of the men here were once poor—all were once young. Youth takes care of itself naturally, the other—that takes, maybe, a little daring." The survey was over, the judgment made.

"What do you do in Attakapas, besides trade furs?"

"I have a farm." The length and depth and breadth of his fields entered Jean-Claude's voice; a man who commanded so much land need stand second to no one, not even a New Orleans dandy in a French shirt and beautifully cut coat. "We bring lumber, cypress, out of the swamp. We have a mill. And you? What business will you and your brother be in?"

"A blacksmith shop," Lafitte said. The cool eyes were amused. Before Jean-Claude could speak, Lafitte said, "You think I give myself airs for a man who is nothing but a smithy."

"I don't judge a man by his business."

"What do you judge him by?"

Jean-Claude, for the second time that day, felt confidence clothe him like a thick woolen cloak. "By his courage. His willingness to face risk—and his ability to take the consequences."

"And honor? Doesn't that matter?"

Jean-Claude sipped his liqueur. That word seemed out of place here, as though belonging to a language not still used. "Honor means different things to different men," he said finally. "But courage—that always means the same."

"So. Perhaps the business my brother and I are really in might interest you. If, in your judgment, you yourself have courage."

"What business might that be?"

"A highly profitable one," Lafitte said. "I will tell you about it someday." The slender hand came out, its strength drawn from the whole lean length of the man. "This is your first visit to New Orleans—I'll wait until you know more of it—and more of yourself."

Jean-Claude took Lafitte's hand. "I know myself now, man."

"Perhaps. But you come from a people who might not view my—business quite as my brother and I do. Now you are testing your new little freedom—I think I'll wait until you know how well you like it before I offer you more."

Jean-Claude watched while Lafitte seated himself at the table, beckoned to a waiter for cognac, picked up the cards. The evening, which had seemed to promise a few hours of diversion only, had opened another road, one that would not curve back around to the same old farm rut. This road Lafitte traveled was not plain—not yet. And Jean-Claude had only the merest foothold on it. But if it led to adventure, riches, if

it led away from plowing and weeding and harvesting—even
if only once in a while—he was damn sure going to follow it.

Noel, on the trip back to Poste des Attakapas, was withdrawn.
Hélène made little effort to take him out of his mood. Her own
thoughts were in New Orleans, in a closely draped room lit
with low-burning candles, where she had lain with François de
la Houssaye. She heard herself saying—"When they marry,
Francis, it will be like incest." And saw again his heavy body
lifted on an elbow, his arm reaching over her to the decanter
of wine on the table next to the bed. His smile when he said—
"What a pity, my dear, that they won't know it."

She shook herself and watched Noel move to the rail and
stare into the water that seemed to roll by as the barge stood
still. "Well," she said, making the web of words wide enough
to follow him, envelop him, "you don't seem very happy,
considering your son's engagement to the daughter of one of
our oldest friends has just been formally announced."

Noel turned and looked at his wife. Did she hear nothing
but flattery, see nothing but this competitor's dress, that one's
jewels? Could she have spent a fortnight in New Orleans and
not have heard one word of the river of power about to be
undammed? "Hélène—" Of what use to be angry. If there ever
was a time for that, it was long, long ago. The heat cooled,
his voice assumed its dull and temperate tones. "You have
heard, I know, that Spain is to cede Louisiana back to France."

"Zut! That is old news. Have they done it, then? Are we
French again? Though that is hardly to be desired, with a
ridiculous peasant parading as an emperor. I heard that Josephine is quite impossible, even some of those who were the
most against royalty sigh for our dear Louis and Marie Antoinette." It was terribly tedious of Noel to go on and on about
politics. One would think that having lost almost all they had
in one political event, he would shut such matters from his
mind forever. Or have the grace to keep them from her.

"No. But it is an open secret that the cession will take place
sometime this year. It is also an open secret that Napoleon then
intends to sell this territory to the Americans."

Noel André, sitting in musing isolation, heard the warning
note in his mother's voice, understood it before he caught the
words.

"But it belongs to us!"

For once, his father did not correct her, did not point out that in her self-absorption, she was forgetting that the territory also belonged to many others. "By right of a grant from the Spanish king."

"The French would honor that—" Noel André had been too small when they had left France to ever remember seeing the effect of exile in his mother's face. He had, growing up, seen what small vexations, minor aggravations, did to that smooth mask that came fresh to meet each day from the ever more numerous pots and jars on her dressing table. Now he saw what real threat, true danger, did. The mask collapsed, it was horribly like seeing a mime age twenty years in fewer seconds; only the eyes, burning, bright, staring out of that wrinkled ruin were alive. "But the Americans may not?"

His father's shoulders lifted. "Who can know what they may do? They have wanted this land, have wheedled grants for the Spanish under conditions far less favorable than ours. Once they own the territory, it is theirs for the taking."

"But surely France can insist—"

"And hold them to that with what? If Napoleon cared to fight on this continent, he would never sell the territory. It is rich, it produces income. The general opinion is that he sells it while he still can, before it becomes spoils of war."

"So before I even have a decent dwelling, we may again be robbed!"

"You have a decent dwelling," Noel said, and stalked to the bow of the boat, where the smoke from his cigar and the mists rising from the water wrapped him in a close veil, blurred his figure, and made him a stranger.

"I don't, you know," Hélène said, seating herself beside her son. "Have a decent dwelling. All those rooms, just added on here and there! You've seen Bocage—and the de Gravelles' house. Now I ask you, Noel André!"

"It sounds as though we might not have land to put it on, Mère." He followed his father to the bow of the boat. "Is there really a chance the Americans won't honor our land grants?"

Again the shrug. "De Gravelle says that the American government is made up of better men than the riffraff that floats down the river. He says they understand honor. And rights. He reminds us that not too many years ago they fought for the right of property—their own right, and that of others. Maybe he's right, Noel André. This American government was begun, after all, by men who pledged their lives, their fortunes, their sacred honor, to the cause they proclaimed. Can they betray all that, not even three decades later?"

The fate of the territory was discussed up and down the bayous. Claude Louis had closed himself in with Jean-Claude upon his return from New Orleans, had listened to the facts, the rumors, Jean-Claude had gleaned. The next Sunday, when the family gathered for dinner, Claude Louis took the opportunity to tell his children, in his own way, of the new threat. Madeline, soon to be confined with her first child, leaned on her husband's arm and chattered with the twins. If Jacques and Madeline were turned from their land, would she give birth by the side of the road, in a field, as her grandmother had? He watched Nicole and Jean compete with each other to tell Madeline about the new lambs, the sow that had produced fifteen fine piglets. A simple family gathering, repeated every Sunday after Mass. That he had expected to be repeated, every Sunday so long as he lived. He sighed. Rapped on the table and waited for quiet. Then he spoke. "There is question as to whether the land titles granted by the Spanish will be recognized by the Americans." At the short bursts of alarm, of worry, he held up his hand. "This is not to say that there is official question. Men who deal with the American government believe it will honor our title. Men who deal with the Americans coming into the territory, eager to have such rich land for themselves—wonder."

"When will we know?" Jean's eyes, direct, dark, close with the small circumference of the world he lived in, fastened themselves on Claude Louis' face.

"Not, I would think, until the Americans take possession."

"And that will be?"

"That will be when the bastard king of Spain and the bastard Napoleon finish, at their leisure, disposing of the lives of thousands of people they have never seen," Jean-Claude said, bursting from the stool near the fire where he sat. "Talk of this cession has gone on for months and months—someone takes a knight here, loses a pawn there. It is a chess game they play, these European rulers, and we are the pieces! Perhaps it will not be so bad to belong to the Americans—they, at least, do not have royalty!"

"That is true," Claude Louis said. "And whatever the citizens of that country may want, its government does speak of justice. One can hope that even if it has no honor it at least does not wish to make a fool of itself, speaking out of both sides of its mouth."

The selfless and selfish reason for behaving well. In spite of his anxiety, Jean-Claude smiled. It had taken him a long while to realize that when his grandmother taught them thus, she was making sure that when there would never be any choice but to behave well. Which now meant, he knew, that he and Jacques and his father and Jean must go about their business, plant their fields, take care of their land, just as though there was no question of who would own the harvest.

As he worked in the fields, turning still cold earth over to be warmed by the fitful spring sun, Jean-Claude dealt with a question he could answer—the question of taking a wife. His mother reported to him after every gathering of the women of the settlement that yet another maman had asked about Jean-Claude. Was he calling on anyone? Had he put his cap outside any particular door? "I can tell you the virtues of every girl in all Attakapas," Cecile said. "Truly, if their mothers are to be believed, you will have a perfect wife no matter whom you choose."

His father, too, had begun to speak of his marrying. "There is more than enough land to farm. Now that we live in papa and maman's house, the small place is empty. And, Jean-Claude—we need more hands."

More hands! That meant children, children he and one of the perfect daughters would produce. To farm the land in their turn, become as tied to it as he was—his thoughts sailed with the March wind to New Orleans, and to Lafitte. A man of business, dependent not on the sun and the rain, the wind and the hailstorms, but on his own wit, his own cunning, for wealth. The soil might be rich, but it would not make them rich. Not if they walked behind a plow a thousand years.

By the end of planting, Jean-Claude had made up his mind. He would marry because he must, and because he knew he could do those things a good husband and father should do. His marriage would be the largest part of his life, that and the eternal farming. But having paid his dues, he would take something for himself. That promised meeting with Lafitte might be a long time coming—but it would come. When it did, Lafitte would learn that Jean-Claude knew himself very well, and that a little freedom had but given him the taste for much, much more. Thus decided, Jean-Claude cast an eye over those daughters whose mamans were so anxious to see them marry him and settled on Marguerite Breaux.

She was quiet, a little plump, serious. Devout, well schooled in the arts of making a home—clearly, she was the most perfect of all those perfect girls. She was also more than a little surprised when Jean-Claude began to pay attention to her. The third Sunday he came to call, riding his best horse, the one obviously set aside for courting, she asked him outright why he was coming. "Is it to tease someone else? Someone you really care for?" They were sitting outside, March having decided to behave itself and act like the beginning of spring.

Jean-Claude was shocked. "Do you think I would do that? Come see you, spend time with you—to make someone else jealous?"

"Why else would you come, then?"

That question, spoken in Marguerite's soft voice, seemed to harden into an arrow that found its way straight into Jean-Claude's heart. He felt suddenly foolish, ridiculous. To pick a wife as he would choose a new plow—or another lot of cattle!

"I—wanted us to know each other. To see if—if perhaps we—" He stopped. He had been coming only to observe the necessary formalities before asking Monsieur Breaux for Marguerite's hand. He had never, not once, doubted the outcome. This quiet girl, who had never been the most sought-after girl at a fête, never had the young men of the district competing for her smiles, would be so grateful that the fine Jean-Claude Langlinais had chosen her that he need not really worry about her again. To find that Marguerite doubted his honesty was bad enough; to know that she had reason for her doubts was worse. He picked up a plump hand, put his other hand over it. "Marguerite. Surely you know that when a young man comes to see a girl—when he is of my age—he means to marry her."

Her hand rested in his so easily, she looked at him with such trust—zut! it would not be possible never to worry about this one. Something in Jean-Claude went out to meet the trust in Marguerite's open face; leaning over, he kissed the hand he held. "You don't mind that I come?"

"Oh, no." Then she smiled, and the light from it made her

cheeks glow. "I like very much that you come, Jean-Claude. I just—I just didn't want to like it too much. If you were going to stop coming."

By the time Jean-Claude could properly ask for Marguerite's hand in marriage, he had indeed come to know her, to see beyond the quiet serious ways to the open nature that, like the sun flitting in and out of April rain clouds, appeared from time to time to light up her whole being. When she put her hand in his, looked up at him and asked one of her earnest questions, he found himself as weak as lust for other women made him. And when his answer made her smile, more, made her laugh and clap her hands, he felt a quick rush of strength—never had Jean-Claude been quiet so manly, quite so in charge, as when he was with Marguerite.

Claude Louis approved his son's choice. "A good family. A good girl," he said. And told himself that Jean-Claude had better sense than he had thought—a young man whose eyes and heart roved was wise to marry someone whose feet were so thoroughly and firmly planted on safe and solid ground. Cecile's head said Jean-Claude had chosen well, her heart yearned for someone a little less serious, a little less plump, a little more like Cecile herself.

"I'm afraid Marguerite will disapprove of me," she said to Hélène one afternoon. Their friendship had a renewed flowering in the time before their sons' weddings—relegated to the uninteresting position of mother of the groom, left out of all the arrangements, they took what pleasure they could from comparing, over cups of coffee and plates of cakes, their observations of everything from the prospective brides to the number of grandchildren each could expect—and how quickly.

"Why should a little pouter pigeon like that disapprove of you?" Hélène said. "If she is as sweet and good as you say she is, surely she will honor and respect you."

Cecile laughed. In Hélène's mouth, words like "sweet" and "good" sounded less than desirable—and while Cecile certainly wished for her grandchildren a sweet and good mother, for herself, she had hoped for a daughter-in-law who enjoyed, once in a while, a little gossip, a little chatter about the peculiarities one noted in one's neighbors. "Oh, I like to sit over coffee like this and gossip a little, Hélène. Nothing bad, nothing wrong— but some things are so funny, or so odd, you know they are, that they have to be told. But Marguerite, I'm afraid, will think I am committing a sin." Cecile pushed the floor, sent the rocker she sat in moving vigorously. "Poor enfant, she is so good, so devout, if she has ever committed a sin it is the sin of worrying too much that she will commit one."

Hélène raised an eyebrow. "I hope Jean-Claude is not marrying someone who has no idea of what marriage is all about."

"I have to say about Marguerite, Hélène, that she is the most perfect housekeeper, the most wonderful cook—" Cecile laughed again. "Now, as you perfectly well know, my house has always been orderly, my children and Claude Louis have always been fed—but, Hélène, I never put my whole mind on it, you know? Whereas Marguerite—her pots almost stand at attention when she looks at them!"

"I didn't mean that," Hélène said. "Does she know what goes on in bed?"

Cecile looked away from the sharp glitter in Hélène's eyes. "Does any bride?"

"Some are more curious than others." When Cecile said nothing, Hélène took another tack. "Aimée, for example. Given the way she has grown up—all that time in the stables, mon Dieu, what an education for a girl!—I imagine she will bring more than curiosity to Noel André's bed."

The strange note in Hélène's voice tugged at Cecile—was Hélène jealous? Of her son's bride? She hurried to speak, to cover that thought with sound. "Ah, well, Hélène, these things have a way of working themselves out. You say she is pretty—"

"Oh, she's pretty enough. Small." The giggle meant Hélène's increasingly ribald wit was about to be shared. "Noel André will have to hunt for her in his bed. When he finds her—well, one hopes she is big enough to hold him!"

"She will be good for Noel André, though. You say she knows a great deal about her father's plantation—and, Hélène, Noel André has always preferred to have his nose in a book, or to be drawing his little pictures, than be on the back of a horse overseeing the fields."

"That's what we have slaves for. As for Aimée—she rides like a man." Hélène's mouth twisted with the disdain of a great beauty for one who threw that advantage away. "She is pretty. She could be more than just pretty—she has a certain style." Hélène's hands went up, a flat gesture of defeat. "But does she use it?" Then, with the old willful toss her head. "At least Aimée has style. From what you tell me, Marguerite has nothing but her pots and pans, her broom and her spinning wheel. And that, I tell you, will be very, very dull!"

Cecile rose, went to Hélène and bent over the rouged cheek. The deep lines around Hélène's mouth were caked with powder; bitterness and resentment were etched against that smooth, smooth mask. "When I admit to myself that there are worse things than dullness, Hélène, I know that I am getting old." She kissed Hélène quickly, pulled her light shawl around her. "But isn't it funny? Even though it takes me longer to catch my breath if I've walked too fast, even though my feet don't keep pace with the fastest tunes now—inside, I don't think I'll ever be much older than I was when I married Claude Louis."

Hélène's mouth curved downward. "You should hear yourself, Cecile. You sound as though marrying a farmer, being stuck out here, was the best thing that ever happened to you." Without waiting for Cecile's answer, Hélène thrust herself out of her chair and went to the gallery railing. "And me—and me—I keep waiting for my life to begin."

Both weddings would be held the last week in October, when the harvest would be over, the cane ground, the sugar made.

"They're making the biggest commotion about all this," Noel André complained to Jean-Claude as they fished together one late summer evening. "Why must a simple wedding consume so much time? Aimée's letters speak of nothing else—I feel like a performer in a circus, that's what—not a man at all."

Jean-Claude laughed. "That's what you get for being rich and proper, Noel André. You have to live with the customs of your people—as I do." He reached forward, baited his hook, cast the line carefully to the center of the bayou. "Of course, our customs are simpler—and perhaps more fun—than yours are."

Noel André's pole drooped limply in his hands. "Are your marriages arranged?"

"By our parents, you mean? Not exactly. Oh, they have to approve. Certainly, the bride's. But I can't imagine anyone *having* to marry someone. Because the parents said so." Jean-Claude looked at Noel André, the pole held straight out in front of him pulled down the weight of a fish that had just taken the bait. "Was your marriage arranged, Noel André? Whether you wanted it or not?"

"No—no, of course not. I—well, of course. I think they hoped we would marry. Maybe even expected us to. But no, Aimée and I—well, it's what we want."

"What else do you want?"

Noel André heard an edge in Jean-Claude's voice; the edge was sharp, barbed—he would be hooked into saying things he preferred not to if he could not evade that trap. "What everyone wants, I suppose. To be happy. Have a good life."

Jean-Claude brought the fish up, twisting the pole to flip the shimmering silver-green body up onto the bank. He brought the heavy end of his knife down on the fish's head, then gutted it. Noel André had watched Jean-Claude do this at least a thousand times. Or bleed a deer. Or pluck a duck. As easily as though he had been born with a hunting knife in one hand and a musket in the other. A half-formed feeling, not strong enough to be envy, came over him. He repeated his words: "To have a good life. That's what I want."

"And how are you going to go about getting it?"

"Getting it? But I'll be married, I'll—I don't understand."

"You'll be married and a good life will just come?" Jean-Claude wrapped the fish in thick leaves, tucked it in his sack, and rebaited the hook. "Like you must think the fish will jump up on the bank without you even trying to catch them? If you don't know what you want, how in the hell will you even know if you have it?"

"I do know what I want." Noel André knew that he was pouting. "I want time to think. Time to make my drawings better. I—I want to enjoy myself."

"You're saying you just want to play all the time? Not ever work?"

Now the pout changed to a scowl. "Why in the hell should I work? My father's rich, slaves work the fields—why should I work?"

Jean-Claude pulled in another fish, a twin to the first. His hands went quickly through the task of stunning it, gutting it. "Trouble with you is, you don't understand what work is. Even fishing—you can sit and let your pole fall in the bayou. But me—I'm supposed to bring home supper. I've heard your papa talk about how he hunted in France—beaters, men to handle the dogs, pick up the game. He didn't even see what he killed until it turned up at his table on a silver platter. But again—we hunt so we can eat better. So we learn to take pleasure from it—but, Noel André, what it mostly is, it's work."

"And that's what you want? A life of work, everything work?"

"No. But I'll tell you something—I'm smart enough to know I'm going to have to put in a lot of work to be able to do other things—things that mean something to me."

Noel André forgot his own problems—was there something Jean-Claude wanted he didn't know how to get? Or couldn't get? "What things? What do you want, if it comes to that?"

Jean-Claude stood tall on the bayou bank, stretched his arms high. "Sometimes I feel like I can't breathe. I want to get away from here—do something besides work day in and day out. But I just can't leave. There's the farm, the land. But once in a while—get away, find something as far from following a plow as I possibly can."

"If you feel that way, why do it just once in a while?"

Jean-Claude'e eyes seemed to be looking at Noel André from a great height; they burned the space between them, burned into Noel André's brain, lighting up the smallness of the thoughts that hid there. "My father depends on me—for much."

"So you'll ruin your life, give up what you really want—be a farmer?"

"It's not as bad a life as your view would have it. I know myself. If I can leave it once in a while—I will probably come to like it very well." He took up his pole, began wrapping the line around it. "At least, Noel André, I can make choices."

"You think I can't?"

"No. I think either you've never had to—or you've never wanted to." Then, with a rapid change of mood, "Until you chose to marry Mademoiselle de la Houssaye." He clasped Noel André's hand. "From that good choice, others will follow."

"I suppose." He had seen Marguerite Breaux, had been baffled at Jean-Claude's choice. When he could have had any of a dozen girls who were prettier, gayer—now, with his own feelings trampled on, bedraggled, he cared little for Jean-Claude's. "Did you make a good choice, though? I've seen Marguerite. Jean-Claude—do you really want her?"

"Want her? As a woman?" Jean-Claude looked so astonished that Noel André felt as he had felt most of their lives—that

Jean-Claude had the only map to the territory, and he must perforce follow his lead blindly. "Look, Noel André, one doesn't marry for that. Marguerite will make good babies. And take care of them. For that, I will love her—protect her. But, Noel André—what you're talking about? How many women could give both? The good mother and still the pleasure in bed? For that—well, there are other women, no?"

"Have you had other women, then?"

"Of course, haven't you?"

Noel André had never really enjoyed a woman, if it came to that. A few encounters in New Orleans, obscured by drink both at the time and certainly in his memory, hardly counted. A local from the other side of the settlement, when he was nineteen, who was perhaps less willing than he would like to believe.

"Yes."

"Well, then." A shrug, a dismissal. What had once been done could be done again.

Noel André watched Jean-Claude walk away, sack of fish slung over one shoulder, pole tilted over the other. He heard Jean-Claude's clear whistle, one of the tunes the fiddlers played at the fais-do-dos. Brought up on the gavottes and waltzes and gallopades his mother adored, he had always considered the Acadian music crude, their dances graceless. But watching the ease for Jean-Claude's body at everything he did, knowing the demands that would be made on him by Aimée de la Houssaye de Clouet in the near future, Noel André heartily wished for a little of that crudity, a little less grace—if it would make him the master.

Aimée Louise de la Houssaye de Clouet turned out to be as brisk and gay in bed as she was in every other activity. Accustomed to finely bred, high-strung animals, sensitive to feelings, she knew that Noel André, for whatever reason, wished to get the whole thing over with as quickly as possible. Her energy was due to great health; the simple novelty of being alone in a bedroom with a handsome young man who said he loved her, whose eyes told her how beautiful she was, was more than enough to arouse her. Noel André's first tentative movements had results that amazed him; almost before he had really made himself realize that he was a married man, that this woman was his wife, he had entered her, had felt her body convulse beneath his, had, in his turn, felt the spasm of passion, and had then gone to sleep with his wife cozily nestled in his arms.

Jean-Claude's wedding night was exactly as he expected. Marguerite knelt to say her prayers, put her hair up in braids, and then slipped between the covers and waited for him, her gray eyes glowing from her calm and trusting face. He was careful to disturb her gown as little as possible, to touch her bare flesh only as necessary to make his act easier for her. He heard a small sigh, felt a tremor in her soft plumpness. When he moved from her and lay beside her, she took his hand and held it to her lips. "You are a good husband, Jean-Claude," she said. She slept with his hand in hers and Jean-Claude went to sleep thanking the Lord for good women.

As the days of the year wound down, the people of the territory felt more and more that the end of this year, the beginning of the new one, must see them safely delivered to their new rulers, with all questions answered, all doubts resolved. The tension that had pulled at them all these long months had not been relieved when the French official who would govern the colony in place of the Spanish intendant arrived in New Orleans in March. After all, Colonial Prefect Pierre Laussat was but a symbol of how kings will flesh out their games to keep the play going. All the while Laussat set up his government, prepared to accept Louisiana for Napoleon, the knowledge that the Americans were waiting to snap them up kept the colonials anxious, irritable, mistrustful.

"It is good that it is finally settled," Noel told Hélène, when de Gravelle wrote that the colony would be officially ceded to France on November 30, and invited the de Clouets to be in the city as his guests. "Many of us have known since winter what was planned—the deliberations of the American Congress are not held on the moon! And of course, since summer, you could find no one who did not know of this infamy."

"Juliette writes that there will be many balls—first for Laussat, and then for the Americans." Hélène laughed, the laugh that could still make silver from empty words, carefully covering them with that light sound until they gleamed and hung in the air, baubles and gauds. "Do you think Americans know how to dance? And do they carry those long guns into the ballroom?"

"I believe you would have watched your queen beheaded if you'd had a new dress to wear!" Noel said. And stormed out to find Joseph to see how the new mare was doing.

"Does that mean we won't go?" Aimée asked Hélène.

"Of course we will go. Noel doesn't think, he has a temper fit about honor while other men take the spoils. No matter if Laussat's rule is brief—he had chosen men of New Orleans to have places in his government. De Gravelle is one of those, Noel knows many of the others. When the Americans come—well, they will need help. Even here. When one has no court, one takes what place one can."

"But how will you get him to change his mind?" Aimée's short acquaintance as an intimate of Hélène's household had fully informed her as to how Hélène got her way. What she really wanted to know was how Hélène viewed her method.

The long silver-blue stare. The still blonde curls tossed over a carefully powdered neck. The slight lift of the bosom. "I am his wife. What more is needed?"

What indeed. "We are going to New Orleans, to obtain a position of importance for your father," Aimée told Noel André later. "There will be women you must flirt with, gentlemen I must please." She climbed into bed next to him, lifted her gown and began to guide him toward her. Always life must be easy for Noel André, never must there be much to decide. "We can do that for your father, can we not?"

Noel André, who found himself wondering over and over if all other women were purposely difficult and only his wife agreeable, or if he truly were the fine lover Aimée said he was, said yes.

For Noel de Clouet, for Claude Louis and Jean-Claude Langlinais, and all the other men of the Louisiana Territory who gathered in New Orleans on November 30 to witness the final lowering of the Spanish flag and the raising of the French tricolor, Laussat's proclamation on that same day constituted the entire reason for their being in New Orleans. Claude Louis, standing with Jean-Claude in the shelter of one of the buildings around the square in front of the cathedral, huddled into his coat. "One hopes this weather is not an omen," he said. An early winter storm had come up the night before, hurtling rain against shuttered windows and rattling loose tiles from rooftops. The rain had stopped, but the wind had not; it blew with constant force across the open area between river and church, chilling them with its damp cold as though it were part of the winter waters flowing past the city.

Jean-Claude was not cold, his blood was too filled with the excitement of this day, the pride in his father, who was being greeted by members of the militia brought in from the various posts for the ceremony. "Did you fight with all these men?" He had listened, astounded, to the tale of one old Acadian who recounted how his father had killed a British scout barehanded on the eve of the battle of Baton Rouge. "And why did you never tell us what you did with Galvez?"

"What I did was not important. What was important was that the British did not win," Claude Louis said. "These trappings, this crowd—" His broad wave took in the square, filled with people, the crowded streets leaning into it, the windows with bodies packed into their small openings, the roofs with their own burden of spectators. "None of this matters. All that maters is whether, when it is all over, we still have our land."

Laussat's proclamation was long, florid, as befitted an official whose moment in history was brief. Its subject immediately gained the attention of his entire audience—he would explain the conditions of the cession of this so newly returned territory to the United States.

"And so he did—with all the usual wordiness, all the usual flesh padded onto the bones," de Gravelle said. He had gathered his male guests around him; if they did not know it, he knew that much of the real power of the territory would lie in the hands of this group, American expectations to the contrary.

Noel de Clouet picked up his glass of wine, savored it on his tongue. He had not so enjoyed wine for days, been so at ease before a fire. "The fifth paragraph alone could have been read," he said. He took up a copy of the proclamation de Gravelle had obtained and began to read that section aloud, giving to each word its own particular inflection. "The article third of the treaty of cession cannot escape your attention. It says: 'That the inhabitants of the ceded territories shall be incorporated into the Union of the United States, and admitted, as soon as possible, according to the principles of the Federal Constitution, to the enjoyment of all the advantages and immunities of citizens of the United States; and that, in the mean-

time, they shall be maintained and protected in the free enjoyment
of their liberties and property, and in the unrestrained exercise
of the religion they profess.' It could not be plainer," he said.
"We are assured of our land."

"And the Americans, how do they perform in the ballroom?"
Cecile asked. She had come at Hélène's invitation to "hear how
the great world lives while we die of boredom in Attakapas."
But it was like hearing fairy tales, complete with handsome
heroes, lovely ladies, and palatial ballrooms, to listen to Hélène
talk. Hélène, one could not help but notice, was always the
center of the stories. Cecile covered a sigh by biting into a
sweetmeat. "Did you dance with any?"

"With Claiborne himself—the new governor, you know.
And with Wilkinson, his chief aide. They are—energetic."
Then Hélène laughed; for the first time since she had been
packed into that stuffy carriage, crammed between the small
wriggling bodies of her children, forced against the stale smell
of Gertrude, she felt really like herself. Claiborne himself had
told her that of all the French ladies, he felt most comfortable
dancing with her. Wilkinson had complimented her on her
command of his language, though her phrases were limited to
the sort of politenesses anyone who had been at a court was
wise enough to master. And Laussat, at the ball he had given
to return the marquis' favor, had led her in the first minuet.

"That ball, the one Laussat gave the marquis, was the most
beautiful," she said. There was new sound in the thinning voice,
the silver had drawn itself into a hard fine core of decision,
authority. "On the supper table, a table set for eighty of us,
you understand, Laussat had had constructed a temple—Cecile, it had columns, it had a dome, it had a statue of a goddess!
It was the temple of Good Faith, something, I don't know. And
then an immense pavilion had been constructed—with tables
for five hundred guests! Oh, Cecile, they say the Americans
are barbarians, but I assure you, until they came, certainly no
one, Spanish or French, bothered with such civilized enter-
tainments!"

"And did Noel get his position?" There had been rumors
that Noel would soon have some importance in Attakapas.

Hélène's voice held that new authority: "He was with de
Gravelle and the other men to whom Laussat had given posi-

tions, responsibilities, constantly. The Americans will need help—de Gravelle assures us we will be among those giving it."

Fairy tales about balls were one thing—this one was quite another. Cecile rose to go. As she bent to kiss Hélène's rouged cheek, she said, "But the United States lets the people choose their rulers, doesn't it? And, Hélène—perhaps you should consider—the people might not choose Noel." She stepped back, watched Hélène's eyes take on the old challenging glitter. "Suppose they want someone else?" Cecile laughed, a laugh that was young with freedom. "They might even want Claude Louis!" At the sudden anger on that stale face, Cecile felt like a mother who has snatched away a baby's favorite toy. Hélène's eyes glittered up at her, cold, piercing. The rush of hatred pushed against Cecile; she moved away, feeling for the stair rail behind her. Then Hélène's powdered eyelids covered her glaring eyes. When she opened them, moments later, the look she gave Cecile was cool, civil.

"Of course that is a risk Noel must take." Hélène lifted herself from the chair, went to Cecile. "As for me—I will be too busy to even think of it again. Noel has finally agreed to build me my house. We're going to build it in that grove of live oaks over there—we'll call it Beau Chêne." The smallest glitter flickered at the back of the ice-blue eyes. "I know you'll be interested. It will be quite the grandest house you've ever seen, you'll learn a great deal about how well people can live."

"Of course, Hélène," Cecile said, tying her bonnet strings. "I have always been so interested in all of you and I have already learned from you a great deal about how well people can live."

# CHAPTER 9

# *Beau Chêne*

Noel André, his mother on his arm, was making the usual late afternoon survey of the day's work on the house. Since the eight columns, soaring a full two stories to support the roof overhanging the upper and lower galleries, had been hauled into place, supplanting the makeshift supports of lesser grace, Beau Chêne had begun to take on the character he and Hélène had envisioned during the tedious time of drawing plans, meeting with builders, convincing Noel that if the de Clouets were finally building their homeplace, to spare expense would dishonor the family name.

Aimée had been no help at all. When she realized, soon after their wedding, that she had more interest in the sugar fields than did her husband, and that Noel André would easily abdicate his place next to his father to her, she had, except for time out—a dismayingly brief time out—to have Noel Troisième, spent most of her time riding the plantation at her father-in-law's side, or huddled in the office, keeping records, making neat entries in the cloth-bound ledgers.

"One can see the face of the house now," Hélène said. She had held out, when they began building two years ago, for a replica of the much romanticized and mourned over château in France. To all of her husband's arguments, she had been resistant. But one afternoon with her son, shut away from the rest of the family in her boudoir, had changed her mind. "Look maman," he said, the long fingers holding his drawing pencil firmly, the slim hand moving lightly over the paper. Under that rapid point of soft lead had grown a house that Hélène immediately saw was right. Noel André placed as many of the tall windows and doors opposite each other as he could, the better to catch any breeze, any small cloud of air, wafting up from Bayou Teche that traveled behind the house. The two-storied gallery in the front, the loggia at the back of both floors, the high-pitched roof—these were other shields against the bombardment the heated heavy air made steadily from late June until early October. But graceful shields, lovely shields, more like an elegant fan lifted to protect a delicate face than the barriers some builders made.

"It is necessary to begin thinking of furnishings," Hélène said. She tugged Noel André's arm slightly, led him to a seat which she had had placed, months ago, in a shaded spot from which she could watch her fantasy take shape, brick by precious brick.

Noel André felt a sigh like one of those small clouds of air from the bayou form. He knew better than to release it. Now that the house was only months away from completion, now that the lines he had drawn on paper were real, he had to force his interest to keep it at the avid pitch his mother demanded. This was, after all, his parents' home. Though he and Aimée and Troi would one day own it—and, if he were not mistaken, Aimée would soon tell him that another infant was on its tedious way—for now, they would continue to live in that first sprawling structure that had begun as a two-room cabin and had ended by accommodating three generations with some privacy and space.

Not that he minded that. The heir did not step into possession until the current owner was dead; he was building a house, not preparing graves. But with this house completed, the enormous sense of life that had taken him these months would go. Once again, he could linger over his café au lait until midmorning, with no task to make him drink a hasty cup, toss a napkin on the table, and rush to the landing to supervise the unloading of yet another barge. His conversation would be, not about the new batch of bricks fired that day from clay dug from the bayou's banks, or about how well the marble floor for the dining room had fit the space laid for it, but about all the trivia he and his mother had discussed for years—he would be relegated to his position of lap dog, and his wife would run the plantation.

He stood, moved his shoulders under the weight of that thought. Aimée did run the plantation, she and his father. If Noel died tonight, fell in his fields of tall cane never more to rise, his son would know next to nothing about how this plantation worked. But Aimée, whose little body still enveloped him with ease, whose small hips had bounced Troi out in so short a time the midwife had allowed herself bawdy comment, would know all.

"Don't fidget," Hélène said. "Gentlemen don't fidget, Noel André, how often must I tell you that?" For how many years had Hélène been correcting him in just such fashion, with just such an indulgent smile? Preparing him for life at a court that had not existed since it was proven with swift finality that royal necks may not bend, but they do sever—and bleed.

"De Gravelle wrote me again last week—he still urges me to study under an architect in New Orleans—develop what he calls my 'fine talent.'" Noel André gave the regulation laugh— gentlemen did not fidget, they also did not need talents, developed fine, or otherwise.

"He presumes on our long friendship," Hélène said. "You've no need of his advice."

"At least he takes my drawing seriously."

"And I don't? Haven't I framed those flower drawings you did, put them in my boudoir?"

"Mère. There's nothing in drawing flowers."

"And there is something in drawing buildings? Hiring out one's talent for beauty?"

"There's a hell of a lot more to it than that, mère. I designed Beau Chêne—why shouldn't I go on doing that, designing houses, buildings—?"

Hélène came closer, touched his cheek with her teasing fingers. "I agree. Why shouldn't you go on doing that? Why study under anyone, when you do so well as you are?"

"De Gravelle says I would learn about stress, how to pitch a roof to achieve a certain balance of the weight, that—"

"Zut! You listen to the opinion of a man who has turned his wife's home into a bank? The man has the mind of a merchant."

"Many men would gladly turn their mother's home into a bank if it were the Louisiana Bank," Noel André said. "Mère— I will never be anything but an amateur playing at being an architect if I don't study with someone."

"And if you study? Are no longer an amateur? Would you really like that life, Noel André? Going to an office, dealing with stupid people who because they pay you think they can tell you what to draw? After all my efforts, are you becoming like that vulgar de Gravelle? A tradesman?"

"Tradesman! He's a banker, on his way to being one of the

wealthiest men in New Orleans. And if you had not insisted
my father put so much money into this house, he'd have been
one of the original investors in de Gravelle's bank. Instead of
getting in later at a higher rate."

"I was not that interested in your father becoming a tradesman. De Clouets have never been tradesmen—why should they
now?"

"In a country where trade is king and merchants the
aristocracy, bankers, ma chère maman, will become the first
nobility." Hélène turned to him, her eyes hot and angry. Rarely
did Noel André get burned by Hélène's wrath—usually he was
its receptacle, taking all the rage, frustration, sulks, she could
draw up each day, cooling that age-fired mixture, giving it back
to her as a smooth drink of flattery and cajolery. "I'm going
to find Aimée," he said, and swung down the alley of oaks
leading up to the house before his mother's tongue could stop
him. As he strode away, he realized that once again Hélène
had managed to detour him into a maze of her own whims—
the question of whether he would go to New Orleans, study
with de Gravelle's friend, had been left in one blind alley, while
he pursued what had appeared to be the clear way out.

The walk under the great trees calmed him. The house had
been set in a grove of live oaks already on the de Clouet land;
Hélène had augmented God's bounty with this alley, having
several slaves spend valuable weeks away from the fields to
dig the deep holes, carry water up from the bayou, wet down
the earth, before going out into the wild forest to bring back
oak saplings as large as could be safely transplanted. When
the inevitable number died, she had called men back from the
planting, the hoeing, to go out and find trees to replace those
that were lost. Finally, her will prevailed even over nature, and
now the double line of trees marched in living rhythm down
to the trail that wound through the territory.

Finding Aimée presented no difficulty—the new mare had
arrived yesterday, and Noel André knew Aimée and his father,
with Joseph, would be down in the pasture, vying to see who
would ride her with that grace, that sense of natural ownership,
that would stamp her as "mine." Aimée, he thought, had not
spoken of her pregnancy because she didn't want him fussing;
even alone, he felt his face redden with her remembered ridicule
after Troi's birth. He had gone to Aimée's room one morning
when their son was but weeks old, expecting to visit his con-

valescent wife. He had found Aimée pulling on her boots, hooking her riding skirt around her still thick waist. When he had protested, speaking of her condition, Aimée had patted his cheek and laughed. "Oh, Noel André! I am healed sufficiently to have you between my legs—cannot I then ride? As for Troi—Marguerite Langlinais nurses him at one breast, her own baby at the other. So what is there left?" And she had strode out of the room, whip in hand, to join Noel, who had, as a small concession to his son's fears, brought round a gentle gelding known as the "invalid's mount." But the next day, Aimée had galloped past him, hair flying, her body tightly molded against the back of her own horse, a huge red stallion that still frightened most of the men and all of the women on the place.

He stopped on a rise of land that looked over the fenced pasture. Two men leaned against the rail fence, their heads turning to follow the circling ride of the woman and horse before them. Noel André didn't have to see their faces; his father's face would look as it always did when he watched Aimé, as though here before him was the most perfect being ever created. As far as Noel André could remember, his wife had never done one single thing that her father-in-law did not find absolutely charming, exceptionally intelligent, or surpassingly brave. Joseph's face would echo Noel's—Joseph had use for no woman except his own mother; he barely spoke to Hélène, but he worshiped Aimée. He would crouch before her, seated on an overturned feed bucket, and talk for hours about this horse's pulled ligament, that one's unhappy tendency to break gait without warning. And while Noel André normally plastered his wounded feelings with poultices contrived of memories of Aimée's body compliant beneath his, he was beginning to believe that she belonged to him in the one way that did not really matter to her.

I'll go see Jean-Claude, he thought, and turned back to the road.

Another figure was watching the scene in the horse pasture, a dark, bold-faced man who stood on the other side of the field, half concealed by shrubs and low-hanging branches. His pose, the leanness of his muscles, the deep brightness of his eyes, spoke of youth. The skin of his face and neck was aged, weathered, like wood left from a building that has lain long in the sun and rain. His close-fitting breeches were tucked in soft

Spanish boots, and he had a blue coat of fine broadcloth slung carelessly over one shoulder. His eyes followed Aimée, their dark lights gleaming as his gaze circled the field. His body seemed almost to imitate the rhythmic movement of the mare as she cantered over the yellowing autumn grass. Then, he turned and vanished into the shadowed woods behind him.

Though Noel André's soul was comforted, fulfilled, by the spacious rooms and ornate design of Beau Chêne, his body found its place in Marguerite Langlinais' kitchen. Since Troi's infancy, when Marguerite's full breast had fed her daughter and his son, Noel André had felt a special bond between him and this placid young woman. And now, though the excuse he gave for his visits to Jean-Claude's farm was always one of business, if he had to leave without a cup of Marguerite's strong coffee, a taste of one of her new-baked loaves, the disappointment was that of a child denied a promised treat.

"I came to ask Jean-Claude if he wants to go to New Orleans with me," he said now, warming his belly with the hot black demitasse and his feet at Marguerite's cooking fire. "Mère is sending me to order the furnishings for the house—I leave next week."

Marguerite rescued Mathilde, toddling near the hearth, from the fire tongs and pulled her to her lap. "Your mother doesn't go herself?" The wonder in Marguerite's voice was all the comment she would ever allow herself about Hélène. Watching her, her smooth dark hair pulled low over her fine forehead, the knot of hair at the back of her neck gleaming in the firelight, Noel André thought again of Jean-Claude's happy acceptance of the fact that few women could give one both excitement in bed and a well-run house. He had thought, when he and Aimée had first been married, and she had so quickly satisfied him, had been so quickly satisfied herself, that that was excitement. Now, his eyes wandering over Marguerite's comfortable plumpness, he thought perhaps it would be more rewarding to have leisurely lovemaking, to have the time to know a lover's body, learn her ways. He sometimes wanted to say to Aimée, "Wait— slow down. Let us take our time, not be in such a hurry." He pushed from his mind the thought that Aimée was not eager, merely bored.

"Jean-Claude will probably go," Marguerite said. "The baby will arrive soon after Christmas, so he must make his big trip now. And Aimée, her baby will arrive not long after mine, isn't that so?" Before he could cover his confusion, Marguerite leaned across the table and patted his hand. "She hasn't told you? Ah, well, that Aimée, she wants to do everything herself, even those things she must very much have help with." She put her child down, lifted one of Jean-Claude's big gray work-shirts from her mending basket. "Tell me, Noel André, did you hear that Adolphe Picou is back?"

A delicious sweetness like that of the sugar melting with coffee at the bottom of his cup came over Noel André. For the next hour, he and Marguerite would take out each event of settlement life and go over it with the same exacting care that Marguerite gave to the garments in her sewing basket. A gossip with his mother left him feeling ill at ease, discontent—and often sullied. Whereas when Marguerite talked of her neighbors' lives, the veil of kindness and compassion she drew over the dark places softened them; in the light of those clear eyes, all life had meaning, all men and women meant good.

Though he very well knew that Adolphe Picou was the errant brother of Joseph, his father's right hand, Noel André gladly took up the formula: "Adolphe Picou, now let me see—Joseph's brother, is he not?"

Marguerite laughed. Her Jean-Claude was a good man, none better. His days were long, spent in the field, or in the swamp marking the huge cypress to be felled and split, or at the mill weighing corn. But when he talked, it was of big things, large things. Her tongue preferred the small stories she and Noel André put together on these afternoons, stories that made an increasingly solid bond between them, like beads slipped on a chain.

"You know they say he is with Lafitte." Her voice hovered over that black name. Privateer, he and his brother called themselves, with letters of marque from the government of the seaport of Cartagena in the province of Colombia. "Pirates," said others, who swore that although the rich booty of Spanish ships filled treasure troves at Barataria, the island stronghold of these men, no prisoners were ever seen—alive.

"He is bringing in slaves," she said, "and two planters from down the bayou went to a big auction Jean and Pierre Lafitte had way back in the swamp to buy some."

Noel André frowned. "If the Americans insist on forbidding

slaves to be brought in legally, they will be smuggled in, Marguerite. What men need, they get. And there is no way to have a sugar plantation without slaves."

"Which is why the Langlinais do not have one," she said. Her voice was still placid, but there was a thin gleam in her eye, like the thin gleam of the needle flashing in and out of the heavy gray cloth.

"Tell me about this Adolphe," he said. Afternoons in this quiet haven were too precious to be disturbed—let others argue over slavery, he would fill his cup, break off another piece of good bread, spread it thickly with blackberry jam, and be happy.

On the edge of the swamp, Jean-Claude cursed as he worked to lead his oxen out of a mud hole. The rough sled full of cypress trunks still sat on the other side of the bog. Thank heaven he had seen the team begin to sink and had cut loose the lines before his load of lumber, too, was in trouble. But this was no way to end the day, no!

"Put that anger into your back instead of your mouth and you might get the bastards out," a lazy voice behind him said.

Now, by heaven, that was too much. Whatever cochon would come onto a man's own land and taunt him deserved all he got. By the time Jean-Claude had turned to confront his visitor, his fists were at the ready, his eyes blazing. The first punch hit solidly in the man's belly, the second his shoulder. There was no third punch. Jean-Claude felt himself caught in two arms that seemed to have the strength of those laboring oxen behind him. The wind was being squeezed from him, he could hear his breath strangling his throat. What, was he being murdered on his land, too? First taunted, then beaten? He gathered himself together, willed field-hard muscles to one effort, one springing explosion of energy. The arms loosed, just enough for him to slide beneath them, reach a swift hand to the knife as his belt. Before the arms could close again, he had danced away to a safe distance, where he stood, knife held low before him, ready to thrust. He drew sweet air and waited.

"So what do you do when a man comes to steal your oxen rather than help you get them out?" The man opposite him shrugged out of his dark blue coat, began to roll up the sleeves of his white linen shirt. "Come, Langlinais, save your temper for a fight that might earn you more than a bloodied head. Now, if we get branches and push them into the mud, make a bridge to land, even these dumb animals might get home for supper—and you and I might have time for a talk."

"Who in the devil are you?" But the anger was gone. He would wait to challenge this man when he had first used his brains—laying branches into the mud, now that wasn't a bad thought, he must remember that. They worked in silence for a time, until one ox, goaded from lethargy by repeated slaps on the rump, reluctantly began to heave itself from the mud and onto the bed of branches. When both oxen stood on firm ground, the man pulled a long silver flask from an inner pocket in his coat.

"Brandy," he said, offering it to Jean-Claude.

"Before I drink, I know your name," Jean-Claude said, his hand at his side not reaching for the flask.

"Damme, Lafitte was right. You are a man for us. You know me, Jean-Claude Langlinais. Or did. I am Adolphe Picou, Joseph's brother."

"You said Lafitte?"

"You remember him?"

"At a quadroon ball. Some years ago."

"Now will you drink? Or must I decide you are not honest, after all? You know my name—"

"And what they say about you," Jean-Claude said. He had taken the flask, was putting it to his lips. With the remembered sting of good brandy, he saw again that dark lean figure, a cutout of black and white against the splendor of the ball.

"That I am becoming rich? Do they say that? What would you say if I told you I have a share in an enterprise that brings me in nearly five hundred dollars a month?"

"That you are either a liar or a thief."

"To which do you object the most?"

Jean-Claude drank again, then handed the flask back to Picou. While the liquid burned itself through his body, his mind pulled up, in rapid order, the bits and pieces he had heard about the Lafittes and their enterprises. Of course they raided Spanish ships. Was not their letter of marque their permission to do so? Of course they sold their booty, smuggling in not only slaves but every other sort of good greedy New Orleanians would buy. Not only New Orleanians dealt with the Lafittes, but planters up and down the bayous, and over to the farther reaches of the Gulf. The Lafitte fleet ventured from its base at Barataria, an island that had slept in the brilliant southern sun for centuries until commandeered by the pirate band. Pirate. That was the word that lay under each tale about the Lafittes. Were they privateers, to be admired, made much of? Or pirates who raped ships and women, stole jewels and virginity, murdered sleep and men?

Jean-Claude shrugged. "It's not up to me to object to what you do. Only to what I do. And me—I do not lie and I do not steal."

"But you would like to have money." Picou slapped one of the mudcaked oxen on the rump. "You won't get five hundred a month fooling with these." His arm went out, waved at the fields. "Or from those fields. No matter how tired and dirty and smelly you get."

"And you can show me how to do better." Jean-Claude's anger was gone. Looking at Picou's clothes, the fine workmanship of his boots, he remembered when no one would have predicted anything but defeat and disgrace for this man—thrown in jail for drunken brawling, with no will to come back, take up his duties and show his people he had repented, Picou had been the terrible example of what could befall a young man led astray by the temptations of New Orleans. And now look at him! Jean-Claude doubted if anyone but Noel de Clouet had a coat of cloth so rich.

"If making a lot of money is doing better—yes, I can."

Jean-Claude thought again of the tales told about Lafitte. The argument over whether the man was a privateer or a pirate had always amused him—what difference did it make what you called something if the thing itself remained the same? To say privateering was all right because it was against "enemies" of the nation giving the letter of marque seemed to be nothing more than a lie—a lie people told themselves so that they could go on stealing and killing. He did not lie. Not to himself, not to anyone else. If he decided to work with Lafitte, he would know exactly what he was doing—and he would be able to live with it.

"What does he want?"

Picou tilted the flask. It was of heavy silver plate, with a delicately traced design coiled around a monogram in the center. The initials, Jean-Claude could see, were WRD—clearly, Picou was not the first owner. Which was, of course, the whole point, as far as he was concerned. By the time men like Lafitte got hold of goods, they had undoubtedly changed hands so many times, spoils in the games the galleons played on every ocean where wind could sail them, that there was no possibility of the rightful owner ever seeing them again. In which case, the riches of the sea belonged to him who could make his claim stick.

"Lafitte needs a place to store goods, goods buyers will come for later. He knows the extent of the land you hold, you and your father. He thought perhaps—deep in the swamp— away from your lumbering—there would be a place?"

"On the water, for the boats?" At Picou's nod, Jean-Claude walked mentally over his land, the map of which was as much a part of his brain as the cells that made him see and hear. "There is a place. An arm of the bayou runs up to it. A boat drawing, maybe, three feet, could get there. The land is high, there are Indian mounds. And heavy wood cover. As yet, we have no use for it."

"You will take me there?"

Jean-Claude glanced at the sky. They were a month into autumn, the sun was speeding its journey across the heavens so that each day it took a shorter time. "Not enough light left today. In the morning. Meet me here."

"You haven't asked the price Lafitte will pay."

Jean-Claude's eyes flicked over Picou's clothes, measured the cut of his coat, the fine thread count of the linen that made his shirt. "I have met Lafitte. The price will be what it should be."

"This should be perfect for Lafitte's purposes," Picou said, surveying the land that rose in a steep slope at the head of the inlet coming in from the bayou. The earth was hard packed by winter rains and the seasonal high waters of the bayou that flooded it; it was massed with scrub brush, swamp grass, and debris left by the movement of water. The trees, except for a few big oaks, were spindly, reaching up through the growth to find sun. "Can you build a shelter?"

"For the goods? Of course. How big?"

Picou moved up the bank to the place where the land leveled off. "If you cut a few of these poplars, those little gums, you'd have a clearing about large enough, I'd think."

"Plenty of cypress for it," Jean-Claude said.

Picou smiled. "What, won't you bring in boards from your sawmill? Or won't you tell your father about this new business?"

"I make up my mind for me. Not for him."

"He might want to get in on this, Jean-Claude. What kind of son keeps his own father from making money?"

Jean-Claude looked at Picou. He had learned some time ago that there were men who were not content with living their own lives, letting you live yours. Picou would not rest, apparently, until he made Jean-Claude out to be as many of the Yankees were reputed to be—so eager for gold that they set no limits on what they would do to get it.

"Picou. One thing you should know. Each man makes his own way. My father stays here in Attakapas, he has always stayed here. I am the one who was sent to New Orleans, who met Lafitte. Do you think I am an infant, that I run home and babble about everything I see, everything I hear? If my father wanted more—he would go look for it."

"But you want more."

"More than money." The air was heavy with swamp-damp. As far back as they were in the swamp, the air never became completely dry. Steam in summer, cold mist in the winter, with only a few days in spring and autumn during which a man could breathe without feeling the moisture coat his lungs. Sometimes Jean-Claude felt that the swamp air had entered him, that he was always smothering in it. To find a place big enough to breathe! He took Picou by the shoulder. "You understand that, Picou. Look, when you got out of jail, in New Orleans, and then didn't come home? He's too ashamed, they said. He can't face his mother, they said. Merde. I knew very well why you didn't come back. You'd escaped, hadn't you? The farm and the plowing and the planting and the sick cows— why in hell would you have come back to that?"

"So you feel that, too." Picou's voice, which yesterday had been taunting, was now calm, stating facts they both knew. Jean-Claude looked into Picou's eyes, fixed so steadily on his face. Those eyes held visions of ships with sails in flames, of women dancing in bright dresses, of glittering jewels, of deep-running blood. What he would give for what Picou had seen! "Maybe—maybe just being Lafitte's storekeeper isn't enough." Picou's eyes were like candles, two burning lights that held Jean-Claude in their promise. He shrugged. "Perhaps you should talk with Lafitte. He seems to like you—who knows? He may give you an opportunity to satisfy both those thirsts of yours—for adventure as well as gold."

"Join Lafitte?" Even as he said the words, he knew how impossible that was. One did not marry a wife, begin a family, and then run off to the sea.

Picou's laugh, hard, full of harsh wisdom, challenged Jean-Claude. "You don't know what you're saying—join Lafitte! Listen—who knows what Lafitte might say? If you want—see him in New Orleans. His blacksmith shop is on Rue de Bourbon. If he's not there, his brother Pierre is."

During the week that followed, Jean-Claude spent as much time as he could at the site he was preparing for Lafitte. And while he cleared underbrush and split cypress, he kept thinking of Picou's words. Lafitte liked him. Lafitte might offer him adventures as well as gold. By the end of the week, he found reason to go to New Orleans. "I should order tools we'll need in the spring. See if I can get a better price for our furs—and," he added, "I can buy you a present."

Marguerite, whose only concern about the proposed trip was that New Orleans was a filthy city and that illness was everywhere, shook her head. "I don't need a present, Jean-Claude. Just don't come back with lung fever. You know how bad the air in New Orleans is." On the day he left, she packed "enough food for an entire boatload of men, even if they were to be gone for weeks," Jean-Claude said, lifting the sack, bulging with cheese and bread and sausages.

"How long will you be gone?"

Jean-Claude looked into her eyes, which had never given back anything but trust. "I promise I'll be home by Christmas," he said.

Noel André took the same boat as Jean-Claude. He, he told Jean-Claude, had an appointment with an American named Grimes, a sugar factor de Gravelle was making much of. Grimes and a few other investors were going to build a sugar mill in Attakapas. And, of course, de Gravelle had urged Noel de Clouet to try to get the mill built on his land.

"A good idea, too," Jean-Claude said.

"A good idea to deal with Americans? Men like de Gravelle are ruining New Orleans," Noel André grumbled to Jean-Claude. "Until the Americans bought the territory, de Gravelle's nose was as high in the air as anyone's—you very well know New Orleans was overrun with those vulgarians for years before the purchase! And would de Gravelle even speak to them? No! But now, now, he courts them, dines with them, even as they take New Orleans from our people."

"He is a banker," Jean-Claude said.

"He has become a merchant," Noel André said. "In France, he would have given up his title if he had behaved as he does here."

Jean-Claude looked around the crowded café on the edge of the cathedral square. Not patronized by any one group, its clientele was as heterogeneous as the population of New Orleans herself. Finely dressed Creoles speaking with elegant precision sat with bearded Americans whose rough voices seemed to carry the vastness of the western prairies and Kentucky mountains from which they came. Acadians up from the bayou country mixed with men whose features carried the stamp of Spanish blood, or the imprint of Indian heritage. "But this is not France," he said, fixing Noel André with a look that, released from the mask of tolerance Jean-Claude usually wore, showed clearly the reality he lived with. "This is part of the United States, where there are no titles."

"I know that—"

"Let me finish. It is also a place where many men are scrambling to become rich, to have what your family had in France. And, Noel André, if you do not do some scrambling, too—"

"We have capital."

Jean-Claude shrugged. "Capital? Your capital depends now on your sugar. And on slaves to grow it. You are no different from anyone else, Noel André. Either you earn enough each year to live on—or you use your capital up. That grand house—"

Finally angered, Noel André drained the last of his wine and rose. "And you? What capital do the Langlinais have?"

Jean-Claude rose also. "The capital we have always had. Our children. Who work in the fields, boys and girls both. Because you, Noel André, recited verse with your tutor, your father had to purchase slaves to do your work. While my father—my father had a son, heir to his land, working beside him. As I will have." He clapped Noel André on the back. "If I were you, Noel André, I would treat this Mr. Grimes well.

Remember, there are many scramblers. And not all will make it."

Watching Jean-Claude move off across the square, Noel André felt his anger die. This was the man who had, throughout their boyhood, taught him—so gently that Noel André was never made to feel as awkward, as ignorant, as he really was—all the things he needed to know to survive in the swamps, the fields. This was the man whose father had offered his food, seed, tools. Langlinais did not speak from envy. And while he did not understand these Acadians, while he did not know how they could watch neighbors who had come to the country years after themselves build fine homes, plant rich fields, without rancor, he knew that it was so—Jean-Claude and the people like him lived with a kind of privacy that made them tend very much to their own business, very little to their neighbors. Even Marguerite, enjoying though she did a good gossip, did not punctuate each story with sly comments, pointed insults, jealous comparisons, as did Hélène. They don't compare themselves to anyone else, Noel André thought. How in the hell do they manage that?

By the time Jean-Claude reached the blacksmith shop on Rue de Bourbon, Noel André and his problems had vanished from his mind. Rarely, very rarely, did he allow himself to advise a de Clouet. Clearly, when people built a house far larger, for grander than those around them, they worked and built not for what they truly needed but for what they thought they wanted. Well, he could do nothing about that.

Jean-Claude stood for a long moment in front of the Lafitte smithy before knocking at the courtyard gate. The high wall, its flat face completely concealing the life within, seemed mysterious, almost threatening. Any dark deed could be performed behind that mask—walls were not only to keep intruders out, but to keep secrets in. Jean-Claude felt something open within him. Behind this gate waited adventure, challenge. Not the challenge of pulling oxen from a bed of mud, or the adventure of bartering for furs deep in the swamp, but the challenge of steel against steel, of cannon fired from a wave-tossed ship, of chests of gold, jewels, silver. He pulled air into his lungs, pushed his body to its full height. Then he lifted the knocker and heard its heavy sound boom throughout the suddenly quiet street.

The woman who answered his knock was dark, with a beauty at once compelling and strange.

"I come to see Monsieur Jean Lafitte," Jean-Claude said. "My name is Jean-Claude Langlinais. From Attakapas."

Her dark body blended with the darkness of the hallway behind her. Jean-Claude could see very little in the small space between the woman and the door frame, but an aroma strong with spices hung around her. The world he had dreamed existed was real—he could smell it, see its power in the woman's face, the way she held her long-muscled body.

"Monsieur Jean is not here."

"Then Pierre Lafitte. Is he here?"

A big voice came from the shadowed darkness. "Who is it?"

The woman turned. "Jean-Claude Langlinais. From Attakapas."

"Bring him back."

The door swung wider, making room for Jean-Claude to enter. Silently, the woman led him into a room where a well-formed man sat playing with a small boy. Jean-Claude walked forward, his hand outstretched. "You are Pierre Lafitte?"

As Lafitte rose, Jean-Claude saw the dark eyes go over him, taking his measure as though he, too, were to be put on an auction block. "Will I do?" he said. There was both laughter and defiance in his voice—this Lafitte could decide which would prevail.

An arm went swiftly around Jean-Claude's shoulders, pulled him to the table. "Sit," Pierre said. He poured wine in a silver cup, handed it to Jean-Claude. "Drink. My brother said we should probably see you." One of the man's black eyebrows lifted, an easy curve of humor in that dark face. "Picou reports that you find it a little—tedious, to be always a farmer."

"I already know how to do that," Jean-Claude said. And when the eyebrow lifted higher—"I'm already good at it—all of it. Farming—lumbering—hunting—fishing—"

"So you want a new game? A man's game, is that it?" Again that measuring look, that weighing. "Jean is at Barataria. You've heard of it?" It was their headquarters, their fortress, their safe haven. As for what Jean-Claude had heard—if only half of it were true, Barataria would live up to its legend. "Why not go there with me? See what games we play."

Jean-Claude saw a flicker in the woman's eyes. Fear? Disapproval? She put a plate of food in front of him and moved to stand in the shadows where the child played. Now the surge of excitement that had begun to open in him when he stood before the gate was like a hole that has been torn into the side of a great dam. And like the waters that rage through the hole, sweeping before them all order, all design, the passion for excitement he suppressed when plowing his fields, grinding his neighbors' corn, rushed up and over him. Gone was Attakapas with its careful life. The world was before him, the open sea, the tropic sun that turned men's skins dark and in whose hellish heat no deed was too violent, no need denied.

"When do we start?"

Pierre smiled. "Now."

Not four squares away, Noel André sulked in Henry Grimes's office. In the first place, Grimes had kept him waiting, kept him sitting in an outer room with other men who, apparently, were accustomed to this unpleasantness and bore it patiently. He, Noel André de Clouet, was not accustomed to being kept waiting, as he had made plain to Grimes. There had been no apology; instead, a level stare until Noel André had made his little speech. Then Grimes had waved him to a chair and begun to talk.

"So, de Clouet, what is your answer?"

Noel André dragged his thoughts back to Grimes. For some forty-five minutes the man had been droning on, his harsh American accent falling gratingly on Noel André's ears. He had pushed graphs, and charts beneath Noel André's nose, pointing to figures with a thick, hairy finger. His shirt cuffs, Noel André saw, were grimy. Noel André had spent a good five minutes of this tedium making jokes about the American's name that he could repest to Marguerite. Now he looked at the man de Gravelle so unaccountably thought so well of. "My answer, Mr. Grimes?"

The face opposite his reddened. It was like watching the glow of the sunset fill an open window, turn everything before it into a roseate reflection of itself. "What the devil do you think you're here for, de Clouet? Didn't de Gravelle tell you what I want?"

Noel André rose. Carefully, he picked up the gloves he had laid, with his hat and cane, on the low table next to his chair. The table did not hold, as would a table in any decent man's office, a decanter of wine, one of brandy. Not even a humidor of cigars. These Americans might be scrambling for money, but they did not go about it with style. De Gravelle must have lost his mind to do business with them.

"Monsieur de Gravelle does not speak for the de Clouets," Noel André said, and wished that Hélène were here. "My father and I will confer. Then we will give you our decision as to whether or not you may build your mill at Beau Chêne." Those silver words rolled on his tongue.

Like a streak of cloud across the sunset, Grimes's white teeth gleamed as he opened his mouth and laughed. Noel André waited for this final rudeness to cease. It did not cease, but grew louder, louder, until Grimes was almost choking on his own full sounds. Furious, Noel André pulled on his gloves, jammed his hat on his head and strode toward the door. As he slammed it behind him, Grimes finally controlled that terrible noise and shouted after Noel André: "You silly young pup, do you think I need the de Clouets? It is de Gravelle who is pushing you—he says you are nearly bankrupt and need a favor. You'll be brankrupt in hell before I help you now."

Blindly walking, almost running, on the banquette outside, Noel André had gone two squares over before he finally slowed himself down. He settled his hat on his head, straightened the ruffles of his shirt and pulled at his vest. Grimes was a liar, as were all Americans. His mother was right. They had left a country to escape rule by peasants to find haven in a country that now belonged to peasants.

"Chéri, there is something wrong? I can cure you." A soft voice near his ear, a scent of violets. Turning, he saw the young round face in the window opening onto the street. Under a thin shawl, he saw a low-cut bodice, with young round breasts swelling above it. Deliberately, the girl took a red rose from her hair and handed it to him. "If you want to return it to me, monsieur, walk through the courtyard and knock at the second door." She reached out, pulled the shutters to. He heard the bar drop down across them. For a moment only, he stood looking at the solid shutters that concealed the girl, the room, from the world outside. Whatever he did behind them would be unseen, unknown. If ever he was to learn what it was like to have time to explore a woman's body, have her explore his, it would be with a girl like this. Aimée was—bored. Marguerite, not possible. He pulled air into his lungs, pushed his body to its full height. Then he went through the courtyard, found the second door, and knocked. Its small sound carried clearly across the suddenly quiet air.

From the time he left New Orleans with Pierre Lafitte, slipping down a maze of water until they reached the Lafitte head-quarters on Grande Terre, Jean-Claude had felt, more and more, that another man had taken over his farmer's body. By the third day at Barataria, that man, whoever he was, had entered into the life there. Under that blistering sun, even in it autumnal mood hot and strong during the middle hours of the day, he had joined the men who lived in palmetto-thatched huts built among the oak trees dwarfed and twisted by the wind, their leaves scalded by the salt spray tossed up from the Gulf. He had sat with them and their women under the oleanders that clustered around each hut, protecting it from the wind blowing in from the Gulf. He had plucked late-hanging oranges from the grove behind the houses, sucking sweet juice. He had feasted with them, drinking from golden goblets, eating from golden plates, served by women whose ill-kept bodies were covered by stained finery, satin and silk and lace gowns whose former owners needed them no more.

At the end of the third day, Lafitte had taken him to the warehouse where their treasures were stored. They had walked across the beach, the sea and sky darkening together as the sun closed down its light. The heavier wind coming in from the gulf had winter's breath on it. Jean-Claude shivered and turned up his coat collar. But once inside the big warehouse, he was warm. The sight of that treasure was like the striking of a flint; fire burned inside him, he stroked the green silk, the crimson velvet and wondered—if a little dove like Marguerite ever saw such splendor, would she, too, yearn to be a bird of paradise? His fingers turned over the emeralds set in filigreed gold, rubies rimmed with diamonds. Chest after chest, casket after casket, barrel after barrel—"Sacrebleu, and have you left the Spaniards anything at all?"

"Those who had these want it no longer," Lafitte said. "Those who would have owned it—have been replaced. The people of Louisiana enjoy fine things also. Isn't that so?" Lafitte went to a small casket, searched through the pieces of jewelry there. He held up a long gold chain, weighted by an ornate gold cross. "Your wife, Marguerite—would this not look well on her?"

Jean-Claude reached out, took the necklace. As though all the light in the warehouse, cast forth by lanterns swinging from the beams or set upon rough shelves, had gathered into one bright eye and focused itself on the shining length in his hand, the links of gold glittered and gleamed until he could see nothing else. The heavy cross moved gently back and forth, drawing his gaze. He was surrounded by the deep gleam of silver, the higher glint of gold, the gaudy sparkle of faceted jewels. Perfume rose from the silks and satins piled around him, from sachets tucked in open trunks. He could imagine that richness on Marguerite, the way the twisted links would lay around the curve of her neck, the way the cross would gleam against the gray and black of her clothes. "I did promise her a present," he said. Then he handed the gold chain back to Lafitte. "But—I do not take such gifts."

"Even when the man giving it has so much?" The careless wave of Lafitte's hand made all that wealth his.

"What does how much you have to do with me?" Jean-Claude said. "I judge by what I am willing to take—not by what you are willing to give."

"So." Lafitte tucked the necklace into an inner pocket. "As you wish. If you earned it? Would you take it then?"

"If the work was worth the payment."

Lafitte laughed. "I can assure you—it will be at least that." He led the way back across the now night-hidden beach to his quarters. They stepped over the bodies of men, sunk in drunken sleep where they lay.

"Don't you sail tomorrow?" Jean-Claude said. He had heard the report of a Spanish galleon, beating her way into Barataria's path. "Will they even be able to board ship?"

Lafitte's hand went briefly to the pistol stuck through his belt. "They will sail," he said. "And you? Will you sail with us?"

Jean-Claude could not see Lafitte's face in the dark that covered even the moon. There had been much teasing, the past few days, about their farmer-sailor. And though Jean-Claude had waited for something to be said, for Jean to fulfill the promises both Picou and Pierre seemed to have made, there had been nothing. Jean-Claude tested Lafitte's voice, the words themselves. "You ask that truly?" he said.

"Lafitte always speaks the truth." Then he laughed. "There are enough lies told about me, I don't need to make more. Yes—I ask you to come with us."

"You spoke of work. What work?"

They were in Lafitte's quarters, sharing a bottle of port and a wedge of Dutch cheese. "There's a great big white Spanish goose out there, Jean-Claude. Waiting for her golden eggs to be taken and for her feathers to be plucked." Lafitte's eyes went over him, that same weighing, measuring gaze. "I don't think you're ready yet to—wring her neck. But the plucking—that I think you will do very well."

Jean-Claude stood on the deck of Lafitte's ship, his eyes reflecting the golden light that poured into the blue waters and then shot back up from the white-tipped waves like a fountain of sparkling dewdrops. The tall masts above him were in full sail; Jean had explained to him that this was a brigantine, and he had begun to talk of mainsails and rigging until Jean-Claude had stopped him. "It is enough I go in this ship, I can't work it, me!" It was more than enough to go in this ship. He had never, in all his life, felt more alive. The ship leaped beneath his feet, eagerly following a path across this stretching blue that led, so Lafitte said, to a rich Spanish prize. Around him, men sharpened knives, rammed oiled cloth down musket barrels, prepared for the fight ahead. The world was bounded now by the circling line of the horizon. It separated him from that insular life in Attakapas, where the sameness of the days, the seasons, drew close around them the protection of routine and the security of repetition.

Now he made a promise to himself. There was a fight ahead, a good one. It was nothing to him whom they fought. That was Lafitte's worry. The treasure back on the island—Jean-Claude had had no part in taking that. But the necklace, the necklace that had been put before him, offered him. If he fought well today, if he deserved Lafitte's trust, the necklace was his, and no man could deny it. His hand went to the knife at his side. Since that day weeks ago when Adolphe Picou had surprised him, his blood had been ready. A man should not have to wait so long to fight, it did him the same harm as when he could not fill other needs.

A hoarse shout came from the lookout high above him; as though the sound were vibrating through each man's head, moving him, the crew ran to their stations. Even before the second shout came, and Jean-Claude heard plainly the words *Infanta* sighted, three leagues west of starboard," guns were being uncovered, blades unsheathed, Jean-Claude had been assigned to a cannon in the bow of the ship, manned by Pierre. He ran quickly to his position, stood at Pierre's side. Ahead of them, sailing as lightly as though she were being drawn to them by a pulley, was a massive ship. She seemed to have a hundred sails, their whiteness gleaming in the white October light. Her proud bow dipped and rose with the crest of the waves, and still she came on.

"Don't they see us?"

"They see us, all right," Pierre said. He sounded different, gone was the careless voice Jean-Claude had heard during that first meeting, when Pierre's son played in the corner, his mistress served the food. This was business, this was work. All the rest—that was what men did when they needed respite. But this—this was life. "They know they can't get away. We're faster than they are—and better sailors. They've got to stand and fight. At least," Pierre said, moving the cannon's barrel to a higher angle, "at least they will die as men."

In the thunder and lightning of the cannon, Jean-Claude learned a new kind of storm. Sheets of fire as a burning sail fell to deck. Streaks of glowing light as powder exploded. Iron falling from the skies. The noise. The cursing, the shouts of warning, cries of pain. "A look at hell," Pierre said. Around them, crew members were using long grappling hooks to bring the ships together. Eager ones were already leaping across the small space that still separated the Lafitte ship and her prey, knives at the ready, faces glaring with light from the havoc before them.

"Who then are the devils?" Jean-Claude asked.

Pierre shot a look at him, heavy, burning, as the shot from their cannon. "All men," he said. Lafitte pulled Jean-Claude out of the fray, took him to his cabin and poured wine.

"I could be fighting," Jean-Claude said. But he did not resist.

"Not with them." A time of silence followed; the shouts, the sound of steel, of pistol fire, was quieter, muffled by the tension in the room. Then Lafitte turned. "You have seen our men, Langlinais. Eaten with them, drunk with them. They are—not quite as you. They do not live among good women, as you do. They do not live to create something, as you do. They live to destroy." He shrugged. "Men like that sometimes do—unnecessary things in battle."

"They are your men," Jean-Claude said. "It is your orders

they follow." Lafitte sounded almost like a de Clouet, talking this way. He must have some Royalist blood; not for the first time, Jean-Claude thanked the good Lord that his blood was simple, his thoughts straight.

Eventually, the noise dimmed, with little sound of exploding gunpowder, fewer shouts from the embattled men. "I think it must be time to begin plucking," Lafitte said. He turned his eyes on Jean-Claude. "You can stay here, if you wish."

"And miss the work you said I would enjoy?" Jean-Claude finished his wine and followed Lafitte onto the empty deck of the ship.

Before him was the havoc wrought by that fire storm from hell. The bleeding bodies of Spanish sailors were everywhere—hanging in the rigging, caught as they fought to get over the rail, at the great steering wheel—everywhere blood ran and steeped the deckboards beneath their feet. One of Lafitte's men, struggling to open a chest brought up from the hold, took a bayonet from a stiffening hand to pry the lock as easily as Jean-Claude would have taken it from his own side. "They live with death," Jean Lafitte said. His voice had the chill of the wind on the beach the night before. Jean-Claude thought of the ballroom, the white, white linen, the slender hands, the elegant ways.

"With cruelty, too," Jean-Claude said. The unneeded hacking. The mutilation.

"The excitement wears off, for some," Lafitte said. "So they need more. Come—we'll go to the captain's cabin. They'll bring the best things there."

And, under the fierce eye of Pierre, they did. Casket after casket of jewels, chest after chest of gold. So much that Jean-Claude wearied of sorting them, counting them. "I've seen enough gold to last a lifetime," he said.

"I wonder," Lafitte said. "A fever for gold—it's like malaria, it comes and goes, but never quite does it die—and always, always it weakens you."

Jean-Claude's eyes went to the chests and caskets, spilling their bounty. A crimson haze seemed to dim the golden sheen; in that dull mist, even the diamonds were without luster, brilliance. "You know the cross? The one you showed me in the warehouse? I think—I think that is enough."

"I told you the work would be worth the payment. Do you sell your effort so cheaply?"

Jean-Claude looked past Lafitte to the porthole giving onto the deck. Though he could not see the dead men nor smell their blood, he didn't have to. "If that cross was bought as this gold was—it was not bought cheaply. It is enough."

Jean-Claude arrived back in New Orleans with the necklace resting safely in a small pouch he wore on a leather thong around his neck and with one of Lafitte's fine white linen handkerchiefs folded and tucked down in his pack. "If you ever need me, tie this to a stick and mount it on the cabin roof at the meeting place in the swamp," Lafitte had said. "The men who go there will see it and tell me."

On going to an inn, there to wait the departure of the boat for Attakapas, Jean-Claude found Noel André still in New Orleans. "Where have you been?" Noel André asked. "How long does it take to order plows? Or whatever it was you had to do."

"There were other things." He signaled a waiter for a coffee. "It's only been three weeks. And you? It takes so long to find furniture?"

Noel André smiled. "As you say—there were other things."

"You've found a woman!" Now that he studied him, Jean-Claude could see there was something different about Noel André. "She must be a fine one."

"Why do you say that?" For his part, Noel André found Jean-Claude different, too. Wherever he had been on this mysterious business, he had returned as though he knew some secret that made him more than other men. But no matter how Noel André pried, hinted, Jean-Claude said nothing, only rattled coins in his pockets and whistled at the sky. Dropping one comment, one remark only. That perhaps Noel André could use his talents for houses in Attakapas as well as in New Orleans. Men other than the de Clouets might also wish to build better homes for their families.

"There is a way a man holds himself when his body is satisfied. That's all." Jean-Claude grinned again. "The rest of your business, it went as well?"

"The furnishings are all ordered. As for Grimes—well, like all Americans, one has to steel one's stomach to his manner—or lack of it! However, I decided to help him a little." Noel André peered into his glass as though studying the sediment in his wine. He's lying, thought Jean-Claude. To himself as well as to me. A mental shrug. It was no more to him if a de Clouet were a liar or a thief than if a Picou were.

"So? And what is this business?"

"A sugar mill. In Attakapas."

Jean-Claude felt the coins in his pocket. A mill. Now that was something that could, almost, turn grain to gold, as in the fairy tales the women told to children. "A sugar mill? And who will own it?"

"Several men."

"You?"

"An interest. It will be on our land." The disturbance in Noel André's face announced that he would say no more. In some way, Noel André's idea of how that business should go had been violated. Jean-Claude sighed. Now the de Clouet pride, that complicated, overstuffed, overfed pride, would once more get between them. If ever these de Clouets learned to be proud of the right things, how much better off they all would be! Behind the disturbed face, Noel André remembered the aftermath of the first visit to Grimes. An abrupt, hardly polite note from de Gravelle, waiting at his rooms when he returned from that first idyll with Yvonne. A note that summoned him to de Gravelle's bank, where he was shown, with now no politeness at all, the state of the de Clouet finances.

"When a woman spends what your mother spends, it has to be made up somewhere. You must learn, de Clouet, that slaves are not serfs. Your serfs in France paid dues, taxes, and cared for themselves. They rented the use of your mills, your wine presses. Your slaves pay nothing—you must feed them, house them, clothe them, medicate them. They work because they must, for no other reason. So if you do not use every means available, every means, I repeat, to replenish your capital, to build an income that will support this life your mother demands, then, Noel André, the dynasty of the de Clouets will have a swift and predictable end." And then the orders, to return to Grimes, to wait even longer in that cold waiting room, to enter that office, hat and gloves in hand, and to beg pardon. To sign an agreement then, at far less favorable terms.

"What I would have paid you in dollars you took out in good will," Grimes said when Noel André protested the change. "If there were any other land in that district so well suited to the mill, believe me, you would not have any part of it."

* * *

"Did you have a good trip?" Marguerite asked Jean-Claude the night of his return. The heavy cross still lay hidden; he would bring it out at the birth of their child.

"Very good." Jean-Claude watched Marguerite move around the room, the room his father and mother had begun their marriage in. It had been understood that two houses, one on the original Langlinais grant and one on the land Claude had brought for his son, would always house the family—sons would be born, would move into the larger, older house, would watch their sons have their families, would die, make way for the next generation— "Marguerite, one would not want a house like Beau Chêne. That is foolish. But a house built all of a piece, not added on to—there is no reason why we should not have that." Jean-Claude did not ask her if she agreed. The price Jean Lafitte would pay him for the storage place was good. With that set aside, he could use what his fields and traps and trees yielded—no wonder men with gold under their pillows or buried behind their chimneys walked taller. When a man didn't have to carry worry as well as work—Jean-Claude pulled Marguerite onto his lap. "You'd like that, wouldn't you, chérie? A nice big house?"

Marguerite leaned against him. She smelled of the bread she had baked, of the spices in the fruit she had been stewing. "Will you be in it?"

"Of course."

"Always?"

He was like a bear now, ready to close in for the winter. He had a store inside him to live on for a long, long while. But if spring came? And all that store was gone? "Well—almost always."

Her laughter tickled his neck. "If you had said 'always' I wouldn't have believed you."

"Did you have a good trip?" The question, put to Noel André almost at the same time by three different tongues, meant three different things. Hélène meant—will the furniture you bought astonish all who see it, fire envy in every woman's heart? Aimée meant—did you do the plantation business that I entrusted to you with care? Did you arrange to replace the slave who ran off? Noel meant—did you sign the contract with Grimes?

Noel André took a bite of food, chewed it carefully, sipped wine. Meals with Yvonne had been a new and wonderful experience. Sitting across from him in her loose robe, her hair curling around her face, her eyes and lips open and ready for him, she had attended to his every wish almost before he knew he had it. She stroked his shoulders when he was tired, rubbed his forehead when he was cross, sang songs for him when he wanted to be gay. Well Jean-Claude was right. No woman could give a man both. Let Aimée run the damn plantation. Let his father do business with a Yankee. Let his mother ruin them all with her dreams of lost grandeur.

"Very good," he said. "And I have decided that de Gravelle is right. I should be an architect. There will be many people here building fine homes. And other buildings will go up. So—" He rose, enjoying the force of three pairs of eyes piercing him, trying to determine what new game this was. "So, I shall spend time in New Orleans, studying under the man de Gravelle recommends. It is not as though I am needed for anything here." He did not ask them if they agreed. As soon as the barges came down the bayou with Hélène's goods, she would be occupied for months. As soon as the plans for the mill arrived, Noel and Aimée would have time for nothing else. "Architecture is, maman, a gentleman's occupation."

# CHAPTER 10

## *White Gold*

The de Clouets and the Langlinaises would have good reason
to mark the year 1807 as a significant one. For the de Clouets,
the year dropped bounty from between the pages of the calendar
as though it were one package of surprises. Beginning with the
birth of the second daughter, Louise, early in the year, continuing with the appointment of Noel as parish judge when the
county of Attakapas became St. Martin Parish, through the
grand opening of Beau Chêne and ending with the start-up of
the sugar mill, the de Clouets could finally breathe, almost
constantly, the rarefied air they so depended on. For Jean-
Claude and Marguerite Langlinais, one event and one event
only was necessary to make 1807 memorable: the birth of a
son.

Cecile Langlinais was, in fact, late for her private viewing
of Beau Chêne because she had stopped to visit her grandson.
"And would you believe it, already we can see he is just like
his grandfather!" She and Hélène were sitting in the de Clouet
drawing room, built on the second floor of the house. Lifted
above the humid air that clung to the soft earth, the drawing
room seemed to soar in a green world of oak boughs and light,
where every possible breath of air dancing by was enticed inside
by the splendor there.

Hélène leaned back in the carved chair and ran a careful
hand over the tapestry that covered it. On the weekend, a party
of their friends would arrive to celebrate the opening of Beau
Chêne. The de Gravells from New Orleans, the de la Houssaye
from down the bayou. Others who had, like the de Clouets,
arrived at some degree of civilized living in the years since
insanity became the rule and the only known order was chaos.
But no matter how Charlotte and Juliette flattered her taste,

she would hear criticism. The only sincere praise this house would receive was Cecile's. As they went from room to room, Hélène watched Cecile's face as each new beauty was revealed. She had seen the knowing fingers testing the smoothness of the silk, the eyes balancing each other, judging, approving.

Now, as they sipped coffee from the elaborately decorated new porcelain, Hélène said, watching the effect of her words on Cecile, "If you are ever reincarnated, Cecile, I hope it is as a great lady. Your taste is too fine to have only one life— and that one in Attakapas." Her laugh was silver still, but more brittle now, more tarnished with the markings of age. "Pardon. In Saint Martin. With Noel as the judge, you would think I could remember." Then the flick of the silver-tipped whip, the glance that reminded that Noel ruled, and others obeyed.

"I hope so, too," Cecile said. She put down her cup, rose, stretched her arms above her head. "I sat too long spinning this morning, my back needs a walk." Her eyes, eyes that still held at times the unknowing, almost unseeing, look of a child, went over the room, stopping now on the gaily painted border that edged the deep crown molding, now on the fine grain of the game table. The gaze came to rest on Hélène. "I hope that if I ever have another life, it will be a life like that of my mother-in-law, Mathilde. Or perhaps my daughter-in-law, Marguerite."

"What? Do you think you are getting old, Cecile? So that you turn to pious thoughts?"

"Maybe I am not getting old so much as finally growing up, Hélène. You remember when you first came here?" The words flowed by, a soft clear stream of thought that, like a spring brook, mirrored the world around it. "You were everything I was not. That Mathilde was not. And we had a good time, did we not? I don't know when I really knew I was a play toy to you, as my ribbons and bits of lace were to me. Maybe after I visited you in New Orleans."

"Good Lord, Cecile, you are getting old. Leave old bones lying." Hélène too rose. She hated these kinds of conversations, she had always hated them. Life was not to be examined, it was to be lived. In fact, if one lived it as one wished to, it did not bear examination.

"These are not old bones. They are what I have lived with for a long time. I didn't want to think about what had happened in New Orleans, Hélène." She paused. "Claude Louis—" Though the voice went on, the soft clear stream washing away the sediment, the decay, that had kept the fresh waters from flowing strongly, Hélène heard it no more. She saw only the light that came into Cecile's face when she said her husband's name. And knew that ever, in her entire life, if she had felt that way about a man for one week, let alone a lifetime, that well of loss in her would have been filled.

"Claude Louis made a safe place for me. He knew there was something wrong, and he tried to keep it from me. I let him, for so long I let him do all the work, all the hard things. I played, and I told myself his mother, and then Marguerite, were stupid, dull."

Hélène yawned, fingers barely covering her wide mouth. "You disappoint me, Cecile. Of course I know there is a great difference between us—but I thought you had a larger view of life than what you say now. Are you telling me your time would have been better spent getting knotted hands and weathered skin? Zut! You Langlinais will never rise in this world if you can't beat down that peasant blood."

Cecile settled her bonnet over her hair, drawn into a low knot on her neck with a few curling tendrils still hovering over her face. The calm in her eyes remained as she looked at Hélène. "My father-in-law had something he used to say, Hélène. That there were two things a man did not betray—his God and his bed. I think it is the same for a woman. And for all my foolishness, all my playing, I have betrayed neither." She moved to the wide doors that led out to the gallery, with stairs leading down to the lower level of the house. "Perhaps to live up to that is all that divides gentlemen and ladies from everyone else. No matter what blood beats through the body. Your house is lovely, Hélène. I hope it brings you great happiness."

Hélène watched the small figure descend the stairs, vanish from her sight. How straight Cecile's back was, how firm her step. As though the fiber that was inside her, a fiber weakened, stunted, by the grim chill of neglect and abuse, had finally responded to the warmth and light Claude Louis brought into her life. Had come out into the sunshine, while the shadows fled.

Hélène strode to the bell pull near the hearth, tugged it violently. A young slave, turban tied hastily around her head, answered. She carried away the coffee tray, returned with a decanter of wine. When Aimée and Noel came in from the mill, they found Hélène asleep by the fire, the decanter at her side half empty, the glass on the table hall full.

Noel filled two glasses with the remaining wine, handed one to Aimée. "Fortunately, nothing is required of Hélène in the coming festivities but that she appear, dressed in a fashion worthy of this house."

"She's bored," Aimée said. She herself was never bored. When Noel André first began his sojourns in New Orleans to study architecture, young wives on neighboring plantations had pitied her. She must be so lonely without her husband. She hardly missed him. She would have no more children, three was plenty. If Noel André left the plantation to her, she could not be a brood mare as well. And why would any woman miss Noel André in bed? As for missing him in any other way—it had been a long time now since she had heard his talk as anything but an interruption of important matters. She cared nothing for the books, the music, the collections of prints Noel André doted on. When he began to speak of a new novel, recently shipped from his bookseller in New Orleans, Aimée would play with her food, lift an eyebrow at Noel, wait for a small break in Noel André's words so that she could turn the conversation back to the progress of the mill, the state of the second barn.

Hélène interested her even less. Hélène was an expensive nuisance, something carried on the plantation books as a complete loss. Aimée knew to a penny what it cost to keep Hélène going; it was the one piece of information concerning their business that she did not share with her father-in-law.

"The party this weekend will entertain her, then," Noel said. He flung himself onto the horsehair sofa opposite the low chair where Aimée sat. "I sometimes think, Aimée, that the system we live by is not a very good one." Aimée's face, known as well to Noel as his own, questioned him. "The reason husbands and wives are chosen—change. If fate, or something, does not intervene—" The question on her face became a statement, he need say no more. Noel knew Aimée shared his astonishment that despite the fact that almost every man seemed to marry precisely the wrong woman for him, and every woman precisely the wrong man, the generation of children, children optimistic about their own chances for a happy life, continued.

"Let us be frivolous for once, Noel. If you were God, creating the first and most perfect woman, what would she be like?"

A vision, so near his consciousness that it needed little to bring it to life, filled Noel's mind. The rhythms of the old Acadian dance he had first danced with Cecile filled his blood. He felt again the slender waist, the sweet breath heavy on his cheek. And felt the slight stiffening in the waist, the slight catch in the breath, when his hand had tightened on her, his arm had drawn her close. He had envied Claude Louis then and nothing that had happened in all these years had changed that. His balance in de Gravelle's bank was low; much more depended on the success of this sugar mill than even Aimée knew. His son, no matter whose house he designed, what building bore his name, would never be the man Claude Louis' son was. There might be glory ahead for the de Clouets, did not everyone say so? But to Noel de Clouet, sitting in his fine home with the position as first judge of St. Martin Parish securely his, the fuel that fed the glory seemed volatile, difficult to control. Whereas the Langlinais flame burned with the steadiness of a fire consuming heartwood.

"Noel?"

He turned. Aimée, at least, was all she had promised to be. With that wiry body galloping at his side, he could carry the de Clouet standard yet another time into battle. "My perfect woman?" The bell sounded faintly in the dining room below them. Before rousing his wife, Noel went to his daughter-in-law, kissed her smooth forehead. "Someone very much like you, my dear Aimée. Very much like you."

The farmer's dictum that it took one season to properly clear a field, another to plant it and a third to harvest it proved equally true for the sugar mill. Not until three years after it began grinding cane did the mill bring the return its builders expected, but with the harvest of 1810, the fields of slender cane, the green-ribbon leaves bending in a constantly changing wave, began to produce a river of white gold.

"We've reached the turnaround," Aimée said, closing the thick ledger and leaning back in her chair. Outside the front door, her children played. Troi sat astride his new pony, a crown of autumn leaves set firmly on his curls. Lélé and Louise had woven leaves also along the bridle and reins, and the red and

gold against the pony's cream coat caught light from the setting
sun. Aimée would never be the kind of mother Marguerite
was, whose five children, very soon to be joined by another,
centered her life. Aimée cared for her children as she did
everything else on the place—with what was due them. And
so the de Clouet daughters and son had a balanced diet, good
sleeping habits, lots of exercise and enough love to keep them
good-tempered—what worked for high-bred horses worked
equally well for high-bred children.

Now she faced Noel. "Do you think I haven't known how
close to ruin this place has been? The size of the notes de
Gravelle held? I may not enjoy the things Hélène does—but
I know what they cost."

"I wonder if you do," Noel said. Then, before the silence
between them could become dangerous, as it had lately had a
habit of doing—"I have a surprise for you. Down in the south
pasture." He rose, held out his hand to her. Her strong slim
hand fit in his; over how many hills had he helped her as they
walked the fields, how many ditches had her short legs leaped,
balanced by his arm? She tucked her arm through his, turned
the oil lamp out, and went with him into the fresh October
afternoon.

"Look, maman, how well I ride." His sisters trailing behind
him, Troi led a parade around the hedged garden opening out
beyond the office door.

"Like a true chevalier," his grandfather said.

"Be sure to brush him well when you finish your ride,"
Aimée said. "People who don't take care of their horses don't
deserve to have them." She saw Tante, the children's nurse,
sitting on a bench nearby, mending in her hand. "Troi may
have three more turns around the garden," she said. "Then take
the girls in and have him take his pony to the barn."

Freed, her thoughts went to the surprise waiting in the pasture. Of course a horse, what else? But what horse? They had
been looking at animals for several months; there was no way
to keep a stable at top form without constantly bringing in new
blood. It wasn't like Noel to choose an important horse without
consulting her. Now which? "What have you gotten me?" she
said. "That big black we saw at LeBeau? Or the roan?"

"A pony," he teased. "The brother to Troi's."

She squeezed his arm, felt the warmth of his body through
his light coat. "Troi is not the only chevalier at Beau Chêne,"

she said. Rising on tiptoe, she kissed his cheek.

His arm came around her. "Aimée—"

But they had broken through the trees that edged the south pasture and she saw what waited there. "Noel!" His name, breathed out in just that way, adoring, delighted, had kept him going through more than one crisis when the red ink in de Gravelle's books had seemed as ready to engulf him as the Red Sea had been to engulf the children of Israel. "Noel!" More softly, her whole being caught up in the splendor of the stallion before her, Aimée repeated his name.

"Well, and how much did that one cost?" The voice cut through them, knifing its way between man and woman, woman and horse, separating them.

Noel turned to his wife. "Not nearly as much as he'll bring in stud fees."

"To think he performs so well he is paid for it," Hélène said. She was closer to them now, they could see the careful lurch in her walk.

I must get Noel André to spend more time here, Noel thought. The more he is in New Orleans, the more his mother drinks.

"Of course our Aimée will ride him," Hélène said. "That makes him worth whatever he cost." Aimée gathered herself in close control. She hated to see Noel embarrassed; what had he done to deserve such a wife?

"No one will ride him until he has settled in," she said quietly. "It wouldn't be safe."

"Safe! Is that what you think about? You and Noel, the hours you spend together, you are thinking about being safe?"

"We are running the plantation," Aimée said. Now she turned away, moved to the rail fence and leaned on it. The stallion saw her and pawed the ground. His head was lifted, testing the scents and sounds of this new place. Forgetting everything but the animal, Aimée gave herself up to the pure joy of seeing perfection. She stood, willing the stallion to know her, to trust her, until the edge of the pasture was blending with the shadows of twilight.

Noel had long since taken Hélène back to the house. Noel André was probably already in his mother's boudoir. Whenever he came back from New Orleans, he went first to Hélène, ready to play all the little games she loved so well. Aimée laughed, a laugh as short and harsh as the sound the stallion made when he tossed that proud neck skyward. How must it be to be serviced by a male who performed so well he was paid for it?

Jean-Claude pushed through the dying swamp grass, ducking as a low branch cut across his face. He rarely visited the spit of land Lafitte used; payment arrived on time each quarter of the year, and, except for an occasional dinner with Jean when they were both in New Orleans at the same time, he had not seen either brother since his first visit to Grande Terre. Adolphe Picou appeared once in a while, his clothes always elegant, his tongue always boasting. "I get more in one month than you earn a year from all your work," Picou would tell him. "If not in one month, then certainly in two."

He didn't need to see the de Clouet books to know that the sugar mill was finally paying off. When Noel André met with him last week to bring plans for the house Jean-Claude had finally decided to build, he moved with the air of a man who could finally afford the way he lived. He had looked over the map of the Langlinais land, studying the spot Jean-Claude had chosen for the house. "I'd no idea you had all this land. Too bad you don't put it in sugar. But then, no matter how many children you Langlinais have, you will never grow sugar. For that, as you have so often told me, Jean-Claude, one must have slaves."

"Since the slave trade has long been forbidden in this territory, that's not possible," Jean-Claude said.

"Is that the reason you don't have them? No moral objection, like your father?"

"I've no idea. It's not a question I've had to answer." Jean-Claude laughed at the look on Noel André's face. "Or a moral decision I've had to make. I don't have the choice my father did—to buy slaves or not."

"What? Are you saying you don't make moral decisions until you have to?"

"Noel André. How would I know a decision was needed, until the occasion arose?"

"Don't be an idiot, Jean-Claude. There are moral laws, ethical laws, things men know and believe whether they ever use them or not!"

"Now you are the idiot, Noel André. Me, I don't bother to learn anything, or believe anything, if I have no use for it."

He smiled at Marguerite, sitting mending by the fire. "Of course, I have my Marguerite. She is my conscience." He went to his wife, turned her face to the light. "As long as her eyes look at me in just that way, I know I'm all right."

Noel André thought of Aimée, who no longer looked at him at all.

"One decision you will have to make—about the house. I'll make some sketches, shall I? And bring them back next week?"

"You're late," Adolphe said when Jean-Claude pushed open the door to the cabin.

"I don't stop my life because you want me."

Adolphe stared at him, the thin mouth setting a line between them. "You say you don't care for luxury. That fine independence of yours may be the costliest thing you have."

"I pay for it."

"It's nothing to me. Now, this is what Lafitte wants." Jean-Claude sat at the table and poured wine. As he listened to Adolphe, the good taste in his mouth became vile. Spitting the wine out, he also spat out a word: "Slaves?"

"There is a market here. Lafitte needs a place for the auction. What better place than this?"

"Our agreement is for storage only. I want no slave buyers on my land."

"Lafitte will triple what he pays you." A silence. Jean-Claude pried the cork from a new bottle of wine. "Besides, what's it to you? Slaves are better treated here than in other places—it's not as though they won't be sold to someone."

"You mean, whether you use my land or not, these—people will still be slaves."

"It is their condition in life. Who are we to argue with that?" Adolphe, too, took more wine. "Lafitte sent you this," he said. A heavy pistol, the grip inlaid with silver, appeared in Adolphe's hand. He slid the weapon across the table. "Lafitte has taken a fancy to you, don't ask me why."

"We understand each other," Jean-Claude said.

"Well, then. If you understand each other, you should understand why Lafitte asks you to let us sell slaves on your land— and he should understand why you say no. Isn't that right?" Picou yawned. He much preferred the company of honest thieves and murderers to men like Jean-Claude Langlinais who fooled themselves into doing things they very well intended to do all along.

"Where are these slaves coming from?"

"Where? How would I know? What difference does that make?" Then Picou laughed. "Wait. I see. What you want to know is—is this the first time they'll be sold? Or have they gone through many owners? You'll be doing wrong and you know it. What you're asking is—how big is the wrong?"

"I'll not buy them."

"You'll make money from their sale."

The plans Noel André had left with them came before him. A house so simple even Marguerite liked it, but so sound, so solid, that Jean-Claude had, for the first time in his life, treated Noel André with respect. The money from the sale would go a long way to getting that house built. And as Picou said— slaves in the district, in neighboring districts, were treated well. If it were a choice between their freedom and slavery—but someone else had already made that decision.

"Tell Lafitte it's all right," Jean-Claude said. "But, Picou— tell him the next time just to bring them in. I don't need to know about it."

"An astonishing thing," Noel André said to Jean-Claude. They had met at the site of the new house so that Noel André could place the stakes marking its precise location, the chill of November surrounding them. "I went to an auction to buy another house servant for mater—and it was on your land!"

"So?"

Noel André set the final stake, stood back and looked at Jean-Claude.

"So, I wanted to ask—have you had to make your moral decision? About slavery, I mean."

"I wasn't there. I own no slaves."

"You made it possible for others to buy them."

Jean-Claude laughed. "I made it possible for other men to make a moral decision. If they decided to own slaves—what is that to me?"

"Is that how it's done, then? The simple goodness my father goes on and on about, admires so in your people? It's not goodness at all, is it, Jean-Claude? It's closing your eyes, holding your nose, not smelling the muck you're in!"

"We've not had the luxury of living far enough above the

muck to get out of it, de Clouet. You learn to live with it."

"And even make money out of it."

"Don't put your rules on me."

Noel André laughed. "My rules? They're not just my rules. But what difference does it make? If you can keep your left hand from knowing what your right hand is doing—and still think you deserve Marguerite's trust—"

"You go too far, de Clouet."

"She is your conscience, isn't she? Does she know how you make the money you'll build her house with?"

"Do you know how your wife makes the money that keeps yours?"

The anger between them, like a charged metal bar, drew them slowly and steadily toward each other. The first blows fell at the same time—Jean-Claude's fist to Noel André's face. Noel André's to Jean-Claude's chest. Jean-Claude fought carefully, placing his blows. He would teach de Clouet a lesson, but not a fatal one. At the end, Noel André was bloody, bruised. But not really hurt. As Jean-Claude turned away, the man on the ground called out. Jean-Claude waited, his back stiff.

"You win with your weapons, peasant. Next time, it will be with mine. And you won't get off so easily."

Jean-Claude turned. "Get off my land." He removed a pouch from his coat pocket, poured gold coins from it into his hand. He strode to where Noel André sat, still catching air back into his lungs in long struggling waves. "Here is your fee." The gold shimmered in one long line from Jean-Claude's hand onto the ground beside Noel André. "Now let's see if aristocrats scramble for gold as do other men." He did not look back.


"What have you done to yourself?" Sacrebleu, he'd forgotten his parents were coming for supper, how his mother as well as Marguerite would fuss over him—and under his father's wise eye, how to explain his face, his scarred knuckles? The women created their usual healing commotion, bringing hot cloths, rubbing salve, pouring wine.

"Did papa fall down and hurt himself?" Mathilde, at six her mother's mirror, hovered.

"No, but I think maybe somebody else did," her grandfather told her. "Mathilde, you go play with your sisters. Your papa's all right." Claude Louis studied his son. "So how does the other man look?"

"Jean-Claude, have you been fighting?" Marguerite's eyes, always large, grew so wide Jean-Claude thought he could fall into them. Before he could speak, she lifted a hand. "No, I don't want to hear about it. If you did fight, you had your reasons." She put her face next to his, kissed his cheek. "You are not hurt, that's all that matters."

"But if you did fight, who was it?" his mother asked. Jean-Claude heard the fear in her voice. Always the dark that lay waiting, always the threat that could devour her.

"Noel André," he said, and waited for the explosion. Marguerite flashed him a look, then bent over her cook pots. Cecile drew in one quick breath. A look of understanding crossed her face, and then she went back to the embroidery in her lap. Only his father seemed to want more. Jean-Claude looked at those questioning eyes. "Later," he said.

They sat on the low porch after the meal and smoked their pipes while the women put the children to bed. "Why did you fight?"

"Noel André got above himself. I took him back down."

Claude Louis leaned back against the porch rail. "Above himself? Or you?"

The afternoon's heat was in Jean-Claude's voice. "He can't get above me."

"Then why fight him?"

The arctic air rushing down the plains seemed to be pushing silence ahead of it, surrounding them. Overhead, the thick sky of summer had given way to the sharp clarity of the coming winter; the moon, unveiled, spilled brilliance over the land. Jean-Claude heard the quiet sureness in his father's voice. "Jean-Claude—there will always be men who try to put themselves above you. There will always men who truly are above you— in how much land they own, how many cattle—and there will always be men who will never be above you. Jean-Claude— if we spend our time trying to bring down those above us— either in their minds or in ours—how is there time for anything else?"

When Noel André came in, blood caking with dirt on his forehead, his cheeks, trousers ruined, shirt stained, Hélène welcomed crisis. "What have you done to yourself?" she said, rising. "Aimée, don't you see that your husband is hurt?"

Aimée put down the book she was reading to Noel. Hélène

knew it was another of the medical works Aimée was newly absorbed in. And though Noel argued that someone had to understand the ailments of the body, Hélène viewed this latest interest as final proof—Aimée de la Houssaye de Clouet, whatever else she was, was no lady. Even though she left her chair and went to her husband, her survey of his wounds was brief. "None of the cuts are deep. They need a good cleaning. I'll ring for Zeke."

"Yes, I suppose a black man can take as good care of your husband as you do," Hélène said. "In all ways."

"Don't ring for Zeke yet, Aimée." Noel's voice had a power Hélène had rarely heard since he had left France. He strode to Noel André, held his face toward the light from a candelabra. "All right. What *have* you done to yourself?"

Noel Andrée jerked his head from his father's grasp, sipped wine and winced as it touched the open cuts on his lips. "Jean-Claude Langlinais took it into his head to go crazy."

"*Jean-Claude* did that to you?"

Noel André looked at his father, his eyes so like Hélène's that Noel's own eyes blanked. "I've no idea why you sanctify those Langlinais, pater. They are just as capable of being wrong as anyone else." He poured more wine, almost enjoying its sting on his bruised mouth. "For example, there was a slave auction on Jean-Claude's land. That's what the fight was about. He didn't like my pointing out the difference between what he preaches and what he does."

"A slave auction? That's against the law! Noel, as judge, you must do something about that." Hélène smiled to herself. How straight would Cecile's back be when her precious son was tried for illegal traffic in slaves?

"Have you both gone mad?" The shadows in the room changed its shape, the colors of its furnishings. This was not the world he lived in, nor these creatures his wife and son. Noel was aware of Aimée, standing quietly near him. He looked at Noel André, then at Hélène. "We owe our lives to Jean-Claude's father. To his family. And if simple gratitude is not enough, let me point out that the house slave you so graciously presented to your mother last week came from that same auction, as you well know. If I try Jean-Claude, you will be behind him."

"Noel—"

For once, that high silver thread would not spin out to its

end. "Enough, Hélène. Enough. You do nothing that is good, not one person on this plantation owes one thing to you. You may live as you please, God knows you have always done so. But you are never to tell me what to do, or what you think of what I do, again."

In the distance, Noel heard a faint bell. Zeke would come, would take Noel André away. Hélène would go to her boudoir. And he and Aimée would have peace. He sank back into his chair. "Where were we?" he said.

"At the beginning of this discussion of yellow fever." Aimée's voice could be the softest quietest, most pleasant sound in the world. He leaned back, closed his eyes. As her voice took up the reading, he heard his wife and son leave.


"I've paid for the plans, I'm damn well going to use them," Jean-Claude said, and hired men to build his house. It went up so quickly that by the time spring planting came, Marguerite and Cecile could plant the house gardens, too. Raised on pillars, with long gables and rambling galleries, it had the style of some of the summer homes wealthy New Orleanians were building in the country. "But it is plenty fancy enough," Marguerite said. While Cecile made aprons for her granddaughters, embroidering wreaths of vines and violets or roses around the tiny skirts, or played with her newest granddaughter, named for her, Marguerite churned the butter and set the bread to rise.

"We won't live with you," Cecile said when Jean-Claude pointed out how much room there was. "But I'll be here so much you'll have to go to my house to be alone. What will you do with your old house?"

"Papa and I will use it for an office," Jean-Claude said. "Get all our records in one place. There's a lot to keep track of." He had said as much to Claude Louis. "We've got to know which thing we do does the best—with the least work, papa."

"The things you do must do very well. For you to build that house."

"I've made contacts in New Orleans. It's a growing city, papa. Lots of opportunities."

"So I've heard," Claude Louis said.


"Why do women always want pretty things and men always want practical ones?" Cecile asked Marguerite. The move to the new house had coincided with the great May feast of Our

Lady; the fête held under the broad oaks and lemon-smelling magnolias and tall pecan trees had honored both.

"But after all that work, we need to sit, yes!" Marguerite had said the next day, and so Cecile had her usually quick-stepping daughter-in-law at her side for all of a spring after-noon. "Maybe the men have to look at practical things so women can have the pretty ones," Marguerite teased. "We couldn't be sitting on this nice gallery if our men didn't work so hard."

The clear sunlight held no shadows; the one that crossed Cecile's face had another source. "Do you think they've had to work too hard?"

"What is too hard? Now Jean-Claude has his office, he can sit and go over his books and count cypress logs and hides—don't you know, mère, Jean-Claude would work that hard whether he had a wife and six children or not?"

"To beat the de Clouets." Cecile said the words as though she were not embroidering a statement in the air where it would hang for all the world to see. At Marguerite's small gesture of denial, she shook her head vigorously. "I know what I'm talking about. Ever since they came here, Noel and Hélène, Claude Louis has known I compared him to Noel, myself to Hélène." And when Marguerite half rose, perhaps to come to her mother-in-law, stop this kind of talk, Cecile held up her hand. "No, let me say it. Everything Hélène had, I wanted. Whether or not my tongue said so, my eyes said so. And so Claude Louis tried. The pieces of lace, the squares of silk. The teapots and tablecloths. More than I could ever, ever use. Never as much as Hélène de Clouet had." Tears slipped from behind the shadow, like rain slipping from a low-hanging spring cloud.

Now Marguerite did go to Cecile, plump arms circling her. "Mère, oh, mère. He worships you, you know that. Anything he gave you he wanted to give you. Don't talk like that, it's foolish."

Cecile pressed a handkerchief to her eyes. "He may worship me—but he doesn't look at me the way his father looked at his mother. Or the way my son looks at you."

"Come, mère, forget this. Look, I'll go make some more coffee, there's still some light bread left, and the new honey—"

"There is a way a man looks at a woman when he knows she lives to thank him for his love. He can never look at me that way." Marguerite hesitated on the threshold. The sounds of her children playing on the back gallery carried through the open hall. She would go get them, have them sing and dance for their grandmother. Zut, Cecile could be like a child, needing to be diverted from her moods! Then she heard a note in Cecile's voice she had not heard before. Quiet, accepting. A small shrug of those still fine shoulders. "Well, that is what I deserve. I shall live with it."

In his office, Jean-Claude totaled up the rows of figures once more. Even with the share of the crop pledged to Émile Leveque, the help of an extra man would make this year one of their best. The speed with which he had been able to build the house tempted him. What if, besides bringing cypress from the swamp, splitting it, selling it, he also built houses? Barns? So local custom still got most of this work done with the free hands of friends and relatives. Those hands were taken from other work to do it. If he could prove that a man was better off having Jean-Claude manage the whole business—his pen tried to follow the schemes of that active mind. Already, Jean-Claude Langlinais had learned something. Well-planned ventures had a much better chance of succeeding than did those in which a man just followed his nose. Look how much finer their house was than one built without plans! And though he still hated the fact that Noel André de Clouet was responsible for its design, he loved the house itself. Simple, comfortable, it achieved exactly what Jean-Claude desired—an exterior that aroused no envy in his neighbors, and an interior that accommodated all his family's needs and provided certain luxuries as well.

"I rode by the Langlinais house this afternoon," Hélène announced at supper. "I think I even saw Cecile and Marguerite sitting on the front gallery—just like the grand ladies they've always wanted to be!" She sent a bright glance to Noel. "Have you been to call, Noel? You seem so concerned always about the Langlinais' feelings!"

"What horse did you ride, Hélène?" Aimée's voice cut across the challenge of Hélène's look. There will be no bitchery here, it plainly said.

"A brown mare. I don't remember her name. Sully. Something."

Noel André's wine sputtered as he choked back a laugh.

"Sulky? You rode Sulky? More like being pulled on a stuffed animal, wasn't it?"

"Your mother hasn't ridden in a long time," Noel said. "She did well to begin on a calm horse."

"Calm unto death," Noel André said. "Well, mater, I think we can finally draw the curtain on your somewhat hectic, but still aristocratic, past. From riding to the hunt with the king of France to plodding along country roads on the fat back of old Sulky is a definite loss of—shall we say style?"

"Your tongue becomes most unpleasant when you've put too much wine past it," Aimée said. She began to talk of something else, another of the endless medical articles she filled one whole bookshelf in the library with. Seemingly unaware of her furious mother-in-law, her pouting husband, she fastened her eyes on Noel's face and spoke as though they two dined alone.

When Hélène's chair hit the floor, the sudden loudness of wood clattering on wood was like a lever changing the balance of force in the room. Hélène flew up, propelled onto her feet by the violence of that change. "You'll see whether it's over," she said. "Whether I'm through." She strode through the door, slamming it shut. Then the rapid sounds of Hélène's heels, tapping down the hall, receded. Another door slammed. And then there was silence.

"Of course," Aimée said after a pause, "there is another opinion. Richardson writing in—"

"I'm going to bed," Noel André said. He bowed elaborately. "Though I know I won't be missed."

Aimée's hand closed on Noel's wrist, slowed the quick blood. "Good night, Noel André," she said. The room's force, temporarily scattered by Hélène, gathered around the magnet in Aimé's voice. Noel André risked one moment of staring her down, then turned away.

"If he were a horse, we'd have gelded him," Noel said into the silence that filled Noel André's exit.

"The children have your blood—and mine."

"Thank God for that."

Noel and Aimée moved to the library, Aimée to write in the plantation journal, Noel to read letters from New Orleans. The moon seemed caught in the low branches of the oaks that towered up to the second-floor gallery, its light illuminating not only the long reaches of the gallery, but the lawn and drive before the house as well. Windows open to the softness of the May night, tall draperies shifting gracefully with the night breeze, the room's tranquility settled over the two.

"The constitutional convention is to be held in November," Noel said, holding a letter from de Gravelle out to Aimée.

Aimée read the letter quickly. "Same old de Gravelle," she said. "He would get in bed with his mistress's maid if he thought he could gain by it." Noel nodded. It was one thing to work for statehood for the territory. It was another to adapt so completely to whoever the ruling powers happened to be—Spanish, American—yes, de Gravelle had forgotten, very easily, who he was and what his family stood for.

A distant sound stopped his thought. Like the bay of a new hound in his kennel, the difficulty in placing the sound, giving a name to it, bothered him. He lifted his head, turned toward the direction of the interruption.

"I think that was the front door," Aimée said. She stood and walked to one of the windows, peered out.

"Is there anyone out there?" He had come up beside her.

"No—"

Then another sound, hooves, galloping hard. Aimée ran to the door leading to the gallery, tugged it open. She reached the gallery railing and leaned forward, her eyes searching a horse and rider.

"There!" Noel's arm lifted, pointed, took her gaze to a figure emerging from the black shadows that ranged around the edge of the moonlit lawn. A small figure was seated on a huge horse and the two were coming forward as though drawn by the magnet of the moon. Behind them, another figure was running, shouting. The horse and rider broke from the darkness into the full light. "My God! It's Hélène!"

"Jupiter!" The name was barely breathed, but Noel caught the fear in Aimée's voice. Now he, too, could see that the horse his wife rode was Aimée's big stallion, the one no one else dared approach save Joseph. "He'll kill her." Now her voice was flat. She leaned far forward, called to the man running behind. "Joseph! Joseph, catch them!" Then she turned and ran down the broad steps leading to the ground, Noel behind her. As his head disappeared below the level of the gallery floor, he caught one last glimpse of Hélène. A long shaft of moonlight pierced through the leaf canopy above her, gilding her hair into the glory of her youth. The shadows that light cast took years from her body and from her face—in that one moment, she and the horse were perfectly matched, one figure, one movement. Then Jupiter tossed that large neck, swerved left, and hurtled down the drive. By the time they reached the lawn, they could see nothing but the empty moon.

Joseph tore by on another horse, his face a blur that vanished like the hot breath of his mount. Without speaking, Noel and Aimée sped to the stable, Noel's arm half supporting her, half urging her on. Swiftly they bridled two horses, mounted bare back and headed after Hélène.

The stallion judged his rider well. He teased her first with an easy ride, a tearing gallop down the straight way of the drive. When they reached the road, his speed increased until the breath was torn from Hélène's body. Only when she was leaning on his neck, gasping, did the stallion make it harder. Without breaking that long stride, he turned toward the fenced pasture that followed the whitely gleaming road. His body lifted, sailed over the tall rails with inches to spare. His feet hit the dew-wet grass still in that mighty stride and his body flowed on, moonlight glinting on his coat, sparking the fury in his eye. At the foot of a fencepost, a small figure lay, the golden light of the hair dimming as the moon chased a cloud.

Three sets of hooves pounded, slowed, stopped. "Her neck is broken," Aimée said, not looking at Noel. "I think she died— right away." She stood, two hands rubbing against each other, feeling still that warm crooked neck. She faced Noel, tried to see his eyes. The light in them too had chased a cloud, and was hidden. Her arms went around him. "She didn't know it, Noel. I'm sure she felt nothing." His stillness frightened her. "Noel—" He moved from her arms, turned, climbed over the fence, mounted his horse and pulled his head toward home.

Remembering them, he looked back. "I'm going for a wagon. For her."

"Oh, Lord, I told her, I told her when I saw it was for her, you know I'd never have saddled Jupiter for her—" God in heaven, Noel in shock, Joseph guilt-stricken.

"Joseph! Of course you didn't know the horse was for Madame de Clouet. I don't want to hear anything about it, do you understand? Nothing. We've enough to bear as it is. Now go back and help Monsieur de Clouet. I'll stay with her."

Aimée swung up to the fence, reached up and loosened her hair. The breeze that blew up from the bayou strengthened with

the rise of the moon; it lifted her hair and stroked her with cool
fingers. Aimée's eyes scanned the pasture, searching for that
loved form. The moon hung high and still. A cloud came down
the sky, hesitated, settled over it. When the cloud drew away,
she saw Jupiter, tall, powerful, full of his dark knowledge. Her
clear high whistle shrilled through the heavy air, making a
chain that caught at the big horse, gentled him, brought him
slowly to her. Aimée leaned her head on his neck, her arms
pulling him to her. "She should have known better than to take
what is mine," she whispered.

The night after her mother-in-law's burial, Aimée watched
her husband drink himself through dinner. She watched him
lurch off to bed. She settled herself opposite her father-in-law
for their usual after-dinner hour. "There's a new journal here,"
she said. "Shall I read to you?"

"Aimée. Look at me."

He was standing before her, his hands stretched out to her.
She felt a rise of joy, as though she were being lifted through
the clear air on Jupiter's strong back. She rose to meet him,
went into the arms that waited. With her face pressed against
his waistcoat, she whispered, "She should have known better
than to take what is mine."

Noel heard only the word "mine." "You are mine," he said.
"Since the minute I saw you at Bocage—"

The laughter was back in her voice. "Mon Dieu," she said,
stretching up to kiss him, "but you've had a long wait!"

"Then don't make it longer, Aimée." He tucked her arms
in his, walked with her through the house, checking bolts,
pulling draperies. When they reached the top of the stairs, they
paused at the ell in the hall leading to Noel André and Aimée's
wing. Then, without another glance, they moved toward Noel's
door.

"I'm suddenly afraid," Noel said, watching her undress.
"It—it's been a very long time."

"For me—it's been never," Aimée said. She slipped into
the bed, held out her arms. "I've never been loved by a man,
Noel." He saw the mischief in her eyes—but something else
as well that stopped his fear. "There's nothing to be afraid of
at all."

Once he was beside her, held her small body in his arms,
he found that she was right.

\* \* \*

The Langlinais, Claude Louis and Cecile, Jean-Claude and Marguerite, had attended Hélène's funeral. They had paid their formal mourning call to the family, the men stiff, the women subdued. "I said my good-byes to Hélène long ago," Cecile told Claude Louis when he asked if this would be too hard for her. It had somehow been possible to avoid speaking directly to Noel André. Jean-Claude said a few words to Noel, a few more to Aimée, and had escaped to the gallery to stand smoking with other men. Claude Louis, after one long moment, had taken Noel into his arms. "If she was not happy, Noel, that cannot be laid at your door." But that meeting came at a time when more than a fight and a death separated them. The river of white gold bore sugar planters on its crest; others still worked in the backwaters, waiting for their own freshet to run.

Jean-Claude had abandoned, at least for the time, the building enterprise. While having an extra hand on the place was a help, still, he learned that men do not work quite so hard on someone else's land. Rather than spend his time and effort getting others to work for him, he would find something in which all of his energy would produce direct—and profitable—results. With an eye to building up his own herd, he purchased a new bull. Not only would his own cows be served, but by allowing neighbors to bring their cows to also be impregnated, he could collect fees, either in stock or trade goods.

The bull arrived at the same time the cattle, which had been grazing loose on the prairies, were being rounded up for slaughter. This was the work of several days, as men and boys corralled the suddenly resistant beasts, separated them by brands, and then drove them to their home place.

"Let's carry some bread and cheese out to the pasture and watch them work," Marguerite said to Cecile. "'Tit Frère doesn't know it, but today his father makes a new brand and begins a herd for our son." She gathered up the children, standing on the broad gallery and clapping her hands. "Mathilde, Nicole, Bernadette!" Three sun-bonneted heads bobbed up from under an oak tree where dolls had set up house. "'Tit Frère, put that pole down before you fall in the well!" Her four-year-old son, stout legs planted firmly, was fishing in the well, his eyes intent on his pole as he had seen his grandfather do. Marguerite scooped up two-year-old Gaston, waited while Cecile went inside to get the baby from her cradle, and then led the small parade down to the pasture near the barn.

Dust fogged the surface of the earth, blurring the swift activity before them. The grunts and heavy protests of the cattle mingled with the shouts of the sweating men; fires for the branding irons glowed through the lowering dust. From a little rise some fifty yards away, Marguerite and Cecile watched with the children. "See, 'Tit Frère," Marguerite said, her arm around her eldest son. "Papa is taking ten of the new cows and marking them with a brand that means they belong to you."

"Why can't I have some cows?" Mathilde asked. Her large eyes fastened on her mother's face. "Can't girls have cows?"

"Girls have chickens," Marguerite said.

It was some time before they realized that Gaston was gone. One moment he was with them, placidly gnawing a piece of cheese, the next moment he was not. His sisters searched first, their mother only standing with a hand shading her eyes directing them. But when a sweep of the immediate ground around them did not reveal Gaston, asleep under a low bush or hiding in the tall grass, Marguerite became alarmed. She hurried down to the men, thinking the child might have toddled off to find his father, while Cecile went the other way, calling his name in a high worried voice.

Cecile heard the two sounds at exactly the same moment; the rough snort of an angry animal, and the low cry of a child. Her eyes turned, found the source of those sounds. Ten yards away, the new bull stood in the strong pen they had put him in on his arrival. And before him, watching him with frightened eyes and crumpling face, cowered Gaston. Without thinking, Cecile whipped off the bright apron tied around her waist. She began flapping it in the air, shouting, running toward the pen. "Gaston, come to grand-mère!" she called. She climbed inside the pen and now the bull's eyes left the child, the great head turned to her.

Cecile felt into the depths of her pocket, found one of the sweets the children loved. "Gaston, look! Candy!" She held it up in one hand, the apron streaming from the other. Then she tossed the candy high in the air and saw, from the corner of her eye, her grandson climb under the low bottom rail of the pen and move to where it fell. She, too, turned to find her way out. But the bull, his morning disturbed, his solitude ruined, had had enough. He lurched forward, his head low. Before she reached the fence, before she could clamber through it, he found her. The sharp horn pierced her side, the heavy body butted her again and again.

After she had been pulled out of the pen Claude Louis knelt beside her on the sweet green grass. That she should die in terror, that the walls he had put around her had not kept her safe! Her eyes opened and looked up at his. He felt a small stirring from the hand he clasped. The words she tried to say were almost drowned in the blood trickling from her mouth. He leaned low over her, struggling to hear. A last effort, her body almost lifting with it. "Claude Louis—I have been happy—because of you." A peace entered her face then, a peace he could feel also on his. His love had walked beside her, then, all the days of her life. If some men had shown her hell, he had shown her heaven.

# CHAPTER 11

## Under One Flag

"Enfin, what I am saying, Noel, is that you should come to New Orleans with all speed. After months of distrust, delay, the people are finally rallying. Only yesterday, I, with eight other men of position, signed a proclamation urging our people to unite, to defend their sovereignty and property to their last extremity. One does not make too much of the British threat, Noel, to say that if they take New Orleans, they will have the key to the entire Lower Mississippi Valley." Noel scanned the rest of de Gravelle's letter and put it aside. "He says Jackson is on his way to New Orleans to prepare the defenses and should arrive the first week of December."

"I don't understand why he thinks you should be in New Orleans. As if we didn't have enough to do here!" For Aimée, the war with the British had, so far, been primarily an inconvenience. With trade routes blocked and disrupted, the river of white gold had been dammed; it was becoming, eight months into the war, more and more difficult to get the things they needed. She looked at Noel sharply. "Is there any real danger New Orleans will fall?"

Noel placed another log on the fire, poked up the coals into flame. "Who knows? Jackson is supposed to be quite a general—but will Frenchmen fight under him? De Gravelle won't admit it, but I've been told a number of New Orleanians have protested to the French consul that they are Frenchmen, not Americans, and should be protected from a foreign war."

Aimée laughed, that short sound that punctuated her normally even voice. "And from that protected place, they can see who emerges the victor—whose boots to lick. Don't go to New Orleans to lick boots, Noel."

He went to her, leaned over her, his hands on her slender

257

shoulders. "If I decide to go, Aimée, it will be to fill the boots of my heritage. You have helped me remember what I had almost forgotten—one may lose a battle, but one does not have to suffer defeat."

The same lithe grace that carried her swinging up into the saddle astride Jupiter carried her up into his arms. "As long as I live, Noel, I will protect Beau Chêne with my life. Go where you must, risk what you must. What you have built here is safe with me."

If neither of them noticed that she spoke as though she, not Hélène, had been at his side from the beginning, it was because that place had been empty until Aimée stood beside him. For so long there had been no interest, no concern, from Hélène that Noel had forgotten how it felt to be a part of a pair, one of two people whose lives were joined, intertwined, entangled. Until Aimée began to ride with him, work with him—and finally, love him. "We are more married than Hélène and I, you and Noel André, ever were," Noel had told her. "Words don't make a marriage—living does."

"I suppose Noel André should go to New Orleans with me. He could at least return here quickly to warn you if there is grave danger."

Aimée pulled back, lifted her eyes to Noel's face. "Yes, do take him. Troi will be a much better protector here than his father—and with Noel André out of the way, perhaps I can get some work done."

A small outbuilding, resembling the dovecotes of France, had been placed to the rear of the formal garden for use as a studio; here Noel André spent most of his days, producing just enough designs to maintain his claim that he was working. And several splendid mansions in the region did give emphatic witness to his talent—Noel André had been able to select his clients after he was commissioned to design Oakgrove Park, the Bayou Teche home of one of the state's founders. But drawing houses for real people, who had strong ideas as to how they wished their homes to look, was not nearly as satisfactory as drawing only for himself. Within the past few years, Noel André had taken up sketching and painting, and the walls of his studio were lined with the results.

A large canvas occupied the rosewood easel placed in the pouring light before the north windows of the studio. Noel could see his son's hand moving, brush going from palette to painting. "What are you working on, now?" he asked. Despite years of isolation from museums and galleries, Noel had not so forgotten good line, composition as not to see that Noel André knew what he was doing. If Aimée had not scorned these hours "playing with paints" as totally without value in a world where all must turn their energies to the fields, he might have made more of Noel André's work, perhaps sponsored him in a showing in New Orleans.

"See for yourself," Noel André said. He stood back from the canvas to make room for Noel. Unsuspecting, glad to put off talk of war for the moment, Noel stepped forward to face the painting. And saw Hélène. Hélène as she was just before the world fell apart. Head lifted, eyes challenging the world to prove her view of it wrong. Hair so golden that it seemed she must carry the secret of the sun inside her. "I modeled it after this," Noel André said, and handed Noel a miniature framed in silver.

It was the one Marie LeBrun, portrait painter for the French court, had painted in preparation for the grand portrait of Hélène Noel had commissioned for their fifth wedding anniversary. He remembered well Hélène's excitement that the woman whose work was demanded by every royal face in Europe wanted to paint her. "She will make me immortal!" Hélène had said. The sketches for that portrait, like many another plan for immortality, had been caught in a whirlwind. But perhaps whirlwinds were not final, perhaps men were not as tempest-tossed as one sometimes thought. "Your mother would be very pleased," Noel said. For a moment, they stood together in a clear, warm night. "Will you hang it in the drawing room?"

"The present chatelaine might object," Noel André said.

"You might ask her."

Noel André dropped the cloth over the canvas, putting out the light between them. "One of the pleasures of my life is that, as things have worked out, Aimée cares no more what I do than I care what she does. I wonder if we ever did—at any rate, I'll keep the portrait here."

"As you wish. It's fine work, Noel André. If we manage to survive this war, perhaps you should travel abroad. I'm told artists should have that experience, if they are to develop."

"It would be wasted on me," Noel André said. He lounged on the day bed near the hearth, smoking a small china pipe. "I should hate money to be invested in me. Aimée would expect a return. As it is, my playing keeps me out of her way—harmlessly."

"No one can call your work play if you do not," Noel said. Every meeting with his son, no matter how it began, ended thus. They had absolutely nothing in common, not even a desire to keep the peace.

Noel had waited, those first weeks after Hélène's death, for Noel André to confront either him or Aimée. Instead, he had, after a decent period during which he helped receive callers, departed for New Orleans, staying there several months. Toward the end of his stay, he had written to Noel. "Cher papa—I hope my absence has given you and my wife time to establish yourselves comfortably. I may be indifferent, but I am not ignorant. Be assured that I have, for a long time, had my own source of—what shall we call it? Love? Satisfaction? No matter. The only cause I have for jealousy is that I have to travel to New Orleans, you and Aimée can stay at home. I am confident that we are all well-bred enough to maintain appearance—for the sake of the children if for nothing else. I shall be back in a fortnight." When Noel showed the letter to Aimée, she had said, "This is the first sign I've seen that Noel André has something of a man's courage, after all." But despite Noel André's acceptance, despite the veneer of civility, the small ties that had held father and son were not strong enough now. They spoke of necessity, that was all.

"What I came to tell you—things are apparently coming to a crisis point. The British will attack New Orleans, and the American general, Jackson, is coming to head the defense. De Gravelle writes that we must go to New Orleans, be part of these efforts."

The smoke rising from Noel André's pipe drifted before Noel's face; his nostrils twitched at the sudden strong odor. "Where in hell do you get your tobacco?" he said, moving away from that thin gray line. "My God, it smells like Aimée's medicine chest." When Noel André said nothing, Noel went back to his first theme. "I know very well you have little or no interest in politics, Noel André. But I won't live forever. If we do manage to beat the British, it won't hurt your chances for position here if you have helped."

"You mean fight under this American? With that conglomerate army which will, I am sure, reflect the flower of that society? Whatever this life has prepared for me, pater, it has not prepared me to stand shoulder to shoulder with a smelly Kentucky woodsman risking my neck for a flag I couldn't draw from memory if I were hanged for it. I shall go with you to New Orleans, it has been a wretched autumn and I'm in need of diversions. But when the bugles are calling the fierce of heart, the ready of hand—I will not answer. And de Gravelle may make of that what he will."

It had been a wretched autumn for Jean-Claude also. For the first time since the war began, traders were not getting through the British blockades. Tall bundles of furs filled the back room of the house he used as his office; he knew exactly the place the money they would bring could be spent, and he intended to sell them, war or no war, redcoat blockade or no. "Damn the British!" But of course. The solution, when it came, was so simple he knew it would work. Taking the monogrammed handkerchief Lafitte had given him over a decade ago, he made his way to the cabin deep in the swamp and tied the square of white linen to a branch which he lashed firmly to the peak of the clapboard roof. Then he went home to wait.

A fortnight later, a man appeared at his office, a man who pronounced himself sent from Jean Lafitte. Small, but broad and strong of shoulder, the man had light hair that sailed atop his sun-darkened face. His name, he said, was Dominique You. Hearing that name, Jean-Claude swung wide the door and opened a better wine. Picou, jealous, sullen, had spoken of this man, whose military career had begun in France during the revolution, continued with a brother-in-law of Napoleon against the black of Haiti, and finally settled into privateering. Alone at first, Dominique You was soon attracted by the greater efficiency and profit of the Lafitte operation. Within a year of his joining Lafitte, You was known as Jean's favorite lieutenant— "a name he deserves," Picou admitted grudgingly.

"Lafitte sends a big gun for a small bird," Jean-Claude said.

Dominique You tilted his glass, emptied it. "You call on Lafitte once in more than ten years—you need something quick. Since he is studying to be a soldier, he sent me." Knowing he had Jean-Claude's complete attention, he went on. "Generals aren't crazy. They know Lafitte can fight. The British have been trying to get him to go on their side." Dominique You threw back his head and laughed with the open pleasure of a child. "They don't know Lafitte. Governor Claiborne, he jailed

Lafitte, he put a price on his head—but Lafitte, he won't sell out. If he fights with anyone, it'll be with the Americans—and Jackson."

But no matter how momentarily interesting Lafitte's games were, there was still the matter of the furs. Jean-Claude outlined his problem—he needed a safe route by water, a route that would take the furs past the British ships to the waiting market. Did Dominique You know such a route? You grinned. "Where You's vessel goes, there is the route." And with the swift decision Jean-Claude remembered from sessions with Lafitte on Grande Terre, You sketched his plan. Drawing a map as he talked, he showed Jean-Claude how they would load the furs onto flatboats, take them west and out the Calcasieu, threading through the maze of islets, bayous and marshes between that river and the Gulf. "Then, we put them on my ship—and no man stops us."

It had been a wretched autumn. Cold, wet, the air outside was like the spirit of the people, who faced another winter of war with little understanding of why it was being fought and little interest in the outcome save for one question—if the British took any part of Louisiana, what would happen to their land? After all, the redcoats had burned Washington to the ground, and still nothing changed. Perhaps the river would be fought over in every generation, and only those who lived farthest from its turbulence would have peace. Jean-Claude was tired of the cold, the wet, the worry. He thought of a ship leaping under his feet, of the open sky, the sea boiling up to meet it. "I'll go with you," he said.

"You will be careful, Jean-Claude," Marguerite said. It didn't surprise her that Jean-Claude had found a way to get his furs to market, nor did the appearance of a stranger with the manners of a gentleman and the fierce eye of a hawk disturb her serenity. She did not even ask who he was or from where he came, only ladled more gumbo into his empty plate and urged yet another piece of apple tart. When he settled near the hearth with the children, making shadows with his hands and teasing them with riddles and jokes, she sat happily by.

"You have a bonne femme," Dominique You told Jean-Claude as they poled their way into the current of the bayou. "A woman like that—one doesn't even have to risk for."

"Which is probably why one does," Jean Claude said. Already, home was behind him, lost behind the curve of the bayou, the thick foliage on its bank. Ahead was a waterpath that led, in ever-widening reaches, to freedom. He loosened the wool scarf, squared his cap on his head. "Tell me more of this general," he said. "This Jackson."

During the last days of November, the Café des Réfugiés was filled with New Orleanians dissecting every rumor, analyzing every alarm, debating every decision made by Governor Claiborne and his staff. Long a meeting place for fugitives from Santo Domingo, as well as certain Baratarians, the café now drew anyone who had an opinion to expound: Lafitte had joined the British navy and was even now showing them a secret route to the city. Lafitte would bargain with Claiborne—his pardon in exchange for military aid. Lafitte had fled and would fight with no one. The British were invincible. The British were tired and had no heart for this war.

Sitting with his father, Noel André moved slightly apart from the group gathered at one of the small tables. He knew their talk by heart, and it interested him no more than it had the first afternoon in New Orleans. Though the city was finally rousing itself, stirred to a resentful defense by the persistence of Claiborne's urging, it was still bitterly divided between those who would fight the British and those who would not. Claiborne, it was reported, had actually written to advise Jackson that the country was filled with traitors and spies, and it was commonly acknowledged that many businessmen would honor any flag under whose protection their trade would flourish and their establishments prosper.

Noel André leaned forward, his attention on a couple standing on the banquette outside the café. It had been two years since he had been with Yvonne. She had found a protector, a gentleman she would not name, but someone "très beau et très gentil." And though he had found another woman, he had not found another Yvonne. He was sure it was she, the slight sideways tilt of the head, the haze of auburn that touched her dark hair with light. And the way she moved, the body so deceptively slender, yet so promisingly full. The tall man with her leaned down, said something that made her laugh. No, there was no possible mistake. How could he forget the way her lips opened and when she laughed, small, pink—rose petals were no sweeter. He drained his wine, whispered to his father, picked up hat and cane and threaded his way through the crowd.

Following several paces behind them, he sauntered after Yvonne and her escort. Until now, her "protector" had been a shadow, someone who paid Yvonne's dressmaker, bought her a house—but did not take her to bed. Now he was real, a man who held her arm possessively, a man who owned, for as long as he chose, those delights Yvonne had given Noel André. Perhaps she still would give—it could not be pleasant for so sweet a girl as Yvonne to feel always bought, always bound to another's whim.

When they turned into a gate, he crossed the street, the better to observe their destination. It was, apparently, a private house. Through the iron grillwork of the gate Noel André could see a courtyard, with camellias in pastel profusion. The blank walls and shuttered windows of the house presented a closed face to passersby. Remembering his own afternoons with Yvonne, Noel André became restless. There was a café on the corner; he entered it, sat at a table with a view of the street, and waited.

The man finally did emerge, shown out by a large Negress whose tignon was borne with the dignity of a queen. Noel André watched him down the street and then finished his wine, contemplating the pleasure ahead. When the Negress answered the bell attached to the gate, he asked to see her mistress, using the tone that almost announced the number of people like herself who called him master. When she hesitated, standing on the far side of that protecting grill, he flung his name at her and ordered her to take it to the lady. The Negress disappeared through a door giving onto the courtyard. The winter afternoon was closing down, the thick gray clouds themselves building a wall around the city. Noel André felt a river of cold air down his neck; the warmth of Yvonne and her bed was suddenly compelling. He took the bell pull in his hand and yanked it over and over again, sending the clamorous vibrations bouncing off the massive air.

A hand on his shoulder spun him around. "What do you want, that you make a disturbance at a lady's home?" It was Yvonne's escort, the man who had so easily entered her home—and, Noel André was sure, so easily entered her.

"You have had your visit," he said. "Are you so greedy that you deny others what you have no immediate need of?"

"You are at the wrong address," the man said. The voice

was long and stiff now, shiny with threat.

Noel André laughed, and the tone of it spoke his opinion of the house, of the woman inside, of the man on the banquette before him. A whipping slap across his cheek cut through the insolent sound. His hand went to his stinging face. A card was pressed into his other hand. "My name, sir. And the place where your second may find me." The man gave one short tug on the bell pull. The Negress glided forth. Without looking at Noel André, she unlocked the gate, opened it just wide enough for the man to slip through. He strode across the courtyard, rapped at a door, and went in. The Negress stood for one long minute, hands on hips, head high. Then she laughed, a short bark so like Aimée's that Noel André felt the heat under the still smarting skin. Before that laugh, and the black look in her eyes, Noel André fled.

"So you've been challenged to a duel." Noel looked sourly at his son. With every other gentleman in New Orleans preparing for the honorable battle ahead, this fool had to get into some brawl. Over a woman, undoubtedly. What sort of woman would be better not to ask. De Gravelle had asked Noel to sit in with the council helping to mobilize the city; Noel André would have to mobilize for this private war on his own. "Well, you got yourself into it. I imagine you're man enough to get through it." He turned back to the desk, began to go over the figures listing food supplies on hand, houses that could be turned into hospitals.

Noel André had no difficulty in finding a second. Despite laws to the contrary, dueling remained a popular pastime for men of all ages and all professions, and, as his second said, "It is a privilege to serve a gentleman, when you thought of all the riffraff taking up dueling just as though they understood the code of honor it defended."

And so, on the morning of December 1, when others were gathering to welcome Jackson to the city, Noel André stood under the tall oaks weeping Spanish moss that had come to mark the accepted spot for these affairs of honor. The weapons were pistols, the distance twenty paces. Though Noel André had, for a while, held out for swords as a more graceful, more elegant, way of doing battle, his second was practical. "Too much can go wrong, Noel André. Your foot slips, your arm falters. Besides, you don't know this man. He could be much, much better than you. It is one thing to defend honor. It is another to die needlessly."

Pistols could kill, too. If the duel ran its course, if nothing ended it on the first shot, or even the second, and it went the entire three firings—then his chances of being hurt, killed, were good.

His opponent was already waiting when Noel André and his second arrived at the secluded place frequented only by duelists, the surgeons whose role in the bloody business well prepared them for the casualties of war, and the ghosts, some said, of men who had died there. The trees were majestic, commanding in their splendid girth and height. Their branches lifted towering bowers of green webbed with curling strands of moss that cast an eerie spell on even the most sun-lit day. It was dark under the oaks: Noel André's imagination found it easy to see the ground dark, too—not with winter's damp, but with old blood.

Then the theatricality of the scene overcame his fear. How his mother would have loved this! He greeted the others with careless grace, took the cup of brandy offered and stood at his ease while the weapons were inspected, the distance paced off, the positions set. As though rising at just the right moment to light up the stage upon which their little scene was played, the sun found an opening in the curtain of green and bathed the clearing with filtered gold. The light glinted off the silver filigree on the pistols' grips, off the long barrels, off the shiny surgeon's tools. It skipped over the healthy pink of fear-warmed skin, softly touched and gilded fine hair lifting in the breeze. And it threw its harsh real light on the two bodies that fell to the waiting earth, each with a blood-welling hole in its violated chest.

Dominique You's ship indeed found a path through the English-guarded sea. Though warships flying the British flag loomed up through the autumn fogs, they sailed past without challenging the Baratarian's brig—"They know we have nothing they want, while they might very well have something we want," You said. "And they still hope Lafitte will join them."

"That he would never do," Jean-Claude said. He had watched Lafitte among the gentlemen of New Orleans, seen the way he was admired by the women. Even an incident a few years ago, when the lone survivor of a pirate attack on an American merchant ship out of Havana had blamed Jean Lafitte for the murderous act, had not tarnished the brilliance of Lafitte's name. For though piracy was despicable, Lafitte was not. And when the Lafitte brothers stood the storm of rumor down, took their casual stroll in the Place d'Armes, tipping fine tall hats to the ladies, exchanging pleasantries with the gentlemen—well, how could such men be pirates? No, Lafitte was bound to New Orleans by more than the ties of business. He would not help the English take her.

The furs safely traded, Dominique You turned the ship's bow toward Grande Terre. And Jean-Claude, his season's work done, was on holiday. He stood with Dominique You, searched the horizon for first sign of that low-lying island. He did not think about St. Martin, or his home there. The crops filled the barn, the land lay at rest. Now was time for change, new scenes. He kept his heart quiet when talk turned to war against the British, but he felt its strong impatience. An urgent wish began to form in him, a wish to fight this arrogant breed of men who appeared on the continent whenever it suited them, threatening all peace, all tranquillity. Merde, but they needed to be taught a long lesson!

He repeated that sentiment to Jean Lafitte the first night in Grande Terre. "I have decided I will help this American general teach them that lesson," Lafitte said.

"Help the general who speaks of us as 'hellish banditti'?" You asked. But he laughed as he spoke. A man's character is often judged by where he stands, beside you or against you. And when Jackson learned from Lafitte that he had hidden in the swamps a large supply of flints and ammunition, a change occurred. Baratarians who had been jailed were freed; Dominique You and other of Lafitte's lieutenants in his enterprise of piracy became captains in Jackson's army. When Jackson wrote in a dispatch of the infusion of fresh troops and supplies, he spoke of Lafitte and his men as "these privateers"—a military about-face from the "hellish banditti" he had once called them. Jackson promptly sent some of the Baratarians to man siege guns at the forts of Petites Coquilles, St. John, and St. Phillip. The rest were ordered up to New Orleans, there to join Jackson's troops defending the city.

* * *

"I see no more that can be done," Noel said, wearily rubbing the back of his neck. He pushed his chair back, rose and stood staring at the crowds filling Rue de Royale.

De Gravelle rose also, came and clapped a hand on Noel's shoulder. "I agree. You have done all that any man could ask." They spoke of the military preparations, but de Gravelle referred also to Noel André's death. After the first shock, Noel had performed almost as though he had known this death would come. He had made arrangements to send the body back to St. Martin, had dispatched a younger de Gravelle to escort it, and had written to Aimée advising her of his decision to remain in New Orleans. "After all," he wrote, "there is really nothing I can do for Noel André, but by remaining here, I feel I am defending his children's heritage." Though he did not write it, Noel could not see himself standing at Aimée's side while his son sank into the winter earth.

Of all the upheavals in his life, all the changes that had rippled through the rich tapestry of his life in France, leaving him a few scraps with which to patch a new one, perhaps the worst was knowing that words like "wife" and "son" held no magic. The innocence with which he had married Hélène—not sexual innocence, hardly that, but an emotional innocence—had soon been corrupted. There was no trust between them, no loyalty, no truth. She had not even wanted there to be. As for his son—Noel remembered his first look at his male heir. The midwife had brought Noel André out, tufts of wet hair sticking to his small round head. "Madame had a good passage for him," she had said. "See how his head stayed nice and shapely." Even as he reached out for his son, Noel had thought she ought to have a good passage. It's been widened by enough use. Had he wondered, holding the baby, if it were really his? Allowed himself to wonder that? He had finally made an act of will. The baby was born in the house, of his lawful wife. He was his son. The head agreed—the heart? Perhaps not.

The sound of a disturbance in the street attracted them. De Gravelle opened the door onto the balcony and stepped out. Two men stood in front of the building, talking earnestly to the guard posted there. "What is it?" de Gravelle called out. One of the men raised his head and looked upward. "Gabriel! What are you doing here?" A torrent of French answered him.

De Gravelle lifted his hand. "Wait, they will let you up. It's all right," he called to the guard. "This is Gabriel Villere. His father is the commanding officer of the militia."

Noel and de Gravelle stood in the room where Villere met Jackson, listening in rigid tension to what he was reporting. Villere had brought an English-speaking friend with him, but even so, the terrible excitement that filled them twisted both tongues, and it was some time before anyone in the room, French or American, understood completely what Villere and Dussau de la Croix were saying. Then it was shatteringly clear. The Twenty-second Light Brigade of the British army, some sixteen hundred men, were even now settling themselves for the night on the Villere plantation, some nine miles south of New Orleans. "And between there and here, monsieur general, there is not so much as one picket!" De la Croix threw up his arms in disbelief. How could the Americans, lauded to the heavens for their military prowess, allow this to happen?

Every eye fastened itself on Jackson, asking that same question. Jackson rose, his malaria-ravaged body stretched to its full height. "Gentlemen, we will engage the British tonight. Now." When the troops left the city, marching between the swamp to the left and the river to the right, shadows cast up from the ground and mist rising from the water drew a heavy veil over them. They disappeared under its cover, a cover that soon became complete. By the time they met the British forces, they fought in a moonless, starless night, and only the glow of campfires and the flash of musket fire lit up the field. When the sun joined the foray again, it found the Americans fallen back to a position along the Rodriguez Canal, where they dug in, in earnest. Across from them, the British army rolled up its sleeves, waded in the gumbo mud, and made its own preparation for victory. In the pocket of its commanding general was a commission for the governorship of Louisiana—in his memory rang the promise of his regent that the fall of New Orleans would raise him to an earldom. Battles are won with far less incentive.

"Mais, what kind of fighting is this?" Jean-Claude said to Dominique You. More than a week had passed since that initial skirmish with the British. The first day of the New Year had been observed; now he expected something to happen. He was tired making gabions, the big wickerwork baskets they used for breastworks. Even the artillery battle on New Year's Day had not fed his fever. Dominique You was a tough commander; the thirty-six Baratarians serving under him at Battery Three found that manning two long twenty-four-pounders became tedious work when the British fire kept coming and coming and coming. "It will not come forever," You said, and kept them working. Until the British guns were silenced, the tide of red-coated soldiers contained—and rain, mud, and cold again took over as prime enemies of their peace and comfort.

You poked up the fire, set the coffeepot over the coals. Jackson, on one of his constant prowls of the camp, had had a cup of You's coffee and termed it the best to be had; only a smuggler could get decent coffee, what with stern British ships monitoring the sea. "Like any fighting. What kind you want?"

"Sea fighting is different. You don't sit around and wait and wait."

"Sure you do. Except you sit on a ship instead of in mud. You mend nets and sails, clean guns. Jean-Claude, this is no fistfight, you understand? Men get killed in this kind of fighting." You poured coffee into two tin cups, handed one to Jean-Claude. He settled himself against the base of one of the big guns. "Maybe you are here for the wrong reason."

"Same reason as anyone." Jean-Claude could feel the little pricks of tension stinging at his nerves. His muscles felt unused and overused, ready to obey him and ready to ignore him.

"No, Jean Lafitte's not your bos, trying to save his skin. You're not in Jackson's army. As for fighting for your country—you're no American. You're an Acadian. Even if these British win"—Dominique slapped the long barrel of the cannon, smiled that fresh grin—"which they will not, but even if they did, they'd have their hands full with a city full of Frenchmen, they wouldn't bother you. So what's your reason?"

The words stared back at Jean-Claude as though a hand had written them in the air between them. "Because I get tired being a farmer." He looked at You. "And what kind of reason is that?"

You threw back his head, roared his great laugh to the sky with the force of the shot his big guns hurled at the British. "An honest one," he said finally. "But Jean-Claude, I tell you the truth, you find another interest, yes? You can excite yourself right into the cemetery doing this."

* * *

Noel was sorry he had not used the excuse of his son's death to leave a city whose intrigues, while not as sophisticated perhaps as those which haunted French courts, had still the power to disrupt the carefully formed alliances so necessary for defense. Only yesterday Jackson had ordered the legislature dissolved until Governor Claiborne could assure him that what he had been told concerning the plans of certain members of that great body to make separate peace with the British on terms favorable to themselves and their business was not correct. And Noel very well knew that even now a delegation of merchants was preparing to go out to the front lines and demand that Jackson tell them if he would burn the city if he were forced to retreat. Sacrebleu, if they would put their courage at Jackson's disposal instead of gathering it up to ask him foolish questions!

Remembering his first meeting with Jackson, Noel could smile. The city officials had brought together as much display as possible to greet Jackson when he arrived in New Orleans. Jackson had ridden into the Place d'Armes, the only military feature about him his blazing eyes and his poker-straight seat on his horse. His short blue cloak in the Spanish style had been faded by weather, his leather boots were unpolished, his leather cap worn. Enfin, he was a scarecrow.

Had there not been the obligatory reception that evening, hosted by Edward Livingston, whose old claim to friendship could not be ignored, Noel knew very well that nothing de Gravelle or any other man said would have marshaled those Frenchmen behind Jackson. Jackson amazed not only the guests at the Livingston home but also his host. "You should have heard him at dinner," Livingston told Noel. "We placed him next to Mademoiselle Eliza Chotard, who speaks English so well. And when she commented to him that she understood he had known me a very long time, do you know what he said?" Livingston paused, then brought out his friend's words, offering them to the company of Frenchmen as though they were a coat-of-arms. "He said—'Yes, Miss Chotard, I had the honor to know Mr. Livingston probably before the world was blessed by your existence.'" Not only from Livingston did the French hear Jackson praised. Their own wives and daughters took up his cause. "So that is the savage Indian fighter you scorn? The rough frontier general? Oh, monsieurs, we assure you, he is a veritable preux chevalier!"

After working with the man, Noel had to agree. He had all those qualities any ruler would value in a general. If these selfish merchants were not so obsessed with saving their investments, Jackson might be able to win. As it was—Noel shrugged. It was one thing for him to be high-minded. His property lay far to the west, protected by distance, and by a mire of swamp no foreign army would attempt. If all he owned were here—Merde. He would go call on Sister St. Paul of the Cross. Claude Louis had sent a package of food to her, and though the nuns devoted themselves to a spiritual life, their stomachs were as empty as anyone else's. He pulled his cloak around him and went out.

A tall Negress stepped toward him. "You are Monsieur Noel de Clouet, the father of Noel André de Clouet?" What now? Noel André was dead, would his mischief never cease? Curtly, Noel acknowledged her address. "I have been sent by my mistress, Madame Henri de la Plante. She requests that you call her at this address. It has to do with your son's death." Without waiting for his answer, the woman turned into the crowd. Noel watched her progress down Rue de Royale, scarlet tignon flaming. He shoved the piece of paper into an inner pocket and continued his way to the Ursuline convent.

Something of the peace of the convent had entered his spirit by the time his visit was over. Sister St. Paul had given him a card, which he now held in his hand. It was the prayer for the dead, copied out in a fine hand, embellished with a careful design of laurel wreaths. His son's name and the date of his death were at the bottom, and then a listing of the days Masses had been said for his soul. Until that moment, Noel had given not one thought to the fate of his son's soul.

Taking the other card from his pocket, the one the Negress had given him, he read the address, paused for a moment, and then plunged into the crowd on the banquette, turning his face in the direction of the home of Madame Henri de la Plante.

"I am glad that you came, monsieur. I was not certain that you would." The woman was beautiful. Her voice was soft, low, so that Noel had to bend forward to hear her. The room they sat in was filled with the kind of feminine fripperies with which Hélène was always surrounded. In this room, they seemed pleasant objects only. They had no life of their own, they were pretty, fun—but their owner's attention, clearly, was on the gentleman opposite her. Noel felt himself relax. Whatever this lady wanted of him, it would not bring him more trouble. He could even feel the beginning of envy for the hours his son had spent with her.

"I had not seen Noel André for some years. You understand, he could not become my protector. And when I met Monsieur de la Plante, my maman urged me to allow him to take care of me." She saw the question in Noel's eyes. "Oh, monsieur, I am not Madame de la Plante. I am . . ." The low voice stopped. Noel remembered his friends, when he first arrived in New Orleans, taunting him because he would not take up with one of the golden women whose bedrooms, he had been assured, were gardens of unique delight.

"You are a beautiful and gracious lady, madame."

Her head came up. "When Tica brought me his card—I didn't know what to do. What purpose was there in seeing him? And yet—" The golden eyes were veiled with a mist of tears. "And yet, Noel André and I had been gay together, happy. I couldn't just send him away." A pause while the veil was blinked away, the clear openness of golden light returned. "While I thought, Monsieur de la Plante returned. You know the rest."

"And now they are both dead," Noel said. He had denied his anger these many days—how could he be angry, furious, ready to strangle a man who was already dead? Now it burst forth, he felt it pushing him to his feet to pace the small quiet room. Her eyes were on him, her face still. She listened to the words coming up from the dark reaches of his soul, all the anger, the grief, over his son that had built through the years of Noel André's useless life. Finally, he said that word, over and over. "Useless. Everything useless."

She waited until he had quieted himself, was seated once more across from her. "No, monsieur, you are quite wrong. Noel André's life was not useless. That is why I sent for you." She rose, went to an armoire in the corner of the room, opened it and removed a thick sheaf of paper. She placed this on a table at Noel's side. "Look through those, monsieur. Just look through those."

They were sketches, sketches of the people and scenes of New Orleans. Here a drawing of the cathedral, there one of an arrogant woman, much like Tica, tignon high, basket balanced on her hip. The life of the city grew in the spare lines and delicate shading; the sketches were the work of a man who loved life, and knew his art. Compared to the work Noel André did at Beau Chêne, these were the work of the master and those of his apprentice.

"He did those during the time we spent together. I couldn't understand, monsieur, why he did not work this way all the time. He sometimes showed me sketches he did at his home— why were they not the same? That puzzled me. But I think, you know, that his wife likes only one kind of man. Some women are like that. They see not the man as he is, but as they think he should be." The round shoulders, firm in the silken dress, lifted. "Madame de Clouet apparently wanted a man of much activity. But she married an artist. It is a pity she did not know how to enjoy him."

"And a blessing that you did," Noel said. "But surely you want these?"

"Oh, no, monsieur. But no. His children should have them. They will not know under what circumstances he did them. Only that he did. They will be proud."

Noel hesitated. He could feel his heart inside him again, he had not felt its presence since the terrible morning he had been told of Noel André's death. And he could feel a stirring in his soul; he knew that when he left here, he would go to the cathedral to light candles for his son. "Madame—with your protector dead—what—what becomes of you?"

"Money is settled on me. This house is mine. That is the custom, monsieur." Then more than a veil of tears covered and blotted the splendor of her eyes. Grief that slept with her and woke with her stared out through her tears seeking solace, surcease from pain. "I have more than enough to keep me alive a very long time in great comfort, monsieur. The knife tearing at my heart is made of gold and studded with jewels. Isn't it strange, monsieur, that it hurts so terribly all the same?"

"Now I think you get your fight," Dominique You said. A week after New Year's Day, life in camp had fallen into a routine. Make meals, clean guns, fight mud. This morning, a British rocket had lit up the fog; the routine had not changed. But when the sun finally got itself up, pushing the fog away as though it were a blanket, something changed. The field between the two armies was no longer empty. The British army was drawn up in two broad columns, a cleared space in the middle allowing for the fire from their artillery. All over the American camp, men were picking up weapons, moving into position. Toward the rear, the municipal band, which had come out to celebrate New Year's and decided to stay, began to play. "That's the kind of hymn to hear on a Sunday!" You said. It was "Yankee Doodle," a tune that would become a death knell for more than three thousand British soldiers that day.

The Kentuckians knew nothing about the traditions of civilized European armies. They did not fire in volleys; each man fired on his own, quickly reloading to fire again. That fire, coming as it did from hundreds of muskets and rifles tightly packed in one small area, made a flame of death that roared over the advancing British. When the crack Twenty-first regiment advanced, nine hundred Highlanders strong, only a hundred and sixty men were alive after that first onslaught from the deadly guns of the mountaineers. And the Baratarians added fuel to the powerful roar of that consuming flame.

Dominique You and the other Lafitte lieutenants were high in Jackson's regard. "I wish I had fifty such guns on this line, with five hundred such devils as those fellows behind them!" he had said after the devastating accuracy of You's fire had so decimated the British artillery on New Year's Day. And later— "If I were ordered to storm the gates of hell, with Captain Dominique as my lieutenant, I would have no misgivings of the result!" Now here was a captain worth obeying—and Jean-Claude did, learning the heavy work of artillery fighting, learning, as You told him, that to harvest victory, one must prepare the field.

Ahead of their battery, the carnage rolled on, propelled by an implacable machine. Suddenly, Dominique ordered the guns silenced. The methodical experienced cursing of an expert sounded in the pocket of quiet. "How can we kill redcoats with this powder?" he said. "Merde, I like Lafitte to be my bos— my captain. He has only the best for his men."

"What! By God, You, why have you ceased firing?" Jackson's voice poured wrath over them. Jean-Claude looked up. The general, face haggard, the only alive feature in that death's-head his fierce eyes, towered over them, his horse tightly reined.

"But, general—you understand, this powder—it is good for nothing. Fit to shoot blackbirds with—not redcoats."

Now the wrath was diverted, poured elsewhere. Turning to

an aide, Jackson spoke: "Tell the ordnance officer he will be shot in five minutes as a traitor if Dominique complains any more of his powder."

"I think," You said when fresh powder had been brought up, tested, proclaimed good, "I think maybe this man Jackson can be like my bos, Lafitte."

Every citizen of New Orleans agreed with Dominique You that Jackson was "bos." At the end of the battle, only eight Americans had been killed, thirteen wounded. The British army was in full retreat, and Andrew Jackson was the darling of the city. The Ursuline nuns left their prayers to turn the convent into a hospital. The women of New Orleans, led by Mrs. Claiborne and Mrs. Livingston, loaded their carriages with bandages and drove to the battlefield. Nothing was too good for their general—and the celebration two weeks after the victory would show it.

"You need to stay for that, Jean-Claude," Dominique argued. They were taking their rest at the blacksmith shop, luxuriating in the knowledge that they, too, deserved the name "hero." Lafitte and his Baratarians had been singled out for compliments by Jackson time and time again; it was good, thought Jean-Claude, not only to win, but to win well. "Jean and Pierre are even going to the grand ball! Now, that will be a sight—those Kentuckians and Creoles together under one roof. That might be a better fight than any you've been in so far."

Jean-Claude lifted his wineglass, stretched his feet to the fire. "There would always be something to stay for, isn't that so? And then, it would somehow not be what you expected—so there would be another thing." He got up. "Don't misunderstand me, Dominique. After I am with my Marguerite, hold my children on my knee, I will look at that mud I must plow when it dries, think of that lumber waiting to be cut, furs waiting to be trapped—and I will sigh. I will know that no matter what I do now, my life is set by a farmer's seasons. And it is boring, Dominique!"

Dominique You looked at the man standing before him. The short body, muscles crowding each other, moving under the weather-darkened skin. Eyes ready to blaze at a moment, with anger, with passion, with joy. "You carry a big life inside you, Langlinais. Someday you will find a way to live that size." He, too, rose. Going to a small leather chest in the corner of the room, he knelt. When he turned, he had a pouch in his hands. He gave it to Jean-Claude. "There are five hundred pieces of gold in that pouch, Jean-Claude. It may help you to find a little space."

# CHAPTER 12

## *Adagio*

There are some lives which seem to begin in the channel most
suited to them, the channel which will be theirs until the course
is run. Marquerite Langlinais' life was one of those. She had
been born into solid domesticity, the secure life of a farm, and,
just as she expected, that life had continued when she married
Jean-Claude. Jean-Claude's ventures into broader rivers, deeper
passages, she accepted. A man must let his rebellion against
duty, rules, responsibility, out every once in a while, that she
understood. So long as he came home again, to be her own
Jean-Claude, her quiet was undisturbed. So settled was she into
her small life that the approaching birth of a grandchild, firstborn of her oldest son, Brother, was treated as though no baby
had ever been born before. The time she did not spend sewing
clothes for the baby, she spent giving her son's bride advice.
When Brother protested, and reminded his mother that Julie
had a mother of her own, Marguerite was firm. "She is under
our protection now, Brother. She is my son's wife. Do I not
take care of her as I do my own?" And when Brother understood
that no young woman waiting the birth of her first child can
have too much attention, too much concern, he went back to
his fields and left the women alone.

If Marguerite's life followed the same even course from
beginning to end, Aimée de la Houssaye de Clouet's did not.
Her years at Beau Chêne had brought out her strength, her
determination to live as she saw fit, no matter what anyone
else was doing—or thinking. Like the current of a flooding
river that cuts new paths when the old ones are too narrow,
Aimée had, when the incompatibility with Noel André became
clear, simply found another way to live.

For many years, that way had been centered on Noel. The

idyll begun with Noel André's death the year of the war with the British lasted a dozen years—and five years after Noel's death, Aimée had still not come to terms with it. Still when the day was ending, she looked at his empty chair and wept. The sole reason she had not gone mad with grief when Noel died was that her son, Troi, was, thank God, his grandfather all over. He not only understood what was needed to make the plantation and the sugar mill produce more and more income each year, he enjoyed doing it. While her sessions in the office with Troi did not have that undercurrent of excitement that had made the recounting of dull figures with Noel take on an air of conspiracy, the results were equally satisfying. At the brink of the third decade of the nineteenth century, the de Clouets were very rich indeed.

Aimée de Clouet rode through the April twilight, her usually straight back slumped in fatigue. The scent of jasmine and sweet olive crowding upon her from the roadside jolted her; she couldn't banish the image of the young dead face she had just left at the Langlinais', eyelids closed over pain-tired eyes, hands so recently clenched in hard spasms of agony relaxed on the still breast. There would be jasmine and sweet olive in the cemetery. One penalty for such profuse flowering was that the same blooms were everywhere; surely something could be saved for joy alone.

Zephyr, the gelding she rode for what she thought of as duty work, had caught his rider's mood and slowed almost to a halt. His hooves were muted by the thick dust in the road, previewing the trappings of the funeral cortege. The earth hung in an azure span of air as though waiting for some direction, some sign, before it would move toward night. Aimée thought again of Julie Vidrine Langlinais, dead in childbirth at the age of eighteen. "At least," she said aloud, slapping Zephyr's rump and giving him his head, "at least the baby lived. There is still a Claude."

She gave Troi the news rapidly, speaking in a low quick voice so that his wife, Annette, should not hear. She had safely delivered her first child, a girl, eight months ago, and was now expecting to be confined again in only six months more. Not everyone was as strong-minded as Aimée—better a young woman with years of childbearing ahead of her know as little as possible about all the things that could go wrong with what should be so natural a process. Aimée handed her bag to one of the house servants, pulled off her bonnet and sank into a chair. "Pour me a little brandy, Troi. It has been a terrible day." She could see her daughter-in-law through the long window fronting on the gallery; Annette was playing with her baby, Germaine, while a nurse stood placidly by, waiting to carry the infant off to bed.

"How is Brother?"

Aimée shrugged. "His mother bore six children and still has the strength of a girl. He doesn't believe it."

"He won't—blame you?"

Aimée looked at her son. Troi had his father's sensitivity without the weakness. It was in his voice as he said, "I mean— there have been—bad feelings between us at times. You do too much for people as it is, I don't want them taking their grief out on you when someone isn't saved."

"The Langlinais have more sense than that. They know I did what could be done—could they have left her to one of these country midwives?" Aimée stood up, stretched her arms high. At forty-six, her figure was still lithe, still graceful. It seemed to her children that each year she took up some new idea, some new thing to study. Her early medical reading had gradually evolved into a kind of informal practice, and more than one family considered Madame de Clouet the equal of all but the finest New Orleans physicians. Her daughters learned it was useless to protest maman's queer occupation, or to be embarrassed. "I am helping heal the sick," she told them. "Is that not God's work?" Since Aimée de Clouet rarely referred to God, on those occasions that she did, she was listened to.

"When is the funeral?"

"Marguerite is sending word to the others. I suppose in a few days."

"But the baby? A boy, you said? He is healthy?"

For the first time in many hours, Aimée smiled. She remembered that feeling, not to be described to someone who has not held new life in his hands, when the blood-stained, wriggling, thrusting little form popped into her waiting arms. For one slow moment, the eyes had been tightly shut, the mouth drawn, the skin gray. Then, with a sudden gasp, the baby had drawn in its first long breath. And then yelled. Loud, angry, protesting, Julie Langlinais took the last breath of her life as her son took his first, but the sweet sound of his birth cry heralded her home. "Yes. And like his father, eager for life."

Aimée watched while Brother Langlinais, surrounded by his mother and four sisters, supported by his brother and father, followed his wife's casket to the small cemetery set to the rear of the first Langlinais homestead. How well she understood the haze of disbelief with which he heard their voices join those of the priest and the other mourners: "May the angels take you into paradise—" Aimée heard those words with more anger than faith. Julie Vidrine and Brother Langlinais had been married not yet two years—they were still in paradise here, that paradise known only to those who are both young and very much in love. What comfort was it to Brother, to think that Julie now knew a paradise he had no part in?

One thing you had always to give the Langlinais, Aimée thought. They behaved well. They gathered around their desolate son and brother, offered him the shelter of their arms and their love—if anyone there had a sorrow in his own life, it was forgotten in their common concern to help Brother heal. She saw Mathilde, the Langlinais daughter who at twenty-eight had long been a confirmed spinster, go to Brother and take his hand. She walked with him to the edge of the grave where he leaned down to put one small dried white rose on top of the coffin. It was from Julie's wedding bouquet, Aimée had seen the rest of it in Julie's room in a blue vase under a glass bell. Marguerite would dry the flowers from Julie's grave and add them to that first brave bouquet. Thinking of the yellow roses that climbed on the trellis outside the office door, the same roses that grew also over the picket fence that separated the plantation cemetery from the fields just beyond, Aimée remembered that it was more than she could bear to decorate the drawing room with flowers that also dipped so carefully to touch Noel's grave. Her heart flew to Brother—he might pray for the day when his memory of his wife would be, like her dead flowers, pale, sweet, and only faintly perfumed with sadness. But unless he knew something she did not about conquering grief, that day would not come.

"Another year better than the one before," Troi said. He closed the ledger, pulled the new one forward, carefully wrote in the date—1832. "And a good thing, too. Annette believes money has but one use—to spend. If she ever knew just how much there is—"

"She doesn't?" Aimée wasn't really surprised. Annette was a doll, a pretty plaything. Had it not been for a certain kind of strength that was not courage, but served just as well, Aimée would have despised her daughter-in-law. Not long after Julie died, Annette had sought Aimée out. "Mère de Clouet. I know you are worried I will be afraid to have this baby, because of Julie. Well, I'm not. I don't worry about things I can't help and I'm not afraid of things I can't do anything about. Besides, your son likes to lie with me—and if I am not to stop that, I must be willing to have all the babies that come." Then she had tossed her hair, that swirling crown of auburn. "But one thing, Mère de Clouet. If I'm going to get fat from having babies, I'm going to do it in New Orleans— and New York—and London—and Paris. Maybe you never wanted to be anywhere but Beau Chêne—but I do—and I will." A last challenging look. "After all, we've lots and lots of money. Isn't that true?"

It was true. The Louisiana Bank held no notes from the de Clouets now, hadn't for several years. The last of Hélène's jewels, the splendid sapphire tiara with matching necklace and bracelets, had been redeemed. And the white gold continued in a molten flood.

There never seemed to be a moment when it was decided that Mathilde would give up the various good works that occupied her days to concentrate her entire attention on the rearing of her nephew. But as the infant Claude nursing at a neighborly breast became a toddling inquisitive boy who spooned her good couche-couche into his never still mouth, Mathilde took on more and more of his care. By the child's second birthday, he called his aunt "maman"; by that time, it also seemed decided that Brother had no thought of marrying again. Aunt Mathilde might just as well be maman, there would be, it seemed, no one else.

"What you give to those horses you should give to a woman," Marguerite said to her son. It was a complaint said almost by rote. She had watched the growing absorption of her husband in horseflesh; she was not surprised that her son filled the space Julie had left with animals on which he could spend affection as well as care.

\* \* \*

Even before Noel's death, the de Clouets had begun to sell off some of the horses from their large stable. When Jean-Claude had taken Marguerite to see the horses he was considering buying from Noel, she had admitted that they were beautiful to watch. "But don't tell how much you pay, no!"

Noel was to concentrate on developing a few strong contenders; "I need money to bring in another stallion, get new stock," he had told Jean-Claude. "Mon Dieu, but I hate to sell any of them. As for Aimée—she won't come out here at all if one is being sold that day."

Jean-Claude had bought two horses. They formed the beginning of his own small stable; the afternoon a Langlinais horse placed first at the Magnolia track at Baton Rouge, he insisted that one round of drinks be downed in honor of Dominique You. Thinking of the gold pieces he had used to purchase those first horses, he lifted his glass high and said, "To my good friend Dominique You, whose advice is as direct a hit as the shot from his big guns."

Now a Langlinais-bred and -trained horse was entered in almost every race at the Magnolia course, and Jean-Claude had set his sights on the tracks at New Orleans. "Let me tell you something," he said to Brother. "Our horses may not have owners with blood that goes back to the kings of France—but the blood they've got, that's as good as any on either the Metairie or Eclipse tracks." Brother had begun working with the horses right after Julie's death. The long hours in the stable, or in the pasture, the patient concentration on the horses' condition, the time spent going over each inch of hide to make sure no small scratch or abrasion could leave a path open to a deadly infection—those hours were hours in which he was not feeling pain. The pain was there, it would leap up as soon as he poured a bucket of water over his dust-grimed head at the end of a long stint—but the close air of the stable was a bandage against it.

"We make a good team, you and me," his father said after the first few months. "You like all that careful work—and me, I like the excitement." It was true. Brother cared little about actually watching a race. For that matter, once the early training was done, he attended few of the timed practices held on a track Jean-Claude laid out near the office. But for Jean-Claude, there was no excitement like watching one of his horses run.

He seemed to feel every exertion of muscle, every deep chest-filling breath. He became the racing animal, feeling the panting heat from the horses around him, taking the shock of pounded earth in his tensed legs. Each win was his, each loss.

"Jean-Claude, you've got horses on your brain to where you forget who you are," Marguerite told him. But—"It's good for Jean-Claude. And for Brother, too," she assured Mathilde during the long evenings when both men were down at the stable or out in the pasture. "Men, just being a husband, a father, it's never enough. Either their work, or some idea they've got—or a woman, even—has to be important. So for them it's horses. That's all right with me."

Aimée had hoped it would be horses for Troi, too. When Noel died, and he made it clear he intended to sell off the stables, keeping only a few for the family's use, Aimée was more than shocked. She was devastated. "But, Troi, these horses—and just when horse racing is coming into its own here—do you realize how much money you can earn with a winning horse?"

"And how much you can lose. No, maman, I'm not in the horse-racing business. I'm in the sugar business. The stable takes too much time, too much money and too much land. That's it."

Aimée still had her fine stallion, and the plantation still boasted good work horses, better riding horses. But the afternoon the last of the great thoroughbreds was led off the place, Aimée shut herself into her room and refused to come down for dinner. "She can't keep getting her way about everything," Troi told Annette, carving the venison roast. "She and grand-père loved horses. I don't."

The rain that had held off all afternoon suddenly split the big pewter plate of sky as though the first crack of thunder had dropped hard and broken it in two. "We waited too long," Jean-Claude said to Brother. "We'd better take shelter, this won't be over for a while." They had been slashing cypress trunks, deadening the trees so that when the spring floods brought high water, the big logs could be floated out. Though the sky had plainly meant rain, they had hoped to get a full afternoon of work done before heading home; it wasn't worth it to come this deep into the swamp for a few hours. "This way," Jean-

Claude said, heading off into the brush around them as though following a clear path.

He was heading for the cabin Lafitte had used. Since the Baratarians had abandoned Grande Terre and set up headquarters at Galveston, no one had come here. And so when they broke through into the small clearing, Jean-Claude thrust out a cautioning arm when he saw smoke erupting from the chimney in short bursts, sucked up and then blown back down by the erratic wind. "Someone else looking for shelter," he said to Brother, but his hand went to the knife in his belt, and he stepped more cautiously over the leaf-sodden ground.

"I'll go first," he said. He thrust the door, heavy with disuse on its leather hinges, ahead of him and moved quickly into the center of the cabin, Brother behind him. The man kneeling at the fire, hands held out before him, half fell back on his heels as he turned at the sound of their entry. "Picou!"

The kneeling man struggled to his feet. "Langlinais, what the hell you doing here?"

Jean-Claude laughed, knife still in his hand. "Me? This is my cabin, isn't it? On my land? Better I ask, what are you doing here?"

Picou sat astride a bench drawn up to the cypress table. "I was surprised, I didn't know anyone came here now."

Jean-Claude moved to the fire, threw another piece of wood on it. "Brother, this is Adolphe Picou. You know his brother, Joseph? At the de Clouets? Adolphe, my son, Claude—we call him Brother."

"Not like it was before," Picou said, moving his eyes over the room with the measured gaze of one who can look at an empty sea and tell by its slight changes, small differences, what is happening miles away. Then, to Brother. "Your father and I, we used to do business. When I was with Lafitte."

"The privateer?" Brother had been steaming his wet jacket at the fire, carefully holding it so that the heavy wool wouldn't scorch.

"You don't say pirate."

"No one did, after New Orleans. Don't think we didn't all grow up on that story! When I was a little boy, I thought Dominique You was some kind of saint."

"Some kind," Adolphe agreed, laughing. "Well, Jean-Claude, so how has it been for you? How many years? Twenty?"

"Twenty-five," Jean-Claude said. The astounding weight of those two words pinned him where he stood—how could it be twenty-five years since he had fought with Lafitte's men at New Orleans?

"Are you still bored?" Brother heard the hook on the smooth words.

Jean-Claude went to a small cabinet built against the side of the chimney, opened it and rummaged at the back. He pulled out a bottle of wine and brought it to the table.

"Now where was that?" Picou said. "I've been here almost a week—I never found it."

"A week?" At the silencing look in Picou's eyes, Jean-Claude turned back to the task of prying the cork from the bottle. "It was behind a brick. We scooped out a kind of cave behind the wall to keep wine in." He passed the bottle around, taking a deep draught first. "Fire on the hearth, wine in the belly—if we had a squirrel, a little bird—"

Picou went to a corner of the cabin, leaned over and picked something up. "I killed this a little while before the rain started. I was going to cook it when the fire got going. You think three can gnaw on these bones?"

Jean-Claude weighed the rabbit with his eyes. "A meal for you. A bite for us. We have supper waiting. So, Picou, what are you doing here?"

Picou spitted the rabbit, placed the spit in the grooves built into the sides of the fireplace. "Hiding. Things haven't been good for a long time. You know Lafitte's dead."

The blazing image of Lafitte towering on the tossed deck on one of his ships, or striding through a ballroom's gaiety, seared itself on Jean-Claude's mind. "Dead? How can he be?"

"Well, he is. In the Yucatán, some say. About fourteen years ago. Anyway, he'd been gone from Campeachy for five years by then."

"The place at Galveston?"

"You heard he burned Galveston? When no one would listen, when crews were pillaging, murdering—" Picou's voice was stopped by the violence his eyes remembered.

"But surely there was still money to be made," Jean-Claude said. Brother, who had sprawled out in front of the fire, arms pillowing his head, heard that distant note in his father's voice.

"It was—no longer worth it."

"What, Adolphe, not for the five hundred a month? Or did

it have to be five hundred a month to be worth it? If you made less, any less, then murder became just—murder, rape just rape, thievery just thievery?"

Picou moved as though each nerve was telling him this place was no longer safe. "Without Lafitte's discipline, the risk was too great. People were getting careless—allowing themselves to do anything they wished. We were hunted, despised."

Now the distant tone had retreated further still from the room they stood in. Jean-Claude seemed to be far, far away, looking at this scene as though it were being played on purpose for him to comment upon. "But could you not have foreseen that, Picou? That when one, or a few, men are murdered, there is then no reason not to murder others? That to prove to oneself that murdering one man was nothing, not bad, not wrong, one must murder still more? Because if one can do that, can repeat the act, and still appear to be a man—you understand me, I mean still eat, and lie with a woman, and pat small children on the head and even give to beggars—then the murder seems not evil. Only necessary."

"You have not been bored," Picou said. His voice was now as distant as Jean-Claude's, but in a different way. It had the distance of something pushed out, fenced off, put outside. "You have been thinking about life." The voice, though distant, could reach a thin blade of disgust across the space between them. "And like all who think about life, you have come up with ideas that serve you quite well. And no one else."

"How does what my father says serve him only?" They had forgotten the young man stretched by the fire. The low coals with only an occasional leaping flame to cast greater light kept him in shadow—he had been so still that if they thought of him at all, they thought him asleep.

Now Picou looked at Brother. "How? By making mock of things he once thought splendid. By making this little life he leads here seem better than the large life he wanted. I'd rather be hiding here, knowing I've spent my life exactly as I've wanted to, than have your father's place, with all the peace and safety that place has. At least, young man, Adolphe Picou has had a life."

Brother sensed a tension, twisting out of those two voices whose distance only increased the pressure each put upon the other. His own muscles drew up, knotting beneath the damp clothing, waiting for a signal to begin. He saw his father make the beginning of a movement, saw a clenched fist start the swing upward—then stop. Fingers opened, flexed. As though his own muscles were in an outer rim of movement that reacted to what Jean-Claude did, Brother felt himself begin to go limp. Jean-Claude moved toward the door. "Brother, I think it stops enough so we can make it home without drowning. Picou, if you have to winter here, all right. But come spring, you go. You hear?" Without waiting for an answer, Jean-Claude went out into the rain-drenched woods.

"Why didn't you hit him, papa?"

"I didn't have to," Jean-Claude said.

Brother took a little side look at his father, noting first the brightness of the eye, then the firm line of the mouth. He laughed, changed the rhythm of his step so that they marched together. "I am looking at you as though I never saw you before."

"Why? You knew I'd known Lafitte, called him friend."

"But this Picou seems to say you wanted to be one of them."

"Does that make your mouth go big and your eyes stare? Has no one ever wanted adventure, excitement? Sacrebleu, Brother, what you think? I have always been fifty-seven years?"

"But, Papa, pirates?"

"I didn't do it, did I?" Jean-Claude slapped at a wet thorn branch that whipped down, leaving a scattering of raindrops across his face.

Brother watched carefully, waiting for the moment to speak as though he were a fighter watching for the time he could get past his opponent's guard. Then—"Are you sorry?"

Turning to face his son, Jean-Claude missed his footing. He went sliding down a mud bank, clutching at branches, saplings, as he fell toward a small bayou rushing through the swamp with the new energy of the downpour. "Merde!" he shouted as he hit the bottom and ended sitting with water up to his waist.

Brother stood at the edge of the bank, searching for a strong branch he could use to pull Jean-Claude by. He kept his eyes anywhere but on his father's face, waiting for the deluge of cursing with which Jean-Claude would relieve his blocked anger. Then he heard Jean-Claude laugh, the big, fine laugh that had echoed down all the years of his childhood. Brother found his pole, shoved it toward his father, whose head was turned up to the darkening sky. Jean-Claude grabbed the branch, used it as he found purchase with his feet, and began slipping, climbing, up the sloping mud. When he finally stood by his son, he took Brother's face in two big muddy hands. "Sorry? Sorry I didn't become a pirate? And miss this life? Out there, one fought other men—and always had the advantage." Jean-Claude turned, spat onto the ground. "Here"—his arm took in the entire circumference of the swamp, the fields beyond— "here one fights this, all of it. Rain when you don't need it. Heat when you don't need it. Neither rain nor heat when you do need it. Mud. Bugs that eat the crops. With no advantage. None at all. Except one, don't forget it, Brother, except just the one."

"What's that?" Brother was balanced carefully on his feet, listening, watching.

"The grace to leave the big things to the bon Dieu—and the larger grace to laugh at the little ones one keeps for oneself." Jean-Claude leaned forward, took his son in his wet arms. "You, you've had a big thing in your life already. And you and your little boy, you got through it, yes? Now, you need to learn to laugh." A hug, strong, yearning. A voice rough against his ear. "I won't always be here to laugh for you."

The rain had ruined more than lumbering that day, it had ruined Aimée's ride. She had gone out to the stable, had her horse saddled. But the rain had kept her imprisoned in the big building, where row after row of empty stalls increased her feeling of having lost any control at Beau Chêne she once had. "Look at them, Joseph! Look at them! Don't you remember when every one was filled with a horse more magnificent than the next?"

She had not wanted to spend the afternoon exchanging stories with Joseph, and had stood in the open door, waiting for the rain to stop. She finally started back to the house when raindrops were still spinning cobwebs around the trees and making veils of gauze to scatter over the dying grass. Her bones ached; all those years of riding, of hurtling herself at fences, ditches, hedges, on the back of a tall horse, had jolted the nerve endings, knotted the muscles, put points of pain in her bones. The cold and damp knew how to find each weakness, how to make her know distant parts of her body by the sharp nearness of the pain. She came to the stile over the fence that divided the stableyard from the lawn approaching the house and climbed the three steps to the top. Standing there, she saw Noel's face before her. How many afternoons had she stood just like this, with him waiting for her to jump into his arms! In a sudden fall of memory, she leaped forward. She hit the ground, left leg twisted under her. Her voice was muffled by the soft wetness around her, and it was not until an hour later that Joseph found her as he walked up to the kitchen for his supper.

"Of course it's broken, Troi, any fool can see that plainly enough." Aimée lay against the pile of pillows, her small body swallowed by the folds of the lace-encrusted gown Annette had helped her into.

"Dr. Forêt can set it, maman."

"Dr. Forêt doesn't know as much as I do," Aimée said.

"I'll send for him right away, maman."

"It won't do any good, Troi. I lay out there too long— there's so much swelling already not even the best New Orleans doctor could set it, much less Gervase Forêt."

"He can try, maman. Don't be so stubborn. There's no disgrace in being the patient for once."

The effort of bearing this pain without crying, without showing weakness, had put her at the edge of her strength. "I will be more than happy to be a patient, Troi. When the swelling has gone down so that treatment is possible." She heard the exhaustion in her voice. She wanted only for them to leave, for night to come, to sleep. And to wake to find two whole legs, a stable filled with horses, and Noel calling her to breakfast. "I want to sleep now." As they were leaving—"Troi, put my bag where I can reach it. If I have trouble sleeping—I'll take a little something for the pain." Ever since she had learned that Noel André had a duplicate key to her medicine chest, and helped himself to the opium stored there, using it to fuel the dreams that filled so many of his days, she had kept such drugs in her bag—and her bag with her. She watched Troi put the bag on the table near her, and, with Annette, leave the room. For some time, Aimée stared ahead of her at the wind-broken trees tossing wildly outside her window. They were in pain, too, they felt the winter descending, stealing life from them. They would struggle back to life in the spring, but some part of them would remain dead, some branches for which the effort was too much would not put out new leaf, would become more and more decayed until they fell from the living trunk and, dropping to the earth, finally became part of it again. Even when the swelling went down, and the leg was set, she knew how little were her chances that it would heal well. At the most, she'd be able to walk, maybe even give up crutches, the cane, after a while. Her eyes looked into the darkness past the trees, saw open spring meadows, herself on the back of a galloping horse, and at her side, Noel.

Aimée's hand went to the bag at her side, opened the familiar clasp, rummaged inside, and found what it wanted. She looked at the pistol in her hand. Small, beautifully designed, capable of killing a man at a short distance. She had carried it for protection when she traveled after dark on one of her cases. The powder and shot were also in the bag. Quickly, she loaded the weapon. Then she turned it to her temple and fired.

"Was that thunder?" Annette asked. It was rather pleasant to have Troi to herself, not to have Aimée seated at the foot of the table opposite him while she, his wife, took a child's seat at his side.

"I shouldn't think so," Troi said. "Don't know what it was." He waited, as though expecting the sound to be repeated, shrugged and took up the conversation again. "Certainly the four oldest children can benefit from having a tutor now, Annette. When we go to New Orleans for Mardi Gras, we will find someone suitable and bring him back with us."

"Oh, Mister Troi!" The slave standing in the flung-open door was rigid with some emotion so strong that, after that first horrified exclamation, he could not speak. Troi rose, responding to the primitive fear he saw in the man's face with a quickened heartbeat, breath that came fast and irregularly.

"What?"

The controlled roar in Troi's voice shook the man into life. "It's Miss Aimée, Mister Troi. Oh, Mister Troi, Miss Aimée's dead!" Then, into Troi's ear: "She done shot herself, Mister Troi."

Troi heard his wife's scream behind him as he tore up the narrow flight of inside stairs. Even before he reached his mother's room, an image of what he would find had come out of the dark places of his brain and was filling the air before him. What he was not prepared for was the look of peace on his mother's face. The entry hole of the bullet was small, and Troi did not lift the head to see the damage done when the bullet emerged. He drew the eyelids down, pulled the lace-edged sheet up over her face.

"Who else saw this?"

The slave stood behind him. The fear had gone from his face into his body, and he trembled like the twigs and leaves on the trees outside. "Only Tante."

"Very well. Neither you nor Tante is to say anything, do you understand that?" Then, taking pity on the man, he said more gently. "Miss Aimée could not be buried in the church if it was known that she had—died this way. You can see how—distressing—that would be."

"Yes, Mister Troi."

"Go start making a coffin, Rafe. And send Tante here."

The night that had descended for Aimée seemed to go on and on for Troi. He sent his wife to bed, telling her only that his mother was very ill, that Tante was sitting with her. He announced her death at midmorning, and then had the doors to her bedroom locked, with Tante on guard outside. "There's no need to see her yet," he said. Only when the coffin was finished, and Aimée's body had been placed inside, with a lacy cap covering that mutilated head, did he allow anyone else's eyes upon her. The darkened parlor, the small glow of the candles set round the coffin, cast shadows that, like the shadow he himself was casting, hid the truth.

"That's an unlucky house for women," Marguerite said. She, Jean-Claude, Brother, and Mathilde were walking back home from the de Clouet cemetery where Aimée had been placed beside her husband. "Madame Hélène broke her neck—Aimée dies of—what did Dr. Forêt say? A piece of blood from the broken leg got in her lungs?"

"Troi says that's what the doctor thinks must have happened. He never saw her. He only went by what Troi told him." Jean-Claude's voice was slow, hesitant.

"I don't know why they didn't send for the doctor right away—she might still be alive." Brother's grief over Julie was back with all the strength of its first happening. Aimée had been a way back to Julie, Aimée had been with Julie when she died, Aimée had helped Julie give him a son.

Marguerite spoke emphatically, making lines under her words. "If they didn't send for the doctor right way, it was because Aimée told them not to. That Aimée, you should re-member, Jean-Claude, that Aimée, she never asked for help if she thought she could take care of something herself."

"Troi, what did your mother really die of?" Annette was indulging herself with a second glass of brandy. It had been a long, long day. People from plantations up and down the bayou, people from the village. People who were friends, people Aimée had treated. The storeroom was filled with offerings, from dried apples to blackberry wine. Listening to the praise heaped, poured, lavished, on her mother-in-law, Annette had felt her smile grow tight. She had accepted Troi's story of his mother's death. But she had known he was lying. Until now, until she had heard a barely dead woman sanctified, she hadn't cared. "Troi, tell me, what did she die of?"

Troi poured his own second glass. What the hell—Annette never liked his mother, but she'd keep quiet for the sake of the family. "She shot herself." He turned and looked at Annette. Her soft features, still finely carved against the background of gradually plumping cheeks, showed nothing. And then, Annette smiled. "Good for her," she said. "There really wasn't anything else for her to do, was there?"

"Good God, Annette—"

"Troi, it was all over for her. All over. So she shot herself." The plump shoulders shrugged.

"You're not shocked."

Annette stood up, began to snuff out the candles. "I'm never shocked when people do what they have to do. Now come to bed, Troi. It's been a long day."

Outside, the moon had climbed above the winter-laden clouds and had opened her lens to the fullest. The land stretched out before her, revealing its features in that clear light. The bayous ran silver, the fields were carved in black. Trees rose up in clumps, or in long curved growth along water. Houses nestled within their frame of oak or pecan or sweet gum. The lens shone on headstones marking the houses of the dead, on Claude and Mathilde, Claude Louis and Cecile, on Julie. On Noel and Hélène, on Noel André and Aimée. Moonlight and wind drift, field and bayou, living and dead—they pulled winter around them, and slept.

# CHAPTER 13

## *Anniversary: 1855*

The high sun of summer still blessed the crops in the fields that stretched away from St. Martinville like velvet casing around a setting of gray and white. From inside the church, the sound of voices rose up into the sweltering air and hung there, imprisoned in the heavy layer of heat that separated earth from colder sky. "Pitié, O Seigneur. Pitíe, O Christ. Pitié. O Seigneur."

Claude Langlinais reached over and took one of the twins into his arms. His eyes surveyed his family, blessing them. His wife, Françoise, held the newest daughter, born just three weeks past, against her breast. Claudette, twin sister to the boy in his arms, crowded close to her mother's skirts. Beyond Françoise, his father, Brother Langlinais, stood. Claude's ears could pick up, from that unified chorus of prayer, the voices of certain friends, neighbors. The priest chanted the first words of the next prayer: "Gloire à Dieu, au plus haut des cieux." The Acadians, gathered in their church this fifth day of September in the year 1855, chanted with him: "Et paix sur la terre aux hommes qu'il aime. Nous te louons, nous te bénissons, nous t'adorons. . . ."

While Claude's tongue spoke the words, his thoughts ignored them. One hundred years since his ancestors, and the ancestors of all who prayed here, had gathered in another church, a church at Grand Pré. And listened in profound shock to what was said there. Martyrdom began in one church, was sanctified in another. Already his family was into its sixth generation in this place, this Acadiana. There was no one left alive who had been part of that exile—but the horror of it still lived. We still protect ourselves, Claude thought, and shifted his son's weight to his other arm.

He thought of his land, delivering up to him each year its fruits, its grains, its fish and game and birds. It had taken them one hundred years. But the Langlinais, and the other exiled people, had found a land and made it theirs. His free arm circled his wife's waist. The infant in her arms stirred, hungry mouth seeking her breast. With all the vigor of his joy, his voice rose above the others: "Toi seul es le Très-Haut Jesus Christ, Avec le Saint-Esprit, Dans la gloire du Père. Amen." The voices stilled, the congregation settled itself to listen to the readings. This is an island still, Claude thought. Surrounded not by the sea, but by bayous and swamps and inlets of water that change with the season. Separated from others not by miles of open ocean, but by our desire to be left alone, to live in peace. Beyond the town, the spikes of sugar cane did make a gray-green sea. The chanting voices of the men and women working in the rows also rose into the sweltering air and hung there, imprisoned in the heavy layer of heat that separated earth from colder sky. They, too, prayed to the Lord. But their prayers did not praise His glory. They asked for deliverance.

Noel André de Clouet IV sat between his father, Troi de Clouet, and Louis Bertaut, sipping the fine bourbon that had come in the last shipment from New Orleans. He had introduced bourbon and the many drinks made from it to Beau Chêne; when his father grumbled that the tuition at the University of Virginia had been meant to pay for a classical education, not one in the use of potables, Noel became deaf. Or mixed a stronger julep.

The Bertauts were visiting to make final arrangements for the marriage of their daughter, Caroline, to Noel IV. It would be held in the spring, when, Caroline said, "God is decorating the outdoors and all maman and I have to worry about is the inside." Simple to be a woman, Noel thought. Being a man was all very well when it meant that amounts of money were spent on his education, his travel; but it was not so pleasant when it meant sitting in on these endless political discussions. "I say, father, you don't really need me here, do you?"

Troi took his attention away from Louis Bertaut. "*I* don't need you." The first word had only the slightest amount more force than did the rest, but even that small strength was sufficient to bring color to Noel's cheeks. "If you are going to someday take my place, *you* need to be here." Again that slight force. Without waiting for Noel's response, Troi turned back to Bertaut. "It's true what you say, Louis. Politics is always a matter of capital, rarely a matter of principle."

"And you don't like it. Well, Troi, I don't like it, either. In one way, I agree with the Democrats about secession. Why should people without our problems tell us what to do? In another way, I can't agree."

"Because we need machines as well as slaves for our sugar, Louis. And the North has the machines." Troi paused, stared at the crystal glass of bourbon in his hand. "Sounds ugly, put just that way."

"If I tried to untangle all the things that sound ugly when you put them just the way they are, Troi—" Bertaut's voice trailed off. He stood, strode to the rail of the fencing that edged the gallery. "Even the Democrats don't agree anymore, not after the Kansas-Nebraska Bill."

"So are you going to support the Know-Nothings?" Troi heard a deeper tone in Noel's voice, a tone that demanded notice.

"What do you know of them?" he asked.

"Only what I hear. Whigs are joining them. Some Democrats. And they do seem to attract men—like ourselves."

"Men like ourselves." Troi joined Bertaut at the gallery rail, stared out into the shimmering haze that hung over his fields. "How much effort goes into making that distinction."

Below, the clear chime of the clock in the office sounded noon. A gust of hot wind brought the smell of cooking from the kitchen that lay to the back of the house. "Time to find the ladies," Troi said. As they went down the gallery steps, Noel took his father's arm, stopped him. "But, father, suppose it doesn't work."

"What?"

"The compromise. The Know-Nothings will run Filmore next year, won't they? For president?"

Troi laughed. "So you did attend a lecture, once in a while. Or at least, kept your ears open. I don't know, Noel. They very well may. But somehow, no matter how much men say they want to compromise, give a little—there is always the question of which side will give first. You know?"

"So if it doesn't work—what then?" Noel realized that his hand was gripping his father's arm, holding on to it as though to a spar in a stormy sea. He relaxed his fingers and then removed them.

"I don't think anyone knows, Noel. I am very much afraid, though, that we are going to find out."

Louis had already joined the ladies, was seating Annette in her place. At the entrance to the dining room, Troi and Noel stood for a moment, not yet part of the group inside. The heavy Waterford chandelier swung its myriad prisms over the long table. Aromatic steam rose from the porcelain tureen one of the house servants was carrying. The butler was pouring wine into the thin Bavarian crystal goblets. "Well," Noel said, his optimism returning, fueled by the familiar splendor of the scene before him—"we have built a pretty tight little kingdom here at Beau Chêne. It should ride out any storm."

# PART TWO
## *1865—1916*

# CHAPTER 14

## *Hurricane*

Among the resorts wealthy Louisianians visited during the golden 1850s was Last Island, a small stretch of land off the Louisiana coast in the Gulf of Mexico. An elaborate resort hotel, many-storied, balconied, its windows opening to the fresh Gulf breeze on one side, to the brackish swamp air on the other, attracted hundreds of pleasure-seekers, who bathed in the waters, strolled on the beaches, and filled the ballroom with swirling skirts and flashing black-trousered legs. Like other sugar planters, Troi and Annette de Clouet were frequent guests at that hotel; Annette often took the children there for several weeks, with Troi joining them for the last fortnight. In August of 1856, Troi and Annette joined a party of friends for a few days at Last Island. While they, with hundreds of other vacationers, danced in the great ballroom, a hurricane lay out in the distant waters, building up the slamming force that would, in one massive blowing squall of wind and rain, sweep the island clear. Among those who died, drowned in waters from the tidal wave that rushed along with the wind, partner in a fatal pas de deux, were Troi and Annette de Clouet.

Their son, Noel André de Clouet IV, called Noel, married to Caroline Bertaut just that spring, took over Beau Chêne, entering into that vast responsibility with a reluctance matched almost by his ignorance. "I can tell you the school, the period, the artist, of almost any painting you show me," he had complained to Caroline. "But I'll be damned if I can tell one variety of cane from another."

"Then you'd better learn," Caroline had said. "Hadn't you?" While she produced a daughter, Marthe, and a son, named for his father and called Nollie, Noel produced a sugar cane and money. By the time another hurricane struck, sweeping with slamming force over those fecund lands its massive blowing squall of artillery fire and cavalry charges, of weary infantry and pillaged citizenry, Beau Chêne was a ripe, a luxurious, a rich, target. In that great blast of destruction, while her master was away with the Washington Artillery, a noted regiment from New Orleans, Beau Chêne fell to her knees.

During those years, women whose lives had been filled with the ordered work of plantations, with the easy gaiety of wealth, learned the grinding despair of struggles to survive. Men hunted, not in sport, but in earnest. Caroline de Clouet faced the death of her world with two defenses: her own will, and the wiliness of Claude Langlinais. Living a scant mile away through the woods between the two landholds, Claude and his wife, Françoise, extended the circle of their concern to take in also Caroline, Marthe, and Nollie.

Before the Teche campaign resulted in a Yankee victory, Claude had fought with the home guard, leaving his fields to do battle much as did the minute men in the Revolution. After that campaign, he left his fields to continue the battle, using his knowledge of the swamps, the back bayous, to work his way through Yankee-occupied territory and out to the Gulf, where he bartered, bought, bargained, to get medicines, food, cloth—any item which would keep two families going. When Françoise would warn of the danger, Claude laughed. "The Yankees are no different from anyone else. As long as they get what they see as their share—I can have the rest."

"And isn't that dangerous? Trading with the enemy? Claude, when people hear—"

"Hear what? That I found my way to food, medicine? Brought it back? Paid a small bit of it to keep the rest—and my head? Françoise, you think it's better to starve? Anyway—" he would say, "anyway, when a man has a wife, five children, he feeds them first. later, he thinks about whether a few pounds of coffee to the Yankee pot, a little tobacco, make a hell of a lot of difference in who wins this war."

By April of 1865, Caroline and her two children knew more about the sheer labor involved in wresting food from the earth than Noel would ever know. By that same year, Caroline knew something else—that principles formed with no attention paid to physical reality may very well be useless, and that people who understood that, as did Claude Langlinais, would survive. Françoise Langlinais, accustomed to survival, planned for more.

Her twins were twelve, Jumie gaining on his sister Claudette in height, Claudette gaining on Jumie in grace. The other three, Francie, Mathilde, and Jean, she wouldn't worry about for now. Her mind, left free by the repetitive tasks of housekeeping, was as busy as her hands. The war would not last forever. Claude had shown her that he could meet obstacles, find his way over them. A man who could run Yankee lines, smuggle in goods, trade with the enemy, and feel all right about it, could do anything. She would tell him what that anything was to be.

Caroline de Clouet's fingers moved swiftly over the bean vine, plucking full pods from the spreading green plant. From the corner of her eye, she could see Marthe squatting in a row several feet away, carefully pulling carrots from the summer-dry earth. "Put your bonnet back on," she called to the child, and paused in her own work until she saw the small brown hands reach back for the sun-faded lavender bonnet and place it firmly on the blond head. Then, with that sudden drop of fear that seemed never to leave her now—"Where's your brother?"

Marthe stood up and rubbed her back. She turned and gazed across the garden at her mother. "Fishing." When she saw the terror that was always in her mother's eyes wash over her face she added, "He's with Jumie, maman. He's all right." She watched her mother put the fear back in its place, in that cave behind her eyes where it could peek out at them, or pounce upon them. It had been a very long time since her mother's eyes had been clear, happy. Maybe never.

There were still tomatoes to pick, and a few ears of corn. If Nollie did catch a fish, or if Jumie Langlinais caught enough so that he could give Nollie one, they would have a good supper. Caroline wouldn't think of the end of summer, when the frost stole into her garden and stripped it of its yield. She had managed to keep them fed, had learned from Françoise Langlinais how to make a garden, how to hoe, to weed, how, finally, to dry whatever they didn't eat. She had not learned to hunt. If Claude, Françoise's husband, had not brought her duck, venison, squirrel, had not shown her how to use roots from swamp plants, they would have starved long ago.

"Someone's coming, maman!" Marthe had caught fear from her in the first year of the war, when Noel was in Virginia with the Washington Artillery, when the slaves were leaving the plantation, stealing away to take freedom even before Lincoln gave it to them. Caroline had brought her children to her own bed, three-year-old Marthe and one-year-old Nollie. The doors were bolted, a lamp lit, and a pistol made a heavy lump under her pillow. At first, the children had slept as easily as if still in their own beds. They lay curled against her own rigid body, coming to her for the warmth, the comfort, she had always given. Nollie had continued to sleep that way. But Marthe, after a few weeks, had become restless. She had demanded more lullabies, yet another story, until Caroline's patience broke. "Only one more, Marthe, and then you must go to sleep. Whatever is the matter with you anyway?" The child had grown almost hysterical then, sobbing in great choking cries against her mother's breast. When Caroline could finally understand what Marthe was saying, she knew what her own fear had done. "When you are singing to me, maman, or saying a story, I forget about the bad man who is coming."

"What bad man, Marthe, what are you talking about?"

The child had stopped crying, had looked at her mother with eyes grown old. "The one you are going to shoot with papa's gun."

Well, the bad man had come. The Yankees had occupied the house, had kept Caroline and the children prisoners on the third floor. When they had finally gone, and she had once more walked the grounds of Beau Chêne as its mistress, she had learned that sometimes one doesn't fear the future enough.

Now she walked to the edge of the garden, hoe in hand, and shaded her eyes against the streaming July sun. The large-brimmed sunbonnet, copied from a pattern of Françoise's, made a tunnel of blue cotton around her face. On either side of that tunnel, the wasted sugar fields lay, weed-choked, the province once more of nesting birds. The slave quarters that stretched in a line behind the great house were empty, too, except for a few sheltering those too old, too ill, or too frightened to leave. The heavy weight of midafternoon sun beat on her, drawing sweat from the thin body clothed in a rough cotton dress. That, too, she owed to Françoise, who had handed it to her along with the first lesson in gardening—"To save your nice gowns until Noel comes home," Françoise had said.

A man was coming up the alley of oaks, moving slowly, as though the air of summer was an obstacle so strong that his own strength could not prevail against it. Caroline shrugged.

A soldier making his way home, hoping to find a meal, fresh water, perhaps a clean bed. She no longer feared them, these men who had begun to straggle along the roads early in May, coming soon after the news of final surrender had also straggled down the bayous. She fed them and gave them water and a bed if they needed it, willing other women to give the same to her Noel. For surely he would come. Surely the emptiness she endured she would not always endure. Surely no letters came, not because Noel no longer lived to write them, but because with everyone in this vast territory of defeat hungry, with many of them homeless, with all of them caught in a grief so encompassing that even birdsong seemed a violation of that silent mourning, the delivery of mail seemed—not important.

"It's papa." The small voice behind her was sure, stating a positive truth.

"Oh, Marthe, no—papa is taller, bigger—"

"It's papa," Marthe said again. She stood stolidly, the basket of carrots gripped tightly, her face blank.

What was the child seeing that Caroline did not see? A sudden jealousy flared; would she not know her husband before a child who was barely three when he left knew her father? Then something, a shattering of the light that fell beneath the full-leafed oaks, changed. The man became Noel.

Like Marthe, Caroline stood, hoe still in her hand. She felt tears rising, fighting to be free of the well she had kept them in, a well covered by discipline, abandoned by necessity, forgotten by will. I won't cry, I haven't cried since the day the Yankees rode in and took over this house. I won't cry. Wells of tears may be kept covered, may be abandoned, may be forgotten, when all a woman needs is courage. When vanity is threatened, no will is strong enough. It isn't fair, it isn't. I've ruined my hands and I don't have shoes on, and I look worse than any fieldhand we ever had—and I've kept one good dress ready, I've hung on to a ribbon for my hair, stockings for my feet. . . . He saw her then. Or saw the two figures, as unmoving as though they had been placed in the garden to frighten crows and hares away. He walked across the tall grass that wandered over the flower beds Hélène had scattered over the close-trimmed lawn like lace medallions stitched onto an emerald silk gown. He climbed the stile separating the house lawn from the beginnings of the kitchen yard. "Caroline?" Her name had not left his heart, but still it was strange to his lips.

The woman hesitated, leaned down, put the hoe on the ground, straightened, and began to come toward him. He could not see beneath the shadows the bonnet cast, and the lines of the figure were not the ones he remembered. It was not until she was but yards away that he saw her face. And then, for the first time, Noel saw defeat.

"You probably should be getting home now," Jumie Langlinais said. He was gutting the catfish he had caught, laying two of the larger ones aside for Nollie to take back to Beau Chêne.

"I didn't catch any fish, Jumie. So I don't get any," Nollie said. But his eyes were following every move the older boy's hands made. It was hard to remember maman's rules when you were hungry.

"You helped. You dug the worms. Now, just find us some big leaves to wrap these in. I've got way more than we can eat, that's for sure."

Jumie lay back and let his ears keep track of Nollie. He hadn't told his own little brother, Jean, he was going fishing, hoping for an afternoon to himself. And then Nollie had turned up! Well, what was he to do? There was no question Madame de Clouet and her children would never have made it if his parents hadn't helped them. Could he enjoy the peace this bayou still gave knowing the de Clouets would go hungry? "But how long can we do this, papa?" he had asked his father. "Suppose Monsieur de Clouet never comes home? Are we just going to take care of his family forever?"

"How long does the bon Dieu take care of us?"

Jumie had waited for his father to say more. When nothing came, he pressed. "We are not the bon Dieu."

His father had put down the ax he was sharpening. He had taken his son's face in his hands, had looked into the eyes that were, everyone said, exactly like his grandfather's. "No, we are not. But we are supposed to imitate Him. Now, go help your grandfather. He's plowing the last field today."

"You probably should be getting home now," Jumie said again. He heard Nollie's small sigh and knew what the child was thinking—the way to the bayou had seemed short enough a few hours ago; now it stretched as long as summer itself. "I'll give you a ride," he said. "And we'll use the shortcut." Nollie watched while Jumie wrapped the cleaned fish in the big sycamore leaves and pierced the leaves with thorns to hold them together. He watched the catch disappear into the pouch Jumie slung over his shoulder. Then, when Jumie stooped, Nollie climbed aboard the offered back and fastened his sunned arms around the older boy's dusty neck. He leaned against the damp hair, sniffling at the unmistakable smell of Jumie.

"I like you, Jumie," he said. "I really do like you a lot."

"I like you, too," Jumie answered, and set off with quick-paced steps into the woods.

Going by the road, the de Clouet place was a good five miles from Jumie's home. Going by the shortcut that bypassed fences and hedgerows, roads and fields, it was just under a mile. The path emerged below the stableyard at Beau Chêne, on the edge of a pasture where Nollie's great-grandmother Aimée had tried new horses. That pasture was grazed now by a few cattle, several sheep, and three or four goats. The stables, long the pride of Beau Chêne, had been used as warehouses by the Union soldiers camping at Beau Chêne, during the Teche campaign. The horses' boxes had been ripped out to make a larger, undivided space, and signs of careless occupation had scarred the remaining walls.

Stopping to get his breath, Jumie looked at the scene before him. The hard glare of a midsummer, midday sun had been tempered by the approach of twilight, but still, the sunbeams that poured from the center of that high flame were surgically unsparing of the house they fell upon. The searching light showed flaking paint on columns, negligent ivy creeping over windows, doors settling off their hinges. Roses tumbled in the garden, some creeping along the weed-spread ground, others peering from the top of spindly stems. "I like our house, don't you, Jumie?" Jumie bent over and with a twist of his back, invited Nollie to hop down. His own house, smaller, less grand, was shining with fresh whitewash. The paths were filled with small gravel raked from the bayou, the door frames were plumb.

"Sure, Nollie, it's a good house." Then Jumie saw a man coming toward them. Clothes of faded homespun hung upon him as though someone, going through the contents of an old trunk, had tossed pants and shirt, shoes and stockings, willy-nilly into the air and they had fallen upon and garbed this man. The hair, newly brushed, lay close to the head in water-induced neatness. The beard could not be tamed with water and comb; it sprang away from the face in defiant clarity. The eyes of the man were fixed on Nollie—finally, it was the eyes Jumie knew.

Not from any real memory of Noel de Clouet, but from the portraits that hung in the de Clouet drawing room. "Monsieur de Clouet?"

"Who are you?" the man said. He stood still, not coming one step closer to where Jumie and Nollie stopped.

"Jumie—Claude Langlinais, monsieur. Called Jumie."

"The boy is my son?"

"Yes." Still no one moved. Jumie could feel the last heat of the day making its insistent presence known upon his neck, his shoulder blades. He could feel the heat going all through him, finally reaching his feet, which it would melt into the ground. He would stand here forever, the three of them would stand here forever, replacing the statues which had been delivered just before the war started, and were, as far as he knew, still junked in a heap, uncrated and unused. He pushed Nollie forward. "That's your papa, Nollie. Your papa's come home."

Nollie's body pressed itself against Jumie, small back against Jumie's belly. "I don't have a papa," Nollie said. Jumie saw a sudden fire in Noel's eyes. It leapt, held, then died.

"And you," Noel said. "Do you have a papa?"

"Yes," Jumie said.

"Home yet?" Then, when Jumie looked a question: "From the war."

"He didn't go," Jumie said. "He was in the home..."

Noel's head jerked back with the rough violence of his laughter. An arm, thin, the sleeve ragged and torn, gestured at the empty fields. "And I suppose his fields are green, his cattle fat. I hope he's grateful for what I bought him."

"Sir..."

Noel waited to hear no more; turning fast, he strode back to the house. In his turn, Jumie sighed. He leaned over and picked Nollie up. "Sure you have a papa," he said, walking slowly in the path de Clouet had just taken. "That's him. Back from helping General Beauregard. You remember when he left, don't you?"

Nollie settled himself against the familiar chest, felt the particular arrangement of bone and muscle that meant Jumie. "I've forgotten, Jumie," he said. "Tell me again."

Noel de Clouet eased himself into the rocker and drew on the pipe Caroline had fixed for him. Cooler air from the bayou was creeping up through the heated breath of summer that had streamed over him all day; outlines of oak and pasture, gallery railing and picket fence were blending together in the muted palette of evening. Almost, he could think this was 1860. Before.

"That was a good supper, Caroline. Thank you." He reached out his hand and took the one she gave him. If Noel had wanted to weep when he saw his wife's face, he wanted to go back to war when he felt her hand. The remembered curves and lines of soft skin were gone. He might have been holding the hand of someone born with a hoe in it. "How bad was it, really?"

The trembling of her hand told him more than her words did. From time to time, so low was that little voice, so hesitant the phrasing, that it seemed as though the falling light took with it Caroline's will to speak, and that she, like other solid objects around them, was blending into an indistinct landscape of shadow and intermittent, capricious light. But Noel knew his wife and the life that was hers—before. This knowledge filled in the gaps, took the difficult jumps she refused to take, until he saw the course her life had taken plain.

The Union army had ridden in early in 1863, had taken over Beau Chêne, had imprisoned Caroline and the two children on the third floor of the house. And there she had stayed until summer of 1864, when, inexplicably, the contingent camped on her grounds had left. Then Françoise Langlinaise had helped her make a late garden, had helped her clean the house. That was all. To each of his questions, his concerns, she answered, "I don't think of it."

"What did they give you for food?"

"I don't think of it."

"Did you have decent beds, did they take your things up . . . ?"

"I don't think of it."

"But the sanitation, your baths, your . . ."

"I don't think of it."

"And the children, they needed to run, they needed . . ."

"I don't think of it."

Then he rose, sent his rocker cracking across the floor of the gallery, went to her, pulled her into his arms. "You will never have to think of it again, Caroline. Nor will you ever live that way again."

She was quiet in his arms, so quiet that another hunger he had long borne seemed too much for what she offered. "I have lived that way once," she said finally. "When you've done it, it doesn't matter if you have to do it again."

He turned her face up. He had not kissed her since he came home; they did not know each other. The scars each had made a fence that crossed between them. Now he touched his lips to her forehead, then moved them down her cheekline. Slowly, the cast of quietude that kept her locked away from him broke. As his lips kissed her throat, then found her mouth, her arms went around his neck, her body found the old curves, the old resting places, the old challenges, of his. "Oh, Noel," she said, and the tears that came told him that now her body could be alive. "Oh, Noel, I thought you'd never, never be with me again."

Lying with Caroline in the pineapple posted bed, enveloped in the scent of vetivert that rose from the heavy linen sheets, Noel could believe that none of the past four years had happened. He had not journeyed to New Orleans to join his friends in the Washington Artillery, he had not fought at Bull Run, nor at any of the less God-ordained battles afterward, he had not learned that aristocratic blood flows just as easily from wounds just as horrible as those of the lowly born. And he had not heard the endless screams of comrades, screams that began on the battlefield and echoed down all his nights thereafter. "Caroline—in all that time—did anyone . . . ?"

Thank the dear God in heaven, she did not say, "I don't think of it." Her thin body convulsed against his. "No. No, Noel, never, never." Stillness. Silence. Then, against his flesh, soft, low. "If that had happened, you would not have found me alive."

The hot smell of frying catfish rose up and took over the air in the kitchen. Françoise Langlinais, her blue homespun dress covered by a huge apron, expertly turned the filets in the big black iron skillet. "Claudette, how are you coming with that cornmeal? It's time to fry it, yes." Claudette's hands, as swift and skilled as her mother's, were stirring chopped onions into the cornmeal mush in the pottery bowl in front of her. A bit of ground red pepper, a little salt—fried in balls in the bacon fat they had cooked the fish in, this cornmeal dish filled bellies and tasted good.

"Here, it's ready," Claudette said. She had been as lean as Jumie at the beginning of May; now, three months later, those stark lines were beginning to soften, her dress to hang, not straight, but in the faintest hint of curve. At least all those soldiers were gone. What mother wanted a girl to become a woman when the countryside was full of men who were far from home, who had forgotten that mothers and sisters are the same the world over, who wanted to remember only that women are the same?

"Madame de Clouet must be happy," Claudette said.

"Yes."

Claudette shot a glance at her mother. Lately, she looked beneath the surface of Françoise's words, knowing another meaning lay there if she but had the tools to get to it. "Don't you think she's happy? To have Monsieur de Clouet home?"

Françoise dropped another ball of cornmeal into the fat, watched it sputter, turned it as it started to brown. "Of course. But—things are not as they were. At Beau Chêne. The slaves are gone. Their sugar fields are ruined. They've almost no stock." Françoise shrugged. "So—she is happy, yes. Her man is alive. But much else is dead."

Claudette lifted a tanned hand, swept these difficulties away. "They can work. Isn't that what everyone does when they have to start all over?"

Françoise set the platter of cornmeal and fish at the back of the stove to keep warm. "Call the men, Claudette. Supper is ready." When her daughter waited, her questions repeated in every line of her body, Françoise measured the girl with her eyes. "What everyone does?" she said. "Not everyone. Some cannot work. Some won't. Some—simply don't ever think it is necessary."

"But Madame de Clouet has worked. Made a garden. Mama? Will they not work? Will they let it all go?"

"That's up to them, isn't it, Claudette? For me, I've got my work. Right now, my work is to feed my family." She slapped the girl's bottom lightly. "And yours is to call them in!" As Claudette stepped out into the yard, she called after her—"And make them wash, Claudette! You hear?"

"The best time of the day," Françoise said. She and Claude sat on the broad front porch, idly fanning themselves with the big fans she made from palmetto leaves. She had ticked off the many duties of her day as she would tick off the beads of her Rosary before she slept; now, with an hour before her, she could gossip with Claude, take her ease. "So what do you think the de Clouets will do? How are they going to make out?"

"The garden is in. They'll have food. They have a house." The smoke from Claude's pipe puffed a veil of protection around them; few mosquitoes braved its pungent odor.

"But, Claude, the de Clouets have never just had food, a house. They've had that grand way of life—now you tell me, how are they going to get it back?"

Claude peered at his wife. "Maybe they won't. That happens, in a war."

Françoise fanned herself rapidly, the light woven shape stirring the pipe smoke, lifting the water-soaked air from her skin. "It's a pity, though, isn't it? They've been something to watch. I don't know . . . like a circus, or one of those puppet shows people go see when they go to the city. A play. Maybe we all watched them like a play." Her tongue was running away with her mind now, putting words out for Claude to look over, pick up, think about, respond to. Her own fancy spurred her on. "Yes, Claude, that's what it is. They have been a play for us, the de Clouets. That big house, like something you'd see in a fine theater. Costumes. Dancing. Music, not the fiddle, but the harpsichord the women play. And always something going on!"

"But for them, Françoise, it has not been a play. It has been their life. Just as what we do each day is our life. Everything changes, for everyone. Will you tell me we have not made changes, suffered?"

She would not look at him. Men of course did not quite understand the fascination that grand life had. One would not want to live it oneself, of course not, how would one manage to live in such a complicated way? How could one remember it all? But it had been nice, knowing that there were people who managed it. She would never leave St. Martinville, that she knew. But if there were people who understood another life, who lived it . . . and if she watched them closely enough, could not her children have some of it?

"Of course we have suffered," she said, rising in that swift movement that made her seem to always be answering some cry for help. "Your father's lumber business will have to be started all over again. And the good God alone knows if the fur trade can ever be set up . . . those poor Indians may have hidden themselves so well, they will never find themselves. But, Claude . . ."

He saw something in her eyes then that he had never seen before. A longing, for something, a wanting, a hope that she had never shared. "But, Claude, it is not as though all that, the lumber, the fur trade, meant anything." Before he could speak, her hand came between them, silencing him. "I mean, Claude, it brought in money. And some of the money was used. But no one went anywhere. The children of this family did not get learning because of the money." The secret thoughts withdrew behind the brighter look that searched out the duties of each day. "We have always lived in a smaller world than the de Clouets, that's all." She vanished into the house, which was already enclosed in darkness.

Claude sat awhile longer on the porch, smoking. A smaller world? For five generations, it had been the Langlinais' pride that their land grant was as large as that later given only to slave owners with stock. The original grant had been expanded by careful purchase; even Françoise probably did not know how much land his father really owned. Of course they did not farm it all; how could they, without slaves? Land was owned for its own sake, it didn't have to do anything. So what was this new idea of Françoise's about a smaller world? "No one went anywhere. The children didn't get learning."

Claude felt a kind of weariness begin to lift itself from his thick-soled shoes in a sigh that would push itself from the entire length of his body. Even sensible women like Françoise were born with a love of trinkets; he supposed men would always have to deal with that. During the war, she had taken on more and more work, driven herself as each day delivered weightier burdens, longer pain. Now the war was over, and zut! just like that, she was speaking of big trinkets like education for the children, journeys for themselves.

Well, God made women the way they were, it must be the task of men to make them happy. A son away at college? A daughter studying with the nuns? Claude got up, set the rockers against the wall of the house, dumped his dying pipe into the flower bed that bordered the porch. If his grandfather could almost become a pirate, he guessed his children could become students. It would need courage, yes. Humor, too. But the Langlinaises, they had more than enough of both.

An aroma at once unfamiliar and overpoweringly remembered was blending with the dried sweet smell of vetivert; Noel at

one moment was in the deepest sleep he'd had in four and a
half years and at the next moment was awake. "Caroline, is
that coffee?" He had not had real coffee, coffee made from
coffee beans, properly roasted, properly ground, for months.
Years? "But where did you get it?"

Caroline took her own cup, perched on the steps pulled up
next to the bed. "Claude Langlinais." Noel caught the note in
her voice as she said that name—In the way the children said,
"Saint Nicholas."

"Where does Langlinais get coffee?" The small frown that
crossed her forehead as a cloudlet chased by a breeze told him
she heard the pique he felt.

"Who knows where he got any of the things he shared with
us? Not a whole lot, Noel, he has a family of his own. But
some coffee now and then, medicines we couldn't have gotten."
A silence while she sipped her coffee. "I could not have lived
if they hadn't helped me, Noel."

The coffee was marvelous; well roasted, freshly ground,
freshly dripped. The thought of Langlinais drinking it in his
kitchen every day while he, Noel, had swill in the open field
angered him. What other prices had he paid so Langlinais could
live so well? "Obviously, I owe Langlinais a great deal," he
said. The cloudlet came back on Caroline's forehead, stronger
than the breeze chasing it.

"You do," she said.

Was that expression on her face, almost of distaste, just a
trick of sunlight through the shuttered window? He drained his
cup, forced his mind to a place it had been avoiding. "The
little I saw yesterday, this place is almost ruined. Is there anything left, Caroline?" He tried to sound matter-of-fact, as though
they were speaking of something unimportant, something that
if it were indeed ruined, if there were little left, it was of no
interest. He heard the lie beneath the matter-of-fact voice; that
was one of the worst things about a war: it put to the test all
those phrases about honor and bravery and loyalty you would
rather die than deny—but how awful when you had to.

"The land is left." She put her cup down and went around
the bedroom, opening the shutters back against the brick exterior walls. The air already smelled of grass heating up. "But
there're no cane fields. Just straggling stands. No stock. What
the Yankees didn't eat, they killed or ran off. I've got a cow
for milk, the Langlinaises gave her to me. And some of the

Langlinaises' sheep and goats graze here. I can have the goats' milk if I want it. And the sheep's wool."

"The Yankees didn't take their stock?"

"Of course they did. But he had already hidden some back in the swamp . . . someplace his family has had back there for a long time. The Yankees never did go in there, why would they? So even though they took what they could find, they didn't find it all."

That was the easy explanation. Why wouldn't Caroline believe it? As another generation had believed Langlinais' grandfather had all the virtues of privateers and none of the vices of pirates. "And the Negroes?" He could hardly say the word. He had not really believed, ever, that the violence of this war, the totality of the South's defeat, rested on the slavery issue. Too many Yankee fortunes had been made, been made up to the very threshold of Fort Sumter, in the slave trade. Hadn't Lafitte himself come to grief, not all that many years ago, because one of his fleet attacked an American merchant ship loaded to every porthole with African slaves? Slavery had been the only issue for many, that he knew. For others—it was a hook, a hook that could be baited with emotional appeals, sordid examples, vivid descriptions of debauched and degraded humanity. Now he could say, along with thousands of men like him, that he had learned one thing: in a game such as this, the fisherman may or may not catch his fish, the fish may or may not get away—but the bait is always eaten.

"And the Negroes? Did they all leave?"

"Not quite all. SuSu is here. And Tatum. Allie. Pete."

Noel laughed. "The lame, the halt and the blind. Fit followers for their humbled leader. And with that, I'll rebuild Beau Chêne?"

Now she came close to him. There was a distance between their bodies, but the burning of her eyes drew him to her until he felt he knew the passion that filled her. "No, not with that, Noel. You will rebuild Beau Chêne because you must. With devotion to duty. To our children. You and I, we will never live the way we lived—before." A simple movement of her shoulders, a simple acceptance. "But we have children. And I will not have them grow up to be peasants! I will not have my daughter hoeing corn, or pulling weeds, do you hear me, Noel, I will not! Our son will go to a university, a good one. I have not sacrificed all this, Noel, to see our children live in poverty.

I don't care how you do it, I don't care what means you use, but you are going to get Beau Chêne back to what it was, Noel. Or I will take our children and get as far from this place as bribery will take me."

He focused on the one word he could let have meaning. "Bribery? With what?"

War had strung out her body, taken her face and with heavy thumbs marked it well. It had not changed those burning eyes. "With silver. With jewelry."

"But didn't the Yankees—"

"It's hidden. Back wherever it is Claude hid his cows." At that quick doubt, that easy anger, she looked at Noel as though he, too, were finally a stranger. "What? Do you think he traded your family's heirlooms for coffee? For medicine? Noel, how could you fight a war if you trust no one?" She didn't wait for an answer. "I'll have breakfast ready by the time you're dressed," she said, picking up the tray. "I've put one of your old suits in your dressing room." Then she laughed, and he knew that perhaps, for all the bitterness each had tasted, all the violence each had felt, the two of them might have a life after all. "It's not the latest fashion, heaven knows. But it's what all the gentlemen of Saint Martin Parish are wearing this summer."

Claude had decided to wait awhile before going to welcome Noel de Clouet home. They had never known each other well; the early closeness between their families, begun so naturally from the need of one great-grandfather, the generosity of the other, had, even as the generations settled themselves into the land, distanced. It was as though in order to have room for these spreading family trees, the Langlinaises and the de Clouets must move from each other's space. But he had learned to respect Caroline. Her home happened to be the one the Union wanted for its field headquarters; she and her children happened to be in the way. Certainly the woman's spirit lived still in an attic, imprisoned, caged, restricted not by the force of arms but by her own unwillingness to risk. She had emerged from that first attic able to work for her children. Whether or not she would emerge from the second depended perhaps more on Noel than on Caroline.

Claude thought about Noel as he took the shortcut to Beau Chêne. The first de Clouet to live in the style the de Clouets expected to be born to, Noel had viewed the world from the backs of thoroughbred horses, the interiors of fine carriages, the galleries and bay windows of tall houses. He was able to focus on those elements of the landscape, those characteristics of the people, that were most pleasing—it had not greatly surprised Claude when Françoise had told him that Caroline spent a great deal of time reading a journal Noel kept of his life, and poring over sketches he drew to illustrate these skimming thoughts.

Claude was shown into the library by Tatum, one of the Beau Chêne Negroes who clung to the plantation even more tenaciously than the wild blackberry and honeysuckle vines twined over the dead fields. Noel was looking through his volumes. "You can't eat books—nor sell them easily. I suppose I have Yankee practicality to thank for my library." Noel had wheeled the tall library steps up against one set of mahogany shelves and was sitting on the top rung. He gestured with the small leather-bound volume in his hand. "I might even have spent some pleasant hours talking with the Union commanding officer, judging from what he read."

Then the look, the look every de Clouet used to signal disapproval, violation of code, came over his face. Almost, Claude thought, as though it were on loan from the face of his grandfather, caught in paint and rigid in a heavy gilt frame. "Of course, I would have much preferred that he not dog-ear these pages, nor underline passages he liked. As for his own comment, scribbled in the margins—" The arm that stretched out to replace the book carried also the motion of a dismissing shrug. Barbarians had lived in his house. If one or more of the barbarians had some pretensions to education, well, one could not expect them to behave as if the education were solid, resting on long-built foundations.

"It's a lot of books," Claude said.

"So why worry about a few scribbles, a few bent corners, is that what you think?" Noel climbed down the ladder, knees bending in hard motion. "Funny how a man can sit on the top of a horse almost night and day for years on end and then hardly be able to walk once it all stops. Have you noticed that, Langlinais?" A pause, another de Clouet look, this one the one that said—"But I'm out of your experience now, you don't know what I'm talking about." Aloud, Noel said, "I'd forgotten. You somehow—escaped the war."

Claude waited while Noel found a chair, lowered himself

into it, and then, after a pause just long enough to underscore their positions, waved to the matching chair opposite him. Claude sat astride the arm of the chair, one leg cocked over the other knee. "I was in the home guard. Most of us in the militia were. We fought. The same Yankees who finally took over your house, de Clouet. When they won, this was occupied territory. It was a different war, that's all."

The thin face across from him was half screened by the wings jutting out from the back of the massive chair. In those depths of black leather, Noel's flesh was an indistinct mask. The voice, when it spoke, seemed detached. His words might almost have been spoken by someone else. "But Madame de Clouet tells me you had access to many goods—things that were scarce, that few people had."

"The only reason she knows that, de Clouet, is because they were shared with her. And with your children."

The mask became clear as Noel pushed himself out of the chair. Though Claude could see no change in the face, some emotion was at work behind it. Hardly looking at Claude, Noel went to the desk and opened a deep drawer. He removed a tall silver flask and poured liquid into two small cups. "I've battlefield manners, which is to say none. The flask went with me through the war, but the bourbon is of less arduous origin. Caro—Madame de Clouet's father somehow got hold of a case and kindly sent me some."

Claude shifted weight from his hip to the leg resting on the floor. "Why will you drink with a man you suspect of dealing with the enemy? Isn't that against your code?"

The mask had color now; red was the color of shame, but it was also the color of offended dignity. "I've accused you of nothing."

Claude stood up, went to the desk and picked up the cup of liquor. "I'm not like you, de Clouet. I don't understand all the ways in which you say something, and yet leave it still unsaid." He touched the cup to his mouth, sipped the bourbon. "You have all kinds of rules about who you eat with, when you drink. Me, I know one thing. Claude Langlinais will not let women and children starve—not his women, his children, not your woman, your children—if he can do something about it. And you know what, de Clouet? If, when I bring in food, medicine, for our people, yours and mine both, some gets— freed—by the Yankees, some bellies wearing blue get fed, what do I care? I've never been rich enough, or grand enough, for your kind of code. And I'll tell you something else. I damn well never will be." He drained the cup, placed it back on the desk.

"All right. So you see things one way, I another." The bourbon had the fire and clarity of well-aged liquor; Bertaut must have sold his grandmother to get it.

"No. You put yourself in a place where you can see things only one way. Me, I live down where life is happening, de Clouet. And sometimes, down where I live, the facts—get in the way of what I might rather see." Claude picked up the silver flask, twisted its cap open and refilled his cup. He put the flask down, just inches away from Noel's hand. "De Clouet—were you ever captured, in the war?"

"No."

"Ever trapped behind enemy lines?"

"No."

"So. Look, you fought. You were in danger of your life, over and over. I respect that. But, man, there were no women, no children." Claude's eyes were back in time, seeing, over and over again, the hungry tears of his children, the bleak despair of his wife. "To take care of them—my family and your family, de Clouet—maybe I had to push some things down, forget about them for a little."

"Things like principles? Like honor? You traded with the Yankees, Langlinais. There were no other ships at this end of the Gulf, how could there be with Farragut ruling it?"

"There were no rules either, de Clouet. The war was over, for us. And there was nothing any of us could do about that. Except survive until it was over everywhere."

Claude's body made a half turn, his arm taking in the rows of books towering to the full height of the ceiling. "I don't think you'll ever understand, de Clouet. We are bothered by different things. It offended you, hurt you, that a man you don't know, a man who had locked up your wife and children, sat here in this room in your chair, reading your books. Not only reading them, but marking in them. Making free with them. Isn't that it, de Clouet? Someone you don't approve of, some man you'd never have a meal with, drink with, made free with your possessions."

Noel's hand crept forward, closed the gap between it and the flask. "Something like that."

"All right. Me, I feel you have made free with something I possess."

Claude watched while Noel carefully poured bourbon into his cup. He held the flask several inches over the rim of the cup so that the sun that groped its way into the dim room could gleam through the golden brown trickle of liquid and light it into the silver bowl shaped below it. "What have I made free with?"

"With the way I live. The way I think. The way I am. You judge me, de Clouet. And you are not my judge."

Noel pushed the chair behind the desk back a little and sprawled his length into it. "When one breaks a code, one must expect to be judged."

"I don't judge you."

Now the mask was dropped. Or perhaps melted in the heat of Noel's astonishment. "Whatever would you judge me for?"

"For owning slaves."

"For owning slaves? What, have you become an abolitionist? Was that indeed the price you paid for food?"

"I have become nothing. No Langlinais has ever owned a slave. Or believed another man should. The trouble with you, de Clouet, is you don't mind other people paying the price for your choices. While me? I pay for my own."

"Come on, Langlinais. If you didn't have slaves it was because you couldn't afford them."

"This land is damn near ruined, de Clouet. Because you and men like you thought you could own other human beings. We've all paid your price."

Noel put down his cup, went to the window overlooking the garden that fell away to where the sugar fields began. "Yes, the land is ruined. Gone back to the wild. And now there are no hands to hoe it, or plow it, or plant it. I'm paying the heaviest price, me and the other planters."

"You should. It's your stiff necks that bring on destruction, time after time after time. Why shouldn't you pay the heaviest price?" Claude went back to the desk and filled both cups. "My people were driven from their land because they believed each man had a right to live, to worship, in his own way—so long as that way allows everyone else to do the same. Your people were driven from their land because they did not believe that, de Clouet."

Noel reached for his cup. "Because they did not believe that rabble knew better than they did how to govern."

Claude shrugged. "No. Because the rabble, as you call them, knew that you did not think they were men. As you did not think the slaves were men. De Clouet, don't you know a man has to have a home? If he is to be a man?"

"You're talking about slaves? Slaves had homes, they weren't worked day and night."

"Home, de Clouet. Home in a place with doors that can be barred, windows that can be shuttered. Home in a place where your woman, the woman you chose, and would have until the bon Dieu took her, cooked for you. Lay with you. Got you children that could not be sold. Home, de Clouet."

Even the click of silver on silver, of silver on wood, as cups were filled again and the empty flask laid down, did not break through the silence. Then Noel spoke. "That's all very well, Claude. But men live in different houses, pay different prices to get them. Whatever the cause of the destruction—it happened. And even if the planters pay the heaviest price, you won't escape. If this state, if this section, doesn't get back to what she was—we all go under. No one lives alone, Claude. Not you, not me."

Claude laughed. "I never thought I did. I've got cousins, neighbors—and I never had sugar. In a little while, we'll start up the lumber, the fur. But you, how are you going to plant those fields, make all that sugar again?"

"Hire Negroes. They've got to eat." A small smile, punctuating the bitterness. "And have homes."

"You'll pay them?"

"With the money I borrow on the jewelry you kept for my wife."

"You believe it's still there?" Claude moved back to the window, to that vista of land covered with thicket, brambles, a tangled maze of shrub. The fields that surrounded the house looked as though the destructive broom that swept across the South, powered by a vengeful arm, had left the tattered debris of men and their symbols in desolate piles, like old dust in a long-empty house. "Suppose there's some missing, out there where I hid it? A few knives here, a platter there, perhaps a string of beads? How will you know if Langlinais took it, sold it, ate it? Or if someone else did?" He swung around, faced Noel. "A man who trades with your enemy would stop at nothing, isn't that it?"

"You'd stop at theft, Langlinais." Noel seemed to retreat; so far had his mask descended that he was no more present than the portrait on the wall.

"You know that? Or you hope it? And what if I did steal? What does your code say then? Would you punish me as a thief? Or consider your jewels and plate just payment for bringing your wife and children through?"

"The two have nothing to do with one another, Langlinais."

Claude picked up his broad straw hat and clapped it on his head. "They have everything to do with one another, de Clouet. Like all men of your kind, you don't see that when a man is true to one big thing, he's too busy to bother being false to little ones."

"I have a hard time, sometimes, seeing the one big thing you're true to, Langlinais."

"I know that. I'll get your treasure, de Clouet. And bring it here. Though where you can use it, even the good Lord may not know. You understand, the banks are ruined."

"Claude . . ."

"Don't apologize. You're not sorry you doubted me—you're just glad you weren't right. This time."

"Our families go way back, Claude. I keep trying to remember that. And to understand you."

Claude crossed the small space between them, put out his hand. "We do go way back. One family teaching, the other learning. But maybe each thinks he is the teacher, the other the student?" He shrugged. "Who knows?"

Noel looked at the hand in front of him, put his forward and clasped Claude's.

"It's a lot to learn, Claude."

"But, Noel—after all this time—wouldn't you think it would get easier?" Claude shook his head. "I don't know. I'm beginning to think either the Langlinais or the de Clouets must be the worst kind of fools. Somebody never learns."

# CHAPTER 15

## *Scourge*

The thin lines of rain, drawn down from a gray layer of cloud that changed neither in density nor in color for days on end, screened each house, each barn, each shed, from all the rest of the world. Françoise, ducking through those evenly spaced, evenly timed, drops of water, ran into the stable where Claude sat mending the plow horses' harness. "Mon Dieu, this rain is enough to make a heathen believe in the Bible!" she said. "Claude, I hope that's an ark you're building, yes!"

"It'll stop. It always stops. Don't pray it away, Françoise. Remember last summer, when the drought killed everything?"

"Crez me zaire de la vie! I don't ask God to change what He's doing. As long as the roof is sound, and the children are well."

She turned the straw in the cow's food trough with one impatient hand. "Zut! That crazy thing! What's she putting a nest in here for?"

Claude looked up. "Your guinea?"

"Of course. Know she's different, I guess. Wants her privacy! Like a fine lady, that one acts." She made a sack with her apron, carefully placed the three small eggs within. "That reminds me. I saw Caroline de Clouet up at church this morning. It's her maman's saint day, she was lighting candles. She said the water's up in Lafourche. Her maman and papa are going up to Natchitoches to stay with her sister—they think maybe there's going to be a crevasse somewhere. What do you think?"

When Françoise looked at him that way, fixed him with her eye as though putting him under a dozen candles all gathered into the same spot, he told her all he knew. "Anytime there's a lot of rain they talk about a crevasse. So last year they didn't. This year they do."

He watched her go to the open doors of the stable. The rain, from that perspective, lit from behind by the hidden fire of the sun, looked like a large flat sheet of wavy metal pressed against the stable door to seal them both within. Though he could not see what Françoise saw, he knew it. Her kitchen garden was already sprouting, and in the fields beyond, corn and rice and sugar cane were planted, ready to cover the earth with their redeeming growth, ready to dress it with ribbons of green and sheaths of gold and tassels of shimmering brown. "Ah, Claude, I think sometimes it's a good thing I was born a Catholic." She didn't wait for an answer; she had learned soon after the baptism of the first infant that to Claude, religion was something you had, like strong muscles or good eyesight. You had it, you took care of it, you used it. He had watched her battles with God for a long time; as long as he did not take sides, she told him, he could find her as amusing as he pleased. "Because if I wasn't, I would wonder about a lot of things."

"What would you wonder about, maman?" Jumie's voice came from somewhere behind them. Claude, peering into the dimness of the corners of the stable, saw a lean shape become his son, sitting with his back against a bale of hay.

"What are you doing there?" Françoise's voice was always on the alert. Even before her eyes followed Claude and she found Jumie, she was ready to catalogue his sins.

"Reading." The boy came into the place of light Claude's lantern made. At fourteen, Jumie had a little more height than his father had at that age; Françoise said he would be as tall as his great-grandfather, the one who fought with Andrew Jackson. When she said this, she would fix her husband with those great sharp eyes. "I have always known this son was special," the eyes said. "See how God is making him tall to do big things."

"One of Noel's books?" Claude laughed to himself at that note in Françoise's voice. She very well knew Jumie had the run of the de Clouet library since Noel's return two years ago, was in and out like a chicken in the corn. Her way of keeping track of the myriad details of her life was to constantly check what she knew with others; though Claude had little time and less interest in worrying about what life meant, he did think, from time to time, that with Françoise asking the questions,

God would surely get worn out and start providing some answers. She stretched out her arm. "What's this one?"

Jumie put the small green book into his mother's hand. "Just some stories. About the Greeks."

"With pictures?" Françoise was flipping through the pages, busy eyes trying to impose her order on what appeared to be a chaos of tiny shapes.

Now Claude laughed out loud, the fullness of the sound reaching into the dim rafters above them. "Françoise, how many times do I tell you? The pictures the words put in Jumie's head are the ones you should think about, not the ones they put in to decorate the book."

"Monsieur de Clouet says I have a fine mind," Jumie said, almost stuttering in his hurry to get another idea before his mother. "A fine mind." He repeated the particular words the man had used, saying them slowly and carefully in case she hadn't heard well the first time.

Françoise closed the book, handed it back. "Well, of course. Do we need a de Clouet to tell us a Langlinais is smart?" But both Claude and Jumie heard her pleasure. Jumie thought it was pleasure for the moment, Claude knew it was much more. Ever since Noel had found out that Jumie could read, and that some of his children's fearful tedium had been relieved by listening to Jumie read, haltingly, inaccurately, but with great enthusiasm, some of the simpler children's books, he had encouraged the boy's interest. It was the hope closest to Françoise's heart, and the one she spoke of the least, that when Jumie was a little older, Noel would help them find a school to send him to.

"So what would you wonder about, maman?"

"What?"

"You were saying to papa that it's a good thing you were born a Catholic, because if you weren't, you'd wonder about a lot of things."

In the stillness of the stable, made more definite by that blanket of rain which wrapped it in silence, Françoise stood looking at her son. Then she went to him, took him in her arms, and pulled him close to her. Claude could not remember when he had seen her pause in her day to touch, to clasp, any of the children. Her love fed them, washed their clothes, brushed and braided their hair, pulled splinters from their feet—it rarely had time for anything else. When she stepped back, let Jumie go, her face was softened as clouds are softened when a power of sun heat suffuses them. "I guess I would wonder about all the things those people in those books wonder about—why does it rain so much that we are afraid of it? Why does the sun burn up our food sometimes? Why is it always the best cow that gets sick? Why do babies die?"

"No one knows, maman." His face, taking the unformed features of childhood and forcing them to become sharp with the thought and feeling of maturity, strained toward her. "I don't think anyone knows."

Françoise laughed, moved toward the stable door. "So! That makes me not care so much I don't read. All that big library at Beau Chêne—and every book nothing but questions with no answers."

They watched her run across the yard and vanish into the house. "Monsieur de Clouet says maman is the most remarkable woman he's ever met," Jumie said. He had a way of making these pronouncements as though he were announcing a discovery that would change their lives. "Papa," he had said to Claude a few months before, "papa, I never thought—I never knew—" Then he had stopped. The sharpness of his mother's eyes was more focused in Jumie. Where Françoise questioned everything with the nervous curiosity of a housewife who knows that what she doesn't see may very well be getting into trouble, Jumie's questions were more deliberate.

"What did you not know?"

Claude remembered the springing enthusiasm that had possessed Jumie then. His disorganized body had suddenly pulled itself together, for one moment the man inside was clear. "I never knew there was more than being the best fisherman, or the best hunter! I never knew—I never knew about *thinking*, you know, papa?"

"Yes," Claude had said, and hugged his son.

Noel de Clouet could well call Françoise Langlinais remarkable. Her visits to Beau Chêne were less frequent after Noel's return, but those she made were no less necessary to the survival of the de Clouet family. Crops, except for the scraggling gardens put in by the women, had not even been planted the year the war ended. The fields were now acres of weeds, their owners exhausted and ill. By working the few Negroes who had stayed at Beau Chêne, by borrowing money from a Philadelphia bank on the sapphires that were the star of the de Clouet women's jewelry to hire other hands, and by finding that he was not yet as exhausted as he was going to be, Noel had managed to clear enough acreage to put in a sugar crop in the spring of 1866. That crop burned in the fields during the summer drought; the little that was left froze in the fields that fall—without a practiced overseer, random hands couldn't work. Wouldn't. Didn't.

Now Noel had promoted Tatum, one of the old Beau Chêne hands, to the overseer's place. At least Tatum remembered how the fields had once been, what they had done to get them that way. Tatum moved into the overseer's house nearest the kitchen yard; Tatum met with Noel every morning in the plantation office to plan the day's work. The morning Caroline came in with a pitcher of lemonade, poured two glasses and handed one to Tatum, Noel remembered the king his forebears had served. "Après moi, le déluge."

"Why wasn't I aware of rain and drought and pests and marauding animals before?" Noel said to Caroline. They were sitting across from each other in the office, the large walnut desk between them. Though Caroline didn't know it, Aimée de la Houssaye de Clouet had sat, morning after morning, in that same chair, pulled to just that angle, across from another Noel, also making entries in the plantation ledgers. But while the air between that earlier pair had been tense with electric passion, there was a thick, dull wall between Noel and Caroline.

"You didn't run the plantation long between your father's death and the war—did you ever run it? Lesage did most of it, didn't he?"

"God, when he was overseer, I wouldn't have given a half dollar for him. Now—" He thrust himself out of his chair and went to the window. "I think there will be a crevasse. Somewhere." A short laugh, announcing his own faithlessness to his peers. "Let's pray that it happens someplace else. If this crop is ruined . . . what a hellacious way to earn a living."

Caroline said nothing. She was tired of Noel's complaints, tired of his continual surprise that the war had wiped out a way of life, that they were like refugees in their own land, that the frustration of plantation owners who could not coax that river of white gold to start up again was the fastest-growing crop in the parish. "It's time for the children's lessons." She rose, closed the ledger. As she went through the door, his voice came from behind her.

"Caroline—Caroline, I'm sorry."

Still turned from him, she spoke. "For what?"

Carefully, he approached her, put his arms around her determined back. "For all that's happened—your hard work—the sacrifice . . ."

He felt the anger in the swiftness of her turn to him. Leaning back against his arms, she stared up at him, her eyes going over his face as though searching for some familiar sign. "Oh, Noel, Noel. Will you remember that the war destroyed *every-thing*? Not just Beau Chêne. Not just your precious way of life. *Everything*. No one is living any better. Do you apologize, Noel, for war?" Her head shook from side to side, negating her disbelief. "Do you really think I am so stupid as to think you had anything to do with bringing this ruin down on us?"

"Langlinais does." He let her go, stepped back to watch her. "He told me that men like me, who owned slaves, were the cause of all of this. It was plain he sees himself as a victim, paying the price for other men's folly."

"At least," Caroline said, "he is still willing to pay it. For others, too."

After Caroline was gone, Noel stood looking out at the rain for a long, long time. Whatever his upbringing had prepared him for, it was not this. Tatum knew far more about how to run the plantation than he did, and what's more, Noel was happy to let him do it. His thoughts traveled over the winter water-laden bayous to New Orleans. The city was still occupied, had been since Farragut's victory in 1862. But the Yankees would not stay there forever. Nor would they always rule the state. De Clouets had long had a hand in Louisiana's business, but if he rotted here at Beau Chêne along with the crops, another tradition would die. He would go to New Orleans, perhaps even live there part of the time. Waiting for nature to help recoup their fortune was futile. It was far better to wrest what he wanted wherever it could be found. Returning to the desk, Noel sat down and wrote a long letter to Étienne de Gravelle, who, he was very sure, was as much a part of the underside of New Orleans political life as his father and grandfather before him.

\*    \*    \*

The Ides of March lived up to their solemn portent that spring of 1867. Though the news of them took its own time to travel to St. Martinville, two acts of the Thirty-ninth Congress, both passed that disastrous month, ended activities in the former Confederate States which were, according to the Union victors, indicative of total unrepentance and continued rebellion. Northern papers, incensed by the Black Codes, the increasing Southern resistance to Negro political equility, editorialized the increasingly general sentiment that two years after losing the war, an unpenitent South was winning the peace. The Reconstruction Acts of 1867 ended any such illusion.

An event that same month of more immediate impact began on March 27, when the long-expected, much discussed crevasse finally broke. Weary from the effort to hold back the torrent of water pouring from the entire midcontinent down the deep-dredging Mississippi, the west-bank levee in Pointe Coupée Parish gave way along a half-mile length. That opening was like blasting a tunnel through a damn—the descending rush of river found it far easier simply to spread through this new outlet, submerging all in its capricious detour, than to keep itself bound in the levee-tight channel. The land between Bayou La Fourche and Bayou Teche became one stretch of roiling, boiling, murderous flood.

"New Iberia's not got one room to let, one bed to spare," Noel reported. When news of the crevasse had reached them, sped as always by messengers more rapid than the newspapers, he had begun a daily trip into New Iberia, fifteen miles away. The steamboat *Teche* had but one route now—over to flooded areas to the east and back to New Iberia, still safe above the rising waters of the bayou. "There must be thousands of people crowded in and around the town," he said.

"But will they be safe? The waters haven't stopped rising yet," Caroline had gone through the small store of linen, medicine, food, at Beau Chêne and sent what she could by Noel to the people who were now, incredibly, even worse off than they had been at the end of the war. She had suggested taking some flood victims in, a suggestion Noel had ignored. "There's no telling how long it will be before these people can go back to their homes," he'd said. "We can scarcely feed ourselves, how can we feed others?"

"Safe? Who or what is safe? So far, the fields on this side of the bayou are still all right. But if New Iberia is flooded—

our sugar is ruined again. You will pardon me, I hope, if my first concern is for my own family."

"I hate this." Caroline, it had seemed to Noel in the almost two years since the war, had given up any negative or angry feeling. She looked upon her past life as something never to occur again; she told Noel, on more than one occasion, that it gave her much happiness to be able to read his journal, look at his sketches, of their former life. "It helps me remember it as it was. It helps me remember that I had more happiness, more luxury, more pleasure, in those years than many people have in all their lives. Or in several lifetimes." But the strength of passion in her voice was the same strength Noel heard in the voices of men who resented every element of their present lives, every affirmation of Negro equality, every proof that they owed their own survival to the whim of the victorious government.

"What do you hate?"

"Having necessity get in the way of what I would like to do. Knowing that the sacrifices we have made to get that crop in, the jewelry borrowed against, the burden of worry we carry always, can be wiped out, made nothing, by one or two feet more of water—water that is dumped on us by the same Yankee states that have already brought us to our knees. And now seem intent on keeping us there."

How astonishing that in the instant she spoke feelings he himself had, he wanted to change her mind. "Don't talk that way, Caroline. It won't be the end of Beau Chêne, flood or no flood. There's more than one way to regain a fortune." It was the first time he had even hinted to her that he had been thinking of what some of those other ways might be.

She came and sat beside him on the horsehair sofa in the upstairs drawing room. "What are you talking about, Noel?"

"I'm going to emulate some of our more impetuous citizens. I am not going to wait for Fate to find me and bless me. I am going to search her out, force her to give back to the de Clouets what she has so wantonly and unjustly taken."

"Oh, Noel, don't talk foolishness. What, are you going to become a bandit? A thief?"

"Perhaps, after all, that is what I am going to do. I am going to become a politician."

"To what purpose? Noel, I don't understand you, I . . ."

Ceremoniously, he went to the cabinet upon which stood a

decanter of brandy. He poured out two small glasses, handed one to his wife. "To what purpose? Why, to the same noble purpose that all men in politics strive—the lining of their own pockets so that the public may be served by men of wealth and position."

"Noel—"

"Don't you be a fool, Caroline. Do you not know that this state is being robbed blind? Are you going to say to me there is anything wrong in my not getting back what I can? From whom will I be stealing, if the kind of graft we are becoming familiar with can be called stealing? Our friends? They've nothing left. Our victims? Where are they? Damn it, Caroline, this is no time for debate about what is right. I'm going to make us safe first, make Beau Chêne safe—then maybe I can sit around and talk about truth, justice, all that." Something tugged at him, a memory of someone else saying those words. Claude? Yes. In that moment, Noel felt a small chill wind of change, a wind he turned his back on and ignored.

"Can you do it?" There was no feeling at all in her voice now. Only the force of her flat question. Don't tell me something if you can't make it happen.

"I believe so."

"And get an education for Nollie? Some kind of life for Marthe?"

"That is part of it, surely."

She looked at him for so long a time that Noel began to feel as though he were being stared at by a stranger. "Am I being measured?" he said finally. And when she said nothing— "As to whether or not I am up to the challenge?"

"Oh, you're up to it. De Clouets have always been up to whatever challenge they face. That's hardly the problem. The problem, Noel, is in getting them to choose to face it."

Toward the end of April, Noel returned from the by now twice-weekly trip into New Iberia to report that one flood had crested less than twenty-four inches from the top of the west bank of Bayou Teche. And that a crevasse carefully arranged by the Congress of the United States had undammed a new kind of flood: the First Reconstruction Act, made law on March 2, had been the explosive powder, the Second Reconstruction Act, made law on March 23, had been the lighted fuse. "And we, Caroline, are left with only the most primitive methods of stopping what is about to happen. I can't wait, I'll have to prepare to go to New Orleans immediately, stay certainly through the summer, perhaps later."

In late July, dread news came to New Iberia in the form of a man traveling through who became ill and died within a day— of yellow fever. The town's four physicians treated fifty cases within the next two weeks; by mid-August, no one went into New Iberia at all. Even the steamboats docked a mile downstream at Mintmère Plantation, daring come no closer to the dying town. And by late August, the scourge had found its way along the Teche to Franklin, to St. Martinville. The Langlinaises stayed close to home, the men and boys taking to the fields early and remaining late, Françoise and her daughters staying indoors. When the priest announced that people were excused from attending Mass on Sunday until the epidemic was over, all meetings ceased, except when people gathered to bury the dead.

At these sad occasions, the only comfort to be had was in the tales of the courage and compassion of the doctors who defied death over and over again to tend yet another victim, hold yet another dying patient's hand. In particular, Dr. Robert Hilliard's name was spoken in tones of reverence normally accorded to canonized saints. "But the man is a saint," Brother Langlinais pronounced, when the story was repeated of Hilliard going without rest for nearly three days during one period when fresh cases were reported faster than the dead could be buried.

With the arrival of September, fewer people took ill. Barred from much direct contact, inhabitants of the plagued region still found ways to communicate; the good news was that both the death toll and the number of new cases were falling. When word came that Dr. Robert Hilliard had finally been attacked by the pest he had fought so bravely, and had died, Brother Langlinais listened to no one. "I will go to his funeral," he said to Claude. "There are things one does."

"Papa, I understand your feeling. But we have been spared so far—it looks as though the epidemic may be almost over. For you to go where it has been the worst—at your age—" At the glare in his father's eyes, Claude stopped. But Françoise was less easily vanquished. She invoked, not only the health of her father-in-law, but that of the children. "Do you want to bring that to your grandchildren? Do you want to put them in that kind of danger?"

"They can stay away from me when I get back," Brother said. "And if I am as old and feeble as you believe, then how much life do I have left?" It was not until he and Claude were harnessing the team that would pull the wagon that he said more. "I have been lonely for a long, long time, Claude. Thirty-seven years since your mother died—not so long to you, you have been busy growing up, marrying, having your family. But me—if by going to bid an old friend good-bye I find my own way home—is that so bad?"

Claude tightened the harness, tested the balance between the two horses. "Why didn't you marry again, papa? You wouldn't have been so alone, you would have had other children—"

His father climbed onto the wagon seat, took up the reins, spoke softly to the team. Then he looked down at his son. "But I had known your mother. There are some women, Claude, who make a man forget everyone else. I haven't needed anyone, Julie has stayed with me." In the early light of morning, Claude saw a glisten of brightness over his father's eyes. "But lately, lately I find I don't remember as well. I need to see her, Claude. I need to see her."

Claude "Brother" Langlinais' death was the last recorded death from yellow fever that year. On All Saints' Day, after visiting his father's grave, Claude took Jumie with him to lay flowers also on the tomb of Dr. Hilliard. "It's what he would have done," he told Françoise, who for once agreed that duty also included those not immediately part of the family. He and Jumie put the wreath Claudette and her sisters had woven on the doctor's tombstone. Leaning over, Jumie read the words carved there. "'He lived without fear and without reproach and fell at his post in the full tide of his usefulness.' Papa, Doctor Hilliard must have been a very great man."

Turning his son to him, Claude studied the face that was so like the grandfather just lost. "What we must work for, son, is a world in which men like Doctor Hilliard and your grandfather are not thought of as very great men, but simply as men."

"You are a great man to me," Jumie said.

"Me? To you, yes, that is good. But the world, I think, looks more to men like Monsieur de Clouet to be what it calls great."

Jumie looked back at the tombstone. "Great like Doctor

Hilliard? But Monsieur de Clouet has no post. I don't understand."

"He has none now. But the epidemic is over, the quarantine long since lifted. He can go to New Orleans now. And there, Jumie, I think he expects to find a post."

Noel de Clouet was already in New Orleans. Held in St. Martinville first by the epidemic and then by the registration of voters required under the Second Reconstruction Act, he had used the time to study well the provisions of the acts, including the Third Reconstruction Act, which had become law in July.

"The first de Clouet to come here at least could leave a land given over to ignorance and violence," he said to Caroline one evening early in October before his departure. Caroline, after her imprisonment, had taken up the Acadian habit of spending as much time as possible on the galleries of her house. "I feel better with much space around me," she said when Noel suggested that the drawing room was more comfortable.

"'Whither thou goest, I will go,'" he said, and had a small smoking table and a cabinet for his brandy installed between their two big rockers. Now he thought that the Acadians knew perhaps more about civilized living than he might have believed. Certainly it was pleasant to sit at his ease in the twilight, feeling the comfort of every stirring of air, able to look down the alley at passersby on the road.

"Are we given over to ignorance and violence?" She was sewing, she seemed always to be busy with her hands these days; she had told him just a few days before that she thought she would like a loom such as the one Françoise Langlinais had. "They're working on Claudette's trousseau—imagine, the loom will make ten blankets at once."

"And will your sisters and aunts come and help you set up the warp? Jumie tells me his mother uses between four hundred and six hundred hand-tied loops to get the loom ready for weaving. That's why, he says, they call that whole laborious process L'amour de Maman." Noel liked showing Caroline that he knew as much about the everyday lives of their neighbors as he did about the everyday lives of the Greeks and Romans. "Not that this knowledge is any more useful," he would say, relegating the Acadians and all their ways to a recalcitrant culture which refused to have very much to do with any other opinions, methods, or ideas. It was one area in which they differed so much that they could hardly speak of it; Caroline remembered that she owed her life and the lives of her children to the shrewd boldness of Claude Langlinais; Noel preferred not to think of that at all.

"Certainly. Can a government run by renegades and illiterates produce anything but ignorance and violence? Surely you've studied these acts, you know what our beneficient Congress has ordered."

"I've been too busy hoeing," Caroline said. "But if you are somehow going to save us all from this, perhaps you'd better explain it to me."

There it was again, the bitter humor that, like good wine slowly turned to vinegar, seemed the only kind of humor Caroline had left. When he had first come home, Noel had thought there would still be some pleasure in their lives together. Now he knew that she had not only given up all wish for pleasure, she had forgotten what it was.

He ignored her tone, paid attention only to the request. "You know we are part of the Fifth Military District, that the general officer and the military courts are over anything our own state courts might rule—and, of course, you know every grown male who could find his way to registrars and had not been disenfranchised because of rebellious activity has now been made a voter—that, my dear, is where the ignorance comes in!"

"I don't understand how you could register and my cousin Henri could not. You were an officer."

"But my commission was from General Beauregard, Caroline. From the Confederacy. Not from the Union army. Had your cousin not so gallantly resigned his captaincy in one army to receive colonel's rank in the opposing one, he, too, could join the illustrious ranks of the newly franchised."

"Noel, how are you going to stand it?"

"What?"

"What's ahead of you. My father doesn't even like to think about what's going on, he detests General Sheridan, some of his best friends were among the aldermen he replaced in New Orleans. He told me there were almost twice as many Negroes registered to vote as whites. Now, Noel, how can you work against that?"

"Not twice as many. About seventy-eight thousand to forty-eight thousand. Damn it, Caroline, what else is there to work with? There's no time to wait for things to get better. Either men like me join together to make them better—or we live in darkness forever."

"And this will happen in New Orleans?"

"It will begin there."

For many observers, what happened in New Orleans at the constitutional convention that opened in late November of 1867 was hardly a beginning, and almost certainly an end. Though the delegates there might try to forget it, serious wounds, inflicted in the summer of 1866, would fester, turn gangrenous, and eventually poison the Louisiana body politic for decades to come. In that second summer of Reconstruction, an attempt was made to reconvene the constitutional convention of 1864. The Democrats, largely ex-Confederates, accustomed to social and political standing, wanted the old order back. The Republicans, reacting to Black Codes the Democratic-controlled legislature had enacted, were equally determined that victory on the battlefield would be transferred to victory in the legislature, in the courthouse, at the polling place. As in any situation where opposing views become causes, causes become fanatically held dogmas, the parties polarized, and certain members became extreme. The Bourbon Democrats would be satisfied with nothing less than disenfranchisement of the Negro, while the Radical Republicans would be satisfied with nothing less than Negro rule. Between these extremes, moderates of both parties groped toward compromise.

But in the streets of New Orleans, that summer of 1866, riots broke out with the quick and senseless violence of the summer heat storms. Thirty-eight died, 146 were wounded. The Democrats, blaming such excesses on the Radicals and Negroes, threw themselves into the fray, more determined than ever to take back their state; Noel de Clouet and Étienne de Gravelle were among them. And in the chaos of those times, few noticed that Reconstruction in Louisiana had been taken out of President Andrew Johnson's steadier hands, and given over to the Radical Republicans, who would ride the state hard toward ten years of hell.

In late November during the constitutional convention, emotions reached the boiling point. The constitution they had convened to ratify would give the Negro the vote and eliminate segregation. Until Louisiana adopted such a constitution, it could not be readmitted to the Union. The press on both sides raged; those who had hoped the Confederate states would be restored to full membership in the Union without punitive measures humiliating them before they could be raised to equality saw the convention as a victory for the Radical Republicans. It was called a base conspiracy against human nature; papers sympathetic to the Democrats wrote that arson, rape, murder, rebellion, and civil war surely lay ahead, with the Negroes openly against the whites, and openly supported by the Northerners flooding into the state. "And I agree," Noel said, slapping the issue of *DeBow's Review* he had been reading. "What goes on down there is enough to make any civilized man who respects the workings of democratic government completely disillusioned."

"What, did you pack your illusions along with fresh linen, de Clouet?" Étienne de Gravelle had survived when New Orleans was so brutally occupied by the Federal troops of General Banks and General Butler; he could outlast Sheridan as well. As necessary as it was to work with any man willing to help hold the line against the increasing strength of the Republicans, he hoped Noel would prove more of an asset than it presently appeared.

"We're left with no party, de Gravelle. Nor will there be any hope of our having one again if this convention achieves its purposes."

Étienne poured another glass of wine, sipped. "Can you doubt that it will achieve its purpose? We will never have statehood if it does not."

"It's a mockery, de Gravelle, doesn't that bother you? The contents of the new constitution have already been ordered and each infamous section will make it even more certain that you and I, de Gravelle, will live in poverty and shame the rest of our days."

"I have no intention of doing either, Noel," Étienne said. "Nor have you. You are like all planters, you think all that is necessary is that a little seed be put into the earth and then God will make the crop grow." He rose, stood over Noel. "Politics is not like planting, de Clouet. Yes, we plow. Yes, we plant. But we stay in the field, we watch, we learn who has power, and why he has it. When the time comes—and believe me,

Noel, it always does—when the time comes—then the harvest."

"In the meantime, we have a constitution that must be approved by a Yankee Congress. In the meantime, we have been forced to ratify the Fourteenth Amendment."

"In the meantime, we regain our statehood. And then, my dear de Clouet—whose impatience seems peculiarly inappropriate to one who must wait an entire summer for his crop to bloom—then we change the rules." He began making orderly stacks of the papers in front of him. "We've worked long enough. A lady I know is preparing a little supper. I believe she has a friend visiting her who will also be present. You will join us?"

Noel thought of Caroline's thin body, which was neither less thin nor more passionate than it had been on his return. "Why not?" he said. It struck him then that Caroline had never asked, during the time he had been back, if he had lain with another woman while he was gone. Because she trusted him? Maybe. More likely, because she didn't care.

Walking through the quiet streets, Noel drew a deep breath. "We can give the Yankees credit for one thing," he said. "At least this city is clean."

Étienne shrugged. "With an army of soldiers to force the work done, certainly it's clean."

"Surely this is an improvement. I can remember walking these streets with a handkerchief held to my face because of the stench. Now it is almost pleasant."

"Even Yankees have virtues," de Gravelle said, pausing at a wooden gate. His hand on the bell, he turned to Noel and laughed. "Cleanliness is one of them, chastity another. Though that second virtue is perhaps not of choice. The ladies of New Orleans have not exactly welcomed our northern brothers."

Marietta and Louisette Ducharme were sisters; they were charming, beautifully dressed in gowns whose necklines were cut away until almost the entire breast was revealed. When Louisette, in the midst of a tale of how she had treated a Yankee major who had dared bow to her on the street, saw Noel's eyes fixed on that line of lace, she tapped his wrist with slender fingers. "Monsieur, do you not have appetizers before the entrée? Well, these stories I tell you are the appetizer—but I assure you, they will be followed by the entrée."

Had de Gravelle not been present, grinning at him, already kissing Marietta's hands, hurrying them all through the court-bouillon, then yawning and saying he was fatigued and must lie down, Noel would have left. When Étienne and Marietta disappeared down the hall, and he heard a door close firmly behind them, he almost did go. It had been a long, long time since he had had to worry about pleasing a woman. Caroline only wanted him to finish, she made that plain. But Louisette— not only would she want more, he wanted to give it to her. "I've been married a long time," he said. "And I was in the war."

"Shh," she said. She snuffed out all but two of the candles, took his hand and led him in turn down the hall. She drew him through an open door, closed it, turned the heavy key in the lock and shot the bolt. Two candles shaded by tall crystal hurricane lamps stood on the mantel. The light they gave pierced the shadows of draperies around the high mahogany bed. "Sit," Louisette said. She pushed him into a low slipper chair, then bent over and removed her shoes. "Watch," she said.

The light had seemed dim, but in the moment he realized she was going to undress for him, the light bloomed and surrounded her. Her hands loosened hooks and ribbons, pulled off the heavy blue dress. Her tightly laced corset pushed her breasts high under the embroidered camisole. Ruffled petticoats cascaded over hips he could almost feel under him. She untied the ribbons of the camisole, drew it over her head. Her breasts were full, round, with a nipple the size of a gold coin tipping each one. He saw her unlace the corset, pull it off, showing the waist that his hands would soon circle. Petticoats fell in a waterfall of softness; she stood naked from the waist up, thin batiste pantaloons covering her long legs. "Why don't you take them off?"

She came close to the chair on which he sat. He reached up, found the band at the top of the garment, began to draw them down over her unresisting hips. Whether it was her breath or his own he heard, her heartbeat or his own he felt, he knew the quickened rhythm of his body was making him hard; by the time the pantaloons touched the floor, he wanted to enter her. "Undo your trousers," she said. And then he felt her come forward on him, lower herself so that she sat astride him. Her hands were guiding him, he felt a thrust, and then he pushed his mouth against her breasts and gave himself up to her.

"Now you can undress," she said. "And we can get into bed. And perhaps go more slowly."

"You see," de Gravelle told him over breakfast, "the Radicals have not managed to ruin everything."

# CHAPTER 16

## *Oasis*

Françoise stood in the center of a cluster of women, blinking against the strong sun. Claudette's banns of marriage to Gaston Thibodeaux had been read for the first time at Mass that morning; as the bride's mother, Françoise took the women's felicitations, eager questions, as her due. She saw Caroline making her way toward the step where Françoise stood. She's almost gotten the dirt out from between her toes, Françoise thought. To think just six years ago Caroline had been grateful for the least little offering—a skinny hen, a half bushel of potatoes, a few eggs. Now the de Clouets were well on their way to being rich again—Claude didn't seem to care one way or another, but every time Françoise thought of how weak Caroline had been, how helpless, her hard anger burned. And look at her now! Fine clothes, fine skin—and that daughter of hers being trained for a New Orleans debut. She turned to a woman beside her, began to speak rapidly of Gaston's farm, his good stand of lumber.

"Françoise! Françoise!" Caroline, behind her, calling. The woman with Françoise put her hand up. "Françoise—Madame de Clouet—she wants you."

In the moment of Françoise's turning, Caroline saw something in those dark eyes that slowed her tongue, made her step back. "Françoise! It's so wonderful about Claudette! I'd not heard, I was so surprised—happy for her." The small group of women were still, attentive. Caroline felt their interest; it was not, she thought, shared by Françoise. "I wanted to offer— I'd like to let Claudette wear—oh, Françoise, I want her to use the veil Noel's grandmother wore when she was married. Aimée's veil, you remember, I showed it to you—"

The dark eyes were cold now, winter lakes under ice. "It's

too grand, Caroline. Claudette would not look well in it."

"But, Françoise—what can be too grand for a bride?"

"Claudette marries a farmer, Caroline. A farmer with good land, yes. But still, a farmer. And farmers' wives don't wear finery they have to borrow." Françoise's smile was only on her lips. "Besides—it's not comme il faut to dress above yourself, is it?"

Another woman interrupted. "Françoise—the wedding, when will it be?" Caroline moved back. She had heard the quick shocked rush of breath at Françoise's words. She hadn't imagined the rudeness, then, the intended slight. As she walked away, she heard Françoise behind her. "In October. After harvest. When else?" Of course, Caroline thought. Of course. Just after harvest. And just before the elections, when Claude would run for justice of the peace and Noel would stand for parish judge. With all Claude's friends and relatives gathering for Claudette's wedding, the papa-candidate could accept congratulations and solicit votes at the same time. And wine and dine prospective voters as well! These people! How easily their lives seemed to work. With no daughter's wedding feast to aid him, Noel would have to go through the course laid out by custom and by dictate of the Constitution. If there were any major fault with democracy, she decided, it was that it took such a lot of time.

Françoise stood at the back door, watching Claudette pick her way through the kitchen garden. She had been hoeing the plot of brown cotton she and her mother planted each year to have the colored thread so needed for their weaving; her sunbonnet had fallen back on her neck, and her work-quickened blood ran close under the heated surface of her skin, bringing a rosy flush to cheeks that still held the curving sweetness of childhood. She's such a baby still, Françoise thought. And yet, she was nineteen, she should have been long since married. "Claudette! Listen, we need to start on your dress. There's that lace from your great-grandmother Cecile—we can trim the bodice with that. Then we can take..."

When Claude and Jumie came in at dusk, the wedding gown had long since been designed. They were now planning the food with Françoise mentally setting aside a certain number of chickens for the gumbo, the yield from a certain row of beans, a certain number of okra plants. "Claude, you will have butchered? By the wedding?"

He looked at his eldest son. It was good to have a son who was almost a man, who could share one's wonderment at how the good Lord could have created so orderly and understandable a universe and then somehow still created woman. "Well, what? You want me to say yes or you want me to say no?"

"Claude! I want you to say which—you will or you won't?"

"We need some meat for the jambalaya," Claudette said. "For the fête."

"We will have butchered," Claude said.

"Jamais de la vie," Françoise said. "I don't see how we're going to make it, me." She lifted one strong hand before them, fingers held stiffly apart. She counted on each as she spoke. "First, we have the harvest. Then, we have the boucherie. Then, we have the wedding. Then, we have the election." Her thumb stood uncounted. Françoise looked at it, observed it. "And, that thumb, it tells me there will be something else! All I have to say is, we better work even when we think there's nothing to do."

"Let's walk down by the bayou," Claudette said to Jumie after supper. Her sisters, Francie and Mathilde, were sitting with their parents on the gallery, embroidery for their own trousseaux in their hands. Jean had slipped off to visit his friend Pierre Labat down the road.

"I think the wedding makes maman happy," Claudette said. They sat on the bench their great-great-grandfather had hewn from swamp cypress, put together so that the swelling of the pieces at the joint held it as strongly as any pegs. "She wanted so much for me. I'm not sure she thinks marrying Gaston Thibodeaux is the way to have it."

"Gaston is a good man. A good farmer." When Claudette said nothing, Jumie, too, went silent. The moon seemed to be pasted to the backdrop of heavy clouds that pressed themselves against the darkening sky. If it rose any higher, it would rise because the cloud it was stuck to rose, drifting into the lighter air above until both cloud and moon were out of sight. Jumie slapped at a hungry mosquito. "Claudette, you do want to marry Gaston?"

"Of course. If maman had never . . . had never talked about anything else . . ."

"I know." Again the silence, a silence that, because of the dual years between them, spoke. "Look at me. Ever since I was a little boy, and learned to read, and began to borrow Monsieur de Clouet's books, and to study, she thought I would go off to school somewhere. I used to think I would, too."

"If you had gone, Jumie—what would you have done, do you think?"

"I don't know. I never thought about doing anything. Just being at a college. With more books even than the de Clouets have. And more people to talk to. I didn't go past that."

"You can still read. And think. And talk."

"To the plow horses? To my friends who like to listen to some of the stories, who are happy I know all that if it makes me happy, but who care nothing for books themselves? Who can I talk to, Claudette?"

"You can talk to me, Jumie." He felt the movement of her arm away from him, saw the shadow of her hand go deep into the pocket of her full skirt. She put a small book into his hand. "I've learned to read, Jumie. Oh, not as well as you. I stumble a lot, and Madame de Clouet has to go over and over some of it—but I've read all of this, and I can talk about it, Jumie, I can."

The cloud holding the moon leaned low enough to let Jumie read the gilt letters curving across the leather cover. *"Lamb's Tales from Shakespeare.* Claudette, you read this?" The familiar rewarding tone in Jumie's voice was all she needed.

"Yes, Jumie, yes. And Madame de Clouet says I can run over to Beau Chêne for more books any time I want!"

Jumie reached over, stroked his sister's heavy curls. "Don't get your head too full of books, Claudette. When you marry Gaston—well, I won't be around to talk to so much."

"I know." She caught at his hand, held it. "Sometimes I wish I didn't have to marry anyone. Not Gaston, not anyone. Just stay with maman and papa and all of you. Why can't I do that, Jumie?"

Jumie put his other hand over hers. "I suppose you could, if you really wanted to, Claudette. But you'll see. You'll like having your own house—your own kitchen!"

Claudette laughed. "Don't think maman won't tell me how to fix it! Oh, I know you're right. It's such a commotion, though—all the goings-on! I just wish it were all over with— I hate having so much attention!"

"It'll be all right, Claudette. You'll see."

The moon shook itself free of the cloud, prepared to soar into its own accustomed place. In the power of its freedom, it lit up the bayou bank, lit up the two figures sitting there. "If it's not—if anything ever isn't all right—will you come help, Jumie?"

Jumie's arm went around Claudette's shoulder, his body formed a protecting bulk. "Help my twin? Claudette, what else am I here for?" He stood and pulled her to her feet. "But, Claudette, listen. Gaston's a good man. There'll never be anything he can't handle."

Marthe de Clouet twisted impatiently. "For heaven's sakes, aren't you *done?*"

The woman kneeling in front of her sat back on her heels, tongue moving expertly around a mouth full of pins. "I never will be done if you can't hold still. How can I pin this hem straight with you wiggling like a monkey in a cage?"

"This dress will look terrible anyway."

Tante Rose picked up a fold of pale green silk, judged the length and stuck a judicious pin. "All thirteen-year-old girls think every gown they have looks terrible. As pretty as you are, Marthe, you will think that until you are about sixteen. Then, you will believe what the beaux tell you. You will think the face in your mirror is the prettiest you ever saw, that every dress you have is beautiful. You will think that because you will be in love."

Marthe stared at the old woman. Tante Rose had been sewing for her for the past two years, ever since papa had begun to have money again. Never had she said anything of the least interest. Marthe had been thoroughly convinced that Tante Rose's world was bound by thread and needles, bolts of cloth, and squares of lace, and that her largest concern was the sharpness of the flashing blades that ruthlessly cut until the design hiding in the fabric emerged. "Who will I be in love with?"

"Who? With no one, with everyone. You will simply be in love. Now mind, Marthe, the thing to pray about is not that you marry, you will do that. After all, you are pretty, your papa is on his way to being rich again. What you are to pray for is that during the time you are always in love, you pledge yourself to someone you will not mind spending your life with."

The hem finished, Tante Rose stretched herself up to fit the

bodice. Her fingers moved over the tucks that filed across
Marthe's bosom. "Humph—so I'd better make these full enough
to let out. You've added almost an inch here since I cut this
gown, do you know that?"

"No." Of course she did. She was too ashamed to confess
to Father Maraist that she sinned by looking at herself naked
in the tall pier glass in her room, but she continued to do it
anyway.

"If you keep on adding, you'll have one of the finest figures
in the Teche. Then you will be pretty and have a rich papa and
a fine figure, too. You will be able to choose a prince."

"Tante Rose, that's silly." Her voice did not quite close the
gate in the fence around her intense privacy.

"No, it isn't. Do you think these boys, these sons of planters
trying to get back on their feet, would not prefer to marry
someone with a little flesh who can also bring a good dowry?"

"You're making that up," she said. "You've never even
married, Tante Rose, how do you know what young men want?"

Tante Rose made a last adjustment, then sat in the low rocker
that stood near the sewing room fireplace. "But I've dressed
many a bride, Marthe. And made dresses to cover their bellies
full with babies. I've been told what these young men want.
Older ones, too. A woman who is a lady in the drawing room
and who is not a lady in the bedroom." The dressmaker's eyes
flashed out with the quickness of her finest German steel needle,
caught Marthe's face on the sharp point. "I tell you this, Marthe,
because I think you are one of those women. If I am right,
then you can, indeed, marry very well. Comprenez-vous?"

Caroline popped her head in the half-open door. "Marthe,
I've just heard from—why, Marthe! You look—so grown up."
She came into the room, circled the silent figure of her daughter.
"Tante Rose, is the dress—too old for Marthe? There's some-
thing—I don't know—"

Tante Rose got up, went to help Marthe out of the dress.
"That something, Madame Caroline, is Marthe's style. And
there is nothing even I can do about that."

"Well—I suppose. Of course, by November, she'll be almost fourteen—oh, that's what I wanted to tell you, Marthe.
The play on opening night will be *Help*. That Maeder thing
Joseph Murphy does so well. The plot's nothing, ridiculous,
really, but he plays so many parts, it shows off his acting quite

well—" The unexpected opulence of her daughter's figure, freed from the lines of green silk, startled her.

"I'm sure I'll enjoy it, maman." Marthe pulled her light gray housedress on, fastened the bow at her waist. "Thank you, Tante Rose, for the dress. And for—such interesting information. I think I shall be quite indebted to you."

"What was that all about?" Caroline wondered that she had ever wanted a wider world for Marthe. The thought of keeping track of her in New Orleans, even for a short visit, seemed difficult enough.

"I was telling her what the ladies are wearing in New Orleans next winter, madame. Now, about that dress for you . . ."

Noel de Clouet and Étienne de Gravelle stood blinking in the clear hot light that beamed up St. Peter Street from the river. "Well, de Clouet, too early for a little wine?"

"Too hot," Noel said. The heavy linen shirt stuck to him unpleasantly, his cravat seemed to strangle his talk-swollen throat.

"Let's walk toward the river. There may be air stirring there. If not, I have a little friend . . ." Then, briskly. "Well, what do you think? Do we have a party?"

"Hardly. We have a ticket," Noel responded.

"Will it win?"

"Warmoth's heading it, isn't he?"

"You speak his name as though it were a particularly unpleasant word, Noel."

"The man's been called everything from a traitor to a thug by his own Republican party. Good Lord, one wing of it read him out of its ranks last year—and what did our own paper say about him? That he'd stabbed public virtue to the heart and trampled it under his feet!"

Étienne ran a thick finger beneath his collar, loosening the damp cloth from his sweating neck. "Oh, well, after all, the editor of the *Bee* gets a little carried away sometimes, Noel. Warmoth's not all that bad."

"I don't agree. I think possibly the second worst thing to happen to this state was the day in 1868 Henry Clay Warmoth became our first postwar governor."

"And the first worst thing?"

Noel heard the amusement in Étienne's voice; stubbornly,

he stared ahead and went on: "The day the first Negro slave set foot here."

"Your family would never have built Beau Chêne without them."

"I've had to rebuilt it without them."

"But then you've been able to hire hands. With the money I make for you."

They had reached the levee, were strolling along its deep grass-covered top. Stray sheep pulled the long blades of toughened grass, their dust-dyed coats thin in the August heat. The river stretched placidly before them; brown, turgid, spreading itself under the sun of late summer with a lethargy that belied the energy it would have come spring.

"You don't think I invest it here? God, no. Never mind, Noel. Those little baubles Caroline was willing to part with to start you up again, the few pieces of plate—they've primed the pump quite well. You'll soon have a river of gold, Noel."

"Honest gold, Étienne?"

Étienne looked away. "What's honest? Does anyone know anymore?"

"I do, I think. I doubt that this bastard ticket we've delivered, this fruit of illicit union, will know it, however."

"Illicit? Do you remember how quickly the Reform party gained strength? From a committee of fifty-one just before Christmas—to over ten thousand supporters by February. If the Democratic party hadn't joined with them..."

"A Democratic party that repudiated Warmoth as soon as he and his friends tried to call themselves Democrats..."

"Noel. Noel. What else could be done to control the man but to run him? He was everywhere! Had his own Liberals going, us going, the Reformers going..."

"Better to have left him to the Liberal Republicans. They fit in neither wing of their party—nor do they fit in this fusion we've made."

"But they're in it, Noel. Along with the Reformers and the old-line Democrats and you and me and anybody else who wants to get back control of our own state."

Noel tossed the end of his cigar toward the river, watched it hang an instant in the still, heavy water near the bank before succumbing to the underwater movement of a current and hesitantly drift to the center of the stream. "Those Enforcement Acts have teeth, Étienne. If any physical threat against voters—

any class of voter, any color voter—is used now as it was in the last election, I think those teeth will be armed. We'll have another war, Étienne."

"Merde! The old one's not over. This state is still occupied, still held by the enemy."

Noel turned his back against the sun so that its blazing spotlight was diffused around his body. "The enemy? The enemy, Étienne? You say that, when we are using one of the most powerful of our enemies—the much revered Warmoth—to help us defeat the Republicans?"

"I'd run the devil himself if that's what it took, Noel. In desperate circumstances, we take allies where we find them."

"Without asking what they stand to gain by allying with us? Or do we hope that we all want the same things? Peace among our neighbors, prosperity for those who—deserve it."

Étienne took Noel's arm and began steering him down the levee. "You've become an awful cynic, de Clouet. What happened to my friend who saw life as he could capture it in pen and ink? I tell you, you were much more amusing then!"

"I agree," Noel said, following Étienne through the gate leading to the house of this latest little friend. "But, then, so was life."

"However," Étienne said, his lips already taking on the shape of pleasure to come, "life is not without its amusing moments now, Noel. If we can blink, you and I, at illicit unions which come from political necessity only, how much more happily can we blink at those we form for more pleasurable necessities."

"I suppose," he answered. But even as he prepared to meet Étienne's friend, who would, inevitably, have a friend, a sister, a cousin, of her own, he felt a sudden jarring, as though he had somehow lost his place. The hot world around him did not seem very real anymore; he knew now what happened in the inner rooms, both those inhabited by politicians and those inhabited by whores. Their activity bore little relationship to the high words of duty, conscience, and honor he had read about in the library at Beau Chêne. Their activity bore less relationship to the ideas he'd had about love between men and women, about chivalry, about chasteness. If he could get rich enough, fast enough, he could go back to Beau Chêne, to that tall quiet library where the only dissension was defined, limited, set forth with reason and ethical appeals. He could take up the sketchbook fallen from his hand when he reached out for a sword.

"Let me offer the first toast," he said when the wine was poured. He gazed into the bed-wise eyes of his companion of the afternoon. "To union," he said.

Étienne's friend paused, frowning. "Why are we drinking to that?" she said. "Are you a Scalawag?"

"That's not the union he means," Étienne said, and winked at the closed door behind him.

"Not a Scalawag—a wag," the woman said, and drained her glass.

The steam slowly rising from the curing moss, imperceptible in the steaming heat that kept the fields from drying but threatened to cook them instead, pushed against Jumie until he threw his pitchfork to the ground and went to the jug of water under an oak tree. He poured water over the handkerchief tied around his neck, mopped his face and throat. Tilting his head back, he let the tepid liquid flow into his mouth, and almost spat it out again as it took with it the taste of dust encrusting his lips.

"You should get Jean to help me with this," he said, picking up the pitchfork and returning to the long row of curing moss that stretched out almost the length of the pasture. "Turning this moss is the worst kind of job, papa. You don't need to be doing it."

"I don't mind it. Besides, your brother's head is never on his work anymore. I'd rather not have to keep reminding him we're drying moss, not making haystacks."

They worked on for perhaps half an hour more, carefully tossing moss up from the bottom of the drying rows, mixing the mass of fiber so that, at the end of the curing period, they would have only the best quality moss and could ship it to New Orleans for sale to upholsterers and mattress makers.

"The girls got a lot of moss from the trees we brought out this spring," Jumie said. "Not as much as we'll gather this winter—but a good bit, all the same." He turned up a last heap, then took off his straw hat and fanned himself. "They'll never work as hard once Claudette's gone. She makes them stick to business. Turn her loose on Jean, papa—then watch him work."

"She's a good girl," his father said. "Gaston's a lucky man." He leaned on his pitchfork, shaded his eyes against the sun.

"I think I'll go back to the house now. Drink a little coffee. You coming?"

"I'll go down to the bayou, maybe fish a little. Or go over to Beau Chêne. Claudette was going there, getting a book she wants."

Claude nodded, moved off. Jumie watched him a minute, then swung down the path that led to the bayou. The walk to Beau Chêne wasn't that long, but still, if he waited, perhaps Claudette would appear. They'd have time to dip into the new book, test out the words still strange to her. But when the stillness of slow summer time passing was unbroken by Claudette's voice calling to him, the sound of her footsteps over the rough grass, he heaved himself up and went to find her. Hadn't he buried himself in that library at Beau Chêne for hours at a time, not knowing if it were winter or summer, past or present, this world or the next!

And indeed, Claudette had been reading in the library for half the afternoon. Coming for one book, she stayed to sample several. Finally, she had settled herself on the floor, and forgotten everything.

The sound of the library door opening roused her; she raised her head to see a large man enter the room. It wasn't Monsieur de Clouet, nor yet anyone she had ever seen here. Perhaps one of those men from New Orleans who sometimes came to Beau Chêne. She'd heard her papa and grandpapa talk about them, some were all right, some they referred to as "canaille." She was embarrassed to be found sprawled on the floor. She pushed herself back into her corner, hoping the man would disappear without noticing her.

For a moment, she thought she was safe. He had found the heavy silver flask on Monsieur de Clouet's desk and was drinking from it, tilting it to his lips with his eyes staring up at the high ceiling. "Fine thing," she heard him mutter. "De Clouet keeps the liquor locked up—but has his own private source, ready to hand." Claudette kept still. He was coarse-sounding and had been drinking. Perhaps he couldn't see. His voice clapped over her head. "And what's this? Another private source? Something else his guests don't have?" She could smell his old sweat as he bent over her and pulled her to her feet. A hand smeared with road-dust caught her chin, turned her face. "Well, well. Waiting for the master, are you? He's not here, didn't you know that? No one is. Here I made a long hot trip out here just to see the high and mighty Noel de Clouet—and not even a nigger around to fix me a glass of water."

Claudette twisted her face against the pressure of his fingers. She remembered Jumie telling them—"Don't waste time yelling for help if no one can hear you. Save your breath to fight." She began tearing at the hands holding her, butting against the large body with her knee. He was much, much stronger than he looked. He looked like a fat pig's bladder, the kind the children played with. But each part of that large fleshy body had strength, she could feel it in his hand that held both of hers in one huge vise. Even her field-hard muscles weakened against that wall of resistant flesh; she knew that she would use every ounce of force she had, and he would still be there, wearing that red mask molded by the heat and colored by liquor.

When his free hand went to the neck of her dress and began to unfasten it, the terror she had fought as she fought him rushed over her. All the small fears and bigger frights of a girl growing up in a land traveled by roaming soldiers, displaced freed slaves, and destitute war victims had waited for this moment. It was the terror finally that defeated her. She went weak with it, destroyed from within by the uncertainty in human goodness that is perhaps the most awful aftermath of war.

Later, when she tried to tell Jumie what had happened, the terrible clarity of her memory silenced her. As though she had been watching in a mirror, she could see him stripping her, see him forcing her down on the floor, forcing her legs apart. The mirror was inside her, inside her head, she would never, never get rid of it.

Finally, trembling, crying against her brother's shoulder, she had said, "He did the worst thing anyone could do to me, Jumie. I can't say any more." And Jumie, who had found Beau Chêne empty, had slipped inside, gone to the library on the chance Claudette was still there, and found his sister huddled under her torn dress, asked nothing else. He had helped her dress, had lifted her in his arms and carried her home to her mother. "Put her to bed," he told Françoise. "Then we'll talk."

With Claude, he went back to Beau Chêne. "But I can't imagine who could have been here," Caroline said. She stood in the open doorway, staring at the two men. "Claude, come in, can't you? Jumie?" She shut the doors behind them. "Noel's in New Orleans still, I went into New Iberia this afternoon, left the children there, as a matter of fact. You say Claudette was here, in the library? And someone frightened her?" Her eyes went over the two faces that made a blank wall against her. "Claude, was it worse than that? Was Claudette—harmed?" She leaned forward, put a hand on Claude's knee. "Claude— after all we've faced together—can't you tell me?" And when he had—"Claude. My God in heaven. Claude." She felt her face grow weak, fought to hold it steady. It is Claudette who weeps, Françoise who weeps. Remember whose burden this is, Caroline.

"You really have no idea who he could have been? A man coming to see Noel? From Baton Rouge?"

"No—no. He's not even here, hasn't been, won't be. Someone to do with those horrible politics, that's all I can think of. Nothing but scum, any of them—" Her eyes went back to Claude's face. "Claude. I have to do something. It was in my house—she should have been safe here."

"No one's safe anymore, Caroline. We were safer in the war. At least the soldiers were disciplined. The rabble running us now? They don't know what rules mean." His voice was dead, he who had laughed and whistled and sung them all through imprisonment and then the hard years afterward.

"What will happen, Claude?" She thought of the wedding gown Françoise was working on. It hung on a frame in the window, you could see its white form from the road.

"To Claudette? We don't know. It's too soon." They rose to go, hats clutched in their fists. As Claude followed Jumie out, he turned to her. "Caroline? Not a word, you hear? To no one. Except Noel. But only to ask him who might have been coming today. Other than that—not a word."

"I promise. But, Claude, let me send something, let me help—"

His warm hand covered hers. "That's nice, Caroline. But you know Françoise. She's not much on taking."

The thick reddened hand of the priest half hid his face; in fact, from the instant it became clear that what Claude had to say would be difficult for them both, they had assumed almost the posture of the confessional, with Claude's face turned away, his voice low and regular. Almost, he expected to hear the familiar number of Paters and Aves to be said on his knees before the Lady altar. Father Chasse moved his hand, met

Claude's eyes with the full pain of an old friend who shared what Claude felt. "The Carmelite sisters have opened a convent in New Iberia, Claude. They've been in New Orleans, Lafayette. Now they are very near us. I will go speak with the mother superior."

"A convent? Claudette will become a sister?"

Chasse smiled; the small curving of his lips only softened the pain in his face. "As I said, I will speak to the mother superior. Claudette may be taken as a novice—after the testing period, if she has a vocation—"

"A vocation to be a nun? But, father, she is to be married..." His voice stopped. Was to have been married. They had said nothing as yet to Gaston, his family. Claudette was still in bed, recovering, they said, from a summer fever. She had made the decision herself, had said she would not marry Gaston, that they were never to speak of that again. And though she looked rested now, eyes no longer blurred with terror, though she spoke quietly and gently, Claude knew his daughter had died; inside where it mattered, she had died.

"Claude. Claude. Do you not know that sometimes a vocation is not only a gift we make to God—but one He sends to us when another way is closed? Pray that He sends this to your child."

Now Claude's face buried itself deeply in those hands that had been hard to any chore, any task, of his life. He could not wrest memories from Claudette's mind, nor put peace there. The safety he had trapped for his family in the swamp, shot from the sky, planted in the fields—none of that was proof against ugliness and fear. "We will pray that she is accepted." He did pray, then. The kind of prayer he thought Françoise prayed most of the time, not the Church's prescribed words, but her own; not the words said by an angel to a Virgin, or given by a young Christ to his followers, but his own ripped words of fear. He knew that Father Chasse was praying, too, and in the silence, felt that the power of their prayers was stronger than their pain, and could lift them above it.

Two weeks later, Claude hitched the team to the caleche, and helped Françoise to her place. Whatever Françoise had said in private—to herself and to her God—to the world she said nothing. She had listened to Claude's report of his conversation with Father Chasse, had repeated it to Claudette—and waited.

When word came that the mother superior of the Carmelite convent was willing to allow Claudette to begin a novitiate, Françoise had listened also to Claude's suggestion to visit the convent, had agreed—and said nothing.

"Would you rather eat a meal at Serret's or at the Two Lions," Claude said as he started the horses toward New Iberia. "Serret's is pleasant because of the bayou, but then, the Two Lions has the patio—maybe you like that better?"

"Claude—" That was all. But the eyes she turned on him were tumbling out messages faster than his own could receive them. Large, dark, intent eyes signaling—how can we eat in a hotel when our daughter is in pain? How can we think of whether the bayou prospect from our table or a Spanish patio is more pleasing when Claudette and Gaston's life is over? The interview with Gaston and his family had been short; its length was no measure of its pain. Claudette had long felt she had a vocation for the Church, but had doubted the truth of her call. She was now certain, she could be the bride of no one but Christ. Françoise's fullest comment had been made after Gaston and his parents had left: "What terrible pain he has to bear. He cannot even hate his rival."

Claude's hand left the reins, covered hers. "Françoise, life goes on. You know that. We do what we can—we take what comes." He risked a smile. "Today comes a good meal, yes!" Then, whistling the team into a trot, "Besides, today we have a little something to celebrate."

"Today?"

"The lumbering has been going well, Françoise. Broussard's sawmill is producing almost fifty thousand feet of lumber every day." Françoise's shoulders lifted, measured the depth of her interest in Monsieur Broussard's business. "And, Françoise, things need to be made from that lumber, you understand?"

"Things? Claude Langlinais, what are you telling me?"

"I've put some money into a new factory over there. It's a sash and blind factory now, but we plan to make mantels, doors, cisterns, gallery rails—anything people need for their houses."

The reins were pulled from his hands, the horses jerked to a stop. He felt her arms close around him, felt her head collapse against his chest. The silence of weeks was broken, the held-in tears flowing over her taut face, making her grief plastic, flexible, bearable. "Oh, Claude. Oh, Claude." He sat holding her, while the older horse of the team turned his head and stared. The small dust of the empty road drifted into the late summer air indolently, curiously, testing its heat. Soon autumn would come, would settle the dust with her rains, would settle their own disorder with her brisk dawns, her clear noons. Claudette would enter the convent, Françoise would turn her energy away from sorrow and back to preserving, salting, weaving, mending. Francie and Mathilde and Jean would learn their lessons, do their chores. Jumie would stand between the world of his brother and sisters and that of his parents, deciding what to take with him, what to leave behind. And he, Claude Langlinais, would be able to sit by the fire when the harvest was in, the butchering done, and know that while he took his ease, even for a short time, other men were working for him, and making him money.

The visit to the convent brought Françoise back to life. The mother superior conducted the tour herself; they saw the room in which the sisters took their recreation, the refectory, the big kitchen that smelled of drying peppers and cinnamon. They drank coffee in the parlor from fragile porcelain cups, knelt in the dim chapel before the altar of Our Lady of Mount Carmel, walked in the enclosed garden. And at the end, just before they left, the mother superior took both of Françoise's hands in her fine slender ones. "My daughter, trust God. If one path is closed to your beloved child, will that not make the path to a deep love of Him more open? And do we not all have to reach that deep love before we join Him?" Then, with a kiss on Françoise's cheeks—"Besides, your sons are blessed to have a sister in the convent praying for them!"

Settled at a table at the Two Lions, spooning up courtbouillon that she critically pronounced not quite as good as hers, but still, very tasty, Françoise recounted to Claude all she had learned from the ladies in the hotel parlor while she waited for him to conclude his business with his new partners. "Claude, listen, while you men try to get these Yankees to go home and let us live our own way, things are going on, yes. A very nice lady who is staying here in the hotel while her husband sees about his business was telling me—Claude, there's a ballroom here, a nice place, you understand, where the young people come on Saturday and Sunday and have a nice time. Well, young, by young I mean people whose feet are young, you understand. But, Claude, we have two daughters, yes? And this Mrs. Boutte, I am given to understand she is very kind, very cheerful—a place for girls to enjoy life a little, isn't that so?" A sip of the courtbouillon, a light frown. "It needs some lemon peel, that's what it needs. But, Claude, this Mrs. Boutte, they call her Gugueche, don't ask me why, she has gumbo at this place, refreshments—it's a nice place, Claude."

Claude's own courtbouillon needed nothing. To have Françoise again making plans, looking forward—he laughed. "So I spend a little of the money I earn here where I earn it. So we bring the children in, Françoise. I don't know about you, but my feet, they're young."

"And, Claude, something else. Your grandfather, he had horses, yes?"

"Horses! Françoise, what you think? We all have horses."

"Claude, no. I mean race horses."

"Sure."

"Well, Claude, the track here—it's running again. Not just for the big horses, either, those horses whose papas' names are longer than their tails. No, farmers, everyone, they bring in their horses from the fields, they match them up. Claude, that could be nice, yes?"

"Françoise, your feet are young, too. And your heart." As the waitress took away their bowls and whisked crumbs of French bread from the heavy white cloth, he lifted her hand to his lips. "If dancing at Mrs. Boutte's and running my plow horse around a track is what you want—Françoise, let me tell you, they will see us here so much they will think we're moving in like the carpetbaggers."

The fair glow of late afternoon spread across the gallery at Beau Chêne. Caroline, rocking slowly, almost asleep, heard light steps behind her. "Caroline!" Her eyes flew open, she bounced to a straight position. Wouldn't Françoise catch her napping!

"Françoise, but how nice, it's been so long since you've come . . ." She stopped. "We'll have tea. You have time?"

"A little. I came to tell you. Claudette and Gaston—they're not marrying." Does she know I know? Françoise's face was smooth, closed. "Instead—Claudette enters the Mount Carmel convent in New Iberia on October first—the month of the Rosary. I believe she will take that name, when she is professed, it is one she is thinking of—Sister Mary of the Rosary."

"I—I shall be glad to think we have Claudette praying for us, Françoise."

Françoise's head came up. "And, of course, not all our work is wasted. The work for her marriage, I mean. A nun has a trousseau, too. She needs linens, petticoats. So we removed the lace, took out the tucks. The embroidered camisoles—well, we save them for her little sisters, isn't that right?"

"Françoise—you won't want me to say it. I will anyway. You are the most courageous woman I've ever known in my entire life."

Françoise looked away from Caroline. The tea Caroline had rung for arrived, the servant had placed the tray on the table between them and left. Without asking, Caroline put sugar and cream into one of the Sèvres teacups, poured in the richly steeped tea. She placed a thin silver spoon on the saucer, handed it to Françoise. Françoise settled herself against the smooth hardness of the rocking chair. The tea seeped into her with its warmth and strength—courageous? Maybe so. But courage was a tiring virtue, yes!

When Françoise had gone, Caroline hitched her rocker out of the path the sun had carved through the shadows the oak cast on the gallery. For a long time, she sat quietly, hands idle in her lap. Noel had, in his words, "searched heaven and hell to find who that monster was." He'd turned up nothing. The night he came back from seeing Claude was worse, far worse, than any night that first terrible year after the war. "My neighbor's daughter was ruined in my house," he said. "In my house. My God, Caroline. The house he kept safe for me." There was nothing to say. Increasingly, there was nothing to say about any of it. Crooks in the statehouse? A thug in the governor's chair? Rabble swarming over the comatose body of the state, raping what was left of her virtue, stealing what was left of her resources? Her body slumped against the high back of the rocker. Not quite a hundred years late, the mob had caught up with the de Clouets.

A movement at the end of the alley of oaks rippled through the air toward her, caught at her stillness, jerked her into life. Rising, she went to the gallery railing. "Marthe! Marthe, come here." Her hand went to the note in her skirt pocket. Heavy, cream-colored, an engraved crest rising under the tip of her thumb, it had arrived that morning from Natalie de Gravelle. There was no fleeing this time, no boat waiting. No new land to begin all over again. This time, the de Clouets would hold fast. If she had to put up with disorder and chaos—she might as well get out of it what she could. "I've heard from Madame de Gravelle. Come quick, Marthe! Oh, what a visit she has planned!"

As Caroline excitedly told her daughter of the de Gravelles' invitation, Marthe began to feel, at last, that life had begun. She thought of the gowns hanging in various degrees of completion in the tall armoire in the sewing room. She thought of the sets of jewels her mother had brought out, holding this gold chain, that cameo locket, against each gown.

Now the final bit of scenery had been chosen; she would sit beside her mother and hear about each set on which she would appear.

"Of course you know we will go to the opening of the season at the Saint Charles, that has long been arranged," Caroline said, with hands so familiar to the task that she didn't even watch their movement smoothing her daughter's springing blonde curls. "But we will go also to the opera! The de Gravelles have a box, naturellement. And, it happens that during the time we are there, an opera suitable for young girls will be sung. It is *The Magic Flute*, of course it will be sung in German—it will be a nice beginning for you."

Marthe lifted her eyes under the fanning screen of her long eyelashes, projecting an eager male face over her mother's oblivious one. "Could I see something besides *The Magic Flute*, mother? That's a fairy story, after all."

"One goes to the opera for the music, not the story, Marthe. The music is quite lovely."

"If one goes for the music, why can't I hear *Romeo and Juliet* then? Or *Faust?*"

"What do you know of those?"

"I read, maman. After all, nothing happens in those stories, why shouldn't I . . . ?"

"Nothing happens! Juliet elopes to marry a man against her parents' wishes, and Marguerite is a fallen woman, Marthe." As Claudette Langlinais is fallen. Brought down by someone she didn't know, had never seen and would do penance for for the rest of her life.

"But we don't see what happens after Romeo and Juliet marry. Or see Marguerite fall," Marthe said. Her shoulders took a pose Caroline had been seeing in Hélène de Clouet's portrait so long that she did not recognize its source.

"You really don't know what you're talking about, Marthe. I advise you not to pretend to knowledge you don't have. It's not only unbecoming—but it can be dangerous."

"Papa would call anyone out who dared insult me, maman. You know that." Marthe saw a sudden darkening in her mother's eyes, a remembered pain. "Maman?" Shadows that had formed during the years of war seemed to gather around them again— "Maman?"

Caroline shook her head, roused herself to the worry in Marthe's voice. "Yes. You're a fortunate young lady. Your father's name and position protect you very well." She stood up, gathered up her skirt so she could descend the stairs. "Be sure, Marthe, that you honor that protection. It's not given to everyone."

"Claudette's entering the convent, did you hear?" she told Noel that night. "I suppose it's as good a solution as any—it still seems so—I don't know. Unnecessary."

Noel took onyx cuff links from his shirt, laid them on his dresser. "What is unnecessary? Her retreat to the convent? Do you really think she could ever allow a man to touch her after that, Caroline? Husband or not?"

Caroline picked up the cuff links, rubbed the smooth black stone. "I suppose not." She looked at Noel. "But sometimes I think an awful lot of fuss is made about it. A woman's virtue. If men don't care about theirs, why should we? Especially when we pay the price for everyone."

Noel went to the open French doors, stood puffing his pipe. "Just don't let our daughter hear you say that. If there was ever a girl made for—marriage, it's Marthe." He turned. "I'll make you a bargain. You keep her a lady long enough to attract the right kind of husband—and I'll do everything in my power to help arrange the marriage." Then he turned from her, and smoke, brown as the smoke drifting up from smoldering leaves, gray as the smoke fog drifting up from the slumbering bayou, hid his face.

# CHAPTER 17

## Cornucopia

Points of light from hundreds of candle flames picked up blue fire of diamonds, green lightning of emeralds, blood lust of rubies. The light collected itself into a pour of gold to fall over deep silks, heavy velvets, close taffetas. The height of the candles marked the hours; as the candles burned lower, the spirits of the assemblage rose.

"So, Noel, are you still sorry I put some of your money into the lottery?" Étienne de Gravelle signaled to the sommelier behind him, gestured at his empty glass. He sniffed the burgundy's bouquet before lifting the filled glass to his busy mouth. Then—"Caroline, at least you are satisfied with the little investment. After all, what other stock gives you not only dividends but rich feasts?"

"Rich? To the point of being ridiculous. Really, Étienne." She picked up the menu beside her plate, read at random. "Turtle soup—snapper *and* flounder—salmon—Maryland terrapin—crayfish—venison—asparagus—really, Étienne."

"You needn't take what you don't like, Caroline."

"Oh, but I do. I don't like my dinner companions, Étienne. Not at all. And I am not free to say so, at least not to them." She raised her lorgnette, peered through it at the long tables with their damask cloths, massive flowers, glittering silver. "By eleven o'clock, these cloths will be ruined—these barbarians practically eat with their fingers, they become drunk, sloven . . ." She tucked her eyeglass back into her evening bag. "If I had fully understood where we were going—"

"I said a banquet at the Saint Charles Hotel."

"You didn't say it was given by the lottery. Look at this riffraff! You know what the *Picayune* has to say about these legislators who share our dinner. 'Renegades, escaped convicts,

361

broken-down gamblers, exhausted inebriates, panderers of all sizes and colors'—surely you must have read that editorial!"

"Do you also recite poetry, Madame de Clouet?" The wine was warm in Étienne's mouth, his words were cold. "Dividends from this lottery saved Beau Chêne, madame. However high-minded you care to be about dining with the men who served you, you cannot escape the fact that they did indeed save you."

"I knew nothing about that, Étienne. Nor did Noel." She turned to her husband, long silent beside her. "You did not, did you?"

"Know that my small funds were being given to the likes of Charles Howard and his friends? It's fraud, pure and simple."

"It's legal, Noel. Licensed by the state—and does a lot of good for the state, as you damn well know." God, the de Clouets were bores, always had been, always would be. He had grown up on stories of the banking relationship between the de Gravelles and the de Clouets, the de Gravelles making money for the de Clouets, the de Clouets holding their aristocratic noses with one hand and taking their riches with the other.

"Forty thousand to the hospital—yes. And highly visible donations for flood relief."

"Come on, Noel. Other things. Money for cotton mills and a sugar refinery—the planters don't object to that, I can tell you."

"Of course not. They don't buy lottery tickets. They're not that stupid. What are the chances of winning? I read something in the *Democrat* the other day. Let me see—seventy-eight numbers in the wheel—the chance of winning even one drawing is one in seventy-six thousand seventy-six. Why, the writer had figured out that if a man buys a ticket every day at every drawing, he will have only one chance in eighty-four years to draw even a small prize of two hundred dollars or so." Noel laughed. "You have to hand it to these writers. They know how to make a point. He said that if Methuselah had bought a ticket every day from his childhood to the day he died, he'd have spent about two hundred fifty thousand dollars and earned back two thousand, six hundred and seventy-eight dollars and eighty-five cents!"

Étienne signaled again to the sommelier. "Leave the bottle," he said. "What the hell do you care, Noel? As you say, you don't buy tickets. Planters don't buy them. In fact, about ninety percent of the tickets for the big drawings are sold out of this state."

"Of course. But the poor of New Orleans provide the money for the daily drawings. I also read bank reports, Étienne. People are taking their savings and buying lottery tickets."

"We have fought for the freedom of all men, regardless of race or station in life, de Clouet. What they do with that freedom is, after all, up to them."

"It's still a fraud."

"Shall I sell your stock? I know a dozen men who would buy it tonight."

In his turn, Noel signaled to the sommelier. A waiter passing with a fresh tray of salmon mistook the gesture, hurried over. Caroline seized the interruption, took salmon, sent the man for more asparagus, fresh hot bread, mayonnaise. "At least," she said, "the Saint Charles Hotel knows how to do things as they should be done. I can forget the company, Étienne, in my enjoyment of the cuisine."

Lowering his voice, Étienne asked, "Is that also Noel's answer?"

"I should hope that it would be," she said. Coolly, she took up the wine bottle standing between them and filled her glass. "It will be expensive to give Marthe seasons in New Orleans. And to send Nollie to a good university. When the cooking is good enough, Étienne, we can—forgive some breaches in the company."

It was after dessert, when the men were gathering for their brandy and cigars and the ladies were retiring to an adjoining parlor for coffee, that Caroline turned to Noel, speaking loudly enough for the de Gravelles to hear: "Noel, darling, I have heard that General Beauregard makes such a fine occasion supervising the drawings—could we not go see that?"

Without shortening the length of his stride to the door, Noel said, "That is one sight, Caroline, I care to neither sketch— nor to carry in my mind." He turned for one look at his wife; its length matched the march of his legs. "I am sure, however, that Étienne will be more than happy to introduce you to the workings of our mutual investment. He has a penchant, it seems, for being most open in imparting information—after the fact."

Étienne watched Noel's broadclothed back disappear through

the ornate double doors. "Well, what can you do, Caroline? He was brought up to believe all of it—honor is possible, truth is possible, trust is possible."

The veil that usually hid Caroline de Clouet lifted. Her voice, clear of its veil, lifted also. "Why, Étienne, are you telling me that they are not?"

He bent over her hand, took it to his lips. "If one is to survive, Madame de Clouet—as you very well know—probably not."

Natalie de Gravelle bustled over. "Heavens, Caroline, come on. You don't want to miss the best part of the evening. Unless your gossip is better?" She looked from her friend's face to her husband's. "Something I should know?"

"No," Étienne said.

Natalie laughed. "Good." She took Caroline's arm, drew her beside her, began strolling toward the parlor. "The nicest thing about being married to a man like Efienne is that he doesn't want to tell me anything, and I don't want to know it. Tell me, is Noel like that?"

Caroline looked past Natalie at Étienne, who stood watching them. Their eyes and lips had, for one moment, the same light, the same curve. "Something like that," she said. "Now, before we go in, you were saying, the Renoudet girl has been in a scandal?"

Marthe declined to attend the lottery drawing: "Maman, why would you possibly care?" she said, dropping lump after lump of sugar into her café au lait.

"All that sugar will make you fat," Caroline said.

"You haven't looked at me lately," Marthe said. "Nothing goes to my stomach, only here." Her hands went to her breasts, loose and full under the material of her nightgown. "Tante Rose said when I returned from New Orleans, she would probably have to let the seams in all my bodices out again."

"Make sure that's all she has to let out," Caroline said. She saw the quick knowledge in Marthe's eyes and turned back to the mirror. "Very well. I have sent a message to Natalie that they must bring her aunt along to chaperone you while we are gone."

Behind her own reflection in the glass, she saw her daughter's pout. "But, maman, I don't need—"

Caroline set her bonnet squarely on her head, tied the ribbons in two firm moves. She rose, pushed away from the dressing table, gave a final tug to the jacket of her new walking suit. It was nice to be rich again, to have her world back. And if the Yankees with all their crude energy had not been able to ruin it for her, this young daughter, whose energy was less crude but no less dangerous, certainly would not. She turned and surveyed the figure in the bed.

Pillows piled high behind her, lace-edged coverlet drawn up to her waist, Marthe looked like nothing so much as a woman who has gone to bed not for sleep but for wide-awake pleasure. Even the careless bows on the bodice of her gown seemed to announce the ease with which they could untied. "You do need a chaperone. You need to be under the eye of a responsible adult woman every moment of every day until you are safely married. And I assure you, your papa and I will do everything in our power to hasten that day."

The de Gravelles' aunt was near sixty, a spinster who had not chosen her state, who arrived with a volume of *Vanity Fair* in her reticule. "I like to be read to," she announced. As Caroline went out the door, she heard Marthe's sulky voice taking up the tale of Amelia and the wicked Becky Sharp. "Marthe is fortunate," she said in tones loud enough to carry back through the open door to her daughter's ears, "to be exposed to such improving literature. She needs a—clearer view of the world."

"Surely New Orleans is nothing like the London of that book," Natalie said.

"Possibly not in setting. Still, there is a lot to be learned from the adventures of Mademoiselle Becky."

"Oh," said Natalie, "I thought surely it was Amelia you expected her to learn from." Natalie's voice was calm, even. So calm and even that Caroline had a quick understanding of why the de Gravelles' younger son, five years older than Marthe, had not yet put in an appearance, no matter how many times the two families met.

They stood with Étienne toward the back of the theater where the lottery drawings were held. "It's like a play, really," Étienne said. He's one of those men who always looks as though he has just been very well fed, or very well bedded, Caroline thought. So how does he manage to also look as though he is still hungry for either or both? "Our two starring actors, General P.G.T. Beauregard and General Jubal Early, of course set the high quality of the proceedings. How could any endeavor graced with the presence of these honorable warriors be the least bit dishonest?"

"But the drawings are honest, aren't they, Étienne?"

Étienne bowed the women into seats from which they had a good view of the stage, where two large wheels had already been put into place. "Of course. Why would they not be? Monsieur Dauphin, our illustrious manager, assures us that they are. After all, we return fifty-two percent of our income to the—investors." The well-fed smile broadened. "With a sure forty-eight percent profit, we can afford to be honest, my dear Caroline."

"Virtue usually is a matter of being able to afford it," she said.

The stir in the audience was like that when a small wind picks it way over a wheat field, taking a path of movement with it. Caroline's eyes shifted back to the stage. Two elderly gentlemen had walked, marched, on stage. "Heavens, how Early has aged," she said to Natalie. Still large, face florid, shrapnel-sharp gray-blue eyes staring out over their heads as though they were so much undisciplined infantry, General Jubal Early stood beside the larger of the two drums, dressed in a well-tailored suit of Confederate gray fabric. The drum at his side was made of mahogany, with glass across the opening. It rested in a stand on which it would be turned. "Early's drum has the lottery numbers in it," Étienne said. "Beauregard's has the amounts winners will receive."

"Well, certainly, no one could doubt the drawing is honest," Caroline said. "It was stroke of genius to hire these two men, Étienne. But I'm amazed that they'll do it. No matter how much ceremony there is—still, there's something—I don't know—unpleasant about them doing this. Selling their honor to make the lottery look good? Is that what I object to?"

"Come on, Caroline. We're still occupied by federal troops, we won't be taken back into the Union until we behave ourselves according to Yankee standards—what other work is there for generals who led the armies that lost? They can't run for office, their land was in just as bad shape as everyone else's—it is the victors that get the spoils, Caroline. By taking them from the losers."

Two small Negro boys hastened on the stage and were

blindfolded before General Early took up the canvas bags holding the lottery numbers and broke the seals, holding each bag up in open view of the audience. "You can feel the greed," Caroline whispered to Natalie. Each member of the audience seemed pulled to the two drums as though by the same instinct that pulls newborn piglets to the heavy waiting teats. A suspension of breathing, a tension of jaws—"I hope the ladies have their smelling salts, or we'll surely have a few swooning."

While the two boys turned the large drum, now full of small white and black cylinders, Beauregard turned the smaller drum. At exactly eleven o'clock, in the hush of morning when the day seems to brace itself for what is yet to come, the two men opened the small trap doors and commanded their young aides-de-camp to each remove a cylinder from a drum. "I must admit. I don't even have a number in that drum, and I am excited," Caroline said.

"Watch out, then," Natalie said. "Too many people get lottery fever in just that way. A tremendous folklore, set of superstitions, has grown up around these numbers. Ridiculous what people will believe! If you see a drunk man, play fourteen. If you dream of a fish, play thirteen. If you see a stray dog, take number six. And would you think it, until the archbishop put a stop to it, Catholics were asking priests to bless their tickets!"

"God helps those who help themselves," Caroline said.

Étienne turned that fed-hungry look on her. "Precisely. Please make your husband understand that."

Early had called out a number—45,168. Beauregard then gave the amount the ticket had won—$200. By the end of an hour, the tension had so heightened that Caroline felt caught in a net.

"Let's leave," she said to Natalie.

"What? Before any of the really large sums—the one-hundred-thousand- and three-hundred-thousand-dollar prizes are drawn?"

"I don't know if I could bear it if anyone won that amount and I had not even bought a ticket," Caroline said.

"Then we must leave," Étienne said. "Noel makes quite enough from his stock in the lottery, Caroline. Those earnings are a much surer bet."

"Yes, but they are his earnings. Not mine."

Étienne stood, put a hand firmly under her elbow, helped her up. "Natalie, dépêche-toi! Quickly, before Caroline contracts a disease that can be her ruin."

Sitting in the hotel café, sipping a glass of anisette, Caroline took up her argument again. "Why are you so anxious to protect me from something you make available to everyone else? If the lottery is as honest as you say—"

"But, Caroline, think. It is still a lottery. A gamble. For you to purchase a ticket, expecting to win, would be folly. Noel's stock—"

"Is Noel's." A silence. Then—"Very well. May I purchase some stock?"

"Lord, Caroline, there's none for sale. No one will let go of what he's got—can you blame us?"

"Anyway, Caroline, what do you want money for?" Natalie sounded bored.

"I don't know. Why shouldn't I have money?"

"But what would you do with it?" A match flame of interest now.

"Do? Nothing, for a while. I would just have it. Then, for another while, I would think about what to do. Then, at some point, I might do it."

Étienne placed his hand, that large hand that looked so fleshily soft, and now felt so challengingly firm, over one of Caroline's. "I'm sure, Caroline, that if you ask Noel very nicely, he will sign a few shares of his stock over to you. How much would depend, I imagine, on how nicely you asked."

Caroline stared down at the hand that covered hers so completely. She felt its strong warmth, felt a kind of demand in its pressure. When she raised her eyes to Étienne's, she saw a look there she had not seen in any man's eyes but Noel's since before the war, since those evenings of flirtatious gaiety, easy laughter, on the long galleries of plantations and in crowded city drawing rooms. Noel no longer looked at her that way; he came to her when he had to, expecting nothing but acquiescence. Lately, he came less. He had found a mistress, she supposed, someone who had not known him when he was rich and powerful and sure. Someone who would accept a small gift, gold coins discreetly hidden under a plate—her eyes met Étienne's once more. Here was a man who had somehow never lost his wealth, his power, his sureness. Men like Étienne liked women and loved praise. A woman who combined charm with flattery could, Caroline well knew, get something of a man's wealth, something of his power. And from that base, build her own. The warmth in Étienne's hand entered her body, swelled through her blood. "If that's all," she said, "it's as good as mine. You see, I know how to ask very nicely indeed."

Jumie Langlinais carefully honed the edge of the big knife's blade on the stone he held between firmly placed feet. He used an easy rhythm that stroked the metal against the stone with no break, no danger of nicking that smooth sharp line. The men would be bringing their stock soon; he had already checked the pen, making sure they wouldn't have to begin the boucherie by rounding up animals. It had been warm for a long time, with only a few cool fingers touching the land, then withdrawing. But this morning, the fog swinging low over the bayou had seemed like a message from the north—following that chill breath would be the heavy fist of winter. He tested the knife with a hair plucked from his head, and thought about the winter to come.

Already, he knew it would be different in many ways from any he had known before. Although the results of the gubernatorial race were being challenged, and there was no assurance that McEnery would take the office his supporters vowed he had fairly and cleanly won, Claude Langlinais had been elected justice of the peace in St. Martin Parish and would soon be sworn in. That position, even if it did involve such small claims, would take time. As would the sash and blind factory. Running the farm would fall to him, Jumie supposed. And seeing to the lumbering in the swamp—they had branched out into the depths of the Atchafalaya last year, sending men in to mark the trees in the fall, and to float them out at high water in the spring. And keep the moss gathering going, and the fur trapping. Zut! He hoped both Mathilde and Francie married men with big arms and fast legs. Younger brothers, whose portion of their own family's holdings would be so small that they would be free to join the Langlinais enterprises. And Jean—Jean would have to work harder, they both would. Which would leave little time for books.

He heard voices on the other side of the shed where the carving would take place; one sounded like his mother's brother, Felix. He took the sharpened knife inside the shed and laid it on the chopping block. Old stains from other boucheries had entered the grain of the wood through the deep cuts the butcher knives made. He knew that when the butchering started to-morrow, the earth under and around the block would seep up the smell, the feel, the color of blood. Of course they would bleed the animals before they were butchered, catching the blood in pans for boudin rouge. He didn't mind the blood, not the smell of it nor the way it looked. Work was work, yesterday it was hoeing, today it was getting ready for the boucherie. It was not the work he minded—only that no matter how it changed, it was always the same.

He walked around the shed. Felix was closing the pen gate on the pig he had brought. "Now, Claude, such a fine pig I brought, every man here will have a good feast from him." Then, seeing Jumie—"So, Jumie, you going to learn to butcher as fine as your father? You'd better, I tell you. Tomorrow is the tenth Saturday in a row he spends the day cutting up meat, and we got, how many, six more to go?"

"You know papa, Uncle Felix. He teaches me what he wants me to learn. When he decides I'm ready to be a butcher, then I'll be a butcher."

Claude was tightening the chains on the crossbar used to hoist the animal up for slaughter and bleeding. Without taking his attention from his work, he said, "Then you won't ever be a butcher. You don't have to be the butcher to take meat home from the boucherie—just bring your animal, your name is in the pot." He made a final test of the chain's strength and vaulted up to the top rail of the pen. "What you are going to be, Jumie, is a man of business. Me, I have decided."

"The only business a man Jumie's age has is finding his woman," Felix said. "Jumie, you're not going to follow your sister into the Church, are you?"

Jumie hardly heard his uncle. "Papa, what's that you said?"

"Let's go drink coffee," Claude said. He looked at the pig, now rooting a place for itself in the far corner of the pen. "Animals can't think, and look what happens to them! Us, we can think, Jumie. If we don't—we can get eaten, too."

"I'll just come have a sip," Felix said. "Duhon, he has a new rooster he says will give my black devil fits. I don't believe it, no, but I tell you, after they fight tonight, Duhon won't either."

"Maybe I'll come watch," Jumie said.

Felix's rough hand clasped Jumie's shoulder. "Mais, what

you going to just watch for? Put a little money on your uncle's rooster, Jumie. It's not gambling when it's my black devil. He wins, sure."

"Like you win in bourré, huh?" Claude stood at the top of the steps and laughed back at Felix. "Jumie, someday your uncle's going to figure it out—you can't beat the odds at the bourré table and the racetrack and the cockpit all at the same time. Lady Luck, she has a few other favorites, yes."

Françoise was stirring a big cast-iron pot and giving orders to Mathilde and Francie in a voice that bubbled with the same hot energy as the gumbo in the pot. "Mathilde, we need lots of green onions, now chop them fine! And, Francie, check that bread—I set it out to rise in a good warm place, it needs punching down by now." She looked up as the men came in. "Felix, you brought me that new quilt pattern Lizette was bragging about? What you want, you want coffee? A little black?" She lifted the pot that sat on the back of the stove the day long, kept warm by the banked coals. At a signal from her mother, Francie had gotten three small cups from a shelf and put them on a clear end of the wooden table. "Sit, sit," Françoise said. She poured coffee, shoved the sugar bowl in front of the men. "Mathilde, while you're checking that bread, you bring in some of those little cakes, I made a big batch for the children coming tomorrow, but these men can have a few—well, so we'll have a good day, isn't that so?"

Felix took his coffee in one large gulp, wiped his mouth and rose. "Françoise, I tell you, your tongue is as long and busy as your cooking spoon. Claude said he was going to drink coffee and talk to Jumie, but I think that's one gamble he lost, yes." His big laugh echoed behind him as he went out and down the steps.

"He didn't bring the quilt pattern," Françoise said. "So he had to get his word in. Well, Claude, if you need to talk to Jumie, what? Can the girls hear? I need my onions chopped, I need some—"

"Everyone can hear," Claude said. He was sipping his coffee with slow ease. That first cup, the one that jolted him awake, he drained standing up before heading for the barn. Later cups, snatched during the day, were taken in to keep his blood churning fast enough to keep up with tasks still before him. But by this time in the afternoon, what had not been done would not get done—at least, not today. A little winding up, a little tidying—and he could sip his coffee, not be in a hurry. Enjoy.

"When I was in New Iberia the other day, I stopped by that new school, the one Father Beaubien started." Claude could feel Jumie's interest now, as though it were like coffee in the cup, first warming, then stirring, the blood. "It's called the Attakapas Commercial and Industrial School." Claude kept his voice even, paced with the sips of hot black coffee. "I met some of the instructors—they've taught at a lot of different places. And let me tell you, they offer a lot of courses!"

Françoise came and stood over Claude, the big wooden spoon lifted like a baton ready to command. "Claude—you take too long! Say what you have to say."

Now he stood, moved to a place where he could see all of them. Could particularly see Jumie, whose eyes were not quite hoping, whose heart was still ready to be quiet, patient. "I said to Jumie, when we were out by the pen, that he is going to be a man of business." A rustle of feminine breath. "But, even me, Claude Langlinais, doesn't make something so just by saying it!" A rise of fond laughter. "So—I think—how can Jumie learn what he has to know to be a man of business, to carry on my part of the work at the sash and blind factory, to represent us in New Orleans?"

He deliberately did not look at either Françoise or Jumie now. After her first burst of hope for her eldest son, Françoise had taken up her mask of practicality, and had spoken no more of college for Jumie, a wider life for the girls. Still without looking directly at her, he said, "New Iberia can offer more than dances and horse races! At this school"—he turned to look at Jumie—"At this school, Jumie you can study book-keeping, the way accounts are kept, commercial law—and other things as well. Chemistry, father said. Algebra, geometry, natural philosophy, stenography, telegraphy—" The syllables came off Claude's tongue like the sounds and shapes of the folk rhymes they'd grown up with. "And"—turning now to Françoise—"and—instruction in French and religion!"

If any member of her family saw the flash of Françoise's apron to her eyes, the small wet blot on its crisp blue breadth, no comment was made. "A man of business! Going to the factory in New Iberia! Going to New Orleans! Well, let me tell you, Jumie, you'll need to know more than that book-keeping and algebra—what papa said—to do that. You'll need to remember who you are, Jumie. Who your people are. You hear me, Jumie? The business part—that's the way you'll help earn money for your family. The man part—that's your real work, Jumie." She lowered the spoon, laid it on the table. Her eyes went past them to the window, to the stretch of land whose curves and low places, shrubs and woods, fertile plots and barren mud holes they each knew as well as they knew the roughness of the wide-planked cypress floor, the deep-steamed scent of garlic and dry peppers and simmered meat, that was the kitchen. "That—and keeping hold of our land."

Marthe held the cluster of pale pink camellias against her dress; behind her own reflection in the mirror was that of her mother, who stood pulling on long white kid gloves. "They don't do anything for this gown," she said. "You're not wearing flowers, why do I have to?"

"I am wearing them, Louisa arranged them in my coiffure." Caroline turned slightly, showing the deep crimson blossoms tucked between the waves and curls of her dark hair. "As for why you have to wear them—you very well know why. Monsieur de Gravelle sent them to us. He is our host, we will not offend him."

"Are you putting lots of sugar lumps in your café au lait, maman?"

"What?"

"Because you're getting fat."

Caroline stared at her daughter's eyes, blazing between the lighted lamps on the dressing table like two wandering candle flames. "Others say I am getting the figure of a girl, Marthe. Your father is waiting. Get your wrap and come."

Even Marthe's blazing eyes were dimmed in the first brilliance of the de Gravelles' home. The sliding doors between the long double parlors were open, with three musicians sheltered from the promenading guests by carefully placed potted palms. Natalie, in lavender silk, stood against the heavy ivory damask draperies and pale toile-papered walls in chosen splendor and greeted the de Clouets with the arm of a beautiful woman on her own home ground. One slender hand twined itself around Noel's black sleeve, the other took Caroline in tow, and the three of them circled the rooms. Her introductions gave precisely the right information in precisely the right tone; Caroline, bowing over her jeweled fan to an elderly lady stuffed into black crêpe, felt the dust of war blown, fanned, lifted, out of her heart. She was not Caroline de Clouet, plower of gardens, hoer of fields. She was Madame de Clouet, wife of a judge and wealthy planter, a member of what the newspaper, in voices both hostile and servile, called the "Bourbon aristocracy." Her chin went up, the Bertaut chin that was the one feature Marthe inherited from her mother. With a grace she thought lost, she took Étienne's arm and led the first quadrille.

"Are you Henri?"

The young man standing at the table in the dining room across a wide hall from the parlors spun as though a thin silver line had skipped through the air, wrapped itself around his tail-coated figure, and turned him like a child's loop.

"Is the daube good?"

The girl opposite him was easily the most beautiful girl he had ever seen in his entire life. She was like one of the rich cakes arranged on the carved silver trays on the buffet; pink and white and rich and creamy, curves and lace and frills and ribbons. "Are you Marthe?"

The teeth were like lumps of fine sugar, the small pink tongue like a trail of icing. "How did you know?" She came forward, took his hand holding the daube and raised it to her mouth. Leaning toward him, she covered the daube with her mouth, pulled it from his fingers. The touch of her lips against his skin chilled him, though his cheeks felt hot. He looked quickly toward the doorway, where his Aunt Hortense stood guard. "You're not supposed to do things like that," he said.

"Did you mind?" When he didn't answer, she said again, "How did you know I was Marthe?"

"Because my mother said you are the most beautiful young girl in New Orleans this season." He looked away; he could lie very easily to Aunt Hortense, who did not matter.

"What did she really say?" Marthe had taken a small plate and was pointing to trays and platters, directing one of the tall black servants to serve her from the array of pastries and cakes and glacées. Seeing him watching her, she laughed. "I won't get fat. I'm like my great-great-grandmother Hélène. I look just like her, she never was fat, not for one minute. Well, maybe when she was going to have a baby." A look shot up from under the guard of her lashes. She watched it find the target, inflict heavy damage. "Do you mind my saying that? Let's go sit down and talk. Or do you want to dance?"

Henri de Gravelle looked into eyes whose store of ammunition was, he knew, far greater than his defenses against her. She knew what he wanted to do, she was urging him to do it. He thought of the conversation he had had with his father on the occasion of his sixteenth birthday. "Between them, the women have us where they want us, Henri. Those beautiful young girls of your own class will flirt with you, promise you, tease you—but they won't do anything else. You'll have to marry one. If you don't, if you flirt and promise and tease— then the old women take over. You lose your entrée, Henri. You may be a beau gentil garçon, but you will find every door in New Orleans closed to you if you treat one of its daughters badly. When you're ready, I'll send you to a woman I know. She'll find a young girl to keep you satisfied until you marry." A silence in which Henri had gazed at his father's books, studied the plume of his father's cigar smoke, looked everywhere but at his father's face. He heard the click of glass on glass, heard his father sigh. "And maybe after you're married, too. Here, son, have some brandy."

There were worse things, then, than having someone like Marthe de Clouet "jeter son gant" at him. He of course remembered what his mother had really said. Behind the door of her boudoir, when she had had no idea that Henri was sitting in the window on the landing outside, sighting along the barrel of his new rifle. Her words had sounded clearly, each one dropping with separate meaning until suddenly, as though they, too, had gone the length of the gun, they gathered together in full force. "Marthe de Clouet is one of those girls that drives men mad and makes women angry," Natalie had said. "I don't think a single man who sees her doesn't put her in bed with him—and I don't think a single woman who sees her doesn't compare Marthe in bed to what she herself is. She might as well go naked and get it over with."

He had been shocked, so shocked to hear his mother speak that way that he had determined to forget it. Until the blonde girl pulled off the long blue velvet cloak and handed it to the waiting maid. Until he saw what his mother meant. He had had that young girl his father promised for two years now. He doubted she would satisfy him again.

"Mademoiselle de Clouet, may I have the pleasure of this waltz?" he said, and took her small gloved hand in his. He knew Aunt Hortense's eyebrows were sending heavy signals to his mother, that in the particular telegraphy code of his women, within half an hour, everyone concerned and not concerned would be whispering behind fans. But he also caught the pulse that beat through the men when they found a clear space and began to dance. That pulse beat in him, too. Henri glanced across the room at his father. Man of the world though he was, he did not, perhaps, know everything. There very well could be women who were mistresses as well as wives. If there were, he'd bet his new hunting dog Marthe de Clouet was one of them.

"They make a fine couple," Étienne said. He and Caroline stood in an alcove sipping wine. Her cheeks took color from the camellias in her hair, her eyes took fire from the diamonds at her throat. "You're looking splendid, Caroline. Quite as you used to look." A pause while his eyes seemed to paint her. Then—"And did Noel give you the stock?"

"No." The word was said so quietly that he had to bend nearer to hear. While he was still close, she said, "But then, I didn't ask."

"You decided you didn't want it after all?"

"I decided I wouldn't ask Noel."

"Someone else? You'll ask someone else?"

The bare shoulders, round again, soft again, lifted. "Maybe. Can you suggest perhaps a stockholder who might accommodate me?"

Now she looked at him, her own decision clear.

"I think perhaps I can, Caroline. But you might have to ask very nicely—you don't mind?"

"What is there to mind, Étienne?"

"Then I'll send you word tomorrow." He saw Noel across the room, returning Natalie's sister to her husband. "Noel will claim you now—but, Caroline, please keep your afternoon free. These transactions can take time."

Books tucked under his arm, Jumie emerged from the school into the December afternoon. Chill air was freezing out the light of the sun, dimming the air, putting a wall of cold between the people hurrying home to warm pots and cozy hearths. He was to meet his father at the Serrett Hotel to ride home; normally, he rode in on his horse, using the travel time to read over his lessons. But Claude had had business in town, there'd been a list of commissions from Françoise—"Zut, it'll take my whole day, we'll take the caleche, Jumie, and have a visit. I never see you anymore!"

And of course, between the farm chores he still performed and the work at the school, there was little time for anything else. The reading he had done in the de Clouet library had prepared him for many of the courses, but nothing had prepared him for bookkeeping, or the theory of accounts. At the end of a day, his fingers were locked into the cramped hold that he used to push his pen down the hard demanding lines of the ledgers, and his head saw numbers tumbling over themselves everywhere he looked. Commercial law was better, a man could make sense of that, could even see, if he looked, some of what Aristotle and Plato preached about justice and ethics. Thinking of the added work, his shortened leisure hours, Jumie wondered if perhaps the reason people thought so much of land they could hand down was that at least each generation would not have to work for it all over again. As he was working for this knowledge.

He had said something like that to Claude, driving in that morning. "I don't know, papa. All this work. Do I need all this, to know about the sash and blind factory?"

Claude had slapped the side of the caleche with the whip-stock, setting the team into a trot. "What you learn isn't just for now. It's going to be something you have. When you know how to make those accounts come out, no one can take that away, can they?"

"I'd like to see him try!"

Now, with the lights of the hotel in view, Jumie laughed. This year it was ledgers, another year it would be something else. There was always just enough challenge to keep them busy, just enough help to keep them hopeful. He swung through the door into the lobby and went into the café. Claude was sitting at a table with a man Jumie didn't know. A woman was sitting between them, her back to the door.

"There he is," Claude said, beckoning to Jumie. And as Jumie approached—"Jumie, I want you to know Gervase Trahan. And his daughter, Mademoiselle Geneviève Trahan."

The woman turned and became a girl. Large gray eyes so clear and deep Jumie thought he would never see all they held. A face that was ready to laugh, ready to hear good words, ready to say yes. Slender, light. A dancer's body. He could imagine her arms swaying, her body turning, her feet carrying her through the crush on Madame Boutte's dance floor. "Do you go to the dances at Madame Gugueche's?" he said.

"Sometimes," she said.

Jumie pulled out a chair and sat down. He drank coffee and sampled cakes, tried to keep his mind on the men's talk.

"Jumie, Gervase raises race horses. He's got a filly he's ready to sell—what you think, you think we need a race horse?"

Jumie laughed. *"Need* a race horse? Only if she wins! You know maman. If we buy that filly, she better run fast, earn her keep."

Gervase Trahan beckoned the waitress for more coffee. "Mais, you can't have her because you want her, because she's pretty? Listen, does everything on your place have to earn its keep being useful?" He looked at his daughter, who was eating her cake quietly, eyes bright beneath the lowered lids. "Geneviève, she knows how to do all the things needed to make a house good. But besides all that, she's pretty, too! Claude, you have daughters. If a man can have a daughter who's good and pretty—he's a lucky man!"

"That filly won't sweep my stable, Gervase," Claude said. "If what we're talking about now is buying something I don't *need*—we better talk about price again."

"You're in politics, Claude. It won't hurt you to have a horse to take around the tracks. Meet a lot of people that way," Gervase said.

"That filly can't vote, either, Gervase," Claude said. "Now, how much did you say?"

On the way home, Claude reached over and clapped Jumie's knee. "Gervase has a pretty daughter. You noticed?"

Jumie's eyes held her image still; it hung in the cold air just ahead of him, just ahead of the trotting horses. "Yes."

There was a note in Jumie's voice that caught Claude's attention. "More than pretty? You think she's more than pretty?"

Jumie faced Claude. "It's not just pretty. It's something else. I don't know. A feeling . . . I can't explain."

Claude shrugged. "Who can?" The clop of the horse hooves on the winter-packed road kept them company. "You going to call on her?" Jumie nodded. Claude flicked the long reins over the horses' backs, urged them to go faster. The road broke through a wooded place, ran now between harvested fields that lay in the moonglow waiting to be silvered into dark silence.

"Jumie—Jumie, we never talked again about things between a man and a woman. Not since all that happened with Claudette." A rapid Sign of the Cross. She was a postulant now, her vocation, it seemed, or so the mother superior told them, firm. "But, Jumie, it—it isn't always easy."

"Being married? You think I can't see that?"

"No. The other. What happens between a man and his wife." The moon slid discreetly behind a cloud, let Claude speak in darkness. "Your maman—now, Jumie, don't mistake me, she's a blessing in my house. Who takes more on herself than Françoise? But too much, maybe, you know? The girls, they can do a lot. If she rested more—I don't know. I watch her at Madame Boutte's, she dances quick, she laughs, she's full of spirit. But, Jumie, sometimes a woman has a body that goes to sleep. You know?" The moon had given them all the time she would, she peeked over the tip of cloud, a blink of warning. "No, I hope you don't know. I hope you never know. That way, I don't think you can find out until it's too late. And maybe that's the way it's supposed to be."

His father meant he couldn't take Geneviève to bed until they'd been to church, been married. And that he might be deceived. The feeling he'd had when he first saw her was strong; he thought again of those clear deep eyes. To dive into her depths might be worth deception.

Françoise was waiting supper for them when they got home. She bustled about the kitchen, filling plates, bringing wine, breaking bread. Her own news filled them; when she portioned it out, giving to each what she thought right, she would ask for their offerings. Finally, she sat. "So, Claude, your business, it went well?"

"I think so. I'm thinking about buying a horse, Françoise. A filly to run at the track. You'd like that?"

"Can she run?"

Claude laughed. "If she can't, I know who will teach her! I haven't bought her, it's Gervase Trahan's horse. We'll go see her, decide." He teased the tip of his tongue with the hot coffee in his cup, teased his wife with his eyes.

"Gervase had his daughter with him, the oldest one. Geneviève, you remember her?" He nodded at Jumie. "I think Jumie could tell you everything about her, after just one look."

"So could a lot of the other boys. That Geneviève, she knows what she does, yes. Don't think I haven't seen her cutting those eyes around! You want to be one of the crowd that clutters up her papa's yard every Sunday, Jumie?"

"You want him to court someone no one else wants, Françoise? Or you think Jumie can't get her, if he courts her?"

"I don't trust girls who want so much attention," Françoise said. She stood up, shook out her apron. "They have so many strings to their bow before they marry, they may not be satisfied with just one after. The man that marries that Geneviève is going to be led a fast run, Jumie."

Jumie looked across the table at his father. "But, maman, a woman doesn't sleep when she's running, does she?"

Françoise shot him a look, then moved decisively to the shelf where the dish basin stood. "When men start making no sense, that's when I go back to my work," she said.

Claude stood, stretched, letting the tight-worked muscles pull against themselves. "Well, time for a walk. You coming?"

Most nights, Jumie didn't. Now he understood those bed-time marches. He followed Claude through the door. "Papa, you think I have a chance with Geneviève Trahan?"

"Gervase isn't stupid, Jumie. A good man like you with good prospects—what else does a father want for a daughter? And he sees how I take care of your maman, Jumie."

They swung into step, started down the path leading to the road. "I wonder about Geneviève. If she'll like me."

"Mais, son, let me tell you. If I knew what pleases women!"

Jumie thought of the hours at the business college, the hours bent over books. Until this afternoon, all that had been done as duty, to please his father. The thought of working to please a woman hadn't occurred to him. But for Geneviève? To buy her expensive trinkets like those the de Clouet women had? To show her off, let people see what a pretty wife he had? That made sense. "Papa, listen, I'll recite my lessons while we walk."

Claude clapped Jumie on the shoulder. "Good. I'll learn something, too."

Later, Jumie said, "How far do you walk, papa? We've been gone a long time."

Claude's eyes closed briefly, his rapid pace slowed. "Until I'm tired enough to sleep, Jumie. Until I'm tired enough to sleep."

# CHAPTER 18

## *Fireworks*

Hot summer air, hot spiced smells brought sweat to skin surface, saliva to tempted mouths. The spitted meat, constantly basted with Charles Clere's own sauce, would, by noonday, be the focus of the thousands of people gathering in New Iberia to celebrate the first centennial of the Declaration of Independence of the United States of America. Now, in midmorning, those thousands were lining Main Street, crowding to watch Grand Marshal D. U. Broussard lead the parade that would be second only to that held in New Orleans on this July 4, 1876.

Clere extended a sauce-coated spoon to Claude. "You think it needs a little more Tabasco?"

Claude broke off a piece of crusty bread, wiped it across the spoon, chewed judiciously. "It tastes good to me. What, you don't grind your own peppers since McIlhenny made up that Tabasco?"

"Why do what someone can do for you, Langlinais. So—talking about that—how's that factory going?"

Claude turned a roasting kid, stroking the heavy sauce over the heat-crinkled skin with the flat edge of a wooden spoon. "With Jumie running it, it goes well."

"You make way for the young early, Claude. What, you ready to stop work?"

"Stop work? What's that you say?" He ladled one last spoon of sauce onto the meat, put the spoon back into the big black kettle and poured himself a cup of coffee from the pot set to the back of the coals. "You want coffee?" They took their cups and sat under one of the oaks spreading shade like a lady's parasol held up defiantly against a relentlessly marching sun. "Look, I've got the farm, I've got the lumber, I've got the moss, I've got my job as justice of the peace—"

"You got your race horse, don't forget," Clere said. "What, is she safe to bet on?"

"Better be. Françoise will take that filly's feed out of my hide if not." Claude's grin was a curtain, pulled swiftly over his face as a woman hides behind a fan.

"I saw Françoise at church this morning—that was a crowd! How many you think came in on the *René Macready?*"

"I don't know. Captain Pharr, he said he stopped along the bayou so much to pick people up last night, that steamboat thought she had something wrong with her."

"Well, it says something. All these people coming to celebrate union—when we fought like the devil himself to get out of it!"

"Still have to fight, Clere. This celebration, I'm for it. Françoise and me, we worked to put Saint Martinville's part in all this together." The grin descended again. "Though I tell you—with Françoise busy, no one else has to do very much! Sometimes I think if God had created her first, he wouldn't have had to work so hard on the rest." He sipped his coffee a moment, letting the warm darkness of it fill him, excuse his silence. Then—"But, Clere, this Reconstruction has to end. Almost every other state has been taken back into the Union with all privileges, like it was before. Clere, we can't go on like we are."

"So, Claude, we work to get out of it. But I tell you the truth—look at the elections coming up. Who stands for what, can you tell me?"

Claude pushed himself to his feet. Though they had only had to harness the team, drive the dozen or so miles to New Iberia, and thus, unlike those who took one of Captain Pharr's steamboats in, had not had to start this day any earlier than was ordinary, he was tired. Forty-four wasn't old; field work kept his legs, his lungs, strong. It was not the work of the years that wore him, it was the lack of ease. He and Françoise lived alone now, the children well settled in their own lives. Surely she had time for him? But as the number of children putting their feet under her table every day dwindled, Françoise opened their doors more and more to others. Claude found himself bringing men he met through his work as justice of the peace home; later, he learned that Françoise had called upon their wives, was making them friends.

"Why are you concerning yourself with all these people? Don't we have enough with our children, their families?"

"Our sons only have one vote, Claude. Our daughters— none. You want to stay a justice of the peace forever?"

"I don't plan to do anything forever, Françoise. It's time soon to give over to the boys—look, we've more money now. You can think about those trips now—not just New Orleans, Françoise, you've probably seen enough of that—but those other places. Françoise?" He had been ready to plead with her, to remind her of those old dreams and young wishes. He saw her own curtain descend across her eyes, shutting dreams, wishes, hopes away from him.

"Travel? Claude, let me tell you, there's plenty work to be done, I agree. You should turn the farm, the lumber, all of it, over to the boys. The sooner the better. While you get some of what's going to be there for the smart taking when the Yankees move out. That can't be long, Claude. You hear me?"

He heard her. That had been in the fall of last year. Now, Jean and his wife, Lizette, occupied a house on one part of their land—Jean ran the farming operations, leaving the lumber, the moss, anything to do with trade, to Jumie. Francie's husband, Pierre Labadie, kept those crews working, meeting with Jumie each week to review what they had already done, plan what lay ahead. Mathilde helped Jumie in the office, keeping the books and accounts under his direction, taking pride in the fact that she understood the talk of the men who dropped in from time to time to do business with her brother.

Now he turned to Clere, answered the question that had hung between them like the limp flags lining the parade route. "Who stands for what? I don't know what anyone else stands for. But I can tell you what I stand for. A government where men like Colonel de Blanc can't be arrested and dragged off to New Orleans because they stand against corruption and tyranny. Clere, no matter how honorable a speech the colonel made, no matter how his release vindicated him—it should not have happened, no."

"If you can find a government where the ins don't persecute and try to weaken—or destroy—the outs, Claude, you'll have looked hard. Almost as hard as we're working on this barbecue! Me, I'm going to let someone else watch the meat—I'm going to watch the parade."

"Me, too," Claude said. He looked at the sky, measured the oak shadow. "I told Françoise I'd meet her—you need me back later?"

"Only to eat."

Pushing his way through the lines of people, Claude knew Françoise by her stance long before he could see her face. The bombardment of sun and wilting air had gradually crumpled the stiffly starched dresses of the other women—but not Françoise's. As though surrounded by air controlled by her order, Françoise was untouched. Her white skirts stood full around her, borne by the quarts of starch she had soaked them in, then flattened into smoothness with the weighty heated iron. Her hair was chiseled on her head, even July's sun could not tempt loose one tendril, could not persuade one wave to relax in the languorous heat. If she perspired, handkerchiefs, sun-bleached and porous, removed the drops before her skin even shone. In the created shade of her large hat, she stood and measured her world.

"It goes well?" He stood slightly away from her, as conscious of how his body infringed on hers as he was in their suddenly too small bed.

A hinted bow of her hat brim, acknowledging his arrival. "The floats are just beginning. You missed the federal soldiers." A hinting smile, acknowledging men's thinking. "We can't stand seeing them in our town every day, so we bring them here and put them on parade!"

"You're the one who tells me not to argue when it doesn't matter. You wanted me to say no?"

But her eyes were on an approaching float, her ears on the music. Claude waited for her to comment on the girls riding by, on the Goddess of Liberty surrounded by her Thirteen Colonies; he waited for her to find at least half the thirty-eight young men marching alongside the float in commemoration of the thirty-eight states in the Union unsuitable for this solemnity. But though her lips were parted, though they seemed as ready to speak, as certain to speak, as at any other moment in their lives together, no sound came. Except a small release of breath.

He had seen her like this before, particularly since he had begun to make his small way into the political circles of the district. When a crowd gathered, whether it was the anniversary fête of the Heberts, married fifty years, or a boucherie, Françoise seemed to be seeing two scenes; the one that was before her, and the one in her head. More and more, Claude was realizing that in the scene in her head, Françoise recast certain people, certain events. She found importance in this one, a way to use that one. And always he, Claude, or her son, Jumie, were starred.

She was silent in her point of sunlight, her focus of sound. Captain Thomas Morse's float, a tribute to *Old Ironsides,* lumbered past, its fourteen young girls smiling and bowing in a confusion of red, white, and blue draperies, red cheeks, white skins, sky-reflecting eyes. Brass bands and fire companies, contingents from up and down the bayou, from Morgan City, Franklin, St. Martinville and Breaux Bridge. Schoolchildren in the van, waving flags, laughing, seeking out their parents along the route. Carriages decorated with flags and flowers; men prancing by on horses of tall splendor. And then the Negro community, a full complement of bands and fire companies, children, carriages, horsemen. "It may yet be possible," Claude said to his distanced wife. He thought of the celebration theme, hammered out of committee meetings, hammered into resisting hearts: "to destroy all national prejudice, to set aside race, and the issues of the day . . . in order to cement hitherto repellent factions into one common and fraternal bond."

As the last of the cavalcade disappeared down Main Street, as the sounds of brass trumpets and rhythmic feet drifted back from Corinne Street, Claude took Françoise's arm. "Françoise!" The gaze she turned on him was sated. "Françoise! I forgot how you love a show, a spectacle. Françoise, you plan a trip, see something."

She blinked, a long, slow blink that, like a switch on a machine, caught her back to life. "I do like a spectacle, Claude." She moved slightly, let the stiff fall of her skirt move into another composition. "I not only watch, I arrange, I know, when something goes on, not just how it works—but that I helped make it work." She began to walk with the crowd that was forming itself into a kind of procession, with the Dupérier Grove near the convent as its destination. "You remember how I used to talk about Beau Chêne? Like it was a big theater just for me to watch? Zut! What an innocent! The de Clouets, people like that, they want us to be so busy watching we never learn how the trick is done."

"Trick?" Claude was nodding, smiling, taking hands held out to him as they walked.

"The trick of making the way they live seem better than anyone else's way. The trick of making their blood seem finer. The trick, Claude, of keeping their heads higher than ours no matter how crooked their bodies."

"You should be on the program, Françoise," he said.

If she heard the heaviness of his voice, she answered only the lightness of his words. "A woman? Women don't even vote, Claude. As in everything else, we have to get what we want by going through men."

"Everything else?"

Now she was bowing, smiling, pressing hands. The Claude Langlinaises were, clearly, known to most of the people in that throng; Claude saw possibilities he had not even thought of before. "Babies. A home. A place in the world. You men can give these to us—or withhold them. Isn't that right?"

Suddenly two arms were circling his body, holding his own arms against him. Then two soft hands holding his face, a soft mouth against his cheek. "Papa!" Jumie released the hug, stepped around to face his father. Geneviève, her sun-fresh skin basted with warm moisture, stepped away to brush Françoise's cheek with her lips. "Papa! Isn't it splendid? Doesn't it make you believe we have one country again?"

"But where are the babies? What have you done with them?"

Geneviève laughed. "Papa! How can I dance and have a good time carrying two babies around all day? Besides, you want them to embarrass us crying during the speeches? They're with their nainaine, back at my mother's." When Claude's eyes went to her full breasts, covered with a tucked and lacy lawn bodice, she laughed again. "Mais, the baby, he's old enough he can do without his mama a little while! I'll go nurse him before the dance." Her soft hand covered his. "Papa! You think I don't know how to take care of my men?"

Françoise had taken Jumie over, had linked her arm through his and pulled him ahead. Claude looked down at his daughter-in-law, whose full young face was framed by white straw so delicate the sunlight filtering through it made shifting patterns across her eyes, now hiding, now revealing, the mischief there. "I know damn well you know how to take care of your men. Now how about taking care of your old father-in-law for a while?"

It was pleasant, more than pleasant, to feel that urgent body close to his. To listen to her voice tripping over her little stories, tales from Geneviève's view of life brought out for his amusement. She could make anything seem funny, he thought, listening to her go on about an encounter with a peddler who had turned up selling trinkets. "Papa, would you believe he flirted with me? Cut his eyes around in his head, kept making remarks about pretty girls and young wives! Papa, I think if I hadn't told him to go, it was time for me to say my rosary, he'd have said something really *bad!*" Her own big eyes cut at Claude. "You know?"

"Now, Geneviève, anytime someone gives you trouble, you ring that big bell." He heard his voice take on the color of protection. How nice to have a young and pretty and helpless woman who looked to him, as well as to her husband, for care. "If Jumie's away, I'll come. No Langlinais woman has to take care of herself, Geneviève, you know that."

"That's why I like to take care of Langlinais men. They pay me back so nicely." Again her eyes cut over to him. He knew the innocence of her flirting, how unconscious she was that men who saw beneath the shimmer of her darting gaze, the quickness of her laughter, the turning grace of her body, envied her Jumie his bed. If she had been asked, questioned as to whether she thought all men had such a woman, her answer would be as careless, as innocent, as her flirting. Other men? What did she know of them? A shrug, a laugh. They had, she supposed, what they wanted.

They heard the choir before they reached the grove, two hundred voices singing the anthem that once again meant "nation" in both north and south. "I wish the speakers would sing instead," Geneviève said as they found Jumie and Françoise. "I get so tired of paying attention! And then when they go on and on and are so solemn and important, I always want to laugh. Don't look at me, Jumie, or I'll laugh sure enough!"

"Maybe you should have stayed with your nainaine as well," Françoise said, and turned her starched marble back.

From under the cascading ruffled cover of her rose-colored parasol, Caroline de Clouet viewed the crowds. "I think they might have put some men from Saint Martin Parish on the program," she said to Noel. "They were glad enough to accept food for the barbecue, help with the planning."

"They've been a separate parish eight years, Caroline. Long enough to enjoy their independence, not long enough to forget how our politics disagreed with them. Besides, be practical. What politician, given this crowd, this occasion, would yield to a possible rival?"

"All politicians are rivals, Noel, isn't that what you tell me? Even within the same party." She took a silk fan, in color one shade deeper than the rose of her dress and parasol, and slowly unfurled it. Noel watched the movement of her slender hand, the way sun and shade played with the fullness of her bare arm. That rough, dried hand he had taken into his the day he came home from the war was soft again, delicate to his touch, delicate in its flirting movements. And the thin, worn body he had taken into his arms the night he came home was also soft again, full, enticing. Like one of her own roses, which had been spindly and pest-ridden with neglect but was now blooming in furious renewal, Caroline had entered a second summer. "Men who aren't my political rivals are rivals for my wife's attention," Noel liked to say. Étienne de Gravelle was careful not to let Noel see his face when he heard those words.

"We've patched up the Democratic party—to a degree. God knows what the Republicans will do. They've been meeting in New Orleans all this week—we should hear their ticket soon. I told Étienne to keep me informed."

Caroline turned back to the speaker, a look of pleasant attentiveness on her face masking the total inattention of her mind. If anyone could keep Noel informed, it was, of course, Étienne. He was like a spider, a queer sea creature with many busy arms—not only in bed but in politics. His reach stretched into the inner chambers of the warring Republicans as well as those of his own reluctantly joined Democrats. He loved to tell her, a hand stroking her breast, about his political struggles. Though earlier proclaiming himself a Bourbon Democrat, a follower of John McEnery and L. A. Wiltz, two men to whom white supremacy was the natural order of things, he now, with the same smooth ease with which he entered Caroline, was penetrating the core of the Nicholls supporters. "How can you say you're going to go along with Francis Nicholls?" Caroline asked him. "You've laughed at him for years, called him Sir Galahad . . . oh, Étienne, have you no principles at all?"

"I can go along with Francis Nicholls because, apparently, he can win the governor's race, Caroline." Étienne lay back, chest and stomach forming a smooth, firm slope. "As for principles—of course I have principles. My principles involve winning, being powerful, being rich."

"Noel says he will support Nicholls because Nicholls is a gentleman, someone who can lead us out of the disgrace we've been in so long . . . give the Negroes a chance."

Étienne's laugh roared up against the canopy topping the four-poster bed. "Of course Noel would say that. He does not have to earn the money that pays for his principles." He reached for her, pulled her to that firm slope. "While you and I do."

The sound of hands beating on hands, of voices raised in salute, broke into Caroline's thoughts. She looked at Noel, standing beside her. Tall, handsome, he could be one of those who knows what's going on rather than one who waits to be told. She sighed. "And when do the Democrats meet? To select the ticket?"

"Later this month. In Baton Rouge." Noel saw the Langlinaises arranging themselves to listen to the speakers. He nodded his head in their direction. "Claude will probably be there. He's beginning to be looked to by quite a few people as one who might be helpful—when the Democrats win."

"Your party is seeking Claude out?"

"My party? The men I would willingly associate myself with, the way our politics are now, number maybe five, ten. I have no party, Caroline. Only an interest to protect. But yes, the conservative Democrats see Claude Langlinais as a possible leader."

Caroline looked at the Langlinaises, grouped under a shading oak. "From this distance, they look almost—like us," Caroline said.

"Meaning?"

"Meaning Claude Langlinais is no fool, Noel. He learns well from those swamp animals he hunts, he knows how to blend into the landscape. I assure you, let Claude become part of the inner workings of Conservative politics—and I think you'll learn what rivalry really means."

"I fought in the war, too, you know." He heard his voice cutting down between them with metallic finality. "Despite the fact that you know more about Claude's heroics than those of your husband, I was not without my own valiant deeds, Caroline."

The look she cast up at him had none of the rosy softness

of the silk-screened sunlight. Her fire had long since returned, it cut through his barriers as fast as he put them up. "No one questions your—manhood, Noel. Or your valor. I am simply telling you—the fact that Claude Langlinais doesn't have your knowledge of political theory doesn't mean he doesn't understand very well how the game is played. He has a certain instinct for it, Noel. An instinct that can be dangerous, if he is not on your side."

"But we are all one happy party, Caroline. All of us, planters and New Orleans merchants who pride ourselves on the purity of our Whig traditions, the zealots who are almost phobic in their hatred of Negroes, and those who form the middle ground we are not clamoring to stand on—we are united in our purpose. Defeat these Radicals and get back our state."

The applause that rose in the sun-scorched air almost covered her words, but Noel, accustomed to those low tones, heard her clearly. "Just be sure, Noel, you don't get it back—and then hand it over to Claude."

Without looking at him again, she closed her fan, tucked it into her reticule, and strolled across the lawn to a small knoll where Marthe and Nollie had settled with a group of young friends. "Marthe, Nollie, if you plan to come back for the ball, we must go home and nap." Noel began to walk toward the place he had ordered Zeke to hold the carriage. Behind him, Marthe would pout and roll her eyes at her companions, asking them to witness this unreasonable mother, who put a nap above a centennial celebration. The young men, heated by the July sun, by the excitement of the occasion, and by Marthe's luxuriant presence, would crowd around Caroline, begging her to allow Marthe—and of course Nollie—to stay just a while more. They would, several of them and all of them, offer to drive the de Clouet children back to Beau Chêne. They would make any promise, swear any vow, for one hour more of Marthe. Nollie would stand by, his eyes sketching scenes in his head, his lips smiling in easy compliance. Caroline would win, she always won. Though there had been a time when Noel feared she might not control Marthe, that there might be a scandal before a courtship, on the surface, Caroline had her daughter well in hand. Now why did he think—on the surface?

"I don't know why you want to come back for the ball," Caroline said when they had finally pulled away from the crowded streets and were on the road home. "A fire company ball for a girl who's going to be presented at Comus?"

"You always tell me to have good manners, maman. Wouldn't it be ill-mannered to refuse to attend a ball given in honor of democracy on the grounds that it is not comme il faut?" Marthe, Noel noted, had two voices. One was clear and even like the carefully released fall of water in the fountain he'd just had installed in Caroline's rose garden. The other, like a natural stream, went where it chose, with its own force. That voice, seldom heard by her parents, cut across any barriers, man-made and otherwise, that did not suit Mademoiselle Marthe's plans. Like many natural forces, she sometimes accomplished her plans by devastating others.

"Oh, Marthe, don't use sophistry on me. There must be some young man you want to dance with, someone new. Heaven knows you've gone through everyone the Teche country has to offer—and it's only early July."

"I don't think always of myself, maman. Actually, it's Nollie I'm thinking of. He's quite enchanted by Mignon Blanchet."

"Nollie is!" The rosy parasol pivoted Caroline's turn as she faced her son. "Nollie is sixteen. Nollie is enrolled at the University of Virginia. Nollie is not enchanted with anyone. Are you, Nollie?"

His large eyes met hers. Already, inside his head Nollie was sorting out the images of the day, bringing a drummer from one band together with a trumpet player from another, taking the smiling face of one beauty, the lithe body of another. Unlike his father, who had uncompromisingly sketched exactly what he saw, Nollie took pictures from his head and made new images. When Marthe was disappointed because his sketches of her birthday fête were not "like it happened, Nollie, not like it happened at all!," he had shrugged. "It's as it should have happened, Marthe. To be art."

"Life isn't art, Nollie, everyone knows that!"

"Should we not then make it so?"

"If you tell me I am not to be enchanted, then of course I shall not be." Caroline stared at him for another moment, then turned away. Later she complained to Noel. "Why is it that when Nollie is so agreeable, does everything I say, I feel so worried?"

The sun, the speeches, the heavy barbecue, had almost drugged Noel. But the sight of Caroline's firm shoulders, emerging from the soft pink of her dress, focused the heaviness.

He went to her, began to undo the ribbons of her camisole. A few years ago, she had begun leaving off her nightgown when she knew he wanted to take her. No longer did he grope through layers of bedclothes, another layer of fabric swathing her legs. She came to him naked, soft, curling against him. When he began to feel certain new movements in her body, certain ways of pulling him deeper into her, he decided she had been reading the collection of erotica on the top-most shelf of the library.

Jumie pulled the gauzy moustiquaire closed and turned to his wife. Small droplets of milk from his son's nursing beaded her nipples, and he leaned over her to touch them with his tongue. "You said you wanted to sleep," she said, and tickled his bare ribs with silken fingers. The movement became more rapid, more questing. As his mouth covered her body, her hands covered his. He felt the quick rise of her belly up against him, felt her legs open, come over him, clasp him to her. Her laughter accompanied the rise and thrust of his body, the softly scored scale of sound setting a rhythm for him.

Lying beside her, he stared into the tester covering the tall bed. They were in Geneviève's old room, the room he had watched her emerge from when they were walking out together. He remembered how his mind had gone through that solid wood door, picturing her dressing, undressing, naked. Being in bed with her here, despite the fact of their marriage, seemed sinful; the acting out of lustful dreams that he had confessed, haltingly and shamed, to the priest. He had said that to her once when she had asked why he seemed so hesitant, so restrained, when they stayed at her parents' home. "Don't you ever feel—well, not married—when we are here?"

She had laughed at that, too. "What fun, Jumie! To have the excitement of the forbidden and the safety of permission!" Kisses all over his face, eager hands teasing him. "I just like what we do, I don't think about it."

Françoise complained that Geneviève thought of very little. "How can she think, she carries on like a little girl, playing, teasing, laughing all the time!"

"She's happy, maman. Our home is as clean as yours, her meals are good, our children cared for. Does she have to sigh and weep over her work for you to think her a woman? Believe me, maman, Geneviève is a woman."

After that, Françoise did not criticize Geneviève directly.

But her own pace, always hard, became harder and faster when Jumie and Geneviève visited. "I can't stop," she would say, lines across her forehead, line of firm mouth. "There's work to do, the sun doesn't stop coming up just because you've come."

The thin curtain of gauze wrapped them in a private place where sleep came easily. The still air in the room bathed them with its warmth, seeking out the moist patches of skin, slowly drying them. Curled against the firm body of his wife, Jumie slept. Geneviève, comfortable in the old hollows of her mattress, the familiar curves of her husband, took one last look at her dress for the ball, hanging on a hook in the open armoire beside her bed. It had, she knew, five more rows of ruffles than the one Françoise would wear. She might be the young Madame Langlinais, taking a second fiddle's place to her fine lady mother-in-law, but what Françoise was building would someday be hers, just as the land, the businesses, the political position, would someday be Jumie's. She reached over and caressed Jumie, feeling the satiated limpness in her hand. A murmur, a question, half formed. "Nothing, Jumie, nothing. I'm happy. Aren't you?"

The centennial committee had hung lanterns in the trees of Weeks Grove, where Fire Company No. 2 was staging its grand ball. Torches stood in open spaces between the trees; the tall points of fire stretched up to meet the diffused glow from the lanterns, making a pattern of shadowed light against which the pale dresses of the women flickered. Geneviève went to the cleared place where the musicians were gathering; "'Tit Nonc, you going to play till I can't lift even one foot, isn't that so?"

The musician carefully settled the strap of his accordion around his neck, balanced the weight. "Mais, Geneviève, I tell you the truth, if I play long enough to tire you out, I think I'll have worn myself out for good."

One of the fiddlers ran his bow over the taut strings. "Geneviève, if your feet move too fast for 'Tit Nonc, I can keep up."

"Just make sure you don't leave the rest behind." She turned to the man playing guitar, leaned over to tap him with her fan.

"That girl probably flirts with the priest when she's in the confession," Caroline said. "She's impossible."

"She's also natural. I don't think for a minute she even knows she's flirting. She thinks everyone enjoys life as much as she does, that's all," Noel said.

"Well, the poor triangle player is completely entranced. Look at him! He'll be fit for nothing but sad love songs."

"Nollie!"

They heard the voice behind them, turned to see Jumie Langlinais approaching their son, who stood slightly away from his parents, eyes pulling lines, form, color, from the swaying figures before him. "Nollie! Well, how long has it been?"

Caroline, seeing the light that poured over Nollie's face at the sight of Jumie, had her own inner images. Jumie, showing a small boy how to fish, how to tell when was the best time to plant beans, potatoes. How to pluck a goose, clean a duck. Jumie, carefully washed finger pointing his eyes' way across the page, carefully formed words interpreting those incomprehensible marks she told him were letters. Jumie, reading to Nollie, making a place of peace in the midst of an uncertain time. "I'd forgotten how close they once were," she said. "There, Noel, it's a waltz, that won't make me too warm." She lifted her arms, stepped into his. She seldom thought of Étienne when she was at Beau Chêne with Noel. Beau Chêne and Noel were one life, New Orleans and Étienne another. He of course had other women when she was away; that had no interest for her. There were people you shared only points of time with; it would be foolish to try to make an entire life from that.

"So, Nollie, you're all grown up. Taller than me, now how did you do that?" Jumie's hand was on Nollie's shoulder, his face beaming. In the staged light of lanterns, torches, they looked very much of an age; the six years disappeared beneath the breadth of shoulders, the line of strong backs. "I see Geneviève has a partner, let's find some beer." He steered Nollie to the edge of the dance area, where the last of the kegs of beer had been set up. "I heard you're going off to college this fall?"

"The University of Virginia. I'm not sure why."

"Mais, if you're not sure, who is?"

"Maman."

"So this is your maman's idea? Not yours? I thought—I remember—we used to talk about college, you and me."

Nollie sipped his beer. He didn't really like it; unlike other common experiences it had to be tasted, it could not just be drawn. "I remember you were maybe more excited about it than I ever was. Too bad life so often works out that way—I don't give a damn about going off to Virginia, and you'd probably love it."

"Not now. I used to think—but look, Nollie, I've got two children, I'm running some of our businesses—" A shyness, something he'd not felt with Nollie before. "Nollie, you know what I'm doing? In the house we use for our office? I'm putting in one whole room of shelves. For books."

"Business must be good if you need a whole room for your books, Jumie. I'm glad."

"No—not for ledgers. For books. Like you have at Beau Chêne." At Nollie's intense look, focused on him instead of the shifting play around them, he added, "Not really like. Your father has some fine editions in his library—your library. My books will be to read, that's all."

"Which is why you don't need to go to college. I don't need to either. To do what I want to do."

"Tell me about it," Jumie said.

Across the grove, Claude Langlinais stood in a cluster of men. He was obviously telling some story, his hands moving ahead of his lips, miming the life of the words. Noel, approaching them, heard the swift leap of laughter at the end of the tale; Claude's own laugh was quicker, higher, than any, his hands raised now in a kind of blessing over his own folly. He leads by making men think he is only one of the pack, Noel thought. And remembered Caroline's warning.

"So, Noel, it's been a good day, isn't it so?" Claude moved slightly, opened the circle. The men fastened one gaze on Noel. "You all know the judge? Noel de Clouet? Noel and me, our families go way back. My great-grandfather and his—learned a lot from each other."

"A happy tradition," Noel said. Something about his stance seemed to announce his intent for private talk; the men scattered, some to follow the quick-stepping dancing couples, others to the beer kegs, where card games, faster paced than the music, were growing increasingly intense.

"What do you think, Noel, you think we can keep this going till November?" Claude's eyes were on the crowd, but his ears were on Noel's answer.

"This common good feeling?" Noel laughed. "You probably know that better than I do, Claude. I seem buried in the inner chambers, you're out where the people are. What do you think?"

Claude plucked a leaf from the tree they stood under, began methodically ripping it into small pieces. "I don't like what I hear. That many men still think the way to win an election is to keep the wrong voters from the polls, not bring the right ones to them."

"We may not have sufficient 'right' ones. You know that."

The bits of leaf fell from Claude's hand in a flutter. "You see that little leaf? Something that small, that unimportant. I tear it up, I throw it away. So the tree makes another one, Noel. But, Noel, some things we tear up, they're not so small, so unimportant. We have to get the Radicals out, yes. But, Noel, could there be a way to do that that didn't tear so much up?"

"Was there a way for King George to get what he wanted without tearing up your people? Was there a way for the French people to get what they wanted without tearing up mine? Or a way to settle the slavery question without tearing up what both you and I built?"

"If there was—"

"No one bothered to look for it. Fists are faster than laws, Claude. God knows I've learned that!"

"But you don't like it?"

"No." Louis Andrépont was beckoning to Noel, gesturing then to a half circle of chairs drawn at the edge of the grove. "But, Claude—I've found out about myself that I can do what I don't like."

Claude looked out at the dancers. "That's important," he said. "And maybe easy." His eyes were on Noel's face now, the expression shielded by the shadowed light. "The hard thing— at least, I've found it hard—is to know the difference between things I don't like to do which I should do—and things I don't like to do which I shouldn't."

"God's laws make those decisions for you surely?" Noel said. He heard his own cynicism, waited for Claude's anger.

"How can God's laws make decisions for me? Noel—laws are nothing if men don't believe them. That's part of the mess we're in now—people pretending to obey the law, uphold it— and all the time trying to find a way around it." Not anger, then, but weary impatience.

"You can't believe what's going on is right—the so-called law we live under."

"I don't. But I don't pretend I do. I don't lie down with those funny bedfellows. They know where Claude Langlinais stands."

"Not all men can afford such a luxurious position, Claude."

The humor that had filled Claude to lightness earlier burst forth. "You mean the richest men in the state can't afford a position I hold? Hell, Noel. If they can't, it's only because they don't have the guts to risk what they've got now to get what they want later." He struck Noel's shoulder lightly with his open hand, a teasing, almost sympathetic, gesture. "Now I go dance with Françoise. Philippe Broussard, he doesn't have enough votes in his pocket he should dance with her twice. You know?"

Noel, who had watched Caroline's carefully balanced choice of partners, laughed. "I know," he said, and struck through the crowd to find Andrépont.

The five or six men sat in small chairs brought over from The Shadows, the Weeks's home across the way. "I hope," Andrépont said when Noel was settled, "that the condition of The Shadows will remind us why we meet—it's not the only plantation that never recovered this Reconstruction—and by God, if we don't get rid of these Radicals, it will be joined by many more."

"The depression didn't help," Noel said. "Some people were just beginning to do better when that hit—"

"That was three years ago, de Clouet. And if it weren't a depression, it would be something else. There'll always be problems. I'm not saying get rid of the Radicals and we'll all be in glory land but get rid of them and we'll think we are."

"I agree, Andrépont. I just don't want to drag every haunt out of the grave, put everything from floods to the boll weevils on Radical backs. They've sins enough of their own, we don't have to invent them."

"We need to begin by running a governor who can win—or at least, bear the victory we get for him."

"Nicholls is our best choice. He's a natural. His record in the war alone will carry most Democrats. As for the Radical voters . . ."

"The White League will take care of them. Noel, I agree, nothing so major as what happened in New Orleans two years ago—but some judicious reminders, some armed rides at night—a hint to those who can think? And, gentlemen, if someone is wise enough to vote, he's wise enough to think. Isn't that so?"

Noel stirred uneasily. "The whole concept of the White League seems incongruous to me. Gentlemen of our—position hiding behind an organization that is, pure and simple, violent in nature and military in purpose."

"Its purpose is to protect the white people of this state against the growing power of the Negroes, Noel. Power given to them by Yankees anxious to keep us helpless, poor, and defeated."

"Noel, I think if you consider the thing fairly, most of the White Leagues outside of New Orleans are purely political. I'll grant the disturbances in New Orleans, the few elsewhere, are distasteful, but . . ."

"But otherwise it remains an organization of civilized and cultured men, is that it?" Noel said. Again he heard the cynicism in his voice, waited for it to cause anger. And again heard only weary impatience.

"Noel, Noel. We're not dealing with civilized, cultured men. We're dealing with barbarians. They understand nothing but methods like their own. When we win—"

"Yes, when we win," Andrépont said. "Now, about the gubernatorial ticket. Remember, we go to Baton Rouge in three weeks. If Nicholls heads it . . ."

Noel heard the weaving sound of words, making a cloth that could be wrapped around the coming election, painted in whatever colors they chose, and named for whatever cause they thought would win. The color should, of course, be pure white. White for the color of their skin, white for the purity of their motives. White for the clarity of their reason. Carpetbaggers and scalawags and freedman alike had almost finished what the war began. Was it not their duty, their honorable task, to rid the state of such?

He watched the weaving forms of dancers, making a tapestry that wrapped the night in romantic beauty, painting it with colors of luxury and gaiety and all the things that really meant life. Honor came and went, depending, it appeared, upon the time, the place, the persons assembled. Honor as he knew it must wait until he and his allies had won—had he not told Claude, just minutes ago, that not all men could afford the position Langlinais held? Heard Claude's unbelieving laughter?

He closed his eyes, heard the music of the quadrille, drew in the heavy lemon magnolia smell. He lifted his silver flask to his lips, sipped. This luxury and gaiety were as real as they had always been. They could be seen and touched and heard and tasted and smelled. While honor? Truth? They were flirts. He had more than his fill of flirtation. And more than his fill of being gulled. He turned his attention back to the group, busy with their plotting, behaving as though they thought only of the good of the state. When each one was fighting for, protecting, only his own stake. Well, he had a stake, too. Beau Chêne, and all that it meant to him. Perhaps the only honor left was to defend it, to work so that he and all that belonged to him could go back in time to before the war, when the art that lent such charm, such grace, to his sketches of their life never lied, never embellished, because the reality was so radiant, so lovely, so rich. If his grandchildren were ever to turn those pages, exclaiming at how exact his pen was, how true his eye, he'd better learn a far more practical art, one that had little to do with truth, or honor.

Marthe, smiling over the edge of her fan, was bored. Her limited visits to New Orleans, never during the ball season, made her training here more urgent: she danced and rode and picnicked with young men from up and down the bayou, but they were practice skirmishes only, war games during which she never lost sight of her ultimate target. She knew, from gleanings from her mother's correspondence with Natalie de Gravelle, that Henri was studying to be a doctor, working hard, "too hard for a wealthy man's son," his mother complained. Good. If he were working and studying, he had no time to be a beau. He was waiting for her, whether he knew it or not. She remembered their first meeting, the knowledge in his eyes. Then she twisted impatiently, almost dropping her fan. Damn! If some other girl was putting that to use . . . She saw her parents signaling her to join them. "I'm desolate," she murmured, shooting a final fusillade from her great armored eyes, "but I'm afraid it's time for me to go."

Nollie had been ready to go for some hours. His eye had become more practiced, his ability to take the essence of a scene and store it away until needed sharper. He was accustomed to that surface vision; what surprised him was that he was able to also to see what was happening underneath all the motion, the chatter, the laughter. Even if he did not seem to know what he was seeing, when he took up his pen, a life he had not suspected took shape. He looked at his finished drawings and knew that what he looked at was real. This ball, now. What a treasure! His fingers gripped an imaginary pen; perhaps if they were not too late getting home, he would draw for an hour, just a few lines, a little shading. He would ask his mother tomorrow about the studio in the garçonnière. His great-grandfather, wasn't it, who was an architect, did his work there? Painted the portrait of Great-great-grandmother Hélène? He moved toward the carriage, nodding at people as he passed. He laughed suddenly, remembering that just the other day, he had been passing the open parlor door when he heard his mother draw in her breath, then exclaim, "Noel, for heaven's sake! Do you see how Marthe is beginning to look just like Hélène?"

She did not, he thought, understand why that bothered her. He knew why it should. The artist who painted Hélène, unschooled in portraiture though he might have been, had been well schooled in women. The slight thrust of the body, the clear tilt of the head, the even stare of the eyes—taken separately, they were features, part of the artistic concept. Taken together—well, even at sixteen, Nollie knew what that portrait made him feel. The University of Virginia might not be so terrible a lot, when he came to think of it. It was near Washington. And not so far from New York. Where everyone did not know Nollie de Clouet, his father, his mother, and every ancestor before him. What fun to finally come out from behind his mask and find out if what his sketches showed him could ever be real.

"I danced so much with that young man, Sean O'Shea, you know the one, Jumie?" They were piled into the caleche, crowding together with disregard for pristine skirts and careful curls.

"O'Shea? That American? Mathilde, what you thinking of, dancing with an American?" Francie and Pierre had come along, Francie taking her position as young married woman with great firmness, commenting on Mathilde's every bow, every ribbon, every ruffle, until Jumie had thought Mathilde would forget herself and commit one of those sins against charity that are so hard to confess because one is almost never contrite and can certainly not vow never to commit again.

"Why should I not dance with an American? This was the centennial, Francie. We are all Americans." Mathilde's tone committed the sin; if one must confess thoughts, must one confess a tone?

"You may be an American. Me, I'm not." Francie put her arm through Pierre's, leaned her head on his shoulder. "I'm Acadian. So is Pierre. And so will our baby be."

"Francie? A baby?" Mathilde forgot insulted ribbons, offended lace. She hugged Francie, kissed Pierre. "But, Francie, think of it. When your baby is born, maybe papa will have gotten rid of the Radicals. Then we can be anything we want again—even Irish-Americans." She leaned toward her sister and whispered. Francie's face remained firm, but her eyes were soft.

"I think, Mathilde, the hair would be red. You know?"

Hot summer air was simmering through the night. The hot summer smells were full of magnolia and roses, yielding earth and hurrying water. The moon was coming down. It was a slip in time, when everything is possible. Even union.

# CHAPTER 19

## Redemption

"Damn!" The explosion of crystal against hard stone followed the explosion of Étienne de Gravelle's anger. "To see everything we've worked for this year lost because Hayes needs every Republican elector he can get—and Louisiana's are up for stealing!"

Noel took a new glass, filled it with claret, handed it to Étienne. "Grant's sending observers to watch the Returning Board—you can't know for certain the results won't be fair."

"God in heaven, de Clouet—all that country air must make your brain slow. That Returning Board has one purpose and one only—to dispute enough Democrat votes to give the governorship to Packard—and the presidency to Hayes."

"They can hardly dispose of Nicholls' victory that easily, Étienne. Look, it's only November fifteenth—let things settle down a bit. After all, the press in every parish, even here in New Orleans, reported quiet, orderly elections. They'll be hard put to prove charges of intimidation, terrorizing."

Étienne snorted. "Hard put? Yes, because there wasn't enough of it. If there had been, we'd not be going through all this. Damn it, Noel, the White League proved it could get rid of Radicals two years ago—we're damn fools to have ever let up."

"There'd have been another war if that rioting had continued—do you really want to take on the federal troops again?"

"We can if we have to. Ogden and Angell still drill their troops, they're still armed."

"Which is one of the biggest reasons the White League has earned a bad name for itself. It's hard to convince people of your peaceful intentions when you're waving a gun at them."

Étienne poured more wine into his glass, walked to the

window that overlooked Esplanade Avenue, and stared out into the street. "I'm not interested in convincing them. If it comes to that, I'm not interested in 'people' at all."

Noel laughed. "You may be a member of the reformed Democratic party, Étienne, but at heart, you're as much a Bourbon elitist as you ever were."

"You're not? Look at them, Noel. Scurrying about their own affairs, the future of this state as much on their minds as if they were geese in the pens at the market." He was pacing tightly in front of the open draperies, tension drawing his muscles into small springs whose work was slowed by his grating anger. "And yet, we're supposed to think about them! See that every freedman gets to vote, that every scrap-penny farmer rooting like his hogs for a living has as much to say about this state's future as you and I, who risk our fortunes constantly because of those damn common fools."

"You didn't really think we could wrest the governor's chair and the state house from the Radicals so easily, did you, Étienne? The Republicans did some fence-mending of their own when they ran Packard instead of Warmoth. Apparently, their fences are stronger."

"Because we didn't use our full force." Étienne grasped the fringed edges of the dull scarlet velvet draperies, pulled them shut in one rapid movement. He turned and glared at Noel. "Why in the hell did you join the White League if you disapprove of its tactics? I'd see the action taken at Coushatta, at Colfax, here at Liberty Place, repeated a dozen times over if it gave us back our state."

"Change made by violence isn't made with much conviction, Étienne. It has to be enforced with more violence—and more. You'd substitute mob rule for democracy."

"Democracy! Government by the people! Isn't that just another way of saying mob rule? What else can you call it when the ignorant poor have more say than those who not only pay the bills but understand what the bills are?" He pulled the finely carved desk chair to the hearth, flung himself into it. "I tell you, Noel, sometimes I think I'll just give it all up. Lord knows I can afford to. Cash in my lottery stock, move a few investments around—take Natalie and leave this whole damn country to the Packards and the Hayeses and all the rest of them. You ever feel that way?"

"It's a familiar feeling. We probably inherited it. From ancestors who did it."

"What does that mean, Noel?"

"I'm not sure. Maybe that time will always run out for men like you and me, Étienne. Not everyone is as tolerant of us as my neighbor, Langlinais."

"You introduced us at the convention in Baton Rouge, didn't you? What's he got to do with all this?"

"He seems to understand us, Étienne. And not let our ways bother him."

"Well, that's kind of him!"

"Don't be an idiot, de Gravelle. Surely you know that having money, living well, isn't much of an advantage in politics anymore. Poor white people don't have Negro slaves to look down on. Not only that, but they're not living much better than the freedmen are, a lot of them. Having a lien on your crop may not be the same as sharecropping—but in my part of the state, the results are often the same."

"Except, I suppose, for that neighbor."

"Not just Claude. People like him. Descendents of the exiles from Nova Scotia. They've kept hold of something—I don't know. A kind of sense of who they are."

"Fine." Étienne rose, gave the bell pull near him a vicious tug. "I'm glad someone knows who he is and likes it. I know who I am, but I don't like it. A man who worked damned hard to get a governor elected in this state who would mind his business only and let you and me take care of the rest. A man whose damned hard work wasn't enough. A man who can't think of one good reason not to tell Ogden and Angell to get their troops ready—we'll put Nicholls in office if we have to kill every damn carpetbagger and scalawag in this state to do it."

A small mulatto woman opened the study door and poked a tentative head in.

"LuBelle, tell your mistress we're dining out." When the woman stayed, disjointed head posing her question, Étienne said, "Yes, I know people are coming to dinner. They'll just have to be gotten rid of. You can tell Louis that the Returning Board won't certify their invitations—and they're all turned out. Understand?"

One more look at Étienne's face sent her running down the

hall; they could hear her knock on Natalie's boudoir door, the rapid low sounds spelling her urgency.

"Natalie'll tear my heart out and have it for déjeuner," Étienne said. "She's had this dinner on for weeks—a victory celebration, some damn thing."

"Who have you asked?"

"Who? The people you'd expect." He rattled off the names.

Noel took the heavily engraved gold watch Caroline had given him for their twentieth wedding anniversary from its pocket and clicked open the monogrammed cover. "There's just time before dinner, Étienne. Tell Natalie you've changed your mind—you are dining at home." When Étienne stared at him, anger finally abandoned in the face of Noel's solid calm, he said, "During all this, Étienne, I have not disagreed with you. I have not said I think what has happened is right—or good. Most importantly, Étienne, I have not said I thought nothing can be done."

"What are you thinking, Noel?" For the first time since his wineglass had left his hand, Étienne looked curious, interested. "What, do you see something I don't see? Noel—"

"Tell Natalie. Then come back and close the door." He heard Étienne charge down the hall, rap abruptly at Natalie's door, thrust open the door, call in a word or two. He was back instantly, closing and locking the walnut door, getting out the decanter of bourbon, fresh glasses.

"For a man so long on words, you talk to your wife very quickly, Étienne."

"I don't need to persuade her. Now—you have a plan?"

"An idea that can become a plan. Clearly, Louisiana's governorship will not be decided by the voters—not in this election anyway. So, since the will of the people cannot be carried out—even honest men are free to take any measure they think necessary to ensure that Nicholls prevails. You would agree with that, would you not, Étienne?"

"If I don't stop at force, I surely don't balk at a little theft, Noel. But you? You surprise me."

Noel leaned against the needlepoint chairback. His hand, almost unconsciously, followed the smooth curve of the chair arm, stroking the polished wood. "My people came to this country with some illusions—and no land. I have land—and no illusions. I have lost one to save the other—having lost them, it really doesn't matter to me what means I take to protect Beau Chêne. God knows, if we don't get some sanity back in office—there'll be nothing."

"Your idea, Noel. I'm waiting."

"Ellis and Gibson can be of use to us, I think. They represent us in Washington—let them begin there."

"In Washington?"

"They have the president's ear. Or can get it. If they were to begin to suggest, quietly, discreetly, that Grant take less interest in what happens here, that matters be allowed to run their course—"

"The course of the Returning Board? That will put Packard in office and send Nicholls back to Saint Mary Parish as quickly as it can?"

"Nicholls isn't the strongest of men, Étienne. But he's brave. And he has honor. Given a little support, he'll fight this insult. Given a lot of support here—and no interference from Washington—I think he'll win."

"So while Ellis and Gibson work on Grant, we work on Nicholls, is that it?"

Noel stood. The setting sun blazed crimson against the closed draperies; the glow, reflected by the low-blazing fire, gilded Noel's head, shadowed his face. "That's it. He is encouraged to hold fast—not only Nicholls, but everyone elected with him. A whole state house elected with him, Étienne."

"Two governors! Two houses convening! Damn it, Noel, it might just work! And if it does—but what does Grant get out of this?"

"We'll have to find out what he wants, won't we?" Noel picked up his tall hat, moved toward the door. "Better lay another place at dinner, Étienne. We'll talk with the others over brandy." He paused, looked back at Étienne, whose face once more had the happy optimism of a well-pampered infant. "Your guest list couldn't serve our purpose better if we'd planned it, Étienne."

Étienne waved, a careless acknowledgment of power. "You never know when someone will be needed, Noel. I make it a practice to keep all my allies friendly—and in debt to me."

"And your friends? What is your practice with them, Étienne?"

The sun was gone, the fire glow too small to light Étienne's eyes. But Noel knew the narrow look of them as Étienne answered. "My friends? Why, Noel. You are one of my oldest, closest friends. And you know how I treat you."

"Yes." The solid sound of the door closing could seal off Étienne's study. It could not seal off what they had begun there. If only he could see the end of all this, feel safe again. Ride his fields, lounge on his gallery. As he called for his carriage, he wondered if the violence he was doing to gain that peace would make it, finally, impossible to enjoy when he had it.

Marthe tossed her book aside, rose and went to the long windows giving onto the upper gallery at Beau Chêne. "These draperies are so faded, maman," she said. She filled her hand with pale blue damask, crushed it into awkward folds. A long glance at Caroline, busy at her escritoire with writing paper and pen. "The de la Houssayes change the draperies in their parlor every other year. Does that mean they're richer than we are?"

"It means Alicia de la Houssaye hasn't had money long enough not to be able to spend it—whether she needs something or not." Caroline could parry Marthe's practice thrusts with reflexed response; her eyes remained on the letter in her hand, as did her attention.

"But we haven't had money very long, maman."

"We haven't had it *again* very long, Marthe. But before the war, we had it. And had had it."

Marthe came and settled herself in a low lady's chair opposite her mother. She wore a loose wrapper, peach velvet with carelessly open ruffles of ivory Belgian lace. With Noel and Nollie both away, Caroline sometimes relaxed their routine and had dinner served to them in her boudoir. "It gives them a free evening," she said. It also gave Marthe an evening free of Caroline—and Caroline an evening free of Marthe.

"You mean people who have always had money don't spend it?"

"Not in ways to let people know what they have. That's not comme il faut, Marthe. Not at all."

"But we do it anyway. Do you think there's a girl on Bayou Teche who doesn't know to the last cent how much I spent on the dress I wore to Mignon Blanchet's birthday fête?"

"There's nothing we can do about that. Certainly, when we see a fine painting, walk on a floor covered by a fine rug, we recognize the quality. Ladies don't look beyond that, Marthe.

They never, never mention price."

Marthe's lancer gaze fastened on a letter that lay among the clutter; the script was dark, thick, with many dashes, question marks. "I've heard you talk about price." Caroline picked up the pen, began writing in her clear, round hand. "About the price of lottery stock. To Monsieur Étienne de Gravelle."

The will that had taken Caroline through months of dark imprisonment kept the pen moving evenly across the page. She could hardly see the words she was writing, could not comprehend any meaning they might have. She had long since seen Marthe as an opponent. She had not defined that opposition as openly hostile. Now she made her hand finish the note to Marguerite Blanchard thanking her for the fête. She felt Marthe's gaze; its heat, she thought, could melt the sealing wax, its force could mark it. Not until she addressed the letter did she lift her face. "It's valuable stock, Marthe. And it pays excellent dividends. I would be foolish not to keep current on such a fine investment."

"Do you care about papa's other investments like that?" Marthe stood up, began to circle the room, weaving through the tables and settees and fire screens, preening herself in a mirror, dancing to remembered or imagined music, forcing her mother to follow her feinting lead.

"Those I understand."

"And you understand the lottery."

"Marthe—"

Marthe's feet could find space in a ballroom, on a terrace, on the deck of a steamboat plying the bayou, could find the precise space that would make her the immediate center of all space around her. She took that circle of attention with her, seemed to have it always to hand, so that no matter how late she arrived at a gathering, how distant she was from the activity, after a kind of lurch that made new rules for time and motion, all revolved around her. Caroline could feel herself being pulled by that centering force; she shook herself, and looked away.

"Because what I thought I heard, I might have been mistaken, what I thought I heard, was that it wasn't papa's lottery stock you and Monsieur de Gravelle were talking about. It was yours." Not even a pause in the weaving, feinting, bobbing moves. "And so I wondered if maybe papa had given you some. And if he had, if maybe he would give me some. For Christmas. Wouldn't that make a nice gift? A practical gift?" Marthe paused.

"Or would anyone give lottery stock away? Well, probably. If the two people were—close. Like papa and me." Pause. "Or papa and you."

"I don't think anyone gives stock, anything really valuable, to silly little girls, Marthe." Caroline stood back from the candlelight, put her face in deliberate shadow. "Or trips to New Orleans either. We didn't go with your father this time because it's all business. As you know, a very grand trip is planned at carnival. When you will be presented at the Comus ball." She gathered up the letters, put them in her leather letter box, turned the small gold key and tucked it deep in her dress. "If, of course, you get completely over being a silly little girl. Mardi Gras may not be real, Marthe, but it is serious."

That night, Caroline decreed they should dress and have dinner just as they did when Noel was home. She sat squarely in her place, back straight, held away from the tall support of her chair. "Let us finish our discussion of the Pope poem," she said. "I'm not sure you really grasp its meaning." Her voice was pleasant, light, courteous. Her face was bright with interest, measuring as it judged, smiling as it praised. Tobias, going to the warming oven for more bread, told Sarah, the cook: "I don't know what Miss Marthe done to get her maman mad at her, but Miss Caroline, she's mad *clear* through."

After dinner, when Caroline had gone back to her boudoir, Marthe slipped out to the cabin where Sarah lived. "What you doing out here, child? Your maman skin you good if she catches you out after dark." But she patted the bench next to her, beckoned Marthe to sit.

"She's ready to skin me anyway, Sarah."

"That's what Toby told me. Now, Miss Marthe, why can't you stop pestering your maman?"

"I don't know. When Nollie went off to Virginia, I thought maman and I'd be together a lot. Doing lady things." She turned quickly, caught the wide smile on Sarah's face. "Now, Sarah. I do know how to be a lady. Whether maman thinks so or not."

Sarah patted Marthe's arm. "I know that, honey. Seems like you and your maman get up on opposite sides every morning of your lives. Happens like that, sometime."

"But, Sarah, wouldn't you think that after all we went through, we'd be closer? I mean, I was old enough to understand what was happening. In the war. Nollie was just a baby, but I *knew*. And I helped as much as I could, Sarah, you know

I did." Tears Marthe held back when near her mother came easily here; she leaned against Sarah's shoulder and let the angry sobs break.

"I know, honey, I know."

"But if I so much as mention the war, all that—she looks at me as if I was a—a—*Yankee.*"

"She don't like to be reminded, Miss Marthe. Your maman, it was hard for her. Not being able to do any better by you children."

Marthe lifted her head. "But she did, Sarah! She did the best she could, we always had food—and clothes—"

"She don't see it that way, your maman. If it hadn't been for those Langlinais—well, Miss Marthe, I guess you all would have gone under. Your maman would, anyway. Little old thin thing . . ." Sarah shook her turbaned head.

"There's nothing wrong with needing help, Sarah."

"Honey, there ain't. But your maman—she's got that stiff-necked pride all them Bertauts do. Lord, they'd rather starve than take help. If it hadn't been for you and Nollie—I think your maman'd just have sat up in that attic with that mouth closed tight and starved herself to death." Sarah cocked her head at the moon, just clearing the top of a wind-bare sycamore tree. "Time you went back, Miss Marthe. I put some of those light rolls up for you—and some preserves. You take some up to bed now."

"Well, if maman thinks she lowered herself somehow to save us—I can't help that."

"No, you can't." Sarah rose, hugged Marthe close. "But, child, you can help riling her. You're getting too big for that, you hear me?"

Up in her boudoir, Caroline opened the letter box, sorted through its contents, and removed three letters. She slipped them between the pages of a book she would take to bed to read; the post at her head was hollow, the pineapple finial easily removed. Étienne's letters would be safe there until she decided she could part with them. As for her stock, it was safe in New Orleans, its dividends paid into an account in Étienne's bank. Marthe would not tell Noel, her quarrel was not with him. They had survived one war, she and Marthe, only to begin another. So far, Caroline was holding her own. But as she undressed, got ready for bed, it occurred to her that she had been so involved in the battles that she did not know the cause. She lay back against her pillows, book unopened in her hand. Thinking back, she could see a kind of pattern emerge. When she and Marthe fought, was it not, no matter the surface issue, at bottom, always, for primacy at Beau Chêne?

The slow gradual warmth of his oiled palm rubbing against the leather seeped up into Jumie's strongly moving arm; he reached over, dipped his hand into the saddle oil, and began to work the other side of the saddle. "Looks like we might need to replace the girth straps," he called to Claude. "Don't want to lose 'cause the saddle falls off."

Claude stepped back from the horse he had been currying, faced her squarely. "Don't even use the word where she can hear you. If she doesn't know the word, she can't do it, isn't that it?"

Jumie joined Claude, fixing a proud eye on the mare before him. "Any horse that looks this good has to win, papa. She has to."

"Looks? Looks don't mean she runs fast, Jumie." But the parry was reflex, Claude's small defense he kept against the surprises one knew were coming—but not when, not where.

Jumie ducked beneath the railed gate, began running his hand over the mare's thick coat. "Not just pretty, papa. But strong. Good muscles." He skimmed over the well-made flanks, the long legs. Lifted each hoof, checked for cuts, bruises on the pads. "I timed her again this morning. She's beat her own best speed three times in a row."

"So. Maybe we take LeBleu's money. You think?"

"And the side bets as well."

Claude took corn from a basket, held it out to the mare. "Don't let your mother know you're betting. You know what she thinks of gambling."

"Sure. Don't do it unless you can fix it to win." He needn't look at his father to see that this was one surprise Claude's defenses hadn't prepared for. "Don't mistake me, papa. I don't say maman cheats. I'm saying she knows some things that look like gambling are really sure to win. Like the lottery is for the de Clouets."

"Not because they gamble on it, Jumie. Because they own some of it."

"Right."

"So how is making side bets on the race a sure thing?

Winning the purse—now that's one thing. Even if we don't win, we haven't lost money. Betting—Jumie, we work too hard, yes. A little here, a little there—what I'd bet at bourré— but you, you're talking big side bets, isn't that it?"

"About two thousand dollars' worth."

Claude's silence took less time and said more than if he had spoken. Then—"Jumie, what you know about this race I don't know?"

"LeBleu's horse is sick." Jumie patted the mare's face, picked a small hay straw from her black mane. He ducked back out of the stall, took Claude's arm, and began walking to the stable door.

"That's reason for him to postpone the race, Jumie. With no penalty."

Jumie stood in the opening, the soft warm darkness of the stable behind him, the hard cold darkness of early December ahead of him. He was almost accustomed to winter again, to the solid chill that descended on his feet the instant he left his bed and Geneviève, to the dim ache in his neck and shoulder muscles from working in air that soaked skin, muscle, and bone and then iced it so deeply that even warm arms, warm breasts, warm Geneviève, could not get him thawed. Until the weather reversed itself, declared a holiday, called back summer's heat, blanketed them with it so quickly that there was no time to throw off heavy clothes and covers, no time to open staled houses, no time for anything but lung fever and chest sickness, rough coughs and fevered nights. If they could get the babies through the winter—

"LeBleu doesn't know the horse is sick. So he won't call off the race."

"Tell me." Claude's tone was even, clearly neutral. Jumie could almost see, could certainly know, how Claude was turning over what Jumie had already said, sorting it, putting it in an arrangement he could understand.

"One of his boys was exercising the horse yesterday, out in their pasture that goes by the road. I stopped to talk, tease him a little. You know. Well, I could hear how that horse was breathing. Beginning to have to work at it, you know? Even in a four-arpent race, she'll never last."

"But, merde, Jumie. LeBleu's no fool. He'll know the horse is sick. He'll hear what you hear."

"It's not that plain. Me—well, I study a lot, papa, you

know that. And the library at Beau Chêne, it's full of books about horses, from when they had that big stable. I could tell, from how the horse sounded—and from other little signs—it's getting sick. Distemper maybe. Won't be really bad for a few days—but she sure as hell won't run her best tomorrow."

"The stars are good tonight," Claude said. Hung against the sky like baubles floating from a broken chain, the winter stars flamed coldly. "My papa used to show me the shapes." He looked at Jumie. "I remember when you brought home that book from Beau Chêne, and all the stars' names were different. I guess papa made up stories and names he thought I'd like to hear. Papa didn't care too much for what other people thought things were. Just what he thought they were." They walked across the rain-packed mud of the stableyard, fastened the thong that closed the gate with particular care, took the path through Françoise's kitchen garden up to the house. "So—you're not going to tell LeBleu?"

"It's his horse. Any man who owns something, he should know how to care for it. Especially when he plans to make money with it." Just before they climbed the steps into Françoise's world, Jumie said, "Papa! It's two thousand dollars. And the purse—that's four hundred more. Not much from anyone. Little here, little there. Like you said, their bourré money. And, papa—who really cares if some farmer from Breaux Bridge gets beat? Now, papa, you know they want Claude Langlinais to win! You want to make everyone sad?"

Françoise's shadow, tall, straight, looming, filled the kitchen window's light. "Me? Make everyone sad? Mais, no, Jumie! Each man makes enough for himself, he needs me to make more?"

"Gumbo?" Françoise held up a bowl, gestured at Jumie.

"Geneviève has supper, maman."

"She has my gumbo?"

"She has her gumbo. Maman, you both make the best gumbo when I'm eating it."

The pull of pleasure at the edge of Françoise's mouth lasted until her lips closed over the edge of the big spoon. Then she said, "But my gumbo—it's the best even when you're not eating it. Claude, you shoot me some ducks tomorrow, I'll make a big gumbo for when those men come out from New Orleans with Noel. You can take a pot over to Beau Chêne, that Sarah, she knows about ovens, but not much about gumbo."

"What men from New Orleans?" Claude took the bowl Françoise handed him, heaped rice into the center of the rich soup. He pinched file between his thumb and forefinger, powdered it over the surface of the gumbo. Breaking off the pointed end of a hot loaf of bread, he went to the table and sat.

"Don't wait for the blessing, Claude. God doesn't like cold food any more than we do. Jumie, if you stay to listen, you stay to eat."

"Françoise, these men—tell me."

Jumie could almost see his mother clamping her mouth over this knowledge as she had clamped it over her big spoon.

"I heard in New Iberia. At the post office, Caroline was there, sending a big box to Nollie. They don't have shops in Virginia! Anyway, she'd just heard from Noel. He's been in New Orleans since way last month. He's coming here tomorrow, bringing some of those men he works with down there. Claude, you know that work."

"His banker is there. They've got the sugar mill—de Gravelle usually comes after grinding season to check it over. I've met him a time or two."

"These other men aren't his bankers. Aren't in the sugar mill. They're up to something, Claude. Something about the election."

"Merde! The election! Once again, we'll have two governors, two legislatures. Until someone convinces the other one to give up. Or bribes him to give up. Or gets rid of his followers. It's no news they're trying to keep Nicholls in. Sacrebleu, I worked for the man myself."

"Caroline kept saying these little things, you know how they do it, a name, a word. If you are smart, you don't let on you know what they're talking about. Claude, it's not just Nicholls and Packard. It's the president, too."

"Tilden? He's in as much trouble as Packard and Nicholls. But they're supporting him, good Democrat that he is." Claude went to the stove, filled his bowl again. "Not much use in that. The Returning Board's run by the Radicals—they'll throw out enough Democrat votes to give Hayes the presidency, isn't that it? Nicholls may as well enjoy himself, he won't last long."

"That's not what it sounded like, Claude. I'm telling you. Get me some ducks, get me some big fish. Jumie's not the only one who eats and listens, too."

"You coming to the race, maman?" Jumie spooned up the

rest of his gumbo, long ready to be gone. One thing to know a horse race could be worked; maman was talking as though any race could be worked. Men didn't think they were gambling when they voted; if enough men agreed with you, you won. If not, you lost. Maybe winning depended not on the number of men agreeing with you but on the force of that number. Horses were easy.

"In this cold? Who ever heard of a race in December?"

"LeBleu wants to try his horse out, see if she runs as fast as he brags she does. Four arpents, maman, that's no time at all. Your nose won't even know it's outside."

"I'll think on it," she said.

Geneviève had not only gumbo steaming on the stove, but a big kettle of water with spices and lemon rind in it. Jumie entered the kitchen as she snatched the kettle from the heat, carried it to a corner where both children were stuffed into one rocking chair, and placed it on a low table before them. She picked up a thick cotton square and made a shield, keeping the aromatic steam headed toward her babies. "Le traiteur gave me some herbs to put in, too," she said. "For their chests." Her smooth round face was so seldom crossed by anything but smiles that the simple absence of her ordinary happiness warned Jumie.

He crossed the space between the door and rocker in long fast steps, bent over the round faces whose high color, he could see now, was more than fire blush or windburn from a cold outing. "What's wrong?"

"They're hot. And they don't breath easily. Hear?"

No coughing yet, only the small pause between each small breath, the sign that muscles would work harder, and still harder, until each forced outrush of air was surrounded by the hard rasp of a slowly closing chest. "Is it lung fever?"

Not just absence of happiness now. Fear. And a helplessness he'd not seen before. "Oh, Jumie," she said, throwing the cotton shield to the floor and herself into his arms. "I'm so afraid!"

No use to say—don't be. Not when some families had a dozen or more graves in their plot, and almost no room taken at all because of the tiny lengths of most coffins. "They're strong babies, Geneviève. Fat, they sleep well—" He pulled her closer into the circle his arms made, looked over her at the little boy and girl slumped against each other in the rocker.

Claudine at two was beginning to look more like her mother, the short fat baby curls lengthening into flirtatious long ones. 'Tit Frère, only one year away from his mother's protective flesh, was heavily surrounded by protective flesh of his own; his width and height were so much the same, his grand-père Claude said, that to get 'Tit Frère from one place to the other, all they had to do was roll him up and give him a gentle shove. The flesh was still there, but it no longer spoke of health. The pink tones were from an alien source, the bright eyes unfocused. "I'll fix more steam," Jumie said, and picked up the kettle.

"No, you sit with them. Tell them a story, Jumie, or sing to them. I—I've been singing all afternoon, they're so fretful, restless . . ."

He saw that her worry fatigued her more than her work. "Good. I will. And maybe if we make some mulled wine—it will help them sleep?"

Both babies were put on the trundle that pulled out from under their parents' bed. "We'll take turns watching," Jumie said. "You'll be no good to them if you get sick, too, Geneviève."

"I'm not going to sleep anyway," she said. "I'm not even going to get undressed."

"Yes, you are. At least you can rest," he said. He lay next to her, holding her, hushing her, stroking her. Then he listened to the hours rasp by on the heated breath of his children.

By dawn, the babies seemed easier. "Maybe it's over," Geneviève said, hovering over the low bed in which they slept. She put a testing hand on their lax cheeks. "They don't feel so warm. Their breathing—is it better?"

"Maybe." He had become so accustomed to the way they sounded, the little girl seeming to lead with her rough exhalations, the baby boy following with hesitant hard sounds of his own, that he couldn't say—yes, better; no, worse. "Well, LeBleu is lucky anyway. He doesn't know to call off the race, but it'll be called off just the same. He'll be saved a lot!"

"The race is today!" Geneviève stopped in the middle of fastening her dress, stared at Jumie. "Oh, Jumie, you can't call it off!"

"But, Geneviève, I can't race today! Leave you? Leave the babies? Geneviève—"

She took his arm, moved him toward the kitchen, made

him sit while she filled a fresh kettle, put coffee beans to roast. "Jumie, the babies seem better, you know they do. Anyway, Jumie, there comes a time we have to decide, isn't that so?"

"Decide whether a horse race is more important than my babies?"

"No. Decide whether we're going to make plans and keep them going—or let things happen any kind of a way." The night must have been even longer for Geneviève than for him; it had given her time enough to age in. "Today the children are sick, so you give up all that money. Money that will buy them good things when they are well again. Another day, Jumie, it will be something else. Jumie"—she came to him, put her hands on his shoulders, looked down at him—"Jumie, you can't stay home and do my work and not do yours."

"It's not doing your work to worry about the children, to think what—might happen while I'm gone."

Now she sat on his lap, leaned herself into the easy slope of his chest. "Jumie. Jumie. Something can always happen while you're gone. Don't you know that?"

He didn't. In this happy house? Where Geneviève played as though her babies were dolls, and her kitchen full of doll's tea things?

"I know that. That's why I make myself happy." She saw the cloud across his eyes, like steam left from the kettles that had filled the night. "Life will find enough to make us sad. So every day, when I say my prayers, I say also—dear God, today I will look for each bit of joy, each piece of beauty, You have put in this world. And, Jumie, I do."

"Is the race joy or beauty?" he said. And laughed softly against her soft neck.

Now they could cross a bridge back from fear. They could grind the beans, make coffee, eat breakfast, tiptoe in to see the sleeping children. When Jumie left to meet his father, Claudine and 'Tit Frère still slept. "It's a good sign," Geneviève said. And—"Don't tell your mother!"

No, don't tell Françoise. she was no traiteur, to come, offer remedies, leave instructions, depart for her next call. Françoise would move in, take over. The children's illness first. Then the children's sleeping quarters. Then the children. Then the house. Then the marriage. Zut! Those men from New Orleans, if they did have some big plan, should include Françoise in their discussions. Her gumbo and courtbouillon wasn't all she could give them, no.

Caroline had drawn upon all the resources of Beau Chêne to welcome Noel and his guests. She had sent the gardener and his two helpers into the woods to cut pine branches and holly; wearing heavy gloves to protect her hands, she had worked along with Nat to make looping lengths of smoky-green to hang along the gallery rail. Marthe had tied the bows, spending hours fussing over the great puffs of scarlet taffeta that she cut into wide strips and turned into flaming points of cheer. Fresh candles had been placed in all the sconces and candelabra; Sarah's ten-year-old daughter, pressed into service in the emergency, had declared herself plumb tuckered from trimming wicks and scraping old wax. Sarah had disappeared into the kitchen as soon as she heard Noel was bringing gentlemen from New Orleans; the louder she sang, the better her cooking was going, Caroline said, and ordered everyone to leave Sarah completely alone.

Now she and Marthe stood in the parlor, a bowl of Nat's late-blooming roses on the table between them. Caroline looked at her small watch, hanging from a heavy gold chain around her lace-collared neck. "They should be here. Sarah's turtle soup will keep, of course, but still . . ."

"Who all's coming anyway?" Marthe smoothed the blue fabric of her dress. For once, she had put on a properly demure gown with no prodding from her mother. She had pulled her rebel curls into a low knot at the nape of her neck, centering that captured gold with a dull clip of onyx and silver. A simple silver locket was her only other ornament; judging herself in the pier mirror in her room, Marthe had tried to see with Caroline's eyes—she was learning that among the other things that displeased her mother, her competing young beauty ranked high.

"Colonel Roberts—"

"The newspaper editor?"

"Yes. And General Richard Taylor. A Mr. E. A. Burke, and Mr. Ellis. He's in Washington, usually. But he works closely with Governor Nicholls—they all do."

"He's not governor yet, is he? Isn't that what all the fuss is about?"

"I'm sure, Marthe, that your father and Étienne de Gravelle would not be going to this amount of effort if they did not have good reason to believe that, in the end, Nicholls most certainly will be the official governor of this state."

"Oh, is Monsieur de Gravelle coming?"

"Yes." Caroline looked at Marthe, her gaze a twin of the one Marthe had measured herself against. "And, I believe, Henri, as well. He has a long Christmas break from his medical studies and needs a change."

"Beau Chêne will certainly be one! I can't think he'd leave New Orleans to come be buried in the country."

"But he can't hunt in New Orleans, Marthe. Or fish. Or do the kind of riding we do here."

Marthe sighed. "Do all men like hunting better than the theater? Fishing better than balls?" She straightened a pink tearose that had slipped from its place in Caroline's arrangement. "Though Henri is very pleasant when he escorts his sisters and me in New Orleans." She glanced at Caroline. "Maman, after I'm presented, do you think maybe Henri will escort me alone?"

Something in her mother's eyes frightened her, a strangeness, a look almost of fear. "Henri? Escort you?" Caroline shook her head, as though clearing it from a heavy veil of spiderwebs. "Marthe, do you say that to tease me?"

Of course. Henri was Étienne de Gravelle's son. Something she knew, but had not put into her fancies, her daydreams. The fear was still in her mother's eyes; it was, Marthe saw, fear of her, of what she knew. The hard weight that filled her chest, made it difficult to be easy with her mother, lightened. How awful to be her mother, to have learned how helpless she was, to have tried to become strong again—and to know that still, she owed her life to others.

"No, maman. No. I—I only thought—since all the de Gravelles, Madame de Gravelle, the girls, all of them, are such great friends of ours—that perhaps Henri would be a proper escort." The fear receded a little, but still, like a small watchful animal when the predator has passed but is not fully gone, it waited. "You know, maman, it isn't always easy, in New Orleans. The other girls talk about things I don't know about, they go out more—Henri is kind. He makes me feel that I am the same as the others. I'm not afraid when I'm with him."

"Afraid!" Caroline moved swiftly to Marthe, caught her in

a quick embrace. "Afraid! But, Marthe, why should you be afraid, ever? You are lovely, charming, everything a young woman should be—"

Marthe felt tears coming; she blinked them back. "Maman—am I really?"

Under the heavy rhythm of a well-matched team striking the gravel drive with pacing hooves, Marthe heard the answer. "Yes."

Caroline went to the window, looked down the long drive between the towering oaks. "There's the carriage—the steamboat must have been on time after all." She opened the French doors, stepped out and began to wave a lace-edged handkerchief.

Marthe followed her, eyes closing briefly against the sudden assault of bright air. "Papa's new team is marvelous, isn't it, maman? I wish we had the race horses again. Did you know the Langlinaises have one now? They're racing her today, a match race over at the track in Breaux Bridge. A four-hundred-dollar purse, and lots more in side bets."

Caroline was pressed against the low railing, watching the carriage move through the banded light of the alley. Something had happened with Marthe, she wasn't sure just what, but some kind of change. Maybe a step toward growing up. Toward letting her mother go. Caroline felt her own beauty surrounding her, giving her the centered place she had thought long passed to Marthe. Maybe they could be two women who liked each other, if they could not successfully be mother and child. "A racing stable again, Marthe? It took your great-grandmother's almost complete attention to keep them going, before the war. Certainly, there's no one here who has the time—or the interest—to do that." The carriage pulled up below them, stopped. Noel descended and shouted a greeting, then turned to help his guests. Marthe followed her mother down the stairs, her thoughts spinning past the meal ahead. For her, the visit would properly begin when the men retired to papa's study, maman retired to her room—and she had Henri to herself.

"We'll leave you to your cigars," Caroline said. Sarah's menu had been a triumph. She had been called to the dining room to be praised by each guest, and Roberts had said that on his return to New Orleans, he would write a piece about a country visit that would carry good word about her cooking to every household where the *Times* was read.

"And will you write about what else is cooked here?" Étienne said. The piquante sauce in which Sarah had presented the squirrel stimulated his digestive juices, but the piquancy of possibly making love to de Clouet's wife in de Clouet's home stimulated him more pleasurably.

"I think the *Times* will wait to join in the glad cries of the rest of the Conservative press when Nicholls is miraculously made our permanent governor," Roberts said.

"So long as we know what we need to make us glad," Ellis said.

"And what we are willing to offer to get it," Noel added.

"Let me outline the situation as we seem to define it," Étienne said. He took up the brandy decanter Zeke had placed near Noel, filled the glass before him. Even seated, almost lounging in the heavy chair, Étienne seemed to assume a lecturer's pose. "As long as Colonel Angell and Colonel Ogden have troops, Packard will rule only by armed force. Grant may have been a victorious general, but I doubt—we all doubt— if he wishes to be remembered as a president who had to use federal troops to keep order more than ten years after the close of hostilities."

"What hostilities have closed? The war has only gone underground, de Gravelle," Taylor said.

"Right. And our good Republican president is well aware of that. After all, what does he care, really, who is governor in an unredeemed state? It is becoming almost an embarrassment to the Republicans that South Carolina, Florida, and Louisiana are still unrepentant, still not back in the fold. So—"

"So," Noel said, taking coffee from the pot that swung in a silver holder over an alcohol flame. "So, we offer Grant— and Hayes—a deal. If they will support Nicholls in the end, we will quietly see to it that resistance to the Returning Board's decision to declare a sufficient number of Democrat votes in Louisiana void is for appearance's sake only."

"We'll damn well ask for more than that," Burke said. "There's a move under way to impeach Grant in the House— which the Democrats control. We can throw that into the pot— and in return, gentlemen, in return for stopping impeachment, we ask for federal subsidies for the Texas-Pacific Railroad, and for restoration and maintenance of our levees."

"There appears to be only one small difficulty in all of this,"

Noel said. "How can one and the same election result in electoral votes for a Republican president and total endorsement of a Democratic governor?"

"Leave that to me," Ellis said. "And to my friend Mr. Burke."

Zeke appeared in the door. "You rang for me, Mister Noel?"

"We're finished here, Zeke. Are these gentlemen's rooms ready?"

"Sarah's child wanting to show them up. Bags already unpacked, dinner clothes laid out."

Noel rose, signaling adjournment. "I'll be in the library the rest of the afternoon, if any of you feel like company. Otherwise, Caroline and I will expect you at six in the parlor. Zeke can get horses saddled, lay out a tour of the grounds. Ring for anything you don't see."

Étienne lingered, circling them in the last fumes of his cigar. "Where is everyone else? My son and your daughter? Caroline?"

"I heard Marthe suggest a ride to Henri. Caroline, I assume, is resting. Did you want her?"

"Don't bother yourself, Noel. Like your other guests, if there's something I want I don't see, I'll ring." He patted his firm stomach, an almost automatic gesture of self-satisfaction and pleasant expectation that satisfaction would always be his state. As he watched Étienne leave, Noel wondered again why he trusted de Gravelle so completely with his business and at the same time disliked him so much.

By the time he and Claude had saddled the mare and the two horses they would ride to the track, Jumie had almost forgotten the children's illness. Geneviève was right, you couldn't worry yourself into a state over each mishap, each setback. Hadn't the children recovered from every little tumble, every encounter with the perils of the world, so far? He crossed himself quickly, said a fervently brief prayer, and set his attention on Jolie Mademoiselle. Her dam was not a thoroughbred, but her sire was; descended from Kentucky stock, he accounted for her proud lines. The dam was good work stock, and though she was relatively short and chunky, her deep chest had translated itself to her daughter, providing the long wind needed for these intense short runs. "So, four arpents, Jolie, two hundred fifty-six yards, you think you can cover that length so fast LeBleu's horse gets mad if he doesn't already have distemper?"

"She says she can," he reported to Claude, who stood finishing a mug of coffee he'd brought out to the stable.

"She damn well better," Claude said. "We're going to have a little more than two thousand dollars in side bets by the time the match starts."

"So if we don't take it, they'll lose it at bourré tonight— or betting on Felix's roosters."

"Maman's not coming?"

"She says she's got things to do. You know your maman— she won't play when she thinks she should be working."

"Maman even works when she plays," Jumie said, and looked away from Claude.

They mounted their horses, Jumie holding Jolie's reins in one hand and those of his own horse in the other. In a small procession, they filed out of the stableyard, down the drive, and onto the road. They turned toward Breaux Bridge, setting an easy pace that would warm Jolie's blood and loosen her muscles. Françoise, hearing the tripled hooves going past under the kitchen window, went to the front door and stood in its high shadow to watch them down the drive. "If he'd put that much work in his politics!" She shrugged, then sent a straightening jerk down her back. Well, he would. He would.

"Pretty country." Henri's eyes were on Marthe while he spoke. They had ridden halfway to New Iberia, then turned back and filled the empty road with the fast sounds of their galloping horses. Now they were on a trail through the thick woods that lay behind Beau Chêne. "Lord, I envy you living out here."

"When you live in New Orleans? Do you love hunting and fishing so much you'd choose it over the theater? And balls? Oh, Henri!"

He guided his horse around a low-hung pine branch, held it back from Marthe's path. "New Orleans is a filthy city. It's been much cleaner since the federal troops have been there— Yankees know how to scrub, believe me. You can actually breathe when walking our streets, I have to say that for them."

"Well, so now it's clean as well as brilliant. What more could you want?" She was searching for another meaning in Henri's words; he must intend her to believe his interest in the country was interest in her, he must mean for her to know that, compared to Marthe, even New Orleans could not place first.

No one preferred existing out here to living in New Orleans!

"This." They had reached the edge of the woods, stood poised at the top of a pasture that swept down to brown-bare fields, littered with the dry leavings of the cane harvest. "Open sky. Fields. A place to work without having to pay heed to all the grand dames and old men. A place to set my own life, not just follow what someone else has already done. And done and done and done."

"But you're the oldest son. Doesn't your father expect you to take his place? Not in the bank, of course not. But in New Orleans—in the things he does."

"I've no idea what my father expects, Marthe. I'm not in personal conversation with him that often." There was none of Étienne's pleasured portliness about his lean son, none of those avid appetites in his eyes. Henri looked at her, the deliberateness of his words scored by the seriousness of his steady gaze. "As for taking his place in New Orleans—I'm not sure I understand what that place is. Or would care for it if I did."

Bother! Marthe thought of the magnificent dress Tante Rose had planned for the Comus ball. It was meant to please Henri, to duplicate the creamy lace she wore the first time they met; to hint, perhaps, in its shimmering folds of white silk, of wedding gowns and solemn vows.

"But you will practice in New Orleans, won't you? Where your friends are? Your family?"

Henri's eyes went back to the field before them. "Is country life really so terrible, Marthe, that you can't endure it?" Then— "Here, we'll put some excitement into it. I'll race you across." Marthe slapped her horse's rump, leaned low over his smooth neck. Henri's sisters might excel in the parlor—but there was no question of who was the better horsewoman. If country life was what charmed Henri—

They pulled up at the fence of the Jumie Langlinais' kitchen garden. Broccoli and greens and cauliflower still grew there, and turnips poked purple noses above the chilled ground. "Who lives there?" The smoke coming from all the chimneys seemed strange; did the Langlinais also have a houseful of guests?

"Jumie and Geneviève Langlinais. His papa owns a lot of land around here, I don't know, a lot of other things, too, I guess. A race horse. Henri, they have a race here. It makes me so mad. I'm going to ask papa for some horses for Christmas. To start the stables again. Beau Chêne used to have won-

derful horses, when my great-grandmother Aimée lived here.
And we still have the building, it wouldn't take much work to
get it ready, and there's a lot of track near here . . ."

"You couldn't have really good stables here if you lived in
New Orleans, Marthe. But you could always live here and go
to New Orleans for the race season. Which is also the ball
season."

She looked at his eyes, much bluer than she had remembered. She looked at his mouth, whose softness she wished
she knew to remember. After all, when one had money, one
took civilization anywhere. "Henri, Geneviève always has hot
coffee and fresh cakes. Let's go see."

Though Geneviève knew the knock at the front door could
not possibly be Jumie returning, she still sent a fear-worded
prayer that it was. When she opened the door and saw Marthe
de Clouet and a young man, she could not for a moment think
of any reason they should be there. Marthe, seeing the deep
marks of worry that were setting Geneviève's face in a mask
stepped immediately inside. "Geneviève, whatever is the matter?"

"The babies—Claudine and 'Tit Frère—oh, Marthe, they're
so sick!"

"Where are they?"

The young man had followed Marthe in. Now he seemed
to fill the space in the center hall, making Geneviève look only
at him. "Where are they?"

"In—in there—" She gestured toward the open bedroom
door, stared as he pushed past her and almost marched down
the hall. "Marthe, who—what is he doing?"

"He's Henri de Gravelle, he's a medical—Geneviève, he's
a medical student! He's almost a doctor! Maybe he can do
something." She took Geneviève by the hand, pulled her along.
By the time they reached the room, Henri was bent over the
babies, ear pressed first to one struggling chest and then the
other.

"I think it's diphtheria," he said without looking up. "They're
strangling."

"My God!"

Geneviève rushed to the bed, tried to take her children into
her arms. "I've tried everything. They were better when Jumie
left, that's why he went. Then after noon, I don't know, they
go worse. So hot! I made steam, I rocked—" Henri's arm came

around her. "Are they going to die?" She would not look at his eyes for the answer, only listen to a voice that might lie to her.

"There is something I can do—I'll have to go back to Beau Chêne, get my kit."

"I'll go! For heaven's sake, Henri, you can't! Where is it?"

"In my room. Ask Zeke, he unpacked my things." He looked at the two children, already pallid with the light blue underlay of dying blood. "Thank God I brought it. Papa teased me, asked me if I were going to go around soliciting patients when I was supposed to be having a good time."

"Your papa's an idiot," Marthe said. "I'll take Brun, he's faster."

"Can you handle him? He's pretty mean—"

"Henri. Do you really ask?" Then she was gone. Henri directed Geneviève in filling more kettles, helping him make a tent over the trundle to keep the steam inside. They draped linen over the mosquito bar, hammered a pie tin into a kind of funnel, fastened it to the spout of the biggest kettle.

"Now while we wait for Marthe to get back, let me tell you what I'm going to do. It's called a tracheotomy, it's a very simple operation, really—"

Geneviève clasped his wrists with hands almost as fevered as her children's brows. "You're going to cut my babies?"

"Here, Madame Langlinais." He pointed to his trachea. "A little incision. So I can place a tube they can breathe through." He saw the terror in her eyes. A rush of sympathy swept over him. And then a firmness, a control. "Madame, trust me. It will make them better."

"Explain it all to me. If I understand what is wrong, and what you will do, then I will have something to think about."

"Good. Then you will be able to help." He picked up Claudine, gave her to Geneviève, took 'Tit Frère in his own arms. "We'll rock them, calm them," he said. "This kettle's steam is gone anyway."

She listened in steady attention as he told her that the inflammation from diphtheria had produced stenosis—"closing, madame"—of the glottis. "Air can't get through," he said. "So—I will take a very sharp knife, cut a small hole in the right place, insert a metal tube that will bring air in and release it—and they will be able to breathe."

"A tube in their necks, Henri? For how long?"

"Four, five days. I'll be with them as long as I'm needed. Believe me, young children get accustomed to these things more easily than adults!"

A silence, while the fire fell over itself in its efforts to keep the heat filling the room. Then—"Won't it hurt? When you cut?"

"For a little. Understand, I could give them chloroform, put them to sleep—but I'd rather not. We will wrap each one in a blanket. You can hold them still, can't you?"

"While you cut their necks?"

"Yes."

Her eyes, in that moment, grew older. "Yes, I can do that."

They heard Brun's hooves pounding, Marthe's boots beating across the gallery floor, Marthe slamming through the front door and down the hall. "Here. Am—am I in time?"

"Marthe needs a big apron, Madame Langlinais. Marthe, you'll have to help. Their mother will hold the babies, you must hand me the instruments. Can you do that?"

Once more, she said, "Henri. Do you really ask?"

While Geneviève brought aprons for both Henri and Marthe, poured hot water into a basin so they could scrub their hands, Henri opened the instrument case he had removed from his kit and selected what he needed. "Here, Marthe, watch," he said, laying out each on the clean towel Geneviève had put across a table. "This is a scalpel. These, the artery clamps. These, the retractors. Here, two pairs of thumb forceps. A grooved director. Here, a tenaculum. Curved scissors, straight scissors. An aneurism needle. Curved needles. Straight needles. The silk and catgut I'll use to suture. The tubes." He looked from the array before them at Marthe. "Remember all that?"

Thank God for hours spent memorizing Alexander Pope! "Shall I repeat it? Quickly, while you wash?" She did, fiercely not letting her tongue trip, not letting her eyes ask for praise.

"Good. Now, Madame Langlinais, the little girl first, I think."

Swiftly, Henri wrapped Claudine in a blanket, pinning her arms against her side. "Hold her just so," he said, stationing Geneviève so that she could control the child's thrusting movements without obstructing his.

When his knife first brought bright blood to the surface, Marthe wanted to leave. Then it spurted over his fingers, staining them, and Claudine began to cry. Marthe looked at Geneviève, whose face grew whiter with each bubble of blood from her child's throat. She saw the firmness of Geneviève's grip, the way her mouth never stopped forming words and sounds of comfort. "Soon, jolie Claudine, soon, maman's baby, soon, soon, you will sleep, you will be happy." Over and over again, a chanting croon, while Henri's hands moved and the baby screamed.

She blinked her eyes, one small escape. Heard silence. Opened them, was Claudine gone? "What's the matter, Henri? She's crying, tears—I can't hear her."

"No air going through the larnyx. We won't hear a sound from her until the tube's out and she's healed. Clamp."

She tried to watch then, follow the progress of Henri's hands. So small was his work area that she missed it; at one moment there was an open wound, at the next a tube protruding from a gauze bandage. "Hold her while we get 'Tit Frère ready and I boil these instruments," Henri said. "Take her and rock her, that's good for her breathing."

Marthe took the child, limp with exhaustion and fear. The small face was wet with tears, sweat, the heat of the room. In a collapse of resistance, Claudine fell against Marthe, reached arms around her neck, nuzzled against her. She carried the child to the rocker set near the fire, settled in and began to rock. She remembered the low crooning Geneviève comforted her babies with and began to hum. I need to learn some lullabies, all I know is waltzes, she thought. By the time Henri needed her, Claudine was asleep, her breath hissing from the open end of the tube with the steady calm of eased pain.

"We're both doing better," she said to Geneviève when Henri began to insert the tube into 'Tit Frère's throat. "You got so white when he was doing Claudine, I thought we'd lose you."

"And you," Geneviève said.

"I knew I wouldn't lose either of you," Henri said.

When 'Tit Frère, too, was asleep, rocked by Marthe at her insistence while Geneviève fixed Henri strong coffee and a thick piece of new bread, Henri sent her home. "I've got to stay, obviously, Marthe. But it's near dark. You need to get back. Besides, you don't want to miss your mother's dinner— visiting with all those New Orleans gentlemen?"

"Dear God in heaven! How can anyone interest me now? After this?" Marthe de Clouet had not blushed, unintentionally, for years. Now, as Henri and Geneviève looked at her, she felt that fresh rush of blood that was, she knew, like running up her flag of surrender. Pulling on her riding gloves, she laughed, fought back the blush. "Anyway, Henri, my great-grandmother Aimée was a traiteur. A folk-doctor. An interest in medicine runs in the family." But that, she saw, only made it worse. "I'll take one last look," she said, and escaped to the babies.

# CHAPTER 20

## *Union*

The wet smell of swamp and bayou had been iced into the air of winter, so that, until the end of February, the hint of sea life would be always with them. Jumie sniffed, tested the wind with a forefinger. "From the east," he said to Claude. "Bringing bad weather by late tonight, tomorrow. We run just in time."

"There's LeBleu," Claude said, pointing across the field surrounding the track to a tall man centering a cluster of people. The long tail of a roan horse protruded from the cluster like a trailing end of string from a package. "Let's go see."

They tied their horses to the fence, and led Jolie Mademoiselle across the open ground. She picked her way through the mud hillocks, stepping as though she were a princess dancing on a rough floor. "Now, Jolie, you dance like a lady now, but I tell you, you run like a street woman from Butler's troops during the race," Claude said.

"So, that's the horse you think's going to beat mine," LeBleu said, stepping toward them.

"Not think, LeBleu. Know." Claude stepped forward, meeting him. "Let's see your horse that thinks she can stay on the same track with Jolie Mademoiselle."

LeBleu gestured to the group around his horse, and they parted the curtain of bodies. A large roan stood there, testing the surface of the ground with a nervous hoof. "You might as well give up, Langlinais. This horse can beat that one without even breathing hard."

Claude looked at Jumie. The look met one from Jumie in midair. Both signaled the same message: Give him a chance? Yes. Claude turned back to LeBleu. "Talking about breathing hard—LeBleu, you run that horse over here? She's breathing a little hard now, isn't it?"

430

LeBleu looked back at the roan, surveyed her. "Sacrebleu, Langlinais, you don't know deep lungs when you hear them? Why are you finding fault with my horse? To make yours look worse when she loses?"

Claude shrugged. "So—let's go."

"Where's your rider?"

"Madame Breaux's littlest boy, he going to ride," Claude said.

"I'm here," a voice piped. Small, wiry, the boy would be like no weight on Jolie's back. She would feel the strength of his hands, that was all.

"What? You're a traitor? You live almost in my backyard and you ride Langlinais' horse?" LeBleu said to the boy.

Claude rubbed the boy's head. "He's my cousin, LeBleu. What do you expect?"

"Langlinais, let me tell you something. Since you become a politician, yes, it seems like you got cousins coming out of every wall."

Claude laughed. "Like they say, LeBleu, the good God gives us our relatives. We pick our friends. Me, He gave me plenty cousins—and I pick some more. Now—the race, LeBleu, the race. I didn't come just to talk."

The track, two lanes wide, had board fences running down the outside edges of the two lanes and the middle as well as a preventive measure to collisions. "What do I do, Mr. Claude?" the Breaux boy asked.

"Just stick to her like a burr on a coon dog," Claude said. He half knelt to give the boy a bent knee to mount from, felt that small weight spring away from him. "And keep your weight off her back!"

They guided Jolie Mademoiselle to the starting line in one of the lanes, and stood holding her in check while LeBleu got his horse in position. When both were ready, the race starter dropped a big red handkerchief. Claude released his hold on Jolie's bridle. Jumie, at her rear, slapped her hard on the rump, and the child on her back, leaning low over her neck, dug his heels into her side. "Go, Jolie!"

Claude and Jumie found places along the railing, moving constantly down in their efforts to keep their horse in sight. "Let's run to the end," Jumie said, and began pushing through the lines of spectators, most of whom were LeBleu partisans. Ahead of them, flashing down the track, were the flowing tails of the two horses. LeBleu's horse was setting a taunting pace, her tail tickling the fence that divided her from Jolie.

"Jumie, can distemper make a horse run better?" Claude said. His own breath was coming hard in the cold air, and from the running. Now he climbed the fence, would see from a height rather than try to keep that fervent pace. Jumie leaped up beside him, hands white on the top board of the fence.

"She'll fade soon."

"Merde. She better. It's hundred yards they've run, and Jolie still eating her tail."

They were stationed about three-fourths down the length of the track, and had a clear view of the finish line. So sure was Jumie that Jolie would win that he almost expected the track to lengthen itself to give her time to do just that. But with only fifty yards left, LeBleu's horse was still ahead. "I've got to see," Jumie said. He vaulted down, ran heavily toward the end of the track.

"Hey, Langlinais, it's your filly, not your son, that's running this race."

He heard the shouts around him, heard the crowd yelling their own horse on. Some farmers from St. Martin had come, eager to see the Langlinais horse win, and to win a few easy dollars as well. Hands reached for him, voices grabbed at him. He pulled even with the finish line, panting. Looked up to see both horses bearing down on the same goal. Jolie closing, coming up, long legs swinging as though on rockers. Swing, close, swing, close. Close. Pass. Pass. Finish.

"Jolie's won!" He pushed around to the end of the track, took her head in his arms. The Breaux child was shouting, waving his cap in the air. LeBleu's horse had stopped, two yards still from the finish. She had stopped, someone was saying, the moment Jolie passed her. She was looking around, confused, not sure of herself or her surroundings. "Is she sick?" "Did she just quit?" voices, questions, LeBleu now saw his horse's head. "LeBleu, is she sick? What's the matter with that horse?" LeBleu was mad, hot mad. But he said, "Sick? No, she's lazy. Who but a lazy horse would quit the minute she could, without even trying to finish? Mais, I tell you, no more lone runs for her. When she practices now, she's going to have another horse setting the pace. Mais, she got to learn what a race is about, yes."

Jumie spoke. "LeBleu, I think maybe she is sick."

"Langlinais, you keep your opinion and your money to yourself. Gravier, he's holding the purse. I know you. You say my horse is sick so we race over again. Now you think your horse will win all the time, you can place more bets. Thank you no, Langlinais. I'm too smart for that, yes."

"So, all right, LeBleu." He found Claude, held in a group of men.

"Your papa's a good man, Jumie. He made us some good money today, with that horse. A man who knows horses—you can trust him, isn't that it?" The men were jubilant. Claude was always a favorite, always welcome. They were past only wanting Claude to win. They now needed him to. "Look, we got jambalaya, some winie—we eat, yes?"

"First we get the purse," Claude said.

And when that was done, $400 of it, and the bets collected, $2,000 worth, they went to the house where the jambalaya steamed next to a pot of duck gumbo and ate away the early afternoon.

Sarah's spiced fruit, stewing slowly to the back of the fire, sent its fragrance through the early cold of afternoon; later, the smell of roasting duck mingled with it. Étienne, in the library with Noel, sniffed. "What a bouquet! Any claret will have a difficult time vying with that. Which reminds me—I brought a case of wine with me, a little gift to your cellar."

"Good," Noel said. "Political fires seem fueled with the flow of wine; I hope, Étienne, the better the wine, the more efficient and constant our efforts."

"Ellis and Burke are not fools. They'll do well in Washington. And what does Hayes really care, if it comes to that? Better the Democrat Nicholls working with him than the renegade Packard kept here by federal force."

The loud slam of the door near the warming kitchen sent shock waves along the aromatic steam of fruit and game.

"Papa! Papa!"

"It's Marthe," Noel said, and moved fast, throwing open the library door, running into the hall, where Marthe fell against him.

"Oh, papa!"

He tried to hold her away form him to see if she were hurt, but her arms clung too closely. She was gasping, trying to say names, words. Satisfied that she, at least, was whole, he led her back into the library, settled her near the fire and handed her brandy. "Drink." he watched her sip, watched her gain control. "All right. Now tell me, what's the matter?"

She told of their visit to Jumie and Geneviève's house, of the sick babies, of Henri's decision. Noel broke through the tumbling words, a dam across that clear stream. "You came back here? For his kit? And didn't ask for help?"

"Oh, papa! As if there was time! By the time maman had finished worrying, and decided what was proper—can't I do anything without asking for help?"

"It doesn't sound as though help was needed," Étienne said. His chest had begun to fill itself to even grander dimensions as Marthe spoke; how wonderful to have one's son be a savior, a hero, on his very first visit to this country! It made St. Martin not solely the province of the de Clouets, it gave one, somehow, a foothold in their territory.

"So Henri stayed?"

"Yes. Until he's sure they're really better. And, I suppose, until Jumie gets home. He's off in Breaux Bridge, racing Jolie Mademoiselle." She thought of the race horses she planned to ask her father for. Henri was right, you could hardly oversee a fine stable if you lived far away. "I'm certain he'll be back for dinner. As for me—I'm going to rest. I did nothing, really, but I am so fatigued!"

Étienne watched her out the door, then went over and closed it softly. He tossed another log on the fire, expertly rearranged the burning ones so that the fresh one would catch properly. "I've grown up on tales of the de Clouet women, Noel, as I suppose you have. For a time, I thought Marthe would be exactly like her great-great-grandmother Hélène, that legendary beauty! And, of course, she has her looks, no question. Now, however, I think maybe she is more like her great-grandmother Aimée—that spirit, that courage."

For Henri, the afternoon was set outside the kind of time he knew. The hands on his watch moved, but the movement meant nothing. It was not important that it was four o'clock, or five o'clock. It was important only that at this moment, fever seemed to burn lower. At this moment, small chests rose and fell more smoothly. The herbs from the kettles, which kept billowing up great moist puffs of aromatic air, made him feel sleepy. How good it would be to crawl between those two sleeping children and, like them, give oneself up to unconscious rest.

A loud, clear thump came through clouds of soft damp cotton. Henri roused, tried to sit up. His head rested on a large pillow Geneviève had tucked between him and the high back of the rocker: a quilt spread over his torso and legs, wrapping him and holding him still. "It's Jumie!" A blur of movement, a body of cold air hitting him, himself struggling out of the quilt and to his feet. Then two large hands gripping him, a man hugging him, kissing him on both cheeks.

"You saved my babies, Monsieur de Gravelle. You saved my babies."

As he rode back to Beau Chêne, the path through the woods lit by the moon and by the lantern Jumie had loaned him, the patter of his horse's hooves said the words, over and over, against the soft deep mud. "You saved my babies. You saved my babies."

And at dinner, though he kept turning the conversation to other matters, it returned again and again to him. The courage, the skill. The wit to do it. Tell us again, how were you sure? What if they had died? No one would allow that, certainly neither Caroline nor Marthe. He kept them from dying, why would they die from what he did? His skill was up to what his courage demanded, it was as simple as that. Finally, he said, "We have had Henri de Gravelle for soup, for salad, for the entree, for the vegetable, for the fish. We shall not have him for dessert!"

"But I want to hear again," Marthe said. They were walking on the lower gallery, outside the dining room. The gentlemen protested to Caroline that they did not want their cigars just yet: they would be in bed early, against the predawn rising for tomorrow's hunt. They would have coffee with her, a little liqueur. As for the young people—let them leave, the adults needed some privacy. Étienne de Gravelle was famous for his stories; some, he said, were suitable for ladies of a certain manner, and he included his hostess in this elegant and sophisticated group. Marthe held Henri's arm more closely, and nodded her head back to the closed dining room door, against which laughter rapped from time to time. "I shouldn't care to hear your father's stories, no matter how sophisticated I become. But your kind of story—tell me again, Henri, from the beginning."

"But you were there for most of it."

"Zut! Too busy to know what was going on. Now, from the beginning."

The cold length of the gallery slipped under their pacing feet a dozen times as Henri spoke. A pieces-of-eight moon hung low enough to shadow Marthe's face, concealing the brightness there. "And that's it," he said. "If all goes well, the tubes will be out and they'll be into everything again in under a week."

"It isn't all. Henri, I've been trying and trying to think, all afternoon, who you remind me of. And I've finally understood. You remind me of Monsieur Claude Langlinais. Of Jumie, too."

"*I* do."

"Let's walk in the alley. I love to look up through the oaks at the moon, don't you?" She led the way across the gravel paths to the ones that ran parallel to the broad drive down to the open road. "You, you remind me of the Langlinais men. Shall I tell you how?"

"Please do!"

"Well, when I was a little girl, what, three? the Yankees came here. They took Beau Chêne, they wanted to live here, have headquarters, something. So they locked us up, maman and Nollie and me, in the attic. You've heard all this, it's part of our history! But maybe you don't know that during all that time, when we were in the attic, and later when we were set free, were starving to death, it was Monsieur Langlinais, and Jumie, too, who kept us alive."

She drew closer to Henri, settling the folds of her wool cloak so that there was less bulky barrier between them. "He brought food, and medicine. When we were still prisoners, he would give some to our guards. But he would stand his ground, not give them even one little bit, until maman had ours in her hands."

"They could have just taken it. Used force—didn't they try?"

"I don't know. I just know we always got our food. And then, when they left, he kept on helping. So did Madame Langlinais. And Jumie. He showed us how to dig the holes for the beans and the corn. To plant when the moon is dark if you want a big crop of what grows under the ground. That kind of thing."

"And I remind you of them? That flatters me, Marthe."

She moved to a marble bench set halfway between house

and road, sat. Henri watched a beam of light find its way through the shadowing branches and mirror its brightness in her hair. "No, don't you see? You know how to do things with your hands, Henri. Not with just money. Or with words. With your hands."

As he sat beside her, she took his hands in hers. "Now papa uses money, and words. For a long time, such a long time, after the war, we kept waiting and waiting, maman and I did, for papa to put everything right. For the sugar fields to be green again. For there to be money again. It didn't happen, Henri."

"It didn't happen for a lot of planters, Marthe."

"I know. But papa couldn't even plow. He didn't know as much about the plantation as Tatum did. If it hadn't been for Tatum—but really, if it hadn't been for the lottery. That's where the money came from."

"So he works better with his head, Marthe."

"Your papa's head. I think that's why he's so interested in politics. It's something he can do for himself." Her hands still held his, so tightly that she might be claiming them against all others. She shook her head, moved it so that the moon ray danced across the curls around her face. "Well. I love papa. He's smart. But he can't do things with his hands. Which is why you remind me of the Langlinais men."

A figure emerged on the top gallery, came forward to the railing. "It's maman," Marthe said. "She'll fuss if I don't go in."

They began walking back to the house, using the drive so that Caroline could see their approach. "I suppose I would miss this space, in the city," Marthe said.

"I think you might."

"Something else. I was on a visit with maman, one of those rounds of duty calls, your sisters must have to make them, too? Anyway. We were visiting a family down the bayou, maman and the lady were talking about an old lady who had died, and how sad her husband was. 'You know, Caroline,' the lady said to maman, 'you know how it is. In the city, the men go off and don't see their wives from morning till night—sometimes not then. But here, they are in and out all day. Close. So close.'" At the entrance to the house, she faced Henri. "And I thought— but if you didn't love your husband, or your wife, would you want to see so much of them? Now, Henri, I can't think of anything better. Can you?"

"I think not," he said.

Caroline, who had descended to the dining room where mulled wine was ready, said to Noel, "We may be going to have something neither of us thought possible, Noel. A daughter who has long been a woman—and is finally a lady."

"Heroes tend to bring out the best in others, too, Caroline."

"You mean Henri? Because of what he did today?"

Noel handed her a glass of the warm spiced wine. Their guests, who had been playing cards in the library, would be joining them for a light supper; he hoped for a private word with de Gravelle. "Well, wasn't that heroic? Saving two babies?"

"Everything a doctor does can seem heroic at times. Étienne said he had told Henri how solemnly devoted to his profession he appeared, carrying his medicines and supplies on a visit! But of course then he was glad. And I reminded him that with all the hazards of hunting—snakes, gunshot wounds, what all doesn't happen!—Henri was hardly being overcautious in being prepared."

"I wonder what Henri would think of a country practice, if it comes to that." Noel lifted the cover on one of the dishes, took a sample of daube on a bit of Sarah's bread. He knew Caroline was paying closest attention to him now, that, with the ordered details of the supper already behind her, her mind was ready to deal with something else. "This is good daube. Though why do we eat so much? Or so often. It can't be good for us."

Caroline straightened one of the beeswax tapers in the four-branched candelabra that flanked the bowl of fresh fruit centering the table. She had made that arrangement herself, copying the form from a still life that illustrated one of Noel's many art books. She liked using those books for ideas of her own; when Nollie came home at Christmas, she would take him over the house, show him in the greatest detail what she would like to do. And then listen and agree to each change he proposed.

"Are you thinking Henri might want to practice here?"

"Why not?"

"Are you thinking any further than that?"

Noel laughed. "What good is thinking when what one thinks about depends on other people?"

"On Marthe? On Henri and Marthe marrying, and settling here?"

"You've thought of it, too."

She moved to a window, looked past the lace curtains that screened the velvet-framed opening into the deep night. "I don't see Nollie really living here. Running the place. Do you?" She hadn't told Noel that practically every book in the library dealing with art was full of Nollie's writing, beginning with the round, innocent judgments of the schoolboy and progressing to the curving, sophisticated critiques of the young man.

"Not really." Noel picked up a carving knife, held a roast pheasant firmly with the matching fork, and began to cut thin, even slices. "Does that surprise you? That I know my son?"

Automatically, Caroline came to help, to arrange the slices around the bird. "No. Of course not. Still, he's very young. He may change."

"If someone else can stay here, keep Beau Chêne going, why should he? God knows, Caroline, we've got to have gone through all this upheaval for something."

"For Nollie to dabble in art? All right, all right. For something more serious, I know. For our children to live as they wish, cushioned by the money their papa plucks from the many golden fowl that presently abound in this state—and from those still, so to speak, in the egg. Is that it?"

"It's what you said you wanted, remember?" A stretch of space and time between them, thought closed. He saw her face admit that wish, and pressed. "Remember? You even said if our children couldn't have a good life here, you'd take them and leave. Sell the jewelry and silver, wasn't that it?"

"I hear them coming, Noel. I'll tell Zeke to bring in the oysters, shall I?"

He watched her move to the door, wondered if it were the sight of that straight back narrowing at her waist, the sight then of the folds of her dress flowing over her hips, yielding to the movement of her body, that made him speak. "Of course, you wouldn't have to sell jewelry now. Silver, either. You've got all the money you make with your lottery stock, don't you?"

Behind him, he heard the door into the hall open, and then heard Étienne de Gravelle's voice. "Noel, they're saying I took unfair advantage because I introduced them to that game your friend Monsieur Langlinais taught me at the convention this summer—bourré, remember it?"

"Enough to know better than to play it with you, Étienne." Noel looked at de Gravelle, sleek in his dinner clothes, helping himself liberally to pheasant. "Don't any of your appetites ever get you into trouble, de Gravelle?"

Étienne took the cup of oyster stew Zeke handed him, put it on his plate. "Should they?" he asked. "After all, I set one appetite off with another. Tomorrow, my appetite for exercise will offset my appetite for food tonight."

And just what, Noel thought, offsets your appetite for women?

Henri called at the Langlinaises' twice a day for the next few days, changing the bandages that protected the incisions, making sure Geneviève understood how to care for his patients. "It's astounding how quickly they have become 'my patients,'" he said to Marthe. "I've never had patients who were only mine before. In training, we watch other doctors with their patients, or diagnose and treat with someone else supervising us. I shall be very sorry when I've no excuse to go see them."

"They'll miss you when you leave, Henri. And Geneviève. She is quite desolate to think you won't always be near when her babies are ill, or hurt themselves in some way."

"So she keeps telling me." They had tethered their horses and were walking, striding over the frost-dry grass of the pasture, testing their house-stale lungs in the frost-fresh air.

"It was here my great-great-grandmother broke her neck," Marthe said, pointing to a place along the rail fence. "She was riding my great-grandmother's horse, a big stallion, and he threw her. Killed her then and there."

"Then even in the country things happen a doctor can't help."

"But so much happens he can help! My great-grandmother, for instance. The one who built the stables up? She fell somehow, broke her leg. She thought no one could set it in time, the doctor was so far—the leg would go bad—so she shot herself."

"She didn't!"

Marthe jumped to the top rail of the fence, perched there in her dark green riding habit. "She did. Of course, it was kept quiet for ages. Still is, I guess. Except that Nollie and I had so much time, when the Yankees left but the war wasn't over, to just poke around by ourselves. Maman was out in the fields, she couldn't see to us. We found all kinds of things. My grandmother's journal tells the whole thing. How they put Aimée de Clouet to bed, and were having dinner, when a servant came to say she'd shot herself. So they covered it all up, no one knew a thing. Know what else we found out?"

"I'd be afraid to guess."

"Aimée's husband smoked opium."

"How in the world did you find that out? Now I'll warrant that wasn't in anyone's diary!"

"Nollie and I found it. That Noel used the garçonnière for a studio, I think they probably built it for him, he was only the second one. Anyway. We thought we'd clean it out, make a fort, something. We found his old paints, all dried up, and the brushes. Canvases rotting out of frames. And a pouch with a funny-smelling powder in it. It smelled like medicine, so we took it to Claude Langlinais. Jumie's father? He kept bringing food and medicines in, running the Yankee blockade and lines, so we thought he'd know what it was. And he did."

"Maybe your great-grandmother, the folk-doctor, used it." He was enjoying this. They had come to some new place, he and Marthe. It was mixed up, he knew, in how she felt about what he'd done for the Langlinais. But that wasn't all of it. In some way, the same incisions that had allowed Claudine and 'Tit Frère to breathe, to have a chance to live, had opened Marthe, too. She flirted still, lifted those great eyes to his, then sheltered them swiftly behind dark lashes. When she played the harpsichord for him, he knew the teasing shadow the ruffles of her neckline made on her shoulders and throat were studied. And he knew the complete grace of her movement, whether entering the parlor where they were all assembled or walking along a leaf-strewn path, was meant to enchant him. This was all the same. But something, something was not the same. Was it that neither of them was any longer afraid?

He could watch the violent tossing of her curls with secure peace. "No, no, her bag, the bag she kept the gun in she used to shoot herself, is a family relic. Believe me, if anyone had taken anything from that bag, he would surely be past any doctor's help! And besides, we found the pipe he smoked it in."

Across the field, their horses lifted heads to the freshened wind. The sun was going down, burning rays severing ballooning clouds filled with cold night air. "We've time for one long run before heading back," she said. "I'm glad they're all going to dinner in New Iberia tonight, aren't you? It'll be lovely, just you and me for dinner."

He made a footrest of his hands to help her mount. "You and me and that lady who came today. What did your mother call her?"

"Tante Rose?" The sun held itself up for one straining moment so that it could backlight Marthe's figure on the tall horse. "Don't mind her. She makes all my dresses and tells me everything about catching a beau. If you are very nice to her, she'll tell you all our secrets."

Henri swung onto his own horse, gathered up the reins. He waited until Marthe had turned her horse to the far end of the field, preparing the run that would build momentum for the leap over the fence. "The only secret I want to know is how to get caught," he called after her, sure the sun would cut the restraining rope on one of those wind-filled clouds and blow his words away.

Françoise pried another perfect pecan half from the cracked shell and added it to those already in the bowl. "So, Claude, those men from New Orleans, they'll be going back tomorrow, and you, do you know any more why they came than before?"

"Maybe they did only come to hunt, Françoise. They've been out every day." He was tired. The race had energized him; thinking now of Jolie's long swinging run, the lifting cheers from the crowd, the feel of congratulating hands on his back, of the money in his hands, he had a moment of renewal.

"Yes, they came to hunt. To hunt ways to steal the election for Nicholls. Claude, people who help them, they'll be rewarded. You know that."

It would take more than one horse race to give him back the strength Françoise took. Never did she seem to understand that the effort he used trying to see her view of his life, trying to understand what she wanted, could be better spent carrying out his own vision, doing what he chose. "I know I don't just barge up to Beau Chêne and tell Noel to bring me into their talk. I know that, Françoise."

She stood up, gathering her shell-filled apron in a tight orderly bundle. She moved to the hearth, reached behind to untie her apron strings, and then emptied the debris of the pecans into the fire. When she turned to speak to him, the low fire behind her cast her shadow the height of the ceiling, filling almost all the space before him. "But, Claude, Monsieur de Gravelle's son has been at our son's house every day. Every day, Claude! He saved your grandchildren's lives!" She came to him, the urgency in her voice doing the touching her hands would not. "Claude, you could go up to the house—thank him? And who knows?—you met that Étienne de Gravelle in Baton Rouge. He will remember—who knows what can come of that, Claude?"

"Françoise, Françoise. You tell me. What could come of it you want?"

He knew she read newspapers now, knew she remembered every word the men who came to eat her gumbo and stayed to talk said about politics. Knew she had ideas, things she wanted. He didn't know how carefully she had put her thoughts together, or what force they had in her life.

"Claude. Think how it was when Noel came back from the war." He could not remember when she had talked to him without being busy also at something else. She had set the half-filled bowl aside, was leaning forward on the table, each word pried from her with conscious effort to keep it perfect, whole. "Beau Chêne was in ruins. The sugar was gone, no slaves, no food. Claude, if it had not been for you, and me, and Jumie—the de Clouets would have starved."

"So?"

"So now look at it! Richer than ever! Sugar cane bursting out of the ground, Noel going higher and higher—and all without him lifting a hand at a snake!"

Now he knew what had cut some root in her, years ago. He had thought her slow loss of interest in his body was due to changes in her own. Had not known that she no longer saw the work his body did as having value, and thus could not value it. He pried a word of his own from his close-kept hoard. "Noel works, Françoise."

"But his work makes him rich!"

"And mine does not?" He would not let his words bend themselves on the strong bar that usually kept them in. They must flow evenly, shifting toward neither criticism nor complaint.

"Claude—your work makes money. But work with the hands—it can only do so much." He saw her hand move up to the medal that hung on a thin chain around her neck, touch it. "Claude, I say these things for your good. You are as smart as Noel de Clouet. Men like you better. Let Jumie do even more than he does. Hire others to do your chores here." Now both hands reached across to him, asked for his. When had her touch grown so cool? "Claude, you use your head. Make money the way Noel makes money."

"So we can be a play, too, Françoise?" Still the words did not bend, were even, smooth.

"A play?"

"Remember? You said once that Beau Chêne was like a play, something to watch. Are the Langlinaises to put on a play for all the people to mock?"

She rose so quickly, jerked herself up so far, that he waited for some loud sound to jolt him, too. "Put on a play? No, Claude, we put on the play. Caroline de Clouet may string greens on her gallery because she has guests coming—I do it for me! Caroline de Clouet may order fancy gowns so everyone will know how rich her husband is—I want them for me! Caroline de Clouet may send her son to the University of Virginia for herself—I wanted my son to go for him! Claude, I put on no play!"

"Françoise, listen to me. Françoise, when have you said you wanted—"

All that careful energy, released in little spurts over the years of days to keep her movement going, was being used up, consumed, in one great fire. "When have I said! Claude, why would I say? Why would I have to say?" She knelt before him, again taking his hands, pulling them against her breast. "Claude, did you say to me, all those years, I want supper, I want coffee, I want clean shirts?"

"But, Françoise, I used to ask you—you know I did—plan a trip, I said. Not just to New Orleans. Françoise, I asked."

The face he looked into accused him, herself, both of them. "Claude, I don't want you to ask. I just want you to do."

He thought he hadn't heard what she said, bent over her. She turned, still kneeling, holding her face away. Repeated in that empty voice—"I just want you to do."

Claude remembered the years when blue-backed Yankee soldiers migrated along the waterways to the Teche, settled in, adapted themselves to the habitat. He had slipped away in the dark to find a way through their territory to a new supply of food. He had slipped back, days later, to find Françoise on a ladder, or nailing a loose cedar shingle into place, or out in the stable, helping a cow calve, or setting a trawl line in the bayou.

When he had praised her on her quickness, her strength, she had turned away from it. Once, he remembered, she had said, words sharp, bitten: "Sometimes I think I have too long a list of things to praise."

He lifted her to her feet, settled her in the chair. "I'll get coffee," he said. He poured two cups, set one in front of her. "What you said—there's a lot in that. For so much work—your work, my work—we could have more." The small move of his head, hardly enough to change his shadow, stopped her words.

"No, Françoise, you are right. We need to stop doing things that always have to be done over again. Or to do more of the things that, once you have done them, make money without any more notice." He sipped his coffee, let the heated strength sit quietly on his tongue. He thought of the land—pasture, swamp, woods, field. He couldn't not pay notice to it—de Clouet didn't. Look at Beau Chêne's sugar fields. They were among the best producers in the state. But Noel de Clouet had almost nothing to do with that. He had an overseer for the fields, a manager for the sugar mill. A gardener for the vegetables. Damn if de Clouet didn't probably make more money in an hour of thinking how to use some other man's work than Claude did in a day of working for himself.

"I'll get Jumie. And Jean. And Pierre. We'll look over what we're doing, make plans." A light that had been so long gone from the back of her eyes he had almost forgotten it seemed to begin a small glow. "But, Françoise, I know what I really need. I need some of the kind of investments de Clouet's got." He went over to his wife, held her gently against him. "Why don't you make some pralines with those pecans, Françoise? I'll go over to Beau Chêne, take Monsieur Henri de Gravelle a little gift, isn't that it? And maybe see his papa?"

Noel had not after all had his private word with de Gravelle, though he suspected that there had been private words, quite private words, between de Gravelle and at least one de Clouet. Nor had he mentioned the lottery stock to Caroline again. It was something he could just let go; his discovery of her shares had been so accidental that he very well knew he had never been intended to know, and if the secret were that darkly kept, what lay behind its depths should probably be left undisturbed.

They spent the last day hunting deer; the combined pressure of a long span of cold December time and shortened sleep had wrapped Noel away from the others as though he were in another atmosphere. Even as they approached Beau Chêne, gleaming gold in the sun rays that shot up from the horizon, he felt separate from his guests. "It looks almost not real in this light," Henri said. His voice seemed to have deepened in the week, his posture to have changed. "This must be one of the most beautiful houses in the state."

Noel looked at the house; it did seem new, unfamiliar. The way the light fell? The way the cold, the fatigue, wrapped him, so that he could not focus, could not see? A feeling of never having lived there at all, of not knowing any of its inhabitants, came over him. He blinked, looked again, and saw Beau Chêne. "Well, Henri," he said, "and how are your patients?"

"I removed the tubes this morning. They're doing very well." Hearing that young struggle with pride, Noel glanced again at the house. He was conscious of Caroline, standing in one of the upper windows watching them come home. Conscious of Étienne's fat voice behind him, recounting some boudoir victory as though it were quite another fellow's story. Who was he to decide what scenes would be played, which actors allowed to play them? If this play did not work out, there were other players in the wings who might make better use of this house, this land. Too many subplots in the one, better leave them alone.

"So, Étienne," he said, dropping back, "how does it feel to be the father of a miracle worker?"

"Why don't you become his father-in-law and find out?" Étienne said.

They were just finishing dinner when Zeke announced Claude. "To see Monsieur de Gravelle and Monsieur Henri," he said.

"The babies' grandfather," Henri said.

"I've met him," Étienne told him. He was interested to see Claude again; he had pieced together, in the time they had been here, enough information about the Langlinaises to be quite, quite curious to take Claude's measure.

If Henri had had to struggle with pride before, he lost the battle under Claude's stream of praise. Étienne, standing to one side, saw the skill with which it was done; Claude said just enough to so overwhelm Henri that flight was his only response. Not ten minutes had passed before Henri, package of pralines in his hands, had been thanked and, in effect, dismissed. Étienne waited.

"Monsieur de Gravelle, you have a minute?"

"Any number of them, Monsieur Langlinais. Noel has an excellent brandy here—you'll join me?"

They settled on either side of the hearth, studied their glasses.

"Monsieur de Gravelle, maybe you don't remember—we met in Baton Rouge?"

"I remember."

"So you know me a little."

"More than a little. I've picked up things since I've been down here."

"Then I talk shorter. Monsieur de Gravelle, most of the ways I make money—take a long time. And men working every day. One of us making them work." He took a mouthful of brandy, swallowed. "So that's better than when the Langlinaises first came here. But not as good as I want it to be. If you could tell me sometime of another way to make money— the kind of ways you and Noel use—your son saved my grand-babies' lives, Monsieur de Gravelle. And you—you know things that could make their lives better."

"Stocks? That sort of thing?"

"If that's what you say."

"And how soon would you want this kind of investment?"

"As soon as you know about it."

"As soon as—tomorrow?"

Claude took those words in, held them, put them away. "Yes."

Étienne stood. "I'm not sure yet—but I may have a very good thing. We're not leaving until early afternoon. I'll ride over, say, midmorning? One way or the other."

"We'll be ready," Claude said. "Jumie and me."

Going home, he knew it was done. Men like Étienne de Gravelle did not say things unless they knew they could make them come true.

The smooth pleasure of victory stroked Étienne like a woman's hand. He would sell Caroline's lottery stock to this Langlinais, and in one lovely coup, make waste of Noel's suspicions and strengthen Claude's hand. Whether that hand would ever be raised against Noel was not the point; certainly, what Claude held, Noel could not, and that was more than sufficient.

Claude stopped at Jumie's to report his talk with de Gravelle. As he entered the house, he heard a sound he thought he should know—what was it? Not until he walked into the big kitchen and saw Claudine and 'Tit Frère did he recognize what he was hearing: the cries of children. "Geneviève—they're crying."

"I know, Papa Langlinais, I know. Crying and making noise! Isn't it the most wonderful sound in the world?"

He took the three of them in his arms. "Geneviève, sometimes when I think of the things we thank God for! Who would have thought I'd get on my knees because 'Tit Frère can blast my ears again?"

A slow wet winter settled in, locking low-lying farms in a fortress of water-pocked mud. Short dark days slipped by, their grayness lit briefly by Christmas, by King's Day. "If it doesn't get to be Mardi Gras soon," Marthe said, "my gown shall have rotted in this awful damp!"

"Zut! Since when do young girls in love notice the damp?" Tante Rose stuck a firm pin into the satin skirt, sat back on her heels. "Turn. Slowly, slowly! How can I see how it falls if you whirl like that?"

"Tante Rose, I'm so *bored!*"

"Now, calm yourself, Marthe. Soon you will be in New Orleans, where I hear all sorts of things are going to happen. You know my sister, Zollie, makes dresses for the Livaudais ladies. Well, she wrote me a letter, let me tell you what the rumor is—"

Caroline, going into the dry-goods store in St. Martinville, met Françoise coming out, arms laden. "For Claudette's profession," she said, pointing at the package. "She'll take her vows at Easter, I'll spend Lent making her dress."

Caroline's thoughts went back to a day, how many years ago? five, already? when she had offered the veil for Claudette's wedding. And in the swift refusal, learned how narrow the bridge between Beau Chêne and the Langlinais place was. She had walked it carefully since then; the days when Françoise showed her how to ease a back worn with bending over young corn were long over, the shared privation that made generosity simple long gone.

"And you, Caroline? You'll spend Lent resting up from all those balls?"

Caroline found a safe place to walk, went softly. "It's Marthe will need the rest. I—I'm an old lady, as far as balls are concerned." She tried to widen the place, make room for Françoise beside her. "Those balls are not nearly as much fun, even for the young people, as the dances your girls go to in New Iberia. I think Marthe may be disappointed."

Françoise shifted the bulky weight. She had bought white silk, pure white, gauze and lace for the veil to whisper over it. Marthe, she knew, would wear white when she was presented at the Comus ball on carnival night. And while Claudette's finery would commemorate her renunciation of the world and all its goods, her betrothal to Christ, Marthe's would celebrate her entry into the world of luxury and gaiety that would continue, be enriched, by her betrothal to some rich man's son. "Oh, I think Marthe will find something to please her in all that splendor, Caroline. What young girl would not?" Then, with the sure instinct of a mother whose children will never be weapons against her—"And Nollie? Will he be at the balls?"

"Why, no. He's at school, it's much too far—"

"I wasn't sure he'd gone back. College doesn't mean much to him, does it, Caroline?" Françoise moved to the buggy tied in front of the store. "Of course, it doesn't have to. Not when he'll inherit Beau Chêne."

The sharp chill of February sounded in Caroline's voice. "As Jumie will inherit Claude's land."

Swinging up to the buggy seat, Françoise lifted the reins. "And perhaps more. But, Caroline—Jumie has been raised to work as if he would get nothing. You know?"

Caroline watched the buggy move off, the horse picking her way through iced-over mud. She stamped her feet, numbed by the damp cold. There was a numbness in her soul, too; she could usually ignore it. But when Françoise said: "Jumie has been raised to work as if he would get nothing," Caroline read the danger for Beau Chêne. Nollie, as far as she knew, avoided, bought his way out of, charmed his way out of, certainly got out of work anyway he could. She had laughed, because of the absurd way he told the tale, at his account of an argument with his painting master at Virginia. "He insists genius without work is not sufficient; I asked him how did he know?" Caroline, picturing the arrogant tilt of Nollie's chin when he said that, the way his gaze would go past the master as though he were not even there, had smiled; in just that way, Nollie had bullied his nurse and, later, his tutor. But his father, sitting across the hearth reading, had said, without looking up, "How would you know either?"

The slow gray of afternoon darkened with the smoke of the low fires. Caroline pulled the heavy draperies. Maybe they were faded after all. She had seen Étienne looking at them, his lips pursed, measuring, pricing. She heard Marthe's step outside, sat at the tea tray and began to pour. "So how is your gown?"

"Marvelous. Maman, you'll never guess what Tante Rose told me. Such a scandal it's going to be! The Momus parade is going to make the Yankees *so* mad! They're dressing up like devils—Beelzebub and Baal and Lucifer and I don't know who all—and, maman—the masks will make them look like President Grant, and Sherman, and who's the secretary of state? It's going to cause the most awful fuss!"

"My word, Marthe, what's come over people? Natale wrote just last week that two invitations to Comus have been stolen, and though they've offered a thousand-dollar reward, neither has been returned."

"Maman! You can't mean people who shouldn't be there might be at my ball!"

"Now, Marthe, they'll do everything they can—after all, it is Comus."

"It's more than that, maman. It's the most exciting night of my whole entire life, and you must tell papa to tell Monsieur de Gravelle that absolutely not one thing must spoil it."

"Marthe, I promise you—no matter what else might be happening, Comus will go on exactly as it always has. Otherwise, it wouldn't be Comus, isn't that right?"

The official government reaction to the Momus parade was swift, definite, and loud. The army, which was doubly humiliated because U.S. troops and an army band marched behind floats whose maskers showed generals and colonels as denizens of Hades, would never again allow any of its soldiers to take part in a carnival parade. If Beelzebub had not been protected by a mask, the officer he caricatured would have shot him; only the fact that identities were unknown kept retribution from being as swift, definite, and loud as the vocal reaction.

"They're really annoyed," Étienne said to Noel. "Listen to this—'Washington is insulted at a display which professes to caricature the president, the general of the army, the ministers, members of the Cabinet, and leading officials of the United States.'"

"I'd no idea anyone outside of New Orleans took carnival so seriously," Noel said. "Nicholls can wait for the right moment and make one of his flowing apologies. None of it means anything, as you well know."

Because as the public display went on, masking another reality, the move to confirm Nicholls and displace Packard rolled forward as though pulled by a team of horses immune to threat, hysteria, disruption. Like two kings on a chessboard, Packard and Nicholls centered their forces and watched their dispersal. Though for several months each seemed held in check, Nicholls found a gambit that led, by the end of April, to checkmate. Using Angell and Ogden as his flanking knights, he surrounded the Cabildo, seat of the state supreme court. Capitulation was quick—the court, led by Chief Justice Ludeling, abandoned their places. With his own appointees in control of the supreme court, Nicholls next took the lower courts, and though Packard put up a stalling defense, the game was clearly over.

On the night of April 26, 1877, Noel and Caroline de Clouet, Claude and Françoise Langlinais, and all those who belonged to them, for the first time in fifteen years, slept as citizens of an unoccupied state of the Union. Governor Francis T. Nicholls occupied the state house, blessed by President Hayes's own commission. Military intervention was over, and hands made restless by years of waiting were ready to take back control.

# CHAPTER 21

## *Discord*

Light beamed straight out from the lamp on the sideboard,
focused on the glass Claude held, and filtered through the heavy
dark of the wine. "I'll let the sediment settle," he said to Jumie,
who sat at the table tasting Françoise's dressing. "Then we'll
see how good this new cask is."

"For what you paid, it should be some of the best."

"Those dividends the lottery pays—they make a difference,
Jumie. Even after I make other investments, there's money to
play a little. Besides, we're drinking to a new decade—1880.
That has a nice sound—a good year for us."

Jumie watched while Claude lifted the glass to his lips, took
a swallow of burgundy, held it in his mouth. He could judge
the smoothness, the richness, of the wine by the pleasure on
his father's face; obviously, this cask would bless many humble
meals with its richness, ornament many fine occasions with its
deep color and fine bouquet.

"Who's the man coming to dinner tomorrow? The one you
were telling maman about?"

"Mr. Clements from New Orleans. He has some job with
the lottery company, I'm not sure."

"Business on New Year's Day?"

Claude handed Jumie a glass of wine. "Taste. See if you
agree it's good. Now, as for Mr. Clements—why should it be
business? I've met him a few times when I've been in New
Orleans. He knows I live in Saint Martin. His letter said only
that he would be passing through and would like to see me.
Jumie, it was me invited him to our dinner—he didn't invite
himself!"

The wine was good. Claude would bottle it tomorrow, after

452

they'd drawn off a supply for the dinner. He would of course give each son, and Pierre as well, a few bottles. The rest would be used here, used probably every day until it was gone and Claude ordered another cask. Jumie took another sip, remembering the times when even a poor cask of wine was made to last. Of course, then they didn't know just how poor the wine they drank was. "A good thing about having money is that you can buy figuring how to get more money out of the sash and blind factory so I can buy my own cask."

"So. Having good things makes you work hard for more, is that it?"

Jumie went to the cask, took more wine. "Why not? As long as what I want I pay for?"

"Truly. Perhaps, Jumie, perhaps Monsieur Clements will have a little business to talk about. I don't know that he will. I'm saying he might."

"If he did, what sort of business might it be, papa?"

Claude stuck a spoon in the bowl of dressing, then put it in his mouth. "Your maman's dressing is the best in the parish, everyone else may as well stop cooking—or, at least, stop bragging on it! Monsieur Clements' business? Well, Jumie, as you know, the lottery has not managed to keep itself out of our politics."

"Hardly!"

Claude looked at Jumie, shrugged. "Did anyone expect they would? This last year now—what a contretemps! First, the legislature says no, no more lotteries, not now, not ever. Then, the convention gets together to make a new constitution, and it says, all right, lotteries, we can have lotteries, but there mustn't just be one. Anyone who wants to have a lottery company can have one."

"Not many people are rushing to have them." Jumie stood, stretched his arms straight over his head, almost touching the low beams above him. "Zut! Heavy talk and heavy air make me sleepy."

"Then wake enough to hear what I tell you. The lottery needed protection—and it got it. Now, Jumie, isn't it reasonable to think that the men who make the lottery work, who run it, are going to keep on playing with politics—now they are getting such a good record?"

"You mean now they know how much it takes to pay who

off? Merde! What was the going price a few years ago, when they needed men in the Packard legislature to go over to Nicholls?"

"Jumie, however they're doing it—they're getting what they want. So—if they hand out a little of their power, spread it around a little—is there any reason a man shouldn't take it?"

As though he had stepped off the end of a boat dock straight into deep cold water whose ice-smooth ice-chill droplets spread over him and tingled every pore of skin into startled attention, Jumie woke up. "Monsieur Clements comes to give you something like that?"

Claude looked behind him, stepped to the door leading into the wide hall. "I want to be sure it will happen before anyone else knows. Jumie, I don't know if you've read the new constitution—"

"Most of it. Not a lot to read, is there? The main thing is, the governor's got more power than he ever did, and the legislature's got less. Where that leaves us—"

"True. One of the powers the governor has now, Jumie, is to appoint police jurors in each parish."

"And you will be appointed? Is that what Clements is coming about?"

"I've been given to understand that it is."

"Why would Wiltz appoint you? A New Orleans banker—how does he know Claude Langlinais?"

"But, Jumie, have you forgotten the other New Orleans banker who does know Claude Langlinais?"

"Étienne de Gravelle? But why you? Why not his friend de Clouet?"

Claude firmly tapped home the cork that plugged the cask. He placed a cover on the bowl of dressing, set the dressing in the safe on the back porch to stay cool. Then he went to the stove, took up the coffeepot, poured himself a mug.

"Maybe de Clouet thinks it's not grand, being a police juror. Maybe de Gravelle doesn't want him. Me, I let them tend to their own pots. I've got plenty of my own to stir. Now, Jumie, don't say a word, you hear? Until it's sure."

Jumie paused in the doorway, outer coat half pulled onto his left arm. "You got room on the stove for all those pots, papa?"

Claude raised his mug, a salute. "Mais, Jumie, so why do

you think I keep telling you all that goes on? Good chefs have
helpers, isn't it? Who watch, who study—and who take over
the kitchen at the right time."

Jumie pulled on his coat, stood buttoning it. "Why, papa?
Why do it?"

"Be a police juror?"

"Not that. Not just that. Get mixed up with all that. The
same names come up, over and over again. Behind the lottery.
Behind the governor. Running the legislature. Why not just let
them? What difference does it make, if you have to have their
approval to even get in? Damn it, papa, since when is a Langlinais not his own man?"

"A Langlinais is always his own man, Jumie."

"Not if you get in with that crew. You think they won't tell
you what to do?"

Claude's eyes, set in deeply wrinkled skin whose lines, like
the rings of a tree, counted the years spent squinting against
the sun, narrowed. "So they have ideas as to what I should do.
So my ideas are different. Whose ideas do you think I'll follow,
Jumie?"

Jumie pulled a chair toward him, straddled it. "All right.
So you let them think you're going along just to get your hand
in the pot—then you go your own way? Papa—those men are
crooked, not stupid."

"Sometimes it's not very far between the two, Jumie. Listen—I know my people, my territory. The first little bit of
power, maybe I have to get from someone else. After that—I
build my own."

"And what will you do with it, papa? The power?"

Claude laughed. "I don't know. I don't have it, yet."

"So you're going to make a deal with that crowd to get
something you're not even sure you want..."

Jumie saw the quick fire in his father's eyes. "Sure! Yes,
I'm sure!" Claude strode forward, leaned toward his son and
put a hand on each of Jumie's shoulders. "I'm sure I want it
because it's something we have to deal with, you and I. We
got rid of the Yankees, got out from under Reconstruction, by
making a deal—remember that, Jumie? Hayes was glad enough
to sell Packard out, let Nicholls be governor—so long as he
got what he wanted." Claude released Jumie, stepped back. "I
learned something then, Jumie. And so did a lot of other people.
Honor is fine. So is truth. And in the way I deal with my wife,

my children, my friends—I can have both. But in politics? In this state?" Claude spat into the fire. "Honor and truth last as long in that dirty game as that little ball of spit lasted in those coals." He swung back to Jumie. "Can't you see we either get into the game—or get run over by it?"

Jumie stood up, pushed the chair away. "Can't we have our own game, papa? Off to the side, minding our own business?"

"Now you sound like Noel de Clouet. The dirt bothers him, too. Offends him. That finicky nose of his may yet cost him a lot, Jumie. Us, we're not so finicky. Inside our house, yes. We keep our air clean, pure—a baby can breathe it. Outside? We hold our noses tight if we have to, wear masks, turn our heads—but, Jumie, we play."

"I don't know, papa. I'm not sure I'll ever want to stir pots that hold someone else's spoils."

"Then let me tell you Jumie. Your land may end up in someone else's pots—and your hand nowhere near the spoon." He shrugged. "Or—you might end up with a hell of a lot more than what we've got now. And, Jumie—even if you don't want it—how do you know your children, your grandchildren, won't? You going to decide that for them?"

"They can decide for themselves, papa, when the time comes."

Claude looked at Jumie, eyes so filled with pity that Jumie turned from his father's gaze. "It doesn't work that way, Jumie. Either you decide now—or it's gone. You know?"

"I know I'd better get home, help Geneviève," Jumie answered. He went out the back door, mounted his horse and wheeled toward the road. Claude watched Jumie's short whip crack in the air above the horse's back, watched the hooves pick up speed.

Galloping down the road toward home, Jumie passed a carriage from the Beau Chêne stable. The man driving it wore the livery Nollie insisted his mother buy; inside, several young men were laughing boisterously, gloved hands bringing silver flasks to their busy mouths. Mud flew up from under the carriage wheels and splashed against Jumie's coat. His hand automatically went to brush it away as he watched the carriage roll toward Beau Chêne. Friends of Nollie's, starting their New Year's rounds early. He thought of the rooms at Beau Chêne, filled with fine furniture and rugs and hangings and paintings. The table at Beau Chêne, set with delicate English china, heavy

French silver, clear Irish crystal. The armoires at Beau Chêne, bursting with silks and satins, laces and velvets. And the stables, where high-strung thoroughbreds were pampered and catered to and made over. Even their horses live better than most of my people, he thought. He looked at the fields on either side of the road, sleeping the exhausted sleep of winter. Thought of the factory in New Iberia, the other small enterprises. They made money, yes. But brought no power. Maybe one without the other was never safe. If so—his whip cracked in the air again, his horse galloped forward.

Caroline pulled a petit-point-covered footstool near with one small, kid-slippered foot. "Watch the cork doesn't hit that vase," she said. "Lovely," she said, sipping the champagne Noel handed to her. "I'm glad we're having a quiet holiday. After all the turmoil of this fall, I don't care if I ever stir from Beau Chêne again."

"After the results of the turmoil, you may very well not," Noel said.

"You don't seem to care."

Noel set the bottle in the silver wine bucket Zeke had placed on the side table. "I find that I don't care, Caroline. About any of it." He sat opposite her, stretching out one leg to rest a foot on the edge of her footstool. "When the constitutional convention repealed the lottery charter, I was relieved, even if I did stand to lose a lot of money. The gambling part of it—I can take that or leave it alone. But the use the lottery makes of its money, the way it buys candidates, elections—I'm not that sold on democracy, Caroline, God knows. But if we're going to have rule by the people, at least let it be by the people. Not by the men behind the lottery."

"Of course, Noel, you should have known they'd never stand for that." Since Étienne had gotten rid of her stock for her, Caroline asked as little about the lottery as possible; certainly, she would not mourn the demise of an institution which no longer made her rich.

"A matter of finding a way to get around it." Noel took a stuffed date from the dish near him, bit through it. "Of course, what better way than to use the election? You can't run for governor without money, and by God, if anyone understands that, the lottery men do. So—easy trade. Swing the convention to the prolottery side, and the people who do the swinging get money to put their man in the governor's chair. Q.E.D. Wiltz and his delegates sold out, and on December third the constitution keeping the lottery was approved, Wiltz was elected—what, Caroline, is there left for me to care about?"

"My baby," someone behind him said. Hands covered his eyes, soft curls brushed against his forehead. "Papa, for heaven's sake, it's the last day of the seventies! And you're going to have a grandchild before the eighties are very old—don't ask me what there is to care about!"

Noel rose, pulled Marthe within the circle of his arms. "From now on, Marthe, I promise you, what happens here at Beau Chêne is all I will care about. And I'm going to propose a toast to just that—Henri, there's more champagne cooling on the gallery. If you'll get another bottle?"

"Where's Nollie? He said he'd spend part of the evening at home, now don't tell me he's gone off without seeing us!"

Marthe lowered herself into the tall rocker Henri placed next to Caroline. Tante Rose had concealed her rounding figure with drapes and carefully released pleats until the last four weeks; now, any eye could see that Marthe was with child. In an effort, as she said, to divert the gaze away from that interesting mound beneath her waist, Marthe had her necklines lowered until her full breasts seemed hardly constrained by the silk and lace covering them. "Marthe, that bodice!"

"Oh, maman, who in the world is there here to be shocked? As for Nollie—he did go off somewhere, but he said he'd be back quickly." She saw Caroline's question forming. "Don't ask me where, I've no idea. And if you don't like to be shocked, I'd advise you not ask him either."

Early in her pregnancy, Marthe had told Henri that it was well worth the nausea, the other discomforts of pregnancy, to be able to speak to her mother on the sure ground of equal knowledge. "She hasn't been able to say to me *once* that it's not *suitable* for me to know something, Henri!"

"If she ever knew how much you do know, Marthe, she might make that same judgment," Henri had answered. And had then laughed so hard he had almost not been able to enter her when she shot back—"I'm not fooled at all, Henri. You are one of those men Tante Rose told me about—you like a lady in the parlor and a woman in the bedroom. And you think everything I know is very suitable indeed."

Noel filled his glass and Caroline's, handed glasses to Henri and Marthe. "It's good for her," Henri said to Caroline. "Too much would not be, of course. But a glass or two—it aids the digestion."

"See how fortunate I am, maman. My husband not only gets me pregnant, he is able to direct its progress."

"But not deliver the baby," Caroline said.

"Maman—"

"This is excellent champagne," Noel said. "But even a fine vintage doesn't keep alive forever. I am going to propose a toast, if you please."

"We'll come to you," Henri said to Marthe, who was attempting to use the sides of the chair to help lift her weight. He and Noel flanked her as Caroline came to close the grouping.

A bead chain of light dropped from the cut-crystal bobeches in the center of the room. It fell over their circle, drawing its leash of diamante brilliance around them. Points of light pierced the thin glasses in their hands; if the champagne found its way through light-splintered glass, it would fall in light.

"I drink first to the past," Noel said. "To all the de Clouets who have lived here before us, who had a vision of this place, and built it, made that vision real. I drink to the present, to those of us who saw that vision destroyed, and who sought to make it real again. I drink to the future de Clouets, who may learn from us one thing—in this world, it is not often possible to make a vision real for someone else. Therefore, on the last night of 1879, I drink to this resolution—that we will not try to make a world in which Beau Chêne is possible, but a Beau Chêne in which the world is possible."

There was a small stillness before Caroline touched her glass to his. "Heavens, Noel, how poetic. But so solemn, dear!" She sipped, leaned forward to kiss his cheek. "Henri? Marthe?" Her little movement, the little sound of glass on glass, roused them. Glass touched glass, lips touched wine. "It's not midnight," Marthe said. "Will we make a gayer toast then?"

"You won't be up at midnight," Henri said.

And when Marthe said nothing, Caroline laughed. "I wish I'd been as persuasive, Henri, when she was under my care."

"Going to bed when you said to wasn't as much fun," Marthe said. "Oh, maman, don't frown. I have beautiful manners when I need them."

"Good. You can help me choose, then. I'm trying to decide what to send the Mouton girl for a wedding gift—come to my boudoir, I have a few things set out."

Henri closed the door behind them, poured more champagne. "I never thought I'd welcome this quiet. How marriage changes a man!"

"That. And responsibility. You work hard, Henri. Your patients may think you make Godlike cures. But medicine is like anything else. Hard work, most of it."

"Not quite everything else, Noel. Politics, now. Is that hard work, most of it?"

Noel was working the cork from another bottle. He kept his eyes fastened on his hands, spoke as though the same effort that released the cork from the bottle neck helped release his thoughts from a tight enclosure. "If anyone but Étienne de Gravelle's son said that to me, I'd say nothing. But when you say it—" The cork popped, was captured in the waiting hand. Noel held his glass under the bubbling fall of liquid, motioned to Henri to bring his. "When you say it, Henri, there is a reason. You wish to discuss what has happened between your father and me?"

"Not especially. Only to say that I respect you both, I admire you both, I have affection for you both."

"I am flattered that you extend those feelings to me." Noel leaned against the mantel, lifting the long skirt of his coat so that the fire warmth could seep through the fabric of his trousers. "A difference of philosophy, I think, Henri. Your father is a pragmatist. And I—I am not."

Henri set his glass down, carefully placing it on a silver coaster. "That's what pater says, oddly enough." He saw the quick motion of Noel's head, knew the eyes had flashed doubt. "That you are the pragmatist. And that he is not."

"My beliefs have not changed, Henri. I am no longer involved with the Democratic party in this state because I can no longer support its policies. When Nicholls was sold down the river, there went any hope for decency toward the Negroes, Henri. You know that."

"You think that shows idealism—that when the faction you belonged to compromised in order to win, you withdrew your support."

"Merde! More than compromised! Henri, the Bourbon Democrats who are so well represented by Wiltz give no value to the Negro at all. Look at the way he is treated—the methods used to scare him from the polls—to keep him ignorant and abused. By heaven, Henri, I've heard men like Hearsey say they won't rest until they are slaves again! And I've read that sentiment in his newspaper."

"But what good can you do here? Out of the fray? What hope that your view, and the view of men like you, will ever be strong enough to make a difference if you don't stay and fight?"

"Against Burke and his ilk? That's not a fight. With lottery money behind him, Wiltz can buy every goddamn vote in the legislature, as many judges as he needs—how in the hell can I fight that?"

"You can't. If you withdraw completely."

The rough low rumble of a heavy carriage rolling over the crushed-stone drive broke through the pattern of their words. Noel went to the window, lifted a deep gold velvet drapery and looked out. "It must be Nollie. We certainly don't expect any visitors." He let the curtain fall, sealing them in a box of light. "Your father is an idealist, then, because he stays on in the middle of defeat? And I am a pragmatist, I assume, because I stay only when I know I can win?"

"Something like that."

The front door slammed to a clutter of voices: Caroline's, querying, Marthe's, teasing, Nollie's, parrying. "You may well be right. Correction. You and your father may well be right. Perhaps he does show idealism, working with men who stand for everything he has fought. Perhaps I am being not only pragmatic but selfish, getting out of it and resolving to damn well stay out of it. I don't know." He smiled suddenly. "But, Henri, thank God, for the first time in years, I'm going to have time to sit in my study, and read, and think, and find out."

Henri went to hold open the door. "Noel—when you do find out—you'll let me know?"

"If you're still interested in the answer." The two men paused in the doorway, framed by its wide, carved moulding. "You made an excellent choice, Henri, when you decided to become a physician," Noel said. He looked at his son-in-law, whose frame was still lightly covered with flesh; the consuming hours of study and hospital work had been succeeded by hours of riding from one farm to the next, hours of sitting in his small office in St. Martinville and steadily taking pulses, looking down frightened open mouths, holding fevered hands. "You are so busy doing work everyone agrees is good that you yourself do not really have to determine its value."

A spatter of laughter came from below; Marthe, laughing at one of Nollie's stories. A small thunder clap of protest from Caroline. A long, low, encompassing rumble from Nollie that caught the other voices up, carried them forward into a cascading flow. "We'd better go down," Henri said, taking Noel's arm. "I think Nollie is trying to corrupt our wives."

Caroline was ladling turtle soup into soup plates, handing them to Nollie and Marthe, who were already seated. "Pardon this breach of manners," she said. "Keeping Nollie still long enough to eat even a little is much more difficult than following your schedule, Henri, erratic as that is." She passed a basket of toasted bread to Nollie, watched him break it into his soup. "Really, Nollie, you don't have to make all your New Year's calls in two days. You've time—how can you enjoy visiting when you go at such a pace?"

Nollie beckoned to Henri and Noel. "This turtle soup is superb. Truly. I recommend it." He seemed not ready to go on with his own meal, his talk, until they were seated, served, and had not only tasted the soup but agreed with his judgment. "Try a little sherry in it, Henri. It adds that touch which brings it to perfection. And, Papa—little chunks of this very dry toast, broken into the soup—wonderful."

"I can't imagine how we've managed to enjoy our meals at Beau Chêne without you to instruct us, Nollie," Noel said.

"You shouldn't have sent him to college, then. What else did he learn there that has any use?" Marthe turned from the deeper color in her mother's eyes that warned—don't tease. She looked at Nollie, half lounging in the chair across from her.

He had his father's height and figure, the brown hair touched with gold that Françoise called "chatin." His eyes, if hidden beneath lowered lids, were dark, deep; only when he chose to come from behind those careful screens did the clear hazel color his gaze. His fellows called him "Marquis," and could recite the names of his tailor, shirtmaker, tabacconer and vintner as monks chanting Compline.

"Ah, but Marthe—the usefulness of what I learned at the university depends entirely on the surroundings. I agree that many of the little details of living that employ my time are not appropriate here, in the country. But in other environs—"

Marthe shifted position, placed a hand in the middle of her back and rubbed firmly. The discomfort found voice. "We are not exactly barbaric at Beau Chêne, my dear brother."

Nollie took the wine that stood near his father's place, filled his glass, drank off half of it, topped the glass again. "I agree. But when I am in France, for example, there will be no question at all of the necessity for the most perfectly formed taste, the most impeccable manners."

"And you, of course, have both! Oh, Nollie!" Henri, listening to Marthe laugh, was pleased. She would take some good deep breaths, expand her lungs, circulate her blood.

"Nollie's manners and taste are equal to anyone's, Marthe. As are yours."

"France? And when are you planning to be in France?"

Noel's voice, heavier, clearer, pushed teasing, defense, aside.

"In about two months, papa, as a matter of fact."

Excitement pumped the blood, but did not expand the lungs. Henri rose, went to Marthe. "Let's walk along the gallery before we take anything else, Marthe. That soup is excellent, but it might rest a bit heavily. Come, Marthe."

"Oh, Henri, can't you ever forget you're a doctor? I can't believe other women walk miles between courses. It's not a bit comme il faut, maman will think Nollie is right, and we are barbarians here."

"She will think nothing of the sort," Henri said. "I'll get your cloak."

"How gallantly he protects her from all unpleasantness," Nollie said as the outer door closed behind Marthe and Henri.

"It would be agreeable of you to do the same for your mother."

Nollie went to the sideboard, helped himself to the thinly carved ham, the hot spiced fruit, the sweet potatoes cooked in brown sugar and butter. "How I missed these little suppers en famille, maman! They have a certain charm . . . but, papa," he said, seating himself again. "Why is my going to France unpleasant for Maman? It isn't as though she hasn't known I was going."

A silence thin and brittle dropped over them, setting them apart from the sounds of the servants at the back of the house, preparing mulled wine and eggnog, sweets and cold meats for New Year's callers.

Noel picked up his spoon, began to eat his soup. "If your mother knows of your plans, Nollie. I suppose she must have shared that knowledge with me—at some point in time." He took a piece of toast, broke it into equal squares, dropped them one at a time into his soup. "I must have either been so distracted by the circumstances in which your mother spoke to me that I have forgotten—understand, Nollie, your mother, as so many women do, sometimes selects occasions for conversation which men find—difficult. Or—I might have found the information of so little interest that I simply failed to remember it." He tasted a square of soup-saturated toast. "You are quite correct, Nollie. The toast is a good addition. Now, if you will just hand me the sherry . . ."

Very early in the morning of the first day of January 1880, Noel knocked at his wife's bedroom door. When Caroline opened it, velvet dressing gown half covering her challis nightdress, he stood quietly, watching her. She opened the door wider. "Well? Are you coming in?"

"Now that you have asked me, yes." He walked past her, sat in a low chair near the fireplace, and began to unfasten his cuff links. "We can talk now—or we can wait until those circumstances you usually choose when you don't really want me to hear what you are telling me."

The deep shrug moved the dressing gown lower on her shoulders; she slipped it off, climbed into her high bed, and piled the pillows behind her. Noel rose, removed coat, waistcoat, shirt. He took off his belt, let his trousers slip down.

"You must be eating too much," Caroline said. "That scar on your left hip doesn't show as much as it used to."

He went around the bed, pulled the covers back, got in beside her. His hands unbuttoned the front of her gown, moved her away from the pillows so that he could take it from her. "Move closer to me," he said. He slid her down beneath him, pushed her legs apart. Her lips started to move, his mouth came down and covered them. He stayed against her, mouth on hers, body pressing her down, until he felt a small shift in her, and she rose to meet him.

He lifted himself off of her, rolled over, took one of her pillows and put it behind her head. "It took me a long while, Caroline, to understand what you were doing. In bed. Either you would say something that would distract me—that about the scar, something like that—or, if that didn't work, you would wait until I was past the point of wanting to think about anything, and then began to talk to me." She was lying very still beside him, very quiet. "At first, I was puzzled. If you had simply grown tired of the whole business, you would never like it at all, isn't that so?" He raised on one elbow, stared at her. "But I have a good memory, Caroline. And I could remember, in very nice detail, too many incidents that said—Caroline is not tired of it at all. So, what could it be? Another man? Nonsense! Not because another man would not want you, Caroline. But because I did not believe you would do such a thing." He reached a hand forward, turned her face so that he could force her to look at him. "Then there was the lottery stock. Which, if you indeed had some, disappeared with as much secrecy as it had appeared." He felt the line of her jaw harden, felt the resistance in her flesh. He released her, lay back against the pillow. "Once I was sure you had been de Gravelle's mistress, might continue to be, even if his son had married your daughter, I decided to forget it. After all, you had wishes, desires—"

"Noel—"

"If I had ever wanted to know your views, Caroline, I would surely have asked you. I have not. I am not. I am saying to you that tonight, at supper, I finally understood what the war had cost me."

"The war?" She jerked forward, sat up, covers falling from her bare breasts. "What does the war have to do with it? That was fifteen years ago, Noel!"

"Yes. The events. But the changes? They go on, and on, and on. Not just in the way we live, how we work our fields, govern our state. Clearly, the changes were deeper, Caroline. You, for instance, kept from me that our son goes to France—for what purpose does he go? to study? to trace our family history?"

"Noel, we've talked many times of sending Nollie abroad—you yourself said that if your money doesn't give our children broader lives, better lives—Noel, it's late. I'm tired. If we have to continue this, cannot it be another time?"

"I'm almost finished, Caroline. What I realized, at supper, was that when I went off to defend this place, our way of life, my ideas—whatever in hell it was I went off to defend—when I did that, you were forced to take my place. Make the decisions. Face the dangers, the discomforts. I was not here to protect you when you needed me, Caroline. And so you went off down another road, a road you were made to take." She could feel his whole body shudder, almost as it had when he lay in her arms the night he returned from war, and defeat.

"Since I was not here to take you down a safer passage, Caroline, I have no right to judge the road you took."

She lay beside him and felt a softness, weakness, enter her. Her husband's warm breath stirred the cold air around her, his warm pulse beat near her. But she was alone, surrounded by a landscape she had not seen before, though she had lived within it a long, long time. "Noel—" She knew he would answer her, would turn to her, hold her. But the language between them was gone, whatever they said to each other, the rest of their lives, would be in a borrowed tongue.

"Why is everyone so cross?" Marthe said. The day had been marked not only the striking gong of the tall mahogany clock in the central hall but by the rolling wheels of carriages the continuing wishes for "Bonne Année!", the steady stream of silver platters and laden cake stands coming from the kitchen to the damask-covered table in the dining room. "Did we use all our gaiety up on our callers?"

"I'm not in the least cross," Nollie said. "A bit subdued from the effects of a particularly fine champagne punch Francis Blanchet concocted—otherwise, I am in the greatest of moods."

Caroline, standing at the hearth poking at the fire, put one arm against the mantel and leaned forward, resting her head on the dark marble. "I don't think I've been so tired in all my life—not even during the war, when I spent each day out in the fields."

Nollie looked up from cutting the pages of a new book. "Dissipation does take a terrible toll, maman. You should leave it to those of us who are young enough to stand the pace." Then, seeing the slackness of her body, the heavy fatigue that pressed on her, he went to her, took her in his arms. "Maman, are you all right? You're not ill?"

She let him lead her to a chair, settle her in it. "No. Only so tired. Isn't it strange, Nollie? When you and Marthe were little, and the Yankees had left, I used to lie in bed, one of you on each side, thinking and thinking how I could get some money to buy you the things you needed." Her head was back against the tall blue silk moive chair; the silk seemed to cast shadowed hues under her eyes, stroke dim shadings into her temples. A sigh, deep, long held back. "Of course, there was no way to get money. I thought then, that if one could always have money, some amount, something—there could be safety."

Nollie glanced at Henri, nodded toward Caroline. "But, maman, we do have money now. A wonderful lot of it. You are safe, maman." He knelt, took her hands in his, began rubbing the thin wrists. Henri came forward, bent over Caroline.

"Are you only tired? You are pale—perhaps I should treat you as a patient, Mère de Clouet."

Another sigh, deep, releasing with that even airstream wishes and dreams, fears and terrors. "No, Henri, I am all right, truly. I think I am just learning how heavy certain ideas can be. I need sleep, that's all."

"I wish I thought you were going to get it," Marthe said. "I've been sitting here for the last hour counting contractions—and I think, maman, that we all have a wakeful night ahead of us."

"Marthe, you're not going to have that baby now!"

Marthe laughed. "My dear brother—I wish I were going to have it *now*—without the hard hours I suspect I'll go through first. I know you have no intention of being anywhere near when your niece or nephew arrives—but you might just go to New Iberia and get Dr. Renoudet. Maman will have a fit if Henri delivers our baby—and I think she has been tried enough today. Dépêche! Go!"

"I'll go get your father, Marthe. Henri, ring for Tilde. She can help Marthe undress."

Caroline hesitated outside the closed door to Noel's study. So tightly did the door fit into the frame that only the thinnest line of faint light gleamed into the dim hall. Just as tightly did the door closed between them fit the frame Noel had made. Whether the thin, faint light left was enough to let them see by—she raised her hand, knocked. Heard his footsteps as he left the thick, muffling Tabriz and walked on the bare floor near the door. Heard him turn the knob. "Caroline?"

"Noel—" She meant to say—"Marthe's baby is coming." "Noel—I—I'd like to find my way back. Would you—do you think you could come help me?"

She felt the depth of his sighing breath as he held her against his chest. "Would that we could all find our way back, Caroline."


Cold air, weighted with moisture from high clouds and low swamps, breathed its billows of fog around the house, up onto the gallery, close against the windows. Françoise pulled aside a woven cotton curtain, rubbed a circle in the frosted glass with the edge of her apron. "Zut! With that fog, I still can't see a thing. Claude, maybe you should go down to the gate, look out for Monsieur Clements."

"The man can find a gatepost, Françoise. Reste tranquille— it's not one o'clock yet, not for half an hour."

"There is someone coming . . . I can just make out the shape of the horse." She enlarged the circle of clear, rubbed glass. "I don't know—something about the horse looks familiar to me. Claude, come see. Who is that?"

"Françoise, if you can wait a few minutes, yes. Whoever it is will be here and we'll know, isn't it?" But he got up from the table and stood looking out into the mist-smeared air. Then he laughed. "That's Jumie, for God's sake, Françoise! I guess you do know him."

She dropped the curtain, twitched at her apron. "I thought Jumie was down in the back helping with the pig. What's he doing riding around?"

"Ask him," Claude said. He had seen, just before Françoise let the curtain fall, another figure, dimmed by the fog, but growing steadily clearer. "Or I will." He pulled a jacket off the hook by the door, and went down the hall to the front door, buttoning the collar high against the damp chill. "Hey, Jumie!" he called from the edge of the gallery, and then ran down the steps to meet the man who had followed so closely on Jumie's path.

"My God, Langlinais, you live in thick soup!" the man said, tying his horse to the rail in front of the house. "Between the mud pulling at my horse's feet and the fog blinding him, I thought I'd never get here."

"Jumie," Claude said, "this is Monsieur Clements. The man I spoke of? Monsieur Clements, my son, Claude Louis Langlinais. Named like me, so we call him Jumie. He's a twin; his sister, Claudette, she's a nun in the convent in New Iberia. But come in, Monsieur Clements, come in. I have a new cask of burgundy that will clear the fog—Jumie, take Monsieur Clements's horse around to the stable. And Jumie—where have you been? I hope you didn't leave Felix watching that pig!"

Jumie took the horse's bridle, began leading him away. "Over at Beau Chêne. I wanted to see Nollie while he's still home. He's going to France, he told me."

"To study more about his painting?"

"I guess." The horse leaned down, nuzzled the gravel drive to find grass. "Hey, you'll get better than that in the stable. Come on, now."

"Nollie—some relation of Noel de Clouet?"

Claude put a hand under Clement's elbow, steered him toward the stairs. "His son."

"The one who studied at University of Virginia?"

"The only son. They just had the two. The girl, Marthe, she's having a baby soon. Her husband—well, you know him! Étienne's boy? Henri? He's some good doctor, let me tell you."

Clements sniffed the rush of warm air that met them when Claude opened the door. "My nose tells me you have more than good wine waiting for me, Claude. Étienne is quite right—having you with us will be a pleasant experience in many, many ways."

"I haven't told you yes, Clements." He could hear Françoise rattling pots in the kitchen, knew she would feel that finger of cold air and come into the hall to meet them, waving them to the table with her big spoon. "I thought de Clouet would be asked to fill his post. Or, at least, put a man of his own in."

"Perhaps he did. Perhaps you are that man." Clements was watching Claude, his smile cutting across his chill-red face.

Claude beckoned Clements in, closed the door. "Monsieur Clements is here, Françoise," he called down the hall. "I'm just going to take him to our room so he can wash, then we come." Then, as he hung Clements's overcoat and long woolen muffler in a tall cypress armoire near the door: "No, Clements, if de Clouet had any say in who was a police juror in his parish, Claude Langlinais would not be one."

Clements followed Claude into the bedroom, took off his coat and rolled up his sleeve. "Nice house, Langlinais. Big, lots of space. But plain. You don't make voters mad with this house. So—you and Noel don't get along?"

"Sure. We get along. Much as two men can when one got his learning in Virginia at the university and the other got his in the swamps and the fields."

Clements scrubbed his face with one of Françoise's woven towels, then took a comb from his vest pocket and carefully parted his hair. He was peering into the mirror hanging over the washstand; he and Claude watched each other in a small rectangular frame that seemed to freeze them in time and space.

"But I understand that if it hadn't been for you, Noel's family wouldn't have lived through the war. Doesn't that put him in your debt?"

"Which is why he'd never name me police juror, even if he could. Men like de Clouet don't pay off personal debts with political favors."

"You astonish me. Are there really men left who live that way?"

"Don't make it sound so good." Claude saw Clement's eyebrows lift; the depth of the mirrored image held his question between them.

Clements reached out, held Claude's arm. "You understand de Clouet pretty well. And does he understand you?"

"What's to understand? A simple farmer—look, Clements, from that big gallery at Beau Chêne, this place looks pretty small."

"The view from that gallery might be misleading, Langlinais."

Claude laughed. "Of course. But it's like Françoise says. Beau Chêne is just a play, something they make up."

"Fine. Let them keep on playing, whatever they want to do." Clements dropped an arm around Claude's shoulders. "Étienne's gotten a little weary of putting up with the de Clouets and their manqué ways. Now with you down here, Claude, it's a different thing. A different thing entirely. We'll have some private time later?"

"We'll go over to the office. I want my son, Jumie, to hear. Because, Clements, I want to tell you something. If I say yes to this job—it's not for me. You think I don't know what happens, the minute a man puts himself before the people like that? Merde! They expect everything!"

"You'll manage that, Claude."

A shrug. Of course. That wasn't questioned. "For one reason. So Jumie can build on me. You understand? Jumie—he didn't get to the university. But 'Tit Frère—now that's one Langlinais that damn well is going to college, Clements!"

They stood in the doorway to the dining room, where Françoise was herding the people streaming in from the backyard. A suckling pig centered the table, the hot rich smell of slow-roasted port hanging in the air. Under it and shot through it, the sharp smell of greens, the sweet smell of yams in syrup, the plain smell of black-eyed peas. "You sit there, Monsieur

Clements," Françoise said. "So you can tell me everything that's going on in New Orleans."

"Is this your little boy?" Clements said to Jumie, who was helping 'Tit Frère pull out his chair. He reached forward, took the child's hand. "I think you may be the most important Langlinais in this room, young man," he said. "At least, as far as your grand-père is concerned!"

The fire, glowing heat over the banked coals, squared light and sent it against oblong shadows. Geneviève moved closer to Jumie, pressed against him. "Maybe we'll make a baby now, Jumie. For the new year? Maybe that brings luck."

"You don't believe Henri?"

He felt her tense denial. "That I won't have any more? Because of the one I lost? Jumie, he's only a doctor. He's not God, no!"

"Geneviève—if there aren't any more—we have two good ones. You heard papa talking! Already, he has 'Tit Frère at Louisiana State University."

"I heard. Though I tell you, I don't understand how just being a police juror is going to make all that money."

"Geneviève, the police jury runs the parish. Men who serve on it—they know where roads are going, things like that."

"Roads? What good is that?"

"Mais, Geneviève—land near a big road has more value."

"So your papa could buy land where a road was going? Before anyone else knew?" She bounced on the moss-filled mattress. "But, Jumie, there's almost never land for sale around here—"

"Sometimes the roads happen to go near land that's already owned—by the jurors." He watched to see how she took that.

Laughter, bouncing up from her full breasts as her body bounced on the mattress. "Oh, Jumie, you mean we can get a road going straight to New Orleans just because of your papa? One passing right in front of my house?" More laughter, full round sounds that filled him. "Mais, that stuck-up Julie Marchant had better mind her manners, yes. If she's not nice to me, I won't let her use my road, no!"

"So you think it's all right."

She sat up, threw her arms straight over her head. "All right? Listen, Jumie—don't you think I want my son to go to college as much as your papa does? Maybe not in Louisiana even. Maybe to one of those grand schools the de Clouets go to."

"If a man wants to get anywhere in politics, Geneviève, he doesn't send his son to university in another state."

"His son? It's your papa is the police juror, not you."

"It'll be me next."

Gevevieve threw herself on top of Jumie, held his face between her hands. "What? He passes it on to you, like the land?"

"Not like the land. But we make sure, Geneviève, we work to make sure that if I want his position, it comes to me. Don't you understand?"

She ran a light finger around his lips, then kissed him. "Maybe. Maybe the Langlinais are getting what the de Clouets lost, all that time ago."

"I don't—"

"Oh, Jumie, I don't want to talk anymore now." She put a little space between them, sat up and unbuttoned her gown. "All right, I'll say it quick while I can think of it." The gown almost smothered the words as she pulled it over her head. "The de Clouets go on and on about the titles, the châteaux, they left in France. Inherited titles, places at court." The gown sailed across the oblong shadows, across the rectangle of light. "So, Jumie, maybe the Langlinais have inherited titles now, isn't it? Don't answer!"

Early sun touched the climbing ivy, still green. Glanced over the camellia bush bursting with pink flowers. Shimmered off the clear fall of water in the garden fountain. Then found an opening into the house through shutters thrown wide and caressed the woman who lay in a big bed, sleeping.

"She's asleep, they both are," Henri said, softly closing the door to Marthe's room and joining Nollie in the hall.

"Look, I'll never get over not getting Renoudet back in time, Henri. You've no idea how useless it makes me feel— one small task, and I didn't get it done."

"I didn't share Mère de Clouet's doubts about my ability to deliver my own child, Nollie. The road's one long mudhole, the fog's been miserable—anyone could have lost his way, Nollie. Come, let's get some coffee."

They sat near the fire, sipping from Caroline's thin Haviland cups. "I'll probably go to Limoges. See how they make this,"

Nollie said. "Maybe even design something special for maman. She'd like that, don't you think?"

"Yes. Not only because you do it. But because what you do is very good, Nollie."

Nollie thrust his legs out in front of him, sank lower in his chair. "That's what everyone says, Henri. The professors at school. The people who've seen my things. So why don't I just settle into it?"

"Isn't that why you're going to France? To study painting?"

"I've no idea. One day I think so—the next I don't know."

Henri pulled his watch from its pocket, clicked open the cover. "I promised Madame Hebert I'd be by before the noon hour. I'd better go—but, Nollie, isn't it time you decide? Marthe and I, we live here—and she knows something of what goes on, I suppose. Though mostly, it's her horses she works with. And now, with the baby—with little Hélène—and I have my practice, Nollie."

"I'll ride along with you, Henri, if I may. Clear my head. What you're saying, as delicately as you can, is that I'd better make up my mind as to whether I'm going to take care of Beau Chêne—is that it?"

"Someone will have to, Nollie. When your father can't."

Nollie stretched, pulling the fine wool of his coat taut across his broad shoulders. "I'll have to decide that someday, Henri, I agree. But, thank the good God, papa is only, what, forty-seven? If the de Clouet men avoid duels and hurricanes, they generally live to a pretty good age. I've years before I have to worry about that. And by then—maybe Marthe will have produced a series of babies, one of whom will relieve his lazy uncle of the choice."

The day before the Feast of the Kings, Claude and Jumie spent all of the morning and most of the afternoon going over the ledgers detailing what their business had made in the year just gone. "It's up again, papa. More than ever before." Jumie closed the last of the big books and replaced it on the shelf. "And with these new plans—papa, do you know we're going to be rich?"

"It seems so."

"Papa—aren't you pleased?"

Claude opened a small cabinet and took out a bottle of wine. "Get some glasses, Jumie. And some cheese. You say—am I pleased? Well, of course. I'm not fou. Money makes money quicker than I can make it for myself. But that makes me a little sad, Jumie. To think that."

Jumie twisted the cork from the bottle, poured wine. "Sad! I don't see that."

Claude cut a slice of cheese, chewed slowly. "Not all farmers can do what we do, Jumie. They don't have so much land— they don't have the mill, the factory—"

"Well, of course. That's the way of things—you don't get big land unless you can pay for it. And you can't keep it if you can't make it pay."

"I'm going to try to change that, Jumie. I don't want to be the big man because everyone else is so little."

Jumie turned down the flame in the lamp burning on the table, began to put his pens away. "Well, papa, if you feel like that—I better feel like that, too. What Geneviève said—it's probably true. One way or another, what the Langlinais get, they hold on to."

"You go on, Jumie. I'm going to stay awhile. Go over some of the old papers, letters. I always knew, Jumie, when it was plowing, or trapping, or cutting trees, what to do. But politics?" He shook his head, Then rubbed heavily at his neck. "Politics? Jumie, this Langlinais may have taken hold of something he's not going to want to keep."

"Maman will never forget it if you don't keep it," Jumie said. He was glad Geneviève didn't have Françoise's ways. Being married was good, having children was good. As long as a wife kept her eyes on the house, the children, a man could stand her eyes being on him when he was home. But eyes that followed him outside? Not for him, no!

When he was certain that Jumie had gone, Claude opened the small cabinet where he stored the wine and took out a square velvet case. He held it in his hand for a long while, stroking the deep pile, fingering the little spring lock. Then he pressed the catch. The lid flew open, and all the light that was left in the room, gathered from dying coals and lowered lamp, hurled itself into one glowing beam to catch the jeweled brooch on startling fire. De Gravelle had outdone himself; the brooch was delicate in design and simple, but the stones were large and fine—while the neighbors might not know how fine, Françoise would. He thought of the Spanish cross the Langlinais women had worn since Lafitte had sent it home with his grandfather. Well, she could wear the cross to church, as she did now. The brooch? De Gravelle had sent word he expected Claude to come to New Orleans within the month. This time, she would go with him. He would not ask. He would tell her.

Claude closed the velvet case, tucked it away in his pocket. So now one pocket could hold the jewels of the Langlinais women—it had taken several heavy casks to contain the de Clouet jewels when he'd hidden them back in the swamp. The weight of the case seemed ominous; this one brooch would be out of place in Françoise's armoire. She would either never wear it, tuck it away somewhere—or want more. Claude sighed. The seat of his chair was suddenly hard, the edge of the desk sharp. He wanted the long muscles of field work, the deep lungs of open air. But that kind of work didn't buy jewels, or education. That kind of work, simple, honest, gave simple, honest rewards. He had learned how little market there was for those.

He stood and went to the door. A fresh wind blew in from the Gulf, far beyond the swamps. It smelled of salt, of the open ocean. High-flying birds tossed themselves against the dark sky, their movement erratic, off course. He remembered his wonder when he'd learned how far the birds came that wintered here. "How do they know where to fly, if they've never come before?" he'd asked. "It's in them. It's part of them, that's all." The old voice of his grandfather, patient, slow. A restlessness caught at him, the familiar protest of once-active muscles made taut by confinement. And if he got off course, if the path he'd charted led to quicksand, to a morass of swamp? Would part of him correct it, tell him he was going wrong? Maybe de Clouet was right, after all. Maybe, if you made everything either black or white, right or wrong, you would be better off.

Then a gust of wind slapped his face, brought his blood to life. Merde! Why moon like a woman? He'd found his way so far, with little help from any man. He wasn't going into this game without knowing the rules. As he closed the door behind him, slipping the wooden latch through the leather thong, he laughed softly. Already, he was figuring ways to get around them.

# CHAPTER 22

## *Vox Populi*

The 1880s were called, rightfully, the Gilded Age in Louisiana. Money flowed—from the fields of sugar, from the pennies and silver dollars bet in the lottery, from the profit made on land, on railroads—and on politics. The Langlinaises were, as usual, too busy with their own concerns to bother with fancy names. They would remember the eighties not as gilded but as a time when their plans, their work, made visible progress. Claude and Jumie, by 1890, were on the board of directors of one of the banks in New Iberia. The small political niche Claude carved with his seat as a police juror had deepened; though to the unobservant eye, Claude's influence seemed narrow, those with sharper vision knew well how wide that influence was, how subtly it was used. As for Jumie, he had long since passed from being a mere watcher. "Those pots Claude doesn't keep going, Jumie fires," people said. While the people of St. Martin who still counted generations back to Nova Scotia smiled and shrugged and said you might as well have a Langlinais whose ways you understood running things as a city fellow who was totally incomprehensible, certain of the "city fellows" and their country counterparts felt no such ease. "Better see what the Langlinaises think," became a watchword for men running the parish—and the state.

What seemed gilded, elaborate, luxuriant, in a city like New Orleans became a golden haze, a glow of security, of pleasant days flowing one into the other, on a plantation like Beau Chêne. With Nollie in Europe, pursuing art, culture, and pleasure, Marthe and her father ran the plantation. Henri's country practice was good—and fatiguing. The round of family life, cushioned by stacks of money in bank vaults, followed the seasons. Country in the summer, and into harvest. A winter season in New Orleans, until Lent. Perhaps travel in the early spring. Then rich summer again. So natural did that pattern seem, so enduring, that no one at Beau Chêne gave thought to the interruptions and disruptions that occur even in nature.

By the summer of 1891, Claudine Langlinais, a dark-eyed sixteen-year-old with her mother's gaiety and her father's sharpness, was enrolled at the Ursuline convent in new Orleans, and her brother, a year younger, was to begin Louisiana State University in Baton rouge. The de Gravelles' children, Hélène, age ten, René, age eight, and Nanette, age six, lived with their parents and their grandparents at beau Chêne. It was all the world they knew, and all, except for certain selected places in new Orleans, their parents cared for them to know.

Puffs of brown dust, speckled with black soot, burst in the humid air and formed a haze that screened the August sun. Claude took his light straw hat from his head and fanned himself vigorously. "Mais, that train better stir a breeze. Geneviève and Claudine will be smothered before they get home." He touched Jumie's arm. "Jumie, you and Geneviève—you're sure you want Claudine to go to school in New Orleans?"

"Where else can she go, papa? And the Ursulines—those nuns will take good care. After all, didn't she have a great-great-great-aunt who was a nun in that very convent?"

The train whistle cut through the heat, the puffing dust. "Jumie—that's not what I meant. Both your children—gone. You know? Claude Louis to Louisiana State—Claudine to New Orleans. Jumie. It's strange, yes, that when a man has money, it brings him many things—but it takes his children."

The train was visible now, black face pushing against the mask of dusted air. Jumie shook his head, laughed. "Papa, what? You want them still on the farm? Claudine following a plow? Papa. What's the point of all our work if it isn't for them?"

The roar of the approaching train blocked Claude's answer; he filled his lungs with air and shouted against the sooty wind— "But, Jumie, a chance for them mustn't be against us—you know? Jumie—we keep that."

They watched the plunging rods thrust the wheels forward, watched the brakes descend, strain, hold. The train slowed, stopped. Two cars down, Geneviève's head appeared. "Here, Jumie! Jumie, bring all your arms! When you see what we bought!"

Claudine jumped down into her grandfather's arms. "Oh, grandpapa! The school is so nice! The mother superior scared me a little, but I pretended she was my Tante Claudette, and that made it all right."

He held her close, felt the warmth of youth. "Now, Claudine," and his voice was stern, "now, Claudine, since when a Langlinais is scared?" Then he kissed her hair and pinched her cheek. "Claudine, anybody in New Orleans scares you, you let your grandpapa know, you hear?"

"Jumie, you'd never guess who we saw at the Saint Charles Hotel when we went for an ice? Papa Claude, guess!"

"Nollie de Clouet," Claude said. He was strapping their bags and boxes in the space at the back of the caleche, tightening buckles, balancing weights.

"Papa Claude! Now how did you know that?"

"Noel, he was going to New Orleans. On business, he said. But also to meet Nollie. And his family."

"What, Mignon, too? And the children? Let's see—how many? Four?" Geneviève held up fingers, began to count. "They had a little boy, Sept, then a girl Lisette—I don't know, I lose count. Marthe, she doesn't like to talk about Nollie. Who knows why?"

Jumie helped Geneviève into the wagon. "Why? When her brother stays over in France, doing who knows what? And her father gets older and older? What? She's going to run Beau Chêne?"

"She's the one lives there," Geneviève said. She brushed her skirt vigorously, rubbed at her face with a linen handkerchief. "Zut! That train, it moves fast, yes, but not so fast it gets ahead of the dirt it makes. Marthe's babies were born at Beau Chêne. She raises her horses at Beau Chêne—why should Nollie run it?"

"Because he's the male heir," Jumie said. "And no matter what the law says, that's the way the de Clouets have always set it up. Beau Chêne goes to the male, other children get something else."

"Well, if that's not just like the de Clouets," Geneviève said. "One law for everybody else, and one for them! Now, Jumie, that doesn't seem right."

"If everyone agreed that what was right for everyone else was also right for them, we wouldn't need government, Geneviève," Claude said.

"Papa Claude!" She took up her fan and tapped his wrist. "My blood is hot from the ride on the train, my head is heavy with heat. Now, don't give me a big idea to put in there—I tell you, there's no room."

An oval of dust, thick, brown, layered from lightest tan where it met the shimmering blue air to deep café au lait where it rose from the dry earth, marked the track laid out behind the stables at Beau Chêne. The dust was stirred into motion, rolled up, forward, cycled, by the pounding galloping hooves of a horse harnessed to a light racing buggy. Marthe, face red behind the dusty veil, leaned forward, cracked a whip in the air above the racing mare. The air rushed past her, coating the wet back of the horse, the long line of leather rein, the rims of wheels, the leather seat, her linen skirt, with sifting dust.

Henri clicked the stem of the stopwatch and marked the time in the notebook Hélène held up to him. "How did she do, papa?"

"Just a hair better than yesterday. But still—better!"

"Is it fast enough to beat Mr. Jumie's horse?" Henri looked at his son, who was peeling the bark from a twig with his pocketknife.

"Hold the blade away from you, René. Beat Jumie's horse?" Henri tucked the stopwatch away and plucked Nanette from the rail where she sat watching her mother talk to the stableman. "Listen—winning a race isn't anything you can count on. Today, she runs well. Very well. Tomorrow?" He shrugged. "Who can tell?"

"But the race isn't tomorrow, papa." The child in his arms put a small hand against his cheek. "All that matters is how she runs that day, isn't it?"

Henri pulled her sunbonnet forward, tightened its ribbons. "Don't get all sunburned, Nanette. Your grand-mère will have a fit."

Nanette squirmed in his arms, turning to face Marthe, who was walking toward them. "Maman doesn't wear a sunbonnet. Her face is sunburned. So is yours. Why doesn't grand-mère fuss at her? At you?"

Henri put her down, sliding her small length down to the

dust-grayed grass. "Grand-mère doesn't fuss at your mother because it wouldn't do any good. She doesn't fuss at me because I'm a man."

Nanette, one foot already positioned to go to her mother, paused. "That's not fair, papa. Don't men ever get fussed at?"

Henri looked at his wife. Sunlight poured on her face, shining-moist with sweat. Wet curls lay close to her cheeks, clung to her forehead. Light as clear and warm as that of the sun poured from her eyes; her smile broke over them and spilled happiness. "Not if they're lucky," he said. Taking Nanette's hand, he went forward to meet her. "She was faster," he said. "By one-half second."

"One-half second!" She pushed hair from her face, reached behind her for the straw hat which had slipped away in the racing wind and hung by blue ribbons down her back. Pulled it off and began to fan herself, the brim rippling with air and movement. "Oh, well—one-half second every day—but, Henri, my first race! I want to win!"

Henri put an arm around her waist. "Hélène and René have carried the picnic basket up to the big oak. Now walk slowly— let your blood cool."

"But it's not your first race, maman. Your horses have won in New Orleans. I've seen the big cups—and the ribbons."

"Oh, Nanette, baby—my stables have run before. But I haven't ever been in a race."

"You don't ride your horses? When you go to New Orleans?"

Marthe turned her face to the sun, meeting its broad face with her own open delight. "Wouldn't maman just have a fit?" She bent and hugged Nanette. "Ladies don't ride in races. It's not—comme il faut."

"Maman—if ladies get fussed at and men don't—if ladies can't ride in races and men can—maman—is being a lady any fun at all?"

"When she lives at Beau Chêne it is." The sweet smell of clover rose around them, flowers crushed under their feet. The swift flash of cardinals, orange-winged blackbirds, bright blue jays; the coo of pigeons, lazy and fat; the deep russet corn silk waving from the next field; the spiky green of cane, reaching toward the sun; the feel of the hot breeze and of dry pasture grass—all the beauty of Beau Chêne surrounded them. Marthe held her arms wide and slowly circled round. Nanette took one of her mother's outstretched hands, wheeling with her. "Oh,

Henri," Marthe said, her voice hot and strong, "if Nollie has come back to live at Beau Chêne—Henri—if he has—what ever will I do?"

She saw a figure standing at the edge of the pasture, held a hand across her forehead to screen out the sky. "Jumie? Jumie?" Dropping Nanette's hand, she ran forward. "What? Are you spying out how fast my horse is? Well, it's no use! She didn't even work up a sweat, I held her in so!"

He laughed back at her. "You'll turn my own tricks against me, Marthe. Serves me right for teaching you everything I know. Look—about the race. The date?"

"Whenever you want. We just need enough time to announce it. And to make a fête."

"I had thought next week. But papa says wait, there may be something we have to do. He doesn't say what." He shrugged. "You know papa. When he doesn't want to talk—even the Yankees can't make him."

She laughed. "Remember how his French would get so thick, his English so impossible, they decided he was fou and didn't bother with him. They should have been so crazy— Well, Jumie—then at the end of the mouth? Just before the children go to school?"

"That should make it." Then—"I hear Nollie's back. With his family." She felt his eyes on her, a steady, clear warmth.

"Oh, Jumie, it's not that I don't love Nollie—of course I do. But he's been in France for over ten years, he's been back to marry Mignon and that's about it—Beau Chêne can't mean to him what it means to me!"

He took her hand and held it. "Marthe, maybe he's just making a family visit." He saw the tears behind her eyes, fought them with a joke. "Marthe—if he does move here—I tell you. I'll sell you the lumber for a new house for you at my cost. And one of Beau Chêne Beauty's foals for the pot."

The tears dropped away. "Oh, Jumie, I'd rather pay the highest price you charge than give you one of her foals that cheaply! Now, if she were running in this race, your team needn't even show up."

"But since she's not—they've got your picnic ready, Marthe. Go eat. Listen, it's set? Last Saturday in August?"

"An historic day! The first time a de Clouet defeats a Lan-glinais."

Their eyes caught, held, in a struggle of tension. His words came soft, carried across the bridge of air. "Has it always been a race, then?"

Noel let his head rest against the high muslin-covered chair. The closed shutters, drawn draperies, so dimmed the day that, beyond the cluster of chairs and small tables grouped around the one he occupied, he saw only looming shapes.

"Pardon our déshabillé," Étienne said. He had let Noel in, then disappeared after gesturing Noel into the darkened parlor. "I know in the country life goes on as usual, even in the deep of summer—but Natalie flees across the lake to Mandeville the end of May, after stripping the house of anything that might harbor a moth." He came across the floors, bare of their Aubusson rugs, covered with light straw ones.

"Caroline can hardly leave in summer, as you say," Noel said. "It's one of the busiest times for us—but, I assure you, the slipcovers descend over everything, we are in an uproar for a few weeks. New Orleans has no prerogative on dust." He frowned, remembering his walk over from the hotel. "You certainly haven't kept this city the way the Yankees left it, Étienne. They're what—a little over a dozen years gone, and already you've forgotten how to keep sewage and stinking rubbish under control? I could hardly breathe coming over."

"If you'd stayed and breathed the stench of politics I've lived in these past ten years, Noel, you'd not even notice raw sewage and rotting garbage." He pulled out a cigar. When Noel's eyebrows went up, he laughed. "No, I'm not going to smoke it in here, even with Natalie gone. Roselle's laying out a light lunch in my study—we'll talk there."

Noel watched Étienne walk down the hall ahead of him, his rounding body balanced on carefully shod feet. Étienne's appetites, Noel knew, had become perhaps less voracious, but no less discriminating. The same money that bought the fine liquors, the best wines, also bought the most delightful—and skillful—women. He thought of Caroline, naked, one of Étienne's toys. The small surge of outrage died as it began. That was certainly long over. Franklin might have found all cats gray in the dark, and recommended older women. But older men, Noel thought, certainly older rakes such as Étienne, were not flattered by such a conquest. They'd rather buy youth than have age given.

"I hope this business you have made so much of is worth

the trip over here, Étienne. Except for grinding season, I couldn't be busier at Beau Chêne." There had been a string of letters from Étienne, each one presenting some decision, some problem. Finally, the suggestion—"Why not run to the city for a few days? Get all this cleared up." Then, when the letter from Nollie came, saying that they would arrive in New Orleans, there to stay a week before proceeding to "the country," he had given in. Clearly, he would spend at least a part of August, the most wretched month of the year, in new Orleans, a city he had come to dislike with as much strength as he had for disliking anything.

"But then you would have come to meet Nollie, anyway. Wouldn't you?"

Of course Étienne knew Nollie was here, he kept forgetting Henri was Étienne's son. They couldn't be more different, thank the Lord. "Yes. He and Mignon and the children arrived two days ago. They'll be with us at Beau Chêne after a visit to the Blanchets."

Étienne was uncorking a chilled white Bordeaux; he puffed the cork, sniffed it, and picked up a glass. "I was surprised when I heard Noel was running an art gallery. Somehow, it didn't seem like the kind of thing you'd invest in. And without your banker's—advice."

"I didn't. His mother did." Noel watched Étienne roll the wine in his mouth, finally swallow it, and then fill two glasses.

"Caroline did. Astonishing." Étienne's voice was like the mousse, cold, creamy, bland, covering everything with a layer of gelatinous smoothness.

Noel sat and began to eat. "She seemed to have a rather large amount of money available to give him." He looked over his wineglass at Étienne. Those large flat brown eyes were staring at him. They seemed to reflect the clear wine, to hold the same kind of intoxicating power. "I've a good idea where she got it—though I wasn't really interested enough to check—either with her or with you."

"Banker's don't reveal clients' secrets, Noel. You ought to know that."

"I don't think you acted solely as her banker in—helping Caroline obtain—whatever made so much money for her."

Étienne shrugged. "So—a little fiscal counsel, a little advice."

"As you said, Étienne—bankers don't reveal their clients'

secrets. Nor do they, I think, tell secrets that would also reflect on them." Étienne's laugh was more alive, at that moment, than were his eyes. "You are either one of the wisest men I have ever known, Noel, or—"

"One of the most foolish? Is that it?"

The smooth layered voice ladled over him, thick, cool. "Not at all. I was going to say—or simply one of the cleverest." Étienne tipped the wine bottle over Noel's glass. "In either case—your talents are needed."

"You said there was business concerning Beau Chêne. If there is not—"

Étienne reached for a crewel-worked bell pull. "This business I have with you concerns Beau Chêne, Noel. And every other plantation in the state." Roselle's café-au-lait face appeared in the door. "Roselle, bring coffee. And later—a tray for juleps."

"You're going to ask me to get involved in the Anti-Lottery League," Noel said. He thought of spending a long humid August afternoon in Étienne's study, listening to that creamy, bland voice spread itself over all the lumps and bits and pieces and show, finally, only a perfectly smooth, perfectly formed, surface. "Donelson Caffery's from my part of the state, Étienne. I may keep out of politics, but I'm not ignorant of what goes on."

"If I thought you were, I'd hardly have brought you all the way here. So what do you think, Noel?"

Roselle set a silver tray in front of Étienne. Noel watched while she carefully prepared the coffee. She handed it to Étienne and watched while he tested. "Perfect, Roselle. Thank you. And now, Noel? Sugar? Cream?"

They watched her leave the room, her slim body shadowed by the sun slanting through the closed shutters. "Roselle is most happy when she pleases," Étienne said.

"I'm sure you manage to see that she is happy, then," Noel said. He rose, set his cup on the tray. "You ask me what I think—whether of the scheme to make the lottery illegal, or the chances of such a scheme succeeding. I've no idea. Therefore, Étienne, I will tell you my opinion of both." He moved to the hearth, filled now with fern spreading from an Italian pot. Taking a position that mocked Étienne's favored stance, Noel looked down at his host. He held up one finger. "First, the scheme itself. It has been decided, I understand, that even with Burke in exile these few years, McEnery, the rest of them, have too much power still. And McLottery, as he is called—justly, I believe—will, with his little crew, continue to keep the ship of state well in hand—so long as there is lottery money flowing to them. And that won't do, will it, Étienne?"

"Those men are without ethics, Noel. Their pretensions for caring about the people, the state—"

"Don't speak of ethics, Étienne. Or pretensions, when it comes to that. For whatever reason, the Lotteryists must go. But since they cannot be gotten rid of so long as that stream of gold keeps pouring, the lottery itself must go. How the goose that gave you all those lovely golden eggs has turned on you, Étienne!"

A soft knock at the door, followed by Roselle, bearing another tray. Sugar, a silver bucket of ice, two silver tumblers. Sprigs of fresh mint. Étienne took the tray while she removed the coffee service. "That will be all, Roselle. I'll be dining out. You can go on home." The fine quickness of her questioning eyes flicked Noel's attention. Ridiculous how Étienne kept all his masks on, no matter who was his audience.

"That same goose has done well by you, Noel. Which brings me to the point. Though I trust you'd prefer to have a man like Murphy Foster succeed our good Governor Nicholls—you might not want to give up your gains."

"You go too fast. Foster? Is he to be the candidate?"

"Perhaps. Nicholls supports him."

"Poor Nicholls. Dragged out every ten years or so to save us from ourselves—"

"He saved us from what the Yankees had done the first time, Noel. As for this second term—thank God, it was his victory that forced Burke out of power."

"And down to Honduras with a million and a quarter from the state treasury. Vice pays well, Étienne. Does virtue?"

"It's too hot for such rhetoric, Noel. We're not discussing vice or virtue—we're discussing political reality."

"And the reality is that you've been dealt out and you want back in."

Étienne handed the julep to Noel and began mixing his own. He shrugged. "Of course. As I've told you before, nothing is accomplished when you're not in the middle of things. This isn't a spectator sport, Noel."

"And what is it you want from me? My respectability?

Campaign funds? I've been raising sugar cane and reading philosophy for ten years, Étienne. What can you want from me?"

"And making money from the lottery." The cold, thick layer was thicker now, almost solid. A wall between them. "Money you won't have, if the lottery is stopped."

"I can get along without it, Étienne."

"They'll tell you you can't. Promise even larger profits."

"Who?"

"McEnery."

"And do you think I'd listen?" Noel's eyes held the heat of the sun, the dark fire of rage.

Étienne's smile chilled him. The icy bourbon had slid between his warm lips, leaving a cold touch on them. "Good. That is what we needed to be sure of. That you are still—a realist."

"While you are the idealist. I remember Henri explaining that to me."

"Oh, yes, Noel, I am most idealistic. I believe all things are possible—while you—you believe only in what you can see. Isn't that so, Noel?"

"What I see now is that I've spent several hours discussing— what? What in hell do you want, Étienne?"

"Exactly what you have given me. Nothing. You are not needed on our side, Noel. But it might have been a bother if you had joined with the opposition. Now that I know you won't—"

The dipping sun concentrated its beams and found a chink between two shutter slats. The beam focused on Étienne's face, cast each feature in full relief. The challenging eyes, the bold mouth. The face that told Noel he had, once again, been de Gravelle's cuckold.

"What you are saying, then, is not that you need me in the league against the lottery. Only that you must be sure I won't back the other side." His voice, accustomed to the murmurous softness of Beau Chêne, seemed lost in these hard surroundings. He reached forward, placed his tumbler on the tray. "I can assure you, Étienne, I side with no one. Not you, not them."

"I never thought you would." Étienne pulled out his watch, clicked it open. "My carriage will be around in a few minutes— may I drop you at your hotel?"

"I'll walk," Noel said.

"Then let me see you out," Étienne said. They went down the hushed hall, passing doors opening onto summer-draped rooms. "Thank heaven summer is almost over, it's such a stupid season. So inactive, don't you think?" He held open the front door, stood surveying Noel. "But I forget—you prefer a passive life, isn't it so? That's what I told them, Caffery and the others, when we discussed whom we could rely upon in Saint Martin. 'I'm sure Noel de Clouet will just sit the whole thing out,' I told them. I know how you hate these things. 'There is a man over that way, though, who might be very useful.'"

"Who is that?"

"Your neighbor. Langlinais?"

"In with Caffery and those other sugar planters? Claude does well, no mistake about that, but—"

Étienne was shaking his head. "Noel, Noel. Of course not. With the Farmer's Alliance. After all, we can't possibly do this alone—and they're getting stronger. Well organized upstate, beginning to make gains along the river—if they can get Claude Langlinais, they'll have several parishes with one handshake."

"Why would Langlinais fool with a thing like the Farmer's Alliance? He's got more than enough to tend to as it is—I don't know how he does it, but he's got more money to invest than any other ten men like him."

"Which is why he will do it. He isn't like any other ten men. Claude will join the alliance for the very same reason you would never join the Anti-Lottery League, Noel. He wants to keep what he's got."

Claudine Langlinais' hand, soft cloth held firmly, moved over the leather cover. "There," she said, putting the book back in its place, "just the one long shelf left and all papa's books will be clean. Then I'll go up and make some lemonade for you, grandpapa."

"Leave that other shelf, chère. Some men are coming in a little bit, your papa and me, we need to talk." Claude looked up from the pamphlet he held in his hand. Silhouetted against the bright square of window light, Claudine was slender, taller than her mother. The sun blacked out the details of her clothes, he could not see the homespun dress, the bare feet, the braided hair. Soon she would be in New Orleans, wearing the lady clothes they'd brought back. He sighed. "Claudine!"

She came to him, breaking away from the square of light, out of silhouette. "Claudine, now listen—when you're in New Orleans..." Her eyes were bright with innocence—Claude sighed again. Might as well try to prepare a lost calf for the yawning mouth of a 'gator, coming out of the swamp. "Claudine, you remember you're a Langlinais, you hear me?"

She had her mother's laughter, her mother's gaiety. Words bubbled through the laughter, through her innocence. "Grandpapa! Now how would I forget who I am?" She bent and kissed his cheek. "Anyway, they already know. When maman and I were at the school, we heard one of the nuns whisper to another—'the child's grandfather is Claude Langlinais, you know, he...' Then maman pulled me away, she said it wasn't nice to listen."

"So I send them a little wine, a little meat. Once a Langlinais was an Ursuline. We don't forget, that's all." Claude pushed her gently. "Now, run! Go get ready for the fais-do-do. I guess we have to watch all your beaux feel bad 'cause they didn't catch you before you went away."

Eyes, big, fresh, young. Cutting at him from under the edge of her sunbonnet.

"Grandpapa! Now you're teasing!"

He heard her laugh flutter behind her as she went down the path that cut across the pasture to the house. He picked up another of the pamphlets that were scattered before him, began to read.

When Jumie came in, Claude motioned to a chair opposite him. "Listen, Jumie, you know that Farmer's Alliance? The Union, they call themselves?"

Jumie reached over, took one of the pamphlets. "This some of their literature? I'd heard they were trying to work their way in around here." He turned the pamphlet over, leafed through it. "All in French. Gone to a lot of trouble, haven't they?"

"They've got over twenty thousand farmers, Jumie. Everywhere in the state but around the gulf."

Jumie threw the pamphlet down. "You know why that is. Catholics can't join secret societies."

"The Farmers' Union isn't the kind of society the Church means, Jumie. Some of their meetings may be—private. But don't tell me you've never belonged to anything that didn't always meet out in the open, everything aboveboard."

Jumie laughed. "So how did you find out about my bourré club?"

Claude shot a quick glance at Jumie. "Maybe it's more like bourré than you think—these politics. Winning is more than just luck, Jumie. It's knowing when to play what card, when to bluff—"

"What cards do these farmers hold, papa? And look—a lot of what the Union says just isn't true." Jumie's hand moved through the pamphlets. "All that about the eastern bankers? And the Congress? Compared to what goes on among the Carondelet Street bankers—and in our legislature—hell, those eastern banks, the Congress, are like convent schools."

"To you, maybe. To me. But, Jumie, how many farmers are like us? Most of them—they've got no say at all in what happens. Between the Bourbon Democrats with all that lottery money, and the big bankers—"

"Who are mostly one and the same as the Bourbon Democrats—"

"Yes. So what chance has the little man got?"

Jumie stood up, stretched his arms high. "All right, papa. I know. It's not that I don't think farmers need a better deal. But, papa. Look at all we have going now. Geneviève and me—we'd like some time to enjoy a little, you know? Take off, go somewhere." He roamed to the book shelves lining the walls, the newly dusted leather gleaming in the deep afternoon sun. "See some of the places I've read about for years. Don't you and maman ever feel that way?"

"You know your maman, Jumie." Claude looked off, politics forgotten. "She'd rather fuss because she doesn't get to do something than do it."

Jumie turned, stared at the back of his father's head. "Is that it, papa? Really?"

Claude's shoulders lifted in a small, defeated shrug. "I suppose. At first, after the war, I thought, well, when we get going, when there's money—then she can have things, do what she wants." Another shrug, a sigh. "But then it was worse. That pin I gave her, remember? The first real piece of jewelry?"

Jumie straddled a chair opposite Claude, fixed his eyes on his father's face. "She hardly wears it."

"No place to wear it, she said. People would think she was putting on airs. Wouldn't wear it to New Orleans because she didn't have other jewelry to go with it—" Claude's mouth clamped shut, teeth biting tight.

Jumie waited while the silence bloomed, covered them. Then, softly. "Papa. Papa, it's all right. I know how maman is. Me and Geneviève—well, we had to understand it, you know?"

"You understand it? Why she fusses, sees the bad things? Because me, I tell you the truth, I look at my good fields, and at money growing in the bank—and I see her mouth get smaller, her eyes get little, too. Her soul shrinks, Jumie. Françoise, she has a little soul now. No room for life anymore."

"She's afraid, papa. Afraid to want—she may not get it. Like she didn't get a college education for me." The last said quickly, thrown down between them before Jumie could think.

"Damn! I have to hear that all my life? How much better could you be doing if you had gone to college, Jumie? Tell me, how much better?"

"Papa! It's not me feels that way. Hell, papa, me shut up in a classroom in Baton Rouge when I could be here?" He reached out, clasped Claude's arm. "But that was a big dream for her. And I think—I think maybe she thought God owed it to her—you know? Because of the war—all she lost. Anyway. She didn't get that big dream. And sometimes I think there's one dream a person has to have—to keep dreaming."

Claude was silent for a moment, and then looked back at the pamphlets. "Which is why I think we need to support this Union, Jumie. To help farmers get a big dream."

"And how many of mine do I have to give up to help them get it?"

Claude heard the bitterness in Jumie's voice, cutting across the lazy ripple of sound from his usually gentle tongue. He let the acrid note hang, blurring the air between them. "The farmers have been patient a long time, Jumie. Something must be done now."

Jumie's eyes went to the open window, to the road leading away from St. Martin, out through the prairies, coming finally to New Orleans. And from there, ships that could cross the oceans, could take him to Dickens's London, to Balzac's Paris.

"Jumie, we can't have more violence. Not like after the war."

Jumie pulled his eyes from the open window, the wide road.

The sun was dipping behind the large oaks, in the fading light the room was small, dark. "You think it will come to that?"

"And why would it not?"

"So what is it you want me to do?" No bitterness, but something else—resignation that replaces bitterness when, clearly, only one course is open.

"Some men are coming today—from the Union. They'll want us to go to the Union convention in Lafayette later this month. Learn our way around, watch, meet people."

"And then?"

"Then there'll be plenty to do."

Jumie went to the door that opened onto the backyard of the office, stood against the bright square. "They have enough strength to beat the Bourbons?"

"They're putting out feelers to the Anti-Lottery League, I'm told. Some pretty big men in that."

The sun hung low, sending beams into the room, marking the papers that covered the desk with a pen of gold.

Still with his back to Claude, Jumie asked, "Is that sure? There's not a word been said in the open, how can you . . . ?"

"Jumie. Felix brags on his roosters before they fight? Look, the lottery has too much power. Men like Caffery—de Gravelle—they don't like not having power." Claude laughed. "Their money what good does it do them without power?"

Jumie swung around. "De Gravelle? In with the Anti-Lottery League? He has to have made more money from the lottery than damn near anyone else—why would he be against it?"

"Some men know how to jump—just ahead of the fire." Claude rose, looked at the clock. "They'll be here pretty quick. So what, Jumie, you're in?"

Jumie came forward slowly. "They're going to run a slate then? In the elections next year?"

"We've got a year, Jumie. If the Farmers' Union and the Anti-Lottery league work together—and there are some Republicans who would probably come in, too—"

"You're talking a third party, papa?"

"If that's what it takes. Jumie, if we could get a governor. Some of the legislators. It would be a beginning—a chance for our people. We've been out of Reconstruction a long time, Jumie—fourteen years it's been. Are things any better?"

Jumie looked past Claude, followed a line of sun out to the

fields that lay open to the falling light. "You never get there, do you?"

"Where?"

"To a place where there isn't anything else to do."

Claude laughed. "If there is, I've never gotten there."

Jumie moved, a quick straightening of his spine. "All right. If I'm not going to be able to take it easy—let's make this worth the effort, papa. A good fight, isn't that it?" A group of men on horseback turned in, started down the drive. "But, papa—I'm going to get my bourré club in with us. A good fight—it needs some people who know how to have fun, too!"

Goldenrod, thick, yellow, tracing a pollen trail in the dust, pushed up through summer weeds and crowded the rail that circled the Beau Chêne track. Claude helped Françoise up to the platform Marthe had had built; there were benches for the children, seats with backs for the women. Françoise spread a cotton coverlet over the raw wood and settled herself, arranging her bonnet against the high morning sun. She took a palmetto fan from Claude and began wafting it to and fro, stirring the air just in front of her face.

"Mais, I tell you, Claude, I hope Jumie doesn't lose in front of all these people." She peered out at the crowd lining the rail. "Some from New Iberia, from Lafayette, from Breaux Bridge—mais, they have nothing better to do than watch two horses work up a sweat?"

"If one is a thoroughbred from Beau Chêne and the other a Langlinais farm horse? Now, Françoise, that's no everyday race!"

The fan moved faster, a protest flag in the wind. "No Langlinais needs to beat a de Clouet to prove—anything."

"One little horse race, Françoise. One little race. Why make such a fuss?"

She leaned back, closed her eyes against the bright light. "I just don't like any Langlinais to be part of the de Clouets' show." Her voice seemed slowed with dust, heat. She opened her eyes, found Marthe and Jumie, leading their horses toward the starting line. "Who can stay on the stage with a de Clouet and not get the worst of it?"

"Mais, Jumie's not lost yet, Françoise!" Claude's arm circled the scene before them, taking in the chattering women, the men lounging against buggies, fence posts, the scampering children. "Look, it's a good day, a bright day, people laughing, happy—Françoise, don't make clouds!"

"I don't feel good about it, somehow." She stood up and began waving. "Geneviève! Geneviève!"

Below, Geneviève turned her head, saw Françoise and waved. She turned back to Jumie, said something in his ear, kissed him and then walked toward the stand. Sun heat warmed her cheeks, excitement sparked her eyes. She walked slowly through the people at the rail, stopping to talk, moving from one small cluster to the next. "She's good for Jumie," Claude said. "With this Farmers' Union business, it's a help to be able to talk to all kinds of people. Those men, a lot of them, are from upstate."

"Jumie—Geneviève. What about Claude and Françoise? I don't know about you, but me I'm not too old to talk, even with hill country farmers."

Claude went forward to help Geneviève into the stand. Just before he reached for her, he turned to Françoise. "Françoise— just because the strings reach long doesn't mean they can't be pulled from here. You know?"

Françoise reached in her deep pocket for her crochet hook and thread. "Something I do know about string, Claude Langlinais. If you don't put the design in yourself, sometimes it doesn't come out the way you thought. This Farmers' Union— can it trust what those league men say?"

Claude's hand touched Geneviève's: she balanced on the step, then jumped lightly to the platform. Claude extended his free hand, opened it. "Françoise—when the day comes we can't trust a man's handshake—Françoise, then we in plenty trouble."

Marthe untied her broad-brimmed straw hat and tossed it to the side of the track. "I don't want anything to catch the wind and slow me down," she said.

Jumie looked up from the harness buckle he was fastening. "Marthe, I have a feeling you're going to win. You know? Just a feeling. And it's about you, not me. I can tell!"

She vaulted over the wheel, placed herself in the center of the narrow seat. "Don't get me so confident I forget to concentrate, Jumie!" She picked up the reins, arranged them in her hands. "Oh, Jumie, I do so want to win!" Her face, open, curls beginning to paste themselves around its edges like a design traced into soft clay, turned to him. Then—"But, Jumie, I don't want to beat you!"

He looked at her for that long moment it took to finish testing his harness. Soft across the space between them came his answer. "But, Marthe, you can't win the race without beating—my horse."

"Your horse. Well, of course." She flicked the reins, straightened in her seat. "It must be almost time. Is it?"

"The starter's waving us up to the line. Yes."

The two buggies moved forward, rolling wheel pacing rolling wheel. They took their positions between the stand and the rail, coming abreast of a line of blue ribbon held by two small Negroes. The line of blue touched the sweat-wet chests of the horses, seemed like the line of the horizon that held steady, fast. Then the starter's pistol cracked, the line of blue dropped, a lift of hooves, a lurch of wheels—then flying.

Dust clouds around her, dust-earth under her horse's feet. Crowd-shapes in the dust, buggy-shape beside her. Marthe heard the dulled sound of hooves touching hard ground through dust layered by summer. She heard the rattle of wheels turning, the small sound of leather seat sighing beneath her shifting weight. Crowd sounds—a voice raised.

She leaned forward, eyes on the horse pulling away from her, pulling away with her. A cut of the eye toward where Jumie should be—if he weren't there, was he behind her, and defeated? Ahead of her, and victorious? She strained to see, dust, sweat, clouding her eyes. Then he was abreast of her, the sounds of his horse, his buggy, meeting hers in a great roar that was dust and heat and motion. She half stood, leaned forward, cracked the whip above that straining body. A small wind—was she running faster? Outrunning the clock Henri was holding? Outrunning the dust, the heat?

A shout, a roar. Again. Again. Her name? Jumie's name? The sun on her bare head boiled her blood, her face was hot, hot. They were past the stand, the race was done. She began to pull slowly on the reins, sank back, drew deep breaths of dust and heated air between parched lips. Then Henri was there, he was reaching up for the reins, steadying the horse, stopping her. His face was worn, tired—had he run this race?

"Henri—Henri—"

His arms were reaching for her, she must not have won, he would have been smiling. She let him help her down. Behind them, people were clustered—congratulating Jumie? "Henri, who won? For God's sake, Henri!"

He held her hands. Tight, so tight. When she was having Hélène, he had held her hands like that. "I—I didn't see." The pressure on her hands meant something else then. Not that she had lost. "I—I was called away. There was an accident, Marthe. Over at the sugar mill."

Someone was coming up behind them, a figure dark, blocking out the sun.

Her mind counted—Hélène, René, Nanette, all on the stand with her parents. Henri, here. Who, then?

"Marthe—it's Nollie. He's dead, Marthe. He was over there—no one quite knows why—sketching, I think. His—pad and pencil were—near him."

"Inside the mill, Henri? Inside the mill?"

"The centrifugal belt—the machinery was on, they were testing it, making sure all is in order—before grinding season. He—got caught, Marthe."

The dust and heat and light rolled around her in a haze of smoke-heat. And then went dark. Then there were voices over her, dimmed with dust, heat. Voices low, not wanting her to hear. "Henri, I just head. Crushed, is that right?" Jumie, low, soft.

"Dead right away. At least—we'll say so." Henri's fingers on her wrist, the slow steadiness of his firm touch.

"Marthe. Marthe." Jumie, calling her up from sleep. Calling her to come hoe tomatoes or pick caterpillars off of corn. She lifted her head, felt it meet, in that small moment, the wall of Nollie's death.

"Maman—papa—do they know?" Her eyes could not see through the dust, nor the tears.

"Yes." Jumie, rubbing her wrists. She saw his eyes above her, reflecting her loss. "I can't do this. I can't do this. I was afraid he wanted Beau Chêne, I didn't want him to leave it—but, oh, my God, not this, not this!"

"Marthe," Henri said, and she heard husband fighting doctor—"Marthe, you didn't—"

"Now, Marthe, we have that again?" Jumie's voice was all Jumie, laughing at her, teasing her. "Marthe, you remember? When the Yankees came? What you said to me?" She lifted her eyes, watched his sureness. "You said"—the softening laughter beneath the voice, making her foolishness all right—you said you were mad at your maman, and had wanted something bad to happen to her because she had spanked you with her slipper. And you thought all those Yankee soldiers were there just to punish your maman! Now, Marthe, remember how long it took for me to make you realize you couldn't do that? Don't do all that again? Marthe?"

She reached out hands, took their support, rose, steadied. "No." She took the handkerchief Henri gave her, began to rub her face.

"Marthe, listen, let me tell you something. Anyone can beat a Langlinais in a match race—she can do anything."

"Beat—Jumie, I won?" A small spirit rose, a small separate space of light. "I won?"

Jumie's smile flashed across the darkness. "Well—your horse did!"

The flickering lights fought off the dark, the shortening twilight closed down with night, filling the spaces between lanternlit windows.

"Not so many lights at Beau Chêne tonight," Geneviève said. They had put Claude Louis and Claudine on the train, dined at the Three Lions, headed home by moonlight. September moon, promising harvest. "I suppose Mignon's gone to her maman's. They'll be alone again."

Jumie slowed the horses, drew up at the roadside near the wide gates of Beau Chêne.

"Marthe's done well. She's strong."

Geneviève leaned against his shoulder. "Mais, of course. And who taught her to be? You and your papa. Don't think I don't know who put the poker down the de Clouet back!" She took his arm, pressed close against it. "Now, Jumie. We just put the two children on the train; we got a big empty house, and me, I'm sad about that. Take me home quick and make me forget I'm lonesome already!"

The moon behind the tall oaks made filigree of their leaves; branches traced against a golden-lit sky, dark, strong. Noel stood at the gallery rail, pipe glowing with the rhythm of his breath. Marthe, a light shawl shimmering on her shoulders, joined him, slipped an arm around him. "What are you thinking, papa?"

Smoke, thin, misty in the moist air, veiled his face. She watched the dull fire of his pipe. "Beau Chêne is beautiful at night, isn't it?" Noel followed her gaze. Shadowed statues, moonlit pebbled paths. Ordered form, commanded bloom.

"That's what I was thinking, Marthe. About Beau Chêne. About beauty. About what happens when the dark comes down."

# CHAPTER 23

## *Cycles*

The Louisiana gubernatorial election of 1900 served as both a review of the politics of the past decade and a preview of the conflicts that lay ahead. The remnants of the old Anti-Lottery League, that battle well won when the U.S. Congress forbade use of the mails to lotteries in 1892, gathered to take on the Bourbon Democrats one more time. And as in 1892 they had sought the help of the Farmers' Union, as in 1896 they had sought the help of the Populist party that grew out of that union—only to betray their word and lose the election—so in 1900 the political nucleus formed around old money and old blood sought help from men like Jumie Langlinais, who represented a new class of both power and money. As for old blood—the Langlinais had been in Louisiana longer than the de Clouets. But that is not what makes blood "old." There were those who, at Governor Murphy Foster's inaugural ball in 1892, shocked at the appearance of Jumie and Geneviève Langlinais. Jumie had had as much to do with Foster's election as anyone else—but the debate about letting just anyone in to the exalted regions where people who could trace their lineage back hundreds of years in France held sway raged on. If they could not be kept out of the political back rooms, they were still kept out of the formal parlors. The Langlinais, however, were too busy building parlors of their own to notice the exclusion.

Of course, the Langlinais did not have to push their way into the back rooms. They were invited, welcomed, and courted. When Jumie Langlinais threw his support to Donelson Caffery, the candidate representing Democrats who feared and fought the growing strength of the New Orleans ward leaders, those wealthy, educated men—the "crème de la crème," as Caroline de Clouet would say—were glad to get him. And if, as he told them, he was a Langlinais first, last, and always, supporting those who supported what was good for him, his land and his children, at least, in March of 1900, he believed that what served him served the rest of the state as well.

His neighbors no longer believed that any cause but that of self-interest would be served by the Louisiana political process. Noel had refused to embrace either branch of the Democratic party—the Bourbons who were strangling the state with their grip on its tax structure and financial bases, or the wing led by Caffery. As a result, while other sugar planters had the assessments on their lands raised by as much as 20 percent by angry Bourbons, Noel escaped with only a token raise. "At least they still know I'm alive," he said to Marthe, and went back to his books.

Marthe, who had more and more taken over the running of Beau Chêne as her father's health and interest in anything but philosophy declined, was caught between Noel's indifference to reality and her mother's ignorance of it. As far as Caroline was concerned, sugar prices were still at a glittering height, that river of white gold still flowing. If she read anything but the society section of the *Times-Picayune,* she would have known that congress had repealed the two-cents-per-pound sugar bounty in 1893, and that that, plus the high assessments, was damming the river to a slower and less bountiful stream.

The only ones really in high cotton are the Langlinais, Marthe told Henri, whose country practice produced hundreds of patients, but little real money. They knew better than to put their economic fate in just one field crop, or one chancy investment. The growing hum of small factories, the growing commerce on farm-to-market roads, the growing tangle of mercantile lines reaching from the southwest corner of Acadiana to the commercial centers of the South—these were powered by Langlinais skill, Langlinais guts, and Langlinais power.

On the edge of a new century, two families stood. One looked back and thought. The other looked forward and planned.

Purple-fuchsia-rose-pink-white azaleas lined the edge of the Beau Chêne cemetery, dividing it from the road. Henri, riding home from his rounds, reined in his horse and dismounted. He opened the low gate set in the iron fence that held the spilling blossoms from making a carpet of crushed color in the rutted road, and strode down the graveled path to Noel's gravesite.

Two men, shovels lifting heavy mud, worked there. Henri stared down into the grave. March rains, joining water seeping up from the earth below, puddled the bottom. The mud was clay-yellow beneath the line of topsoil; raw, ugly, dead.

"Line it with a good layer of pine needles," he said. "I don't want Madame de Clouet seeing that mess."

"Mister Henri, I hope Miss Marthe don't get her dander up when she sees where we putting Mister Noel. She said not to put him too close to Mister Nollie, but Miss Caroline, she wanted them joined right near."

"Miss Marthe's got too much on her mind to give any thought to that, Armand."

"Mister Noel was a good man, Mister Henri. A good man to work for. Mister Henri, who's going to run Beau Chêne now?"

Henri turned over a lump of mud with the toe of his boot. The black loam that covered the clay took seed easily, fed it, nurtured it. There was no difficulty in making things grow at Beau Chêne. The difficulty was seeing to everything else. "I don't know, Armand. Mister Nollie's son is next in line. Whether he'll take over—" His shoulders shrugged, trying to dislodge the weariness that he could never seem to lose. He turned and picked his way across the wet path.

Jumie Langlinais was waiting for him, astride the new stallion that Henri judged cost at least as much as what Marthe had paid for her last stud—business and farming must pay better than doctoring, and not be nearly so tiring—Jumie looked as he always did, as though he had slept twelve hours without a single twisting dream.

"I heard about Noel last night. I was in a meeting with Caffery, someone sent him word. I came to see what we can do."

Henri took the outstretched hand. "He went quickly," he said, swinging into the saddle. They began picking their way along the rain-marked road toward the main gates of Beau Chêne. "His heart, finally."

"Marthe found him?"

"In his study. He'd climbed to get a book—apparently had an attack, fell." When Marthe had called him, he had run down the hall at the sound of that particular cry, at its shrilling urgency. She was bending over Noel, rubbing his hands, speaking his name. He had lifted her away and listened to Noel's silent heart. Marthe had picked up the book that had tumbled from Noel's hand as he fell and read its title. "Schopenhauer," she had said, and climbed to put it back in its place. Then—"Poor papa. I hope he's found his Nirvana."

"Is she all right?" Of course he meant Marthe. Not the widow, who had gone immediately to her room and had not yet emerged. "Yes. She's busy, that helps. Nanette, thank God, is here. We're trying to reach Hèléne—she's visiting over in Franklin, we sent word." He thought of René, who had, apparently, begun dulling the pain of his loss with liquor, and who had arrived on the late train so drunk he had been put to bed without even visiting his bereaved grandmother—if he roused before dusk, it would be with a hangover so immense that he would be absolutely useless. "Marthe's got more than enough to do, she doesn't need this."

Jumie looked at the house, looming white against the blaze of azaleas set between the oaks. "Noel lived a long life. A good life. Better than many."

"You say that? That's surprising."

Jumie shot a look at Henri. "You think he didn't? Lead a good life?"

"A passive life. He made no contribution—even when he could."

"Henri, because Noel couldn't compromise—"

A short laugh, like a rein pulled against a running horse. "I won't go on and on about it. But twenty years is a long time to sulk. Noel was wealthy, educated—he profited by the system but he damn well wouldn't do anything to improve anyone else's life."

Jumie looked again at the house, settled now into a graceful middle age. He saw a woman's figure at one of the long windows in the dining room and lifted an arm in greeting. "Oh, I don't know, Henri. Somehow, it's given me something to think about, all these years. The way Beau Chêne was more important to Noel than anything else. The way he wouldn't abandon what he believed it stands for—"

"Even if that stubbornness threatened Beau Chêne, everything?"

Jumie pulled up, dismounted. Marthe was coming to meet them, a light shawl wrapped around her shoulders. Her eyes were huge in her face, which seemed shrunk with fatigue and grief. "Some men think, some act." He laughed. "Some do both. Caffery, now—"

"You're supporting him? When he represents a group that sold your union out as fast as it possibly could?"

"That was four years ago, Henri. And I'm not supporting Caffery, necessarily. I'm supporting the Populist cause. He just happens to be that candidate as well as the Republican-Fusionist's."

"And will he win?"

Jumie laughed again. "Win? How in the hell should I know? Me, I don't have to know I'll win to make a fight." He went to Marthe, took her hands in his. "Geneviève is stirring every pot she has. I told her you couldn't possibly use all she's cooking, but you know Geneviève. The more she cares, the more she cooks."

Her smile was smaller. "I won't say we can't use it, Jumie. With so many people coming . . ." Her voice trailed away, taken by the wind gusting around the corner of the house. Jumie saw its hands run over her, shake her with its chill.

"Get out of this wind, Marthe. Your hands are like ice already."

"I can't seem to get warm anymore," she said. She sank into a chair pulled up to the study fire. "Of course I'm tired— and I'm not eating."

"Ring for some hot water and lemons, Marthe. I know where the bourbon is," Jumie said. He opened the cabinet, took out a decanter. "Remember the toddies papa used to fix for you and your maman? When you were so tired, or your stomach was picky?"

He took the tray from Sarah, stirred sugar into the steaming water, squeezed lemon, topped it with the golden bourbon.

"Do you have any other magic cures, Dr. Langlinais?" Henri asked, watching the glow from the glass, the fire, begin to pink his wife's pale cheeks.

"Nothing so magic as saving two babies' lives, Henri. Now, Marthe, you need to eat. I'll tell Sarah on my way out."

Marthe looked at him over the rim of the glass. Her eyes belonged in her face now. "Jumie, when I was a little girl and you were forever telling me what to do, I used to think the day would come when I would be as big as you were, and I'd never have to listen to you again."

"Mais, Marthe," Jumie said as he turned to leave. "Who says you have to listen? All you have to do is eat."

"I don't think I can do this, Henri."

"The funeral?" He sat beside her, picked up one of her hands and began to stroke it.

"Not that. The rest of it." The smooth face, caught by a force as cold and strong as the blustering wind outside, crumpled as though it were one of the azalea blossoms being tossed to the ground. "Henri, you know Beau Chêne will go to Sept now. And Henri—I won't be able to bear that. Ever."

Geneviève held out a spoon. "Taste!" She watched Jumie's face. "It's good?"

Jumie slapped her round bottom, then hugged her. "Will I say it's not?" And when she raised the spoon, frowned at him, he laughed. "It's good. Where's maman?"

Geneviève turned back to the gumbo. "In her room." She shook her head. "I tell you, Jumie, I never thought I'd see the day I'd rather she was in my kitchen hanging over my pots, sniffing my seasoning than being so quiet and polite all the time. Since Papa Claude died Jumie, she doesn't care about telling anybody anything. You know?"

Jumie poured coffee, carried it to the kitchen table. "The only person she cared about hearing her is gone, Geneviève. I don't know. Maybe that was the way she showed she loved him."

"What, fussing about everything like a hen in the wrong nest?"

"Trying to make him as great as she thought he could be. I don't know—"

"Your papa was plenty great. I'll bet there's not half as much people at Noel's funeral as there were at your papa's. Lord, Jumie! Remember? The church full, people all out in the yard—" She brought her own coffee and sat. "He was plenty great, your papa."

"He didn't always win, Geneviève."

"Zut alors! Win? Well, of course not! Who said he had to?" She put a hand on Jumie's arm. "And you. You don't have to always win, either. To be great to me."

Jumie rose, went to the window and looked out across the fields that ran between his house and the woods. On the other side of the leafing trees, Beau Chêne was readying its master for burial. And the new master, was he already ordering cards bearing his new address? "Good. Because there's every chance Caffery won't win. Which means I lose, too."

Geneviève laughed. "I know you too well, Jumie. If you think there's a chance you're going to lose here—you're already planning how to win someplace else." She got up. "Come help me get this ready to take to Beau Chêne. And Jumie, you think Sept will be there yet? I mean—he could be our new neighbor, it would be nice to know who he is, yes?"

Azaleas, like sentinels in formal dress, lined the drive between the oaks of Beau Chêne. Visitors to the house were met with full mourning inside—mirrors covered, Caroline, Marthe, and her daughters in deepest black, clock chimes muffled, harpsichord closed. Outside, color rioted, leaves greened, a haze of life covered the fields, and violets bloomed near Noel's grave.

Henri took on the task of escorting Caroline daily to her husband's tomb. She had wearied early of the mourning callers, rarely left her room except to go the cemetery, her veil pulled over her face, her weight heavy on Henri's arm.

"Who is here now?" she asked, her voice tight against intrusion. Henri helped her down from the light buggy, then surveyed the carriages standing in the drive.

"Probably the lawyers, Mére de Clouet. They wrote they'd be here this week."

"I've no interest in lawyers," Caroline said.

"But you must hear the will read," Henri said. And when he felt the resistance in her, he added, "It would be not comme il faut for you to avoid it, mère."

Mignon and her children had been summoned; they sat slightly apart from the others, they had a somewhat foreign air, and Lisette and Anastasie were not wearing black. "I don't like black on pretty young girls," Mignon had said, and pulled Lisette's curls farther around her face.

Immediately after the lawyers had finished, Caroline retreated to her room. If she understood or cared exactly what the lawyers had read, certainly she gave no sign. Marthe, after one long look at Sept, lounging against the mantel with a thin black cigarette in his mouth, had beckoned to Henri and gone to the study, where they sat for long hours, with only the thin rectangle of light from behind the door betraying the time they worked there.

Mignon announced that she had a headache and would go to bed; her maid spent the rest of the evening trotting back and forth between Mignon's room and the pantry, ordering one dainty after the other, asking for a small pillow, a light coverlet—anything, as Hélène said, to make a nuisance of herself.

Left to themselves, the cousins settled in the parlor, de Gravelles on one side, de Clouets on the other. "You'll have to redo this room entirely, Sept, when you live here," Lisette said. She looked at Hélène from under lashes so long and thick Hélène would have liked to snatch them from her eyelids. "Pardonez-moi, but you understand, when one has lived in Paris—one has certain tastes."

"I should think, then, one would find living in the country, living here, utterly stupid," Hélène said. She could not believe that they would have to leave Beau Chêne, that this incredibly horrible young man would own it, simply because he was male.

Maman had assured them they would build another house, not far from here at all, on some land that would come to her. But she had been able to tell, from the way maman said it, that she had not thought that would ever have to be. "Surely," Hélène had heard maman say to papa, "surely, Henri, when Nollie died, papa must have changed his will. Left Beau Chêne to me, other property to Sept. It would be madness to have that fop run this plantation! I don't think he'd know what sugar cane was if he found it in bed with him."

But grand-père had not changed his will, had not, perhaps, even thought of it. Hélène saw Lisette open the harpsichord, sit as though to play. "Stop!" she said. Lisette's hands descended, but Nanette was quicker. Her two strong hands closed over her cousin's wrists, she lifted those stubborn hands, put them in Lisette's lap, closed the instrument's lid and turned the key. And pocketed it. "You will observe our customs while you are here," she said. "If you do not mourn grand-père, it is because you somehow could never be here for all the family days, all the times we spent together." The thin body, wiry, tough, stood tall. "It is interesting that when you smell money, land, you can find the way easily enough."

"I do hope you girls are not going to fight," Pierre said. He had been strolling around the room, studying the paintings. He stood beneath the portrait of Hélène now, head cocked to one side, eyes narrowed. "Rather rough technique, but quite expressive," he said. "Say, Sept, maybe you'll let me have this, won't you? You've got enough beauties in the flesh, you don't need portraits."

"I think you're upsetting our cousins," Anastasie said. She had seated herself in Marthe's favorite low chair, kicked off her shoes and stretched her feet out to the fire. "As dear grandmère would say, it isn't comme il faut to divide the spoils before the body is cold." And then she laughed, a thin, stiletto-like laugh that pierced easily through the shield Hélène had put between herself and these people. Her sister's laughter, low, filled with knowledge so old, so disgraceful that Hélène wanted to clap her hands over her ears, came in under that high, thin sound. And then Sept and Pierre began to laugh, too. Hélène saw Nanette's face go pale, saw her lips start to open—she stammered something, some protesting cry that met that curtain of laughter and was smothered in it. Hélène reached out and grabbed her sister's hand. "Nanette, come!" They fled the room, slamming the doors behind them, running down the hall to Hélène's bedroom, where they cowered together in the big bed and tried to shut out that terrible noise that seemed to resonate now around all the walls of the house.

Marthe pushed a ledger page over to Henri. "There," she said. "Shouldn't that do it?" She had never felt such tension, such tautness throughout her entire body. Her skin seemed to have a separate life, to be able to creep away from the muscles underneath, her lungs were either filled with air, holding it, keeping it tightly in, or empty, gasping. She thought of the biggest races she'd ever entered, the way she felt waiting for the starting gun, the way her body seemed to freeze in the minutes it took for the horses to circle the track, the way her eyes could focus only on the silks of Beau Chêne, deep green, brilliant scarlet.

"He'd be a fool not to take this offer," Henri said. His eyes moved over the rows of figures. "But, Marthe, you'll strip yourself of practically every other investment. You'll have Beau Chêne, the land—he'll have everything else."

"I'll have the only thing I want," she said. "And, Henri, the plantation makes money. And the mill—Henri, we will certainly be all right."

He put the page between them, went to the fireplace and threw on a small log. "A country medical practice doesn't make much—but between us, we should be all right. Yes." He stood, back to her, face bent to the leaping flames. "It's times like this I could strangle my father—if he hadn't already done it for me. How could he have been so irresponsible, so dishonorable?"

She thought of the *Picayune* headlines, the scandal that had reached down the bayous, had hung over their lives like the parasitic moss in the oaks for one whole awful summer. In 1894, with the lottery dead, his political power gone, "and only honest work left," as someone had said, Étienne had fled the country, a mistress on one arm, a satchel of embezzled money dangling from the other. "There's no good thinking of it, Henri."

She saw the tired slump of his shoulders, the way the fire-glow touched his graying hair. "I try not to." He turned. His face was shadowed, his voice came out of darkness. "But it is sometimes difficult to forget not only the dishonor of what he did, but that he left my mother to face ruin. And me to an inheritance of debt."

"It's all been paid, Henri."

"Yes." He came to her and pulled her against him. She saw their shadows loom against the towering rows of books, darken the pictures on the walls. "But it would be nice, wouldn't it, if we had something to fall back on? If Sept does sell you Beau Chêne, Marthe, you'll have to take it on. God knows I'd be of no help to you, even if I had the time."

Their two shadows made a large figure, one surely large enough to fall over this stretch of land, care for it, nurture its yield.

"I've spent a great deal of time in papa's office, Henri. Working on the stable books, taking care of my own business. I've picked up a lot over the years—Henri, I'm not stupid!"

His lips against hers seemed dry, thin. For the first time, she knew that Henri would get old.

The fall after Noel de Clouet's death, the Beau Chêne stables entered the opening day races at the New Orleans track—but the owner was not present. "I can't possibly go, Henri," Marthe said. "We're in the middle of grinding season, it's the worst time of the year for me to be away."

Her trainer found himself waiting to see her; if the overseer and the trainer both needed her advice, the overseer came first. Weeks went by when Marthe hardly had time to visit the stables, much less know each horse. Two years after Noel's death, she sold off half the horses. Three years after his death, she sold the stables. She was in New Orleans at a sugar planters' association meeting when the last thoroughbred was taken away by its new owner. On her return, she strode through the vast empty stable, overseer at her side. "Have this building cleaned," she said, tossing away a bit of straw that clung to her skirt. "I've brought back plans to have it converted into a plantation store for the workers and more office space." Her eyes lifted to the high rafters where pigeons and doves nested. "This is the twentieth century, after all. We can't waste space on games." One final look. Then—"Have a small stable built for the family horses. We'll need every bit of this room for work."

When Alice Marie DeBlanc, of the Ville Platte DeBlancs, met Claude Louis Langlinais while on a summer visit to her godmother in New Iberia, she immediately canceled plans for a stay on the Gulf Coast and settled into the round of Sunday afternoon picnics, Saturday night dances, and Friday fish fries that kept the area's young people entertained. Claude, who was accustomed to flattering female attention, waited for the new summer visitor to center her light chatter, her quick smiles, her bright glances, on him. At the end of the third week, when Alice paid him no more attention than she paid the cousin who introduced her around, Claude made a formal afternoon call and invited her for a drive. Toward the end of that drive, when Alice was still cool, still no more than pleasantly friendly, Claude had slapped the reins against the front of the buggy and blazed at her: "Why did you come with me if I'm no more to you than a fencepost?" Then he did have her whole attention. Her dark gray eyes looked over him, seeming to measure his easy handsome looks against some inner image. Then she shrugged, a small lift of slender shoulders beneath the fine veiling of her tucked batiste blouse. "But Mr. Langlinais. What a terrible waste of time it would be to pay attention to you." Now the eyes glanced up from beneath long dark lashes. "After all, everyone knows you're going to be a rich old bachelor. And I have absolutely no intention of being an old maid." Then she had turned away, spotted flowers growing in a field, and asked him to pull up so she could pick some. "What, are you going to marry just anybody who'll ask you?" he asked, reaching up to help her down from the buggy. He felt her light frame against him, her warm breath on his neck. She stared at him and laughed. "I don't have to marry just *anybody*," she said, and began filling her arms with the black-eyed susans and Queen Anne's lace that crowded around her feet. When he saw her in Joe Arceneaux's arms at the dance that Saturday night, he suddenly wanted to sweep Alice up and carry her off. By the end of July, he knew that the only way he would get more of Alice's smiles, more of her attention, would be to marry her. Their engagement could not be announced, Alice said, until after Christmas—they'd not known each other nearly long enough. She removed herself to Ville Platte and began completing her trousseau, writing to Claude every day in her graceful convent-trained hand, making plans, behaving, in fact, as though every event of her life leading up to her engagement was preparing her for just that sentimental role. In later years, Claude would put an affectionate arm around Alice's waist and say, "I chased her and chased her until she caught me." Then, he only knew that until he was absolutely first with Alice Marie DeBlanc, nothing else mattered at all.

They were married in the summer of 1901; Alice had a son in the spring of 1902, a daughter a year later. "We'll call him Beau," she said, when his name, Claude Louis Langlinais, was entered in the church's baptismal records. "Beau?" Geneviève said to Jumie. "What kind of name is Beau?" "The name Alice gives her baby," Jumie said. The girl was named for her mother; Alice gave way to Claude, who insisted on Marie rather the Allie Alice favored. "Girls don't need fancy-dan names," he said, chucking his daughter under her fat chins. "Especially this little girl. She's got her papa to make her way for her—she doesn't need anything else."

And though Alice and Claude and the children were settled in next door, in the traditional "bride and groom house on the Langlinais place, Geneviève complained to Jumie more and more frequently that the way Alice drove into town all the time, Claude would have to buy more horses just to keep from wearing the ones he had out. "They're young, Geneviève. They like to have a good time." Geneviève was not convinced. "That Alice. She likes to go so much, if someone was having a dogfight and she didn't get invited, her nose would be out of joint." By the time they had been married five years, the names of Claude and Alice Langlinais were mentioned so often in the lists of guests at parties up and down the Bayou Teche that Geneviève gave up keeping up with the clippings and only kept the pictures that were also appearing, with almost embarrassing regularity, on the social pages of the area newspapers. "What, no one else will be in the pictures?" Geneviève fussed to Claude. He laughed, that lazy laugh so impossible to resist. "Maman. Alice is always the prettiest girl at the party—and I'm always one of the richest men. Why wouldn't they ask us?"

Geneviève set the last plate on the table and stood back to study the effect. "Alice," she called, "come see how my new dishes look." Alice, carrying Marie and holding Beau by the hand, came in from the kitchen. She wore a white dress, with a circlet of white camellias set on her black hair. "You look pretty like a bride," Geneviève said. "Who would know you've been married five years today? Now, Alice, what you think? You like my dishes?"

Alice set the baby down and walked slowly around the table. Her eyes went over each dish, following the scalloped edges of the plates, the curve of the serving pieces. "You could decorate with the platter," she said. "Or the tureen. Like in the magazines. They pile fruit in a dish like this one"—she picked up an oval meat platter, held it out—"then they put it on a sideboard. Or set a tureen out with flowers in it."

"Alice! Flowers instead of soup? Fruit to look at, not eat? Alice, the good God expects us to eat the food He gives us, not let it rot from being looked at. Now, Alice, for your anniversary, Jumie and me, we're going to give you new dishes. But, Alice—pick something you like to use, not just put in your armoires!"

Alice's armoires were her pride and her mother-in-law's penance. "Jumie, I tell you, I run over to Alice's to drink a little coffee, see my grandbabies, and what do I have to do? I have to watch her open her armoires, show me how she has her tableclothes, her sheets, he covers, her spreads, all so neat. And a list on each shelf. Jumie, I tell you, you need to put Alice to work in your business. What Alice likes is lists, lists of everything she has. She doesn't want to use it, no, she just wants to know she has it."

Now she picked up her granddaughter and kissed the fat

cheeks. "Marie, let's you and me look out the window for grandpapa and your papa. Alice, I tell you, you'd think they'd get here before the company comes."

"Claude said they were going to get a surprise." Alice was working at the table, carefully squaring edges of napkins, setting forks and knives in perfect alignment.

"Alice is a good housekeeper, I can't say she's not," Geneviève told Jumie. "But, Jumie, she cleans so it will look like a picture in a magazine, you know? I'm not sure about what doesn't show!"

A sound of wheels, a noise as though a small sugar mill were starting up, working—then a loud blare of sound, repeated, longer each time. "Mais, what in the world?" Geneviève lifted the curtain, peered out. "Alice, would you come look!"

They stared as Jumie and Claude jumped down from a new black automobile, its silvery trim glimmering in the sun. "Now what have they gone and done!" But Alice was already out of the room, running down the hall, through the front door. Geneviève saw her dart down the steps, go up to Claude, began to chatter. "Well, babies, I guess we go see, too," she said, and took Beau's hand.

She circled the automobile, standing away from it. "Jumie, now, Jumie, don't tell me you've gone and bought this thing."

"Geneviève, how I'm going to sell to other people what I don't use myself?"

"Sell? Jumie, you going to sell automobiles?"

"Not me. Or Claude. But we put some money into a place over in Abbeville. Listen, Geneviève, people are going to buy these things—so why should someone else make that money?"

Geneviève raised a hand, began to count on her fingers. "Jumie, you have business in New Iberia, business in St. Martinville, business now in Abbeville, business in Lafayette—Jumie, there's not enough work around here, do you have to keep finding more?"

"But think of all the money it makes," Alice said. She was already sitting in the high front seat, teasing Claude to show her how to drive.

"Money. Listen, Alice, money buys dishes, it buys automobiles—Alice, there's more going on than all that."

The young eyes, studying, taking apart Geneviève's words,

looked at her from the leather roof. "But, Maman Langlinais— then why do they go to so much trouble to make such a lot of it?"

"Why? You just heard *why*. Because, like Jumie says, if people are going to buy these things, why let someone else make that money? Now, listen, don't make a big thing of this automobile, at the fête. You saw how foolish Honoré made himself, making everyone go see his new automobile? Don't be like that!" A last look before she ushered them ahead of her—"But, Jumie, I think maybe I like ours better, you know? His—it didn't look so good."

They drove to New Iberia late that afternoon, Beau between his grandparents, Marie on her mother's lap. On the way home, Claude said, "Let's drive through town—there's something we want you to see."

"An automobile's not enough of a surprise, there's something else?" Geneviève looked at Jumie. "Jumie, you know?"

Jumie shook his head, and followed the directions Claude gave him. They turned down a street two blocks from the church, a street with tall frame houses whose windows glinted rainbows in the afternoon sun. "Stop here," Claude said. It was an empty piece of land, with several trees scattered over its width near the front line. Across the back, a low hedge had been planted; behind that, they could see the shuttered windows of another house.

"We want to buy this, Alice and I," Claude said. "Build a house."

Geneviève stared at him. "Live in town? Claude, live in town?"

Alice, one foot poised to descend from the automobile, patted Geneviève's shoulder. "Maman Langlinais, it's only a few miles. That's no distance at all."

"But in town!" She took Jumie's hand, got out of the automobile and stood looking at the lot. "Alice, Alice, see how small it is. Alice, no room for vegetables, just a few tomatoes, maybe, a little beans. And, Alice, where would you put chickens, a yard small like this?"

"I don't plan to have chickens. Or a vegetable garden either. Claude can put someone on our farm—they can send what I need in. Killed, plucked, and gutted, Mama Langlinais." Alice's hands made a small dainty movement in the air. "I'll have flowers, of course—a small fountain, maybe." She walked away from them, and the sun's light caught the glint of auburn in her dark hair, lit a nimbus of glowing gold around her head. "The parlor will be here," she said, pacing off a square. "And a big hall here . . ."

They watched her build her house, a child making lines in the dirt. "Seems to me like you've already bought it," Jumie said. "Alice's mind is made up, isn't it?"

"You'll see, papa. It'll be good for business. I might even get a little office in town—not spend so much time out there."

"Work in town, too? Now, Claude, I tell you the truth, if I had known when we sent you off to Baton Rouge to school you were going to come back liking a city!" Geneviève's hands were on her hips, her eyes fussing at her son.

His arms came around her, his quick laugh engulfed her. "Oh, maman! St. Martinville's not a city yet, I guess. And you'll see—our house will be so grand, you'll love it."

"And, Alice, what are you going to do all day, with no garden, no chickens?"

Alice's smile took in the ground before her, the houses on either side, the trimmed lawns, the gaslights on the street corner. "I'm going to buy a piano and learn to play, I'm going to go to my cousin Bessie's literary society, I'm going to take excursions to New Orleans—oh, Maman Langlinais, I'm going to have a wonderful time!"

"Mais, Alice—fun? You say you just going to have fun? That's not all life is about, Alice."

Now Alice's eyes fussed at Geneviève, but the smiling mouth spoke sweetly. "Oh, Mama Langlinais, what's the use of being rich if you don't enjoy it?"

"You don't see Marthe de Clouet running around all the time. And if the de Clouets aren't rich, who is?"

"The Langlinais," Alice said.

Marthe pulled at the reins, slowed her horse, stopped him. A small boy ran up to the buggy and took the reins from her. "I'll drive it on around back," he said. "You go on in."

"Heavens," Hélène said, "Alice even has someone for the carriages. Well, haven't they done well for themselves?"

"I hope I'm dressed enough for her tea—her first big party in the house, I certainly don't want to be underdressed." Marthe ran a hand over her gray skirt, pulled the lace-edged jabot of her blouse straight. "Is my hat all right?" Her hand went to the gray velvet hat, tugged it straight.

"You look perfectly fine, mama."

"The meeting at the bank took so long..."

Hélène looked at her watch. "Yes, I thought we'd get here earlier. I'm meeting Charles's train in New Iberia, I can only stay about forty minutes."

"Well, Thanksgiving week—they know everyone's involved." As she went through the low iron gate, Marthe looked up at the house. "Goodness! It is grand, isn't it? Geneviève's been telling me about it—but I'd no idea it was to be so large!"

"It's charming, perfectly charming, Geneviève," Marthe said. Hélène was talking with Alice, who glowed in the center of her square front hall like a ruby blazing in a finely tooled box.

"Well, of course, how could it not be, Alice used up a whole library of magazines getting her ideas—listen, if Claude didn't have the patience of a saint, I don't know how he could put up with it. One week this, the next week another idea—me, I'm glad I just moved into a house that was already done!"

Marthe took the tea Geneviève handed her and glanced around. "Can we sit a minute? Just the thought of a good cup of tea gives me a lift! I'm so tired all the time, it's ridiculous—Henri says I work too hard, but, really, Geneviève, when it's there to be done..."

"You know who won't get tired? Alice! Marthe, think, she has a girl in to help her every day! Marthe, she lives in a house so new the dust hasn't had time to find the corners yet, she has someone to help. Help do what, Alice? I asked her." Geneviève shook her head. "The day I don't keep up my house! Hélène looks good. She likes New Orleans?"

"Loves it. She hardly ever comes here anymore, and you know how crazy she was about Beau Chêne."

"But, Marthe, she has a husband, her little girl—Caroline is how old now? Beau's age?"

"Five in February."

"That's right—Beau was born first, she came six weeks later. But they'll all be here for Thanksgiving?"

Marthe's face, warmed by the glowing fires, the rich flowers, the heavy scent of perfume, the sweet, spiced tea, was suddenly radiant, young. "Oh, yes. Geneviève, even René! He sailed from Paris a month ago, has been making his way home—Geneviève, I haven't seen him in over a year, it seems impossible, but it's been since September a year ago—"

"So. He comes to stay? To learn to run Beau Chêne?"

Some of the youth was lost in the lines that marked her frown. "I don't know. He didn't say—and I haven't asked. For now—for now, Geneviève, I'll have everyone here, Nanette home from school, my grandbaby—I'll not let tomorrow bother me."

Geneviève patted Marthe's hand. "And me. Listen, Claudine is coming, too. Imagine, her husband bought his own pharmacy, Alice's children, they're all excited, it has a soda fountain like Estorge's and they say they're going to go to New Orleans and eat all the ice cream they want and not pay a penny."

"It's a lovely party, Geneviève. Lovely."

Geneviève bit into a small tart. "But the pastry. Alice is a good cook, but she has a heavy hand with her pastry. Alice, I tell her, after you add all the water, you can't stir much, no!"

"So where will you have dinner, Thanksgiving?"

"Where? At my house! What, eat in town where you can smell your neighbors' dinners, they live so close? Besides"— Geneviève rose with Marthe, walked with her to the door— "besides, Alice uses her dishes for flowers, to put fruit in, to put fern—Marthe, she might not have any left to eat on, you know?"

The fire box of the engine sent out a roar of heat; René slammed the door shut and yelled—"All aboard! All aboard!" He turned to Hélène, who crowded next to him in the cab. "Everyone in?"

She looked down the line of cars behind them, lined with hay, filled with people. "Looks like it. Lord, maman must have asked everyone for fifty miles around."

"Pull the whistle, Hélène. Remember how we used to fight to do that?"

The long, shrill whistle split the cold November air in two, sending the vibrating molecules far out over the harvested fields. René leaned against the side of the cab and looked down the track. "Funny thing—I told some girl last year we had a railroad—she thought I was like Jay Gould or something." He laughed, a short laugh that seemed like someone else's, someone Hélène wasn't sure she knew. "I didn't disillusion her— then."

"Well, it is a railroad. And I'd rather have this little old thirty-six-gauge sugar railroad than any other one in the whole world."

"Nice sentiment, but not very practical." René took out a cigarette and lit it. "Big railroads bring big money—and money is what I'd rather have than any other thing in the world."

"Have you already run through what you got when grand-mère died? René, really! What do you do over there with that horrid Sept, anyway?"

René blew smoke; it lifted and met the pluming black smoke from the little engine, clouding back over the string of cars. "As little as possible, my dear sister. As little as possible."

Marthe watched the flame crackle up the pyramid of wood, set the bonfire blazing. "I'm sorry we missed grinding season—remember how much you all loved going out to the sugarhouse and drinking cane juice? And dipping popcorn balls in that good fresh hot syrup?"

René put an arm around her. "If you remembered your famous chicken salad sandwiches, I'll forgo the cane juice. And though I can't remember when I've last touched milk, if you brought hot chocolate, I'll make an exception and drink that, too."

"I wish you'd come home to stay, René. Your French must be marvelous, Charles was saying just the other day he could get you into an export firm in New Orleans where French would be most useful—or you could come home to Beau Chêne." She heard the words rushing away from her, said much too quickly, much too soon. She raised a hand. "Don't tell me 'no,' now. Let me pretend you're going to say 'yes.'"

He sent his cigarette sailing toward the fire, its trail of sparks arcing across the air. "Look, maman, I think Nanette had better find some farmer type at college and marry him. I can't see myself in the role. Really."

"You haven't heard Nanette's plans?"

"I've heard so much in the few days I've been home—I might have—"

"You'd remember this. She's decided to study medicine."

A log broke under the weight of its own burning, fell forward, sending up a blaze of light. Marthe saw the shock on René's face. "Medicine? Nanette? Maman, that's disgusting! How can you allow it? Maman, she can't!"

Marthe thought of the stories that were whispered about Sept de Clouet. The gambling debts. The parties that went on, sometimes, for days. The rush from one end of Europe to the other, ragtag followers picked up at every stop, all looking for "fun," a new thrill. She remembered how, in letters home, René had first described his cousin as "a revolting kind of fellow, not our sort at all," and had then, over the long Paris stay, begun to refer to Sept from time to time as "an amusing kind of chap, once you get to know him."

"There's nothing disgusting about healing people," she said. Firelight did a lot of things, made old people look younger, softened ugliness, lit up beauty. But it couldn't hide the look in her son's eyes that had nothing to do with age, everything to do with experience. "It's taken your father every connection he can think of to get her in—but she'll be at Jefferson Medical College in Philadelphia next fall—and knowing Nanette, I think she'll be able to stick it out."

The little shrug of ennui, the lids of the eyes closing down. "Well. Chacun à son goût. It seems strange, that's all. My little sister with her own cadaver. Will she name it, do you think? I've heard they do."

Marthe watched René go off. Even though the bonfire was at its height, consuming the high-piled wood with frenzied flames, she felt chilled. She thought of the land stretching away from them in the dark. Remembered the price she had paid for it. For whom? Not René, that was clear. Hélène? She'd never leave New Orleans, she had moved into the Livaudais house in the Garden District, moved into the round of theater and balls and dinners and receptions. Beau Chêne was a place to visit, a place to bring Caroline for fresh air—but a place to live? Never. Nanette? By the time she finished her training, poor Henri would be glad of a partner in his practice, a successor. But run Beau Chêne? She reached down and picked up a stray stalk of sugar cane, litter from the just finished grinding. Got a knife from the refreshment table, began to peel away the deep purple stalk with long, sure strokes.

"What are you doing, maman?" Nanette had come up, cheeks bright against her wind-blown hair.

"I'm cutting some cane to chew," Marthe said. "I want to see if it tastes as good as I remember."

"It's a wonderful party, maman. I wish papa could come, though."

Marthe reached out and pulled Nanette to her. "Oh, so do I. But, Nanette—listen. That's what it's like, you know. Being a doctor. You don't get to do a lot for yourself. Pleasure, I mean."

Nanette stepped back. The bonfire was lower now, dying against the darkness. But its gleam caught in Nanette's dark eyes, it lit up the passion there. "But, maman—that's just it. I can't think of anything I'd rather do. Ever. I can't imagine doing anything else."

Marthe laughed. "Isn't it lucky? That's how I feel about running Beau Chêne—I can't imagine doing anything else."

It's good to see so many lights at Beau Chêne, Jumie thought. He'd been squirrel hunting in the woods between the houses, had seen the lamps flare against the coming dark. It's a house that needs a lot of people, somehow. It seems to go cold so quick. He picked up his pace, striding ahead of the descending night. His own kitchen lights shone bright. Inside, he'd find warmth. Food. Geneviève.

Later, when he sat cleaning his guns, making ready for another hunt, he heard a whistle send its long shrill call over the fields where rabbits nested, where small rodents hid. An owl called back, soft, questioning. "Must be running the railroad over at Beau Chêne," Jumie said. He looked up from the shells he was loading. "Sugarhouse party, probably."

"Marthe said she was going to have one, while everyone was home." Geneviève picked up her crochet, cast on another row. "Listen, Alice likes everything to match, I'm making her some potholders, you think her pots will care?"

"Too bad young René won't stay. She ought to have some help with that place. She hasn't had a decent overseer since Hebert left—that man she has now, is he any good?"

Geneviève shrugged. "Who knows? Marthe says it's hard to get a man who wants to work for a woman—but that boy of hers? Listen, Jumie, he wouldn't help. I don't know, I don't like to talk against a neighbor—but, Jumie, I don't think René, he's—nice. You know?"

"You heard Nanette's going to be a doctor?"

Geneviève's hand flew up, made a quick Sign of the Cross. "That she doesn't catch something awful they don't know how to cure! But, Jumie, that Nanette, she's like her maman. Strong, you know? And a head like a pig!" The whistle sounded again, coming over the cold empty fields. "That Marthe. All that company, running that big plantation, a good party—she keeps everything going anyhow."

Jumie finished loading the last shell, carefully put his tools away. "I don't know. I hope so."

"Now what does that mean?"

"Just what I said. I hope she does keep it all going."

Geneviève set a completed potholder aside. "So I used all the ends in the basket—Alice thinks it doesn't match something, it can find its way home. Jumie, what do you know about Marthe you're not telling me?"

Jumie rattled the coffee pot. "You want coffee? I'll drip a little more."

"Stop making up things to talk about. Something from the bank? From the meeting?"

"Geneviève, I don't tell you what I learn at the bank."

"So don't tell me where you learned it. Jumie, is Marthe in trouble?"

The last lingering cry from the whistle hung just above the roof, then died.

"She's been borrowing money. On Beau Chêne."

"Jumie! On her land? Money on her land? Now, Jumie, you've got to tell Marthe not to do that!"

Jumie began to drip the boiling water from a big spoon into the ground coffee. "I don't tell Marthe what to do."

"Oh, Jumie. Since when? Since when? Now, Jumie, you've got to help Marthe. Jumie, it's a lot of money?"

He poured two cups of coffee, carried one to her. "Enough. The mill needed new machinery, the house needed some repairs—Nanette's school isn't cheap, I wouldn't imagine. And to keep René in Paris the way he likes—it takes a lot of money, Geneviève."

"But look how much sugar she raises! Jumie, that's a big place!"

"With a big payroll and overseers who come and go— Marthe's smart, she's stubborn, and she's good. But she's a woman, Geneviève. And she gets taken advantage of."

"Mais, that I don't like! Jumie, do something, you hear?"

Jumie finished his coffee, stood up and stretched. He bent over Geneviève, kissed her. "You think I don't have enough to do, I take on Beau Chêne, too?"

Geneviève came up into his arms. "Mais, Jumie, somebody's got to. And I tell you the truth, around here? When somebody's got to do something, that somebody is usually a Langlinais, yes."

# CHAPTER 24
# *Seedlings*

Though the Louisiana lottery was dead by 1893, the lessons it taught were not. And with the resounding defeat of the Populist movement in the elections of 1896, the victorious Bourbon Democrats went back to the old text, there to learn the principles, not only of winning, but of maintaining control. The result was the beginning of New Orleans machine politics—with the formation in 1897 of the New Orleans Choctaw Club, the Ring, or the Old Regulars, as they were familiarly called, a powerful combine of strength in the New Orleans wards and a following in the country ended the Louisiana political arena. The intraparty battles were bitter and divisive; they also perpetuated the "king-makers," the men behind the scenes who ran the state, no matter who held the governor's chair. By 1910, responding to cries against the corruption and inefficiency in state government, John M. Parker helped form the Good Government League, established first to effect better government in New Orleans—with the statehouse as a later goal. In the same year, President William H. Taft established the Commission of Economy and Efficiency in Government—businessmen, following the slogan, "Let's make government more businesslike," emerged as a positive political force. And in Louisiana, any man of business not allied with the Old Regulars was a candidate for membership in the Good Government League.

The rush of sound surrounded them; Jumie looked up and pointed—"Wood ducks. About twenty of them."

The man beside him in the blind reared up, raised his gun, sighted, shot. Jumie's gun echoed his; the symmetry of the flight was broken as the two lead ducks met the exploding shells, were hit, stopped, and then plummeted to the waiting bayou.

The dog at Jumie's feet leaped forward, hit the water in a flat plunging dive, and swam out to where the ducks floated. "How'd you know they were wood ducks? That far off?"

"The way they sound. Like a train's roar, almost. Mallards, pintails, teal—they glide down. Not wood ducks. They fly faster, for one thing. Really beat the air. When they want to stop—they cup their wings, brake against the air. That's what makes the noise." Jumie reached out and took the duck from the dog's mouth. His hand caressed the black fur, digging deeply into the dog's massive neck.

"Really know your country, don't you?" his companion said.

Jumie laughed. "Man, my people been here since almost two hundred years—I guess I do know it."

The man, reloading his shotgun, paused. "Which is why we want to get you and your son involved with the league. The Langlinaises—they're something to be reckoned with around here."

Jumie raised his hand, shook his head. "Look, duck hunting? It's serious business. I don't talk about anything much when I'm hunting." He looked up at the sky, gray night coming to life with the rose blush of dawn. "Mallards coming in. Good for roasting, good for gumbo. Geneviève'll make oyster dressing. First we hunt, then we eat—then, maybe, we talk."

Around them, the spiky marsh weeds stood dry and brown. The bayou, settling in for a winter of sluggish cold, sudden heat, presented its dull brown face to the rising sun. A smell of wood smoke drifted to them. And in the sky over them, a flock of mallards, brilliant green heads burning in the early sun, paused, settled into a long glide, and then floated silently through the still autumn air.

Marthe closed the ledger, put it away, and picked up the stack of letters Berthe had brought in to her. An announcement of a planters' association meeting, a letter from Nanette—she put that aside to read when work was over—an invitation to a bride's tea, a bill for the new conveyor belt—she sorted through the stack, suddenly restless. The early mist had burned away; when she stepped out the front door early, seeing Henri off, she had known this was going to be a perfect October day—

crisp, clear, earth colors blazing, sky a cold cobalt blue. No day to be inside worrying with bills, meetings—anything!

She put the mail, unopened, back in the letter rack, locked her desk and left the study. She'd pack a picnic, put on good walking shoes, spend a few hours in the woods. She caught a glance at herself in the pier mirror in the hall—was she really that old? But when she stepped out the back door, went through the kitchen garden with tomatoes still clinging to vines, broccoli and cauliflower growing, she forgot age, aches, worries. Autumn was in the woods, spending her glories recklessly before the cold ruled against pleasure. And for a few hours, she would play.

The poplars had turned a deep crimson; their small white seed clusters, like popcorn strung against a field of red, shook in the skipping wind. Pine turned darker green, sent gray-brown cones clattering through the squirrel-heavy branches. Marthe turned over the leaves covering the ground beneath a pecan tree, her boot tip finding the green-hulled nuts. She filled her pockets and walked on. I should do this more often, she thought. It's ridiculous to live in the country if you can't enjoy it. Hélène had said the same thing, writing from New Orleans. "If you're not going to get out more, keep up with your old friends, at least, maman, get out at Beau Chêne. Ride again. Or walk! Papa has always looked tired, but you never have. I worry!"

Hélène had not meant to be amusing, but her mother had laughed. Running a plantation did not, it seemed, mix with being a lady. There might well be gentlemen farmers, Marthe did not think there were lady equivalents. To drive into New Iberia for a morning coffee, go to a luncheon in St. Martinville, took, it seemed, the entire day. And, increasingly, she had found little to say to these women she had known all her life. Talk of grandchildren—well, how much could she say about Caroline, whom she saw far less than she wished to? Talk of new draperies? It had been a long time since she had thought new draperies were important—certainly not as important as new machinery, better fertilizer.

She had complained to Jumie, running across him in the post office. "At the Gautier's dinner the other night, Jumie, I found myself discussing sugar yield and cane diseases with the men while the other women flirted with them! Now, really!" She had begun to laugh. "Jumie, when I think what a little

minx I was—now I sound like something out of the farm
journal."

"Marthe, nobody who looks the way you do is out of the
farm journal," he'd said. "But you do look tired." His smile
always was like the sun. "Marthe, pretty, you look pretty—
but tired. That overseer? He's working out all right?"

"I think so. I know more, of course—so I'm better to work
for. But, Jumie—if I had known ten years ago what I know
now—I wonder if I'd have bought Beau Chêne."

"You need to pleasure yourself more, Marthe."

"Stop telling me what to do!" she'd said. But she'd joined
him for coffee at the café near the church, laughed at his hunting
stories, felt, for a while, like a woman.

The big oak with branches curved low enough to the earth
to make a staircase loomed ahead of her—she had a rush of
wanting, to climb into that spreading tree, settle into the old
familiar seat where she'd spent hours and hours, first as a
frightened child, then as a dreaming girl. "Mais, Marthe, you're
not going to chop our old friend for firewood, are you?"

She whirled, saw Jumie behind her. "You been studying
him for a good five minutes—measuring or thinking?"

"Thinking. Remembering. Even after the Yankees left, I
used to hide up there. You always knew where I was, I used
to think you had eyes everywhere."

"I do. For instance, I saw your picnic basket from a mile
away and came out to see what lady farmers eat when they
finally take some time off."

"God knows I've got enough. Really. Berthe must have
hoped I'd stay gone for days." She took a cloth from the wicker
basket, spread it over the ground. "Let's see—here's chicken—
apples—a loaf of new bread—butter—blackberry jam—
stuffed eggs—wine—my Lord, Jumie, you'd better help me."

"I will." They set out the food, settled on the bed of leaves
that cushioned the earth.

"I couldn't stand to stay inside today. I'd reached the point
where if I opened one more letter that presented something I
had to see about, I'd scream. At least if I scream out here, no
one will hear me."

"I don't know, Marthe. It all keeps coming close—take
now. We got some men from New Orleans at the house, one
I do business with, some friends of his. Came to hunt, they

said. But already, already, they've got a project. Something to talk to me and Claude about. Marthe, I tell you, how come when you got plenty to do, people always think you can do more?"

She sliced an apple, releasing the crisp, tart scent, and handed him a slice. "I don't know. Probably because you never say no, Jumie." And when she saw the protest coming—"You don't. You never have. Not that I know of."

"Maybe I just don't say no to you, Marthe."

She lay back against the scarlet and gold and orange and brown scattered leaves. Looked up through branches and leaves at the high blue sky. "When Henri's father did that terrible thing—and Henri was so mad at him? So humiliated? Jumie, it's awful to say it—but you know, I almost didn't blame him? I know, it was dishonorable. But, Jumie I could perfectly well understand why he wanted to spend the rest of his life being pampered. Instead of more of the same!"

"Marthe, your fields are producing well, though, aren't they?"

"I guess." She flopped over, propped her face in her hands. "Isn't it funny, I'm supposed to be an old lady? Instead, on a day like this, I'm about sixteen."

"And me." His voice was low, quiet. She sat up, began to put the food away.

"Well. Someday one of Henri's colleagues will find a way to bottle a day like today. Then we can take a spoon of it and be restored!" She took his outstretched hand, let herself be pulled up.

"Mais, Marthe, when even nature comes in a bottle, me, I give up."

"I'm glad you came out, Jumie. We haven't been on a picnic together since—right after the war?"

"A long time, Marthe. A long time."

He watched her walk through the afternoon-lighted woods, sun caressing her hair with gold. One thing you can say about those de Clouet women, he thought, seeing the graceful lift of Marthe's head, the easy swing of her walk—they don't ever lose their style.

Geneviève poked her head around the parlor door. "Listen, you've got about five minutes, Jumie. Before the ducks, they're ready to walk on Claude, you open up some of that good red wine." They heard her quick steps down the hall, the far-off rattle of pots in the kitchen.

"I realize you don't like to mix business with pleasure, Jumie. But we'll be going back in the morning. And I'd like to think we've at least explained our position, gotten a good hearing."

"Look, a little politics won't ruin the ducks—or my stomach, either, I guess. Claude. What you think?"

"Sounds like another chapter in an old, old story. Mon Dieu, last time it was the Farmers' Union and the Anti-Lottery League. And look what happened then." Claude turned to Jumie. "Being sold down the river like that might not have killed grandpapa— but it didn't help."

"Now, Claude. Papa understood what happened. The union candidate could never have won. Foster could—and did."

"But the way it was set up. Fooling people into thinking the union would pick the gubernatorial candidate—then pulling the switch." He looked at the men clustered around the hearth. "Is that what we can expect from this Good Government group?"

"John Parker has one goal in mind, Claude. To break the back of the machine that's running this state."

"And the Anti-Lottery League had one goal—to break the back of that little group."

"The lottery did get defeated."

"Because the Congress forbade it to use the federal mails. Look, I'm all for good government. What does the president say? Run government like we run business? But down here, down where I come from, we can trust a man's word. You know? It doesn't take ten lawyers to draw up a contract."

"Why do you think we're here, Langlinais? That's the kind of men we need, too. Men whose word can be trusted. Look— if we're going to elect a Good Government governor in 1912, we'll need some strong local candidate on our side. I'll admit— when we came down here, it was to ask your papa to run for the legislature." The man shot a look at Jumie. "But he cut that off at the tap. Said you were our man." He fixed his eyes on Claude. "That give you any trouble? That we asked you second?"

"Second? I am second to my papa, man. If you'd not asked him first—I'd have thought you were crazy. Dumb crazy, too." Claude pushed away from the table. "Maman gave us five minutes. Me, I'm not keeping her waiting." He moved toward the doorway, then stopped, turned. "I don't think you know what you're asking me to do, that's all."

"Run for the legislature? Of course we know . . ."

Claude laughed. "Not run, man. Be in the legislature. Because if I run, I'll win. That's right, papa?"

"That's right."

Something leaped from father to son and back again. One of the men near the fire shifted his weight; what was this force these people had? To look at them, khaki shirts open, faded work pants, you'd not know they had two dimes to rub together. He thought of the heavily starched shirts, the silk ties, the well-tailored suits, the New Orleans crowd wore when they stuffed themselves on turtle soup and Trout Margeray at Galatoire's. They'd better get in training if they wanted to even stay in the same ring with these fellows.

"What's the matter with being in the legislature, then?"

Claude's eyes went to the windows, to the land beyond the thin fog that veiled them. His arm lifted, moved in a slow half circle. "You've never lived down here, man. You don't know what it's like." That lazy smile. "I told Father Pequet the other day, I said, God has a fight on His hands to make heaven better than living here." He looked back at the men. "I went to school in Baton Rouge, remember? Look, that's not much of a place to live, you know? I mean—not if you've lived here."

"It doesn't mean anything else, then? Being in the legislature?"

"What else? Power? Political power?" Only the smile on Claude's face kept the words from being an insult. "That kind of power—that's what other people either let you have—or you take from them. You know? Either way—it's something you have to keep taking care of, making deals about—hell. What do I need that for?" He turned, left the room.

Jumie moved forward. "He's right, you know. He really doesn't need it."

An arm reached toward Jumie, a firm hand grasped him. "What does he need?"

"What?"

"What could convince Claude to run? What would it take?"

"Nothing. Claude—if he decides to run, he will. But don't say anything else. Don't offer him anything. You hear? Because Claude—he likes to think what he does is his idea. Done for his own reasons. Not yours. Not even mine." He gently moved from the man's grip. "Now—I don't know about anybody else. But me—I'm hungry for ducks."

Marthe put the mail on her supper tray, carried it to the fire in her bedroom and sifted through the envelopes while she sipped soup. Henri had come home for an early meal, gone back to the hospital to deliver a first baby. "Don't wait up," he'd said. She put the bills, the business letters aside. Sufficient to each day, after all. But Nanette's letter, the personal things—she picked up a light gray envelope, addressed with heavy black ink in strong, angular strokes. Turned it over, read the return address. Sept, for heaven's sake. She slit the envelope open, pulled out the single page. "Leontine and I have descended on her parents for a month or so—by some coincidence of unkind Fate, my sisters and Pierre are also in New Orleans. We thought we'd run down to the country, pop in on you. Expect us toward the end of the month—this entourage travels somewhat capriciously, but we'll send more definite word."

Oh, fine. She had met Sept's wife for the only time at their wedding three years ago; Leontine was a thin, dark-haired girl whose life, even at that early stage, seemed to have been curiously disordered. She had studied art at Newcomb, left to work in Paris—apparently met Sept there, brought him back to New Orleans for the wedding, which, as Marthe remembered it, had been odd, eccentric, almost pagan in its absence of tradition and ritual.

As for the rest of them—Anastasie had married some minor English lord, Lisette had run off with an actor, Pierre was still playing at being the artist—well, she'd give them dinner and send them packing. And if they had not been her dead brother's children, she'd not have done even that.

True to their word, Sept and his entourage appeared several weeks later.

"Tonight would be an excellent night to have a meeting at the hospital—or a lazy baby," Marthe said to Henri the afternoon they were to arrive. "They're coming for dinner—and I can't imagine you want to be here."

"Wouldn't think of having you face that menagerie alone," he said. "At least they'll have to behave themselves with me around."

And, in the beginning at least, they were not so bad. They had arrived in a large touring car, Sept at the wheel, the women spilling scarves and furs and cigarette smoke out the sides. Lisette's husband, Enrico, was fat, Italian, and amusing. Lisette was beginning to be plump, her breasts strained against the silk print bodice, and her face was blurring with extra flesh. Anastasie's conversation consisted primarily of gossip about English royalty; Pierre, Marthe noticed, encouraged her, laughing at each detail, winking at the others—"and taking mental notes the entire time," Marthe said to Henri.

They had cocktails in the parlor, and Sept was so pleasant, so civilized, that for a while Marthe hoped the evening would pass quietly, they would eat their dinner, mind their manners— and go home. "René is doing very well," Sept said, scooping up deviled oysters from the chafing dish set on the long table behind the sofa. "He's running a repertory company now, did you know? Some friends of Enrico's put him on to it—it should be a very good thing."

"I'd no idea René knew enough about the theater to run a company," Marthe said. She looked at her husband, whose face was turned just far enough away that he could pretend not to hear what Sept was saying.

"Oh, well, there's a fellow—this friend of Enrico's—who does that kind of thing. René provides the—well, the business sense. You know?"

Acres and acres of green cane, ripening for harvest. Cane joints laid in the earth, sprouting for next year's crop. Transformed into sugar, into syrup—into, apparently, confections for the French stage. "I know," she said.

As the levels in the wine bottles dropped, the barriers set on their tongues dropped also. Marthe, serving charlotte russe into the fine thin crystal dessert glasses, heard Anastasie begin another tale of an unfaithful wife; this one took her architect-lover down to her country house under the pretext of making sketches for a gazebo. "He made sketches, all right," Anastasie said. "Of his mistress. In poses he copied from some book of Oriental erotica. There was one in particular, remember, Pierre, the one . . ." Her voice dropped a little, took on an ugly hoarseness.

Marthe shoved the filled glass at Sept, sitting at her right. "Tell your sister to remember where she is, Sept. I won't allow that kind of talk at my table."

"Anastasie. Our aunt is not amused by your stories. A little restraint, please." He smiled amiably at Marthe, lifted his wine-glass. "We forget how provincial you are out here."

"Bosh." Lisette rose. The light from the candelabra before her touched the deep brightness of the silk stretched across her breasts, lit the firm points of her nipples. She doesn't even wear a chemise, Marthe thought. She looked at the charlotte russe and wondered why she'd bothered to order such an elaborate meal. Far better to have handed them bread and cheese and sent them on their way—or ash cakes. Wasn't that what unwelcome visitors were given? Bitter ale and ash cakes? And here they were swilling Henri's best Bourdeaux!

Lisette had moved away from the table now, was working her way toward Henri, whose attention had long since been focused on his plate. "Henri's a doctor, isn't he? And Marthe, you breed horses, don't you?" She fastened small, glittering eyes on Henri's weary face. "You know all about how it works, don't you, Henri? I mean, you were looking at dirty pictures in medical books when everyone else had to use their imagination. I've always wanted to ask a doctor—does knowing all that make it more fun?" Now the glittering eyes were licking over Marthe. "Or should I ask you?"

Marthe turned to Enrico. "I've been wondering, all evening, Enrico, just what roles Lisette could play in your little troupe. Not the ingenue, that would never do." She stood, tapped her glass. "And now I see it perfectly. She is, of course, the enfant terrible." She stared across the candlelight at Lisette. "An aging enfant terrible—but I suppose makeup takes care of that." Then, briskly, "We'll have coffee in the parlor—it's late, Henri is tired. I'm sure you will excuse him if he doesn't join us."

It's only for this one evening, Marthe told herself. She climbed the stairs slowly, hearing the gabble of voices ahead of her. By the time she reached the parlor, it had already begun to change. Lisette, at the harpsichord, was playing some cabaret song, her carved ivory cigarette holder protruding form scarlet lips. Enrico had removed his coat, loosened his collar, and was lounging at the fire, a snifter of brandy in his hand. Anastasie, already dazed, silent with liquor, sat in the wing chair, steadily sipping the cut-crystal tumbler of bourbon Sept had poured for her. Sept and Leontine were quarreling about something, Pierre was listening and laughing—Marthe watched the soft colors of the room change, saw shadows leap, give contorted shapes to familiar forms. She walked over to a lamp and turned the gas high.

"Oh, God, that's so bright!" Leontine said. "For God's sake, Marthe, turn that down. It's killing my eyes." She turned to Marthe, her great strange eyes, pupils wide, dark, staring.

"I'll light candles," Sept said. "It's much more romantic, much more appropriate, don't you think?"

"I don't want to be inhospitable," Marthe said. "But we keep very early hours here, Sept. I have to be at my desk early, I've got a meeting at the bank—"

His arm, smooth in its well-cut coat, slid around her. His fingers seemed to probe for weakness. "And you want to go to bed? But, my dear aunt, of course. We'll just have our brandy and then slip away—so quietly you won't even know we've gone."

"But, Sept—" A flicker of light crossed his face, and she saw Nollie. Her brother's son. He was a de Clouet, after all. And he seemed still in control, still sober. "All right. But, Sept, please—please don't be long."

He escorted her to the parlor doors, bent to kiss her cheek. "Dear Aunt Marthe," he said. Behind him, Marthe heard Leontine laugh. The laugh rippled around the room, seemed to quiver up and down Marthe's spine.

"Is Leontine all right? She seems, I don't know—"

"A bit nervy. Gets like this once in a while. Jagged around the edges. But she has something to take for it." Sept laughed. "A number of things to take for it." He put his hands on Marthe's shoulders, pushed her through the door. "If she lived in this peaceful country, she'd get over all that in a minute. Country air, isn't that good for everything?"

"I think you'd stifle in it," Marthe said. She heard him close the doors behind her, heard the tinkle of the harpsichord become muted. Pushing back the disquiet that tugged at her like a restless child who won't be pacified, she made ready for bed. How terrible to think that these people were the sort her son considered his kind. Maybe in Paris, or in those Italian resorts they were forever discovering, this behavior was just a game, a play, an extension of their theatricals. They can't give up an audience, that's all. Silly children, full of themselves, showing off. She slipped into the smooth sheets, turned her pillow under her cheek. Trying to shock the grown-ups. It was, when she thought about it, a little sad.

When she woke later, she knew they were still in the house. The heavy doors, the length of hall between parlor and her room, had allowed her to sleep. But there was a new sound, from a new place—she sat up, pulled the covers around her, and listened.

On the gallery? Were they on the gallery? She heard the silver chime of her mantel clock—three o'clock, that was ridiculous. She found her slippers, pulled on her wool robe. Thank God Henri's room was at the back of the house; he, at least, wouldn't be disturbed.

Moonlight filled every corner of the parlor when she opened the door and went in. In that clear light, the progress of the evening was plain. Pieces of glass crunched beneath her feet; she looked down, saw broken stems of wineglasses, shards of etched glass. Looked at the door behind her, saw the wine stains covering it. Candelabra were webbed with wax, long strands of it falling from solid pools that spilled over the silver lips. The fire smoldered, giving off a thick, dense smoke. And from out on the gallery, through the long open doors, a tinkling sound, a staccato sound. She went forward.

Enrico learned against a column, banjo cradled in his arms. His fingers plucked at the strings, pulling those tinkling, teasing, sounds from their pliant length. Lisette sat on a cushion taken from the sofa; she was supporting herself on both arms, thrusting her round breasts up just beneath Enrico's moving hands. Pierre had a pad in his hand, a pencil moved over it. She couldn't see Anastasie, but she could hear her voice, twisted now with liquor, muffled, singing some high refrain. And still that staccato sound, a sound she couldn't understand.

She heard Sept's voice, then Leontine's. They were at the other end of the gallery, quarreling. She stayed back, waiting. Then something sailed through the air, slithered past her, fell. A woman's dress. Then a slip, then, silken, stockings, long, lifeless, curving through the air. She moved onto the gallery just as Sept walked toward her. "Aunt Marthe! So lovely you could join us after all." She felt his hands gripping her arms, pulling her forward. "Leontine is going to dance for us, come where you can see her." His voice was still amiable, agreeable. His face in the moonlight seemed calm, controlled.

"Sept—" She tried to break from his grasp. "Sept—"

The eyes he turned to her were dark. There had been no light in those eyes for a long, long time—not the light of innocence, nor the light of hope. "Yes, Aunt Marthe?" The low, even voice. So quiet, so reassuring. She remembered Henri, discussing a patient he'd seen presented at a meeting in New Orleans. "She looks like anyone else," Henri had said. "Speaks pleasantly, too. Sounds as sane as you or I." He'd shaken his head. "But there's nothing there. It's all gone. She feels nothing. Knows nothing, really. Maybe that's better."

Marthe's eyes went quickly over the figures on the gallery. And what were they shutting out, these nieces and nephews of hers? What world was so terrible that the grotesque one they created was better? Looking down the gallery, she saw a thin figure wrapped in a crimson shawl moving toward them, high heels on bare legs clicking, clicking, fingers clicking castanets. The banjo music bounced from the teased strings, took the insistent rhythm of Enrico's plump fingers and met the tapping of Leontine's feet. "Sept, let's get her to bed. All of you. In the morning—"

The crimson shawl flashed open on bare white skin, closed, then slipped to Leontine's waist, and in a final free movement, fell to the floor. Marthe felt Sept move away from her. His eyes were on his wife, who had danced away from the sheltering shadows of the columns. The moon, like a bright lantern in the sky, was held high to light Leontine's path. Her body was thin, gleaming, with the dark triangle of hair shadowing her belly. Her breasts moved with the rhythm of the music, her crimson heels tapped, her crimson lips parted in that insistent laugh. Marthe was at their wedding again, Leontine's and Sept's, in that strange dark house on Calliope Street, with a minister whose church they never knew chanting words they couldn't understand. "He's sort of a Theist," Sept had said, waving it off. "Or is it Theosophist? No matter. Leontine's very bright. Very avant-garde. Sets her own rules, really." He'd poured more champagne, smiled over the rim of the glass. "Which is why we'll live in Europe. She really doesn't fit in here too well. New Orleans—a little too straitlaced, a little too far behind."

Marthe lunged forward, snatched up the crimson shawl and reached for the dancing figure. Leontine darted away, naked body weaving in the shadowed light. Marthe lunged again, was blocked by Enrico, who moved between them. Sept was just ahead of Marthe, pushing through the others who clustered toward Leontine. She was running now, down to the end of the gallery. Marthe heard a voice raised, a scream. Her voice, screaming at Leontine to stop, stop. She heard her voice soar over the sound of running feet and tried to follow. But now there was something white standing next to one of the far columns; like a column of silk, it swayed. Marthe saw Leontine climb onto the railing, stand there, pose. Then she laughed, reached out over the darkness—and jumped. As the dark closed around her, Marthe heard Enrico's voice. "You shouldn't ever frighten a person in a trance, madam. See what happens?"

Geneviève spooned grits onto Jumie's plate, slid eggs into place. "Listen, tell Claude, if he comes out today, take some boudin to Alice. Wait, do you hear somebody? At the back door?" She set his plate in front of him, tossed her long braid back over her shoulder and went to the door. "Marthe! Marthe, mais, chère, you're frozen, yes. Marthe, what's wrong?" Jumie saw Marthe's face, sealed against some terror still fresh. Geneviève helped her in, sat her in the rocker by the fire. "Marthe, Marthe, is it Henri?"

The eyes were large, staring at them, filled with darkness. "Leontine—" The voice seemed to creak from that tight throat, seemed to push past muscles tired from screaming. She coughed, tried again. "Leontine—Sept's wife—she killed herself."

Geneviève's hand flew up, made the Sign of the Cross. "Mon Dieu! When? Marthe—"

The eyes stared against the dark; almost, as she spoke, Jumie could see what they tried not to. "Last night—at Beau Chêne. They'd—come for dinner. She—jumped off the gallery."

"At Beau Chêne? Marthe, at Beau Chêne? Oh, Marthe, no!" Geneviève took Marthe's hands in hers, began to rub. "Jumie, put some brandy in the coffee—quick!"

Marthe sipped, small, slow sips. "She—broke her neck. Henri—Henri says she was full of laudanum. Crazy with it."

Geneviève refilled the cups. "Listen, Marthe, from what you told me before, that Leontine, she was crazy anyway. That wedding, didn't you tell me? No proper priest, they made up their own words—"

"They're going to cremate her. Scatter her ashes in Lake Pontchartrain." Jumie heard the dull weight in Marthe's voice.

"Oh, Marthe, they're not only crazy, they're bad!"

The weight was too much, it broke through the last of her strength. She slumped forward, tears masking her face. "But they say I made her, that I frightened her, screaming at her. They blame me, they've been awful, awful, when Henri rode in with the—body, they began, they waited until he left, but I couldn't stand it, I couldn't, I grabbed my coat, I ran all the way—"

"Now, Marthe. Now, Marthe." Jumie heard the soft croon in Geneviève's voice, saw her stroking hands settle into a slow rhythm. Hurt children, weeping children, made better by that soft crooning voice, those slowly stroking hands. "Marthe, nobody makes anybody do anything, don't mothers know that? Didn't Claudine marry a pharmacist from New Orleans instead of a nice boy from here? And didn't Claude and Alice pick up and move to town where I never see them at all? Marthe, listen. If people we love, people we care about, if they don't listen to us, if we can't make *them* do what we want, why do you think crazy bad people like that listen? Marthe, chère. You didn't make that woman jump."

"But I did scream at her, I did run toward her—it was awful, she was so naked, so terrible—dancing like that. At Beau Chêne. At Beau Chêne." Her voice was lower, spun out with tiredness. "And Sept—he's all gone inside. I don't know. It's all gone." Geneviève looked at Jumie, raised her eyebrows.

"Marthe, listen, they won't let you sleep over there, you're going to bed here—all right, not long, I'll wake you up when Henri gets back—how will I know? Because"—Geneviève's braid swung with her anger—"because I'm going to put on my clothes and go over there and straighten those people out!"

The yellow dog lifted his head, sniffed, then pointed toward a clump of brush. Claude waited while the covey of birds flew up, then fired. He stuffed the small bodies down into his canvas bag. "You like doves for breakfast? Wrapped with lean bacon? Alice'll fix some."

"I want a decision for breakfast, Claude." Fred Hargrove patted the dog's broad head. "What kind of dog did you say this is?"

"Catahoula hound," Jumie said. "Claude, he carries on about that big retriever of his—but me, I'll take this one any time."

"Thoroughbred?"

"Cornbread," Jumie said, and laughed. "My joke. You never fix cornbread for your hunting dogs? Listen, it's good for them. I make it up with clabber, my little grandson, Claude's boy, he was over at the house one afternoon and he sees a big pan of cornbread on the stove and he cuts a piece and pours syrup over it and he takes a bite, and then he spits it out and he looks at me and says, 'Grandpapa, why didn't you tell me the dogs were coming for supper?'"

Hargrove waited for their laughter to finish. Then—"Langlinais, you all ever just get to the point down here? Without telling jokes, stories, going hunting, eating?"

"That is the point, down here," Jumie said. He slapped Fred's back.

They went across the furrowed field, the dog making a zigzag path ahead of them. "Pick up a few rabbits, Claude," Jumie said. "Maman'll make some stew."

"What's that house? Over there?"

Jumie followed the pointing finger. "Beau Chêne. The de Clouet place. Well, she's a de Clouet. Married Henri de Gravelle from New Orleans."

"Étienne de Gravelle's son?"

"But that fruit fell far from the tree, let me tell you. That Henri, he's a good man. Good doctor. Their oldest girl lives in New Orleans—maybe you know her husband? Charles Livaudais?"

His smile said more than his words. "Lawyer, isn't he? Represents a big utility company."

"According to what Marthe says, Charles thinks those companies have more than just electric power—buy legislators, buy governors."

"Well, papa, why not? Before the lottery, it was the carpetbaggers. After the lottery, the machine—and always money to oil the wheels, make the work quiet." Claude picked up a lump of mud, skimmed it toward a ditch cutting through the field.

"I'll bet no one would buy you, Langlinais." Jumie watched Fred's eyes narrow, focus on Claude's face. He felt again the web that stretched from New Orleans, wound out and up the river, down the bayous, across the state. He watched Claude's quick anger, then saw the laughter start.

"Hell, man," Claude said, and his voice seemed to float across the evening sky—"hell, man, is there that much money in the world?"

"Then will you run?"

"Alice says I should."

"Your wife wants you to run?"

Claude glanced at Jumie. "You know how it is. Even women who get along with their mothers-in-law like to get ahead of them. Everything Alice does, maman's already done, you know? So if she can be a legislator's wife—it gives her a little something her own. And besides"—another glance at Jumie, longer, steady—"besides, papa and I have been talking. The way things are, industry coming in, things building up—there's going to be all kinds of laws going on the books, changing the way we can do business. The way we run our banks. Way we see it, we better have a Langlinais in on all that." He checked his gun to make sure it was empty, slung it from a strap across his shoulder. He reached the free hand out. "So if what you want is a Langlinais running for the legislature in 1912—I guess you've got him."

Hargrove took Claude's hand. "You won't be sorry."

"Sure of that? Never mind. Different things make people sorry. The kind of things you're talking about, the kind of things Alice thinks about—well, that'll be all right." He lifted his head, breathed in a full chest of air. "The rest of it? Having less time to be here? Live the way I like?" Again the long look between father and son. "Well, papa knows what I mean. But I guess what it comes to, finally, is how much you can give up—in order to hang on to the rest."

Light pouring from the fast-setting sun seemed to ladle molten gold over the windows of Beau Chêne, seal them in a sheath of gleaming metal. Shining, blank, they looked out upon the browning fields, the darkening sky. Then the sun dropped, the metal shield dulled, faded. Windows, blank, empty, dull, blinked at him. Jumie had turned away, started to follow Claude and the man, when a moving shadow caught his glance. A small coupe, dusty, battered, was pulling into the stableyard. It was Sept de Clouet. Now what in the hell did he want? Jumie stepped behind a small tree, watched Sept take out a cigarette, light it, then stride toward the house. Years went, dropping away like the sun. He was a young boy, sent to slip past the Yankees with food for the family at Beau Chêne. He moved forward, working his way up to the back door.

"That Mister Sept is here," Berthe said to Marthe. "I told him you were busy, but he said come tell you anyhow."

Berthe's voice ranked Sept's presence—well below a peddler, just barely above a thief. "Is—is Doctor back yet?"

"No, ma'am. You want me to get one of the men?" Berthe's

face was fierce, worried. She stood in the door, blocking it.

"Oh, Berthe, I'll see him. He's an awful nuisance, if he stays more than ten minutes, I'll ring—and you can get Nat to put him out." She smiled against her fear. Sept was rude, ugly, unpleasant, decadent, corrupt—but nothing to be afraid of. She closed the books she was working on, straightened her spine against her chair back, and smoothed her face into a neutral look. Ten minutes she'd give him—ten minutes.

Jumie could see Berthe through the kitchen window, slicing ham. She kept looking at the door into the hall as though expecting someone; once, she left the kitchen, vanished, and then came back frowning. He reached up and knocked on the window, beckoned her to let him in. "I saw that no-good Sept de Clouet drive in and I decided to poke my nose in. What's he up to, Berthe?"

"He's making a lot of noise in there. I can't tell what he's saying, but it don't sound good. Miss Marthe, she told me she'd give him ten minutes, but it don't sound like he's thinking about leaving."

"I'll just check on them, Berthe. Miss Marthe's had about enough of that crew for a while, wouldn't you say?"

"Mister Jumie, we had enough of those people before they ever came here. Trash. Nothing but white trash."

He could hear the voices as he went down the hall. Marthe's raised, angry. Sept's loud, demanding. He opened the door without knocking, walked in. "Evening, Marthe. I was out hunting—thought I saw something scoot in here."

"Jumie—Jumie—he's asking for money."

"From you?"

"He—he says I cheated him—when I bought Beau Chêne. That he was too young to know what it was worth—the things in the house—the land."

"And now he's all grown up, is he? And run out of money?"

"My dear departed's parents are not inclined, it seems, to continue an allowance now that their daughter is—no longer with us," Sept said. He had not moved since Jumie entered the room, had stood as still as one of the field rodents outwaiting a dog. Only his eyes moved, searching Jumie's face, his strength.

"And the money you got for Beau Chêne—that gone, too?"

"Perhaps you can live on very little out here. I've no idea. But in Paris—I have expensive tastes."

"He says he's found a lawyer in New Orleans who will file

suit—for fraud. And—and for manslaughter."

"What?" Jumie's voice boomed against the ceilings, re-sounded in her ears. "What?" Marthe saw Jumie's eyes find the riding whip she'd used in their race, kept with her other trophies. His hand sought the grip, closed on it. He walked toward Sept, the whip end held in his other hand. "Get out," he said. The big booming voice was gathered in now, cased like gunpowder in a shell. If it exploded again, the whip would explode, flailing over Sept's back, striking his face.

"Don't interfere in what doesn't concern you, Langlinais," Sept said. His body still did not move, but the eyes were darting to the door, measuring the distance.

"Like hell it doesn't concern me!" The whip end streaked across the air, hissed down, struck. Was raised, came down, struck. Sept grabbed at it, tried to catch that long thin tail. Then turned, ran for the door, Jumie hard after him. She heard them down the hall, heard the clatter of boots, heavy hard shoes. Curses. Shouts. Then a door slammed and there was silence. He must be making sure he's gone, she thought. A sound of an auto motor catching, then settling into a roar.

"Marthe, let me tell you something, your dogs are getting lazy, yes—they don't keep the tramps out. Marthe, listen, my anger, it's young—but my arm, it's old. Listen, I can't whip every canaille that comes to bother you."

He knew she was crying, knew that if she raised her bent head, tears would veil her eyes. "Marthe, don't cry. Look, I can take Yankees, snakes, manqués like Sept—Marthe, damn it, don't cry."

"Then fix me a toddy, Jumie." She dabbed at her eyes. "But the lawyer—Jumie, what about that?"

"Damn, Marthe, what kind of a lawyer you think a bastard—pardon, Marthe—a canaille like that can get? Your son-in-law, he can take care of that. Or Claude. Claude just did a big favor for some people down there, let's see if they can do one back. Listen, don't worry about any lawyer, Marthe."

"I don't want to worry about anything, Jumie. Ever again. I'm old and I'm tired and Henri is old and he's tired . . ."

Jumie handed her the toddy. "You need a little trip. Make a visit to Hélène, go see Caroline. She's pretty like her grand-mama, Marthe?"

He watched the softness come back into her face. "She's the most beautiful little girl you ever saw in your life, Jumie."

She turned to him, and the old radiance he remembered, the shimmering happiness, glowed. "And, oh, Jumie, she loves it here at Beau Chêne. When I see how much—it almost makes it all worth it—you know?"

In the election of 1912, the Good Government candidate, Judge Luther Egbert Hall, was elected governor on the Reform ticket. And in St. Martin Parish, Claude Louis Langlinais was elected to the House of Representatives. His wife, Alice, celebrated by adding a music room to the house. Her gown for the inaugural ball was made by a New Orleans modiste, it cost, Geneviève told Marthe, as much as Jumie made the first year he opened the sash and blind factory.

# CHAPTER 25

## *Harvest*

It was Christmas Eve in 1916, and all the bounty of the seasons—and all the seasons of Langlinais work—seemed to be theirs.

Alice came out into the front hall, tying her apron over her green challis dress. "Claude, what, more presents? Listen, they think you can't feed your family?" She took the box from his hands, studied it. "Cheese, fruit, wine—Claude, if everybody in the legislature gets so much for Christmas, you don't need to get paid, too!"

"I'll take this box over to the convent for the sisters. You sent that ham out to maman?"

Alice laughed. "You know your maman. She called me up and asked why we had to get ham from Virginia, didn't people know we did a boucheria, had all the pig we wanted?"

"Beau out there?"

"Thanking his grandpapa for his new gun." She shook her head. "Claude, you think that war will be over before he's old enough to go? He's sixteen, it wouldn't be much more..."

"Who can tell that, Alice?" His arms came around her, a big hand pressed her face against his shoulder. "Langlinaises have been in wars before, Alice."

"But never across an ocean! Never so far! Claude, I'm afraid."

He pulled her under the mistletoe hanging from the Tiffany chandelier. "On Christmas Eve? Alice, today is a special time— a time for good things. Alice, for today—no one's afraid."

He felt her lips moving under his, curving into a smile. She pulled away, tugged her apron straight. "One thing I can be afraid of—your maman won't like my new recipe for cranberry compote. Now, listen, Claude, if anyone else comes this morning, say I'm not here! If I don't go rattle my pots fast, I'll never get through."

"I think I'll run out to papa's, see what's going on. Everybody going to Mass tonight?"

"The children have a party at the Boudreauxs'. Then back here to meet us for church. Now, Claude, listen, Miss Bessie's going to sing, and Claude, be a good example for your children. Claude, don't laugh!"

But he will, she thought, hearing him laugh as he went down the walk. He and his papa. Rolling their eyes and laughing. She shook her head. Who could understand men? Like little boys, with their guns and their jokes—until the games turned to war. If all she knew about Claude's work done in Baton Rouge was the funny stories he told, she'd think that was a game, too. Except that the newspapers had begun to quote him, follow him, watch him. When John Parker didn't win for governor, one New Orleans paper had written: "The cause of Good Government suffered a blow when Parker lost to Pleasant, but since men like Claude Langlinais of St. Martin Parish were reelected, the blow is not mortal." She began to hum, Claude was right. Today was a time for good things, not to be afraid.

Marthe pulled the vase of roses toward her, put her face close to them, and breathed in their sweetness. A warm, almost summery day. Not like Christmas at all. Which might make the first Christmas without Henri a little easier. She looked at the pile of documents on her desk. If he'd had any idea the mess his death would leave her in—taxes to pay, René wanting shares of his father's estate right away—and what was his father's estate anyway? Half of Beau Chêne, half of the property of the community. For each of them, a fourth of Henri's half. But her son couldn't fund a literary magazine with a bunch of Russian émigrés unless he had cash. And she couldn't pay inheritance taxes without cash. Which meant selling land. And how untangle, in the maze of mortgages, those overlapping notes, how much to sell? She had decided, finally, to sell it all, everything but the plot the house stood on. The hell with it.

The telephone at her elbow rang. Hélène, calling from New Orleans. "We just got so worried about you, staying out there all alone, mama. I know you're coming in on King's Day. But

Christmas alone! So, mama, I'm sending you a present. Charles just put Caroline on the train, can you meet her?" Marthe hardly heard the rest. A quiet Christmas, because of papa, Hélène was saying. And a happy one, now that mama would have company. Caroline for Christmas! "The loveliest present you could give me, darling. The loveliest in the world."

She went down the hall to find Berthe. "Caroline's coming, Berthe! We'll put her in her mother's old room—the train comes right after lunch, she'll be starving, is there some of that chicken left? Oh, Berthe, I feel like Christmas, after all!"

"You heard from Miss Nanette yet?"

"I'm sure there'll be a letter, something. Africa is a long way, Berthe."

"Humph. Can't see why a nice little girl like Miss Nanette has to go off to a place like that. Why can't she be a doctor here, like her papa?"

"A doctor she very much admired at Jefferson is a medical missionary. He asked her to work with him. She says the experience will be invaluable."

Berthe picked up a carving knife, began to chop celery. "Anybody eat Miss Nanette, he has me to answer to. Don't they have cannibals out there?"

"Oh, God, Berthe, let's hope not." Marthe laughed. "Anyway, I think Miss Nanette is too skinny and too tough to make anybody's dinner." She looked at her watch. "I've still got a little work to do. And I'd better call Anne and tell her Caroline will be with me tomorrow."

"You going to Miz Forêt's for dinner? That's nice, Miss Marthe. You'll have a good day." Berthe patted Marthe's arm. "Seems like it's time something nice happened for you, Miss Marthe."

"It has! Caroline's coming!"

The clean crack of rifle fire echoed through the woods. The tin cans lined upon a fence rail sang as the bullets struck them, their pocked sides glittering in the sun. "Damn, Beau, you're almost as good as your grandpapa," Jumie said. "You wouldn't beat an old man, would you?"

"It's this gun," Beau said. "She's a honey." He was tall, muscled, with a clear open face, strong gray eyes, hair that fell from a cowlick over his forehead. "Already the girls are chasing him," Alice complained to Geneviève. "Don't think I

don't see them batting their eyes at him, even in church!"
Geneviève had laughed. "You ever know a Langlinais the women
didn't like? And didn't like women? Alice, be glad!"

"We'll do a little hunting this week." Jumie scratched the
head of the dog sitting next to him. "You know how long I
been hunting around here? Damn near fifty-five years—since
I was just a little boy. That's a hell of a long time to be doing
anything, Beau." He looked at the dog. "Lots of fine dogs went
with me, too. You, fellow, you got a big tradition to follow!"

"I know how that feels!" Beau said. He raised his rifle,
sighted, fired. The tin cans jumped. "At school? I'm Claude's
son, Jumie's grandson. I thought when I put on long pants, I'd
be me!"

His grandfather's arm covered his shoulders. "So who are
you, if you're not you? Listen, we've had a Claude every
generation since the Langlinaises came here—and if the good
Lord wills it, I guess we always will." He turned the boy to
him, held his face between his hands. "Each one of us—we
find our own way. Like your papa? Look at him in the legislature! The only thing, we find our way without bringing shame
on the name."

Beau laughed. "No way I can do that, grandpapa. Even if
I wanted to we're too well known! Last week? I was at a party
in New Iberia, one of the boys there got a little rowdy—well,
who wants a scene at a party? So I just kind of escorted him
out, you know? And by the time I get home, someone has
already called maman to tell her. 'I hear you behaved very
nicely,' she said. And gave me that look that says—see, I
know what goes on, even in New Iberia."

"Those women! You know what your grandmama says—
if you don't behave well for the good reason of doing right,
then behave well for the reason I'll know if you don't!"

They heard a shout from across the field, looked to see
Claude waving. "Go see your papa," Jumie said. "Clutter up
your grandmama's kitchen awhile. I think I'll walk on over to
Beau Chêne, see how Marthe's doing. It's been a long fall for
her."

"Maman was saying Doctor Henri probably would have
lived longer if he hadn't worked so hard all the time. Worked
himself to death, she said."

"He was a good man. Saved my babies' lives." Jumie's eyes
were staring back into time, watching two babies struggle for

breath. "Nothing I could do could ever repay that."

Beau picked up the tin cans, stuffed them in a sack. "I'll throw these away up at the house. Thanks for the rifle, grand-papa." He grinned. "That's pretty nice of you, giving me a gun I can outshoot you with." He ran from the shower of leaves Jumie tossed at him, then slowed to a walk. Jumie watched him go toward Claude, who stood waiting at the gate. Like watching himself. The boy moving to manhood, the man mov-ing to old age. He was Henri's age, you couldn't say sixty-three was old—but when a friend, a neighbor, just dropped one day, stethoscope falling from his hand, it made you think. At least Geneviève wouldn't be in the fix he imagined Marthe was. She wouldn't have to worry about one damn thing, he'd seen to that.

He set off through the woods, taking the path they'd cut through to Beau Chêne all those years ago. The squirrels were taking advantage of the warmth, scampering through the trees, running over the ground looking for acorns, pecans. It had rained for several days before the warm spell came; the leaves beneath his feet were soft, damp, rotting underneath to become part of the rich earth. The rain had beaten off most of the leaves from the big gums; their branches hung bare against the sky, spiky gum balls clinging to long thin twigs. He spied a cluster of mistletoe high in a gum tree and thought of Marthe. Raised his rifle, fired. The bullets cut through the small branch holding the mistletoe, cracked it away from the larger lump. He took out his pocketknife and cut a thick piece, picking a branch with the waxy white berries full.

No smoke rising from Beau Chêne today; just that one thing made the big house seem so silent, so still, so empty. He thought of his own house, Geneviève bustling around, Claude and Beau drinking coffee, Claudine and her family trimming the tree. And tomorrow, a house full, cousins, aunts, uncles, one of the priests from the church—and a couple of strays Geneviève always managed to find who wouldn't have anywhere else to go.

Berthe looked up as she opened the kitchen door. "Miss Marthe's in her study, Mister Jumie. You want coffee?"

"No, I want some of your eggnog, Berthe. You got time to make me some?"

"I ever not have time on Christmas Eve to make eggnog? I'll bring it, you go on."

"Working on Christmas Eve? Now, Marthe!" He went in, held the mistletoe out to her.

"Oh, Jumie, it's lovely. Caroline will love it—Jumie, she's coming, Charles put her on the train this morning—I'd no idea how much I dreaded Christmas alone until I knew she was coming."

He sat in the chair opposite her, cocking a knee over the arm. "So you should be getting ready for your grandbaby, not fooling with all that."

"The sale has to be concluded before the first, Jumie. I was just looking over the papers." She had pushed the curtains back and opened the windows, letting in the soft morning warmth. In that winter light, the room they sat in seemed softened, too. Colors of book bindings and old rugs blended into shades of rose and crimson and ivory. The sun touched the silver frames of photographs lining the mantel, hovered over Marthe's racing trophies, danced on to light her fair hair. And what will keep all this up, Jumie thought, when she's sold her fields, no longer has the sugar? Has she even thought of that?

"It's too bad this happened now, Marthe. Sugar prices are so high, what with the war. But not high enough?"

"If Henri hadn't died, Jumie. These last two years, prices have been high. God knows I don't want this war to go on—while it does, we're making money. I had even managed to get those notes down. And with Nanette finished school—it looked like we had some breathing time." Her smile reminded him that Marthe was used to trouble, accustomed to facing it. "But—the best laid plans—"

"So how much are you selling?"

She looked away from him, followed the line of sun out to the garden outside. A cardinal was playing in the fountain; the crimson feathers glistened in the spray. "All of it. Except what the house stands on."

"All of it!" His hand moved to the papers in front of her. "Let me see this."

Berthe came in, two steaming tumblers borne on a silver tray. "I didn't put the nog in, Mister Jumie. I guess you can tend to that. I cut some of our fruitcake, too. It's got enough bourbon in it to where you don't need much in that eggnog."

"I won't disgrace you, Berthe," Jumie said. He went to the cabinet, got bourbon, poured it in each glass. "Now let's see what you're doing." He began to read, eyes running over the closely written lines. From time to time, he made a note on the pad Marthe had been using. She watched him, and felt a warmth that had nothing to do with the sun's heat or that of the eggnog. Then, from habit. "Don't tell me what to do, Jumie."

"I won't tell you what to do. Just make a few suggestions. It's my fault you're a smart woman and know good advice when you hear it? Now look—you need to keep some land around the house, Marthe. Hold back fifty acres. Marthe, you need room for some vegetables, a few cows, a few horses. What, you're going to go in to town, buy your food? And, Marthe—keep the mineral rights."

"Jumie, I don't know if they'll go for that—we're so far along in the sale, I realize I should keep these rights, after Solange's find last spring, of course we all expect to be oil barons—"

"Well. Anse la Butte's been producing for years. Marthe, keep the mineral rights."

"And if they say no?"

"Damn, Marthe, a big agriculture combine's buying your land. They don't need to fool with what's under it—may not even be anything there."

She fiddled with the pen in front of her. "Gulf Oil thinks there is."

He sipped his eggnog, searched her calm face. "They do?"

"They're ready to sign a lease. I—I suppose I should tell the buyers."

He slammed down the glass, stood up "Marthe! Damn it! Don't tell them a damn thing!"

"They're not offering that much now—Gulf Oil, I mean. But the royalties, if they brought in some wells—oh, Jumie, I'd never have to worry again!" Her face was like the December weather, changeable, going from soft radiant to worrying chill.

"Marthe, let me tell you a story. A long time ago, papa and me, we raced a horse against Le Bleu, over in Breaux Bridge. You remember that? Well, listen, I was sure—almost sure—that LeBleu's horse was sick, getting distemper, probably. Papa and me, we talked about whether we should tell him. What was right to do?" He laughed, remembering. "Finally we decided if a man has a horse, races her, he should know if she's sick. We gave him one little chance—he didn't take it. So—tant pis."

"The buyers' little chance is if they've picked up word about the lease?"

He shrugged. "Sure. But let me tell you, they cut their chance to nothing when they picked Alcide LeBlanc for their agent. He's dumb, yes. Makes a big show, drives around in his big car, has a fancy office in New Iberia—but, Marthe, the man's dumb. The best thing could happen to you is Alcide making the deal."

"Is even Alcide that dumb? That he wouldn't hear about the lease?"

"He didn't put it in here—about the mineral rights. And that's dumb."

"So if I have it rewritten? And put it in? What will he think?"

"What you tell him to think. That the price per acre is for the top only. Nothing underneath."

"And if they say no? Jumie, I owe money, the interest alone—and René is after me, when can he have his inheritance—"

"He's not still in France?"

"Oh, no. Safe in London. You know René. If there's one thing he knows, it's when to get out. But, Jumie—this sale—"

"If they give you any trouble—tell them you have another offer. Someone who will snap it up, at a better price per acre, only what's on top, the minute the deadline for the act of sale passes."

"But, Jumie, I don't have a buyer—not at this price. Jumie—"

"Like hell you don't," he said. He came to her, held mistletoe over her head, kissed her cheek. "But, Marthe, be a good poker player, all right? Claude and me, we got enough to do without taking on Beau Chêne."

The platform in New Iberia was almost empty; most Christmas traveling had been done earlier. Marthe stood peering down the track; why did you think looking for a train would make it come faster? The times she'd taken that very train back and forth—time rushed over you at Christmas, roaring down, bringing load after load of memories. Her own holidays at Beau Chêne, the house filled with light and music and people. Her children growing up there, singing in the parlor, hanging stockings, trimming the tree. She and Caroline could do that tonight, before Mass. Nat had found a pretty pine, cut it right after Hélène called, and had its stand built before she left for the station. Thank goodness she'd not sent her gifts to New Orleans, planning on giving them on King's Day. She thought of the pearls for Caroline. Creamy, lustrous—how many de Clouet women had worn them, had heard their mamans say, "You're too young for stones. Pearls are for young girls."

Then the train was there, had roared in, stopped. The bright blonde hair, the big blue eyes—Caroline!

Caroline chattered all the way back to Beau Chêne, a stream of light words, silver laughter, that polished the day, made it a mirror of all the happy Christmases from all the years before. "And just think, grandmère, maman's going on a trip during Lent, to rest up after all the balls, and she said if the sisters at Sacred Heart would let me miss a few weeks of school, I can come stay with you! They will, don't you think? I could go to school here, in St. Martinville, couldn't I?" She leaned out the open automobile window, stretched out her arms. "I love it out here. It's so wonderful to live at Beau Chêne, grand-mère. Don't you think so?"

"I can't imagine living anywhere else," Marthe said. And when they turned in the big gates, and the house gleamed at them from the end of the oak alley, she thought with deep happiness that thanks to Jumie Langlinais, she'd never have to.

The tree stood as tall as the ceiling, sixteen feet high. Claude climbed the ladder, star in his hand. "Now, Claude, don't you fall and break your neck. It's Christmas, who wants to go to the hospital?" Alice grasped the ladder firmly and braced herself against it. She watched him put the star in place, moved so he could climb down. She stood close to him, arm around him. "But it's pretty, isn't it? The prettiest tree we've ever had."

"You always say that," he said.

"And the presents! Claude, the children will be spoiled."

"Now, Alice. You can't spoil good children. Alice, it's Christmas."

The December afternoon slipped way, became a clear, starry night. "I think a little front may be coming in," Claude said, sniffing the air. "I can smell the swamp." He watched his children go down the walk, candles in hand. "Listen, be careful with those candles. And sing good, you hear?"

"We'll come by here," Marie said. Beau walked between his sisters, one on each arm. They're good-looking children, Claude thought. Pretty girls.

Fourteen-year-old Marie had at least one beau already, and he had seen twelve-year-old Francie blush when the Trahan boy next door came to bring Christmas candy from his maman. As for Beau—he thought of the hours in the legislature, in long, wearing committee meetings, tedious debates on the floor. He'd kept his mouth pretty much shut that first four years—lie low and find out the way things work before you make your move. And he'd been surprised at how things did work. A lot of it as bad as he'd been told. Lot of buying and selling going on. Lot of people looking out for themselves and damn the rest of the state. A lot of poor people out there who damn near didn't have anyone looking out for them at all. Too bad about the Farmer's Union, the People's Party it supported. Maybe another time. Well. They'd made some progress, he and papa. Beau would make more. They were Langlinais, weren't they? And down here, that meant something.

Far down the street, he heard the sounds of carolers. He'd go find Alice, help fix cocoa and cookies for when they came here. Fix ambrosia for dinner tomorrow. He thought about the long velvet box that nestled in a pile of tissue paper, buried in the depths of the big package he'd wrapped to tease Alice. The jeweler had said diamonds were always in good taste, no matter what. One thing about Alice—she had good taste.

The people of St. Martinville gathered in their church, filling the pews with sleeping babies, nodding grandparents, restless children. They filed before the manger, knelt and prayed. Geneviève looked down the Langlinais pew, counted heads. Jumie. Claudine, her family. Claude. Alice. Their children. She leaned around Jumie, straightened his grandchild's collar, that one's hair. "Stand straight!" she whispered to Marie. "Don't slump!"

The organist began playing, rippling chords that found the melody, held. Miss Bessie's voice rose over them, high, quavering. Geneviève nudged Jumie, saw Alice nudge Claude. "Don't laugh!"

There was a rustle in the aisle and a whiff of perfume. She saw Marthe and Caroline genuflect and enter the de Clouet pew. "But, Jumie, look what a beauty Caroline is!"

From down the pew, Beau saw the girl with Mrs. de Gravelle. Slender, pretty. Long blonde curls, dark eyelashes. Fair skin, pink cheeks. She turned, saw him watching her. He felt himself dissolving in her huge eyes. He straightened his shoulders. Mrs. de Gravelle liked ducks, he remembered. Maybe he'd take some over there tomorrow. After all, they didn't have anyone to hunt for them now.

The priest, vestments shining white, gleaming with gold, stood before them. "Gloria Patri, et Filio, et Spiritui Sancto."

High above the altar, the crucifix hung. But attention was on the Christ Child who lay in the manger and promised peace. They rose for the Gospel, for words old and forever new— "Do not be afraid, for behold, I bring you good news of great joy which shall be to all the people; for today in the town of David a Savior has been born to you, Who is Christ the Lord."

The bells rang out, pealing over the sleeping earth. They rang over field and swamp, woods and bayou, farm and town. And if in the church below them, memory of another church stirred, memory of a church far away, of a time far away, when the people of Grand Pré gathered to hear words of another kind—if that memory stirred, it heard the bells, and slept. For tonight they came to celebrate their joy, to give thanks for their God's goodness; tonight they were in a happy land.

## Sweeping Stories of Captivating Romance

| | | |
|---|---|---|
| ☐23925-0 | **THE FIRST DAUGHTER** Whitney Stine | $3.95 |
| ☐20548-8 | **THE EMPEROR'S LADY** Diana Summers | $3.50 |
| ☐69659-7 | **QUEEN OF PARIS** Christina Nicholson | $3.95 |
| ☐86072-9 | **THE VELVET HART** Felicia Andrews | $3.95 |
| ☐05321-1 | **BELOVED CAPTIVE** Iris Gower | $2.95 |
| ☐79121-2 | **SWEET LOVE SURVIVE** Susan Johnson | $3.50 |
| ☐52092-8 | **FORGET ME NOT** Gabrielle DuPre | $3.95 |
| ☐09023-0 | **CAJUN** Elizabeth Nell Dubus | $4.50 |

Prices may be slightly higher in Canada.

Available wherever paperbacks are sold or use this coupon.

# Bestselling Books
# from Berkley